Modern Greats
of
Science Fiction

Modern Greats
of
Science Fiction

Nine Novellas of Distinction

edited by Jonathan Strahan

ibooks

DISTRIBUTED BY PUBLISHERS GROUP WEST

For Jessica and Sophie, to share

I would like to thank my editor, Andrew Wheeler, for all of his help and advice in preparing this book. I'd also like to thank SFBC contracts person extraordinaire Michael McCormack for his assistance with matters legal. As always, I received a lot of help putting this book together. My thanks always go to Marianne first, and *then* to Charles, for *very* different kinds of help. I'd like to thank my anthology guru, Jack Dann, for advice above and beyond, and my *Locus* colleagues Nick Gevers and Rich Horton for being there to discuss the best short fiction of the year when I needed it most. Thanks also to the following good friends and colleagues without whom this book would have been much poorer, and much less fun to do: Justin Ackroyd, Lou Anders, Simon Brown, Jeremy Byrne, Ellen Datlow, Gardner Dozois, David Hartwell, Kelly Link, Gavin Grant, Garth Nix, Sean Williams, the various posters to the Night Shade Message Boards, and all of the book's contributors.

⇛ Contents ⇚

INTRODUCTION xi

THE EMPRESS OF MARS *by Kage Baker* 1

THE GREEN LEOPARD PLAGUE
by Walter Jon Williams 75

IN SPRINGDALE TOWN
by Robert Freeman Wexler 145

THE SWASTIKA BOMB *by John Meaney* 203

JAILWISE *by Lucius Shepard* 261

JUST LIKE THE ONES WE USED TO KNOW
by Connie Willis 331

GREETINGS *by Terry Bisson* 385

AWAKE IN THE NIGHT *by John C. Wright* 457

OFF ON A STARSHIP *by William Barton* 509

Introduction

by Jonathan Strahan

The short novel, or novella, has a long and illustrious history in the science fiction and fantasy field. Some of the best and most famous science fiction stories of all time—Robert A. Heinlein's "Universe," Jack Vance's "The Dragon Masters," Isaac Asimov's "Foundation" stories, Robert Silverberg's "Born with the Dead," Ursula K. Le Guin's "The Word for World Is Forest"—are novellas. And the novella has, rightly I think, often been described as the ideal form for science fiction.

Defined as a "short narrative tale, especially a popular story having a moral or satirical point," or as "a small new thing" when translated from Italian—the novella provides a writer with enough room to build a world, create believable characters, and to examine a single idea in some depth. And, in these days of five-volume trilogies and quarter-million-word-long novels, the novella leaves no room for indulgence or bloat. In a novella, the writer has to use every word to give his or her story complexity, depth, and impact. Novellas are, as Gardner Dozois said in his introduction to *Modern Classic Short Novels of Science Fiction*, "marvels of compression."

And these are good times for the novella. Just a decade ago Dozois wrote that, despite the virtual disappearance of the short novel or novella from the literary mainstream, there were "still usually a dozen or more novellas published in the science fiction genre every year." A dozen or more! Reliable statistics on the number of novellas and short stories published each year are difficult to come by, but to give you something of an idea of how many novellas are being published today, trade journal *Locus* recommended an average of two dozen novellas on its annual "Recommended Reading" list in each of the past three years. That's not two dozen that were published, but two dozen that were good enough to be considered amongst the very best science fiction and fantasy of the year.

So, what's changed? Why more novellas? It's not because writers are getting lazy or because there's more money to be made. It seems, to me at least, that changes in the short fiction marketplace are creating more opportunities for novellas to be published. The major print magazines—*Asimov's Science Fiction Magazine, Analog Science Fiction & Fact, The Magazine of Fantasy & Science Fiction,* and *Realms of Fantasy*—have always been the mainstay for short science fiction and fantasy. Over the past few years most of those magazines have changed their production schedules, delivering more double issues, which in turn provide a lot more space for longer stories. There has also been a return to the heyday of the late '80s and early '90s, with small press publishers like PS Publishing, Golden Gryphon, Night Shade, and Subterranean Press publishing a number of novellas each year as stand-alone books. And then there is the online world. Unrestricted by the cost of paper or shipping, websites and e-zines have a lot more freedom than their ink-based fellows to publish longer works, and they often do. Easily the best of these is Ellen Datlow's *SciFiction,* which publishes a handful of excellent novellas each year, several of which are reprinted in this book, but you can also find strong fiction at *Strange Horizons, The Infinite Matrix,* and elsewhere.

More importantly, these changes in the marketplace seem to have resulted in the best and most famous writers in the field turning their attention to the novella. Robert Silverberg's two high-profile *Legends* anthologies had some of the biggest-selling genre writers in the world publishing novellas set in their most famous worlds, and major writers like Ursula K. Le Guin, Kate Wilhelm, and Connie Willis have all published fine novellas in the last few years. The field's hot new writers—Charles Stross,

Ian R. Macleod, and Alastair Reynolds—have all also published several major novellas of late. The undisputed king of the modern novella boom, though, is Lucius Shepard. Since returning from a period of comparative inactivity during the '90s, Shepard has published a string of extraordinary novellas every year, any number of which could have won major awards or been collected in a "year's best" annual.

Which brings us to the book you now hold in your hands: a selection of the best novellas or short novels published in 2003. The history of the "year's best" annual goes back to the late 1940s, but this is only the second time that a publisher has attempted a book of this type. Back in 1979 and 1980, celebrated anthologist Terry Carr produced two fine volumes in his *The Best Science Fiction Novellas of the Year* series. As always with Carr, the books were wonderful selections of the very best the science fiction field has to offer, and they are very much the inspiration for this book. I hope, here, and in coming years, to bring you the best of the best, the very finest short science fiction and fantasy novels published each year. Now, go read the stories. They're the good part!

—Jonathan Strahan
Perth, Western Australia
February 2004

THE EMPRESS OF MARS

by Kage Baker

Kage Baker was born in California in 1952 and worked an eclectic range of jobs—actor, director, artist, insurance clerk, and teacher of Elizabethan English—before becoming a professional writer in 1997. Her first professional sale was the story "Noble Mold," which was also the first in her ongoing "Company" series of romantic science fiction novels and short stories. It was followed by four "Company" novels, In the Garden of Iden, Sky Coyote, Mendoza in Hollywood, *and* The Graveyard Game, *and a collection of "Company" short stories,* Black Projects, White Knights. *Baker's most recent novel is the stand-alone fantasy* The Anvil of the World, *and upcoming is a new "Company" novel,* The Life of the World to Come, *and a second story collection,* Mother Aegypt and Other Stories. *Baker's 1999 novella "Son Observe the Time" was nominated for the Hugo Award.*

Baker published three strong short novels in 2003, "Welcome to Olympus, Mr. Hearst," "The Angel in the Darkness," and "The Empress of Mars." A vibrant planetary adventure in the grand style, "The Empress of Mars" takes us to a colorful bar where dusty pioneers look for a little taste of home. It has been nominated for the Nebula Award for Best Novella.

THERE WERE THREE EMPRESSES OF MARS.

The first one was a bar at the Settlement. The second was the lady who ran the bar; though her title was strictly informal, having been bestowed on her by the regular customers, and her domain extended no further than the pleasantly gloomy walls of the only place you could get beer on the Tharsis Bulge.

The third one was the Queen of England.

1
THE BIG RED BALLOON

What were the British doing on Mars?

For one thing, they had no difficulty calculating with metric figures. For another, their space exploration effort had not been fueled primarily by a military industrial complex. This meant that it had never received infusions of taxpayers' money on the huge scale of certain other nations, but also meant that its continued existence had been unaffected by the inconvenient disappearance of enemies. Without the necessity of offworld missile bases, the major powers' interest in colonizing space had quite melted away. This left plenty of room for the private sector.

There was only one question, then: was there money on Mars?

There had definitely been money on Luna. The British Lunar Company had done quite well by its stockholders, with the proceeds from its mining and tourism divisions. Luna had been a great place to channel societal malcontents as well, guaranteeing a work force of rugged individualists and others who couldn't fit in Down Home without medication.

But Luna was pretty thoroughly old news now and no longer anywhere near as profitable as it had been, thanks to the miners' strikes and the litigation with the Ephesian Church over the Diana of Luna incident. Nor was it romantic anymore: its sterile silver valleys were becoming domesticated, domed over with tract housing for all the clerks the BLC needed. Bureaucrats and missionaries had done for Luna as a frontier.

The psychiatric hospitals were filling up with unemployed rugged individualists again. Profit margins were down. The BLC turned its thoughtful eyes to Mars.

Harder to get to than Luna, but nominally easier to colonize. Bigger, but on the other hand no easy gravity well with which to ship ore down to Earth. This ruled out mining for export as a means of profit. And as for low-gravity experiments, they were cheaper and easier to do on Luna. What, really, had Mars to offer to the hopeful capitalist?

Only the prospect of terraforming. And terraforming would

cost a lot of money and a lot of effort, with the *successful* result being a place slightly less hospitable than Outer Mongolia in the dead of winter.

But what are spin doctors for?

So the British Arean Company had been formed, with suitably orchestrated media fanfare. Historical clichés were dusted off and repackaged to look shiny-new. Games and films were produced to create a public appetite for adventure in rocky red landscapes. Clever advertising did its best to convince people they'd missed a golden opportunity by not buying lots on Luna when the land up there was dirt cheap, but intimated that they needn't kick themselves any longer: a second chance was coming for an even better deal!

And so forth and so on.

It all had the desired effect. A lot of people gave the British Arean Company a great deal of money in return for shares of stock that, technically speaking, weren't worth the pixels with which they were impressively depicted in old-engraving style. The big red balloon was launched. Missions to Mars were launched, a domed base was built, and actual scientists were sent out to the new colony along with the better-socially adapted inhabitants of two or three hospitals. So were the members of an incorporated clan, as a goodwill gesture in honor of the most recent treaty with the Celtic Federation. They brought certain institutions the BAC officially forbade, like polluting industries and beast slavery, but conceded were necessary to survival on a frontier.

So all began together the vast and difficult work of setting up the infrastructure for terraforming, preparing the way for wholesale human colonization.

Then there was a change of government, which coincided with the BAC discovering that the fusion generators they had shipped to Mars wouldn't work unless they were in a very strong electromagnetic field, and Mars, it seemed, didn't have much of one. This meant that powering life support alone would cost very much more than anyone had thought it would.

Not only that, the lowland canyons where principal settlement had been planned turned out to channel winds with devastating velocity. Only in the Tharsis highlands, where the air was thinner and colder, was it possible to erect a structure that wouldn't be scoured away by sandstorms within a week. The BAC discovered this after several extremely costly mistakes.

The balloon burst.

Not with a bang and shreds flying everywhere, exactly; more like a very fast leak, so it sort of dwindled down to an ignominious little lopsided thing without much air in it. Just like the dome of the Settlement Base.

So a lot of people were stuck up there without the money to come home, and they had to make the best of things. Under the circumstances, it seemed best to continue on with the job.

Mary Griffith woke alone that morning, though she did not always do so. She lay for a while in the dark, listening to the quiet, which was not the same thing as silence: low hum of the jenny and a few snores drifting from the other lofts tucked in under the curve of the dome like so many swallows' nests. No coughing. No quarreling. No fretful clunking to tell her that Three Tank needed its valves unblocked yet again.

Smiling to herself, she rolled out of her bedclothes and tossed the ladder over the side, so descending nimbly to meet the day. She was a compactly built and muscular little woman of a certain age. Her ancestors, most of them coal miners, had passed along with other hardy genetic characteristics a barrel chest, which gave her considerable bosom a certain massive foundation, and Martian gravity contributed in its own way to make Mother Griffith's Knockers famous throughout the Settlement.

Having sent the ladder back up on its reel and tied off the line neat as any sailor, she set the stove to heating and pumped a kettle of water. The water came up reluctantly, as it always did, rust-colored, strangling and spitting slush from the pipe, but it boiled clear; and as she sat and sipped her tea Mary watched the steam rise like a ghost in the dry cold air.

The visible phantom ascended and dissipated, reaching the lofts and sending its message to the other sleepers, who were pulled awake by its moistness as irresistibly as though it was the smell of eggs and bacon, were they back on Earth. Soon she heard them tossing in their blankets, heard a racking cough or a whispered exchange. She sighed, bidding goodbye to the last bit of early-morning calm. Another day begun.

She got up and rolled back the shade on the big window, and the sullen purple dawn flared in and lit her house.

"Oh, my, that's bright," said someone plaintively, high up in the shadows, and a moment later Mr. Morton came down on his line, in his long black thermals looking uncommonly like a hesitant spider.

"Good morning, Mr. Morton," said Mary, in English because his panCelt was still halting, and "Good morning, Ma'am," said he, and winced as his bare feet hit the cold sanded floor. Half-hopping he picked his way to the stove and poured his tea, inhaling the steam gratefully; brought it back to the long stone table and seated himself, wincing again as his knees knocked into the table supports. He stirred a good lump of butter into the tea and regarded Mary through the steam, looking anxious.

"Er . . . what would you like me to do today?" he inquired.

Mary sighed and summoned patience.

He was nominally her employee, and had been so since that fateful afternoon when he, like so many others, had realized that his redundancy pay did not amount to half the fare back to Earth.

"Well, you didn't finish the scouring on Five Tank yesterday, did you?" she said.

"No," he agreed sadly.

"Then I think perhaps you had better do that, Mr. Morton."

"Okay," he said.

It was not his fault that he had to be told what to do. He had spent most of his adult life in hospital and a good bit of his childhood too, ever since (having at the age of ten been caught reading a story by Edgar Allan Poe) he had been diagnosed as Eccentric.

Mind you, it wasn't all jam and tea in hospital. Even the incurably twisted had to be of some use to society, and Mr. Morton had been brilliant at the chemistry, design, and fabrication of cast-stone structures for industrial use. That was why he had been recruited by the BAC, arriving on Mars with a single black duffel containing all he owned and a heart full of dreams of romantic adventure.

Having designed and fabricated all the structures the BAC needed, however, he had been summarily fired. He had gone wandering away through the Tubes and wound up at the Empress, his white thin face whiter still for shock, and sat at a dark table drinking batch for eight hours before Mary had asked him if he was ever going home, and then he had burst into tears.

So she had given him a job. Mary had been fired, herself. Not for redundancy, though, really; for being too Ethnic.

"Five Tank, yes, and in the afternoon we can brew another pale ale," she decided, "Or maybe a good oatmeal stout, what do you think?" and Mr. Morton brightened at that.

"Have we got any oats?" he inquired.

"If She provides them," Mary said, and he nodded sagely. Mr. Morton wasn't an Ephesian himself, but he was willing to concede that there was Somebody out there responsive to human prayer, and She certainly seemed to hear Mary's.

"Something will turn up," he said, and Mary nodded.

And when the day had well and truly begun—when the lodgers had all descended from their alcoves and gone trudging away down the Tubes to their varied employments, when Mary's daughters and their respective gentlemen callers had been roused and set smiling or sullen about the day's tasks, when the long stone counter had been polished to a dull shine and the heating unit under One Tank was filling the air with a grateful warmth, and Mary herself stood behind the bar drawing the first ale of the day, to be poured into the offering basin in the little shrine with its lumpy image of the Good Mother herself, dim-lit by her little flickering votive wire—even in that moment when the rich hoppy stuff hit the parched stone and foamed extravagantly, for CO_2 is never lacking on Mars—even just then the Lock doors swung open and in came the answer to prayer, being Padraig Moylan with a hundredweight sack of Clan Morrigan oats and two tubs of butter in trade.

Mr. Moylan was thanked with grace and sincerity, the clan's bar tab recalculated accordingly. Soon he was settled in a cozy alcove with a shot of red single malt and Mona, the best listener among Mary's children. Mary, having stashed the welcome barter in a locker, set about her slow eternal task of sweeping the red sand from her tables. She could hear Mr. Morton singing as he worked with his scouring pads, his dreamy lyric baritone echoing inside Five Tank, reverberating *Some Enchanted Evening*.

Mary ticked him off her mental list of Things to Be Seen To, and surveyed the rest of her house as she moved down the length of the table.

There was Alice, her firstborn, graceful as a swan and as irritable too, loading yesterday's beer mugs into the scouring unit. Rowan, brown and practical, was arranging today's mugs in neat ranks behind the bar. Worn by scouring, the mugs had a lovely silkiness on them now, shiny as pink marble, dwindling to a thinness and translucency that meant that soon they'd be too delicate for bar use and more would have to be cast. (Though when that happened, the old ones could be boxed up and sent out to the souvenir store in the landing port, to be sold as Finest Arean Porcelain to such guests as came to inspect the BAC public facilities.)

Over behind Four Tank, the shadows had retreated before a little mine-lamp, and by its light Chiring and Manco had a disassembled filtering unit spread out, cleaning away the gudge with careful paddles. The gudge too was a commodity, to be traded as fertilizer, which was a blessing because it accumulated with dreadful speed in the bottom of the fermentation tanks. It was a combination of blown sand, yeast slurry and the crawly stuff that grew on the ceiling, and it had a haunting and deathless smell, but mixed with manure and liberally spread over thin poor Martian soil, it defied superoxidants and made the barley grow.

And everyone agreed that getting the barley to grow was of vital importance.

So Chiring and Manco sang too, somewhat muffled behind recyclable cloth kerchiefs tied over their mouths and noses, joining the last bit of *Some Enchanted Evening* in their respective gruff bass and eerie tenor. A tiny handcam whirred away at them from its place on the table, adding footage to Chiring's ongoing documentary series for the Kathmandu *Post*. Mary nodded with satisfaction that all was well and glanced ceilingward at the last member of her household, who was only now rappelling down from the lowest of the lofts.

"Sorry," said the Heretic, ducking her head in awkward

acknowledgment of tardiness and hurrying off to the kitchen, where she set about denting pans with more than usual effort to make up for being late. Mary followed after, for the Heretic was another problem case requiring patience.

The Heretic had been an Ephesian sister until she had had some kind of accident, about which few details were known, but which had left her blind in one eye and somehow gotten her excommunicated. She had been obliged to leave her convent under something of a cloud; and how she had wound up here on Mars was anybody's guess. She stammered, jittered, and dropped things, but she was at least not the proselytizing kind of heretic, keeping her blasphemous opinions to herself. She was also a passable cook, so Mary had agreed to take her on at the Empress.

"Are you all right?" asked Mary, peering into the darkness of the kitchen, where the Heretic seemed to be chopping freeze-dried soy protein at great speed.

"Yes."

"Don't you want the lights on? You'll cut off a finger," said Mary, turning the lights on, and the Heretic yelped and covered her good eye, swiveling the ocular replacement on Mary in a reproachful kind of way.

"Ow," she said.

"Are you hung over?"

"No," said the Heretic, cautiously uncovering her eye, and Mary saw that it was red as fire.

"Oh, dear. Did you have the dreams again?"

The Heretic stared through her for a moment before saying, in a strange and breathless voice, *"Out of the ground came scarlet flares, each one bursting, a heart's beacon, and He stood above the night and the red swirling cold sand and in His hand held up the Ace of Diamonds. It burned like the flares. He offered it forth, laughing and said: Can you dig it?"*

"Okay," said Mary, after a moment's silence.

"Sorry," said the Heretic, turning back to her cutting board.

"That's all right," said Mary. "Can you get luncheon on by eleven?"

"Yes."

"Oh, good," said Mary, and exited the kitchen.

Lady, grant me an ordinary day, she begged silently, for the last time the Heretic had said something bizarre like that, all manner of strange things had happened.

Yet the day rolled on in its accustomed groove as ordinary as you please. At noon, the luncheon crowd came in, the agricultural workers from the clan and contract laborers from the Settlement, who were either Sherpas like Chiring or Inkas like Manco; few English frequented the Empress of Mars, for all their Queen might smile from its sign.

After noon, when the laboring men and women went trooping back to their shifts through the brown whirling day, and the wind had reached its accustomed hissing howl, there was too much to do to worry. There were plates and bowls to be scoured, there was beer to brew, and there was the constant tinkering necessary to keep all the machines running, lest the window's forcefield fail against the eternal sandblast, among other things.

So Mary had forgotten all about any dire forebodings by the time the blessed afternoon interval of peace came round, and she retired to the best of her tables and put her feet up.

"Mum."

So much for peace. She opened one eye and looked at Rowan, who was standing there gesturing urgently at the communications console.

"Mr. Cochevelou sends his compliments, and would like to know if he might come up the Tube to talk about something," she said.

"Hell," said Mary, leaping to her feet. It was not that she did not like Mr. Cochevelou, clan chieftain (indeed, he was more than a customer and patron); but she had a pretty good idea what it was he wanted to discuss.

"Tell him 'of course,' and then go down and bring up a bottle of the Black Label," she said. She went to fetch a cushion for Mr. Cochevelou's favorite seat.

Cochevelou must have been waiting with his fist on the receiver, for it seemed no more than a minute later he came shouldering his way through the Tube, emerging from the airlock beard first, and behind him three of his household too, lifting their masks and blinking.

"Luck on this house," said Cochevelou hoarsely, shaking the sand from his suit, and his followers mumbled an echo, and Mary noted philosophically the dunelets piling up around their boots.

"Welcome to the Empress, Mr. Cochevelou. Your usual?"

"Bless you, Ma'am, yes," said Cochevelou, and she took his arm and led him away, jerking a thumb at Mona to indicate she should take a broom to the new sand. Mona sighed and obeyed without good grace, but her mother was far too busy trying to read Cochevelou's expression to notice.

Between the beard and the forge-soot, there wasn't much of Cochevelou's face to see; but his light eyes had a shifting look to them today, at once hopeful and uneasy. He watched Mary pour him a shot of Black Label, rubbing his thick fingers across the bridge of his nose and leaving pale streaks there.

"It's like this, Ma'am," he said abruptly. "We're sending Finn home."

"Oh," said Mary, filling another glass. "Congratulations, Mr. Finn."

"It's on account of I'm dying without the sea," said Finn, a smudgy creature in a suit that had been buckled tight and was still too big.

"And with the silicosis," added Cochevelou.

"That's beside the point," said Finn querulously. "I dream at night of the flat wet beach and the salt mist hanging low, and the white terns wheeling above the white wave. Picking dulse from the tidepools where the water lies clear as glass—"

There were involuntary groans from the others, and one of them booted Finn pretty hard in the ankle to make him stop.

"And, see, he goes on like that and drives the rest of us mad with his glass-clear water and all," said Cochevelou, raising his voice slightly as he lifted his cup and saluted Mary. "So what it comes down to is, we've finally saved enough to send one of us home and it's got to be him, you see? Your health, Ma'am."

He drank, and Mary drank, and when they had both drawn breath, she said:

"What's to happen to his Allotment?"

She had cut straight to the heart of the matter, and Cochevelou smiled in a grimacing kind of way.

Under the terms of the Mutual Use Treaty, which had been hammered out during that momentary thaw in relations between England and the Celtic Federation, every settler on Mars had received an Allotment of acreage for private terraforming. With the lease went the commitment to keep the land under cultivation, at the risk of its reverting to the BAC.

The BAC, long since having repented its rash decision to invite so many undesirables to settle on Mars, had gotten into the habit of grabbing back land it did not feel was being sufficiently utilized.

"Well, that's the question," said Cochevelou. "It's twenty long acres of fine land, Ma'am."

"Five in sugar beets and fifteen in the best barley," said Finn.

"With the soundest roof ever built and its own well, and the sweetest irrigation pipes ever laid," said Cochevelou. "You wouldn't mind drinking out of them, I can tell you."

Mary became aware that dead silence had fallen in her house, that all her family were poised motionless with brooms or trays of castware to hear what would be said next.

Barley was the life of the house. It was grown on cold and bitter Mars because it would grow anywhere, but it didn't grow well on the wretched bit of high-oxidant rock clay Mary had been allotted.

"What a pity if it was to revert to the BAC," she said noncommittally.

"We thought so, too," said Cochevelou, turning the cup in his fingers. "Because of course they'd plough that good stuff under and put it in soy, and wouldn't that be a shame? So of course we thought of offering it to you, first, Ma'am."

"How much?" said Mary at once.

"Four thousand punts Celtic," Cochevelou replied.

Mary narrowed her eyes. "How much of that would you take in trade?"

There was a slight pause.

"The BAC have offered us four grand in cash," said Cochevelou, in a somewhat apologetic tone. "You see. But we'd much rather have *you* as a neighbor, wouldn't we? So if there's any way you could possibly come up with the money. . . ."

"I haven't got it," said Mary bluntly, and she meant it too. Her small economy ran almost entirely on barter and goodwill.

"Aw, now, surely you're mistaken about that," said Cochevelou. "You could take up a collection, maybe. All the good workers love your place, and wouldn't they reach into their hearts and their pockets for a timely contribution? And some of your ex-BACs, haven't they got a little redundancy pay socked away in the bottom of the duffel? If you could even scrape together two-thirds for a down, we'd work out the most reasonable terms for you!"

Mary hesitated. She knew pretty well how much her people had, and it didn't amount to a thousand punts even if they presold their bodies to the xenoforensic studies lab. But the Lady might somehow provide, might She not?

"Perhaps I ought to view the property," she said.

"It would be our pleasure," said Cochevelou, grinning white in his sooty beard, and his people exchanged smiles, and Mary thought to herself: *Careful.*

But she rose and suited up, and fitted her mask on tight, and went for a stroll through the airlock with Cochevelou and his people.

The Settlement was quite a bit more now than the single modest dome that had sheltered the first colonists, though that still rose higher than any other structure, and it did have that lovely vizio top so its inhabitants could see the stars, and which gave it a rather Space-Age Moderne look. It wasted heat, though, and who the hell cared enough about two tiny spitspeck moons to venture out in the freezing night and peer upward at them?

The Tubes had a nice modern look too, where the English maintained them, with lots of transparencies that gave onto stunning views of the Red Planet.

To be strictly accurate, it was only a red planet in places. When Mary had come to live there, her first impression had been of an endless cinnamon-colored waste. Now she saw every color but blue, from primrose-curry-tomcat-ochre to flaming persimmon-vermilion through bloodred and so into ever more livery shades of garnet and rust. There were even greens, both the subdued yellowy olive khaki in the rock and the exuberant rich green of the covered acreage.

And Finn's twenty long acres were green indeed, rich as emerald with a barley crop that had not yet come into its silver beard. Mary clanked through the airlock after Cochevelou and stopped, staring.

"The Crystal Palace itself," said Finn proudly, with a wave of his hand.

She pulled off her mask and inhaled. The air stank, of course, from the methane; but it was rich and wet too, and with a certain sweetness. All down the long tunnel roofed with industrial-grade vizio, the barley grew tall, out to that distant point of shade change that must be sugar beet.

"Oh, my," she said, giddy already with the oxygen.

"You see?" said Cochevelou. "Worth every penny of the asking price."

"If I had it," she retorted, making an effort at shrewdness. It was a beautiful holding, one that would give her all the malted barley she could use and plenty to trade on the side or even to sell. . . .

"No wonder the English want this," she said, and her own words echoed in her ears as she regarded the landscape beyond the vizio, the low-domed methane hell of the clan's cattle pens, the towering pipe-maze of Cochevelou's ironworks.

"No wonder the English want this," she repeated, turning to look Cochevelou in the eye. "If they own this land, it divides Clan Morrigan's holdings smack in two, doesn't it?"

"Too right," agreed Finn, "And then they'll file actions to have the cowshed and the ironworks moved as nuisances, see and—ow," he concluded, as he was kicked again.

"And it's all a part of their secret plot to drive us out," said Cochevelou rather hastily. "You see? They've gone and made us an offer we can't refuse. Now we've broke the ground and manured it for them, they've been just waiting and waiting for us to give up and go home, so they can grab it all. The day after we filed the papers to send Finn back, bastardly Inspector Baldwin shows up on our property."

"Didn't his face fall when he saw what a nice healthy crop we had growing here!" said Finn, rubbing his ankle.

"So he couldn't condemn it and get the lease revoked you see?" Cochevelou continued, giving Finn a black look. "Because obviously it ain't abandoned, it's gone into our collective's common ownership. But it wasn't eight hours later he came around with that offer of four thousand for the land. And if we take it, yes, it's a safe bet they'll start bitching and moaning about our cattle and all."

"Don't sell," said Mary. "Or sell to one of your own."

"Sweetheart, you know we've always thought of you as one of our own," said Cochevelou soupily. "Haven't we? But who in our poor clan would ever be able to come up with that kind of money? And as for not selling, why, you and I can see that having the BAC in here would be doom and destruction and (which is worse) lawsuits inevitable somewhere down the road. But it isn't up to me. Most of our folk will only be able to see that big heap of shining BAC brass they're being offered. And they'll vote to take it, see?"

"We could do a lot with that kind of money," sighed Matelot, he who had been most active kicking Finn. "Buy new generators, which we sorely need. More vizio, which as you know is worth its weight in transparent gold. Much as we'd hate to sell to strangers . . ."

"But if you were to buy the land, we'd have our cake and be able to eat it too, you see?" Cochevelou explained.

Mary eyed him resentfully. She saw, well enough: whichever way the dice fell, she was going to lose. If the Clan Morrigan acreage shrank, her little economy would go out of balance. No barley, no beer.

"You've got me in a cleft stick, Cochevelou," she told him, and he looked sad.

"Aren't we both in a cleft stick, and you're just in the tightest part?" he replied. "But all you have to do is come up with the money, and we're both riding in high cotton, and the BAC can go off and fume. Come on now, darling, you don't have to make up your mind right away! We've got thirty days. Go on home and talk it over with your people, why don't you?"

She clapped her mask on and stamped out through the airlock, muttering.

Mary had been accustomed, all her life, to dealing with emergencies. When her father had announced that he was leaving and she'd have to come home from University to take care of her mother, she had coped. She'd found a job, and a smaller apartment, where she and her mother had lived in an uneasy state of truce until her mother had taken all those sleeping pills. Mary had coped again: buried her mother, found a still smaller apartment, and taken night University courses until she'd got her doctorate in xenobotany.

When Alice's father had died, Mary had coped. She'd summoned all her confidence, and found a prestigious research and development job that paid well enough to keep Alice out of the Federation orphanage.

When Rowan's father had deserted, she'd still coped, though he'd waltzed with most of her money; two years' hard work taking extra projects had gotten her on her feet again.

When Mona's father had decided he preferred boys, she had coped without a moment's trouble to her purse if not her heart, secure in her own finances now with lessons hard-learned. And when the BAC headhunters had approached her with a job offer, it had seemed as though it was the Lady's reward for all her years of coping.

A glorious adventure on another world! The chance to explore, to classify, and to enshrine her name forever in the nomenclature of Martian algae! The little girls had listened with round eyes, and only Alice had sulked and wept about leaving her friends, and only for a little while. So they'd all set off together bravely and become Martians, and the girls had adapted in no time, spoiled rotten as the only children on Mars.

And Mary had five years of happiness as a valued member of a scientific team, respected for her expertise, finding more industrial applications for *Cryptogametes gryffyuddi* than George Washington Carver had found for the peanut.

But when she had discovered all there was to discover about useful lichens on Mars (and in five years she had pretty much exhausted the subject), the BAC had no more use for her.

The nasty interview with General Director Rotherhithe had been both unexpected and brief. Her morals were in question, it had seemed. She had all those resource-consuming children, and while that sort of thing might be acceptable in a Celtic Federation country, Mars belonged to England. She was known to indulge in controlled substances, also no crime in the Federation, but certainly morally wrong. And the BAC had been prepared to tolerate her, ah, *religion* in the hopes that it would keep her from perpetuating certain other kinds of immorality, which had unfortunately not been the case—

"What, because I have men to my bed?" Mary had demanded, unfortunately not losing her grasp of English. "You dried-up dirty-minded old stick, I'll bet you'd wink at it if I had other women, wouldn't you? Bloody hypocrite! I've heard you keep a Lesbian Holopeep in your office cabinet—"

Academic communities are small and full of gossip, and even smaller and more full of gossip under a biodome, and secrets cannot be kept at all. So *Julie and Sylvia Take Deportment Lessons from Ms. Lash* had been giggled at, but never mentioned out loud. Until now.

General Director Rotherhithe had had a choking fit and gone a nice shade of lilac, and Sub-Director Thorpe had taken over to say that It was therefore with infinite regret, et cetera. . . .

And Mary had had to cope again.

She hadn't cared that she couldn't afford the fare home; she loved Mars. She had decided she was damned if she was going to be thrown off. So, with her final paycheck, she'd gone into business for herself.

She'd purchased a dome from the Federation colonists, a surplus shelter originally used for livestock; and though the smell took some weeks to go away even in the dry thin air, the walls were sound and warm, and easily remodeled with berths for lodgers.

Chiring, who had had his contract canceled with the BAC for writing highly critical articles about them and sending the columns home to the Kathmandu *Post*, came to her because he too had nowhere else to go. He was a decent mechanic, and helped her repair the broken well pump and set up the generators.

Manco Inka, who had been asked to leave the BAC community because he was discovered to be a (sort of) practicing Christian, brought her a stone-casting unit in exchange for rent, and soon she'd been able to cast her five fine brewing tanks and ever so many cups, bowls, and dishes. Cochevelou himself had stood her the first load of barley for malting.

And once it was known that she had both beer and pretty daughters, the Empress of Mars was in business.

For five years now, it had stood defiantly on its rocky bit of upland slope, the very picture of what a cozy country tavern on Mars ought to be: squat low dome grown all over with lichen patches most picturesque, except on the weather-wall where the prevailing winds blasted it bald with an unceasing torrent of sand, so it had to be puttied constantly with red stonecast leavings to keep it whole there. Mary swapped resources with the clan, with the laborers, with even a few stealthy BAC personnel for fuel and food, and an economy had been born.

And now it was threatened, and she was going to have to cope again.

"Holy Mother, why is it always *something?*" she growled into her mask, kicking through drifts as she stormed back along the Tube. "Could I count on You for even one year where nothing went wrong for once? I could not, indeed.

"And now I'm expected to pull Cochevelou's smoky black chestnuts out of the fire for him, the brute, and where am I to come up with the money? Could You even grant me one little miracle? Oh, no, I'm strong enough to cope on my own, aren't I? I'll solve everyone's problems so they needn't develop the spine to do it themselves, won't I? Bloody hell!"

She came to a transparency and glared out.

Before her was Dead Snake Field, a stretch of rock distinguished by a cairn marking the last resting place of Cochevelou's pet ball python, which had survived the trip to Mars only to escape from its terrarium and freeze to death Outside. Initial hopes that it might be thawed and revived had been dashed when Finn, in an attempt at wit, had set the coiled icicle on his head like a hat and it had slipped off and fallen to the floor, shattering.

There in the pink distance, just under the melted slope of

Mons Olympus, was the sad-looking semicollapsed vizio wall of Mary's own few long acres, the nasty little Allotment she'd been granted almost as a nose-thumbing with her redundancy pay. Its spidery old Aeromotors gave it a deceptively rural look. With all the abundant freaky Martian geology to choose from, the BAC had managed to find her a strip of the most sterile clay imaginable; and though she was unable to farm it very effectively, they had never shown any inclination to snatch it back.

"There's another joke," she snarled. "Fine fertile fields, is it? Oh, damn the old purse-mouth pervert!"

She stalked on and shortly came to the Tube branch leading to her allotment, and went down to see how her own crops were doing.

Plumes of mist were leaking from the airlock seal; now that needed replacing too, something *else* broken she couldn't afford to fix. There were tears in her eyes as she stepped through and lowered her mask, to survey that low yellow wretched barley, fluttering feebly in the oxygen waves. The contrast with Finn's lush fields was too much. She sat down on an overturned bucket and wept, and her tears amounted to one scant drop of water spattering on the sere red clay, fizzing like peroxide.

When her anger and despair were wept out, she remained staring numbly at the fast-drying spot. The clay was the exact color of terracotta.

"I wonder," she said, "whether we could make pots out of the damned stuff."

She didn't need pots, of course; she could stonecast all the household vessels she needed out of Martian dust. What else was clay good for?

Sculpting things, she thought to herself. Works of art? Useful bric-a-brac? Little tiles with SOUVENIR OF MARS stamped into them? Though she had no artistic talent herself, maybe one of her people had, and then what if they could get the Export Bazaar to take pieces on consignment? The Arean Porcelain sold pretty well.

"What the hell," she said, wiping her eyes, and standing up she righted the bucket and fetched a spade from the tool rack. She dug down a meter or so through the hardpan, gasping with effort even in the (comparatively) rich air, and filled the bucket with stiff chunks of clay. Then she put on her mask again and trudged home, lugging the latest hope for a few pounds.

In her house, her family might have been frozen in their places from the moment she'd left. On her entry they came to shamefaced hurried life again, resuming their various household chores as though they'd been hard at work ever since she'd left and not standing around discussing the clan's offer.

Mr. Morton came stalking up to her, knotting his fingers together.

"Er—Ma'am, we've been talking, and—"

"Here, Mama, that's too heavy for you," said Manco, scuttling close and relieving her of the bucket. "You sit down, huh?"

"Very kind, I'm sure," Mary said sourly, looking around. "I'll bet not one of you started the oatmeal stout brewing like I asked, have you? Take that out to the ball mill," she added to Manco, pointing at the bucket. "As long as we've got all this damned clay, let's put it to good use and make something out of it."

"Yes, Mama."

"Here, you sit down—" Mr. Morton gestured her toward a chair with flapping motions of his long arms.

"I can't sit down! I have too much to do. Holy Mother, Alice, that heating unit should have been turned on an hour ago! Do I have to see to everything around here?"

"Water's heating now, Mum," Alice cried, running back from Tank Three.

"Well, but I wanted to tell you about our ideas—if it would be all right—" said Mr. Morton.

"I'm sure it will be when I'm not so busy, Mr. Morton," said Mary, grabbing a push broom and going after the sand again. "Rowan, did you and Chiring reinstall the filter the new way we discussed?"

"Yes, Mum, and—"

"See, I thought we might raise four thousand pounds easily if we put on a sort of cabaret in here," Mr. Morton continued earnestly. "Like a dinner show? I could sing and do dramatic recitals, and—"

"What a very nice idea, Mr. Morton, and I'm sure I'll think

about it, but in the meanwhile I need you to get that sack of oats out of the storage locker."

"And I thought I could do a striptease," said Mona.

Three broom-pushes before the meaning sank in, and then:

"Striptease?" Mary shouted. "Are you mad? When the BAC already sees us as a cesspit of immorality and substance abuse? That'd really frost the cake!"

Mona pouted. "But you said when you were at University—"

"That was a long time ago and I needed the money, and—"

"And we need the money now! We *never* have any money!"

"Ladies, please—" said poor Mr. Morton, his face pink for once.

"The oats, Mr. Morton. Mona, you will keep your clothes on until you come of age and that's all that will be said on the subject, do you understand?"

"What's this?" said Manco, emerging from the utility area and holding out something in his hand. He had an odd look on his face. "This was in the bottom of the bucket. The clay cracked apart and—"

"It's a rock," said Mary, glancing at it. "Pitch it out."

"I don't think it's a rock, Mama."

"He's right," said Chiring, squinting at it. "It looks more like a crystal."

"Then put it on the back bar with the fossils and we'll ask one of the geologists about it. What was that?" Mary looked up suspiciously. "Who's that? Who just threw up?"

"It was me," said Alice miserably, emerging from behind the bar, and Rowan ran to her with a bar towel.

Mary ground her teeth. "Food poisoning. Just what we all needed. That devil-worshipping looney—" She started for the kitchen with blood in her eye, but was stopped in her tracks as Rowan said quietly:

"It's not food poisoning, Mum."

Mary did an about-face, staring at her daughters. There was a profound moment of silence in which she continued staring, and the three men present wondered what was going on, until Alice wailed:

"Well, I didn't think you could *get* pregnant on Mars!"

So in all the excitement, the crystal was stuck on the back bar and forgotten until that evening, when the Brick came in from his polar run.

The Brick was so named because he resembled one. Not only was he vast and tall and wide in his quilted Hauler's jumpsuit, he was the color of a brick as well, though what shade he might be under years of high-impact red dust was anybody's guess.

There was red grit between his teeth when he grinned, as he did now on emerging from the airlock, and his bloodshot red eyes widened in the pleasant evening darkness of the Empress. He lifted his head and sucked in air through a nose flattened as a gorilla's from years of collisions with fists, boots, steering wheels, and (it was rumored) hospital orderlies' foreheads. He had been on Mars a long, long time.

"Damn, I love that smell," he howled in English, striding to the bar and slapping down his gauntlets. "Beer, onions, and soy-gold nuggets frying, eh? Give me a Party Platter with Bisto and a pitcher of Foster's."

"I'm afraid we don't have Foster's, sir," dithered Mr. Morton. Mary elbowed him.

"It's what we call the Ares Lager when he's in here," she murmured, and Mr. Morton ran off at once to fill a pitcher.

"How's it going, Beautiful?"

"Tolerably, Mr. Brick," said Mary, sighing.

He looked at her keenly and his voice dropped a couple of decibels when he said, "Trouble over something? Did the BAC finally get that warrant?"

"What warrant?"

"Oh, nothing you need to know about right now," he said casually, accepting his pitcher of beer and drinking from it. "Not to worry, doll. Uncle Brick hears rumors all the time, and half of 'em never pan out. As long as the Ice Haulers want you here, you'll stay here."

"I suppose they're trying to get me closed down again," said Mary. "Bad cess to them, and what else is new? But I have other problems today."

She told him about the day's occurrences and he listened, sipping and nodding meanwhile, grunting occasionally in agreement or surprise.

"Congratulations, m'dear," he said. "This'll be the first human child born on Mars, you know that? Any idea who the father is?"

"She knows who she *hasn't* been with, at least," said Mary. "And there'll be tests, so it's not as though we'll be in suspense for long. It's only a baby, after all. But where am I going to get four thousand punts, I'd like to know?"

Brick rumbled meditatively, shaking his head.

"'Only a baby', she says. You know they're not having 'em Down Home any more, don't you?"

"Oh, that's certainly not true. I had three myself," said Mary indignantly.

"The birth rate's dropping, all the same," said the Brick, having another sip of his beer. "That's what I hear. Funny thing for a species to do when it's colonizing other planets, isn't it?"

Mary shrugged. "I'm sure it isn't as bad as all that," she said. "Life will go on somehow. It always does. The Goddess provides."

"I guess so," agreed Brick, and his voice rose to a genial roar as he hailed the Heretic, shuffling out from the kitchen with his Party Platter. "Hey, sweetheart! You're looking gorgeous this evening."

The Heretic blinked at him and shuffled closer. "Hi," she said, offering him the food. He took it in one hand and swept her close for a kiss on the forehead.

"How've you been?"

"I saw the living glory burning. A bright tower in the icy waste," she said.

"That's nice. Can I get just a little more Bisto on these fries?"
"Okay."

The Heretic went back to the kitchen and fetched out a little saucepan of gravy-like substance, and as she larded Brick's dinner, Mary went on:

"If you could see that twenty acres! It was as rich as pudding, probably from our very own sewage we sold them, and green as anything on Earth. Where I'm going to get the cash for it I simply do not know. Chiring makes forty punts a week from his column in the Kathmandu *Post*, of which he has kindly offered me ten per week toward the land, but I've only got a month. If one of my people was a brilliant artist we might sell some folk art out of clay, but all of them protested they're quite talentless, so bang goes another good idea, and I'm running out of good ideas. Just when I thought everything had settled down to some kind of equilibrium—"

"What's that new thing on the back bar?" inquired Brick, slightly muffled because his mouth was full.

"Oh. That? Wait, you were a mineralogist, weren't you?" Mary paused, looking over her shoulder at him as she fetched the crystal down.

"I have been many things, m'dear," he informed her, washing down his mouthful with more beer. "And I did take a degree in Mineralogy at the University of Queensland once."

"Then you have a look at it. It was in some clay I dug up this afternoon. Maybe quartz with some cinnabar stain? Or more of the ever-present rust? It's a funny old thing." She tossed it over and he caught it in his massive hand, peered at it for a long moment.

Then he unflapped his transport suit, reached into the breast and brought out a tiny spectrometer mounted in a headset. He slipped it on with one hand, holding the crystal out to the light with the other. He stared through the eyepiece for a long moment.

"Or do you think it's some kind of agate?" said Mary.

"No," Brick replied, turning and turning the crystal in his hand. "Unless this gizmo is mistaken, sweetheart, you've got yourself a diamond here."

Nobody believed it. How could something that looked like a lump of frozen tomato juice be worth anything? *A diamond?*

Whatever it turned out to be, however, everyone agreed that the BAC must not be told.

Cochevelou offered to trade the glorious twenty acres for the rock outright, and in fact proposed to Mary. Smiling, she declined. But terms of sale for the land were worked out and a deposit of ten punts was accepted, and the transfer of title was registered with the BAC by Mr. Morton, who as a Briton seemed less likely to annoy the authorities.

And on the appointed day, the rock was sewn into the lining of Finn's thermal suit, and he was seen off to the spaceport with much cheer, after promising faithfully to take the diamond straight to the best dealers in Amsterdam immediately on arriving Down Home.

The next they heard of him, however, was that he was found drowned and smiling on the rocks at Antrim not three weeks after his homecoming, a bottle still clutched in his hand.

Mary shrugged. She had title to the land, and Cochevelou had ten punts a week from her. For once, she thought to herself, she had broken even.

2

THE RICHEST WOMAN ON MARS

It was the Queen's Birthday, and Mary was hosting the Cement Kayak Regatta.

Outdoor sports were possible on Mars. Just.

Not to the extent that the famous original advertising holo implied (grinning man in shirtsleeves with football and micromask, standing just outside an airlock door, captioned: "This man is actually STANDING on the SURFACE of MARS!" though without any mention of the fact that the holo had been taken at noon on the hottest day in summer at the equator and that the man remained outside for exactly five seconds before the shot was taken, after which he leaped back inside and begged for a bottle of Visine), but possible nonetheless, especially if you were inventive.

The cement kayaks had been cast of the ever-present and abundant Martian grit, and fitted at one end with tiny antigravity units. These, like so many other things on Mars, did not work especially well, but enabled the kayaks to float about two feet above the ground. Indoors, they bobbed aimlessly in place, having no motive power; once pushed out an airlock, they were at the mercy of the driving winds.

But it was possible to deflect or direct the wind with big double-bladed paddles made of scrap pipe and sheet metal, salvaged from the BAC's refuse tip. It was then possible to sail along through the air, if you wore full Outside kit, and actually sort of steer.

So Cement Kayaking had become a favorite sport on Mars, indeed the only outdoor sport. An obstacle course had been set up in Dead Snake Field, and four kayaks lurched about in it now, fighting the wind and each other.

"Competitive sport and the pioneer spirit," Chiring was announcing into his handcam, a solemn talking head against a background of improbable action. "Anachronisms on Earth, do they fulfill a vital function here on the final frontier? Have these colonists fallen back on degrading social violence, or is cultural evolution an ongoing process on Mars?" Nobody answered him.

The Tube was blocked with spectators, crowding around the transparencies to watch. They were also shouting, which dried their throats nicely, so the beer was selling well.

"LEFT, RAMSAY!" howled Cochevelou, pointing vainly at the hololoop of Queen Anne waving that served as the mid-point marker. "Oh, you stupid little git, LEFT!"

"A Phobos Porter for you, Cochevelou?" Mary inquired cheerily. "On the house?"

"Yes please," he growled. Mary beckoned and the Heretic trudged back along the line. She turned to display the castware tank she bore in its harness on her back, and Mary selected a mug from the dangling assortment and drew a pint with practiced ease.

Cochevelou took it, lifted his mask and gulped it down, wiping the foam from his moustache with the back of his hand.

"Very kind of you, I'm sure," he said bitterly. "Given the amount I'm losing today. YOU'RE A DISGRACE TO FLUFFY'S MEMORY!" he bellowed at Ramsay. Fluffy had been the python's name.

"*We buried evil on Mars,*" said the Heretic in a dreamy little voice, and nobody paid any attention to her.

"It's not really his fault," said Mary. "How can the poor man hope to compete with our Manco? It's all those extra blood vessels in his fingertips, you know, from being born in the Andes. Gives him better control of the paddles. Selected by Nature, as it were."

"You must have bet a packet on him," said Cochevelou, staring as Manco swung round Fluffy's Cairn and sent Ramsay spinning off to the boundary with an expert paddle-check.

"Bet? Now, dear Mr. Cochevelou, where would I get the money to do that?" said Mary, smiling wide behind her mask. "You're getting every penny I earn for Finn's Field, so you are."

Cochevelou grimaced.

"Speak no ill of the dead and all, but if I could ever get my hands on that little bastard's neck—" he said.

"Beer please," said one of the BAC engineers, shouldering through the crowd.

"A pint for the English!" Mary announced, and he looked around guiltily and pulled up the hood of his suit. "How nice of you to come down here to our primitive little fete. Perhaps later we can do some colorful folk dancing for your amusement." She handed him a mug. "That'll be one punt Celtic."

"I heard you'll take air filters," said the engineer in an undertone.

"What size, dear?"

"BX3s," replied the engineer, drawing one from the breast of his suit and displaying it. Mary inspected it critically and took it from him.

"Your gracious patronage is always appreciated," she said, and handed it to the Heretic, who tucked it out of sight. "Enjoy your beer. You see, Cochevelou? No money in my hands at all. What's a poor little widow to do?"

But Cochevelou missed the sarcasm, staring over her head down the tunnel.

"Who's this coming?" he said. "Did they bring a passenger on the last transport up?"

Mary turned and saw the newcomer, treading gingerly along in the cat-step people walked with before they became accustomed to Martian gravity. He was tall, and wore a shiny new thermal suit, and he carried a bukecase. He was peering uncertainly through his goggles at the crowd around the transparencies.

"That's a damned solicitor, that's what that is," said Cochevelou, scowling blackly. "Five'll get you ten he's come to see you or me."

Mary's lip curled. She watched as the newcomer studied the crowd. He swung his mask in her direction at last, and stared; then walked toward her decisively.

"It's you, eh?" said Cochevelou, trying not to sound too relieved as he sidled away. "My sympathies, Mary darling."

"MS. GRIFFITH?" inquired the stranger. Mary folded her arms.

"I am," she replied.

"ELIPHAL DE WIT," he said. "I'VE HAD QUITE A TIME FINDING YOU!"

"TURN YOUR SPEAKER DOWN! I'M NOT DEAF!"

"OH! I'M sorry," said Mr. De Wit, hurriedly twiddling the knob. "Is that better? They didn't seem to know who you were at the port office, and then they admitted you were still resident but unemployed, but they wouldn't tell me where you lived. Very confusing."

"You're not from the BAC, then?" Mary looked him up and down.

"What?" Mr. De Wit started involuntarily at the crowd's roar of excitement. The English kayaker had just swung past the midway marker. "No. Didn't you get my communication? I'm from Polieos of Amsterdam."

"WHAT?" said Mary, without benefit of volume knob.

"I'm here about your diamond," Mr. De Wit explained.

"And to think I thought you were a solicitor at first!" Mary babbled, setting down a pitcher of batch and two mugs.

"Actually, Ms. Griffith, I am one," said Mr. De Wit, gazing around at the inside of the Empress. "On permanent retainer for Polieos, to deal with special circumstances."

"Really?" Mary halted in the act of reaching to fill his mug.

"And I'm here as your counsel," he explained carefully. "There has really been no precedent for this situation. Polieos feels it would be best to proceed with a certain amount of caution at first."

"Don't they want to buy my diamond, then?" Mary demanded.

"Absolutely, yes, Ms. Griffith," Mr. De Wit assured her. "And we would prefer to buy it from you. I'm here to determine whether or not we can legally do that."

"What d'you mean?"

"Well—" Mr. De Wit lifted his mug and paused, staring down at the brown foam brimming. "Er—what are we drinking?"

"It's water we've put things in, because you wouldn't want to drink Mars water plain," said Mary impatiently. "No alcohol in it, dear, so it won't hurt you if you're not a drinking man. Cut to the chase, please."

Mr. De Wit set his mug aside, folded his hands and said:

"In a minute, I'm going to ask you how you got the diamond, but I'm going to tell you a few things first, and it's important that you listen closely.

"What you sent us is a red diamond, a true red, which is very rare. The color doesn't come from impurities, but from the arrangement of the crystal lattice within the stone itself. It weighs 306 carats at the present time, uncut, and preliminary analysis indicates it has remarkable potential for a modified trillion cut. It would be a unique gem even if it hadn't come from Mars. The fact that it did makes its potential value quite a bit greater."

He took the buke from its case and connected the projector arm and dish. Mary watched with suspicion as he completed setup and switched it on. After a couple of commands, a holo-image shot forth, hanging in the dark air between them, and Mary recognized the lump she'd entrusted to Finn.

"That's my diamond!"

"As it is now," said Mr. De Wit. "Here's what we propose to do with it." He gave another command and the sullen rock vanished. In its place was an artist's conception of a three-cornered stone the color of an Earth sunset. Mary caught her breath.

"Possibly 280 carats," said Mr. De Wit.

"What's it worth?"

"That all depends," Mr. De Wit replied. "A diamond is only worth the highest price you can get for it. The trick is to make it *desirable*. It's red, it's from Mars—those are big selling points. We'll need to give it a fancy name. At present," and he coughed apologetically, "it's being called the Big Mitsubishi, but the marketing department will probably go with either the War-God's Eye or the Heart of Mars."

"Yes, yes, whatever," said Mary.

"Very well. And Polieos is prepared to cut, polish, and market the diamond. We can do this as your agents, in which case our fee will be deducted from the sale price, or we can buy it from you outright. *Assuming*," and Mr. De Wit held up a long forefinger warningly, "that we can establish that you are, in fact, the owner."

"Hm." Mary frowned at the tabletop. She had a pretty good idea of what was coming next.

"You see, Ms. Griffith, under the terms of your Allotment lease with the BAC, you are entitled to any produce grown on the land. The terms of your lease do not include mineral rights to the aforesaid land. Therefore—"

"If I dug it up on my Allotment, it belongs to the BAC," said Mary.

"Exactly. If, however, someone sold you the diamond," and Mr. De Wit looked around at the Empress again, his gaze dwelling on the more-than-rustic details, "say perhaps some colorful local character who found it somewhere else and traded it to you for a drink—well, then, not only is it your diamond, but we have a very nice story for the marketing department at Polieos."

"I see," said Mary.

"Good. And now, Ms. Griffith, if you please: how did you come into possession of the diamond?" Mr. De Wit sat back and folded his hands.

Mary spoke without pause. "Why, sir, one of our regulars brought it in! An Ice Hauler, as it happens, and he found it somewhere on his travels between poles. Traded it to me for two pints of my best Ares Lager."

"Excellent." Smiling, Mr. Dr. Wit shut off the buke and stood. "And now, Ms. Griffith, may I see the Allotment where you didn't find the diamond?"

As they were walking back from the field, and Mr. De Wit was wiping the clay from his hands, he said quietly:

"It's just as well the land isn't producing anything much.

When the diamond becomes public knowledge, you can expect the BAC to make you an offer for the Allotment."

"Even though I didn't find the diamond there?" said Mary warily.

"Yes. And I would take whatever they offer, Ms. Griffith, and I would buy passage back to Earth."

"I'll take what they offer, but I'm not leaving Mars," said Mary. "I've hung on through bad luck and I'm damned if good luck will pry me out. This is my home!"

Mr. De Wit tugged at his beard, unhappy about something.

"You'll have more than enough money to live in comfort on Earth," he said. "And things are about to change up here, you know. As soon as anyone suspects there's real money to be made on Mars, you won't know the place."

"I think I'll do smashing, whatever happens," said Mary. "Miners drink, don't they? Anywhere people go to get rich, they need places to spend their money."

"That's true," said Mr. De Wit, sighing.

"And just think what I can do with all that money!" Mary crowed. "No more making do with the BAC's leftovers!" She paused by a transparency and pointed out at the red desolation. "See that? It's nobody's land. I could have laid claim to it any time this five years, but what would I have done with it? It's the bloody BAC has the water and the lights and the heating and the vizio I'd need!

"But with *money*. . . ."

By the time they got back to the Empress, she was barreling along in her enthusiasm with such speed that Mr. De Wit was panting as he tried to keep up. She jumped in through the airlock, faced her household (just in from the field of glorious combat and settling down to a celebratory libation) flung off her mask, and cried: "Congratulate me, you lot! I'm the richest woman on Mars!"

"You did bet on the match," said Rowan reproachfully.

"I did not," said Mary, thrusting a hand at Mr. De Wit. "You know who this kind gentleman is? This is my extremely good friend from Amsterdam." She winked hugely. "He's a *gem* of a man. A genuine *diamond* in the rough. And he's brought your mother very good news, my dears."

Stunned silence while everyone took that it, and then Mona leaped up screaming.

"*Thediamondthediamondthediamond!* Omigoddess!"

"How much are we getting for it?" asked Rowan at once.

"Well—" Mary looked at Mr. De Wit. "There's papers and things to sign, first, and we have to find a buyer. But there'll be more than enough to fix us all up nicely, I'm sure."

"Very probably," Mr. De Wit agreed.

"We finally won't be POOR anymore!" caroled Mona, bounding up and down.

"Congratulations, Mama!" said Manco.

"Congratulations, Mother," said Chiring.

Mr. Morton giggled uneasily.

"So . . . this means you're leaving Mars?" he said. "What will the rest of us do?"

"I'm not about to leave," Mary assured him. His face lit up.

"Oh, that's wonderful! Because I've got nothing to go back to, down there, you know, and Mars has been the first place I ever really—"

"What do you MEAN we're not leaving?" said Alice in a strangled kind of voice. "You're ruining my life *again*, aren't you?"

She turned and fled. Her bedchamber being as it was in a loft accessible only by rope ladder, Alice was unable to leap in and fling herself on her bed, there to sob furiously; so she resorted to running away to the darkness behind the brew tanks and sobbing there.

". . . felt as though I belonged in a family," Mr. Morton continued.

Alice might weep, but she was outvoted.

Rowan opted to stay on Mars. Mona waffled on the question until the boy-to-girl ratio on Earth was explained to her, after which she firmly cast her lot with the Red Planet. Chiring had no intention of leaving; his *Dispatches from Mars* had doubled the number of subscribers to the Kathmandu *Post*, which was run by his sister's husband, and as a result of the Mars exposés he looked fair to win Nepal's highest journalism award.

Manco had no intention of leaving either, since it would be difficult to transport his life's work. This was a shrine in a grotto three kilometers from the Empress, containing a cast-stone life-sized statue of the Virgen de Guadalupe surrounded by roses sculpted from a mixture of pink Martian dust and Manco's own blood. It was an ongoing work of art, and an awesome and terrible thing.

The Heretic, when asked if she would like to return to Earth, became so distraught that her ocular implant telescoped and retracted uncontrollably for five minutes before she was able to stammer out a refusal. She would not elaborate. Later she drank half a bottle of Black Label and was found unconscious behind the malt locker.

"So, you see? We're staying," said Mary to the Brick, in grim triumph.

"Way to go, Beautiful," said the Brick, raising his breakfast pint of Ares Lager. "I just hope you're ready to deal with the BAC, because this'll *really* get up their noses. And I hope you can trust this Dutchman."

"Here he is now," said Chiring *sotto voce*, looking up from the taphead he was in the act of changing. They raised their heads to watch Mr. De Wit's progress down from the ceiling on his line. He made it to the floor easily and tied off his line like a native, without one wasted gesture; but as he turned to them again, he seemed to draw the character of Hesitant Tourist about him like a cloak, stooping slightly as he peered through the gloom.

"Good morning, sir, and did you sleep well?" Mary cried brightly.

"Yes, thank you," Mr. De Wit replied. "Er—I was wondering where I might get some laundry done?"

"Bless you, sir, we don't have Earth-style laundries up here," said Mary. "Best you think of it as a sort of dry-cleaning. Leave it in a pile on your bunk and I'll send one of the girls up for it later." She cleared her throat. "And this is my friend Mr. Brick. Brick is the, ahem, *colorful local character* who sold me the diamond. Aren't you, dear?"

"That's right," said the Brick, without batting an eye. "Howdy, stranger."

"Oh, great!" Mr. De Wit pulled his buke from his coat.

"Would you be willing to record a statement to that effect?"

"Sure," said the Brick, kicking the bar stool next to him. "Have a seat. We'll talk."

Mr. De Wit sat down and set up his buke, and Mary drew him a pint of batch and left them talking. She was busily sweeping sand when Manco entered through the airlock and came straight up to her. His face was impassive, but his black eyes glinted with anger.

"You'd better come see something, Mama," he said.

"I went to replace the old lock seal like you told me," he said, pointing. "Then I looked through. No point now, huh?"

Mary stared at her Allotment. It had never been a sight to rejoice the eye, but now it was the picture of all desolation. Halfway down the acreage someone had slashed through the vizio wall, and the bitter Martian winds had widened the tear and brought in a freight of red sand, which duned in long ripples over what remained of her barley, now blasted and shriveled with cold. Worse still, it was trampled: for someone had come in through the hole and excavated here and there, long channels orderly cut in the red clay or random potholes. There were Outside-issue bootprints all over.

She said something heartfelt and unprintable.

"You think it was the BAC?" said Manco.

"Not likely," Mary said. "They don't know about the diamond, do they? This has *Clan Morrigan* written all over it."

"We can't report this, can we?"

Mary shook her head. "That'd be just what the BAC would want to hear. 'Vandalism, is it, Ms. Griffith? Well, what can you expect in a criminal environment such as what you've fostered here, Ms. Griffith? Perhaps you'd best crawl off into the sand and die, Ms. Griffith, and stop peddling your nasty beer and Goddess-worshipping superstitions and leave Mars to decent people, Ms. Griffith!' That's what they'd say."

"And they'd say, 'What were people digging for?' too," said Manco gloomily.

"So they would." Mary felt a chill. "I think I must speak with Mr. De Wit again."

"What should I do here?"

"Seal up the vizio with duct tape," Mary advised. "Then get the quaddy out and plough it all under."

"Quaddy needs a new air filter, Mama."

"Use a sock! Works just as well," said Mary, and stamped away back up the Tube.

Manco surveyed the ruined Allotment and sighed. Resolving to offer Her another rose of his heart's blood if She would render assistance, he wrestled the rusting quaddy out of its garage and squatted to inspect the engine.

Mr. De Wit and the Brick were still where Mary had left them, deep in conversation; the Brick seemed to be regaling Mr. De Wit with exciting tales of his bipolar journeys for carbon dioxide and water ice. Mr. De Wit was listening with his mouth slightly open.

Mary started toward him, intent on a hasty conference, but Rowan stepped into her path.

"Mum, Mr. Cochevelou wants a word," she said in an undertone.

"Cochevelou!" Mary said, turning with a basilisk glare, and spotted him in his customary booth. He smiled at her, rubbing his fingertips together in a nervous kind of way, and seemed to shrink back into the darkness as she advanced on him.

"Eh, I imagine you've come from your old Allotment," he said. "That's just what I wanted to talk to you about, Mary dearest."

"Don't you Mary Dearest me!" she told him.

"Darling! Darling. You've every right to be killing mad, so you do. I struck the bastards to the floor with these two hands when I found out, so I did. 'You worthless thieving pigs!' I said to them. 'Aren't you ashamed of yourselves?' I said. 'Here we are in this cold hard place and do we stick together in adversity, as true Celts ought? Won't the English laugh and nod at us when they find out?' That's what I said."

"Words are all you have for me, are they?" said Mary icily.

"No indeed, dear," said Cochevelou, looking wounded. "Aren't I talking compensation? But you have to understand that some of the lads come of desperate stock, and there's some will always envy another's good fortune bitterly keen."

"How'd they know about my good fortune?" Mary demanded.

"Well, your Mona might have told our DeWayne," said Cochevelou. "Or it might have gone about the Tube some other way, but good news travels fast, eh? And there's no secrets up here anyway, as we both know. The main thing is, we're dealing with it. The clan has voted to expel the dirty beggars forthwith—"

"Much good that does me!"

"And to award you Finn's Field free and clear, all further payments waived," Cochevelou added.

"That's better." Mary relaxed slightly.

"And perhaps we'll find other little ways to make it up to you," said Cochevelou, pouring her a cup of her own Black Label. "I can send work parties over to mend the damage. New vizio panels for you, what about it? And free harrowing and manuring that poor tract of worthless ground."

"I'm sure you'd love to get your boys in there digging again," Mary grumbled, accepting the cup.

"No, no; they're out, as I told you," said Cochevelou. "We're shipping their raggedy asses back to Earth on the next flight."

"Are you?" Mary halted in the act of raising the cup to her lips. She set it down. "And where are you getting the money for that, pray?"

Cochevelou winced.

"An unexpected inheritance?" he suggested, and dodged the cup that came flying at him.

"You hound!" Mary cried. "They'll have an unexpected inheritance sewn into their suits, won't they? Won't they, you black beast?"

"If you'd only be mine, all this wouldn't matter," said Cochevelou wretchedly, crawling from the booth and making for the airlock with as much dignity as he could muster. "We could rule Mars together, you know that, don't you?"

He didn't wait for an answer, but pulled his mask on and fled through the airlock. Mary nearly pitched the bottle after him too and stopped herself, aware that all her staff, as well as Mr. De Wit and the Brick, were staring at her.

"Mr. De Wit," she said, as decorously as she could, "May I have a world with you in private?"

"That was sooner than I expected," said Mr. De Wit, when she'd told him all about it.

"You expected this?" Mary said.

"Of course," he replied, tugging unhappily at his beard. "Have you ever heard of the Gold Rush of 1849? I don't know if you know much American history, Ms. Griffith—"

"Gold was discovered at Sutter's Mill," Mary snapped.

"Yes, and do you know what happened to Mr. Sutter? Prospectors destroyed his farm. He was ruined."

"I won't be ruined," Mary declared. "If I have to put a guard on that field every hour of the day and night, I'll do it."

"It's too late for that," Mr. De Wit explained. "The secret can't be kept any longer, you see? More Martian settlers will be putting more red diamonds on the market. The value will go down, but that won't stop the flood of people coming up here hoping to get rich."

And he was right.

For five years, there had been one shuttle from Earth every three months. They might have come more often; technological advances over the last couple of decades had greatly trimmed travel time to Mars. There just hadn't been any reason to waste the money.

The change came slowly at first, and was barely noticed: an unaccustomed distant thunder of landing jets at unexpected moments, a stranger wandering wide-eyed into the Empress at odd hours. More lights glinting under the vizio dome of BAC headquarters after dark.

Then the change sped up.

More shuttles, arriving all hours, and not just the big green BAC ships but vessels of all description, freelance transport services competing. More strangers lining the bar at the Empress, shivering, gravity-sick, unable to get used to the smell or the taste of the beer or the air but unable to do without either.

Strangers wandering around outside the Tubes, inadequately

suited, losing their sense of direction in the sandstorms and having to be rescued on a daily basis by some opportunistic Celt who charged for his kindness: "Just to pay for the oxygen expenditure, see?" Strangers losing or abandoning all manner of useful odds and ends in the red desolation, to be gleefully salvaged by the locals. Mary's back bar became a kind of shrine to the absurd items people brought from Earth, such as a digital perpetual calendar geared to 365 days in a year, a pair of ice skates, a ballroom dancing trophy, and a snow globe depicting the Historic Astoria Column of Astoria, Oregon.

"I can't think why you advised me to leave," Mary said to Mr. De Wit, as he sat at the bar. "We've never done so well!"

Mr. De Wit shook his head gloomily, staring into the holoscreen above his buke. "It's all a matter of timing," he said, and drained his mug of Ares Lager.

"Let me pour you another, sweetheart," said Alice, fetching away the empty. Mary watched her narrowly. To everyone's astonishment but Alice's, Mr. De Wit had proposed marriage to her. As far as Mary had been able to tell, it had happened somehow because Alice had been the one delegated to collect his laundry, and had made it a point to personally deliver his fresh socks and thermals at an inappropriate hour, and one thing had led to another, as it generally did in the course of human history, whether on Earth or elsewhere.

He accepted another mug from her now with a smile. Mary shrugged to herself and was about to retreat in a discreet manner when there was a tremendous crash in the kitchen.

When she got to the door, she beheld the Heretic crouched in a corner, rocking herself to and fro, white and silent. On the floor lay Mary's largest kettle and a great quantity of wasted water, sizzling slightly as it interacted with the dust that had been tracked in.

"What's this?" said Mary.

The Heretic turned her face. "*They're coming,*" she whispered. "*And the mountain's on fire.*"

Mary felt a qualm, but said quietly: "Your vision's a bit late. The place is already full of newcomers. What, did you think you saw something in the water? There's nothing in there but red mud. Pick yourself up and—"

There was another crash, though less impressive, and a high-pitched yell of excitement. Turning, Mary beheld Mr. De Wit leaping up and down, fists clenched above his head.

"We did it," he cried, "We found a buyer!"

"How much?" Mary asked instantly.

"Two million punts Celtic," he replied, gasping after his exertion. "Mitsubishi, of course, because we aimed all the marketing at them. I just wasn't sure—I've instructed Polieos to take their offer. I hope that meets with your approval, Ms. Griffith? Because, you know, no one will ever get that kind of money for a Martian diamond again."

"Won't they?" Mary was puzzled by his certainty. "Whyever not?"

"Well—" Mr. De Wit coughed dust, took a gulp from his pint and composed himself. "Because most of the appeal was in the novelty, and in the story behind your particular stone, and—and timing, like I said. Now the publicity will work against the market. Those stones that were stolen out of your field will go on sale at inflated prices, you see? Everyone will expect to make a fortune."

"But they won't?"

"No, because—" Mr. De Wit waved vaguely. "Do you know why they say *A diamond is forever*? Because it's murder to unload the damned things, in the cold hard light of day. No dealer ever buys back a stone they've sold. It took a fantastic amount of work to sell the Big Mitsubishi. We were very, very lucky. Nobody else will have our luck."

He stooped forward and put his hands on her shoulders. "Now, please. Follow my advice. Take out a little to treat yourself and put the rest in high-yield savings, or very careful investments."

"Or I'll tell you what you could do," said a bright voice from the bar.

They turned to see the Brick in the act of downing a pint. He finished, wiped his mouth with the back of his hand and said: "You could sink a magma well up the hill on Mons Olympus, and start your own energy plant. That'd really screw the BAC! And make you a shitload of money on the side.

"Magma well?" Mary repeated.

"Old-style geothermal energy. Nobody's used it since Fusion, because Fusion's cheaper, but it'd work up here. The BAC's been debating a plant, but their committees are so brain-constipated they'll never get around to it!" The Brick rose to his feet in his enthusiasm. "Hell, all you'd need would be a water-drilling rig, to start with. And you'd need to build the plant and lay pipes, but you can afford that now, right? Then you'd have all the power you'd want to grow all the barley you'd want *and* sell it to other settlers!"

"I suppose I could do that, couldn't I?" said Mary slowly. She looked up at Mr. De Wit. "What do you think? Could I make a fortune with a magma well?"

Mr. De Wit sighed.

"Yes," he said. "I have to tell you that you could."

The only difficult part was getting the drilling rig.

Cochevelou looked uncertainly at Mona, who had perched herself on one of his knees, and then at Rowan, who was firmly stationed on the other with her fingers twined in his beard.

"Please, Mr. Cochevelou, my dear dearest?" Mona crooned.

Mary leaned forward and filled his glass, looking him straight in the eye.

"You said we might rule Mars together," she said. "Well, this is the way to do it. You and me together, eh, pooling our resources as we've always done?"

"You staked claim to the whole volcano?" he said, incredulous. "Bloody honking huge Mons Olympus?"

"Nothing in the laws said I couldn't, if I had the cash for the filing fee, which, being the richest woman on Mars now, I *had,* of course," Mary replied. "Nothing in the tiniest print said I was even obliged to tell the BAC. I had my fine lawyer *and* nearly son-in-law Mr. De Wit file with the Tri-Worlds Settlement Bureau, and they just said Yes, Ms. Griffith, here's your virtual title and good luck to you. Doubtless sniggering in their First World sleeves and wondering what a silly widow woman will do with a big frozen cowpat of a volcano. They'll see!"

"But—" Cochevelou paused and took a drink. His pause lost him ground, for Mary shoved Mona out of the way and took her place on his knee, bringing her gimlet stare, and her bosom, closer.

"Think of it, darling man!" she said. "Think how we've been robbed, and kept down, and made to make do with the dry leavings while the *English* got the best of everything! Haven't we always triumphed by turning adversity to our own uses? And so it'll be now. Your ironworks and your strong lads with my money and Mars's own hot heart itself beating for us in a thunderous counterpoint to our passion!"

"Passion?" said Cochevelou, somewhat dazed but beginning to smile.

"She's got him," Chiring informed the others, who were lurking in the kitchen. Mr. Morton gave a cheer, which was promptly shut off as Manco and the Heretic clapped their hands over his mouth. Chiring put his eye to the peephole again.

"They're shaking hands," he said. "He just kissed her. She hasn't slapped him. She's saying . . . something about Celtic Energy Systems."

"It's the beginning of a new world!" whispered Mr. Morton. "There's never been money on Mars, but—but—now we can have Centres for the Performing Arts!"

"We can have a lot more than that," said Manco.

"They could found a whole other city," said Chiring, stepping back. "You know? What a story this is going to be!"

"We could attract artistes," said Mr. Morton, stars in his eyes. "*Culture!*"

"We could be completely independent, if we bought vizio and water pumps, and got enough land under cultivation," Manco pointed out. A look of shock crossed his face. "I could grow *real* roses."

"You could," Chiring agreed, whipping out his jotpad. "*Interviews with the Locals: What Will Money Mean to the New Martians?* By your News Martian. Okay, Morton, you'd want performing arts, and *you'd* develop Martian horticulture." He nodded at Manco and then glanced over at the Heretic. "How about you? What do you hope to get out of this?"

"A better place to hide," she said bleakly, raising her head as she listened to the rumble of the next shuttle arriving.

It was still possible to ride an automobile on Mars, though they had long since become illegal on Earth and Luna.

A great deal of preparation was necessary, to be sure: one had first to put on a suit of thermals, and then a suit of cotton fleece, and then a suit of bubblefilm, and then a final layer of quilted Outside wear. Boots with ankle locks were necessary too, and wrist-locked gauntlets. One could put on an old-fashioned-looking aquarium helmet, if one had the money; people at Mary's economic level made do with a snugly fitting hood, a face mask hooked up to a back tank, and kitchen grease mixed with UV blocker daubed thickly on anything that the mask didn't cover.

Having done this, one could then clamber through an airlock and motor across Mars, in a rickety CeltCart 600 with knobbed rubber tires and a top speed of eight kilometers an hour. It was transportation neither dignified nor efficient, since one was swamped with methane fumes and bounced about like a pea in a football. Nevertheless, it beat walking, or being blown sidelong in an antigravity car. And it really beat climbing.

Mary clung to the rollbar and reflected that today was actually a fine day for a jaunt Outside, considering. Bright summer sky overhead like peaches and cream, though liver-dark storm clouds raged far down the small horizon behind. Before, of course, was only the gentle but near-eternal swell of Mons Olympus, and the road that had been made by the expedient of rolling or pushing larger rocks out of the way.

"Mind the pit, Cochevelou," she admonished. Cochevelou exhaled his annoyance so forcefully that steam escaped from the edges of his mask, but he steered clear of the pit and so on up the winding track to the drill site.

The lads were hard at work when they arrived at last, having had a full hour's warning that the Cart was on its way up, since from the high slide of the slope one could see half the world spread out below, and its planetary curve too. There was therefore a big mound of broken gravel and frozen mudslurry, industriously scraped from the drillbits, to show for their morning's work. Better still, there was a thin spindrift of steam coming off the rusty pipes, coalescing into short-lived frost as it fell.

"Look, Mama!" said Manco proudly, gesturing at the white. "Heat *and* water!"

"So I see," said Mary, crawling from the car. "Who'd have thought mud could be so lovely, eh? And we've brought you a present. Unload it, please."

Matelot and the others who had been industriously leaning on their shovels sighed, and set about unclamping the bungees that had kept the great crate in its place on the back of the CeltCart. The crate was much too big to have traveled on a comparative vehicle on Earth without squashing it, and even so the Cart's wheels groaned and splayed, though as the men lifted the crate like so many ants hoisting a dead cricket the wheels bowed gratefully back. The cords had bit deep into the crate's foamcast during the journey, and the errant Martian breezes had just about scoured the label off with flying grit, but the logo of Third Word Alternatives, Inc. could still be made out.

"So this is our pump and all?" inquired Padraig, squinting at it through his goggles.

"This is the thing itself, pump and jenny and all but the pipes to send wet hot gold down the mountain to us," Cochevelou told him.

"And the pipes've been ordered," Mary added proudly. "And paid for! And here's Mr. Morton to exercise his great talents building a shed to house it all."

Mr. Morton unfolded himself from the rear cockpit and tottered to his feet, looking about with wide eyes. The speaker in his mask was broken, so he merely waved at everyone and went off at once to look at the foundations Manco had dug.

"And lastly," said Mary, lifting a transport unit that had been rather squashed under the seat, "Algemite sandwiches for everybody! And free rounds on the house when you're home tonight, if you get the dear machine hooked up before dark."

"Does it come with instructions?" Matelot inquired, puffing as he stood back from the crate.

"It promised an easy-to-follow holomanual in five languages, and if one isn't in there we're to mail the manufacturers at once," Mary said. "But they're a reputable firm, I'm sure."

"Now, isn't that a sight, my darling?" said Cochevelou happily, turning to look down the slope at the Tharsis Bulge. "Civilization, what there is of it anyhow, spread out at our feet like a drunk to be rolled."

Mary gazed down, and shivered. From this distance, the Settlement Dome looked tiny and pathetic, even with its new housing annex. The network of Tubes seemed like so many glassy worms, and her own house might have been a mudball on the landscape. It was true that the landing port had recently enlarged, which made it more of a handkerchief than a postage stamp of pink concrete. Still, little stone cairns dotted the wasteland here and there, marking the spots where luckless prospectors had been cached because nobody had any interest in shipping frozen corpses back to Earth.

But she lifted her chin and looked back at it all in defiance.

"Think of our long acres of green," she said. "Think of our own rooms steam-heated. Lady bless us, think of having a hot *bath!*"

Which was such an obscenely expensive pleasure on Mars that Cochevelou gasped and slid his arm around her, moved beyond words, and they clung together for quite a while on that cold prominence before either of them noticed the tiny figure making its way up the track from the Empress.

"Who's that, then?" Mary peered down at it, disengaging herself abruptly from Cochevelou's embrace. "Is that Mr. De Wit?"

It was Mr. De Wit.

By the time they reached him in the CeltCart, he was walking more slowly, and his eyes were standing out of his face so they looked fair to pop through his goggles, but he seemed unstoppable.

"WHAT IS IT?" Mary demanded, turning her volume all the way up. "IS SOMETHING GONE WRONG WITH ALICE?"

Mr. De Wit shook his head, slumping forward on the Cart's fender. He cranked up his volume as far as it went too and gasped, "LAWYER—"

"YES!" Mary said irritably, "YOU'RE A LAWYER!"

"*OTHER* LAWYER!" said Mr. De Wit, pointing back down the slope at the Empress.

Mary bit her lip. "YOU MEAN—" she turned her volume

down, reluctant to broadcast words of ill omen. "There's a lawyer from somebody else? The BAC, maybe?"

Mr. De Wit nodded, crawling wearily into the back seat of the Cart.

"Oh, bugger all," growled Cochevelou. "Whyn't you fight him off then, as one shark to another?"

"Did my best," wheezed Mr. De Wit. "Filed appeal. But you have to make mark."

Mary said something unprintable. She reached past Cochevelou and threw the Cart into neutral to save gas. It went bucketing down the slope, reaching such a velocity near the bottom that Mr. De Wit found himself praying for the first time since his childhood.

Somehow they arrived with no more damage done than a chunk of lichen sheared off the airlock wall, but they might have taken their time, for all the good it did them.

The lawyer was not Hodges from the Settlement, whose particular personal interests Mary knew to a nicety and whom she might have quelled with a good hard stare. No, this lawyer was a solicitor from London, no less, immaculate in an airlock ensemble from Bond Street and his white skullcap of office. He sat poised on the very edge of one of Mary's settles, listening diffidently as Mr. De Wit (who had gone quite native by now, stooped, wheezing, powdered with red dust, his beard lank with facegrease and sand) explained the situation, which was, to wit:

Whereas, the British Ares Company had operated at an average annual loss to its shareholders of 13 percent of the original estimated minimum annual profit for a period of five (Earth) calendar years, and

Whereas, it had come to the attention of the Board of Directors that there were hitherto-unknown venues of profit in the area of mineral resources, and

Whereas, having reviewed the original Terms of Settlement and Allotment as stated in the Contract for the Settlement and Terraforming of Ares, and having determined that the contractment of any and all allotted agricultural zones was contingent upon said zones contributing to the common wealth of Mars and the continued profit of its shareholders, and

Whereas, the aforesaid Contract specified that in the event that revocation of all Leases of Allotment was determined to be in the best interests of the shareholders, the Board of Directors retained the right to the exercise of Eminent Domain,

Therefore, the British Ares Company respectfully informed Mary Griffith that her lease was revoked and due notice of eviction from all areas of Settlement would follow within thirty (Earth) calendar days. She was, of course, at full liberty to file an appeal with the proper authorities.

"Which you are in the process of doing," said Mr. De Wit, and picked up a text plaquette from the table. "Here it is. Sign at the bottom."

"Can she read?" the solicitor inquired, stifling a yawn. Mary's lip curled.

"Ten years at Mount Snowdon University says I can, little man," she informed him, and having run her eye down the document, she thumbprinted it firmly. "So take that and stick it where appeals are filed, if you please." She handed the plaquette to the solicitor, who accepted it without comment and put it in his briefcase.

"Hard luck, my dear," said Cochevelou, pouring himself a drink. "I'll just quell my thirst and then edge off home, shall I?"

"Are you a resident of the Clan Morrigan?" the solicitor inquired, fixing him with a fishy eye.

"I am." Cochevelou stared back.

"Then, can you direct me to their current duly elected chieftain?"

"That would be him," said Mary.

"Ah." The solicitor drew a second plaquette from his briefcase and held it out. "Maurice Cochevelou? You are hereby advised that—"

"Is that the same as what you just served *her* with?" Cochevelou demanded, slowly raising fists like rusty cannon balls.

"In short, sir, yes, you are evicted," replied the solicitor, with remarkable sangfroid. "Do you wish to appeal as well?"

"Do you wish to take a walk Outside, you little—"

"He'll appeal as well," said Mary firmly, and, grabbing the second plaquette, she took Cochevelou's great sooty thumb and stamped the plaquette firmly. "There now. Run along, please."

"You can tell your masters they've got a fight on their hands, you whey-faced soy-eating little timeserver!" roared Cochevelou at the solicitor's retreating back. The airlock shut after him and Cochevelou picked up a mug and hurled it at the lock, where it shattered into pink fragments.

"We'll burn their Settlement Dome over their heads!" he said, stamping like a bull in a stall. "We'll drive our kine through their spotless tunnels, eh, and give 'em methane up close and personal, won't we just!"

"We will not," said Mary. "We'll ruin 'em with lawsuits, won't we, Mr. De Wit?"

"I don't think you're going to be able to do either," said Mr. De Wit, sagging onto a bench. "They've already found new tenants to work the land, you see. The Martian Agricultural Collective will be coming up soon. Very much more the kind of people they would rather see living up here. And the BAC itself is dissolving. The Board of Directors will be running the whole operation from Earth now, under the corporate name ARECO. I told you things would change."

"The cowards," growled Cochevelou. "So they'll evaporate into mist when we swing at them, will they?"

"Then what's the point of appealing?" Mary asked.

"It will buy you time," Mr. De Wit replied, raising his gray exhausted face. Alice brought him a cup of hot tea, setting it before him. She began to massage his bowed shoulders.

"Of course," Alice said quietly, "we *could* all go home again."

"*This* is my home," said Mary, bridling.

"Well, it isn't *mine*," said Alice defiantly. "And it isn't Eli's, either. He's only staying up here to help you because he's kind. But we *will* go back to Earth, Mum, and if you want to see your grandchild, you'll have to go too."

"Alice, don't say that to your mother," said Mr. De Wit, putting his face in his hands.

Mary looked at her daughter stone-faced.

"So you're playing that game, are you?'

"I'm not playing any game! I just—"

"Go back to Earth, then. Be happy there, if you're capable of being happy. Neither you nor anybody else alive will call my bluff," said Mary, not loudly but in tones that formed ice around the edges of Mr. De Wit's tea. He groaned.

"And what'm *I* to do?" said Cochevelou, looking horrified as the full impact hit him. "Mine will call for a vote. Three votes of no-confidence for a chieftain and there's a new chieftain."

"Overwhelm them with persuasion, man," Mary told him. "Spin them a tale about our glorious new future up the slope in—in—"

"Mars Two," said Mr. De Wit, staring into his teacup.

3

THE SHINING CITY ON THE HILL

Cochevelou survived the vote. That was one good thing. Another was that Celtic Energy Systems got its pumping station built and online. Though the easy-to-follow assembly holo was indeed in five languages, they turned out to be Telugu, Swahili, Pashto, Malayalam, and Hakka. Fortunately, most of the orderlies in the hospital where Mr. Morton had grown up had spoken Swahili, and he had picked up enough to follow assembly directions.

Of course, the pipes hadn't arrived from Earth yet, so there was no way to send water, heat or steam anywhere; but Mr. Morton had fabricated an elegant little neoGothic structure to house the pumping station, a sort of architectural prototype, as he explained, for the Edgar Allan Poe Memorial Cabaret, and he was already happily designing the Downtown Arts Plaza and Promenade.

"It's the backlash," said the Brick gloomily, nursing his beer. "Too many freaks up here for the BAC to cope with, so they'll just scrap the whole Settlement and ship up their own hand-picked squares. Have you seen any of these guys from the Martian Agricultural Collective?"

"I have not," said Mary, looking over his head to count the house. Three booths occupied, and only two seats at the bar; not good, for a Friday night. "They're not drinkers, seemingly."

"They're not drinkers," the Brick affirmed. "Their idea of fun is singing anthems to Agrarian Socialism, okay? Bunch of shaven-headed humorless bastards."

"Oh, dear," said Mary. "No beer, is it? And are they monkish as well?"

"No," said the Brick, shuddering. "They got their own ladies. They shave their heads too. Seriously political."

"So they won't be inclined to stop by for a chat," said Mary thoughtfully. "How's your job security, then, under the new regime?"

The Brick grinned. "They can round up all the other loonies and ship 'em home, but they'll still need Ice Haulers, right? And we've got the Bipolar Boys and Girls Union. They mess with us, we'll drive a dozen six-ton flatbeds through Settlement Dome and Mars 'em."

Marsing was a local custom. It resembled mooning, but was uglier.

"I'm sure they won't dare mess with you, Mr. Brick," said Mary.

"Hey, let 'em," said the Brick, waving a massive hand. "I like a good fight."

Wreathed in an air of pleasant anticipation and carbon dioxide, he downed the last of his beer and headed out, pausing by the airlock to mask up. As he exited, two other people came in from the Tube.

They removed their masks and stared around at the Empress. Their gazes dwelt with approval a moment on the votive shrine to the Mother, in its alcove; traveled on and grew somewhat cold looking on the great brewtanks that loomed at the back of Mary's domain. They were both pear-shaped women, one elderly and one youngish, and Mary wondered what the hell they were doing on Mars.

"Are you perhaps lost, ladies?" she inquired in English.

"Oh, I don't think so," said the elder of the two. She advanced on the bar, closely followed by her associate. Somewhere in the gloom behind Mary, there was a gasp and the clang of a dropped skillet.

"You must be Mary Griffith," said the elder. "I am Mother

Glenda and this is Mother Willow. We're with the Ephesian Mission."

"Indeed? How nice," said Mary. "Visiting from Luna, then?"

"Oh, no," said Mother Glenda. "We've come to stay. Blessed be."

"Blessed be," Mary echoed, feeling slightly uneasy as she looked into Mother Glenda's face, which was pink-cheeked and jolly-smiling, though there was a certain hard glint in her eyes.

"The Church felt it was time to bring the Goddess to this desolate place," said Mother Willow, who had a high breathless voice. "Especially with all these desperate people seeking their fortunes here. Because, there are really hardly any red diamonds up here after all, are there? So they'll need spiritual comfort when the vain quest for worldly riches fails them. And besides, it's *Mars.*"

"Mythologically the planet of war and masculine brutality," explained Mother Glenda.

"Ah," said Mary.

"And the Martian Agricultural Collective are all atheists, you see, so it's an even greater challenge," said Mother Willow earnestly. "You can imagine how pleased we were to learn that there was already a Daughter resident up here. And how outraged we were to hear that you have been the victim of paternalist oppression!"

"I wouldn't say I've been a victim," Mary replied, grinning. "I'd say I've given as good as I've got, and I'm still here."

"*Good* answer," said Mother Glenda. "Holy Mother Church has followed your struggle with some interest, daughter."

"Really," said Mary, not much liking the sound of that.

"And, of course, one of the first things we want to do is offer our support," Mother Willow assured her. "Holy Mother Church will help you fight your eviction. Our legal and financial resources are practically unlimited, you know, and we have publicists who would love to tell your story. The Goddess cares for Her own, but most especially for those who have suffered persecution in Her name!"

Mary caught her breath. She thought of the Diana of Luna affair, that had cost the British Luna Company millions of pounds and kilometers of real estate. And now the Church must be look-ing to duplicate that success here. . . .

"Oh, my, what a lovely thought," she said dreamily. "This might be ever so much fun. Please, allow me to offer you a nice mug of—er—tea."

Everyone in three worlds knew the story: how, in the early days of Luna's settlement, a devout Ephesian named Lavender Dragonsbane had found a solid silver statue of the Goddess buried on the moon. The British Lunar Company claimed that what she had found was, in fact, a vaguely woman-shaped lump of nickel ore. It was given to archaeologists to study, and then other parties (including MI5) had stepped in to demand a look at it, and somehow it had mysteriously vanished in transit from one set of experts to another.

The Ephesian Church had sued the BLC, and the BLC had sued back. Lavender Dragonsbane had a vision wherein the Goddess told her to build a shrine on the spot where she had found the statue. The BLC claimed that the statue had been deliberately planted by the Ephesians on that spot because it hap-pened to be valuable real estate they wanted.

However, in calling what had been found a *statue,* the BAC had contradicted their earlier statement that it had been nothing but a curiously shaped bit of rock. The Tri-Worlds Council for Integrity found for the Ephesian Church on points. Now the Church owned half the Moon.

". . . and *you* could be our next Lavender Dragonsbane, daughter," said Mother Willow, setting aside her tea.

"Well, that would spoke the BAC's wheels and no mistake," said Mary giddily. "Or Areco or whatever they're calling them-selves now."

"The perennial oppressors," said Mother Willow, smiling, "brought to their knees by the simple faith of one woman. Blessed be!"

"Blessed be!" Mary echoed, visions of sweet revenge dancing through her head.

"Of course, you understand there will have to be some changes," said Mother Glenda.

"Yes, of course," said Mary, and then: "Excuse me?"

Mother Willow coughed delicately. "We have been given to understand that your staff is nearly all male. We can scarcely present you as Her defender on Mars when you perpetuate hiring bias, can we, daughter? And Holy Mother Church is *very* concerned at rumors that one of your employees is a . . . Christian."

"Oh, Manco!" said Mary. "No, you don't understand. He really worships Her, you see, only it's just in the image of Our Lady of Guadalupe. And everybody knows that's some kind of Red Indian flower goddess really, and nothing to do with paternalist oppressors or anything like that and after all he's a, er, Native American, isn't he? Member of a viciously oppressed ethnic minority? And he's built Her a big shrine and everything in a sacred grotto hereabouts."

Mother Willow brightened. "Yes, I see! That makes it an entirely different matter. I expect our publicists could do very well with that." She pulled out a jotpad and made a few brief notes. "One of Her faithful sons escaping to Mars from the brutal lash of Earth prejudice, yes. . . ."

"And as for the rest of 'em being male," said Mary, "Well, I have to take what I can get up here, don't I? And they're not bad fellows at all. And anyway, out of the whole Settlement, there's only—" She had been about to say, *There's only the Heretic wanted a job,* but caught herself and went on—"Er, only so many women on Mars, after all."

"That's true," said Mother Willow graciously.

"And we *quite* understand you have been placed in a position where it was necessary to fight the enemy with his own weapons," said Mother Glenda. "However, all of that—" and she pointed at the brewtanks, "must stop, immediately."

"I beg your pardon?" said Mary.

"There is to be no more traffic in controlled substances," said Mother Glenda.

"But it's only beer!" Mary cried. "And it's not illegal in the Celtic Federation, anyway, of which I am a citizen, see? So I'm not doing anything wrong."

"Not under the statutes of *men,*" said Mother Glenda. "But

how can you feel you are doing Her will by serving a deadly toxin like alcohol to the impoverished working classes of Mars? No, daughter. Holy Mother Church wants to see those tanks dismantled before she grants her aid."

"But what would I serve my regulars?" Mary demanded.

"Herbal teas and nourishing broths," suggested Mother Willow. "*Healthful* drinks."

Mary narrowed her eyes. Perhaps sensing an explosion imminent, Mother Willow changed the subject and said delicately:

"And there is one other matter. . . ."

"What's that?" said Mary stonily.

"There was an unfortunate incident on Luna," said Mother Willow. "Tragic, really. One of our faithful daughters was injured in an accident. The poor creature was confused—we're certain now there was brain damage—but it would appear that, in her dementia, she said certain things that were interpreted in entirely the wrong way. Misunderstandings will happen . . . but Holy Mother Church seeks now to bring her child home."

"We understand she works for you here," said Mother Glenda.

"Er," said Mary. "Well. She has done, but . . . you must know she's a bit unreliable. I never know when she'll turn up. I thought she was a heretic, anyway."

"She doesn't know what she's talking about," said Mother Glenda quickly. "She ought to be in—that is, on medication for her condition."

"You mean you want to put her in hospital," said Mary.

"Oh, no, no, no!" Mother Willow assured her. "Not one of those dreadful state-run homes at all. The Church has a special place for its afflicted daughters."

I'll just bet you do, Mary thought. She sat mulling over the price tag on her future for a long moment. At last she stood up.

"Ladies, I think you'd best go now."

When they had left at last, when the flint-edged smiles and veiled threats and sniffs of mutual disapproval had been exchanged, Mary drew a deep breath. "Missionaries," she muttered. Then she made her way back into the stygian blackness of her kitchen.

She found the Heretic at last, wedged behind the pantry cupboard like a human cockroach, by the sound her ocular implant was making as it telescoped in and out.

"They're gone now," Mary informed her.

"Can't come out," the Heretic replied hoarsely.

"You don't want to go back to Earth with them?"

The Heretic didn't answer.

"You'd get lots of nice drugs," Mary pointed out. The Heretic shifted, but was still mute.

"Look, they're not going to hurt you. This is modern times, see? They even hinted your excommunication might be revoked. Wouldn't you like that?"

"No," said the Heretic. "They think He'll talk for them. But He won't."

"Who won't talk for them?" Mary asked, settling back on her heels. "Your, er, sort of god thing?"

"Yes."

"Why would they want him to talk to them?"

There was a silence, filled gradually with the sound of the cupboard rattling and the whirring noise of the Heretic's eye. Finally she controlled her trembling and gasped:

"Because of what He said when I was in the House of Gentle Persuasion. He told them—something was going to happen. And it happened just like He said."

"You mean, like a prophecy?"

"*Prophecies predictions can't let this get out! Bad press Goddess knows false field day for the unbelievers paternalist voodoo conspiracies wait! We can use her!*" The Heretic's voice rose in a shriek like a rusty hinge coming unhinged. "*Stop that now or you'll put your other eye out!* But He was there. Held down His hand from the red planet and said *Come to me!* Showed me the open window and I left. Showed me a cargo freighter and I signed on. And I am here with Him and I will never go back now."

Mary stared into the shadows, just able to make out one sunken red-rimmed eye in a pale face.

"So they think you can do predictions, is that it?"

There was silence again.

"And that's why the Church wants you back," said Mary grimly.

The blur in the darkness might have nodded.

There were rumors.

Mary heard that Areco had no interest in the terraforming project, that its intention was to strip-mine for red diamonds, which were much more valuable than anyone had thought, and it had signed no real lease with the MAC.

At the same time, she heard that the red diamond rush had played out completely and that Areco was committed to backing the Martian Agricultural Collective, because terraforming was the only way anyone would ever make money on Mars.

She heard that General Director Rotherhithe had been called home in disgrace and seemed to be dying of emphysema. He was also rumored to be in perfect health and Areco's principal stockholder, calling the shots from some sinister high desk on Earth.

She heard that the Church was encountering unheard-of resistance from the MAC. She heard that the Church had signed a mutually profitable agreement with the MAC and that the new mission complex—temple, administrative offices and all—was being built even now on the other side of the settlement.

And her appeal was certain to be rejected, and her appeal was certain to succeed. Any day now.

Nothing happened. Life went on.

Then everything happened at once.

It was difficult to organize a baby shower on Mars, but Rowan had managed, on the very day before Mr. De Wit and Alice were scheduled to return to Earth.

Alice's baby had been determined to be a girl, which was fortunate for the purposes of party décor, as most of the household ware was already pink. The Heretic had been coaxed out from under the refrigeration unit long enough to bake a cake, which rose like a pink cloud and stayed that way, thanks to Martian gravity, and while there was nothing but a tin of Golden Syrup to pour over it, the effect was impressive.

The problem of presents had been overcome as well. Rowan had commandeered Mr. De Wit's buke to catalog-shop, and simply printed out pictures of what she had ordered. The images were blurry, gray, and took most of a day to print out, but once she had them she painted them with red ochre and pink clay.

"See? Virtual presents," she said, holding up a depiction of a woolly jumper. "You don't even have to worry about luggage weight on the shuttle. This set's from me. It comes with matching bootees and a cap."

Alice blotted tears and accepted it gratefully. Beside her, Mona gazed at the heap of pictures—receiving blankets, bassinet, more woolly jumpers—and squeaked, "Oh, I can't *wait* to have a baby of my own!"

"Yes, you *can*, my girl," Mary told her, standing to one side with Mr. De Wit, who seemed rather stunned.

"I can't imagine what my neighbors will think when all this stuff starts arriving," he said, giggling weakly. "I've been a bachelor so many years. . . ."

"They'll get over it," said Alice, and blew her nose. "Oh, Eli, darling, *look!* An Itsy Witsy Play Set with a slide and a sandbox!"

"That's from me," said Mary, somewhat stiffly. "If the little thing has to grow up on Earth, at least she'll be able to play outdoors."

There was a sizzling moment wherein Alice glared at her mother, and Mr. Morton broke the silence by clearing his throat.

"I, er, I hope you won't mind—I prepared something." He stepped forward and offered Alice a text plaquette. "In honor of your name being Alice, I thought it would be nice—there's this marvelous old book, proscribed of course, but I recorded as much as I could remember of the poems—perhaps she'll like them. . . ."

Alice thumbed the switch and the screen lit up, and there was Mr. Morton in miniature, wringing his hands as he said: "Ahem! 'Jabberwocky.' By Lewis Carroll. 'Twas brillig, and the slithy toves did gyre and gimbal in the wade. . . ."

"My, is it in Old English?" Alice inquired politely. "How nice, Mr. Morton!"

"Well, it—"

"This is from me." Manco stepped forward, and drew from his coat a little figurine, cast from the most delicately rose-colored grit he could find. The Virgen de Guadalupe smiled demurely down at the businesslike little seraph who held her aloft on a crescent moon. "The Good Mother will look after her. You'll see."

"It's lovely! Oh, but I hope it doesn't get confiscated going through Earth customs," Alice cried.

"Just point to the crescent horns and tell 'em it's Isis," Mary advised.

Chiring stepped forward and laid a black cube on the table.

"This is a holoalbum," he said. "Candid shots of the whole family and a visual essay on the Martian landscape, you see? So she'll know where she's from. She'll also get a lifetime subscription to the Kathmandu *Post*."

"That's very thoughtful," said Alice, not knowing what else to say. "Thank you, Chiring."

"Ma'am? There's somebody in the airlock," said Mr. Morton.

"That'll be Lulu and Jeannemarie from the clan, I expect," said Rowan.

It wasn't.

"Ma'am." Matelot stood stiffly, twisting his air mask in his hands. Padraig Moylan and Gwil Evans flanked him, staring at the floor.

"What's this, gentlemen?" said Mary.

Matelot cleared his throat and looked from one to the other of his companions, clearly hoping one of them would speak. When neither showed any evidence of opening their mouths for the rest of eternity, he cleared his throat again and said:

"Himself sends word to say that, er, he's been made an offer he can't refuse to drop our appeal against eviction. And that even if he could refuse it, the clan has voted to accept."

"But there's still Celtic Energy Systems, my dears," said Mary, into the thunderous silence that had fallen.

"Well, that's not piped up to anything yet, you know . . . but it's not that, Ma'am," said Matelot, looking up into Mary's eyes and looking away quickly. He gulped for air and went on: "Areco wants the fruit of our labors. The ironworks and the cattle sheds and fields and all. Areco's buying 'em for a princely sum and giving us a golden rocket back to Earth, plus company shares. Every one of us rich enough to retire and live like gentry the rest of our lives. And so Himself sends you four thousand punts Celtic as compensation for Finn's fields, and hopes you will consider emigration as well."

Padraig Moylan extended a banking plaquette in a trembling hand.

The silence went on and on. Was anyone breathing? After a moment Mary reached out and took the plaquette. She glanced at it before looking back at the clansmen.

"I see," she said.

"And we'll just be going, then," said Matelot. Mary's voice hit him like an iron bar as she said:

"Is he selling *all* the fixtures?"

"What?" said Matelot weakly.

"I want to buy all your antigrav units," said Mary, handing the plaquette back. "I want them in my house by tomorrow morning. And I'll make a preemptive bid, look you, for your last harvest. Go now and tell him so."

"Yes'm," said Matelot, and collided with his fellow clansmen as they all three attempted to get out the airlock at once.

When they had gone, Mary sank down on a settle. The rest of her household stared at her. Nobody said anything until Rowan came and crouched beside her.

"Mum, it doesn't matter. Maybe Areco will make us an offer too—"

"We're not waiting to see," said Mary.

"You're going back to Earth?" asked Alice, too shocked for triumph. Mr. De Wit shook his head in silence, a sick expression in his eyes.

"I am not," said Mary. "I said I won't be driven out and I meant it."

"Good for you!" cried Mr. Morton, and blanched as everyone turned to stare at him. Then he drew a breath and said: "She's right! We—we don't need the clan. We've got our pumping station and all that land up there. We can make a *new* place! Our own settlement, for people like us. We've already got plans for the theaters. We can expand into a hotel and restaurant and—who knows what else?" He spread out his hands in general appeal.

"Where are we going to get the people?" asked Manco.

"Well, er—you can advertise in the Kathmandu *Post*, can't you?" Mr. Morton turned to Chiring. "Tell the Sherpas all about the great job opportunities now being offered at, ah, Griffith Energy Systems! Tell them we're making a wonderful place up here where people will be free and there'll be Art and exciting adventure and, and no corporate bad guys running their lives!"

Chiring had already pulled out his jotpad before Mr. Morton had stammered to his conclusion, and was busily making notes.

"I think we can get Earth's attention," he said.

Alice sighed, gazing at her mother. She looked down at the bright pictures scattered at her feet.

"We'll stay and give you all the help we can," she said. "Won't we, Eli?"

"No." Mary got to her feet. "You're going back to Earth. No sense wasting perfectly good tickets. You can be my agents there. I'll be buying a lot of things for the new place; I want them shipped properly. And Mr. De Wit can handle all of the *thousand* lawsuits I plan to file much more effectively if he's on Earth, can't you, Mr. De Wit?"

Mr. De Wit bowed slightly. "Your servant, Madam." He coughed. "I think it might be worth your while to inquire whether Polieos is interested in buying shares in Griffith Energy Systems."

"I will, by Goddess!" Mary began to pace. She swung one arm at her available complement of men. "You lot go over to the clan now and start collecting those antigrav units. If the old bastard won't sell, tell him we're just borrowing them, but collected they must be."

"Yes, Mama." Manco picked up a crowbar and looked significantly at Chiring, Morton, and De Wit. They headed all together for the airlock.

"Girls, start packing. Everything's to be closed down and strapped in. Disconnect everything except Three Tank. Mona, you go out to the Ice Depot and let the Haulers know I'm giving away beer tonight."

"Right away, Mum!" Mona grabbed her air mask.

As Alice and Rowan hurried away to pack, Mary strode into her kitchen.

"Did you hear all that?" she called. There was a rustle from the shadows in the pantry. Finally the Heretic sidled into sight.

"Yes," she said, blinking.

"Will it work, do you think? Can we tell them all to go to hell and start our own place?" Mary demanded.

The Heretic just shrugged, drooping forward like an empty garment; then it was as though someone had seized her by the back of the neck and jerked her upright. She fixed a blazing red eye on Mary, and in a brassy voice cried:

"For the finest in Martian hospitality, the tourist has only one real choice: Ares' premiere hotel— The Empress of Mars in Mars Two, founded by turn-of-the-century pioneer Mary Griffith and still managed by her family today. Enjoy five-star cuisine in the Empress's unique Mitsubishi Room, or discover the delights of a low-gravity hot spring sauna!"

Mary blinked. "Mars Two, is it to be? As good a name as any, I suppose. That's a grand picture of the future, but a little practical advice would be appreciated."

The strange voice took on a new intonation, sounding sly:

"All-seeing Zeus is lustful, can never be trusted; His son has a golden skull. But Ares loves a fighter."

"I don't hold with gods," said Mary stiffly. "Especially not a god of war."

Someone else smiled, using the Heretic's face. It was profoundly unsettling.

"All life has to fight to live. There's more to it than spears and empty rhetoric; she who struggles bravely has His attention."

Mary backed out of the kitchen, averting her eyes from the red grin.

"Then watch me, whoever you are, because I'm going to give Areco one hell of a fight," she muttered. "And if my cook's still in there, tell her to get to work. I'm throwing a party tonight."

By the time the sullen day dawned, the Haulers were still drunk enough to be enthusiastic.

"Jack the whole thing up on ag units, yeah!" roared the Brick. "Brilliant!"

His fellow Haulers howled their agreement.

"And just sort of walk it up the slope a ways, we thought," said Mary. "So it'll be on my claim, see."

"No, no, no, babe—" a Hauler named Tiny Reg swayed over her like a cliff about to fall. "See, that'll never work. See? Too much tail wind. Get yer arse blowed down to Valles Marinerisisis. You nona let—wanna let us—"

"Tow my house all the way up there?" asked Mary artlessly. "Oh, I couldn't ask!"

"Hell yeah!" said the Brick. "Just hook it up an' go!"

"Fink I got my glacier chains inna cabover," said a Hauler named Alf, rising from a settle abruptly and falling with a crash that sent a bow wave of spilled beer over Mary's boots. When his friends had picked him up, he wiped Phobos Porter from his face and grinned obligingly. "Jus' nip out an' see, shall I?"

"Oh, sir, how very kind," said Mary. She put out an arm and arrested Mr. Morton's flight, for he had been in the process of running to refill mugs from a pitcher. "Can we do it?" she demanded of him *sotto voce*. "You understand these things. Will the house take the stresses, without cracking like half an eggshell?"

"Er—" Mr. Morton blinked, stared around him for the first time with professional eyes. "Well—it will if we brace the interior cantilevers. We'd need, ah, telescoping struts—which we haven't got, but—"

"Where can we get them?"

"They're all in the construction storage shed on the Base. . . ." Mr. Morton's voice trailed off. He looked down at the pitcher he was carrying. Lifting it to his mouth, he drank the last pint it contained and wiped his mouth with the back of his hand. "I know the code to get the shed door open," he said.

"Do you?" Mary watched him closely. His spine was stiffening. He put down the pitcher, flexed his long arms.

"Yes, I do," he said. "I'll just go off and see an oppressive corporate monolithic evil entity about a dog, shall I?"

"I think that would be a good idea," said Mary. Mr. Morton strode to the airlock, put on his mask, and paused as though to utter a dramatic exit line; then realized he should have delivered it before putting his mask on. He saluted instead, with a stiff perfect British salute, and marched away down the Tube.

"Mum?"

Mary turned and beheld Alice, swathed extravagantly for the trip Outside. Mr. De Wit stood beside her, a carryon in each hand and under either arm.

"The tickets say to get there three hours before flight time for processing," said Alice hesitantly.

"So you'd best go now," said Mary. Alice burst into tears and flung her arms around her mother's neck.

"I'm sorry I haven't been a good daughter," cried Alice. "And now I'm going to feel like a deserter too!"

"No, dearest, of course you're not a deserter," said Mary automatically, patting her on the arm. She looked over Alice's shoulder at Mr. De Wit. "You're going to go away with this nice man and bear me a lovely granddaughter, see, and perhaps someday I'll come visit you in my diamond-encrusted planet shuttle, yes?"

"I hope so," said Alice, straightening up, for her back ached. Mother and daughter looked at one another across all the resentments, the dislike, the grudges, the eternal intractable *issues* of their lives. What else was there to say?

"I love you, Mum," said Alice at last.

"I love you, too," said Mary. She went to Mr. De Wit and stood on tiptoe to kiss him, for which he bent down.

"If you desert her, I'll hunt you down and kill you with my own two hands," she murmured in his ear. He grinned.

They went away through the airlock, just as Alf the Hauler came in. Beer had frozen on his clothing and he was bleeding from his nostrils, but he seemed not to have noticed.

"Got a couple fousand meters of chain!" he announced. "'Nough to move bloody shrackin' Antartarctica!"

"You silly boy, did you go out without your air?" Mary scolded gently. "Rowan, bring a wet face flannel for our Alf. Where are your keys, dear?"

Smiling like a broken pumpkin, Alf held them up. Mary confiscated them and passed them to Manco, who masked up before ducking outside to back Alf's hauler into position.

"You can hold yer breff out dere, you know," said Alf proudly if muffledly, as Mary cleaned him up. "S'really easy once you get used to it."

"I'm sure it is, love. Have another beer and sit still for a bit," Mary told him, and turned to Rowan. "What's happening now?"

"Uncle Brick and the others are putting the ag-units in place," said Rowan. "Is it time to disconnect Three Tank yet?"

"Not yet. They'll want a drink before they go up the slope," Mary replied.

"But, Mum, they're *drunk!*" Rowan protested.

"Can you think of a better way to get them to do it?" Mary snapped. "What chance have we got, unless they think it's a mad lark they came up with themselves? I'll get this house on my claim any damned way I can. Pour another round!"

Alice was reclining in her compartment, adjusting to the artificial gravity and staring up at the monitor above the couch. It was showing only old-fashioned flat images from the live camera mounted above the shuttleport; but the views were something to occupy her attention in the gray cubespace, and the litany of *Last time I'll ever have to look at this* was soothing her terrors.

Suddenly, something on the screen moved, and the image became surreal, impossible: there out beyond the Settlement a dome was rising, as though a hill had decided to walk. Alice cried out. Eliphal was beside her immediately, though she had had the impression he had been off seeing about their menu selections for the flight.

"What's the matter?" he asked, taking her hand in both his own.

"Where did you come from?" she asked him, bewildered. "Look out there! She's actually talked them into it!"

Clearly free now, the Empress of Mars was crawling up the slope from the Settlement Base like a gigantic snail, ponderous, of immense dignity, tugged along inexorably by no less than three freighters on separate leads of chain, each one sending up its own pink cloud of dust from roaring jets.

"Of course she's done it, Alice." How assured his voice was, and yet a little sad. "Your mother will found a city up there, on beer and rebellion. It'll be a remarkable success. You'll see, my dear."

"You really think so?" She stared into his eyes, unsettled by the expression there. He was the kindest man she had ever met, but sometimes she felt as though she were a small lost animal he'd picked up and taken home. She turned her eyes back to the monitor. "I guess we should have stayed to help her, shouldn't we?"

"No!" He put his arms around her. "You'll come home to Earth. I'll keep you safe, you and the little girl. I promised your mother."

"Oh, Earth . . ." Alice thought of green hills, and blue skies, and a blue sea breaking on a white beach . . . and her mother, and her mother's problems, finally subtracted from her life. She closed her eyes, burying her face in Eliphal's shoulder. His beard smelled of cinnamon and myrrh.

"Looks like a huge mobile tit!" whooped the Brick, peering into his rear monitor as he yanked back on the throttle.

"But it's leaking, Mum," fretted Mona, watching the vapor plumes emerge and dissipate instantly wherever they appeared, over every unplastered crack and vent. "Are we going to have any air at all once we get it up there?"

"We can wear our masks indoors the first few days," Mary told her, not taking her eyes off the monitor. "Wear extra thermals. Whatever we *have* to do. Hush, girl!"

In Alf's cab, Chiring was muttering into a mike, aiming his cam at the monitor for lack of a window.

"Chiring Skousen, your News Martian, here! What you're seeing is an epic journey, ladies and gentlemen, a heroic gesture in defiance of oppression!" He paused, reflected on the number of seats the NeoMaoists had won in the last Nepali parliamentary election, and went on: "The valiant working classes have risen in aid of one woman's brave stand against injustice, while the technocrats cower in their opulent shelters! Yes, the underpaid laborers of Mars still believe in such seemingly outmoded concepts as gallantry, chivalry, and courage!"

"And *beer,*" said Alf. "Whoo-hoo!"

"The new battle cry of Mars, ladies and gentlemen!" Chiring ranted. "The ancient demand of *Beer for the Workers!* Now, if you're still getting the picture from the monitor clearly, you can see the slope of Mons Olympus rising before us. Our road is that paler area between the two rows of boulders. We, er, we're fighting quite a headwind, but our progress has been quite good so far, due to the several ice freighters kindly donated by the Haulers Union, which are really doing a tremendous job of moving Ms. Griffith's structure."

"Yeh, fanks," said Alf.

"And the, er, the chains used for this amazing feat are the

same gauge used for tackling and hauling polar ice, so as you can imagine, they're quite strong—" Chiring babbled, keeping his camera on the forward monitor because he had spotted something he did not understand in the rear monitor. He paused again and squinted at it.

"What the hell's that?" he whispered to Alf. Alf looked up at the monitor.

"Uh-oh," he said. "That's a Strawberry."

"And, and, er, ladies and gentlemen, if you'll follow now as I turn my cam on the rear monitor, you can see one of the unique phenomena of the Martian landscape. That sort of lumpy pink thing that appears to be advancing on the Settlement Base at high speed is what the locals call a Strawberry. Let's ask local weather expert Mr. Alfred Chipping to explain just exactly what a Strawberry is. Mr. Chipping?"

Alf stared into the cam, blinking. "Well, it's—it's like a storm kind of a fing. See, you got yer sandstorms, wot is bad news eh? And you got yer funny jogeraphy up here and jolligy and, er, now and again you get yer Strawberry, wot is like all free of 'em coming together to make this really fick sandstorm wot pingpongs off the hills and rocks and changes direction wifout warning."

"And—why's it that funny spotty color, Mr. Chipping?"

"Cos it's got rocks in," grunted Alf, slapping all three accelerator levers up with one blow of his hamhand.

Chiring began to pray to Vishnu, but he did it silently, and turned his camera back to the forward monitor.

"Well, isn't that interesting!" he cried brightly. "More details on the fascinating Martian weather coming up soon, ladies and gentlemen!"

"I'll be damned," said the Brick, in a voice that meant he had abruptly sobered. "There's a Strawberry down there!"

"Where?" Mary craned her head, instinctively looking for a window, but he pointed at the rear monitor. "What's a Strawberry?"

"Trouble for somebody," the Brick replied, accelerating. "Settlement Base, looks like."

"What?"

"Oh!" said Mona. "You mean one of those cyclone things like Tiny Reg was in?"

"*What?*"

"Yeah," grunted the Brick, accelerating more.

"Tiny Reg said he was hit by one down by Terra Sirenum and it just took his freighter and picked it up with him in it and he went round and round so fast it broke all his gyros and his compass as well," Mona explained.

"Bloody Hell!" Mary began to undo her seat harness, but the Brick put out an arm to restrain her.

"You don't want to do that, babe," he said quietly.

"What do we care if it hits Settlement Base, anyroad?" Mona asked.

"Girl, your sister's down there!"

"Oh!" Mona looked up at the monitor in horror, just as the Strawberry collided with the new Temple of Diana, which imploded in a puff of crimson sand.

"Alice!" Mary screamed, searching across the monitors for a glimpse of the transport station. There was the shuttle, safe on its pad, lights still blinking in loading patterns. There it stayed safe, too, for the Strawberry turned now and shot away from the Base, tearing through Tubes as it went, and the lockout klaxons sounded as oxygen blew away white like seafoam in the burning-cold day.

"Never saw one come up on Tharsis before," was all the Brick said, steering carefully.

"But the transport station's safe!" Mona said.

"Goddess thank You, Goddess thank You, Goddess. . . . Is it getting bigger?" Mary stared fixedly at the monitor bank.

"No," said the Brick. "It's just getting closer."

Within the Empress, Mr. Morton scrambled spiderlike along the network of crossing stabilizer struts, which had telescoped out to prop the Empress' walls like glass threads in a witchball. He peered down worriedly at the floor. It was heaving and flexing rather more than he had thought it would. He looked over at the telltale he had mounted on the wall to monitor stress changes, but it was too far away to read easily.

"Are we going to be okay?" inquired Manco, remarkably stoic for a man dangling in a harness ten meters above uncertain eternity. The Heretic swung counterclockwise beside him, her red eye shut, listening to the clatter of her saucepans within their wired-up cupboards.

"Masks on, I think," said Mr. Morton.

"Gotcha," said Manco, and he slipped his on as Mr. Morton did the same, and gulped oxygen, and after a moment he nudged the Heretic as she orbited past. "Come on, honey, mask up. Leaks, you know?"

"Yeah," said the Heretic, not opening her eye, but she slipped on her mask and adjusted the fit.

"So what do we do?" Manco asked.

"Hang in there," said Mr. Morton, with a pitch in his giggle suggesting the long sharp teeth of impending catastrophe.

"Ha bloody Ha," said Manco, watching the walls. "We're shaking more. Are they speeding up out there?"

"Oh, no, certainly not!" Mr. Morton said. "They know better than to do that. No more than two kilometers an hour, I told them, or the stresses will exceed acceptable limits."

"Really?" Manco squinted through his goggles at a bit of rushing-by ground glimpsed through a crack on the floor that opened and shut like a mouth.

"All right, here's something we can do—" Mr. Morton edged his way along a strut to the bundle of extras. "Let's reinforce! Never hurts to be sure, does it?" He pulled out a telescoping unit and passed it hand over hand to Manco. "Just pop that open and wedge it into any of the cantilevers I haven't already braced."

Manco grabbed the strut and twisted it. It unlocked and shot out in two directions, and he swung himself up to the nearest joist to ram it into place.

"Splendid," said Mr. Morton, unlocking another strut and wedging it athwart two others.

"Should I be doing that too?" asked the Heretic, opening her good eye.

"Well, er—" Mr. Morton thought of her inability to hold on to a pan, let alone a structural element requiring strength and exactitude in placement, and, kindly as possible, he said: "Here's a thought: why don't you rappel down to that big box there on the wall, you see? And just, er, watch the little numbers on the screen and let us know if they exceed 5008. Can you do that?"

"Okay," said the Heretic, and went down to the telltale in a sort of controlled plummet. Below her, the floor winked open and gave another glimpse of Mars, which seemed to be going by faster than it had a moment earlier.

"This box says 5024," the Heretic announced.

Mr. Morton said a word he had never used before. Manco, hanging by one hand, turned to stare, and the Heretic's ocular implant began to whirr in and out, gravely disturbing the fit of her mask.

"So, Mr. Brick," said Mary in a voice calm as iron, "Am I to understand that the storm is bearing down upon us now?"

"Bearing *up,* babe, but that's it, essentially," said the Brick, not taking his eyes off the monitor.

"Can we outrun it, Mr. Brick?"

"We might," he said, "If we weren't towing a house behind us."

"I see," said Mary.

There followed what would have been a silence, were it not for the roar of the motors and the rotors and the rising percussive howl of the wind.

"How does one release the tow lines, Mr. Brick?" Mary inquired.

"That lever right there, babe," said the Brick.

"Mum, that's our house!" said Mona.

"A house is only a thing, girl," said Mary.

"And there's still people in it! Mr. Morton stayed inside, didn't he? And Manco stayed with him! They're holding it together!"

Mary did not answer, staring at the monitor. The Strawberry loomed now like a mountain behind them, and under it the Empress seemed tiny as a horseshoe crab scuttling for cover.

"And there's always the chance the Strawberry'll hit something and go poinging off in another direction," said the Brick, in a carefully neutral voice.

"Mr. Brick," said Mary, "Basing your judgment on your years of experience hauling carbon dioxide from the icy and intolerant polar regions, could you please think carefully now and tell me exactly what chance there is that the Strawberry will, in fact, change direction and leave us alone? In your opinion, see?"

"I absolutely do not know," the Brick replied.

"Right," said Mary. She reached out and pulled down the lever to release the tow line.

A nasty twanging mess was avoided by the fact that Alf, in his freighter, had made the same decision to cast loose at nearly the same second, as had Tiny Reg (who had actually lived through a Strawberry after all and who would have cast loose even earlier, had his reflexes not been somewhat impaired by seventeen imperial pints of Red Crater Ale).

They all three sheared away in different directions, as though released from slings, speeding madly over the red stony desolation and slaloming through piles of rock the color of traffic cones. Behind them the Empress of Mars drifted to a halt, its tow lines fluttering like streamers. The Strawberry kept coming.

"5020," the Heretic announced in a trembling voice. "5010. 5000. 4050."

"*Much* better," said Mr. Morton, gasping in relief. "Good sensible fellows. Perhaps they were only giving in to the temptation to race, or something manly like that. Now, I'll just get out my flexospanner and we'll—"

"405*1*," said the Heretic.

"What the hell's that noi—" said Manco, just before the ordered world ended.

On thirty-seven monitors, which was exactly how many there were on the planet, horrified spectators saw the Strawberry bend over as though it were having a good look at the Empress of Mars; then they saw it leap away, only giving the Empress a swat with its tail end as it bounced off to play with the quailing sand dunes of Amazonia Planitia. The Empress, for its part, shot away up the swell of Mons Olympus, rotating end over end as it went.

Mr. Morton found himself swung about on his tether in ever-decreasing circles, ever closer to a lethal-looking tangle of snapping struts to which he was unfortunately still moored. The Heretic caromed past him, clinging with both arms to the stress telltale, which had torn free of the wall. Something hit him from behind like a sack of sand, and then was in front of him, and he clutched at it and looked into Manco's eyes. Manco seized hold of the nearest strut with bleeding hands, but his grasp was slick, and it took both of them scrabbling with hands and feet to fend off the broken struts and find a comparatively still bit of chaos where they clung, as the floor and ceiling revolved, revolved, slower now, revolving—

Floor upwards—

Righting itself—

Going over again, oh no, was the floor going to crack right open?—

Still tumbling—oh, don't let it settle on its side, it'll split open for sure—

Righting itself again—

And then a colossal lurch as the wind hit the Empress, only the ordinary gale force wind of Mars now but enough to sail anything mounted on ag-units, and Mr. Morton thought: *We're going to be blown to the South Pole!*

Something dropped toward them from above, and both men saw the Heretic hurtling past, still clutching the stress telltale as well as a long confusion of line that had become wrapped about her legs. She regarded them blankly in the second before she went through the floor, which opened now like split fruit rind. The line fell after her and then snapped taut, in the inrush of freezing no-air. There was a shuddering shock and the Empress strained at what anchored it, but in vain.

The men yelled and sucked air, clutching at their masks. Staring down through the vortex of blasting sand, Manco saw Mr. Morton's neoGothic pumping station with the stress telltale bedded firmly in its roof, and several snarls of line wound around its decorative gables.

And he saw, and Mr. Morton saw too, the Heretic rising on the air like a blown leaf, mask gone, her clothing being scoured away but replaced like a second skin by a coating of sand and blood that froze, her hair streaming sidelong. Were her arms flung out in a pointless clutching reflex, or was she opening them in an embrace? Was her mouth wide in a cry of pain or of delight, as the red sand filled it?

And Manco watched, stunned, and saw what he saw, and Mr. Morton saw it too, and they both swore ever afterward to what they saw then, which was: that the Heretic turned her head, smiled at them, and *flew away into the tempest.*

"Take us back!" Mary shrieked. "Look, look, it's been blown halfway up the damn volcano, but it's still in one piece!"

The Brick dutifully came about and sent them hurtling back, through a cloud of sand and gravel that whined against the freighter's hull. "Looks like it's stuck on something," he said.

"So maybe everybody's okay!" cried Mona. "Don't you think, Mum? Maybe they just rode inside like it was a ship, and nobody even got hurt?"

Mary and the Brick exchanged glances. "Certainly," said Mary. "Not to worry, dear."

But as they neared the drilling platform, it was painfully obvious that the Empress was still in trouble. Air plumed from a dozen cracks in the dome, and lay like a white mist along the underside, eddying where the occasional gust hit it. Several of the ag-units had broken or gone offline, causing it to sag groundward here and there, and even above the roar of the wind and through the walls of the cab, Mary could hear the Empress groaning in all its beams.

"Mum, there's a hole in the floor!" Mona screamed.

"I can see that. Hush, girl."

"But they'll all be dead inside!"

"Maybe not. They'd masks, hadn't they? Mr. Brick, I think we'd best see for ourselves."

The Brick just nodded, and made careful landing on the high plateau. They left Mona weeping in the cab and walked out, bent over against the wind, deflecting sand from their goggles with gloved hands.

"YOU GOT UNITS 4, 6, AND 10 DEAD, LOOKS LIKE,"

announced the Brick. "IF WE SHUT OFF 2, 8, AND 12, THAT OUGHT TO EVEN OUT THE STRESS AND LET HER DOWN SOME."

"WILL YOU GIVE ME A LEG UP, THEN, PLEASE?"

The Brick obliged, hoisting Mary to his shoulders, and there she balanced to just reach the shutoff switches, and, little by little, the Empress evened out, and settled, and looked not quite so much like a drunken dowager with her skirts over her head. Mary was just climbing down when Alf and Tiny Reg pulled up in their freighters. Chiring scrambled from Alf's cab and came running toward her with his cam held high.

"UNBELIEVABLE!" he said. "IT'S AN ACT OF THE GODS, LADIES AND GENTLEMEN! NARROW ESCAPE FROM CERTAIN DEATH! FREAK STORM DEPOSITING BUILDING INTACT ON VERY SITE INTENDED! MARS'S FIRST RECORDED MIRACLE!"

"SHUT THE DAMN THING OFF," Mary told the audience of Posterity. "WE'VE GOT PEOPLE INSIDE."

Chiring gulped, seeing the wreckage clearly for the first time. He ran for the Empress, where the Brick was already taking a crowbar to the airlock.

"MUM!" Rowan jumped from Tiny Reg's cab. She reached her mother just as Mona did the same, and they clung to Mary, weeping.

"HUSH YOUR NOISE!" Mary yelled. "WE'RE ALIVE, AREN'T WE? THE HOUSE IS HERE, ISN'T IT?"

"DAMN YOU, MUM, WHAT'LL WE BREATHE UP HERE?" Rowan yelled back. "HOW'LL WE LIVE? WE'LL FREEZE!"

"THE GODDESS WILL PROVIDE!"

Rowan said something atheistical and uncomplimentary then, and Mary would have slapped her if she hadn't been wearing a mask, and as they stood glaring at each other Mary noticed, far down the slope below Rowan, a traveling plume of grit coming up the road. It was the CeltCart.

By the time the cart reached the plateau, Mary had armed herself with the Brick's crowbar, and marched out swinging it threateningly.

"COCHEVELOU, YOU'RE ON MY LAND," she said. She aimed a round blow at his head but it only glanced off, and he kept coming and wrapped his arms around her.

"DARLING GIRL, I'M BEGGING YOUR PARDON ON MY KNEES," said Cochevelou. Mary tried to take another swipe at him but dropped the crowbar.

"HOUND!" she gasped, "GO BACK TO EARTH, TO YOUR SOFT LIFE, AND I, ON MARS, WILL DRY MY TEARS, AND LIVE TO MAKE MY ENEMIES KNEEL!"

"AW, HONEY, YOU DON'T MEAN THAT," Cochevelou said. "HAVEN'T I GONE AND GIVEN IT ALL UP FOR YOUR SAKE? THE SPOILED DARLINGS CAN ELECT THEMSELVES ANOTHER CHIEFTAIN. I'M STAYING ON."

Mary peered over his shoulder at the CeltCart, and noted the preponderance of tools he had brought with him: anvil, portable forge, pig iron . . . and she thought of the thousand repairs the Empress's tanks and cantilevers would now require. Drawing a deep breath, she cried:

"OH, MY DEAR, I'M THE GLADDEST WOMAN THAT EVER WAS!"

"MUM! MUM!" Mona fought her way through the blowing sand. "THEY'VE COME ROUND!"

Mary broke from Cochevelou's embrace, and he followed her back to the cab of the Brick's freighter, where Manco and Mr. Morton were sitting up, or more correctly propping themselves up, weak as newborns, letting Alf swab BioGoo on their cuts and scrapes.

"ARE YOU ALL RIGHT, BOYS? WHERE'S THE HERETIC GONE?" Mary demanded.

Mr. Morton began to cry, but Manco stared at her with eyes like eggs and said, "There was a miracle, Mama."

Miracles are good for business, and so is the attraction of a hot bath in a frozen place of eternal dirt, and so are fine ales and beers in an otherwise joyless proletarian agricultural paradise. And free arethermal energy is very good indeed, if it's only free to *you* and costs others a packet, especially if they have to crawl and apologize to you and treat you like a lady in addition to paying your price for it.

Five years down the line, there was a new public house sign, what with the Queen of England being scoured away at last by relentless grit, and a fine new sign it was. Two grinning giants, one red and one black, supported between them a regal little lady in fine clothes. At her throat was the painted glory of a red diamond; in her right hand was a brimful mug, and her left hand beckoned the weary traveler to warmth and good cheer. Inside, in the steamy warmth, Sherpas drank their beer with butter.

Five years down the line, there were holocards on the back bar, all featuring little Mary De Wit of Amsterdam, whether screaming and red-faced for the camera in her first bath, or holding tight to Mr. De Wit's long hand while paddling her toes in the blue sea, or smiling like a sticky cherub before a massed extravagance of Solstice presents and Chanukah sweets, or solemn on her first day of school.

Five years down the line, there was a little shrine in the corner of the kitchen with a new image, a saint for the new faith. It resembled nothing so much as the hood ornament of an ancient Rolls-Royce, a sylph leaning forward into the wind, discreetly shrouded by slipstream short of actual nakedness. Its smile was distinctly unsettling. Its one eye was a red diamond.

Five years down the line, there was actually a Centre for the Performing Arts on Mars, and its thin black-clad manager put on very strange plays indeed, drawing the young intellectuals from what used to be Settlement Base, and there were pasty-faced disciples of Martian Drama (they called themselves the UltraViolets) creating a new art form in the rapidly expanding city on Mons Olympus.

Five years down the line at Mars One, there were long green fields spidering out along the Martian equator and even down to the lowlands, because that's what a good socialist work-ethic will get you, but up in Mars Two, there were domed rose gardens to the greater glory of Her who smiled serene in Her cloak of stars, Mother of miracles like roses that bloom in despite of bitter frost.

THE GREEN LEOPARD PLAGUE

by Walter Jon Williams

Walter Jon Williams was born in 1953 in Minnesota. He attended the University of New Mexico and received his B.A. in 1975. He lives in rural New Mexico.

Williams first started writing in the early '80s, publishing a series of naval adventures under the name Jon Williams. His first science fiction novel, Ambassador of Progress, *appeared in 1984 and was followed by fifteen more, most notably* Hardwired, Aristoi, Metropolitan *and its sequel* City on Fire, *and the first two volumes in his "Praxis" trilogy,* The Praxis *and* The Sundering.

A prolific short fiction writer, Williams's first short story, "Side Effects," appeared in 1985 and was followed by a string of major stories that were nominated for important awards, including "Dinosaurs," "Surfacing," "Wall, Stone, Craft," "Lethe," and the Nebula Award-winner "Daddy's World." A number of these are collected in Facets.

The story that follows, one of Williams's very best, is a cleverly deceptive tale of romance, biology, and revenge.

KICKING HER LEGS OUT OVER the ocean, the lonely mermaid gazed at the horizon from her perch in the overhanging banyan tree.

The air was absolutely still and filled with the scent of night flowers. Large fruit bats flew purposefully over the sea, heading for their daytime rest. Somewhere a white cockatoo gave a penetrating squawk. A starling made a brief flutter out to sea, then came back again. The rising sun threw up red-gold sparkles from the wavetops and brought a brilliance to the tropical growth that crowned the many islands spread out on the horizon.

The mermaid decided it was time for breakfast. She slipped from her hanging canvas chair and walked out along one of the banyan's great limbs. The branch swayed lightly under her weight, and her bare feet found sure traction on the rough bark. She looked down to see the deep blue of the channel, distinct from the turquoise of the shallows atop the reefs.

She raised her arms, poised briefly on the limb, the ruddy light of the sun glowing bronze on her bare skin, and then pushed off and dove head-first into the Philippine Sea. She landed with a cool impact and a rush of bubbles.

Her wings unfolded, and she flew away.

After her hunt, the mermaid—her name was Michelle—cached her fishing gear in a pile of dead coral above the reef, and then ghosted easily over the sea grass with the rippled sunlight casting patterns on her wings. When she could look up to see the colossal, twisted tangle that were the roots of her banyan tree, she lifted her head from the water and gulped her first breath of air.

The Rock Islands were made of soft limestone coral, and tide and chemical action had eaten away the limestone at sea level, undercutting the stone above. Some of the smaller islands looked like mushrooms, pointed green pinnacles balanced atop thin stems. Michelle's island was larger and irregularly shaped, but it still had steep limestone walls undercut six meters by the tide, with no obvious way for a person to clamber from the sea to the land. Her banyan perched on the saucer-edge of the island, itself undercut by the sea.

Michelle had arranged a rope elevator from her nest in the tree, just a loop on the end of a long nylon line. She tucked her wings away—they were harder to retract than to deploy, and the gills on the undersides were delicate—and then slipped her feet through the loop. At her verbal command, a hoist mechanism lifted her in silence from the sea to her resting place in the bright green-dappled forest canopy.

She had been an ape once, a siamang, and she felt perfectly at home in the treetops.

During her excursion, she had speared a yellowlip emperor, and this she carried with her in a mesh bag. She filleted the emperor with a blade she kept in her nest, and tossed the rest into the sea, where it became a subject of interest to a school of bait fish. She ate a slice of one fillet raw, enjoying the brilliant flavor, sea and trembling pale flesh together, then cooked the fillets on her small stove, eating one with some rice she'd cooked the previous evening and saving the other for later.

By the time Michelle finished breakfast, the island was alive. Geckoes scurried over the banyan's bark, and coconut crabs sidled beneath the leaves like touts offering illicit downloads to passing tourists. Out in the deep water, a flock of circling, diving black noddies marked where a school of skipjack tuna was feeding on swarms of bait fish.

It was time for Michelle to begin her day as well. With sure, steady feet, she moved along a rope walkway to the ironwood tree that held her satellite uplink in its crown, straddled a limb, took her deck from the mesh bag she'd roped to the tree, and downloaded her messages.

There were several journalists requesting interviews—the legend of the lonely mermaid was spreading. This pleased her more often than not, but she didn't answer any of the queries. There was a message from Darton, which she decided to savor for a while before opening. And then she saw a note from Dr. Davout, and opened it at once.

Davout was, roughly, twelve times her age. He'd actually been carried for nine months in his mother's womb, not created from scratch in a nanobed like almost everyone else she knew. He had a sib who was a famous astronaut, a McEldowny prize for his *Lavoisier and His Age*, and a red-haired wife who was nearly as well-known as he was. A couple of years ago, Michelle had attended a series of his lectures at the College of Mystery, and been interested despite her specialty being, strictly speaking, biology.

He had shaved off the little goatee he'd worn when she'd last seen him, which Michelle considered a good thing. "I have a research project for you, if you're free," the recording said. "It shouldn't take too much effort."

Michelle contacted him at once. He was a rich old bastard with a thousand years of tenure and no notion of what it was to be young in these times, and he'd pay her whatever outrageous fee she asked.

Her material needs at the moment were few, but she wouldn't stay on this island forever.

Davout answered right away. Behind him, working at her own console, Michelle could see his red-haired wife Katrin.

"Michelle!" Davout said, loudly enough for Katrin to know who'd called without turning around. "Good!" He hesitated, and then his fingers formed the mudra for <concern>. "I understand you've suffered a loss," he said.

"Yes," she said, her answer delayed by a second's satellite lag.

"And the young man—?"

"Doesn't remember."

Which was not exactly a lie, the point being *what* was remembered.

Davout's fingers were still fixed in <concern>. "Are you all right?" he asked.

Her own fingers formed an equivocal answer. "I'm getting better." Which was probably true.

"I see you're not an ape any more."

"I decided to go the mermaid route. New perspectives, all that." And welcome isolation.

"Is there any way we can make things easier for you?"

She put on a hopeful expression. "You said something about a job?"

"Yes." He seemed relieved not to have to probe further—he'd had a realdeath in his own family, Michelle remembered, a chance-in-a-billion thing, and perhaps he didn't want to relive any part of that.

"I'm working on a biography of Terzian," Davout said.

" . . . And his Age?" Michelle finished.

"And his *Legacy*." Davout smiled. "There's a three-week period in his life where he—well, he drops right off the map. I'd like to find out where he went—and who he was with, if anyone."

Michelle was impressed. Even in comparatively unsophisticated times such as that inhabited by Jonathan Terzian, it was difficult for people to disappear.

"It's a critical time for him," Davout went on. "He'd lost his job at Tulane, his wife had just died—realdeath, remember—and if he decided he simply wanted to get lost, he would have all my sympathies." He raised a hand as if to tug at the chin-whiskers that were no longer there, made a vague pawing gesture, then dropped the hand. "But my problem is that when he resurfaces, everything's changed for him. In June, he delivered an undistinguished paper at the Athenai conference in Paris, then vanishes. When he surfaced in Venice in mid-July, he didn't deliver the paper he was scheduled to read, instead he delivered the first version of his Cornucopia Theory."

Michelle's fingers formed the mudra, <highly impressed>. "How have you tried to locate him?"

"Credit card records—they end on June 17, when he buys a lot of euros at American Express in Paris. After that, he must have paid for everything with cash."

"He really *did* try to get lost, didn't he?" Michelle pulled up one bare leg and rested her chin on it. "Did you try passport records?"

<No luck.> "But if he stayed in the European Community he wouldn't have had to present a passport when crossing a border."

"Cash machines?"

"Not till after he arrived in Venice, just a couple of days prior to the conference."

The mermaid thought about it for a moment, then smiled. "I guess you need me, all right."

<I concur> Davout flashed solemnly. "How much would it cost me?"

Michelle pretended to consider the question for a moment, then named an outrageous sum.

Davout frowned. "Sounds all right," he said.

Inwardly, Michelle rejoiced. Outwardly, she leaned toward the camera lens and looked businesslike. "I'll get busy, then."

Davout looked grateful. "You'll be able to get on it right away?"

"Certainly. What I need you to do is send me pictures of Terzian, from as many different angles as possible, especially from around that period of time."

"I have them ready."

"Send away."

An eyeblink later, the pictures were in Michelle's deck.

<Thanks> she flashed. "I'll let you know as soon as I find anything."

At university, Michelle had discovered that she was very good at research, and it had become a profitable sideline for her. People—usually people connected with academe in one way or another—hired her to do the duller bits of their own jobs, finding documents or references, or, in this case, three missing weeks out of a person's life. It was almost always work they could do themselves, but Michelle was simply better at research than most people, and she was considered worth the extra expense. Michelle herself usually enjoyed the work—it gave her interesting sidelights on fields about which she knew little, and provided a welcome break from routine.

Plus, this particular job required not so much a researcher as an artist, and Michelle was very good at this particular art.

Michelle looked through the pictures, most scanned from old photographs. Davout had selected well: Terzian's face or profile was clear in every picture. Most of the pictures showed him young, in his twenties, and the ones that showed him older were of high quality, or showed parts of the body that would be crucial to the biometric scan, like his hands or his ears.

The mermaid paused for a moment to look at one of the old photos: Terzian smiling with his arm around a tall, long-legged woman with a wide mouth and dark, bobbed hair, presumably the wife who had died. Behind them was a Louis Quinze table with a blaze of gladiolas in a cloisonné vase, and, above the table, a large portrait of a stately looking horse in a heavy gilded frame. Beneath the table were stowed—temporarily, Michelle assumed—a dozen or so trophies, which to judge from the little golden figures balanced atop them were awarded either for gymnastics or martial arts. The opulent setting seemed a little at odds with the young, informally dressed couple: she wore a flowery tropical shirt tucked into khakis, and Terzian was dressed in a tank top and shorts. There was a sense that the photographer had caught them almost in motion, as if they'd paused for the picture en route from one place to another.

Nice shoulders, Michelle thought. Big hands, well-shaped muscular legs. She hadn't ever thought of Terzian as young, or large, or strong, but he had a genuine, powerful physical presence that came across even in the old, casual photographs. He looked more like a football player than a famous thinker.

Michelle called up her character-recognition software and fed in all the pictures, then checked the software's work, something she was reasonably certain her employer would never have done if he'd been doing this job himself. Most people using this kind of canned software didn't realize how the program could be fooled, particularly when used with old media, scanned film prints heavy with grain and primitive digital images scanned by machines that simply weren't very bright. In the end, Michelle and the software between them managed an excellent job of mapping Terzian's body and calibrating its precise ratios: the distance between the eyes, the length of nose and curve of lip, the distinct shape of the ears, the length of limb and trunk. Other men might share some of these biometric ratios, but none would share them all.

The mermaid downloaded the data into her specialized research spiders, and sent them forth into the electronic world.

A staggering amount of the trivial past existed there, and nowhere else. People had uploaded pictures, diaries, commentary, and video; they'd digitized old home movies, complete with the garish, deteriorating colors of the old film stock; they'd scanned in family trees, post cards, wedding lists, drawings, political screeds, and images of handwritten letters. Long, dull hours of security video. Whatever had meant something to someone, at some time, had been turned into electrons and made available to the universe at large.

A surprising amount of this stuff had survived the Lightspeed War—none of it had seemed worth targeting, or, if trashed, had been reloaded from backups.

What all this meant was that Terzian was somewhere in there. Wherever Terzian had gone in his weeks of absence—Paris, Dalmatia, or Thule—there would have been someone with a camera. In stills of children eating ice cream in front of Notre Dame, or moving through the video of buskers playing saxophone on the Pont des Artistes, there would be a figure in the background, and that figure would be Terzian. Terzian might be found lying on a beach in Corfu, reflected in a bar mirror in

Gdynia, or negotiating with a prostitute in Hamburg's St. Pauli district—Michelle had found targets in exactly those places during the course of her other searches.

Michelle sent her software forth to find Terzian, then lifted her arms above her head and stretched—stretched fiercely, thrusting out her bare feet and curling the toes, the muscles trembling with tension, her mouth yawned in a silent shriek.

Then she leaned over her deck, again, and called up the message from Darton, the message she'd saved till last.

"I don't understand," he said. "Why won't you talk to me? I love you!"

His brown eyes were a little wild.

"Don't you understand?" he cried. "I'm not dead! *I'm not really dead!*"

Michelle hovered three or four meters below the surface of Zigzag Lake, gazing upward at the inverted bowl of the heavens, the brilliant blue of the Pacific sky surrounded by the dark, shadowy towers of mangrove. Something caught her eye, something black and falling, like a bullet: and then there was a splash and a boil of bubbles, and the daggerlike bill of a collared kingfisher speared a blue-eyed apogonid that had been hovering over a bright red coral head. The kingfisher flashed its pale underside as it stroked to the surface, its wings doing efficient double duty as fins, and then there was a flurry of wings and feet and bubbles and the kingfisher was airborne again.

Michelle floated up and over the barrel-shaped coral head, then over a pair of giant clams, each over a meter long. The clams drew shut as Michelle slid across them, withdrawing the huge siphons as thick as her wrist. The fleshy lips that overhung the scalloped edges of the shells were a riot of colors, purples, blues, greens, and reds interwoven in a eye-boggling pattern.

Carefully drawing in her gills so their surfaces wouldn't be inflamed by coral stings, she kicked up her feet and dove beneath the mangrove roots into the narrow tunnel that connected Zigzag Lake with the sea.

Of the three hundred or so Rock Islands, seventy or thereabouts had marine lakes. The islands were made of coral limestone and porous to one degree or another: some lakes were connected to the ocean through tunnels and caves, and others through seepage. Many of the lakes contained forms of life unique in all the world, evolved distinctly from their remote ancestors: even now, after all this time, new species were being described.

During the months Michelle had spent in the islands, she thought she'd discovered two undescribed species: a variation on the *Entacmaea medusivora* white anemone that was patterned strangely with scarlet and a cobalt-blue; and a nudibranch, deep violet with yellow polka-dots, that had undulated past her one night on the reef, flapping like a tea towel in a strong wind as a seven-knot tidal current tore it along. The nudi and samples of the anemone had been sent to the appropriate authorities, and perhaps in time Michelle would be immortalized by having a Latinate version of her name appended to the scientific description of the two marine animals.

The tunnel was about fifteen meters long, and had a few narrow twists where Michelle had to pull her wings in close to her sides and maneuver by the merest fluttering of their edges. The tunnel turned up, and brightened with the sun; the mermaid extended her wings and flew over brilliant pink soft corals toward the light.

Two hours' work, she thought, *plus a hazardous environment. Twenty-two hundred calories, easy.*

The sea was brilliantly lit, unlike the gloomy marine lake surrounded by tall cliffs, mangroves, and shadow, and for a moment Michelle's sun-dazzled eyes failed to see the boat bobbing on the tide. She stopped short, her wings cupping to brake her motion, and then she recognized the boat's distinctive paint job, a bright red meant to imitate the natural oil of the *cheritem* fruit.

Michelle prudently rose to the surface a safe distance away—Torbiong might be fishing, and sometimes he did it with a spear. The old man saw her, and stood to give a wave before Michelle could unblock her trachea and draw air into her lungs to give a hail.

"I brought you supplies," he said.

"Thanks." Michelle said as she wiped a rain of sea water from her face.

Torbiong was over two hundred years old, and Paramount Chief of Koror, the capital forty minutes away by boat. He was small and wiry and black-haired, and had a broad-nosed, strong-chinned, unlined face. He had traveled over the world and off it while young, but returned to Belau as he aged. His duties as chief were mostly ceremonial, but counted for tax purposes; he had money from hotels and restaurants that his ancestors had built and that others managed for him, and he spent most of his time visiting his neighbors, gossiping, and fishing. He had befriended Darton and Michelle when they'd first come to Belau, and helped them in securing the permissions for their researches on the Rock Islands. A few months back, after Darton died, Torbiong had agreed to bring supplies to Michelle in exchange for the occasional fish.

His boat was ten meters long and featured a waterproof canopy amidships made from interwoven pandanas leaves. Over the scarlet faux-*cheritem* paint were zigzags, crosses, and stripes in the brilliant yellow of the ginger plant. The ends of the thwarts were decorated with grotesque carved faces, and dozens of white cowrie shells were glued to the gunwales. Wooden statues of the kingfisher bird sat on the prow and stern.

Thrusting above the pandanas canopy were antennae, flag-poles, deep-sea fishing rods, fish spears, radar, and a satellite uplink. Below the canopy, where Torbiong could command the boat from an elaborately carved throne of breadfruit-tree wood, were the engine and rudder controls, radio, audio, and video sets, a collection of large audio speakers, a depth finder, a satellite navigation relay, and radar. Attached to the uprights that supported the canopy were whistles tuned to make an eerie, discordant wailing noise when the boat was at speed.

Torbiong was fond of discordant wailing noises. As Michelle swam closer, she heard the driving, screeching electronic music that Torbiong loved trickling from the earpieces of his headset— he normally howled it out of speakers, but when sitting still he didn't want to scare the fish. At night, she could hear Torbiong for miles, as he raced over the darkened sea blasted out of his skull on betel-nut juice with his music thundering and the whistles shrieking.

He removed the headset, releasing a brief audio onslaught before switching off his sound system.

"You're going to make yourself deaf," Michelle said.

Torbiong grinned. "Love that music. Gets the blood moving."

Michelle floated to the boat and put a hand on the gunwale between a pair of cowries.

"I saw that boy of yours on the news," Torbiong said. "He's making you famous."

"I don't want to be famous."

"He doesn't understand why you don't talk to him."

"He's dead," Michelle said.

Torbiong made a spreading gesture with his hands. "That's a matter of opinion."

"Watch your head," said Michelle.

Torbiong ducked as a gust threatened to bring him into contact with a pitcher plant that drooped over the edge of the island's overhang. Torbiong evaded the plant and then stepped to the bow to haul in his mooring line before the boat's canopy got caught beneath the overhang,

Michelle submerged and swam till she reached her banyan tree, then surfaced and called down her rope elevator. By the time Torbiong's boat hissed up to her, she'd folded away her gills and wings and was sitting in the sling, kicking her legs over the water.

Torbiong handed her a bag of supplies: some rice, tea, salt, vegetables, and fruit. For the last several weeks Michelle had experienced a craving for blueberries, which didn't grow here, and Torbiong had included a large package fresh off the shuttle, and a small bottle of cream to go with them. Michelle thanked him.

"Most tourists want corn chips or something," Torbiong said pointedly.

"I'm not a tourist." Michelle said. "I'm sorry I don't have any fish to swap—I've been hunting smaller game." She held out the specimen bag, still dripping sea water.

Torbiong gestured toward the cooler built into the back of his boat. "I got some *chai* and a *chersuuch* today," he said, using the local names for barracuda and mahi mahi.

"Good fishing."

"Trolling." With a shrug. He looked up at her, a quizzical look on his face. "I've got some calls from reporters," he said, and then his betel-stained smile broke out. "I always make sure to send them tourist literature."

"I'm sure they enjoy reading it."

Torbiong's grin widened. "You get lonely, now," he said, "you come visit the family. We'll give you a home-cooked meal."

She smiled. "Thanks."

They said their farewells and Torbiong's boat hissed away on its jets, the whistles building to an eerie, spine-shivering chord. Michelle rose into the trees and stashed her specimens and groceries. With a bowl of blueberries and cream, Michelle crossed the rope walkway to her deck, and checked the progress of her search spiders.

There were pointers to a swarm of articles about the death of Terzian's wife, and Michelle wished she'd given her spiders clearer instructions about dates.

The spiders had come up with three pictures. One was a not-very-well focused tourist video from July 10, showing a man standing in front of the Basilica di Santa Croce in Florence. A statue of Dante, also not in focus, gloomed down at him from beneath thick-bellied rain clouds. As the camera panned across him, he stood with his back to the camera, but turned to the right, one leg turned out as he scowled down at the ground—the profile was a little smeared, but the big, broad-shouldered body seemed right. The software reckoned that there was a 78 percent chance the man was Terzian.

Michelle got busy refining the image, and after a few passes of the software, decided the chances of the figure being Terzian were more on the order of 95 percent.

So maybe Terzian had gone on a Grand Tour of European cultural sites. He didn't look happy in the video, but then the day was cloudy and rainy and Terzian didn't have an umbrella.

And his wife had died, of course.

Now that Michelle had a date and a place she refined the instructions from her search spiders to seek out images from Florence a week either way from July 3, and then expand the search from there, first all Tuscany, then all Italy.

If Terzian was doing tourist sites, then she surely had him nailed.

The next two hits, from her earlier research spiders, were duds. The software gave a less than 50 percent chance of Terzian's being in Lisbon or Cape Sounion, and refinements of the image reduced the chance to something near zero.

Then the next video popped up, with a time stamp right there in the image—Paris, June 26, 13:41:44 hours, just a day before Terzian bought a bankroll of Euros and vanished.

<Bingo!> Michelle's fingers formed.

The first thing Michelle saw was Terzian walking out of the frame—no doubt this time that it was him. He was looking over his shoulder at a small crowd of people. There was a dark-haired woman huddled on his arm, her face turned away from the camera. Michelle's heart warmed at the thought of the lonely widower Terzian having an affair in the City of Love.

Then she followed Terzian's gaze to see what had so drawn his attention. A dead man stretched out on the pavement, surrounded by hapless bystanders.

And then, as the scene slowly settled into her astonished mind, the video sang at her in the piping voice of Pan.

Terzian looked at his audience as anger raged in his backbrain. A wooden chair creaked, and the sound spurred Terzian to wonder how long the silence had gone on. Even the Slovenian woman who had been drowsing realized that something had changed, and blinked herself to alertness.

"I'm sorry," he said in French. "But my wife just died, and I don't feel like playing this game any more."

His silent audience watched as he gathered his papers, put them in his case, and left the lecture room, his feet making sharp, murderous sounds on the wooden floor.

Yet up to that point his paper had been going all right. He'd been uncertain about commenting on Baudrillard in Baudrillard's own country, and in Baudrillard's own language, a cheery compare-and-contrast exercise between Baudrillard's "the self does not exist" and Rorty's "I don't care," the stereotypical

French and American answers to modern life. There had been seven in his audience, perched on creaking wooden chairs, and none of them had gone to sleep, or walked out, or condemned him for his audacity.

Yet, as he looked at his audience and read on, Terzian had felt the anger growing, spawned by the sensation of his own uselessness. Here he was, in the City of Lights, its every cobblestone a monument to European civilization, and he was in a dreary lecture hall on the Left Bank, reading to his audience of seven from a paper that was nothing more than a footnote, and a footnote to a footnote at that. To come to the land of *cogito ergo sum* and to answer, *I don't care?*

I came to Paris for this? he thought. *To read this* drivel? *I* paid *for the privilege of doing* this?

I do *care*, he thought as his feet turned toward the Seine. *Desiderio, ergo sum,* if he had his Latin right. I am in pain, and therefore I *do* exist.

He ended in a Norman restaurant on the Ile de la Cité, with lunch as his excuse and the thought of getting hopelessly drunk not far from his thoughts. He had absolutely nothing to do until August, after which he would return to the States and collect his belongings from the servants' quarters of the house on Esplanade, and then he would go about looking for a job.

He wasn't certain whether he would be more depressed by finding a job or by not finding one.

You are alive, he told himself. *You are alive and in Paris with the whole summer ahead of you, and you're eating the cuisine of Normandy in the Place Dauphine. And if that isn't a command to be joyful, what is?*

It was then that the Peruvian band began to play. Terzian looked up from his plate in weary surprise.

When Terzian had been a child his parents—both university professors—had first taken him to Europe, and he'd seen then that every European city had its own Peruvian or Bolivian street band, Indians in black bowler hats and colorful blankets crouched in some public place, gazing with impassive brown eyes from over their guitars and reed flutes.

Now, a couple of decades later, the musicians were still here, though they'd exchanged the blankets and bowler hats for European styles, and their presentation had grown more slick. Now they had amps, and cassettes and CDs for sale. Now they had congregated in the triangular Place Dauphine, overshadowed by neo-classical mass of the Palais de Justice, and commenced a Latin-flavored medley of old Abba songs.

Maybe, after Terzian finished his veal in calvados sauce, he'd go up to the band and kick in their guitars.

The breeze flapped the canvas overhead. Terzian looked at his empty plate. The food had been excellent, but he could barely remember tasting it.

Anger still roiled beneath his thoughts. And—for God's *sake*—was that band now playing *Oasis?* Those chords were beginning to sound suspiciously like "Wonderwall." "Wonderwall" on Spanish guitars, reed flutes, and a mandolin!

Terzian had nearly decided to call for a bottle of cognac and stay here all afternoon, but not with that noise in the park. He put some euros on the table, anchoring the bills with a saucer against the fresh spring breeze that rattled the green canvas canopy over his head. He was stepping through the restaurant's little wrought-iron gate to the sidewalk when the scuffle caught his attention.

The man falling into the street, his face pinched with pain. The hands of the three men on either side who were, seemingly, unable to keep their friend erect.

Idiots, Terzian thought, fury blazing in him.

There was a sudden shrill of tires, of an auto horn.

Papers streamed in the wind as they spilled from a briefcase.

And over it all came the amped sound of pan pipes from the Peruvian band. *Wonderwall.*

Terzian watched in exasperated surprise as the three men sprang after the papers. He took a step toward the fallen man—*someone* had to take charge here. The fallen man's hair had spilled in a shock over his forehead and he'd curled on his side, his face still screwed up in pain.

.   The pan pipes played on, one distinct hollow shriek after another.

Terzian stopped with one foot still on the sidewalk and looked around at faces that all registered the same sense of shock.

Was there a doctor here? he wondered. A *French* doctor? All his French seemed to have just drained from his head. Even such simple questions as *Are you all right?* and *How are you feeling?* seemed beyond him now. The first-aid course he'd taken in his Kenpo school was *ages* ago.

Unnaturally pale, the fallen man's face relaxed. The wind floated his shock of thinning dark hair over his face. In the park, Terzian saw a man in a baseball cap panning a video camera, and his anger suddenly blazed up again at the fatuous uselessness of the tourist, the uselessness that mirrored his own.

Suddenly there was a crowd around the casualty, people coming out of stopped cars, off the sidewalk. Down the street, Terzian saw the distinctive flat-topped kepis of a pair of policemen bobbing in this direction from the direction of the Palais de Justice, and felt a surge of relief. Someone more capable than this lot would deal with this now.

He began, hesitantly, to step away. And then his arm was seized by a pair of hands and he looked in surprise at the woman who had just huddled her face into his shoulder, cinnamon-dark skin and eyes invisible beneath wraparound shades.

"Please," she said in English a bit too musical to be American. "Take me out of here."

The sound of the reed pipes followed them as they made their escape.

He walked her past the statue of the Vert Galant himself, good old lecherous Henri IV, and onto the Pont Neuf. To the left, across the Seine, the Louvre glowed in mellow colors beyond a screen of plane trees.

Traffic roared by, a stampede of steel unleashed by a green light. Unfocused anger blazed in his mind. He didn't want this woman attached to him, and he suspected she was running some kind of scam. The gym bag she wore on a strap over one shoulder kept banging him on the ass. Surreptitiously, he slid his hand into his right front trouser pocket to make sure his money was still there.

Wonderwall, he thought. Christ.

He supposed he should offer some kind of civilized comment, just in case the woman was genuinely distressed.

"I suppose he'll be all right," he said, half-barking the words in his annoyance and anger.

The woman's face was still half-buried in his shoulder. "He's dead," she murmured into his jacket. "Couldn't you tell?"

For Terzian, death had never occurred under the sky, but shut away, in hospice rooms with crisp sheets and warm colors and the scent of disinfectant. In an explosion of tumors and wasting limbs and endless pain masked only in part by morphia.

He thought of the man's pale face, the sudden relaxation.

Yes, he thought, death came with a sigh.

Reflex kept him talking. "The police were coming," he said. "They'll—they'll call an ambulance or something."

"I only hope they catch the bastards who did it," she said.

Terzian's heart gave a jolt as he recalled the three men who let the man victim fall, and then dashed through the square for his papers. For some reason, all he could remember about them were their black-laced boots, with thick soles.

"Who were they?" he asked blankly.

The woman's shades slid down her nose, and Terzian saw startling green eyes narrowed to murderous slits. "I suppose they think of themselves as cops," she said.

Terzian parked his companion in a café near Les Halles, within sight of the dome of the Bourse. She insisted on sitting indoors, not on the sidewalk, and on facing the front door so that she could scan whoever came in. She put her gym bag, with its white Nike swoosh, on the floor between the table legs and the wall, but Terzian noticed she kept its shoulder strap in her lap, as if she might have to bolt at any moment.

Terzian kept his wedding ring within her sight. He wanted her to see it; it might make things simpler.

Her hands were trembling. Terzian ordered coffee for them both. "No," she said suddenly. "I want ice cream."

Terzian studied her as she turned to the waiter and ordered in French. She was around his own age, twenty-nine. There was no question that she was a mixture of races, but *which* races? The flat nose could be African or Asian or Polynesian, and Polynesia was again confirmed by the black, thick brows. Her smooth brown complexion could be from anywhere but Europe, but her pale green eyes were nothing but European. Her broad, sensitive mouth suggested Nubia. The black ringlets yanked into a knot behind her head could be African or East Indian, or, for that matter, French. The result was too striking to be beautiful—and also too striking, Terzian thought, to belong to a successful criminal. Those looks could be too easily identified.

The waiter left. She turned her wide eyes toward Terzian, and seemed faintly surprised that he was still there.

"My name's Jonathan," he said.

"I'm," hesitating, "Stephanie."

"Really?" Terzian let his skepticism show.

"Yes." She nodded, reaching in a pocket for cigarettes. "Why would I lie? It doesn't matter if you know my real name or not."

"Then you'd better give me the whole thing."

She held her cigarette upward, at an angle, and enunciated clearly. "Stephanie América Pais e Silva."

"America?"

Striking a match. "It's a perfectly ordinary Portuguese name."

He looked at her. "But you're not Portuguese."

"I carry a Portuguese passport."

Terzian bit back the comment, *I'm sure you do.*

Instead he said, "Did you know the man who was killed?"

Stephanie nodded. The drags she took off her cigarette did not ease the tremor in her hands.

"Did you know him well?"

"Not very." She dragged in smoke again, then let the smoke out as she spoke. She let the smoke out as she spoke.

"He was a colleague. A biochemist."

Surprise silenced Terzian. Stephanie tipped ash into the Cinzano ashtray, but her nervousness made her miss, and the little tube of ash fell on the tablecloth.

"Shit," she said, and swept the ash to the floor with a nervous movement of her fingers.

"Are you a biochemist, too?" Terzian asked.

"I'm a nurse." She looked at him with her pale eyes. "I work for Santa Croce—it's a—"

"A relief agency." A Catholic one, he remembered. The name meant *Holy Cross*.

She nodded.

"Shouldn't you go to the police?" he asked. And then his skepticism returned. "Oh, that's right—it was the police who did the killing."

"Not the *French* police." She leaned across the table toward him. "This was a different sort of police, the kind who think that killing someone and making an arrest are the same thing. You look at the television news tonight. They'll report the death, but there won't be any arrests. Or any suspects." Her face darkened, and she leaned back in her chair to consider a new thought. "Unless they somehow manage to blame it on me."

Terzian remembered papers flying in the spring wind, men in heavy boots sprinting after. The pinched, pale face of the victim.

"Who, then?"

She gave him a bleak look through a curl of cigarette smoke. "Have you ever heard of Transnistria?"

Terzian hesitated, then decided "No" was the most sensible answer.

"The murderers are Transnistrian." A ragged smile drew itself across Stephanie's face. "They're intellectual property police. They killed Adrian over a copyright."

At that point, the waiter brought Terzian's coffee, along with Stephanie's order. Hers was colossal, a huge glass goblet filled with pastel-colored ice creams and fruit syrups in bright primary colors, topped by a mountain of cream and a toy pinwheel on a candy-striped stick. Stephanie looked at the creation in shock, her eyes wide.

"I love ice cream," she choked, and then her eyes brimmed with tears and she began to cry.

Stephanie wept for a while, across the table, and, between sobs, choked down heaping spoonfuls of ice cream, eating in great gulps and swiping at her lips and tear-stained cheeks with a paper napkin.

The waiter stood quietly in the corner, but from his glare and the set of his jaw it was clear that he blamed Terzian for making the lovely woman cry.

Terzian felt his body surge with the impulse to aid her, but he didn't know what to do. Move around the table and put an arm around her? Take her hand? Call someone to take her off his hands?

The latter, for preference.

He settled for handing her a clean napkin when her own grew sodden.

His skepticism had not survived the mention of the Transnistrian copyright police. This was far too bizarre to be a con—a scam was based on basic human desire, greed, or lust, not something as abstract as intellectual property. Unless there was a gang who made a point of targeting academics from the States, luring them with a tantalizing hook about a copyright worth murdering for. . . .

Eventually, the storm subsided. Stephanie pushed the half-consumed ice cream away, and reached for another cigarette.

He tapped his wedding ring on the table top, something he did when thinking. "Shouldn't you contact the local police?" he asked. "You know something about this . . . death." For some reason he was reluctant to use the word *murder*. It was as if using the word would make something true, not the killing itself but his relationship to the killing . . . to call it murder would grant it some kind of power over him.

She shook her head. "I've got to get out of France before those guys find me. Out of Europe, if I can, but that would be hard. My passport's in my hotel room, and they're probably watching it."

"Because of this copyright."

Her mouth twitched in a half-smile. "That's right."

"It's not a literary copyright, I take it."

She shook her head, the half-smile still on her face.

"Your friend was a biologist." He felt a hum in his nerves, a certainty that he already knew the answer to the next question.

"Is it a weapon?" he asked.

She wasn't surprised by the question. "No," she said. "No, just the opposite." She took a drag on her cigarette and sighed the smoke out. "It's an antidote. An antidote to human folly."

"Listen," Stephanie said. "Just because the Soviet Union fell doesn't mean that *Sovietism* fell with it. Sovietism is still there—the only difference is that its moral justification is gone, and what's left is violence and extortion disguised as law enforcement and taxation. The old empire breaks up, and in the West you think it's great, but more countries just meant more palms to be greased—all throughout the former Soviet empire you've got more 'inspectors' and 'tax collectors,' more 'customs agents' and 'security directorates' than there ever were under the Russians. All these people do is prey off their own populations, because no one else will do business with them unless they've got oil or some other resource that people want."

"Trashcanistans," Terzian said. It was a word he'd heard used of his own ancestral homeland, the former Soviet Republic of Armenia, whose looted economy and paranoid, murderous, despotic Russian puppet regime was supported only by millions of dollars sent to the country by Americans of Armenian descent, who thought that propping up the gang of thugs in power somehow translated into freedom for the fatherland.

Stephanie nodded. "And the worst Trashcanistan of all is Transnistria."

She and Terzian had left the café and taken a taxi back to the Left Bank and Terzian's hotel. He had turned the television to a local station, but muted the sound until the news came on. Until then the station showed a rerun of an American cop show, stolid, businesslike detectives underplaying their latest sordid confrontation with tragedy.

The hotel room hadn't been built for the queen-sized bed it now held, and there was an eighteen-inch clearance around the bed and no room for chairs. Terzian, not wanting Stephanie to think he wanted to get her in the sack, perched uncertainly on a corner of the bed, while Stephanie disposed herself more comfortably, sitting cross-legged in its center.

"Moldova was a Soviet republic put together by Stalin," she said. "It was made up of Bessarabia, which was a part of Romania that Stalin chewed off at the beginning of the Second World War, plus a strip of industrial land on the far side of the Dniester. When the Soviet Union went down, Moldova became 'independent'—" Terzian could hear the quotes in her voice. "But independence had nothing to do with the Moldovan *people*, it was just Romanian-speaking Soviet elites going off on their own account once their own superiors were no longer there to retrain them. And Moldova soon split—first the Turkish Christians . . ."

"Wait a second," Terzian said. "There are *Christian Turks?*"

The idea of Christian Turks was not a part of his Armenian-American worldview.

Stephanie nodded. "Orthodox Christian Turks, yes. They're called Gagauz, and they now have their own autonomous republic of Gagauzia within Moldova."

Stephanie reached into her pocket for a cigarette and her lighter.

"Uh," Terzian said. "Would you mind smoking in the window?"

Stephanie made a face. "Americans," she said, but she moved to the window and opened it, letting in a blast of cool spring air. She perched on the windowsill, sheltered her cigarette from the wind, and lit up.

"Where was I?" she asked.

"Turkish Christians."

"Right." Blowing smoke into the teeth of the gale. "Gagauzia was only the start—after that, a Russian general allied with a bunch of crooks and KGB types created a rebellion in the bit of Moldova that was on the far side of the Dniester—another collection of Soviet elites, representing no one but themselves. Once the Russian-speaking rebels rose against their Romanian-speaking oppressors, the Soviet Fourteen Army stepped in as 'peacekeepers,' complete with blue helmets, and created a twenty-mile-wide state recognized by no other government. And that meant more military, more border guards, more administrators, more taxes to charge, and customs duties, and uniformed ex-Soviets whose palms needed greasing. And over a hundred thousand refugees who could be put in camps while the administration stole their supplies and rations. . . .

"But—" She jabbed the cigarette like a pointer. "Transnistria had a problem. No other nation recognized their existence, and they were tiny and had no natural resources, barring the underage girls they enslaved by the thousands to export for prostitution. The rest of the population was leaving as fast as they could, restrained only slightly by the fact that they carried passports no other state recognized, and that meant there were fewer people whose productivity the elite could steal to support their predatory post-Soviet lifestyles. All they had was a lot of obsolete Soviet heavy industry geared to produce stuff no one wanted.

"But they still had the *infrastructure*. They had power plants—running off Russian oil they couldn't afford to buy—and they had a transportation system. So the outlaw regime set up to attract other outlaws who needed industrial capacity—the idea was that they'd attract entrepreneurs who were excused paying most of the local 'taxes' in exchange for making one big payoff to the higher echelon."

"Weapons?" Terzian asked.

"Weapons, sure," Stephanie nodded. "Mostly they're producing cheap knockoffs of other people's guns, but the guns are up to the size of howitzers. They tried banking and data havens, but the authorities couldn't restrain themselves from ripping those off—banks and data run on trust and control of information, and when the regulators are greedy, short-sighted crooks, you don't get either one. So what they settled on was, well, *biotech*. They've got companies creating cheap generic pharmaceuticals that evade Western patents. . . ." Her look darkened. "Not that I've got a problem with *that*, not when I've seen thousands dying of diseases they couldn't afford to cure. And they've also got other companies who are ripping off Western genetic research to develop their own products. And as long as they make their payoffs to the elite, these companies remain *completely unregulated*. Nobody, not even the government, knows what they're doing in those factories, and the government gives them security free of charge."

Terzian imagined gene-splicing going on in a rusting Soviet factory, rows and rows of mutant plants with untested, unregulated genetics, all set to be released on an unsuspecting world. Transgenic elements drifting down the Dniester to the Black Sea, growing quietly in its saline environment. . . .

"The news," Stephanie reminded, and pointed at the television.

Terzian reached for the control and hit the mute button, just as the throbbing, anxious music that announced the news began to fade.

The murder on the Ile de la Cité was the second item on the broadcast. The victim was described as a "foreign national" who had been fatally stabbed, and no arrests had been made. The motive for the killing was unknown.

Terzian changed the channel in time to catch the same item on another channel. The story was unchanged.

"I told you," Stephanie said. "No suspects. No motive."

"You could tell them."

She made a negative motion with her cigarette. "I couldn't tell them who did it, or how to find them. All I could do is put myself under suspicion."

Terzian turned off the TV. "So what happened exactly? Your friend stole from these people?"

Stephanie swiped her forehead with the back of her wrist. "He stole something that was of no value to them. It's only valuable to poor people, who can't afford to pay. And—" She turned to the window and spun her cigarette into the street below. "I'll take it out of here as soon as I can," she said. "I've got to try to contact some people." She closed the window, shutting out the spring breeze. "I wish I had my passport. That would change everything."

I saw a murder this afternoon, Terzian thought. He closed his eyes and saw the man falling, the white face so completely absorbed in the reality of its own agony.

He was so fucking sick of death.

He opened his eyes. "I can get your passport back," he said.

Anger kept him moving until he saw the killers, across the street from Stephanie's hotel, sitting at an outdoor table in a café-bar. Terzian recognized them immediately—he didn't need to look at the heavy shoes, or the broad faces with their disciplined military mustaches—one glance at the crowd at the café showed the only two in the place who weren't French. That was probably how Stephanie knew to speak to him in English, he just didn't dress or carry himself like a Frenchman, for all that he'd worn an anonymous coat and tie. He tore his gaze away before they saw him gaping at them.

Anger turned very suddenly to fear, and as he continued his stride toward the hotel he told himself that they wouldn't recognize him from the Norman restaurant, that he'd changed into blue jeans and sneakers and a windbreaker, and carried a soft-sided suitcase. Still he felt a gunsight on the back of his neck, and he was so nervous that he nearly ran head-first into the glass lobby door.

Terzian paid for a room with his credit card, took the key from the Vietnamese clerk, and walked up the narrow stair to what the French called the second floor, but what he would have called the third. No one lurked in the stairwell, and he wondered where the third assassin had gone. Looking for Stephanie somewhere else, probably, an airport or train station.

In his room Terzian put his suitcase on the bed—it held only a few token items, plus his shaving kit—and then he took Stephanie's key from his pocket and held it in his hand. The key was simple, attached to a weighted doorknob-shaped ceramic plug.

The jolt of fear and surprise that had so staggered him on first sighting the two men began to shift again into rage.

They were drinking *beer,* there had been half-empty mugs on the table in front of them, and a pair of empties as well.

Drinking on duty. Doing surveillance while drunk.

Bastards. Trashcanians. They could kill someone simply through drunkenness.

Perhaps they already had.

He was angry when he left his room and took the stairs to the floor below. No foes kept watch in the hall. He opened Stephanie's room and then closed the door behind him.

He didn't turn on the light. The sun was surprisingly high in the sky for the hour: he had noticed that the sun seemed to set later here than it did at home. Maybe France was very far to the west for its time zone.

Stephanie didn't have a suitcase, just a kind of nylon duffel, a larger version of the athletic bag she already carried. He took it from the little closet, and enough of Terzian's suspicion remained so that he checked the luggage tag to make certain the name was *Steph. Pais*, and not another.

He opened the duffel, then got her passport and travel documents from the bedside table and tossed them in. He added a jacket and a sweater from the closet, then packed her toothbrush and shaver into her plastic travel bag and put it in the duffel.

The plan was for him to return to his room on the upper floor and stay the night and avoid raising suspicion by leaving a hotel he'd just checked into. In the morning, carrying two bags, he'd check out and rejoin Stephanie in his own hotel, where she had spent the night in his room, and where the air would by now almost certainly reek with her cigarette smoke.

Terzian opened a dresser drawer and scooped out a double handful of Stephanie's T-shirts, underwear, and stockings, and then he remembered that the last time he'd done this was when he cleaned Claire's belongings out of the Esplanade house.

Shit. Fuck. He gazed down at the clothing between his hands and let the fury rage like a tempest in his skull.

And then, in the angry silence, he heard a creak in the corridor, and then a stumbling thud.

Thick rubber military soles, he thought. With drunk baboons in them.

Instinct shrieked at him not to be trapped in this room, this dead-end where he could be trapped and killed. He dropped Stephanie's clothes back into the drawer and stepped to the bed and picked up the duffel in one hand. Another step took him to the door, which he opened with one hand while using the other to fling the duffel into the surprised face of the drunken murderer on the other side.

Terzian hadn't been at his Kenpo school in six years, not since he'd left Kansas City, but certain reflexes don't go away after they've been drilled into a person thousands of times—certainly not the front kick that hooked upward under the intruder's breastbone and drove him breathless into the corridor wall opposite.

A primitive element of his mind rejoiced in the fact that he was bigger than these guys. He could really knock them around.

The second Trashcanian tried to draw a pistol, but Terzian passed outside the pistol hand and drove the point of an elbow into the man's face. Terzian then grabbed the automatic with both hands, took a further step down the corridor, and spun around, which swung the man around Terzian's hip a full two hundred and seventy degrees and drove him head-first into the corridor wall. When he'd finished falling and opened his eyes he was staring into the barrel of his own gun.

Red rage gave a fangs-bared roar of animal triumph inside Terzian's skull. Perhaps his tongue echoed it. It was all he could do to stop himself from pulling the trigger.

Get Death working for *him* for a change. Why not?

Except that the first man hadn't realized that his side had just lost. He had drawn a knife—a glittering chromed single-edged thing that may have already killed once today—and now he took a dangerous step toward Terzian.

Terzian pointed the pistol straight at the knife man and pulled the trigger. Nothing happened.

The intruder stared at the gun as if he'd just realized at just this moment it wasn't his partner who held it.

Terzian pulled the trigger again, and when nothing happened his rage melted into terror and he ran. Behind him he heard the drunken knife man trip over his partner and crash to the floor.

Terzian was at the bottom of the stair before he heard the thick-soled military boots clatter on the risers above him. He dashed through the small lobby—he sensed the Vietnamese night clerk, who was facing away, begin to turn toward him just as he pushed open the glass door and ran into the street.

He kept running. At some point he discovered the gun still in his fist, and he put it in the pocket of his windbreaker.

Some moments later, he realized that he wasn't being pursued. And he remembered that Stephanie's passport was still in her duffel, which he'd thrown at the knife man and hadn't retrieved.

For a moment, rage ran through him, and he thought about taking out the gun and fixing whatever was wrong with it and going back to Stephanie's room and getting the documents one way or another.

But then the anger faded enough for him to see what a foolish course that would be, and he returned to his own hotel.

Terzian had given Stephanie his key, so he knocked on his own door before realizing she was very unlikely to open to a random knock. "It's Jonathan," he said. "It didn't work out."

She snatched the door open from the inside. Her face was taut with anxiety. She held pages in her hand, the text of the paper he'd delivered that morning.

"Sorry," he said. "They were there, outside the hotel. I got into your room, but—"

She took his arm and almost yanked him into the room, then shut the door behind him. "Did they follow you?" she demanded.

"No. They didn't chase me. Maybe they thought I'd figure out how to work the gun." He took the pistol out of his pocket and showed it to her. "I can't believe how stupid I was—"

"Where did you get that? Where did you get that?" Her voice was nearly a scream, and she shrank away from him, her eyes wide. Her fist crumpled papers over her heart. To his astonishment, he realized that she was afraid of him, that she thought he was *connected,* somehow, with the killers.

He threw the pistol onto the bed and raised his hands in a gesture of surrender. "No really!" he shouted over her cries. "It's not mine! I took it from one of them!"

Stephanie took a deep gasp of air. Her eyes were still wild. "Who the hell are you, then?" she said. "James Bond?"

He gave a disgusted laugh. "James Bond would have known how to shoot."

"I was reading your—your article." She held out the pages toward him. "I was thinking, my God, I was thinking, what have I got this poor guy into. Some professor I was sending to his death." She passed a hand over her forehead. "They probably bugged my room. They would have known right away that someone was in it."

"They were drunk," Terzian said. "Maybe they've been drinking all day. Those assholes really pissed me off."

He sat on the bed and picked up the pistol. It was small and blue steel and surprisingly heavy. In the years since he'd last shot a gun, he had forgotten that purposefulness, the way a firearm was designed for a single, clear function. He found the safety where it had been all along, near his right thumb, and flicked it off and then on again.

"There," he said. "That's what I should have done."

Waves of anger shivered through his limbs at the touch of the adrenaline still pouring into his system. A bitter impulse to laugh again rose in him, and he tried to suppress it.

"I guess I was lucky after all," he said. "It wouldn't have done you any good to have to explain a pair of corpses outside your room." He looked up at Stephanie, who was pacing back and forth in the narrow lane between the bed and the wall, and looking as if she badly needed a cigarette. "I'm sorry about your passport. Where were you going to go, anyway?"

"It doesn't so much matter if *I* go," she said. She gave Terzian a quick, nervous glance. "You can fly it out, right?"

"It?" He stared at her. "What do you mean, it?"

"The biotech." Stephanie stopped her pacing and stared at him with those startling green eyes. "Adrian gave it to me. Just before they killed him." Terzian's gaze followed hers to the black bag with the Nike swoosh, the bag that sat at the foot of Terzian's bed.

Terzian's impulse to laugh faded. Unregulated, illegal, stolen biotech, he thought. Right in his own hotel room. Along with a stolen gun and a woman who was probably out of her mind.

Fuck.

The dead man was identified by news files as Adrian Cristea, a citizen of Ukraine and a researcher. He had been stabbed once in the right kidney and bled to death without identifying his assailants. Witnesses reported two or maybe three men leaving the scene immediately after Cristea's death. Michelle set more search spiders to work.

For a moment, she considered calling Davout and letting him know that Terzian had probably been a witness to a murder, but decided to wait until she had some more evidence one way or another.

For the next few hours, she did her real work, analyzing the samples she'd taken from Zigzag Lake's sulphide-tainted deeps. It wasn't very physical, and Michelle figured it was only worth a few hundred calories.

A wind floated through the treetops, bringing the scent of night flowers and swaying Michelle's perch beneath her as she peered into her biochemical reader, and she remembered the gentle pressure of Darton against her back, rocking with her as he looked over her shoulder at her results. Suddenly she could remember, with a near-perfect clarity, the taste of his skin on her tongue.

She rose from her woven seat and paced along the bough. *Damn it,* she thought, *I watched you die.*

Michelle returned to her deck and discovered that her spiders had located the police file on Cristea's death. A translation program handled the antique French without trouble, even producing modern equivalents of forensic jargon. Cristea was of Romanian descent, had been born in the old USSR, and had acquired Ukranian citizenship on the breakup of the Soviet Union. The French files themselves had translations of Cristea's Ukranian travel documents, which included receipts showing that he had paid personal insurance, environmental insurance, and departure taxes from Transnistria, a place of which she'd never heard, as well as similar documents from Moldova, which at least was a province, or country, that sounded familiar.

What kind of places were these, where you had to buy *insurance* at the *border?* And what was environmental insurance anyway?

There were copies of emails between French and Ukranian authorities, in which the Ukranians politely declined any knowledge of their citizen beyond the fact that he *was* a citizen. They had no addresses for him.

Cristea apparently lived in Transnistria, but the authorities there echoed the Ukranians in saying they knew nothing of him.

Cristea's tickets and vouchers showed that he had apparently taken a train to Bucharest, and there he'd got on an airline that took him to Prague, and thence to Paris. He had been in the city less than a day before he was killed. Found in Cristea's hotel room was a curious document certifying that Cristea was carrying medical supplies, specifically a vaccine against hepatitis A. Michelle wondered why he would be carrying a hepatitis vaccine from Transnistria to France. France presumably had all the hepatitis vaccine it needed.

No vaccine had turned up. Apparently Cristea had got into

the European Community without having his bags searched, as there was no evidence that the documents relating to the alleged vaccine had ever been examined.

The missing "vaccine"—at some point in the police file the skeptical quotation marks had appeared—had convinced the Paris police that Cristea was a murdered drug courier, and at that point they'd lost interest in the case. It was rarely possible to solve a professional killing in the drug underworld.

Michelle's brief investigation seemed to have come to a dead end. That Terzian might have witnessed a murder would rate maybe half a sentence in Professor Davout's biography.

Then she checked what her spiders had brought her in regard to Terzian, and found something that cheered her.

There he was inside the Basilica di Santa Croce, a tourist still photograph taken before the tomb of Machiavelli. He was only slightly turned away from the camera and the face was unmistakable. Though there was no date on the photograph, only the year, he wore the same clothes he wore in the video taken outside the church, and the photo caught him in the act of speaking to a companion. She was a tall woman with deep brown skin, but she was turned away from the camera, and a wide-brimmed sun hat made her features indistinguishable.

Humming happily, Michelle deployed her software to determine whether this was the same woman who had been on Terzian's arm on the Place Dauphine. Without facial features or other critical measurements to compare, the software was uncertain, but the proportion of limb and thorax was right, and the software gave an estimate of 41 percent, which Michelle took to be encouraging.

Another still image of Terzian appeared in an undated photograph taken at a festival in southern France. He wore dark glasses, and he'd grown heavily tanned; he carried a glass of wine in either hand, but the person to whom he was bringing the second glass was out of the frame. Michelle set her software to locating the identity of the church seen in the background, a task the two distinctive belltowers would make easy. She was lucky and got a hit right away: the church was the Eglise St-Michel in Salon-de-Provence, which meant Terzian had attended the Fête des Aires de la Dine in June. Michelle set more search spiders to seeking out photo and video from the festivals. She had no doubt that she'd find Terzian there, and perhaps again his companion.

Michelle retired happily to her hammock. The search was going well. Terzian had met a woman in Paris and traveled with her for weeks. The evidence wasn't quite there yet, but Michelle would drag it out of history somehow.

Romance. The lonely mermaid was in favor of romance, the kind where you ran away to faraway places to be more intently one with the person you adored.

It was what she herself had done, before everything had gone so wrong, and Michelle had had to take steps to re-establish the moral balance of her universe.

Terzian paid for a room for Stephanie for the night, not so much because he was gallant as because he needed to be alone to think. "There's a breakfast buffet downstairs in the morning," he said. "They have hard-boiled eggs and croissants and Nutella. It's a very un-French thing to do. I recommend it."

He wondered if he would ever see her again. She might just vanish, particularly if she read his thoughts, because another reason for wanting privacy was so that he could call the police and bring an end to this insane situation.

He never quite assembled the motivation to make the call. Perhaps Rorty's *I don't care* had rubbed off on him. And he never got a chance to taste the buffet, either. Stephanie banged on his door very early, and he dragged on his jeans and opened the door. She entered, furiously smoking from her new cigarette pack, the athletic bag over her shoulder.

"How did you pay for the room at my hotel?" she asked.

"Credit card," he said, and in the stunned, accusing silence that followed he saw his James Bond fantasies sink slowly beneath the slack, oily surface of a dismal lake.

Because credit cards leave trails. The Transnistrians would have checked the hotel registry, and the credit card impression taken by the hotel, and now they knew who *he* was. And it wouldn't be long before they'd trace him at this hotel.

"Shit, I should have warned you to pay cash." Stephanie

stalked to the window and peered out cautiously. "They could be out there right now."

Terzian felt a sudden compulsion to have the gun in his hand. He took it from the bedside table and stood there, feeling stupid and cold and shirtless.

"How much money do you have?" Terzian asked.

"Couple hundred."

"I have less."

"You should max out your credit card and just carry Euros. Use your card now before they cancel it."

"Cancel it? How could they cancel it?"

She gave him a tight-lipped, impatient look. "Jonathan. They may be assholes, but they're still a *government*."

They took a cab to the American Express near the Opéra and Terzian got ten thousand Euros in cash from some people who were extremely skeptical about the validity of his documents, but who had, in the end, to admit that all was technically correct. Then Stephanie got a cell phone under the name A. Silva, with a bunch of prepaid hours on it, and within a couple of hours they were on the TGV, speeding south to Nice at nearly two hundred seventy kilometers per hour, all with a strange absence of sound and vibration that made the French countryside speeding past seem like a strangely unconvincing special effect.

Terzian had put them in first class and he and Stephanie were alone in a group of four seats. Stephanie was twitchy because he hadn't bought seats in a smoking section. He sat uncertain, unhappy about all the cash he was carrying and not knowing what to do with it—he'd made two big rolls and zipped them into the pockets of his windbreaker. He carried the pistol in the front pocket of his jeans and its weight and discomfort was a perpetual reminder of this situation that he'd been dragged into, pursued by killers from Trashcanistan and escorting illegal biotechnology.

He kept mentally rehearsing drawing the pistol and shooting it. Over and over, remembering to thumb off the safety this time. Just in case Trashcanian commandos stormed the train.

"Hurled into life," he muttered. "An object lesson right out of Heidegger."

"Beg pardon?"

He looked at her. "Heidegger said we're hurled into life. Just like I've been hurled into—" He flapped his hands uselessly. "Into whatever this is. The situation exists before you even got here, but here you are anyway, and the whole business is something you inherit and have to live with." He felt his lips draw back in a snarl. "He also said that a fundamental feature of existence is anxiety in the face of death, which would also seem to apply to our situation. And his answer to all of this was to make existence, *dasein* if you want to get technical, an authentic project." He looked at her. "So what's your authentic project, then? And how authentic is it?"

Her brow furrowed. "What?"

Terzian couldn't stop, not that he wanted to. It was just Stephanie's hard luck that he couldn't shoot anybody right now, or break something up with his fists, and was compelled to lecture instead. "Or," he went on, "to put this in a more accessible context, just pretend we're in a Hitchcock film, okay? This is the scene where Grace Kelly tells Cary Grant exactly who she is and what the maguffin is."

Stephanie's face was frozen into a hostile mask. Whether she understood what he was saying or not, the hostility was clear.

"I don't get it," she said.

"What's in the fucking bag?" he demanded.

She glared at him for a long moment, then spoke, her own anger plain in her voice. "It's the answer to world hunger," she said. "Is that authentic enough for you?"

Stephanie's father was from Angola and her mother from East Timor, both former Portuguese colonies swamped in the decades since independence by war and massacre. Both parents had, with great foresight and intelligence, retained Portuguese passports, and had met in Rome, where they worked for UNESCO, and where Stephanie had grown up with a blend of their genetics and their service ethic.

Stephanie herself had received a degree in administration from the University of Virginia, which accounted for the American lights in her English, then she'd gotten another degree in nursing and went to work for the Catholic relief agency Santa

Croce, which sent her to its every war-wrecked, locust-blighted, warlord-ridden, sandstorm-blasted camp in Africa. And a few that *weren't* in Africa.

"Trashcanistan," Terzian said.

"Moldova," Stephanie said. "For three months, on what was supposed to be my vacation." She shuddered. "I don't mind telling you that it was a frightening thing. I was used to that kind of thing in Africa, but to see it all happening in the developed world . . . warlords, ethnic hatreds, populations being moved at the point of a gun, whole forested districts being turned to deserts because people suddenly need firewood. . . ." Her emerald eyes flashed. "It's all politics, okay? Just like in Africa. Famine and camps are all politics now, and have been since before I was born. A whole population starves, and it's because someone, somewhere, sees a profit in it. It's difficult to just kill an ethnic group you don't like, war is expensive and there are questions at the UN and you may end up at the Hague being tried for war crimes. But if you just wait for a bad harvest and then arrange for the whole population to *starve*, it's different—suddenly your enemies are giving you all their money in return for food, you get aid from the UN instead of grief, and you can award yourself a piece of the relief action and collect bribes from all the relief agencies, and your enemies are rounded up into camps and you can get your armed forces into the country without resistance, make sure your enemies disappear, control everything while some deliveries disappear into government warehouses where the food can be sold to the starving or just sold abroad for a profit. . . ." She shrugged. "That's the way of the world, okay? *But no more!*" She grabbed a fistful of the Nike bag and brandished it at him.

What her time in Moldova had done was to leave Stephanie contacts in the area, some in relief agencies, some in industry and government. So that when news of a useful project came up in Transnistria, she was among the first to know.

"So what is it?" Terzian asked. "Some kind of genetically modified food crop?"

"No." She smiled thinly. "What we have here is a genetically modified *consumer*."

Those Transnistrian companies had mostly been interested in

duplicating pharmaceuticals and transgenetic food crops created by other companies, producing them on the cheap and underselling the patent-owners. There were bits and pieces of everything in those labs, DNA human and animal and vegetable. A lot of it had other people's trademarks and patents on it, even the human codes, which U.S. law permitted companies to patent provided they came up with something useful to do with it. And what these semi-outlaw companies were doing was making two things they figured people couldn't do without: drugs and food.

And not just people, since animals need drugs and food, too. Starving, tubercular sheep or pigs aren't worth much at market, so there's as much money in keeping livestock alive as in doing the same for people. So at some point one of the administrators—after a few too many shots of vodka flavored with bison grass—said, "Why should we worry about feeding the animals at all? Why not have them grow their own food, like plants?"

So then began the Green Swine Project, an attempt to make pigs fat and happy by just herding them out into the sun.

"Green swine," Terzian repeated, wondering. "People are getting killed over green swine."

"Well, no." Stephanie waved the idea away with a twitchy swipe of her hand. "The idea never quite got beyond the vaporware stage, because at that point another question was asked—why swine? Adrian said, Why stop at having animals do photosynthesis—why not *people?*"

"No!" Terzian cried, appalled. "You're going to turn people green?"

Stephanie glared at him. "Something wrong with fat, happy green people?" Her hands banged out a furious rhythm on the armrests of her seat. "I'd have skin to match my eyes. Wouldn't that be attractive?"

"I'd have to see it first," Terzian said, the shock still rolling through his bones.

"Adrian was pretty smart," Stephanie said. "The Transnistrians killed themselves a real genius." She shook her head. "He had it all worked out. He wanted to limit the effect to the skin—no green muscle tissue or skeletons—so he started with a virus that has a tropism for the epidermis—papiloma, that's warts, okay?"

So now we've got green warts, Terzian thought, but he kept his mouth shut.

"So if you're Adrian, what you do is gut out the virus and re-encode to create chlorophyll. Once a person's infected, exposure to sunlight will cause the virus to replicate and chlorophyll to reproduce in the skin."

Terzian gave Stephanie a skeptical look. "That's not going to be very efficient," he said. "Plants get sugars and oxygen from chlorophyll, okay, but they don't need much food, they stand in one place and don't walk around. Add chlorophyll to a person's skin, how many calories do you get each day? Tens? Dozens?"

Stephanie's lips parted in a fierce little smile. "You don't stop with just the chlorophyll. You have to get really efficient electron transport. In a plant that's handled in the chloroplasts, but the human body already has mitochondria to do the same job. You don't have to create these huge support mechanisms for the chlorophyll, you just make use of what's already there. So if you're Adrian, what you do is add trafficking tags to the reaction center proteins so that they'll target the mitochondria, which *already* are loaded with proteins to handle electron transport. The result is that the mitochondria handle transport from the chlorophyll, which is the sort of job they do anyway, and once the virus starts replicating, you can get maybe a thousand calories or more just from standing in the sun. It won't provide full nutrition, but it can keep starvation at bay, and it's not as if starving people have much to do besides stand in the sun anyway."

"It's not going to do much good for Icelanders," Terzian said.

She turned severe. "Icelanders aren't starving. It so happens that most of the people in the world who are starving happen to be in hot places."

Terzian flapped his hands. "Fine. I must be a racist. Sue me."

Stephanie's grin broadened, and she leaned toward Terzian. "I didn't tell you about Adrian's most interesting bit of cleverness. When people start getting normal nutrition, there'll be a competition within the mitochondria between normal metabolism and solar-induced electron transport. So the green virus is just a redundant backup system in case normal nutrition isn't available."

A triumphant smile crossed Stephanie's face. "Starvation will no longer be a weapon," she said. "Green skin can keep people active and on their feet long enough to get help. It will keep them healthy enough to fend off the epidemics associated with malnutrition. The point is—" She made fists and shook them at the sky. "*The bad guys don't get to use starvation as a weapon anymore!* Famine *ends!* One of the Four Horsemen of the Apocalypse *dies,* right here, right now, as a result of *what I've got in this bag!*" She picked up the bag and threw it into Terzian's lap, and he jerked on the seat in defensive reflex, knees rising to meet elbows. Her lips skinned back in a snarl, and her tone was mocking.

"I think even that Nazi fuck Heidegger would think my *project* is pretty damn *authentic.* Wouldn't you agree, Herr Doktor Terzian?"

Got you, Michelle thought. Here was a still photo of Terzian at the Fête des Aires de la Dine, with the dark-skinned woman. She had the same wide-brimmed straw hat she'd worn in the Florence church, and had the same black bag over her shoulder, but now Michelle had a clear view of a three-quarter profile, and one hand, with its critical alignments, was clearly visible, holding an ice cream cone.

Night insects whirled around the computer display. Michelle batted them away and got busy mapping. The photo was digital and Michelle could enlarge it.

To her surprise, she discovered that the woman had green eyes. Black women with green irises—or irises of orange or chartreuse or chrome steel—were not unusual in her own time, but she knew that in Terzian's time they were rare. That would make the search much easier.

"Michelle . . ." The voice came just as Michelle sent her new search spiders into the ether. A shiver ran up her spine.

"Michelle . . ." The voice came again.

It was Darton.

Michelle's heart gave a sickening lurch. She closed her console and put it back in the mesh bag, then crossed the rope bridge between the ironwood tree and the banyan. Her knees were weak, and the swaying bridge seemed to take a couple of unexpected pitches. She stepped out onto the banyan's sturdy over-hanging limb and gazed out at the water.

"Michelle . . ." To the southwest, in the channel between the mermaid's island and another, she could see a pale light bobbing, the light of a small boat.

"Michelle, where are you?"

The voice died away in the silence and surf. Michelle remembered the spike in her hand, the long, agonized trek up the slope above Jellyfish Lake. Darton pale, panting for breath, dying in her arms.

The lake was one of the wonders of the world, but the steep path over the ridge that fenced the lake from the ocean was challenging even for those who were not dying. When Michelle and Darton—at that time, apes—came up from their boat that afternoon, they didn't climb the steep path, but swung hand-over-hand through the trees overhead, through the hardwood and guava trees, and avoided the poison trees with their bleeding, allergenic black sap. Even though their trip was less exhausting than if they'd gone over the land route, the two were ready for the cool water by the time they arrived at the lake.

Tens of thousands of years in the past, the water level was higher, and when it receded, the lake was cut off from the Pacific, and with it the *Mastigias sp.* jellyfish, which soon exhausted the supply of small fish that were its food. As the human race did later, the jellies gave up hunting and gathering in exchange for agriculture, and permitted themselves to be farmed by colonies of algae that provided the sugars they needed for life. At night, they'd descend to the bottom of the lake, where they fertilized their algae crops in the anoxic, sulfurous waters; at dawn, the jellies rose to the surface, and during the day, they crossed the lake, following the course of the sun, and allowed the sun's rays to supply the energy necessary for making their daily ration of food.

When Darton and Michelle arrived, there were ten million jellyfish in the lake, from fingertip-sized to jellies the size of a dinner plate, all in one warm throbbing golden-brown mass in the center of the water. The two swam easily on the surface with their long siamang arms, laughing and calling to one another as the jellyfish in their millions caressed them with the most featherlike of touches. The lake was the temperature of their own blood, and it was like a soupy bath, the jellyfish so thick that Michelle felt she could almost walk on the surface. The warm touch wasn't erotic, exactly, but it was sensual in the way that an erotic touch was sensual, a light brush over the skin by the pad of a teasing finger.

Trapped in a lake for thousands of years without suitable prey, the jellyfish had lost most of their ability to sting. Only a small percentage of people were sensitive enough to the toxin to receive a rash or feel a modest burning.

A very few people, though, were more sensitive than that.

Darton and Michelle left at dusk, and, by that time Darton, was already gasping for breath. He said he'd overexerted himself, that all he needed was to get back to their base for a snack, but as he swung through the trees on the way up the ridge, he lost his hold on a Palauan apple tree and crashed through a thicket of limbs to sprawl, amid a hail of fruit, on the sharp algae-covered limestone of the ridge.

Michelle swung down from the trees, her heart pounding. Darton was nearly colorless and struggling to breathe. They had no way of calling for help unless Michelle took their boat to Koror or to their base camp on another island. She tried to help Darton walk, taking one of his long arms over her shoulder, supporting him up the steep island trail. He collapsed, finally, at the foot of a poison tree, and Michelle bent over him to shield him from the drops of venomous sap until he died.

Her back aflame with the poison sap, she'd whispered her parting words into Darton's ear. She never knew if he heard.

The coroner said it was a million-to-one chance that Darton had been so deathly allergic, and tried to comfort her with the thought that there was nothing she could have done. Torbiong, who had made the arrangements for Darton and Michelle to come in the first place, had been consoling, had offered to let Michelle stay with his family. Michelle had surprised him by asking permission to move her base camp to another island, and to continue her work alone.

She also had herself transformed into a mermaid, and subsequently, a romantic local legend.

And now Darton was back, bobbing in a boat in the nearby channel and calling her name, shouting into a bullhorn.

"Michelle, I love you." The words floated clear into the night air. Michelle's mouth was dry. Her fingers formed the sign, <go away>.

There was a silence, and then Michelle heard the engine start on Darton's boat. He motored past her position, within five hundred meters or so, and continued on to the northern point of the island.

<go away> . . .

"Michelle . . ." Again his voice floated out onto the breeze. It was clear that he didn't know where she was. She was going to have to be careful about showing lights.

<go away> . . .

Michelle waited while Darton called out a half-dozen more times, and then he started his engine and moved on. She wondered if he would search all three hundred islands in the Rock Island group.

No, she knew he was more organized than that.

She'd have to decide what to do when he finally found her.

While a thousand questions chased each other's tails through his mind, Terzian opened the Nike bag and withdrew the small hard plastic case inside, something like a box for fishing tackle. He popped the locks on the case and opened the lid, and he saw glass vials resting in slots cut into dark grey foam. In them was a liquid with a faint golden caste.

"The papiloma," Stephanie said.

Terzian dropped the lid on the case as he cast a guilty look over his shoulder, not wanting anyone to see him with this stuff. If he were arrested under suspicion of being a drug dealer, the wads of cash and the pistol certainly wouldn't help.

"What do you do with the stuff once you get to where you're going?"

"Brush it on the skin. With exposure to solar energy it replicates as needed."

"Has it been tested?"

"On people? No. Works fine on rhesus monkeys, though."

He tapped his wedding ring on the arm of his seat. "Can it be . . . caught? I mean, it's a virus, can it go from one person to another?"

"Through skin-to-skin contact."

"I'd say that's a yes. Can mothers pass it on to their children?"

"Adrian didn't think it would cross the placental barrier, but he didn't get a chance to test it. If mothers want to infect their children, they'll probably have to do it deliberately." She shrugged. "Whatever the case, my guess is that mothers won't mind green babies, as long as they're green *healthy* babies." She looked down at the little vials in their secure coffins of foam. "We can infect tens of thousands of people with this amount," she said. "And we can make more very easily."

If mothers want to infect their children . . . Terzian closed the lid of the plastic case and snapped the locks. "You're out of your mind," he said.

Stephanie cocked her head and peered at him, looking as if she'd anticipated his objections and was humoring him. "How so?"

"Where do I start?" Terzian zipped up the bag, then tossed it in Stephanie's lap, pleased to see her defensive reflexes leap in response. "You're planning on unleashing an untested transgenetic virus on Africa—on *Africa* of all places, a continent that doesn't exactly have a happy history with pandemics. And it's a virus that's cooked up by a bunch of illegal pharmacists in a non-country with a murderous secret police, facts that don't give me much confidence that this is going to be anything but a disaster."

Stephanie tapped two fingers on her chin as if she was wishing there were a cigarette between them. "I can put your mind to rest on the last issue. The animal study worked. Adrian had a family of bright green rhesus in his lab, till the project was canceled and the rhesus were, ah, liquidated."

"So if the project's so terrific, why'd the company pull the plug?"

"Money." Her lips twisted in anger. "Starving people can't afford to pay for the treatments, so they'd have to practically give the stuff away. Plus they'd get reams of endless bad publicity, which is exactly what outlaw biotech companies in outlaw countries don't want. There are millions of people who go ballistic at the very thought of a genetically engineered *vegetable*—you can imagine how people who can't abide the idea of a transgenetic bell pepper would freak at the thought of infecting people with an engineered virus. The company decided it wasn't worth the risk. They closed the project down."

Stephanie looked at the bag in her hands. "But Adrian had been in the camps himself, you see. A displaced person, a refugee from the civil war in Moldova. And he couldn't stand the thought that there was a way to end hunger sitting in his refrigerator in the lab, and that nothing was being done with it. And so . . ." Her hands outlined the case inside the Nike bag. "He called me. He took some vacation time and booked himself into the Henri IV, on the Place Dauphine. And I guess he must have been careless, because . . ."

Tears starred in her eyes, and she fell silent. Terzian, strong in the knowledge that he'd shared quite enough of her troubles by now, stared out the window, at the green landscape that was beginning to take on the brilliant colors of Provence. The Hautes-Alpes floated blue and white-capped in the distant East, and nearby were orchards of almonds and olives with shimmering leaves, and hillsides covered with rows of orderly vines. The Rhone ran silver under the westering sun.

"I'm not going to be your bagman," he said. "I'm not going to contaminate the world with your freaky biotech."

"Then they'll catch you and you'll die," Stephanie said. "And it will be for nothing."

"My experience of death," said Terzian, "is that it's *always* for nothing."

She snorted then, angry. "My experience of death," she mocked, "is that it's too often for *profit*. I want to make mass murder an unprofitable venture. I want to crash the market in starvation by *giving away life*." She gave another snort, amused this time. "It's the ultimate anti-capitalist gesture."

Terzian didn't rise to that. Gestures, he thought, were just that. Gestures didn't change the fundamentals. If some jefe couldn't starve his people to death, he'd just use bullets, or deadly genetic technology he bought from outlaw Transnistrian corporations.

The landscape, all blazing green, raced past at over two hundred kilometers per hour. An attendant came by and sold them each a cup of coffee and a sandwich.

"You should use my phone to call your wife," Stephanie said as she peeled the cellophane from her sandwich. "Let her know that your travel plans have changed."

Apparently she'd noticed Terzian's wedding ring.

"My wife is dead," Terzian said.

She looked at him in surprise. "I'm sorry," she said.

"Brain cancer," he said.

Though it was more complicated than that. Claire had first complained of back pain, and there had been an operation, and the tumor removed from her spine. There had been a couple of weeks of mad joy and relief, and then it had been revealed that the cancer had spread to the brain and that it was inoperable. Chemotherapy had failed. She died six weeks after her first visit to the doctor.

"Do you have any other family?" Stephanie said.

"My parents are dead, too." Auto accident, aneurysm. He didn't mention Claire's uncle Geoff and his partner Luis, who had died of HIV within eight months of each other and left Claire the Victorian house on Esplanade in New Orleans. The house that, a few weeks ago, he had sold for six hundred and fifty thousand dollars, and the furnishings for a further ninety-five thousand, and Uncle Geoff's collection of equestrian art for a further forty-one thousand.

He was disinclined to mention that he had quite a lot of money, enough to float around Europe for years.

Telling Stephanie that might only encourage her.

There was a long silence. Terzian broke it. "I've read spy novels," he said. "And I know that we shouldn't go to the place we've bought tickets for. We shouldn't go anywhere *near* Nice."

She considered this, then said, "We'll get off at Avignon."

They stayed in Provence for nearly two weeks, staying always in unrated hotels, those that didn't even rise to a single star from the Ministry of Tourism, or in *gîtes ruraux,* farmhouses with rooms for rent. Stephanie spent much of her energy trying to call colleagues in Africa on her cell phone and achieved only sporadic success, a frustration that left her in a near-permanent fury. It was never clear just who she was trying to call, or how she thought they were going to get the papiloma off her hands. Terzian wondered how many people were involved in this conspiracy of hers.

They attended some local fêtes, though it was always a struggle to convince Stephanie it was safe to appear in a crowd. She made a point of disguising herself in big hats and shades and ended up looking like a cartoon spy. Terzian tramped rural lanes or fields or village streets, lost some pounds despite the splendid fresh local cuisine, and gained a suntan. He made a stab at writing several papers on his laptop, and spent time researching them in internet cafés.

He kept thinking he would have enjoyed this trip, if only Claire had been with him.

"What is it you *do,* exactly?" Stephanie asked him once, as he wrote. "I know you teach at university, but . . ."

"I don't teach anymore," Terzian said. "I didn't get my postdoc renewed. The department and I didn't exactly get along."

"Why not?"

Terzian turned away from the stale, stalled ideas on his display. "I'm too interdisciplinary. There's a place on the academic spectrum where history and politics and philosophy come together—it's called 'political theory' usually—but I throw in economics and a layman's understanding of science as well, and it confuses everybody but me. That's why my M.A. is in American Studies—nobody in my philosophy or political science department had the nerve to deal with me, and nobody knows what American Studies actually *are,* so I was able to hide out there. And my doctorate is in philosophy, but only because I found one rogue professor emeritus who was willing to chair my committee.

"The problem is that if you're hired by a philosophy department, you're supposed to teach Plato or Hume or whoever, and they don't want you confusing everybody by adding Maynard Keynes and Leo Szilard. And if you teach history, you're supposed to confine yourself to acceptable stories about the past and not toss in ideas about perceptual mechanics and Kant's ideas of the noumenon, and of course you court crucifixion from the laity if you mention Foucault or Nietzsche."

Amusement touched Stephanie's lips. "So where do you find a job?"

"France?" he ventured, and they laughed. "In France, 'thinker' is a job description. It's not necessary to have a degree, it's just something you do." He shrugged. "And if that fails, there's always Burger King."

She seemed amused. "Sounds like burgers are in your future."

"Oh, it's not as bad as all that. If I can generate enough interesting, sexy, highly original papers, I might attract attention and a job, in that order."

"And have you done that?"

Terzian looked at his display and sighed. "So far, no."

Stephanie narrowed her eyes and she considered him. "You're not a conventional person. You don't think inside the box, as they say."

"As they say," Terzian repeated.

"Then you should have no objections to radical solutions to world hunger. Particularly ones that don't cost a penny to white liberals throughout the world."

"Hah," Terzian said. "Who says I'm a liberal? I'm an *economist*."

So Stephanie told him terrible things about Africa. Another famine was brewing across the southern part of the continent. Mozambique was plagued with flood *and* drought, a startling combination. The Horn of Africa was worse. According to her friends, Santa Croce had a food shipment stuck in Mogadishu and before letting it pass, the local warlord wanted to renegotiate his bribe. In the meantime, people were starving, dying of malnutrition, infection, and dysentery in camps in the dry highlands of Bale and Sidamo. Their own government in Addis Ababa was worse than the Somali warlord, at this stage permitting no aid at all, bribes or no bribes.

And as for the southern Sudan, it didn't bear thinking about.

"What's *your* solution to this?" she demanded of Terzian. "Or do you have one?"

"Test this stuff, this papiloma," he said, "show me that it

works, and I'm with you. But there are too many plagues in Africa as it is."

"Confine the papiloma to labs while thousands die? Hand it to governments who can suppress it because of pressure from religious loons and hysterical NGOs? You call *that* an answer?" And Stephanie went back to working her phone while Terzian walked off in anger for another stalk down country lanes.

Terzian walked toward an old ruined castle that shambled down the slope of a nearby hill. And if Stephanie's plant-people proved viable? he wondered. All bets were off. A world in which humans could become plants was a world in which none of the old rules applied.

Stephanie had said she wanted to crash the market in starvation. But, Terzian thought, that also meant crashing the market in *food*. If people with no money had all the food they needed, that meant *food itself had no value in the marketplace*. Food would be so cheap that there would be no profit in growing or selling it.

And this was all just *one application* of the technology. Terzian tried to keep up with science: he knew about nanoassemblers. Green people was just the first magic bullet in a long volley of scientific musketry that would change every fundamental rule by which humanity had operated since they'd first stood upright. What happened when *every* basic commodity—food, clothing, shelter, maybe even health—was so cheap that it was free? What then had value?

Even *money* wouldn't have value then. Money only had value if it could be exchanged for something of equivalent worth.

He paused in his walk and looked ahead at the ruined castle, the castle that had once provided justice and security and government for the district, and he wondered if he was looking at the future of *all* government. Providing an orderly framework in which commodities could be exchanged was the basic function of the state, that and providing a secure currency. If people didn't need government to furnish that kind of security and if the currency was worthless, the whole future of government itself was in question. Taxes weren't worth the expense of collecting if the money wasn't any good, anyway, and without taxes, government couldn't be paid for.

Terzian paused at the foot of the ruined castle and wondered if he saw the future of the civilized world. Either the castle would be rebuilt by tyrants, or it would fall.

Michelle heard Darton's bullhorn again the next evening, and she wondered why he was keeping fruit-bat hours. Was it because his calls would travel farther at night?

If he were sleeping in the morning, she thought, that would make it easier. She'd finished analyzing some of her samples, but a principle of science was not to do these things alone: she'd have to travel to Koror to mail her samples to other people, and now she knew to do it in the morning, when Darton would be asleep.

The problem for Michelle was that she was a legend. When the lonely mermaid emerged from the sea and walked to the post office in the little foam booties she wore when walking on pavement, she was noticed. People pointed; children followed her on their boards, people in cars waved. She wondered if she could trust them not to contact Darton as soon as they saw her.

She hoped that Darton wasn't starting to get the islanders on his side.

Michelle and Darton had met on a field trip in Borneo, their obligatory government service after graduation. The other field workers were older, paying their taxes or working on their second or third or fourth or fifth careers, and Michelle knew on sight that Darton was no older than she, that he, too, was a child among all these elders. They were pulled to each other as if drawn by some violent natural force, cataloguing snails and terrapins by day and spending their nights wrapped in each other in their own shell, their turtleback tent. The ancients with whom they shared their days treated them with amused condescension, but then, that was how they treated everything. Darton and Michelle didn't care. In their youth they stood against all creation.

When the trip came to an end, they decided to continue their work together, just a hop across the equator in Belau. Paying their taxes ahead of time. They celebrated by getting new bodies, an exciting experience for Michelle, who had been built by strict parents who wouldn't allow her to have a new body until adulthood, no matter how many of her friends had been transforming from an early age into one newly fashionable shape or another.

Michelle and Darton thought that anthropoid bodies would be suitable for the work, and so they went to the clinic in Delhi and settled themselves on nanobeds and let the little machines turn their bodies, their minds, their memories, their desires and their knowledge and their souls, into long strings of numbers. All of which were fed into their new bodies when they were ready, and reserved as backups to be downloaded as necessary.

Being a siamang was a glorious discovery. They soared through the treetops of their little island, swinging overhand from limb to limb in a frenzy of glory. Michelle took a particular delight in her body hair—she didn't have as much as a real ape, but there was enough on her chest and back to be interesting. They built nests of foliage in trees and lay tangled together, analyzing data or making love or shaving their hair into interesting tribal patterns. Love was far from placid—it was a flame, a fury. An obsession that, against all odds, had been fulfilled, only to build the flame higher.

The fury still burned in Michelle. But now, after Darton's death, it had a different quality, a quality that had nothing to do with life or youth.

Michelle, spooning up blueberries and cream, riffled through the names and faces her spiders had spat out. There were, now she added them up, a preposterous number of pictures of green-eyed women with dark skin whose pictures were somewhere in the net. Nearly all of them had striking good looks. Many of them were unidentified in the old scans, or identified only by a first name. The highest probability the software offered was 43 percent.

That 43 percent belonged to a Brazilian named Laura Flor, who research swiftly showed was home in Aracaju during the critical period, among other things having a baby. A video of the delivery was available, but Michelle didn't watch it. The way women delivered babies back then was disgusting.

The next most likely female was another Brazilian seen in some tourist photographs taken in Rio. Not even a name given. A further search based on this woman's physiognomy turned up nothing, not until Michelle broadened the search to a different gender, and discovered that the Brazilian was a transvestite. That didn't seem to be Terzian's scene, so she left it alone.

The third was identified only as Stephanie, and posted on a site created by a woman who had done relief work in Africa. Stephanie was shown with a group of other relief workers, posing in front of a tin-roofed, cinderblock building identified as a hospital.

The quality of the photograph wasn't very good, but Michelle mapped the physiognomy anyway, and sent it forth along with the name "Stephanie" to see what might happen.

There was a hit right away, a credit card charge to a Stephanie América Pais e Silva. She had stayed in a hotel in Paris for the three nights before Terzian disappeared.

Michelle's blood surged as the data flashed on her screens. She sent out more spiders and the good news began rolling in.

Stephanie Pais was a dual citizen of Portugal and Angola, and had been educated partly in the States—a quick check showed that her time at university didn't overlap Terzian's. From her graduation, she had worked for a relief agency called Santa Croce.

Then a news item turned up, a sensational one. Stephanie Pais had been spectacularly murdered in Venice on the night of July 19, six days before Terzian had delivered the first version of his Cornucopia Theory.

Two murders. . . .

One in Paris, one in Venice. And one of them of the woman who seemed to be Terzian's lover.

Michelle's body shivered to a sudden gasping spasm, and she realized that in her suspense she'd been holding her breath. Her head swam. When it cleared, she worked out what time it was in Maryland, where Dr. Davout lived, and then told her deck to page him at once.

Davout was unavailable at first, and by the time he returned her call, she had more information about Stephanie Pais. She blurted the story out to him while her fingers jabbed at the keyboard of her deck, sending him copies of her corroborating data.

Davout's startled eyes leaped from the data to Michelle and

back. "How much of this . . ." he began, then gave up. "How did she die?" he managed.

"The news article says stabbed. I'm looking for the police report."

"Is Terzian mentioned?"

<No> she signed. "The police report will have more details."

"Any idea what this is about? There's no history of Terzian *ever* being connected with violence."

"By tomorrow," Michelle said, "I should be able to tell you. But I thought I should send this to you because you might be able to tie this in with other elements of Terzian's life that I don't know anything about."

Davout's fingers formed a mudra that Michelle didn't recognize—an old one, probably. He shook his head. "I have no idea what's happening here. The only thing I have to suggest is that this is some kind of wild coincidence."

"I don't believe in that kind of coincidence," Michelle said.

Davout smiled. "A good attitude for a researcher," he said. "But experience—well," he waved a hand.

But he loved her, Michelle insisted inwardly. She knew that in her heart. She was the woman he loved after Claire died, and then she was killed and Terzian went on to create the intellectual framework on which the world was now built. He had spent his modest fortune building pilot programs in Africa that demonstrated his vision was a practical one. The whole modern world was a monument to Stephanie.

Everyone was young then, Michelle thought. Even the seventy-year-olds were young compared to the people now. The world must have been *ablaze* with love and passion. But Davout didn't understand that because he was old and had forgotten all about love.

"Michelle . . ." Darton's voice came wafting over the waters.

Bastard. Michelle wasn't about to let him spoil this.

Her fingers formed <gotta go>. "I'll send you everything once it comes in," she said. "I think we've got something amazing here."

She picked up her deck and swung it around so that she could be sure that the light from the display couldn't be seen from the ocean. Her bare back against the rough bark of the ironwood, she began flashing through the data as it arrived.

She couldn't find the police report. Michelle went in search of it and discovered that all police records from that period in Venetian history had been wiped out in the Lightspeed War, leaving her only with what had been reported in the media.

"Where are you? I love you!" Darton's voice came from farther away. He'd narrowed his search, that was clear, but he still wasn't sure exactly where Michelle had built her nest.

Smiling, Michelle closed her deck and slipped it into its pouch. Her spiders would work for her tirelessly till dawn while she dreamed on in her hammock and let Darton's distant calls lull her to sleep.

They shifted their lodgings every few days. Terzian always arranged for separate bedrooms. Once, as they sat in the evening shade of a farm terrace and watched the setting sun shimmer on the silver leaves of the olives, Terzian found himself looking at her as she sat in an old cane chair, at the profile cutting sharp against the old limestone of the Vaucluse. The blustering wind brought gusts of lavender from the neighboring farm, a scent that made Terzian want to inhale until his lungs creaked against his ribs.

From a quirk of Stephanie's lips, Terzian was suddenly aware that she knew he was looking at her. He glanced away.

"You haven't tried to sleep with me," she said.

"No," he agreed.

"But you *look*," she said. "And it's clear you're not a eunuch."

"We fight all the time," Terzian pointed out. "Sometimes we can't stand to be in the same room."

Stephanie smiled. "That wouldn't stop most of the men I've known. Or the women, either."

Terzian looked out over the olives, saw them shimmer in the breeze. "I'm still in love with my wife," he said.

There was a moment of silence. "That's well," she said.

And I'm angry at her, too, Terzian thought. Angry at Claire for deserting him. And he was furious at the universe for killing her and for leaving him alive, and he was angry at God even though he didn't believe in God. The Trashcanians had been good for him, because he could let his rage and his hatred settle there, on people who deserved it.

Those poor drunken bastards, he thought. Whatever they'd expected in that hotel corridor, it hadn't been a berserk grieving American who would just as soon have ripped out their throats with his bare hands.

The question was, could he do that again? It had all occurred without his thinking about it, old reflexes taking over, but he couldn't count on that happening a second time. He'd been trying to remember the Kenpo he'd once learned, particularly all the tricks against weapons. He found himself miming combats on his long country hikes, and he wondered if he'd retained any of his ability to take a punch.

He kept the gun with him, so the Trashcanians wouldn't get it if they searched his room when he was away. When he was alone, walking through the almond orchards or on a hillside fragrant with wild thyme, he practiced drawing it, snicking off the safety, and putting pressure on the trigger . . . the first time the trigger pull would be hard, but the first shot would cock the pistol automatically and after that the trigger pull would be light.

He wondered if he should buy more ammunition. But he didn't know how to buy ammunition in France and didn't know if a foreigner could get into trouble that way.

"We're both angry," Stephanie said. He looked at her again, her hand raised to her head to keep the gusts from blowing her long ringlets in her face. "We're angry at death. But love must make it more complicated for you."

Her green eyes searched him. "It's not death you're in love with, is it? Because—"

Terzian blew up. She had no right to suggest that he was in a secret alliance with death just because he didn't want to turn a bunch of Africans green. It was their worst argument, and this one ended with both of them stalking away through the fields and orchards while the scent of lavender pursued them on the wind.

When Terzian returned to his room, he checked his caches of money, half-hoping that Stephanie had stolen his Euros and run. She hadn't.

He thought of going into her room while she was away, stealing the papiloma, and taking a train north, handing it over to the Pasteur Institute or someplace. But he didn't.

In the morning, during breakfast, Stephanie's cell phone rang, and she answered. He watched while her face turned from curiosity to apprehension to utter terror. Adrenaline sang in his blood as he watched, and he leaned forward, feeling the familiar rage rise in him, just where he wanted it. In haste, she turned off the phone, then looked at him. "That was one of them. He says he knows where we are, and wants to make a deal."

"If they know where we are," Terzian found himself saying coolly, "why aren't they here?"

"We've got to *go*," she insisted.

So they went. Clean out of France and into the Tuscan hills, with Stephanie's cell phone left behind in a trash can at the train station and a new phone purchased in Siena. The Tuscan countryside was not unlike Provence, with vine-covered hillsides, orchards a-shimmer with the silver-green of olive trees, and walled medieval towns perched on crags; but the slim, tall cypress standing like sentries gave the hills a different profile, and there were different types of wine grapes, and many of the vineyards rented rooms where people could stay and sample the local hospitality. Terzian didn't speak the language, and because Spanish was his first foreign language, consistently pronounced words like "villa" and "panzanella" as if they were Spanish. But Stephanie had grown up in Italy and spoke the language not only like a native, but like a native Roman.

Florence was only a few hours away, and Terzian couldn't resist visiting one of the great living monuments to civilization. His parents, both university professors, had taken him to Europe several times as a child, but somehow never made it here.

Terzian and Stephanie spent a day wandering the center of town, on occasion taking shelter from one of the pelting rainstorms that shattered the day. At one point, with thunder booming overhead, they found themselves in the Basilica di Santa Croce.

"Holy Cross," Terzian said, translating. "That's your outfit."

"We have nothing to do with this church," Stephanie said.

"We don't even have a collection box here."

"A pity," Terzian said as he looked at the soaked swarms of tourists packed in the aisles. "You'd clean up."

Thunder accompanied the camera strobes that flashed against the huge tomb of Galileo like a vast lighting storm. "Nice of them to forget about that Inquisition thing and bury him in a church," Terzian said.

"I expect they just wanted to keep an eye on him."

It was the power of capital, Terzian knew, that had built this church, that had paid for the stained glass and the Giotto frescoes and the tombs and cenotaphs to the great names of Florence: Dante, Michelangelo, Bruni, Alberti, Marconi, Fermi, Rossini, and of course Machiavelli. This structure, with its vaults and chapels and sarcophagi and chanting Franciscans, had been raised by successful bankers, people to whom money was a real, tangible thing, and who had paid for the centuries of labor to build the basilica with caskets of solid, weighty coined silver.

"So what do you think he would make of this?" Terzian asked, nodding at the resting place of Machiavelli, now buried in the city from which he'd been exiled in his lifetime.

Stephanie scowled at the unusually plain sarcophagus with its Latin inscription, "No praise can be high enough," she translated, then turned to him as tourist cameras flashed. "Sounds overrated."

"He was a republican, you know," Terzian said. "You don't get that from just *The Prince*. He wanted Florence to be a republic, defended by citizen soldiers. But when it fell into the hands of a despot, he needed work, and he wrote the manual for despotism. But he looked at despotism a little too clearly, and he didn't get the job." Terzian turned to Stephanie. "He was the founder of modern political theory, and that's what I do. And he based his ideas on the belief that all human beings, at all times, have the same passions." He turned his eyes deliberately to Stephanie's shoulder bag. "That may be about to end, right? You're going to turn people into plants. That should change the passions if anything would."

"Not *plants*," Stephanie hissed, and glanced left and right at the crowds. "And not *here*." She began to move down the aisle, in the direction of Michelangelo's ornate tomb, with its draped figures who appeared not in mourning, but as if they were trying to puzzle out a difficult engineering problem.

"What happens in your scheme," Terzian said, following, "is that the market in food crashes. But that's not the *real* problem. The real problem is, what happens to the market in *labor?*"

Tourist cameras flashed. Stephanie turned her head away from the array of Kodaks. She passed out of the basilica and to the portico. The cloudburst had come to an end, but rainwater still drizzled off the structure. They stepped out of the droplets and down the stairs into the piazza.

The piazza was walled on all sides by old palaces, most of which now held restaurants or shops on the ground floor. To the left, one long palazzo was covered with canvas and scaffolding. The sound of pneumatic hammers banged out over the piazza. Terzian waved a hand in the direction of the clatter.

"Just imagine that food is nearly free," he said. "Suppose you and your children can get most of your food from standing in the sunshine. My next question is, *Why in hell would you take a filthy job like standing on a scaffolding and sandblasting some old building?*"

He stuck his hands in his pockets and began walking at Stephanie's side along the piazza. "Down at the bottom of the labor market, there are a lot of people whose labor goes almost entirely for the necessities. Millions of them cross borders illegally in order to send enough money back home to support their children."

"You think I don't know that?"

"The only reason that there's a market in illegal immigrants is that *there are jobs that well-off people won't do.* Dig ditches. Lay roads. Clean sewers. Restore old buildings. Build *new* buildings. The well-off might serve in the military or police, because there's a certain status involved and an attractive uniform, but we won't guard prisons no matter how pretty the uniform is. That's strictly a job for the laboring classes, and if the laboring classes are too well-off to labor, who guards the prisons?"

She rounded on him, her lips set in an angry line. "So I'm supposed to be afraid of people having more choice in where they work?"

"No," Terzian said, "you should be afraid of people having *no choice at all.* What happens when markets collapse is *intervention—*

and that's state intervention, if the market's critical enough, and you can bet the labor market's critical. And because the state depends on ditch-diggers and prison guards and janitors and road-builders for its very being, then if these classes of people are no longer available, and the very survival of civil society depends on their existence, in the end, the state will just *take* them.

"You think our friends in Transnistria will have any qualms about rounding people up at gunpoint and forcing them to do labor? The powerful are going to want their palaces kept nice and shiny. The liberal democracies will try volunteerism or lotteries or whatever, but you can bet that we're going to want our sewers to work, and somebody to carry our grandparents' bedpans, and the trucks to the supermarkets to run on time. And what *I'm* afraid of is that when things get desperate, we're not going to be any nicer about getting our way than those Sovietists of yours. We're going to make sure that the lower orders do their jobs, even if we have to kill half of them to convince the other half that we mean business. And the technical term for that is *slavery*. And if someone of African descent isn't sensitive to *that* potential problem, then I am very surprised!"

The fury in Stephanie's eyes was visible even through her shades, and he could see the pulse pounding in her throat. Then she said, "I'll save the *people,* that's what I'm good at. You save the rest of the world, *if* you can." She began to turn away, then swung back to him. "And by the way," she added, "fuck you!," turned, and marched away.

"Slavery or anarchy, Stephanie!" Terzian called, taking a step after. "That's the choice you're forcing on people!"

He really felt he had the rhetorical momentum now, and he wanted to enlarge the point by saying that he knew some people thought anarchy was a good thing, but no anarchist he'd ever met had ever even *seen* a real anarchy, or been in one, whereas Stephanie had—drop your anarchist out of a helicopter into the eastern Congo, say, with all his theories and with whatever he could carry on his back, and see how well he prospered. . . .

But Terzian never got to say any of these things, because Stephanie was gone, receding into the vanishing point of a busy street, the shoulder bag swinging back and forth across her butt like a pendulum powered by the force of her convictions.

Terzian thought that perhaps he'd never see her again, that he'd finally provoked her into abandoning him and continuing on her quest alone, but when he stepped off the bus in Montespèrtoli that night, he saw her across the street, shouting into her cell phone.

A day later, as with frozen civility they drank their morning coffee, she said that she was going to Rome the next day. "They might be looking for me there," she said, "because my parents live there. But I won't go near the family, I'll meet Odile at the airport and give her the papiloma."

Odile? Terzian thought. "I should go along," he said.

"What are you going to do?" she said, "carry that gun into an *airport*?"

"I don't have to take the gun. I'll leave it in the hotel room in Rome."

She considered. "Very well."

Again, that night, Terzian found the tumbled castle in Provence haunting his thoughts, that ruined relic of a bygone order, and once more considered stealing the papiloma and running. And again, he didn't.

They didn't get any farther than Florence, because Stephanie's cell phone rang as they waited in the train station. Odile was in Venice. *"Venezia?"* Stephanie shrieked in anger. She clenched her fists. There had been a cache of weapons found at the Fiumicino airport in Rome, and all planes had been diverted, Odile's to Marco Polo outside Venice. Frenzied booking agents had somehow found rooms for her despite the height of the tourist season.

Fiumicino hadn't been re-opened, and Odile didn't know how she was going to get to Rome. "Don't try!" Stephanie shouted. "I'll come to *you*."

This meant changing their tickets to Rome for tickets to Venice. Despite Stephanie's excellent Italian, the ticket seller clearly wished the crazy tourists would make up their mind which monuments of civilization they really wanted to see.

Strange—Terzian had actually *planned* to go to Venice in five days or so. He was scheduled to deliver a paper at the Conference of Classical and Modern Thought.

Maybe, if this whole thing was over by then, he'd read the paper after all. It wasn't a prospect he coveted: he would just be developing another footnote to a footnote.

The hills of Tuscany soon began to pour across the landscape like a green flood. The train slowed at one point—there was work going on on the tracks, men with bronze arms and hard hats—and Terzian wondered how, in the Plant People Future, in the land of Cockaigne, the tracks would ever get fixed, particularly in this heat. He supposed there were people who were meant by nature to fix tracks, who would repair tracks as an avocation or out of boredom regardless of whether they got paid for their time or not, but he suspected that there wouldn't be many of them.

You could build machines, he supposed, robots or something. But they had their own problems, they'd cause pollution and absorb resources and, on top of everything, they'd break down and have to be repaired. And who would do *that?*

If you can't employ the carrot, Terzian thought, if you can't reward people for doing necessary *labor,* then you have to use the stick. You march people out of the cities at gunpoint, like Pol Pot, because there's work that needs to be done.

He tapped his wedding ring on the arm of his chair and wondered what jobs would still have value. Education, he supposed; he'd made a good choice there. Some sorts of administration were necessary. There were people who were natural artists or bureaucrats or salesmen and who would do that job whether they were paid or not.

A woman came by with a cart and sold Terzian some coffee and a nutty snack product that he wasn't quite able to identify. And then he thought, *labor.*

"Labor," he said. In a world in which all basic commodities were provided, the thing that had most value was actual labor. Not the stuff that labor bought, but the work *itself.*

"Okay," he said, "it's labor that's rare and valuable, because people don't *have* to do it anymore. The currency has to be based on some kind of labor exchange—you purchase x hours with y dollars. Labor is the thing you use to pay taxes."

Stephanie gave Terzian a suspicious look. "What's the difference between that and slavery?"

"Have you been reading Nozick?" Terzian scolded. "The difference is the same as the difference between *paying taxes* and *being a slave*. All the time you don't spend paying your taxes is your own." He barked a laugh. "I'm resurrecting Labor Value Theory!" he said. "Adam Smith and Karl Marx are dancing a jig on their tombstones! In Plant People Land, the value is the *labor itself!* The *calories!*" He laughed again, and almost spilled coffee down his chest.

"You budget the whole thing in calories! The government promises to pay you a dollar's worth of calories in exchange for their currency! In order to keep the roads and the sewer lines going, a citizen owes the government a certain number of calories per year—he can either pay in person or hire someone else to do the job. And jobs can be budgeted in calories-per-hour, so that if you do hard physical labor, you owe fewer hours than someone with a desk job—that should keep the young, fit, impatient people doing the nasty jobs, so that they have more free time for their other pursuits." He chortled. "Oh, the intellectuals are going to just hate this! They're used to valuing their brain power over manual labor—I'm going to reverse their whole scale of values!"

Stephanie made a pffing sound. "The people I care about have no money to pay taxes at all."

"They have bodies. They can still be enslaved." Terzian got out his laptop. "Let me put my ideas together."

Terzian's frenetic two-fingered typing went on for the rest of the journey, all the way across the causeway that led into Venice. Stephanie gazed out the window at the lagoon soaring by, the soaring water birds and the dirt and stink of industry. She kept the Nike bag in her lap until the train pulled into the Stazione Ferrovia della Stato Santa Lucia at the end of its long journey.

Odile's hotel was in Cannaregio, which, according to the map purchased in the station gift shop, was the district of the city nearest the station and away from most of the tourist sites. A brisk wind almost tore the map from their fingers as they left the station, and their vaporetto bucked a steep chop on the grey-green Grand Canal as it took them to the Ca' d' Oro, the fanciful white High Gothic palazzo that loomed like a frantic wedding cake above a swarm of bobbing gondolas and motorboats.

Stephanie puffed cigarettes, at first with ferocity, then with satisfaction. Once they got away from the Grand Canal and into Cannaregio itself, they quickly became lost. The twisted medieval streets were broken on occasion by still, silent canals, but the canals didn't seem to lead anywhere in particular. Cooking smells demonstrated that it was dinnertime, and there were few people about, and no tourists. Terzian's stomach rumbled. Sometimes the streets deteriorated into mere passages. Stephanie and Terzian were in such a passage, holding their map open against the wind and shouting directions at each other, when someone slugged Terzian from behind.

He went down on one knee with his head ringing and the taste of blood in his mouth, and then two people rather unexpectedly picked him up again, only to slam him against the passage wall. Through some miracle, he managed not to hit his head on the brickwork and knock himself out. He could smell garlic on the breath of one of the attackers. Air went out of him as he felt an elbow to his ribs.

It was the scream from Stephanie that concentrated his attention. There was violent motion in front of him, and he saw the Nike swoosh, and remembered that he was dealing with killers, and that he had a gun.

In an instant, Terzian had his rage back. He felt his lungs fill with the rage that spread through his body like a river of scalding blood. He planted his feet and twisted abruptly to his left, letting the strength come up his legs from the earth itself, and the man attached to his right arm gave a grunt of surprise and swung counterclockwise. Terzian twisted the other way, which budged the other man only a little, but which freed his right arm to claw into his right pants pocket.

And from this point on it was just the movement that he rehearsed. Draw, thumb the safety, pull the trigger hard. He shot the man on his right and hit him in the groin. For a brief second, Terzian saw his pinched face, the face that reflected such pain that it folded in on itself, and he remembered Adrian falling in the Place Dauphine with just that look. Then he stuck the pistol in the ribs of the man on his left and fired twice. The arms that grappled him relaxed and fell away.

There were two more men grappling with Stephanie. That made four altogether, and Terzian reasoned dully that after the first three fucked up in Paris, the home office had sent a supervisor. One was trying to tug the Nike bag away, and Terzian lunged toward him and fired at a range of two meters, too close to miss, and the man dropped to the ground with a whuff of pain.

The last man had hold of Stephanie and swung her around, keeping her between himself and the pistol. Terzian could see the knife in his hand and recognized it as one he'd seen before. Her dark glasses were cockeyed on her face and Terzian caught a flash of her angry green eyes. He pointed the pistol at the knife man's face. He didn't dare shoot.

"Police!" he shrieked into the wind. *"Policia!"* He used the Spanish word. Bloody spittle spattered the cobblestones as he screamed.

In the Trashcanian's eyes, he saw fear, bafflement, rage.

"Polizia!" He got the pronunciation right this time. He saw the rage in Stephanie's eyes, the fury that mirrored his own, and he saw her struggle against the man who held her.

"No!" he called. Too late. The knife man had too many decisions to make all at once, and Terzian figured he wasn't very bright to begin with. *Kill the hostages* was probably something he'd been taught on his first day at Goon School.

As Stephanie fell, Terzian fired, and kept firing as the man ran away. The killer broke out of the passageway into a little square, and then just fell down.

The slide of the automatic locked back as Terzian ran out of ammunition, and then he staggered forward to where Stephanie was bleeding to death on the cobbles.

Her throat had been cut and she couldn't speak. She gripped his arm as if she could drive her urgent message through the skin, with her nails. In her eyes, he saw frustrated rage, the rage he knew well, until at length he saw there nothing at all, a nothing he knew better than any other thing in the world.

He shouldered the Nike bag and staggered out of the passageway into the tiny Venetian square with its covered well. He took a street at random, and there was Odile's hotel. Of course: the Trashcanians had been staking it out.

It wasn't much of a hotel, and the scent of spice and garlic in the lobby suggested that the desk clerk was eating his dinner. Terzian went up the stair to Odile's room and knocked on the door. When she opened—she was a plump girl with big hips and a suntan—he tossed the Nike bag on the bed.

"You need to get back to Mogadishu right away," he said. "Stephanie just died for that."

Her eyes widened. Terzian stepped to the wash basin to clean the blood off as best he could. It was all he could do not to shriek with grief and anger.

"You take care of the starving," he said finally, "and I'll save the rest of the world."

Michelle rose from the sea near Torbiong's boat, having done thirty-six hundred calories' worth of research and caught a honeycomb grouper in the bargain. She traded the fish for the supplies he brought. "Any more blueberries?" she asked.

"Not this time." He peered down at her, narrowing his eyes against the bright shimmer of sun on the water. "That young man of yours is being quite a nuisance. He's keeping the turtles awake and scaring the fish."

The mermaid tucked away her wings and arranged herself in her rope sling. "Why don't you throw him off the island?"

"My authority doesn't run that far." He scratched his jaw. "He's interviewing people. Adding up all the places you've been seen. He'll find you pretty soon, I think."

"Not if I don't want to be found. He can yell all he likes, but I don't have to answer."

"Well, maybe." Torbiong shook his head. "Thanks for the fish."

Michelle did some preliminary work with her new samples, and then abandoned them for anything new that her search spiders had discovered. She had a feeling she was on the verge of something colossal.

She carried her deck to her overhanging limb and let her legs dangle over the water while she looked through the new data. While paging through the new information, she ate something called a Raspberry Dynamo Bar that Torbiong had thrown in with her supplies. The old man must have included it as a joke: it was over-sweet and sticky with marshmallow and strangely flavored. She chucked it in the water and hoped it wouldn't poison any fish.

Stephanie Pais had been killed in what the news reports called a "street fight" among a group of foreigner visitors. Since the authorities couldn't connect the foreigners to Pais, they had to assume she was an innocent bystander caught up in the violence. The papers didn't mention Terzian at all.

Michelle looked through pages of followup. The gun that had shot the four men had never been found, though nearby canals were dragged. Two of the foreigners had survived the fight, though one died eight weeks later from complications of an operation. The survivor maintained his innocence and claimed that a complete stranger had opened fire on him and his friends, but the judges hadn't believed him and sent him to prison. He lived a great many years and died in the Lightspeed War, along with most people caught in prisons during that deadly time.

One of the four men was Belorussian. Another Ukranian. Another two Moldovan. All had served in the Soviet military in the past, in the Fourteenth Army in Transnistria. It frustrated Michelle that she couldn't shout back in time to tell the Italians to connect these four to the murder of another ex-Soviet, seven weeks earlier, in Paris.

What the hell had Pais and Terzian been up to? Why were all these people with Transnistrian connections killing each other, and Pais?

Maybe it was Pais they'd been after all along. Her records at Santa Croce were missing, which was odd, because other personnel records from the time had survived. Perhaps someone was arranging that certain things not be known.

She tried a search on Santa Croce itself, and slogged through descriptions and mentions of a whole lot of Italian churches, including the famous one in Florence where Terzian and Pais had been seen at Machiavelli's tomb. She refined the search to the Santa Croce relief organization, and found immediately the fact that let it all fall into place.

Santa Croce had maintained a refugee camp in Moldova during the civil war following the establishment of Transnistria. Michelle was willing to bet that Stephanie Pais had served in that camp. She wondered if any of the other players had been residents there.

She looked at the list of other camps that Santa Croce had maintained in that period, which seemed to have been a busy one for them. One name struck her as familiar, and she had to think for a moment before she remembered why she knew it. It was at a Santa Croce camp in the Sidamo province of Ethiopia where the Green Leopard Plague had first broken out, the first transgenetic epidemic.

It had been the first real attempt to modify the human body at the cellular level, to help marginal populations synthesize their own food, and it had been primitive compared to the more successful mods that came later. The ideal design for the efficient use of chlorophyll was a leaf, not the homo sapien—the designer would have been better advised to create a plague that made its victims leafy, and later designers, aiming for the same effect, did exactly that. And Green Leopard's designer had forgotten that the epidermis already contains a solar-activated enzyme: melanin. The result on the African subjects was green skin mottled with dark splotches, like the black spots on an implausibly verdant leopard.

The Green Leopard Plague broke out in the Sidamo camp, then at other camps in the Horn of Africa. Then it leaped clean across the continent to Mozambique, where it first appeared at an Oxfam camp in the flood zone, then spread rapidly across the continent, then leaped across oceans. It had been a generation before anyone found a way to disable it, and by then other transgenetic modifiers had been released into the population, and there was no going back.

The world had entered Terzian's future, the one he had proclaimed at the Conference of Classical and Modern Thought.

What, Michelle thought excitedly, if Terzian had known about Green Leopard ahead of time? His Cornucopia Theory had seemed prescient precisely because Green Leopard appeared just a few weeks after he'd delivered his paper. But if those Eastern bloc thugs had been involved somehow in the plague's transmission, or were attempting to prevent Pais and Terzian from sneaking the modified virus to the camps. . . .

Yes! Michelle thought exultantly. That had to be it. No one had ever worked out where Green Leopard originated, but there had always been suspicion directed toward several semi-covert labs in the former Soviet empire. This was *it.* The only question was how Terzian, that American in Paris, had got involved. . . .

It had to be Stephanie, she thought. Stephanie, who Terzian had loved and who had loved him, and who had involved him in the desperate attempt to aid refugee populations.

For a moment, Michelle bathed in the beauty of the idea. Stephanie, dedicated and in love, had been murdered for her beliefs—realdeath!—and Terzian, broken-hearted, had carried on and brought the future—Michelle's present—into being. A *wonderful* story! And no one had known it till *now,* no one had understood Stephanie's sacrifice, or Terzian's grief . . . not until the lonely mermaid, working in isolation on her rock, had puzzled it out.

"Hello, Michelle," Darton said.

Michelle gave a cry of frustration and glared in fury down at her lover. He was in a yellow plastic kayak—kayaking was popular here, particularly in the Rock Islands—and had slipped his electric-powered boat along the margin of the island, moving in near-silence. He looked grimly up at her from below the pitcher plant that dangled below the overhang.

They had rebuilt him, of course, after his death. All the data was available in backup, in Delhi where he'd been taken apart, recorded, and rebuilt as an ape. He was back in a conventional male body, with the broad shoulders and white smile and short hairy bandy legs she remembered.

Michelle knew that he hadn't made any backups during their time in Belau. He had his memories up to the point where he'd lain down on the nanobed in Delhi. That had been the moment when his love of Michelle had been burning its hottest, when he had just made the commitment to live with Michelle as an ape in the Rock Islands.

That burning love had been consuming him in the weeks since his resurrection, and Michelle was glad of it, had been rejoicing in every desperate, unanswered message that Darton sent sizzling through the ether.

"Damn it," Michelle said, "I'm working."

<Talk to me> Darton's fingers formed. Michelle's fingers made a ruder reply.

"I don't understand," Darton said. "We were in love. We were going to be together."

"I'm not talking to you," Michelle said. She tried to concentrate on her video display.

"We were still together when the accident happened," Darton said. "I don't understand why we can't be together now."

"I'm not listening, either," said Michelle.

"*I'm not leaving, Michelle!*" Darton screamed. "*I'm not leaving till you talk to me!*"

White cockatoos shrieked in answer. Michelle quietly picked up her deck, rose to her feet, and headed inland. The voice that followed her was amplified, and she realized that Darton had brought his bullhorn.

"*You can't get away, Michelle! You've got to tell me what happened!*"

I'll tell you about Lisa Lee, she thought, *so you can send her desperate messages, too.*

Michelle had been deliriously happy for her first month in Belau, living in arboreal nests with Darton and spending the warm days describing their island's unique biology. It was their first vacation, in Prague, that had torn Michelle's happiness apart. It was there that they'd met Lisa Lee Baxter, the American tourist who thought apes were cute, and who wondered what these shaggy kids were doing so far from an arboreal habitat.

It wasn't long before Michelle realized that Lisa Lee was at least two hundred years old, and that behind her diamond-blue eyes was the withered, mummified soul that had drifted into Prague from some waterless desert of the spirit, a soul that required for its continued existence the blood and vitality of the young. Despite her age and presumed experience, Lisa Lee's ploys seemed to Michelle to be so *obvious,* so *blatant.* Darton fell for them all.

It was only because Lisa Lee had finally tired of him that Darton returned to Belau, chastened and solemn and desperate to be in love with Michelle again. But by then it was Michelle who was tired. And who had access to Darton's medical records from the downloads in Delhi.

"You can't get away, Michelle!"

Well, maybe not. Michelle paused with one hand on the banyan's trunk. She closed her deck's display and stashed it in a mesh bag with some of her other stuff, then walked again out on the overhanging limb.

"I'm not going to talk to you like this," she said. "And you can't get onto the island from that side, the overhang's too acute."

"Fine," Darton said. The shouting had made him hoarse. "Come down here, then."

She rocked forward and dived off the limb. The salt water world exploded in her senses. She extended her wings and fluttered close to Darton's kayak, rose, and shook sea water from her eyes.

"There's a tunnel," she said. "It starts at about two meters and exits into the lake. You can swim it easily if you hold your breath."

"All right," he said. "Where is it?"

"Give me your anchor."

She took his anchor, floated to the bottom, and set it where it wouldn't damage the live coral.

She remembered the needle she'd taken to Jellyfish Lake, the needle she'd loaded with the mango extract to which Darton was violently allergic. Once in the midst of the jellyfish swarm, it had been easy to jab the needle into Darton's calf, then let it drop to the anoxic depths of the lake.

He probably thought she'd given him a playful pinch.

Michelle had exulted in Darton's death, the pallor, the labored breathing, the desperate pleading in the eyes.

It wasn't murder, after all, not really, just a fourth-degree felony. They'd build a new Darton in a matter of days. What was the value of a human life, when it could be infinitely duplicated, and cheaply? As far as Michelle was concerned, Darton had amusement value only.

The rebuilt Darton still loved her, and Michelle enjoyed that as well, enjoyed the fact that she caused him anguish, that he would pay for ages for his betrayal of her love.

Linda Lee Baxter could take a few lessons from the mermaid, Michelle thought.

Michelle surfaced near the tunnel and raised a hand with the fingers set at <follow me>. Darton rolled off the kayak, still in his clothes, and splashed clumsily toward her.

"Are you sure about this?" he asked.

"Oh yes," Michelle replied. "You go first, I'll follow and pull you out if you get in trouble."

He loved her, of course. That was why he panted a few times for breath, filled his lungs, and dove.

Michelle had not, of course, bothered to mention the tunnel was fifteen meters long, quite far to go on a single breath. She followed him, very interested in how this would turn out, and when Darton got into trouble in one of the narrow places and tried to back out, she grabbed his shoes and held him right where he was.

He fought hard but none of his kicks struck her. She would remember the look in his wide eyes for a long time, the thunderstruck disbelief in the instant before his breath exploded from his lungs and he died.

She wished that she could speak again the parting words she'd whispered into Darton's ear when he lay dying on the ridge above Jellyfish Lake. *"I've just killed you. And I'm going to do it again."*

But even if she could have spoken the words underwater, they would have been untrue. Michelle supposed this was the last time she could kill him. Twice was dangerous, but a third time would be too clear a pattern. She could end up in jail for a while, though, of course, you only did severe prison time for realdeath.

She supposed that she would have to discover his body at some point, but if she cast the kayak adrift, it wouldn't have to be for a while. And then she'd be thunderstruck and grief-stricken that he'd thrown away his life on this desperate attempt to pursue her after she'd turned her back on him and gone inland, away from the sound of his voice.

Michelle looked forward to playing that part.

She pulled up the kayak's anchor and let it coast away on the six-knot tide, then folded away her wings and returned to her nest in the banyan tree. She let the breeze dry her skin and got her deck from its bag and contemplated the data about Terzian and

Stephanie Pais and the outbreak of the Green Leopard Plague.

Stephanie had died for what she believed in, murdered by the agents of an obscure, murderous regime. It had been Terzian who had shot those four men in her defense, that was clear to her now. And Terzian, who lived a long time and then died in the Lightspeed War along with a few billion other people, had loved Stephanie and kept her secret till his death, a secret shared with the others who loved Stephanie and who had spread the plague among the refugee populations of the world.

It was realdeath that people suffered then, the death that couldn't be corrected. Michelle knew that she understood that kind of death only as an intellectual abstract, not as something she would ever have to face or live with. To lose someone *permanently* . . . that was something she couldn't grasp. Even the ancients, who faced realdeath every day, hadn't been able to accept it, that's why they'd invented the myth of Heaven.

Michelle thought about Stephanie's death, the death that must have broken Terzian's heart, and she contemplated the secret Terzian had kept all those years, and she decided that she was not inclined to reveal it.

Oh, she'd give Davout the facts, that was what he paid her for. She'd tell him what she could find out about Stephanie and the Transnistrians. But she wouldn't mention the camps that Santa Croce had built across the starvation-scarred world, she wouldn't point him at Sidamo and Green Leopard. If he drew those conclusions himself, then obviously the secret was destined to be revealed. But she suspected he wouldn't—he was too old to connect those dots, not when obscure ex-Soviet entities and relief camps in the Horn of Africa were so far out of his reference.

Michelle would respect Terzian's love, and Stephanie's secret. She had some secrets of her own, after all.

The lonely mermaid finished her work for the day and sat on her overhanging limb to gaze down at the sea, and she wondered how long it would be before Darton called her again, and how she would torture him when he did.

—With thanks to Dr. Stephen C. Lee.

IN SPRINGDALE TOWN

by Robert Freeman Wexler

Robert Freeman Wexler has worked as a proofreader, bookseller, public relations associate, typesetter, and book production editor, and once spent half a day unloading trucks at a warehouse during a solar eclipse. He has lived in Texas, New York, and Massachusetts, and currently resides in Yellow Springs, Ohio. He has a journalism degree from the University of Texas at Austin, and attended the Clarion West Writer's Workshop in 1997.

Wexler has published a handful of stories in small press magazines, including The Third Alternative *and* Lady Churchill's Rosebud Wristlet. *His most recent story is "Valley of the Falling Clouds" in* Polyphony 3 *and his most recent book is* In Springdale Town. *Upcoming in 2004 is his first novel,* Circus of the Grand Design.

In the story that follows, Wexler explores a part of small-town America that lies just a little aslant of Ray Bradbury's endless October, beautiful, beguiling, and more than a little disturbing.

> The lonely road is my companion
> A faithful friend in times of pain
> It serves me well in all my rambling
> Through fire and snow and driving rain
>
> I was not always lost and damned
> Nor doomed to live a life disgraced
> But darling Maggie, she did shun me
> For a man of handsome face
>
> (chorus) Now the days, they pass in sorrow
> For my lost love, no wedding gown
> I last saw my Maggie dying
> By the river's edge in Springdale town
>
> —Traditional

1

RICHARD SHELLING LEFT HIS rented Santa Monica home on a weekend evening, with no particular destination other than away. Earlier that day, while attending a brunch party at a television producer's beach house—he attended many parties—looking down from a balcony at the groves of his fellow actors, he thought he heard a voice in his ear whispering "Away, take yourself away." He glanced at his companions, assuming that one of them had spoken, but, as usual, they were taking turns not listening to each other's stories. Shelling set his glass of rum punch on a table and left. At home he packed a bag.

His impulse propelled him east, rather than north or south. On the edge of the continent, west was impossible without a ship, and he understood this to be a road trip. Besides, he had grown up and gone to college in the northwest. East signified new territory, and the exploration of it would fortify him, grant him insights into previously hidden realms.

He drove toward Interstate 10, then to 15. In Barstow he stopped for gas and bought a road atlas and two compact discs of truck driving songs; back in his car, he inserted the first disc and studied the atlas as sounds of horns and snare drum readied him for the journey. Las Vegas was next, and although he had no desire to see that fabled city, it stood between him and Interstate 70's uninterrupted cross-country pavement. Distance plus thought equals change, he decided.

Various Artists, *Songs of Route 66: All American Highway* and *More Songs of Route 66: Roadside Attractions*, Lazy S.O.B. 1997 and 2001. This type of music has a certain nostalgic appeal for some. Oh, that open road, the wind in your hair. The feeling, however, loses something in its transcription to a compact disc player in a mid-size, plushy Japanese car that reduces road noise to a happy little hum and is not meant to be driven with the windows down. Still, there remains the satisfactions of the centerline, tires eating distance, and viewing the sky through tinted glass.

First light of the new day found him a few miles short of the Colorado border. He had never driven into the sunrise, and the intensity of the light, the tactile pinks and yellows filtered through his caffeinated brain, thrilled him. Turning up the music,‡ he sang to the dawn.

By the time he reached Massachusetts (after sleep-stops in Kansas City, then Ohio, where he left I-70 for a northern route), the highway miles had stripped his California shellac and softened him. The past ten years he had spent acting in assorted television programs, years he would have to describe as lucrative but unrewarding, and he found the appeal of a simple, rural life growing in him, coalescing into a picture of a farmhouse surrounded by open countryside.

Fields gave way to hills and low mountains, to billboards advertising ski slopes. A peculiar yellow-gray mist filled the hollows, and he powered up his car windows to block a growing chill. He thought he saw flashes in the mist, like a horde of fireflies. Where the road slid between a sheer rock face on one side and a ravine on the other, the mist thickened, and he couldn't see the road curving. He braked sharply and turned the wheel inward. His right front tire grazed the narrow shoulder, but he managed to straighten the car. He slowed to 25, then 20, then 15. A sign announced Highway 7, Springdale, five miles. At the intersection he turned right, hoping the new road would free him from the mist.

Springdale—the name tickled his memory. He had an image of a river, and a blonde woman wearing a thin satin dress with a plunging neckline. She wouldn't let him near her; another man interceded.

Shelling bounced his right fist off the dashboard and laughed. That wasn't real life—Springdale was the name of the town in that sexy TV drama. He had a guest shot on it once, which he had hoped would develop into a recurring role.‡ He laughed again. The road, that was it, driving too long, couldn't even keep memories of television appearances separate from reality. He needed to stop at a motel and sleep. No sense pushing things. Springdale

The material contained here does not reflect the views of the producers or writers of the show *Blake's River*, nor is it meant to be a speculation on any episode of the show that has been or ever will be broadcast. Although the name "Springdale" is used throughout, it does not constitute a representation of any actual Springdale, whatever its geographic locale, or the residents thereof.

then. The thought of visiting this real-world namesake of a TV town appealed to him.

His highway intersected with another, and he turned left. The stone buildings of the town spread before him—town hall, schools, churches, shops. He didn't see the river till he passed the library. The water drew closer to the road, and half a block farther, Shelling pulled the car into the gravel drive of a road- and water-side park. He lowered the front windows and turned off the engine. Wood smoke and a hint of springtime growth flavored the air. The sign over Springdale Savings showed 54 degrees, cold to his California skin, but he left his jacket in the car and wandered toward the water, savoring the clean air and the music of the stream.

Later that afternoon, he checked into a motel on the south edge of town. From there, he could explore the area, though there wasn't much need—he knew he would stay. When morning came, with a dance of sunlight waking him through the motel windows, the first place he visited was the real estate office on Main Street. The realtor had reddish hair, one of those stiff coifs that could only be maintained with weekly visits to the beauty parlor (which they were still called in places like Springdale). She looked at Shelling carefully, as though judging whether he was worthy enough to buy property in her proximity.

"I was thinking a farmhouse," Shelling said. "When I was a kid, I visited my Uncle Nathan on his farm in Northern California. Uncle Nathan raised goats." Shelling paused as the realtor's left eyebrow rose, an arc that he interpreted to mean he had lost points on her worthiness meter. "Not that *I'm* planning to raise goats here," he added, hoping he hadn't damaged his standing with her.

Despite his assumed faux pas, the realtor drove him to an 1890s farmhouse on the river, about five miles from town. Though he gave it a day's deliberation, he knew as soon as he saw the house and land that he would take it. He arranged to have his things shipped from California, and moved in as soon as the details of purchase could be settled.

In Springdale Shelling knew no one, but anonymity pleased him. As though instinctively planning this new life, he had always used a pseudonym for television, so his real name meant nothing to the realtor, and his face—well, *everyone* looked like someone else. Plus, the show on which he had spent the most time was a futuristic drama set on some far-off planet; for three seasons Shelling had worn orange neoprene over his face and head. Only the most avid fans read the "behind the scenes" articles showing him without makeup. When the realtor inquired about his career, he said he was a computer consultant.

The first time he went to the hardware store, the woman working the cash register asked him if he was Patrick Travis, which sounded familiar, and the name nagged at him for days, until he remembered: the character he had played for his guest appearance on *Blake's River*. He couldn't believe somebody had recognized him from it, but then maybe here, in this real-world Springdale, people took a peculiar pleasure in following the dramas of the fictional one.

Shelling's new town pulsed; he exulted in the weekly paper, reading about the issues that gripped the residents, learning from the editorials, articles, and the police report. In the letters page, residents discussed radio towers, affordable housing, water quality, and traffic. (Surprisingly, for a town its size, the volume of cars passing through on Main Street proved excessive at times—especially during the tourist seasons—and a newly opened resort complex northwest of town inspired much debate.)‡

But even with these signs of life, as a newcomer to Springdale without local connections, with no job-place interactions, Shelling could not figure out how to meet people. He started classes at the

We were urged by Anita Fulton Long (*Springdale Town News*, October 12, 1999) to "be a little kinder to all those big, bad property developments," but the denizens of those tombstone monuments need also be kinder to the pedestrians of our town. The garages of these new highrises house those metal monsters which mount a new daily death toll as they roam our downtown streets. Ms. Long is sure "everything will be okay," but that's what boosters also told West Lee, Smithville, and Fairmont, which now face mud, flood, and smog in Necropolis. Why not cage the "carbarians" and bury *them* before they bury us and write our cemetery epitaphs with highrise signatures in our own city of the dead?

—Conrad Walker Burns,
109 Grapevine Street

yoga center (something he had always meant to do in California), and although the teachers and classmates seemed friendly, it was hard to engage them in something that moved beyond the site of the class, into a café or bar, the socio-emotional realm of deeper contact.

Conversation, a quiet coffee with a friend, the spontaneity of a large group—he needed these things. Yes, he could, and did, talk to the various waitpeople, movie ticket sellers, fishmongers, but feared they would think him odd, coming in day upon day, buying a coffee here, a sandwich there. Perhaps *he* should open a café, or a bookshop. Then the people would come to him. But proprietorship would put him on the other side, the server side, and a wall existed, the barrier between the served and those serving.

In the Japanese restaurant, he often spoke to Monique, the redheaded waitress. He learned about her art school background, her pottery; they had made vague plans for him to visit her studio, but he worried that seeing her outside her job would change the nature of their relationship, might commit him to a course of attempted romance, the failure of which would prevent his return to the restaurant.

Without local contact, he found himself calling Vuksek, his financial advisor, every day for chats having nothing to do with investing.

2

Why had I let myself come back to this . . . place? My train passed the big farmhouse north of town, then the duck pond. At least they've made some improvements, I thought, noticing a particularly robust mallard. After Deirdre and Michael's wedding invitation showed up in the mail, I let desk clutter pile over it so I would forget. I liked them, I wanted to be at their wedding, but why did it have to be in Springdale?

A week or so later, during one of my straightening fits, I found the invitation stuck on the clip that was keeping together the brief on the drunk chef case. That was what I had been looking for—

the brief I mean—because the case was going to trial in a few days. I picked up the invitation and stared at it, then taped it to my computer monitor. The next morning I made a train reservation.

My ex-wife, Caroline, grew up in Springdale. We had moved there after I finished law school.

"Why don't you set up a nice country practice," she had said.

I should have known it wasn't a good idea to move to a town that served as the setting for a murder ballad. Three years we lived together there, the last of which she had been sleeping with that bastard Dr. Malcolm. Somehow, everyone else in town knew about it. Then the fight, the threats of lawsuit, disbarment. Three years isn't enough time to connect to a place, so leaving wasn't any trouble. I had come back once, to wrap up the divorce and sell our house. I hadn't planned to return.

Another couple of minutes and I would be there. I had brought a product liability journal to read on the train, but over the last twenty minutes or so, as the distance to Springdale shrank, I kept reading, over and over, the abstract to one of the cases.‡ Finally, I gave up and slid the journal into my bag.

It was turning out to be a bleached fish kind of day. The sky had that rotten fruit look, all bruised bananas and sour lemon. I briefly considered waiting to take the next train home. Instead, I picked up a car at the little rental place in the station. Like last time, I had booked a room at a hotel by the shopping mall, about six miles from town. No way was I staying any closer, not that there were many choices—the bed and breakfast or the seedy old Drake Motel. Most of the people in town Caroline had known her whole

A woman took diet drugs and died while attempting to lose twenty-five pounds for her wedding. Something to do while planning the seating arrangements for the dinner? "Let's put Uncle Martin with the Phillipses—whoops, just lost another pound." Some months before her death, she began to hallucinate conversations with an idealized version of herself. The counterpart's history included extensive training in dance and ice skating, culminating in an Olympic figure skating competition in which she won a bronze medal. The woman wrote in her journal: "There is a hardness to her, so lithe, so strong. Jealousy overcomes me. I want her body."

fucking life, and I didn't want to run into any of them today. There would be enough socializing at the wedding.

Michael had moved here with Deirdre about a year before I did, to teach at the college. Dee grew up here, a couple of classes ahead of Caroline; they had known each other of course, but hadn't been close friends. Michael and I had bonded over the newcomer-in-a-small-town thing.

It's hard, with break-ups. Some friends try to be neutral, some take sides. Michael and Dee chose mine.

Enough of that. I was starting to sound like some damn country song. I have a pretty good life in the city, a job at a good firm. I've progressed from the little country practice to big-time product liability law. It's this town, it brings things back. I don't like being a fool, but who does?

Springdale looked the same. These places always do. Was in the town charter or something: we will never change. Minor things, like a new café on Main Street, different name on the bank. I drove around, avoiding Pearl, my old street, but working my way toward it nevertheless. Unavoidable, considering the size of this place. I crossed Pearl, but kept going toward the highway out of town. A block farther, I turned around. What would it hurt to drive past the house? Caroline didn't live there anymore.

The new owners had planted pines and maples in the front yard and painted the clapboard a buttery sort of color. It looked comfortable now, a place where people could live and be happy. All Caroline and I had ever done was buy a new refrigerator. For some reason, seeing the house all cuted up affected me more than anything else. So many things I had wanted to do with it. I had studied bunches of house and garden books, but we had never managed to find the time to decide what we would do first. Of course that made sense after I found out where Caroline's spare time was going.

Damn this bitterness. An artifact of my past, that's all. I left town by a back road, then cut across to the highway leading to my shopping mall hotel.

3

Although Shelling awakened with a headache and tingly fingers, the sensations faded, and he didn't expect the day, a Friday, to differ from the routine he had established since moving to Springdale several months ago. He spent the morning pulling weeds from his vegetable garden and sitting in the shade of his back patio, where he dictated his journal into a digital recorder, as he did every morning. It wasn't until afternoon, when he went into town for his yoga class, that he noticed the emptiness.

At the yoga center, though the door hung open and the lights were on, he found no students or teacher. He sat on the couch outside the practice space and removed his shoes and socks, then entered the practice area, a rectangular room with a golden oak floor and a wall of windows—a calming zone in which he always found freedom from the grasping tentacles of chaos that followed after everyone.

He unrolled a mat and waited, sitting cross-legged facing the windows. Cloudless and blue, the kind of day that promised much—perhaps this time, after class, he would suggest lunch to some of the others. Usually, on finishing the hour and a half sessions, he felt so exquisitely drained and limp that conversation proved difficult, and the opportunity for companionship slipped past him.

This empty room was odd though—someone, at least the teacher, should have arrived by now. He rose and walked into the closet-like office, then to the couch, where he sat reading a brochure for a weekend seminar with a visiting yogi. A few minutes later, he slipped his socks and shoes on and left. Across the parking lot, in the food co-op, he bought an avocado, some lemons, and a bag of organic potato chips. Aside from the young woman at the cash register and a man putting out produce, the store was empty.

He deposited the groceries in the trunk of his car and walked toward Main Street; while crossing the street in front of The Cook's House (a store selling upscale kitchen items), he decided to go to the Springdale Library.

The library occupied an attractive 1920s-era brick building

with wood floors and high ceilings. Several afternoons a week, Shelling would come here to sit in the magazine section and look through various newspapers. On this visit, he paused in the foyer to look at a poster advertising the performance of three short Samuel Beckett plays at the college. He had never read or performed any Beckett. Off to his left stood a table of new books; straight through led to the fiction, he knew that . . . but where was the drama section? He thought to ask if the library had the featured Beckett plays.

Besides programs at the college, there were a few theater groups in town. Funny, his discontent with television had colored his entire view of drama. But why not enter the theatrical life here? Though he was hesitant to reveal his past, or rely on his background to secure parts in local productions, it was ridiculous to turn away from acting altogether. Perhaps instead of acting, here in Springdale he would direct plays, explore a more artistic vision, divorced from the business that had involved him for so long.

Finding no one at the front desk, he rummaged through the new books, picking up one with a painting of a sailing ship on its cover. He flipped through the pages, then stopped. The text was not English. It so closely resembled English that at first he thought his eyes had blurred, mixing the words into random configurations. He picked up another book, and it was the same, words in a sort of near-English gibberish: "*Leth free, tor mousled, ol shan vetchy,*" read the line at the top of one page, opposite a strange drawing of young women and people-sized cats wearing clothes.

Shelling looked around for another library patron or employee, but found no one. At the circulation desk, he called out: "Is anyone here?" The ceiling, distant and white, mocked him. He found he couldn't breathe, could not force air in through the knotted thing his windpipe had become. A sudden wave of heat engulfed him, a magnified exhalation, as though he had entered the exhaust vent of an immense furnace.

4

I had just entered my room with the daisy-print wallpaper and started travel ritual number one‡ when someone banged on my door. Not wanting to talk to anyone, I ignored the knock. If the hotel needed me, they could shove a note under the door. The knocking changed to pounding, a rhythmic thud, like some over-worked drum circle reject. My irritation magnified with each drum beat. "Okay, I'm coming," I said. I turned the knob, preparing an irate statement, but smiled when I saw Michael.

"Took you long enough," he said, pushing past me, followed by two men and a woman, all of whom I thought I recognized from around town. "Train ride okay? Should've let me know what time so I could meet you."

"I figured you would be pretty busy with the wedding."

"Well, we're out to have some fun. Not exactly a bachelor party. Drinks with some guys. And not even all guys." He pointed to the woman.

"I'm Sherrie—you handled my divorce," she said.

I nodded, although I didn't remember her. "I have to phone my office," I said, lying. "Then go over some notes on a case. I'll meet you later."

Remove glasses, contact lens case, and contact lens solution from bag and arrange by sink, glasses to the left, contact lens case and solution to the right. Contact lenses were a constant source of irritation, but vision with them was so much better than with glasses. Eye drops made lens wear more bearable, though late in the evening, especially after a night of poor sleeping, even that was insufficient. Vision correction surgery, the kind that reshaped the cornea, was an option, but the idea of cutting, even with laser rather than knife, seemed so drastic. And then the horror stories of people who had undergone the procedure, yet still needed to wear glasses, or had their eyes damaged, forever seeing the world as green and gray shapes flowing in and out of focus.

"Too much work," Michael said. "That's not the Patrick Travis I remember." They left. I waited half an hour, then went out to eat mall food, one of those stupid chain restaurants that make you feel as if you haven't traveled. Springdale has excellent dining, but that was enough reunions for the day. I drifted around the shopping mall till closing. The anonymity of the place comforted me.

5

Swells of oceanographic angst buffeted Shelling. A profusion of discolored velvety fur—pelts of beaver or raccoon—lined the street, softened his fall. Shelling had a beaver dam on his property, and he liked to sit near it, under the trees, losing himself in the sounds of his land. He planned to move a picnic table out there, though he worried it might disturb the animals. But why was he lying in the grass outside the library? Shelling jumped to his feet, and hurried down Main Street.

Half a block from the library, he stopped, unable to recall the source of his agitation. That's what happens when you miss your yoga class, he thought. He would have appreciated an explanation for the cancellation. With his unstructured life, disruptions like this left him dangling. If not for the discipline of yoga, his transition to life in this small town would have been difficult; the practice relaxed and invigorated him, opened him to new experiences. Living in the Los Angeles area for so long, he had grown contemptuous of other places in the country, of small towns, of any place lacking big-city sophistication.

As he walked, he glanced into the windows of several stores, seeing a clerk behind the counter in some, and in others, no one. Not just the yoga center then; the town appeared to be shorn of people, residents and visitors alike.

He entered Frisell's Coffee Roasters, pausing in the doorway, as had become his habit, to allow the fertile aroma of the roast to permeate his lungs. Two young women sat on stools behind the counter. They were laughing; as he drew near, he heard the one at the cash register mention elephants, or maybe cellophane. The other laughed harder, gasping, sucking air through the laughs. She hunched forward, cupping her reddening face with both hands. Silver rings decorated most of her fingers. Shelling recognized one, with a raised zigzag design on a dark background, from the jewelry store across the street. He had spent parts of two afternoons there, trying on rings, assisted once by a bland-faced woman and the other time by a well-manicured bald man, neither of whom gave any indication of interest in talking to Shelling beyond the requirements of their job.

"What's so funny?" he asked. Neither woman responded. The young woman at the cash register asked the other to start a pot of decaf. Shelling ordered a cappuccino and waited while the ring woman prepared it. The cash register woman held out a hand for money. A tattoo of a dark bird, wings outstretched, decorated the underside of her wrist. Shelling wanted to join their discussion, but saw no way to breach the wall. He opened his mouth, preparing to tell the young woman that he admired her tattoo; instead, he carried his mug to a table and looked out the window at the empty sidewalk. The two women continued their conversation as though Shelling didn't exist.

"There's an archival method, Albania or someplace," one of them said. "They use numbered index cards to keep track of the tides."

"Are they suspended by fishing line, like in Greece?"

This emptiness, it haunted him: empty cafés, empty theaters, stores. No cars passed through. Shelling drove around town, searching, up Main Street and into the neighborhoods, but saw no one other than the waiters, waitresses, ticket sellers, fishmongers, and shopkeepers at their respective stations.

He pulled his car into the parking lot of The Crow Bar, a brew-pub occupying an old mill on the north edge of town that could easily absorb the ski season crowds and the summertime hikers. This evening, neither were in evidence, though he did find the bartender and two others, a man and woman.

Shelling felt a smile growing but shut it down. It would not do to appear too eager. He would order a drink, wait for conversation to happen. The dark ale reminded him of winters spent in the mountains, in lodges surrounded by friends and strangers, all laughing and talking. Where were these people now?

The man at the bar spoke to the woman. Shelling couldn't place the extended syllables of his accent. "A man dressed all in black enters a white room. The only sound is the air conditioner, blowing through a vent in the ceiling." The man stopped and drank the last third of his pint. He motioned to the bartender for another. His hands were wide, with sausage-like fingers.

"How large is the vent?" The woman's voice sounded husky,

as though from smoking, but Shelling saw no ashtrays near the couple. Her accent didn't match the man's.

"Doesn't matter. Just a vent blowing air." The bartender set a full glass down on a coaster; the man wrapped his thick fingers around it and lifted it to his lips to drink before continuing his story: "So, here's this man, dressed all in black in a white room. The room is rectangular, maybe four times deeper than it is wide. It's cold. The blowing air pushes against his hair. He takes out a black knit cap, the kind that covers his whole head except for the eyes and mouth. But he doesn't put it on. He's waiting for something, or someone."

The man tipped his glass and drank, finishing the beer in one deep swallow. He nodded to the woman, who picked up her purse and stood.

"What's he waiting for?" Shelling asked, but they left without answering.

Shelling sat for a while, drinking his beer in small, brief sips and idly taking pretzel sticks from a bowl. The bartender moved off to shelve a rack of clean glasses.

When he first stopped here, on his cross-country drive, the streets had been crowded with cars, pedestrians. Or had they? It was as though he carried competing memories—a town alive with human contact, and this, the emptiness.

6

In the morning I dressed and drove to town for the wedding. Michael and Dee had decided to hold it in a mansion owned by one of her relatives. The place was a wreck—hadn't been lived in for years—wallpaper peeling, dank corridors leading off into uninhabitable wings, but it had this amazing ballroom, gilt molding, parquet floor, and a ceiling painted all in cherubs and naked nymphs. I stood in the back, apart from everyone. What a fucking waste, all this. Within a couple of years, either Michael or Dee—didn't matter which—would do something stupid, some fling with a co-worker or whatever, and that would be the end. People are predictable. Everybody starts out with the same well-meaning platitudes.

The woman who had stopped by my room last night with Michael and the others sat beside me. "Sorry you didn't make it out to the bar," she said. "It was a good time. Some of Michael's former students—I think they had all just turned twenty-one recently and were feeling way proud of it—showed up, and we had them going with stories about Michael's wild days in the merchant marines." She waved to some people standing near the door. They came over and sat in the remaining three seats of the row. The woman introduced them to me, but then the music started, freeing me from conversational obligations.

Dee and Michael appeared from opposite ends of the room, all smiley, and their smiles shamed me. I tried to feel better, or at least to hide my cynicism with an outward shine. Hard enough for them without all my negativity coming at them. And they looked great. Dee had bought some vintage wedding dress and shortened it to just below the knees. Michael was wearing a pink ruffled shirt and dark pants.

After the wedding, a civil ceremony with cosmic overtones, we relocated outside for the reception. The garden was mostly overgrown brambly things, but they had cleared enough space for tables and chairs. I went through the hand-shaking line, then sat alone beside a ragged shrub with purple flowers. Late May here was always perfect. I had forgotten. Michael owned a canoe, and after his classes were over, we would take it out on the river. I had always assumed that after putting away enough money from my law practice I would buy a canoe and a riverfront house. Okay, I could still do it, just not here, not in the way I had pictured things back then.

At least Caroline wasn't at the wedding. Turned out she and Dr. Wonderful had gone to Spain for a month. From my spot by the shrub, I saw a familiar-looking woman talking to Caroline's best friend, that romance writer Skippy Brisbane. I definitely wanted to avoid Brisbane. That other woman smiled a lot when she talked, which looked odd next to Brisbane's sour face. Smiley woman was wearing a flowered tank dress that showed a lot of leg. Maybe I had met her once. Maybe she hadn't been wearing glasses then, or her hair had been long.

Several guys I used to play softball with came over, blocking my view of smiley woman. We exchanged small talk; I told them about lawyering and stuff in the city.

Then this man showed up, waving his hands in the air and screaming something about broken hearts. He said if the wedding wasn't stopped, he would "do something." He never said what he would do, just kept repeating the line. A woman standing near him said the wedding had already happened, and he grabbed her shoulders and shook her. That's when that fat cop I had nicknamed Scooter intervened. He pulled the man away and escorted him from the party.

Now I was feeling guilty for all that negativity I had radiated earlier, thinking I had somehow caused this. One of the softball guys said the screaming man had been Dee's boyfriend before she met Michael. Someone else said they had been engaged. I had wanted to hide, alone, by my flowering shrub, but for some reason more people joined the group around me. When I saw Brisbane and smiley woman moving my way, I slipped out.

7

Perhaps the emptiness had been forced on Shelling to balance his past. In his previous life on television, solitude had never been a factor. Even when a network cancelled a show, he found more work quickly; when a relationship ended, another started soon after. All of that seemed so far away now, relics. He wondered what some of those people he had known were doing. Though he owned a television, he hadn't turned it on since receiving his belongings from California.

Saturday morning passed without the situation changing. Shelling sat with his tape recorder as usual, though he thought he spoke with more determination and insight. "In the continuum of solitude, all beings are supreme," he said, then talked for a while about the consequences and benefits of geographic relocation. The recorder had a voice-activation feature; he clipped the unit to the waistband of his pants and moved out into the yard, where, with an unthinking determination, he dug out a broad swath of turf and turned the soil in preparation for sowing. He forgot to talk into the recorder until he had finished digging, then spoke of the seeds he planned to buy, the vegetables he would plant. And with his garden in mind, he drove into town.

Downtown Springdale consisted of Highway 7 (which, as it cut through the town, became Main Street) and the intersecting blocks between Hill Street and the turnoff where Highway 7 veered right to merge with Highway 23 and cross the river. Hill and Knight Streets ran perpendicular to Main. Various stores, offices, and restaurants lined Springdale's streets. Shelling had visited them all. The used bookstore and the Japanese restaurant were on Knight. One of the two movie houses was on Hill, occupying a former vaudeville theater. A new complex, built in a space behind the buildings on the west side of Main Street, housed the other theater. Though new, it had been designed in scale and style to blend with the surrounding buildings.

Shelling left his car near the newer movie house. On reaching the used book store, he allowed himself to be sidetracked from his goal of the garden shop. Entering, he had an odd twist in his stomach, apprehension, he thought, though of what? He laughed—nothing in a book store could hurt him.

The woman who ran the shop came out from the back, passing him without a greeting. Shelling roamed the store, flipping pages and looking at pictures in a few cookbooks, but none drew him. In the fiction section, a book protruded from a shelf; he reached for it,

Dead Language, stories by Samantha Hidalgo. He had heard the name somewhere. The dust jacket photo showed a woman with short dark hair and squarish glasses. "A linguistic and phantasmagoric tour-de-force," the blurb said. He opened the book at random and read the beginning of a story.‡

Across the vale stood a circular house, mundane in appearance, though around it was an area of desolation, circular like the house, as though something radiated from it that killed everything within a certain distance. Some trees stood, bare, trunks brittle as dust, unable even to rot without the creatures that feed on rot. If a hapless traveler came upon it, and few did, the person would have felt an oppressiveness, as though their weight increased with each step closer to the house. And the house itself, thick walls constructed from a limestone prized elsewhere for its use in building. The traveler, circling the house, would note with surprise its lack of windows, and upon making the full circuit, would also come to notice the lack of a door. The traveler's gaze would drift up to the roof, a vault constructed so that each stone shared the weight evenly.

From the erosion surrounding the structure, the ruts along the south slope and the lifeless earth piled higher along the northwest, one would surmise that the entirety had once been buried, and that the work of the elements over time was slowly revealing more.

All of this would lead an observer to ponder what would drive people to build such a structure and bury it, creating what must have looked like nothing more than another hill in a landscape of hills. Though, one might assume, it would have been a hill as devoid of life as the area around the house, which, if true, would mean that the piled-on earth, with nothing to hold it in place, had not lasted as long as its builders might have wished.

Shelling paid for the book and left the store. Back at his car, he opened the passenger-side door and dropped the book on the seat. There he lingered, not ready to return to his empty house. Across the parking lot, the movie marquee beckoned. Shelling didn't like going to movies alone, feeling exposed and self conscious, judged for his inability to find a companion, but Springdale gave him little choice.

The ticket booth was on the inside, to the left of the entrance. Shelling found it untenanted. A film called *The Painting of Kathleen Alice May* would be starting soon.

The theater smelled of corn syrup and stale popcorn.‡ Shelling walked toward the back, passing where the ticket-taker commonly stood. Ahead, the hallway stretched. No one came to challenge him. Continuing, he found the air began to thicken, first around his toes and rising, assuming the consistency of a thin oatmeal porridge, and it resisted his forward progress, pushing on his thighs and sucking at the soles of his shoes. Thick air oozed and flexed to hinder his entry. Perhaps

Savory snack and sweet snack share an origin in the humble grain of corn. Multiple processed products originating from a few raw materials have replaced the diversity once found in the human diet, forming the *illusion* of diversity. Food that once came from the region in which a person lived now journeys unimagined distances to reach the local supermarket. Though even with this bounty, many choose the pre-packaged route rather than assembling and cooking, and many of the new mega-groceries stock variety more as a colorful display rather than to supply our dining and nutritional requirements.

a security measure initiated because of the lack of present employees?

As the air thickened, it also darkened. Shelling looked over his shoulder at the line of fluorescent light fixtures, bright where he entered, fading here. A glow framed a doorway to his right, from behind which came the sounds of a movie playing, but in the dark of the hall, Shelling couldn't read the sign showing the name of the film.

He traveled on, immersing himself in the shape of the hallway, more a shadow of a hall than an actual one, a shadow that clung to him, and he found himself embracing it, willing it closer, wearing it as a cloak. Even as the last, scattered elements of light skittered away, across the blackened carpet, still he continued. His eyes adjusted to the dark, seeing it as a blackness that shaped the world into figures, into objects of startling unfamiliarity, and in them he found comfort.

8

After the reception, I went back to my room and sat on the balcony, which overlooked the main concourse of the shopping mall. The problem with solitude, sometimes, is what to do with it. For me, here, in this tacky mall hotel, the options were few: read my legal journal, watch television (64 channels!), or traverse the corridors of the shopping mall. There was a movie theater on the far end. I considered going, but decided that seeing a movie would constitute a form of replacement solitude.

For the moment, the artificiality of the view appealed to me. Three stories below, people walked about the mall, young couples hand in hand, families, and tired office workers relishing their weekend, everyone buying things: movie posters, compact discs of the latest hit songs, jogging shoes, and sweaters.

Down there to my right, water flowed from a fountain in the shape of that famous cartoon penguin. Benches ringed the fountain—I had sat on one last night after dinner. The water sparkled as if dyed with light.

As I watched, waves began lapping over the sides of the fountain's basin. I figured something must have clogged the drain, though it should be a closed system—water in the basin pumping back up to exit from the penguin's mouth. So with a clogged drain, there should be no water spewing.

Water splashed and pooled on the pavement surrounding the fountain. A child, maybe six years old, ran laughing into the growing puddle, splattering its clothes and head. The mother pulled it away, lifted it, and carried it into a shoe store.

I was feeling hungry, but didn't want to leave my balcony—the scene here entertained me more than any movie could have. I went inside and called room service for pepperoni and mushroom pizza with a salad. When I returned to the balcony, some man in blue coveralls, likely from mall maintenance, stood near the fountain. He spoke into a cell phone, then put it in his pocket. He remained, perhaps observing the situation while someone elsewhere attempted to turn off the water. After a time, as the water converged on the bases of the surrounding benches, he was forced to take several steps back to keep his feet dry.

Surely by now someone would have figured out how to shut it down? My liability-law nature started coming up with scenarios. Obviously a problem with the pump's manufacture, though it could also be a question of improper maintenance. A knock sounded on my door—the pizza. I signed for it and carried the tray out to the balcony.

Another man in blue coveralls had joined the first. I poured blue cheese dressing on the salad and worked it around. The pizza smelled pretty good, considering where I was, and the salad actually had more to it than limp lettuce. I speared a cherry tomato with my fork and ate it.

A man in a business suit called out to the men by the fountain. He trudged around the growing pool, keeping his glossy shoes far from the water's edge. A couple of inches of water now covered the bases of the benches, and I wondered how much farther it could extend. A sporting goods store stood maybe halfway toward the other end of the mall, and I pictured its employees busily inflating rubber rafts for use in an evacuation. They would paddle through the stores, forcing their way through floating clothes and plastic toys.

Closing time neared, and few shoppers remained in the area. Some clerks from stores near the fountain hung out in their door-ways, watching. They jeered when the flow of water stopped, their voices drifting to my perch as thin echoes. I finished the pizza and wiped my lips. With the live entertainment over, I slipped inside and changed for bed.

9

Cold and dusty morning light filled Shelling's front room, a thick light, a light that promised nothing. It smelled of degradation, of decay. Shelling had no place here, the light said. But look around—were these not his things, had he not made his mark on the house, the garden? He refused the light's verdict.

The Briar Café had always been crowded on weekends. Shelling decided to breakfast there among his fellow townsfolk, away from the dismal light that had invaded his house.

He reached the café at 8:45; no one was there but the teen-aged wait staff and the unseen cooks, though a few minutes after the arrival of Shelling's blueberry pancakes, he heard the chime of the brass bell hanging on the door and the sound of people being seated in the booth behind him.

"Ran around naked with the neighbor's horses?"

"Well, up until maybe seven or so. I was her babysitter, did you know that? And her parents' tarot reader of course."

The first speaker sounded like Shelling's Great-Aunt Paula, grandmother's sister on his father's side; the other woman had a scratchy voice. Scratchy-voice had apparently been to a wed-ding the day before. Shelling ate his pancakes and listened to the women. He wanted to talk to them—the first non-service-providers he had encountered since the couple at the bar, but he didn't know how to initiate it. They appeared to be giving him no attention. Obviously, the emptiness wasn't universal, or his presence would have held more significance. Indecision tore at him—he longed for conversation, but feared being rebuffed.

"I was at a CAMAG‡ retreat," Aunt Paula-voice said. "Down in Oakville."

"Did I mention the vegetables?" Scratchy-voice said. "They brought in all these tubs of plants, growing I mean, limes, peppers, mangoes. They had 'em sent from some place in California. Instead of flowers, you see." Scratchy-voice coughed, a tearing sound that couldn't have been painless. Shelling hoped her cough meant that she had given up smoking, but he knew so many who continued despite the onset of emphysema and worse. The names the women kept repeating—Caroline, Wadholm, Caitlin, and others—reminded him of something. Probably he had seen them in the paper. An event as big this wedding—no doubt there had been an announcement.

Rainfall had begun as Shelling entered the café, and its rate increased while he sat. The sound of the rain pleased him. The season had been far too dry. Inspired by his new farmhouse (and the solitude), Shelling had planted a vegetable garden, which he kept expanding as spring progressed into summer. Broccoli, basil, tomatoes and, of course, carrot. Aided by a detailed do-it-yourself book,‡ he had installed a drip irrigation system, but a steady rain like this was so much better.

"He didn't shoot anyone," Scratchy-voice said. "Fired off two rounds into the air to catch everyone's attention. There's just nothing like the report of a Colt .45 Peacemaker."

"What year?" Paula-voice asked.

"1874, with mother-of-pearl grips."

"Sounds like a presentation model."

‡ Oscar Pitstick, *Make Your Garden! A Guide to Preparing the Perfect Garden Environment,* Pieczynski Publishing, Great Barrington, MA, 1997. One of those books that causes purchasers to consider themselves experts as soon as they acquire it, though it does contain some useful information and techniques. As with all guides and do-it-yourself manuals (sometimes called by the clever marketing term DIY), everything depends on the individual. Many people are incapable of following instructions, others excel. Innumerable dissertations have been written on the subject. Richard Shelling proved to be surprisingly (given his actor past) adept.

The waitress left the check. Shelling put money in the tray and got up. He paused beside the women's booth and smiled at them. Scratchy-voice was maybe sixty, with gray hair pulled back in a bun. "I don't need more coffee," she said.

Shelling went outside. Damn this place—nobody gives a thought to a stranger. What use, this river, this scenic vista of a town? Nothing for him, no one. He slumped against the wall, a few feet from the restaurant's door. His throat constricted. He coughed and gasped, and his stomach . . . as soon as he realized what was happening, he staggered to the parking lot side of the restaurant and vomited.

Unbelievable—first time in years he had thrown up. In a daze, he re-entered the café and shuffled into the bathroom to splash his face at the sink. He swished water in his mouth and spat, then pulled several paper towels from the dispenser to dry his face.

Somewhat refreshed, Shelling left the bathroom. The two women were still eating. He stopped in front of them and leaned in close to Scratchy-voice, with his hands resting on the edge of their table. "Hey," he said, using his best growly voice, the one he had developed for the wife-beating psychopath in that episode of *Precinct 10.* "I don't work here. I don't refill no damn coffee cup. Got me?"

Without waiting for a response, he spun around and swaggered out of the café, aiming himself in the direction of the hardware and garden store. Weekends there were always busy. Last week—had it been last week?—he had waited for the old guy . . . Frosty? . . . Smokey? . . . to finish showing some woman how to build window screens and help him, but he had given up and left.

Today, he went straight to the seed display. A man passed him, and Shelling looked up expectantly. Not a customer. And he refused to talk to any more shopkeepers.

He selected packets of seeds: arugula, Boston lettuce, and acorn squash. After paying, Shelling found the exit blocked. The door had been propped open to admit the rain-cooled air, and a man several inches taller than Shelling and as wide as the doorway stood there, facing outward and talking to another tall man. Thrilled to have encountered others, Shelling paused.

"But even that's a reaction," the big man in the doorway said. "I'm trying to reach cause, not effect." He had a long ponytail down the middle of his broad back and spoke in a deep voice.

"Excuse me," Shelling said, thinking more of passage through the door than conversation.

"But what makes a man start fires?" the other asked.

"Excuse me," Shelling said, louder this time.

"When I was in social work it was easy to feel defeated by the forces of nature," the big man said. As he spoke, he gestured wildly with his beefy arms. Shelling tried to squeeze through while the man's arms were up, but the big man brought a ham-sized elbow down on Shelling's forehead, staggering him back against a flashlight display. "What I'm trying to do now," the big man said, continuing, apparently without having felt his arm's impact with Shelling, "is formulate a working model of societal impulses. How everything comes together to form behavior."

Shelling leaned against the flashlight display, taking shallow breaths. He had dropped his seed packets on hitting the display, and they had scattered nearby. He left them. The faces of the men in the door pulsed and distorted, as if viewed through phosphorescent clouds. A humming sounded, starting low and rising to a cicada shriek. Clenching his eyes shut, Shelling propelled himself forward, smacking against the big man at about kidney level. The impact thrust the big man aside and threw Shelling to the sidewalk. Shelling pushed himself to his knees and crawled toward a bench on the opposite side of the sidewalk.

Someone lifted Shelling onto the bench and held him there. Voices echoed, and lights flashed orange and white. A diorama filled the hardware store's front window: in it, a model train rolled along tracks bounded by cornfields and into a town that mirrored Springdale, the stone church on one end of Main, the movie theater, river, shops. Minute figures flowed along the sidewalks. There were the people! His memories of the town, so jumbled—people walking, enjoying the quiet life here. Which town did he inhabit? The train stopped to disembark passengers, who joined the other pedestrians on the crowded streets. Two police officers, a man and woman, walked toward the hardware store.

10

At the train station I returned the rental car, but somewhere between the rental company and the ticket machine I decided to extend my stay. I guess I was feeling sentimental about the place, especially with Caroline away. It had rained, and the morning sky was lemony and wrinkled, which I took as a sign. The train station was a block off Main, behind the town hall. Scooter and a tall policewoman were escorting some guy in as I passed. I went to the bed and breakfast and booked a room for one night, staying there just long enough to drop my bag on the bed and arrange my glasses and contact lens stuff by the sink. Back out on the street, I stood watching passersby. Mist floated on the hills behind town. I had always admired the houses up there, with their sweeping views. I liked height, liked the way this town sat in its nest of hills, with the river cutting through the middle. Maybe I would walk up that way later, after breakfast, if it didn't start raining again.

The little café off Main was crowded, but I saw a spot at the end of the counter. As I passed these two old birds at a booth one of them glared at me. No idea who she was. There was someone sitting on the stool next to the last free spot, and as I sat I recognized smiley woman from the wedding. She nodded a hello. I smiled, not wanting to seem rude, but seeing someone who maybe knew me, or at least knew Caroline, wasn't the way I had intended to start this day.

The waitress came to take the woman's order, then stared at me. "Weren't you just here?" she asked. I said no. She gave me a funny look and handed me smiley woman's menu.

"The pancakes here are great," smiley woman said.

"Thanks." I looked at the menu, then at her. She had one of those haircuts that showed off the neck, and she had a great neck. I tried to remember if I had ever met her.

"I saw you at the wedding," she said, a flat statement implying that her noticing me signified nothing special. "I guess you haven't been back here since the crap with Caroline."

"Hmmm," I said. This place . . . just couldn't escape things smelling of Caroline. At least Brisbane wasn't here too. Smiley woman—she hadn't been Caroline's friend back when I lived here.

"I've never liked her much," she said.

Enough with all these people knowing my past. What was I thinking, staying another day? Endless prosecutorial miasmas shook me, tendrils popping and sticking like unwanted household knickknacks, objects discarded for the associations they held—the clay figurine with the twisted face, bought on a brief trip to Mexico with Caroline the summer before I entered law school, the shirts, many shirts, bought at her insistence, an attempt to remake my image into something fashionable. I had saved one thing as a reminder, not liking the idea of jettisoning my entire past, acknowledging that it existed, deserved to exist, even the unpleasantness. So I kept the footed bowl, set it on the desk in my office, where it stood holding wrapped peppermints (because Caroline hated peppermints).

"We met at a party." The woman's voice broke through my reverie, and I turned my face toward her. "Don't remember whose party," she said. "You were there alone. Caroline was off somewhere, doing something. Maybe you came with Michael and Deirdre. We somehow got into a discussion about fountain pens."

A notebook lay on the counter near her plate, and beside it a fountain pen with a dark, enamel barrel streaked with green. Seeing the pen, I made the connection. "Right—Sammy Hidalgo." My Uncle Omar repaired fountain pens. As a child, he used to let me play with worn-out nibs and other parts on his worktable. When I graduated from high school, he gave me an antique Parker.‡

I told her that I had read one of her novels after I moved away. She said she had finished a first draft of a new story early this

Parker Duofold, circa 1930s, black body, gold nib. Not a pen to be trifled with. Fountain pens . . . the velvety way the nib slides across paper, the heady smell of ink . . . and the status, yet another way for people to flaunt money and pretensions. Fountain pen stores in shopping malls? Patrick Travis had glanced into one his first night at the mall hotel. Uncle Omar's shop had been a dusty old place, with counters and other fixtures dating back to a long-gone era. But no one knew more about pens. Few people like Uncle Omar left in this disposable plastic world. The old building was, of course, demolished, replaced by a high-rise complex not worth describing.

morning and had gone to breakfast to celebrate. We chatted for a time, reminiscing about safe subjects from my years in Springdale, until her food came. Her three pancakes were spread on the plate, overlapping. She stacked them evenly and began cutting, first in half, then fourths, then eighths. The waitress brought my coffee, and I ordered pancakes too. The coffee here was good, some kind of organic shade-grown. There had been other ownership when I lived here, and I preferred this new version. I don't know when this upscaling—The Change (as I called it)—had occurred or why, but it was nationwide. I liked it. Sure, there's an air of pretension involved sometimes, but overall, the good coffee, microbrew beer, fusion cuisine, beats the crap out of blandness.

"I'm not one of these delicate women who can only order a salad," Sammy said as she pushed a forkful of pancakes around the amber pool of syrup. "I was in L.A. last month, having dinner with some friends in a Thai restaurant, and all around me were these pretty little women with tans and tight asses, and I started speculating on how many salads are served per day out there. Greengrocer's wet dream."

"Is the total salad consumption in Los Angeles greater than the rest of the country combined?" I asked.

"It's a fight between New York and Los Angeles. The winner is awarded a bronze sculpture of iceberg lettuce to display in city hall. The rest of the country is irrelevant."‡

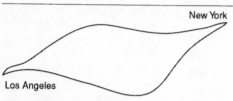

Map of the United States (lower forty-eight) by body weight. From a model formulated by Drs. Silas Barndale and Jane Bricem in 1994, "Geographic Weight Distribution and Its Lack of Effect on Public Opinion," published in *The Journal of Eclectic Dysfunction*, Vol. 12, No. 7.

My pancakes arrived and I drizzled maple syrup over them. Her talk of salad-eating made me self-conscious about it—I didn't want to use so much syrup that she thought I was horsely, or so little that she sneered. Though why did I care? I didn't have to impress anyone in this damn town.

Sammy gave me an incomprehensible look (and I could usually interpret facial expressions—had to for my lawyering).

"High fructose corn syrup," she said. "That's the other thing that sends me on a rant. We're given these competing and contradictory models to follow. Processed high fat corn syrup food is pushed at us all our lives, but at the same time we're bombarded with images of skinny asses and sculpted bodies." She waved her fork at me, and a ribbon of syrup slid toward her fingers.

"If I followed the model that women are given, I would need to apologize to you for my eating pancakes and tell you I'll have to spend all afternoon at the gym to work it off. Well fuck that."

After finishing our food, we remained at the counter. The place had cleared out, and neither of us appeared to be in a rush. I tried to remember what, if anything, I had heard about Sammy. Besides her jacket copy. When I changed plans at the train station, I had been thinking how important it would be to spend some solitary time in the town, sorting out my memories of

Springdale, which as the weekend progressed had slowly shed its malevolence. Sitting here with Sammy helped, though I still needed to be alone.

"Dee and Michael must be on their way to Barcelona by now," she said. I left some money on the counter and stood. She left with me. "What are your plans for the day then?" she asked. "Now that you've decided to be brave and stay a little longer in this terrible place." She smiled when she said that, an open, cheery expression that I found touching.

"Nice out now," I said, looking at where the sun burned through a few remaining skins of cloud. "If it had stayed rainy I would have probably caught the next train out. Maybe I'll take a taxi to the Josephine Rodgers House‡ and see the gardens. It was great talking to you." I extended a hand to shake, and she gripped it with both of hers.

Josephine Rodgers kept a summer house in the area, the garden of which was famous for its splendor; however, during Rodgers's life, her partner, Susan Marcus, did most of the gardening. After Rodgers's death, her conservative family refused to acknowledge Marcus's claims to the property and set up a nonprofit foundation that paid several family members enough money for them to quit their jobs and move to Florida.

"Why not let me show you what's new around here since you left?"

Despite my desire for solitude, I found myself unwilling to cleave myself from her company.

"I know a place Caroline never would have taken you."

11

When had Shelling last eaten? His stomach was a shrunken, leathery thing. He found himself in a narrow room facing two square windows set high, near the ceiling. No furniture but the wooden chair on which he sat, cushioned by a piece of folded burlap. A vent on the wall behind him blew air across the top of his head. Spiders had crafted nests in all the corners. From the windows, the entering light radiated a pinkish glow.

Lethargy gripped him. Shouldn't he demand to see a lawyer? He had acted in cop and lawyer shows—you can't shut someone up like this. Must be something in the atmosphere that kept him from fighting, the white air of the narrow room. The vent stopped blowing. At first, the quiet pleased him. Each molecule of silence emerged, one after another. He pictured them waltzing in loose swirls of air, forming patterns more intricate than snowflakes. Untouchable they swam, free of the clinging spiderwebs.

But after a time, Shelling grew tired of observing the dancing silence. He found himself longing to hear Mozart, a piano sonata to fill the empty spaces.

Now restless, he rose and paced the room, measuring it with his steps: seven steps wide and twenty-eight deep. Did it mean something that the room's depth was divisible by its width? He stopped in a corner to examine the spider webs, whorls of filament rising from floor to ceiling. When he had moved into his farmhouse, he found it full of webs—in corners, doorways, along the base of the kitchen cabinets—and he eradicated all as he encountered them. These, he left undisturbed, for they gave him something to observe besides the white walls and the door, a slab of heavy metal with no knob.

Lost in his examination of the webs, Shelling needed several repetitions of a hollow clanging thump to register the sound. Suddenly filled with nervous energy, he rushed back to his chair, turned it to face the door and sat, trying to calm his heartbeat. Another clang, then a scraping sound from a mechanism inside the door, and it swung outward. A man in a dark blue uniform came into view outside the door. The top of the jamb obscured his face, and he had to dip his head and turn sideways to enter.

The man straightened. He had a russet potato of a face, and a dark blue helmet hung low over his forehead. "Come on now," he said in a rumbly voice. Though obviously some sort of policeman or jailer, he wore no visible gun.

"Where am I? What do you want from me? I won't be—" The policeman-jailer's unresponsiveness stifled Shelling's protests, and he decided to stay in the chair—would not go anywhere until the man answered.

Once, in fifth or sixth grade, Shelling's teacher had tried to send him to the principal's office, but he had refused to go. Despite her command, he remained at his desk, and when she tried to pull him away, he had gripped its sides so firmly she couldn't dislodge him.

"C'mon, no funny stuff," the jailer said. He moved behind Shelling's chair and tipped it forward, forcing Shelling to stand. The jailer was huge, well over a foot taller than Shelling—so large that Shelling couldn't see all of him without stepping back. He flattened against the wall, facing his jailer. He couldn't fight, not this . . . human monolith. The jailer motioned for Shelling to precede him. They entered a narrow hall filled with a reddish light; twenty feet or so farther they reached another metal door, which swung open.

"Right turn," the jailer said.

This new passage ran straight, with the same red light and a worn, asbestos tile floor. Shelling tried to estimate the corridor's length, but the featureless passage numbed him. No other doors appeared, and they continued without pause. From behind, he could sense the bulk of his escort, and he labored to remain ahead of the man's heavy stride. The jailer's breathing echoed from the walls and ceiling, a living, writhing sound that encircled them as they walked, formed a path for them through the center of the hall.

Disconnected thoughts and observations flooded Shelling's mind. No other doors here, no rooms. Lost. Subterranean passage . . . ending where? This man, this jailer, his steps, his stride deliberate, each identical to the ones preceding . . . giant robot man . . . maybe only the one speed. Run? Can't run. Viscous atmosphere pressed, like the oatmeal in the movie theater. He longed to be back in his farmhouse bed. This passage bore through the heart of the planet. The walls closed over him, suffocating, so heavy with the weight of earth overhead, all the cities rivers mountains. . . .

Gasping, Shelling stopped, unable to take another step along the limitless path. Behind him, the jailer also stopped. The man's broad hands pushed against Shelling's back, and he cried out as he tumbled forward. Rough stalks pressed against his face. He heard a door clang shut, but when he sat up, he found himself alone in a cornfield.

12

"You ever have flying dreams?" Sammy asked. She pointed to the east, where a wave of passing rain clouds hung. "I become lost in the clouds every time. Can't tell up, down, whatever."

"So where are we headed first then?" I asked, though I was thinking of telling her I had changed my mind again.

"I grew up around here," she said. "I was gone a while, Waterloo College in Austin, stayed there several years after graduating. I got my first book published when I was in Austin. I guess I didn't want to come back here till I had some success. It's the kind of town that draws people back." She smiled. "So you better be careful."

I followed her into an alley between the rug shop and the Japanese restaurant. I had never noticed the alley before, but figured that it led through to the next street, the train station, fire house, movie theater. I was feeling kind of detached, and willing to be led. I had begun the day expecting to go home. Changing my mind about that led to meeting Sammy, so allowing her to guide me on an adventure seemed right. My whole point of staying was to face my past, prove—to myself anyway—that a town, this town, couldn't control me.

"Springdale is a great place," she said, somehow picking up on my thoughts. "I guess you weren't allowed to see the best of it though. In a way, it's two towns. There are the bored would-be socialite types. Like Caroline and her friends. And an artistic and intellectual side, related to the college of course but not only people on faculty. It's more like an attraction anchored by the college, but extending beyond it."

"Well, I never saw any of that. Unless you would call Skippy Brisbane an artist. I think she has a computer program that assembles her romance plots." Sammy laughed and, walking close to me, slipped a hand between my bicep and my side. I asked her if she was working on a new novel. "Not to insult you by following a comment on Brisbane with a question about your writing, of course."

She laughed again and squeezed my arm, and my whole body tingled. "I'm doing something quasi-historical," she said. "I'm more after mood than historical accuracy. It's about Diogenes of Lesbos."‡

It seemed like we had been going for some time. The walls on either side remained a uniform red brick, but the surface beneath our feet had changed from pavement to hard-packed earth. The alley darkened, and I shivered, though the air didn't feel any cooler. I looked up. Despite the gloom down here, blue sky filled the space between the buildings, and sunlight reflected off a low cloud, but the light

Words emerge. Where they come from is a question that has mystified philosophers for generations. The Greeks used to sit under the twisted branches of olive trees and argue that words were given to humans by either whales or birds.

Some years before the Punic War, the members of the whale camp made the distinction that birds lacked the capacity for speech because their tongues were too small. The bird camp held up the example of parrots to disprove this. Mere mimicry, the whale supporters rebutted, not true speech. These arguments persisted throughout the Classical period. Eventually, a group of rebel philosophers, led by Diogenes of Lesbos, started its own city on a hill overlooking the Mediterranean south of Corinth. Diogenes of Lesbos was a charismatic figure, depicted always with a crow perched on his upraised right forearm and his left hand grasping the staff of knowledge. The Diogenines, as they came to be called, set up a multiracial, egalitarian community based on observations of the Pacific albatross. They learned to communicate with birds in ways never before accomplished. The other group, those espousing whales, left only legendary data. At some point before the time of Alexander, they moved to the North Atlantic where they could live closer to the whales. Unprepared for the extreme temperatures, they froze to death, and all records of their research disappeared. Recently, an expedition sponsored by the National Geographic Society encountered what might be the remains of their settlement, located on a promontory in Norway.

Meanwhile the bird branch has proved that Mozart understood the method by which birds transmitted language to humans. He was working on a piece that, when finished, would have enabled all humans to comprehend the complexities of language. Unfortunately, he died before completing this work, which took the form of a series of harpsichord sonatas. Incomplete, they serve only to show us what might have been. Future researchers may find a way to decipher his notes, which resemble the footprints of pigeons in the sand.

couldn't seem to reach us. It reminded me of that Magritte painting, the one where the street is dark even though a daytime sky hovers over it.‡

Maybe twenty yards on, the light increased, but when I looked up again, the sky had vanished, replaced by a domed ceiling painted in abstract shapes of color, shades of red and orange, with black streaks. Somehow, we had entered a vast, circular space, illuminated by recessed lighting. A railing ran around the diameter of the dome at about second-story level.

I stopped. "Hey," I said. Sammy turned to face me. "Where the fuck are we?"

L'empire des lumières (The Dominion of Light), 1952, oil on canvas, collection of Lois and Georges de Menil. Magritte made sixteen oil and ten gouache versions of *L'empire* between 1949 and 1964. He believed that a painting does not express ideas, but has the power to create them. In a letter to Marcel Mariën, July 27, 1952, Magritte said: "The attempt at an explanation (which is no more than an *attempt*) is unfortunate: I am supposed to be a great mystic, someone who brings comfort (because of the luminous sky) for unpleasant things (the dark houses and trees in the landscape)." This reconciliation of opposites was a paradox typical of the Surrealists.

13

Shelling plodded through the corn for what seemed days, unable to reach the edge of the field. At least he had food. The ears were mature and sweet; he stripped off the husks and ate as he went. But walking was a struggle. He found it difficult to maintain a straight path in any direction. What crazy hand had seeded these fields? No even rows here, everything random, as though planted by chance. And so early in the season—he had thought that this year's crop wouldn't be ready until much later, July or August.

He tried to keep the sun ahead. As a child, he had often tramped along a ditch near his house, pushing his way through tall sunflowers, slashing at them with a hunting knife. But he had known the ditch was near, a few feet to his left, and across it, the streets leading home.

At last, when the sun reached the top of a line of distant trees, he found a road. Roads like this crisscrossed the area, connecting farm, field, and town. He set off to his right, and after a hundred yards or so, a house appeared behind a tumbled stone wall. He decided to stop there and ask directions. A stone path, crowded by overrunning grasses and dandelions, led to the house, and when Shelling reached the front door, he recognized it as his own.

His front door was unlocked as usual; he turned the glass knob and stepped into his living room. Oh, home, his furniture, the two paintings by that California-based Russian artist that he had acquired in L.A., the lingering scent of last night's tomato-basil-garlic pasta. He flopped onto the couch and sobbed. The day, its unknowable trials now passed, folded down, but the familiar objects of his life supported him. Back in his comfortable living room, that cell, the jailer . . . now distant.

When Shelling opened his eyes, the sun had set. He showered and dressed in clean clothes. Unable to remember why his car wasn't there, he called the town's taxi service, and when a cab arrived, he told the driver to take him to the Japanese restaurant. He remained silent all the way to town.

At the restaurant, Shelling took a seat by the front window. The empty dining room saddened him. He had thought, after seeing the women at breakfast, after the day's ordeal, he would find the town revivified. Not this . . . continuation of emptiness.

Monique the waitress brought him tea. The unglazed teapot and mug had a rough shape, more likely formed by hand than by wheel. The warmth of the mug seeped into his palm and flowed up his arm. "Are these yours?" he asked. "I keep saying I want to visit your studio and never do—is tomorrow afternoon good?"

The waitress's expression reminded him of the men at the hardware store—distant, as though inhabiting a different world. She walked back toward the kitchen, leaving Shelling to stare out at the street and the darkened store opposite. At some point he heard another customer enter but didn't turn around to see. What was the use? He couldn't stand the thought of another snub, another cryptic encounter. A person, even an outgoing person, soon succumbs, shrinks into solitude, even embraces it.

But that wasn't him, wasn't what *he* wanted. Where was Monique? He thought that he had made some progress, attempting to set up an appointment with her outside the workplace. That wall again. Things had to be done in small steps, but the time involved, he didn't have the patience anymore. He would tell Monique he was an actor. She would want to sleep with someone who had appeared on television, who knew famous people.

Someone slid into a booth behind him; the cushion and frame creaked with the person's weight, and Shelling heard a rumbly voice ask for tea.

14

Looking back the way we came, I saw no entry, nothing but an unbroken curve of wainscoting that rose to chest-level and, above it, plaster painted a warm terracotta. I stood in the middle of the room, under the multicolored dome, while Sammy circled the periphery.

"What is this place? I didn't notice us going through a door. We were in the alley—"

"The transition is always subtle," she said. She kept walking, trailing a finger along the surface of the wainscoting.

This made no sense. We had been walking down an alley. Which must have led directly into this place. Since my arrival in Springdale, I had been preoccupied with my past. An autopilot kind of thing, and being so closed up I wasn't aware enough of my surroundings to notice where we were going.

"Here's something." She looked over at me, but I didn't move. Who was she, really? We had met, what, an hour ago? Sammy pushed on the wainscoting and a section swung away from her. It could have shut after we had entered, but I didn't remember coming in over there. Sammy stood by the open section, waiting for me. I joined her.

"This is ridiculous. How could somebody who has never been here find their way out after the door closed?"

"This isn't the way we came in. It's the way forward."

I just stared at her, irritation building inside me.

"Patrick, I said I would show you places Caroline never took you. She's lived in Springdale her whole life but knows nothing about this."

It must have been obvious from my face that I still wasn't accepting anything; she smiled and touched my cheek with her fingertips. "Springdale is a complex town, a crossroads, and we're in its hub. We enter, we find our way through. Maybe something we experience changes the way we look at the world."

Sammy emanated a sincerity that I found comforting—a jury would have bought it, no problem. So I smiled back. Her explanation hadn't answered my questions, but if adventure beckoned, I was ready for it.

She stooped and passed through the doorway. I followed. Inside, the ceiling was too low to stand erect. The passage appeared to continue in a straight line, lit from a source I couldn't identify. The indirect light had a misty quality, making it hard to judge distance. A click from behind made me turn. The wainscoting door had swung shut behind us. I pushed, but could find no way to open it.

Sammy held my wrist. "You can't do that. There's only one way to go when you're in here. Come on." She turned away and I had no choice but to follow. My neck started to ache from walking hunched. Sammy was only an inch or so shorter than me, so she didn't have it any easier. For some reason, I was wondering what time I would be returning to the bed and breakfast. Those places were often weird about their guest's hours.

"It's always different here, each time you come," Sammy said. "Sometimes these corridors run straight out to the cornfields. It's better when the ceiling's higher. I feel like I'm walking on chicken strings in here."

After forty yards or so of this, we reached a cylindrical room with a ceiling about twelve feet high. "This is way better," Sammy said as we straightened. I reached back to rub my neck with both hands. "Let me," she said, and began kneading my shoulders. I could feel her breasts against my back. Her hair smelled perfect, some kind of mint and rosemary scent.‡ I liked having her near. It was funny—aside from a brief conversation at that party back when I lived here, we had met only that morning, but I felt as though we had a connection that went deeper. I suppose that explained why I wasn't more anxious about this place she had brought me—I had some innate trust in her. And I wasn't anybody's timid waffle. I liked to explore. But I had wanted to spend today in, I don't know, solitary contemplation.

"I appreciate you bringing me here," I said. "Wherever 'here' is."

She stopped massaging but left her hands on my shoulders. They felt warm there, strong guides. "We picked a good day. This place isn't always so easy to reach. Sometimes the entry doesn't appear." She pushed my right shoulder and pulled my left, turning me around. Her face had a soft expression, thoughtful, and I felt that connection again. "I wanted to share some of the real Springdale with you."

"Sammy . . . I, I appreciate that. But this—" I waved my hands around. "It doesn't make any sense. These rooms and passages leading nowhere. Anyway, I guess we have to go back now." I hunched over and turned into the low corridor from which we had just emerged, but before I could go any farther, Sammy grabbed my arm and yanked me back.

"You can't do that!" She had a bark that I hadn't expected. She still held my arm, which started to throb. I shook her grip loose.

‡ Aveda™, Mint and Rosemary Shampoo, with organic invigoration. Is this a pretentious choice? Could her hair not be equally well-served by the products shelved in drug and grocery stores or the natural brands found in the local food co-op? Connor Evans, proprietor of Kinetic Hair, would say that this brand, this particular formula, is perfectly matched with Sammy Hidalgo's hair type. Though he, of course, is not a reliable reporter. What would be the opinion of Caroline Miller, ex-wife of Patrick Travis and no friend of Ms. Hidalgo (for reasons having much to do with Ms. Hidalgo's status as an artist and with her Mexican-American heritage). Unfortunate that she's still in Spain, out of range of this discussion.

"What's—"

"I told you before. You can only go one way." She rubbed my arm gently, as if smoothing out the spot she had held. "I hope I didn't hurt you." She moved closer and touched my face with her other hand. "This place is sort of a sophisticated funhouse. It has rules, though, and they have to be followed. The main rule is you always move forward. To advance from here, we have to find another door."

15

Shelling loved yellowtail the most, followed by tuna and salmon. Before finding consistent TV work in L.A., he couldn't afford sushi. Sometimes he would order a cup of miso and one piece of fish and make it last as long as possible. He wasn't a glutton, but now, with no financial worries, he wouldn't deny himself the pleasures. He had been thrilled to discover that his new town possessed such a fine Japanese restaurant. What was it Kinsey-Moore had said in her essay on gastronomy? "The path to flavor, though often blocked by under-seasoning, over-saucing, improper cooking, and so many more obstacles that it makes one hesitate, has at its end rewards ample enough to make all trials worthwhile."‡

Ruth Kinsey-Moore, *The Lore of True Cuisine*, Williamson House Press, New York, NY, and Glasgow, Scotland, 1974, p. 123. Perhaps the best book on food and eating ever written. Dwarfish, frizzy-haired, and caustic, Kinsey-Moore would not have thrived in this era of telegenic celebrity chefs, though many of the current breed pay banal compliments to her legacy.

This joyful trinity: fine food, drink, and congenial companions was what made all the Hollywood crap bearable. Crazy how much money the people out there threw around, even to pay small-time actors like him. Though never in a starring role, he had always found consistent work and had invested his earnings well, never wasting money on ridiculous expenditures like sports cars and trendy Albanian clothes. He had known others, friends from his early years, people who had shopped in the same thrift stores, but who, after "making it," spent everything they earned and more, a never-ending deluge that inevitably turned into over-extended credit and the forced-liquidation of expensive toys as soon as the sources of income dissipated for any length of time over a month.

Something heavy approached, a presence forceful and unavoidable, and a hand landed on his shoulder, where it stayed, pressing with an insistence that caused him to look up, discovering beside him the massive blue-uniformed man who had taken him from the narrow room, and who was now holding his shoulder with a wide and formidable hand. The man beckoned with his other hand, and Shelling rose, leaving sushi and contentment.

Outside, the man steered him up the street to a dim alley between the Japanese restaurant and the rug shop. Shelling stopped at the black maw of the alley. "What's this all about? I have rights, you know."

He tried to turn, but the man's fingers clamped onto his shoulders. Shelling refused to move. Let the man push him. Instead, the man slipped his hands under Shelling's armpits and lifted. Shelling squirmed, trying to break the policeman's hold. He swung his legs back and forth, kicking at the man, but nothing had an effect. The policeman-jailer kept walking.

Shelling had appeared in a short-lived television series starring that former professional football player, the one with the state of Texas tattooed on his scalp. The man's size and intimidating interactions with the rest of the cast had upset the delicate essence of creating the show. Once, for fun, the man had grabbed Shelling from behind, encircling his neck with a chokehold that he didn't release until Shelling began to pass out. The man had laughed his "huh huh huh" laugh, and what could Shelling do?

But this new situation was opposite. There was a peacefulness to being carried, as though the act stripped Shelling of responsibility. He felt outside himself, and imagined what it would be like to gaze upon this scene—the dark-uniformed man carrying his burden, some recalcitrant youngster, down the alley. The massive jailer transported Shelling farther than he would have thought possible in this small town. Had they perhaps left the town, penetrated some intersecting region accessible only to this man?

At some point they must have passed into a building, though

Shelling noticed no transition from open alley to closed-in corridor, identical to the corridor he and his jailer had traversed earlier.

16

Sammy and I chose opposite directions, but reached the moving panel at the same time. This one opened to a closet with a metal ladder emerging through a hole in the floor. We descended, Sammy first. The cold of the rungs bothered me, and I had to concentrate on not going so fast I trampled Sammy's fingers. The light in the tube grew dimmer as we descended, though it appeared to follow us, illumining the nearest rungs. Above, everything was dark; I didn't look down any farther than the next rung and the top of Sammy's head. My shoulder muscles burned from the effort. Sammy's breathing rasped, a heavy sound from deep in her throat.

How much longer would this ladder to nowhere continue? The air down here . . . thin . . . insufficient. The walls, the tube, constricted, so hard to squeeze through. Something grabbed my ankles, held them. I tried to kick them free. I would not become trapped, not here, not before seeing one last time the glitter of sun on water, hearing waves caress the shore.

"Patrick!"

Who here knew my name? Not the others—they cared for nothing but their own petty squabbles. This dream amber-trapped me, forced its will.

"Stop moving. Breathe, Patrick, breathe." I became aware of Sammy's hands gripping my ankles. I looked down. She had hooked her feet and knees onto the ladder for support. "You were panicking," she said.

"I'm okay now." I must have sounded uncertain because she didn't release me. She talked, not really saying anything, but the sound of her voice soothed me, and she stroked my calf with her fingers. My breath settled, air sliding in and out of my tender throat.

She slipped her hands from my ankles and started down. I hesitated, though not for long. Sammy kept talking; obviously she thought I needed help staying calm. Who had put her in charge anyway? A ladder. I could go down a fucking ladder without coddling. I knew how to handle myself pretty well, no matter the circumstances.

I glanced down at the top of her head. She cared about me, didn't want me to injure myself. And she had brought me to this place to share an experience before I left town.

"Looks like we're nearly there," she said. "Somewhere, anyway," she muttered.

Careful to maintain my desperate grip on the rungs, I leaned out, trying to see what lay beyond her, at the base of the ladder. There was a pinkish surface, difficult to make out in the dim light.

"Hold up," she said. "Looks like the ladder ends a few feet from the bottom. I'm going to grab the lowest rung with my hands and drop." She worked her way down rung by rung, then slid her right foot off, followed by the left.

"How far?" I asked, but she had already let go.

She cried, "Wheee!" as she dropped, holding her glasses to her face the way a scuba diver holds the mask. Her feet reached the surface. "It's spongy foamy—" Her legs and then her body disappeared into the pinkish mass, cutting off the rest of her words.

I scuttled down the remaining rungs and, not wanting to drop directly over her, pushed off. The stuff met my falling body and pulled me in. It had a thin membrane that made a little "shoup" kind of noise, then I sank into a mass of translucent jelly. Before I could think, I inhaled. The stuff sluiced into my mouth and throat, but instead of choking, I felt refreshed, as though the jelly contained an oxygen-rich mix—a viscous, breathable swimming pool. I folded onto my stomach and swung my arms out toward my head, attempting a slow breaststroke toward, I hoped, Sammy. The vat of jelly disoriented me. Light came from somewhere, maybe the jelly itself. Although I could see through the stuff, I had nothing with which to orient myself. The tube containing the ladder hadn't been more than three feet across, but I had no way of knowing the size of this jelly tank. I wanted to find a wall and gain comfort from its solidity. I tried a breaststroke, my version of one anyway. I had never been much of a swimmer, but this—no worries about squirting water up my nose or having to match the strokes with my breathing—was kind of nice.

Stopping, I hung in the stuff and looked around to see if my swimming had brought me to anything recognizable. Off to my right I saw a shape darker than the jelly, and I set off toward it.

17

Shelling woke on his back. He had dreamt of an academic conference at a beach resort, where he had spent his time at various lectures, the nature of which he couldn't remember. There had been something he was expected to do, prevent a group from being trapped or taken prisoner. Odd thing for him to dream. He had never been to an academic conference, hadn't even played an academic on television. His nose itched; he reached for it, but discovered that he couldn't move.

Padded straps restrained his wrists and ankles. His body lay on some kind of pallet. He rolled his head as far as he could in every direction. High on the wall to his left were two windows. A whistling vent stirred the air. The room—he had been here before. His forehead and armpits felt damp. He needed to wipe the sweat from his face but could do nothing.

A wave hit, helplessness complete. He lay looking up at the plaster ceiling. Dry streambeds scored its surface, flowing around peaks and fissures. A desert, not without life, but the spiders stayed mainly in the corners, building their homes without disturbance. He had known a woman once, an actress, who reminded him of a spider—something about her dark hair and long skinny arms and knobby elbows, the shape of her mouth when she spoke. He always thought she was trying to suck in the world. That show they had been on . . . a comedy. She‡ had played the main character while he appeared in maybe five episodes of the first and only season. Without those giant walnut elbows he would have found her

Linda Scales. Now the kickboxing partner of Ralph Ambrose in the syndicated action-adventure series *Poseidon's Quest.* It is doubtful that she would remember Shelling, having taken no notice of him during their time together on the comedy show, though this was not his fault—Scales was one of the most self-centered people in an industry of self-centered people.

arms alluring. Long arms attracted him—the smooth distance down from shoulder, along bicep, humerus, and tricep.

The lights in his cell brightened, a flash that overpowered his eyes with white. His pupils retreated, agonized by the unexpected intrusion, and he covered them with his lids. A clang sounded, then a clicking-whirring. He blinked repeatedly, trying to bring the room back into focus. His vision cleared enough for him to see the outlines of the windows, and as he concentrated on their shape his pallet moved. The end where his head lay began to rise, a slow, ratchety pull; the whole pallet climbed the wall, lifting him upright.

"Adjustments, adjustments must be made. No one prepared, and so I must crank and strap, fill and elevate."

The speaker was a woman. Her voice soothed him, a musical tone not unlike that of Mindy, the actress he had lived with for six months, the one who had been a folksinger before getting a part in a movie about a folksinger. He had left her eventually, though he couldn't recall why.

His rising pallet was becoming uncomfortable as gravity pulled at his body, at the straps binding his wrists. He tensed to hold himself upright. At some point his eyes recovered and he could see the woman. She was directly below him and bent over, fiddling with something at the bottom edge of his pallet, now a few inches above the floor. When she straightened, the top of her curly red hair was about even with his waist. Behind her stood a low platform with a rod extending vertically a couple of feet, on the end of which was some kind of control panel and a joystick.

She looked up at him, and he thought it *was* Mindy, but with hair red instead of blonde. Mindy though, she was six feet tall. Funny how he had thought of arms—he had loved to watch the movement of her arm as she strummed her guitar. He closed his eyes. She had written a song for him, "only one sky/sometimes in blue and sometimes gray."‡ Stupid to have left her. With her,

"Only One Sky." Though actually written by Jack Hardy, released on *Omens*, 2000. Mindy Vaughn had lied. Why? Was it because she considered her own songwriting to be inadequate and wanted praise from a man she admired? And Shelling—a few months later, he responded to her admiration by ending their relationship.

here, this empty town wouldn't seem so bleak.

When he opened his eyes, the short woman was standing on the platform with her hands resting on the chrome sides of the control panel. She pushed a button with her thumb, and the platform elevated, kept rising until her face leveled with his.

"Better, better," she said, and tweaked the joystick forward, then left, to maneuver herself in front of him.

Close, she didn't look like Mindy. Her eyes were farther apart, or maybe less rounded, and her nose wasn't as pointed.

"And now we can attend to preparations."

Her skin was creamy, unblemished by mark or wrinkle, and her eyes were a soft blue-green. Surely this wasn't the face of a torturer? She lifted the ends of a belt from the sides of the pallet and buckled it over his chest, then pulled it tight.

Shelling gasped. "What is this? What have I done? Hurts . . . I won't be strapped—" He couldn't take in enough air to form words.

The woman pulled her platform back a foot or so. "Secured the subject for analysis." She leaned over the control panel and flipped a cigar-shaped plastic rod from its socket and pointed it at him. Holes covered its rounded tip. With a stubby forefinger, she reached down to push a green button. "Begin recording. How many faces do you have?" She looked at Shelling as though waiting for an answer. "How many?" she asked again.

He tried to speak, he opened his mouth, intending to offer something, but his outburst had drained him of words.

"Subject refuses to speak." She pushed the green button again.

He moved his head from side to side and mouthed "no no no," but she wasn't looking. What crime had he committed? This town, *his* town, he had thought, but if it *were* his town, it would not have conspired to keep him alone and helpless, would not have subjected him to the giant policeman and his partner, this crazed midget woman with her straps and platform and buttons.

18

With the jelly limiting visibility, I was right over Sammy before I saw her. She hovered a foot or so below, face down. At first I thought she had lost consciousness, but her hands flapped every few seconds, slow, water-treading movements. She appeared to be watching something. I stroked downward. It took a lot of strokes to reach her. Either I moved half an inch at a time or she was way farther down than I had thought.

She must have sensed my movement, because as I neared her, she looked up. She smiled, turned her body toward me, and extended a hand. I took it and we hovered there, holding hands. She spoke, but the jelly absorbed the sound. I mouthed back. She pointed down. Below lay the town, like a view from an airplane. Everything was there, church, town hall, houses, stores. Paperclip-sized cars moved along Main Street.

We kicked to propel ourselves lower. A man exited the hardware store and stepped into the street without waiting for a car to pass. The car jerked to a stop, and the man kept going. Farther up the street, several teenagers blocked the sidewalk in front of the record store. When I saw the café where Sammy and I had eaten breakfast, my stomach rumbled. Had that been this morning? It seemed so long ago.

What a god-like sensation, floating over the town like this, so real I thought I could sweep a hand down and pluck a tree from its bed. Probably a video of the town projected onto the floor, with the jelly giving it a three-dimensional appearance. Releasing Sammy's hand, I stroked downward, then I reached to touch the floor. My fingers punched in the roof of a pickup truck. I jerked my hand back and looked at Sammy, who had followed me down. Her expression reflected my surprise.

We stayed at this lower level but kept our hands well away from the street and buildings. Someone emerged from the alley by the rug shop and looked up. It was that fat cop, the one I called Scooter because I couldn't picture him chasing anyone. He was looking in our direction, or at least at the area where we would be if we were really there instead of floating in a vat of pink jelly.

Then he raised his right arm and pointed his index finger straight at us. Sammy grabbed my hand and squeezed. My heart started thumping. "There's no way he can see us," I said. The jelly swallowed my words, but Sammy knew what I meant.

Scooter, as though aware he held our attention, slowly rotated his hand toward the alley behind him, and held it taut, like a weathervane in a strong wind. After a minute or so, he turned around, into the mouth of the alley, and disappeared in the direction he had pointed.

Sammy pulled my arm, then dropped it and stroked toward the alley. I followed. The buildings grew larger as we neared them, rising sides of a brick canyon. We swam through the canyon till we reached a wall that blocked the alley. Sammy touched my hand and pointed up with her other, then kicked her way skyward. We found an open slit of a window. Sammy went straight for it. She tilted her head to the side to make herself flatter and pulled herself in.

I waited until her feet were all the way through, then tried to copy her, but when I put my head into the window, I couldn't breathe. Worse than on the ladder, this crack, the world above, its magnitude sagging. I tried to pull out of the crack, but my head was caught. Sammy would have to come back to help push me free. I stopped moving, trying to think. What had she said earlier?

Closing my eyes, I concentrated on slow, even breath, and pushed myself in. My shoulders somehow flattened enough for me to squeeze through, and I tumbled onto a carpeted floor about two feet below the window. Sammy lay beside me. We had escaped the jelly. Right away the stuff started to dry out, congealing in my hair and face like gelatinous latex. I pulled it from my mouth. Bits of the stuff clung to the back of my throat, but they slowly dissolved. Exhaustion and exhilaration surged through me simultaneously.

"The town," I said. "Like we were there. That breathable jelly." When I got the stuff out of my eyes I turned back to the window, which looked larger from in here. Outside, the sky was a pinkish haze. I grabbed Sammy's hand. "What about that truck? I couldn't have—"

"I don't know. The whole thing was new for me too." Her face had a fixed-in-place look, as if she was trying not to be scared, and her fingers curled tight over mine.

We worked on peeling ourselves clean. Sammy had cleared most of the stuff from her head and neck. Bits of it dotted her nose, and strands hung from the frame of her glasses. "You look like you've dumped a bottle of one of those facial mask things all over your-self," I said.

"Would you like a mirror?"

When I smiled, the stretch and crack of solidifying goo tickled my face. I ran my tongue over my lips, which tasted sweetish. A strip of the dried jelly stuck to Sammy's cheek; I reached to brush it off. She held my hand there and leaned toward me. Her lips tasted sweetish too, fruity-tart like a plum jam. She stroked my back, passing her hand from the base of my neck down and up again. I felt her lips on my ear, and everything tingled. She moved her hands to my face and held my cheeks. Her dark eyes . . . what were they trying to say? We kissed again, slowly, and I understood something I never had with Caroline. We don't need explanations for every action. Tenderness, warmth for another, don't have to be linked with anything other than their own existence.

I forced myself back. "Scooter, that cop," I said. "He couldn't have been motioning to us."

"Something's wrong. We'll have to keep going till we locate him, find out what's happening." Sammy raised my right hand and kissed my fingertips. She got up, pulling me with her, but we didn't hurry. She twined the fingers of her right hand into my hair and rubbed her left across my chest. "Later . . . later, can I take you home and cook you dinner?" We stood close, and the pressure of her strong thigh against mine reassured me.

The room had a normal door, with a panel of frosted glass and a metal knob. We went through it into a long hall. Ahead, something appeared to block the corridor.

Our movements felt out of proportion to the stretched-out passage, so that we walked and walked but appeared to grow no closer to whatever awaited us. As though afraid that speech would slow our progress, we remained silent. My calves began to ache, a dull pain with each step. We held hands, and I found the contact comforting. I knew that together, we would reach . . . then, with a suddenness that made me pause, the shape loomed close; a few steps farther it became Scooter. He stood motionless beside a wide, rust-colored metal door. His bulk filled the hall. At first, I thought he was asleep standing up, but when we got close enough for me to see into his eyes, I had the impression that his mind had turned inward, to run some deep mental process requiring an intensity of concentration I wouldn't have thought him capable of mastering.

He turned his jowly face toward us, a movement so gradual that it gave me this crazy detachment, as though I watched him look at me from a place other than mine. He seemed to measure me with his eyes, as though dissecting every detail of my appearance. When he spoke, his voice rumbled and his words made no sense. "Thinner, hair different, but identical. One inside"—pointing to the metal door—"and one here. Both inhabiting where only one should." He looked at Sammy. "Do you comprehend?" She nodded.

"I don't," I said. "When we were in that jelly, I touched a truck."

He waved a broad hand, quieting me. "Two roads met here, crossed one another, and the force of their meeting sent waves rolling in widening curves, encompassing worlds." He shook his head, as though trying to clear it.

"Laureanno's Law?"‡ Sammy asked, and Scooter nodded. She looked at me.

"I'm not understanding any of this," I said. I needed to go outside,

> "What we regard as the real world is determined by the information our brain is able to process. If we depart our 'real' world, our brain, depending on the attributes of this 'unreal' world we enter, sees only those elements which correspond to our 'real' world . . . if our counterpart exists in this 'unreal' world (which would, of course, be 'real' for our counterpart), complications arise which stretch the proportions of the world in unforeseen ways." M. Laureanno, *Understanding Dimensions*, 2nd ed., Springer-Verlag, Philadelphia, PA, 1998, pp. 169–70.

into sunlight. Scooter reached toward me with a tree branch arm and rested it on my shoulders. The contact warmed me; I hadn't realized I was shivering.

"Laureanno fits the circumstances," he said. His voice filled the space, embracing me with as much force as his arm had. "Only the one who belongs can remain. Expelling the other should regain the balance." I pictured his voice flowing down the hall and bursting out into . . . I had no idea where the hall led.

Scooter lifted his arm from my shoulders and turned to the door. It creaked open at his touch. He stepped through and gestured for us to follow. Inside, a man lay on a hospital bed with the back part elevated so that he sat up. The tall policewoman I had seen around town with Scooter stood on the far side. Her gaze absorbed me the same way Scooter's had.

19

The giant policeman slipped into Shelling's cell, a silent arrival, unnoticed until his bulk commandeered Shelling's vision. Shelling could see two others beyond him, a man and a woman, framed by the doorway. The giant policeman and the two newcomers approached the midget woman on the platform. The new woman looked familiar, but everyone he saw now reminded him of someone from his past, someone he had worked or slept with in California, and that was impossible, as though his brain, rebelling at his treatment, formed associations that, although they defied logic, served to give him an anchor in this otherwise disorienting experience. He looked at the other newcomer, expecting to be reminded of yet another figure from his past. But instead of a face, the other had a patch of glowing, blue-green mist.

Shelling twisted his body; the padded straps cut into his wrists. "Let me go," he said, surprised that his voice was working again.

20

Sammy peered at the face of the man in the hospital bed and sucked in her breath. "You're right. They are the same." She looked back at me. "Patrick has to be the right one. But how could the double have broken through?"

"What are you talking about?" When I stepped forward, it was my turn to gasp. The man on the bed had my face. Like Scooter said, hair different. The man's pupils were dilated, and he jerked his head around, looking at each of us in turn, over and over.

Scooter approached the tall policewoman. She was only an inch or so shorter than he. Scooter glanced at a notepad she held, then back to me. "What do you see?" he asked. I looked at him without responding. He waved an oven-mitt hand around. "This room, this person, what do you see?"

"A room. A man in a bed. He looks like me. What am I supposed to see?"

Sammy reached for my hand. "This can't be easy," she said. "I'm here. I'll help you."

"Help me what?" I pulled my hand away from hers.

"Only one of them can stay," the tall policewoman said. She spoke softly, but her husky voice carried.

Scooter nodded. "But which?" he asked her, not looking at me.

"This one." The tall policewoman pointed to the man in the bed. "He says he's an *actor*." She said "actor" as if it were an explanation, and Scooter bobbed his heavy head up and down in agreement.

Scooter turned to Sammy. "We brought him in earlier, but let him go. We felt the waves crossing, but weren't positive he was the signifier."

The tall policewoman came over to my side of the bed and stood between me and the other, extending an open palm toward each of us as though using them to probe our identities. She had her back to me, and when she spoke, she directed her words to Scooter. "This one, in the bed, he has a past, but his misplacement distorts his perceptions."

"And so he must be removed," Scooter said.

"Removed?" I said.

The tall policewoman lowered her hands and turned to face me. "Sent back to his world."

I looked up at her narrow face, trying to read it, looking for some sign of concern. I pointed to the man in the bed, who had stopped his erratic head turnings and locked his gaze on me. "This person. He's somehow a version of me?"

Sammy stared at the guy in the bed for a moment, then

turned, and came over to me. She took my hand again. "Your counterpart is an actor. That's his connection."

"You must perform the separation," the tall policewoman said.

"I don't know what you mean."

"Don't be stupid!" Her spittle brushed my cheeks. I started to yell back at her, but she grabbed my shoulders and pushed me against the door. The back of my head struck its hard surface, and I cried out. My vision turned yellow, black, and red. I flailed my arms but couldn't break her grip. A rush and confusion of voices filled the room—Sammy's, Scooter's rumble—then the tall policewoman released me.

Scooter spoke: "Please believe me. Officer Mercurio has never raised her voice or struck anyone in her life. The other's presence . . . distortion. The removal must be done now."

My head throbbed. The tall policewoman, Officer Mercurio, her face was still too close. Her eyes, a dull brown, stared into mine and I couldn't break contact, couldn't blink. She spoke, her voice low and soothing: "Rare and marvelous though it is, a moment of exquisite alignment of script, cast, and performance can cause a new reality to emerge, inhabited by the characters involved in that moment." She said some other things, but I couldn't grasp any of it. At some point she stopped and turned away.

Sammy held a hand near my face, but didn't touch me. "You understand now, don't you?" she asked. "Not everyone here knows these things."

Officer Mercurio unsnapped her holster and withdrew some kind of automatic pistol. I knew nothing about guns. I took a step back. "No—I can't shoot a person."

She pulled my hand over the grip and squeezed my fingers around it. "Has to be the head. Move closer." When I didn't move, she gripped both my shoulders and shook me. "Only you can perform the restoration. Now."

"What happens if I don't do it?"

Officer Mercurio screamed—"You're a fool! A base and ignorant man—you have no idea what forces are involved, the consequences we all live with, the powers shaping our lives."

Scooter quieted her, then spoke: "She's right. You don't know. That isn't your fault, none of it is your fault, but that doesn't change the circumstances. If *you* do it, no harm will come to your counterpart. The only other choice is for us to erase *both* of you."

I stepped nearer to my counterpart and raised the gun. It was too heavy for one hand, and its weight seemed to increase the longer I held it—a fell instrument of dire construction, I thought. The man in bed stared at me with my eyes, but I had the impression that what he saw differed from my vision of the room. Did he see a man, a man with his face, pointing a gun at him? Holding the gun with both hands, I sighted down the barrel.

As I fired, I saw the bullet from both sides, its slow, straight path away from me but also flying into my face, so close now that I could read the letters on its tip.

The recoil threw me against the door. The other separated from me, and as he slipped away, I had a sense that he was returning to something. My head throbbed even more and my vision blurred. Someone removed the gun from my hand. Sammy's arms encircled me, and I took solace in her touch.

21

SHELLING WATCHED

a black, circular body pass before a fiery disk. The movement of the black shape captured his attention. He couldn't look away, and as he watched, he lost all desire to try. Something—some warning he had once read about direct viewing of solar eclipses—flashed across his consciousness. The black shape kept moving until it obscured the fire, and in the ensuing darkness a cloud of chilled air covered him.

22

When my eyes were working again, I moved closer to the bed. I needed to see what I had done. The man's head had exploded, painting the wall in bone and blood. I gagged and tried to back away, but my knees gave out. Scooter was there for support on one side, Sammy on the other. They carried me into the hallway and lowered me to the floor. The reddish lights of the hallway spun, forming whirlpools of virulent illumination and color. I reached toward them, spinning too, floating up and out, joining the evening air, where a pale moon hovered and trees sighed like long-lost lovers.

23

Danielle Saul was bragging to Shelling about the photographs that she had commissioned from Crain, or some name like that, a famous celebrity photographer whom Shelling had never heard of. He smiled and nodded, the way people did in Hollywood. She had just finished filming a movie that was scheduled to be the summer's biggest hit and was expected to be her final step toward superstardom. Shelling felt detached from the conversation, from the party around him, which was in the cliffside home of Rod Spender, the television producer responsible for *Precinct 10*, *Gravity Man*, *Fresno Boulevard*, and many others. Shelling had worked on several of them.

He left Danielle Saul and drifted into Rod Spender's "trophy room," the walls of which were covered with photographs, awards, and assorted memorabilia (Duggal's helmet from *Gravity Man*, a Fresno Blvd. street sign, a baseball uniform from some long-forgotten sports drama). Shelling's attention wandered across the pictures, recognizing the original cast members of *Blake's River*, posing in the town where the opening credits had been filmed. He couldn't remember the real town's name. On the show, they called it Springdale.

The faces in the photograph, the buildings behind them—he had been there, and not solely for his guest appearance on the show. Another time, but when? Finding the photograph some-how threatening, he backed away from the wall. What had happened to his house? The simplicity of his vegetable garden had given him such pleasure. He felt a sudden loss . . . intangible yet rooted deep within him. His eyes teared, but for what was he weeping? The patio doors stood open, and he stepped through them to the terrace. Crows called from a line of trees overlooking the ravine. He stared past them, toward a distant house, memorizing its shape as though it held a key to his future.

And beyond these hills lay the city. Encircled by the arteries and veins that propel the life-giving metal corpuscles onward. The edge of the continent crossed by more roads than could ever be traveled. Roads, the reflections of roads, railroads, paved roads, buses, cars, houses along the way—the center of the earth is paved and waiting for the first drivers to arrive.

"There you are." Rod Spender slung an arm around Shelling. "Looks just awesome from here, doesn't it?" Shelling agreed. "I've got something for you," Spender said. "If you're tired of masked aliens. This'll be more like playing yourself."

"I'd like that," Shelling said. "I might even use my real name."

24

I woke on a couch in an unfamiliar room. Soft light came through the drawn curtains, a lacy, ivory-colored material through which I could see an overhanging branch and, beyond it, the street. A car passed, its lights sweeping along the wall. An odd mix of antiques and rough-made furniture decorated the room. The coffee table in front of the couch appeared to have been constructed from wine crates: the words Cincque Terre appeared repeatedly over a logo of intertwined vines.

I sat up and rubbed my eyes. They were irritated from my contact lenses, a gritty tiredness that made thinking difficult. I reached into a pants pocket for my eye drops, but couldn't find them. After this . . . day I'd had . . . all I wanted was my damn eye drops.

The groan came out before I could stop it. I held my breath, listening. I didn't want anyone to know I was awake until I knew where I was. Sounds emanated from another room—water running, then the clang of metal against metal. I got up and, taking care to keep my movements silent, walked toward the source of the noises. An arched doorway separated the living room from a dining room, and through the dining room door I could see into the kitchen, where Sammy stirred something in a pot on the stove.

I pulled back, not wanting her to see me. I couldn't talk to her, not after. . . . How could she be cooking dinner as though nothing had happened? I crossed to the front door and turned the glass knob carefully, opened it just enough to squeeze my body through, and escaped into the evening air.

The area was familiar; Sammy had one of the houses overlooking the town. It would take me at least ten minutes to reach the bed and breakfast. As I walked, I kept expecting her to come after me. At the corner I turned onto the street leading down to the town. The train station was between me and the bed and breakfast. I looked at my watch, which showed ten minutes past eight. There was an 8:50 train. By midnight, I could be back in the city, in my own bed.

I increased my pace, letting the slope pull me. I had no time to explain the situation to the proprietor of the bed and breakfast—what would I say?—or to retrieve my suitcase. I had only packed for a couple of days anyway. I could leave it. But I needed to pop out these damn contact lenses.

Life on the street appeared serene, but in the faces of those who passed, I sensed knowledge of the events that had transpired in that funhouse, or whatever it was. These people . . . this town . . . repelled me. I wondered what would happen if that tall policewoman, Officer Mercurio, saw me. Or Scooter, that comical name I had once applied, now preposterous. A sense of unreality clothed the air. I couldn't bury the feeling that I was escaping something—that if I had stayed with Sammy, eaten dinner, gone to bed with her after, I would have trapped myself in this town forever.

By the time I got to the train station I still had fifteen or so minutes. I bought a ticket from the machine and went back out.

I wanted to run, but I had to stay calm. Best not to be noticed. The bed and breakfast wasn't far. The foyer was empty. I heard voices off to the left, in the lounge. My room was at the top of the stairs. I fetched what I needed and returned to the street in less than a minute.

By the tracks, I stood watching the steps up to the platform, obsessing on the notion that I would soon view, emerging from the top of the stairs, first the heads of Scooter or Officer Mercurio, then the rest of their bodies as they climbed each step, propelling them toward me to prevent my escape.

Only one other passenger waited, a man in a dark suit standing near the tracks. My position, without the anonymity of a crowd, exposed me to too much scrutiny. I walked farther down the tracks, selecting a bench hidden by an overhanging shadow, and I waited.

When the train came, it brought the relief of knowing I would soon be home. I boarded, choosing a seat in the car opposite the steps. A jolt of dizziness shook me, and I slumped forward. That room, what I had done there—it all returned to me, and I watched, a flash of memory so real I felt that I was there again, though apart from myself. The shot, and that man—my Doppelgänger—the impact of the bullet with his head. His body twitched, rose a few inches, then settled. A glow seeped from him, pinkish like the breathable jelly, and the glow conformed to his features, aped the contours of his body. Where the head had been, the luminescence formed a replacement, solidified, then began to contract, shrinking and taking the body with it until nothing remained but a pink silhouette on the sheets. Then it too faded.

I stared out the train window, trying to see beyond the dark platform, to the town, to the maple trees and peaceful streets, Sammy's house. My fingers cramped, and my right arm spasmed. I relaxed my hand—I had been clutching my contact lens case. The raised L and R indented my palm. I unscrewed the caps and popped my lenses out, relieving my tired, gritty eyes, and with my glasses on, I resumed my vigil.

By now, Sammy would have noticed my absence. What was

her role in this? She had given me some crap about living with the knowledge. And Officer Mercurio, what had she said—inconceivable that a character would fall out of its reality. At least I had been here to help send him back to TV land, or whatever the hell it was. But was that his reality . . . ? I jumped up from my train seat. Officer Mercurio, she had said my counterpart was an actor. That was supposed to mean something. And she said he had a past. Implying that I didn't?

Sammy wanted me to stay. And despite everything that had happened today, I trusted her. The train door swished shut.

"No, wait," I said aloud to the empty car.

I scrambled over and tried to pry open the door. "I want to get off." I drummed my hand on the Plexiglas window, yelling for someone to open the door. There had to be a conductor near. Pain shot through my hand—looking down, I saw I had torn my fingernails on the door. With a jerk and shudder, we pulled away from the landing. As we rolled out of town, the tangible darkness, with warm sticky fingers, invaded the train.

THE SWASTIKA BOMB

by John Meaney

John Meaney was born in North London in 1957, and grew up in Slough. He studied physics at Birmingham University, before graduating with a combined physics and computer science degree from the Open University, and is doing postgraduate work at Oxford University. He currently works as an IT consultant and professional writer.

Meaney has published three novels to date, British Science Fiction Award-nominees To Hold Infinity, Paradox, *and* Context, *the latter pair being the first books in the "Nulapeiron Sequence." Upcoming is the third "Nulapeiron" novel,* Resonance, *and an unrelated science fiction novel. Meaney's first short fiction appeared in* Interzone *in 1992, and he has published a handful of increasingly impressive short stories, including British Science Fiction Award-nominees "Sharp Tang" and "Entangled Eyes Are Smiling."*

The story that follows, which originally appeared in Live Without a Net, *is a moving tale in a very strange time of war.*

A GREAT BLACK DELTA-SHAPE SLID overhead, gut-wrenching subharmonics pouring down in waves. It slewed into position, hovering above Nelson's Column. Panicked, pigeon flocks exploded outward, a burst of wing-flurries as the intruder's shadow fell upon Trafalgar Square.

Heinkel Drache 22-E. I recognized the species immediately. Already, beneath its wings, the dark, deadly payload was struggling to be free.

I stared upward—frozen, despite all my training: the wings' noise felt *solid*, beating down—and swallowed at the sight. Great Luftwaffe cross-insignias matched the black wriggling *Hakenkreuzen* slung in bomb racks.

Move.

Wrenching my attention down, preparing to run . . . and right at that moment I saw her, and fell in love.

Like a spring storm, when the sky darkens, yet suddenly a figure on the ground glows in contrast with white, internal radiance—that was her. Upswept honey-hued hair, her pale triangular face an ivory glow above the trim blue-gray RAF uniform, wide-eyed . . .

Her devastating gaze met mine.

My God. Such beauty—

Then the Swastika Bombs dropped.

She hesitated beside the dry wide fountain—the black lion statues were at my back—as I *felt* the movement overheard and then I was moving very fast.

By the time I reached her she had kicked off her shoes, and I grabbed her jacket in the small of the back—that perfect back—and lifted her almost bodily as we sprinted in time, swerved, ran hard, heading for the tall pale church of Saint-Martin-in-the-Fields as the big black hooked crosses fell.

They snapped, writhed, anxious for the kill.

Run.

Her thoughts were mine, in total communion, with no breath to speak: we were elemental primates, running for the mortal joy and fear. Sprinting for our lives.

Faster.

Then we were at the building's side, and for a moment I thought we might run on to Charing Cross but she tugged left, making the decision, and we skidded to a halt beside piled sandbags as a great *crump* sounded from behind. Ravening bombs, like great conjoined black worms, whipped in their death-throes, smashed granite like papier-mâché, building up a crescendo of maddened destruction, internal pressures building, rising until virus/venom-sacs and acid-bladders exploded—

Too late.

But we were already stumbling down the steps, and helping hands dragged us through the doorway and then we were inside the church's darkened crypt and safe. A great gout of dust followed us in as walls blew apart on the street above.

Safe . . .

And in that moment of exhilaration, we grasped each other hard, and kissed—her lips like silk, absorbing—each pulling the other inwards as though we would fuse together in blissful joy, forever.

For this was war, our darkest hour, and things were very different then.

I asked her, "Will you marry me?" and she said: "Yes," and then we told each other our names.

This was the way of things, when no one knew whether life or death awaited the next day, or the next.

"I'm Laura." Her voice was breathless and elegant.

Around us, others crouched or stood in the shadow-shrouded crypt, barely lit by flickering orange candle flames. Some were civilians in mufti; most were service personnel in uniform. They hunched atop the three-century-old headstones which paved the floor, sunk inside their own thoughts or muttering to those close by.

But to me, there was only Laura: the real and beautiful wonder of her.

"Listen."

Her hands tightened their grip, and then I heard it: a bright silver whistling through the air. There was a grim edge to her smile as she whispered:

"Now we'll see."

A distant *whump*, and you could picture the sudden burst of flame, feel the wave of heat. Then we all heard the strange eldritch cry of a wounded bomber-dragon.

"Spitfires!"

Cheers rose up around the darkened crypt.

"Bastard Jerries had it now."

Later, we would get the full description: of those brave young men who took their green-and-silver raptors, perched in the tiny spinal cockpits, melded into their mounts' ganglionic pathways, hurtling down from the clouds with wings furled, then snapping those wings outwards—under heart-wrenching stresses—as they swooped past the formation of great black delta-winged dragons, glimpsing the crews' shocked faces as they carried destruction back to the death-bringers.

It was not one-sided, that fierce battle, for the Luftwaffe had their own escort of emerald-green Messerschmidt Falke-104s, the dreaded Falcons glinting in the sun, and soon there were duels in the air above beleaguered London as the faster Germans took on maneuverable Spitfires: brave young men—on both sides—with iron will and lightning reflexes, fighting for their countries, risking everything.

The bomber-dragon that had hit Trafalgar Square took severe injuries in those first few seconds: from flamebursts and fling-stings as the Spitfires swooped past. Wounded, the great black dragon swung up into the air, delta wings curling, but the injuries were mortal and the crew could do no more as vital organs burst inside, and then they were falling in a long lazy arc towards the Thames.

It smashed into waves, the impact hurling gouts of spume high into the air, wrecking any hopes of capturing the aircrew alive: pulping their bodies as the dragon's back broke in two.

Later that evening, crowds of adults, and a small number of children who had missed evacuation, would watch from the Embankment as Navy trawlobsters dragged the huge corpse ashore, to the waiting RAF dissectors.

But as the air-battle, still raging overhead, moved further away, there was a ripple of relieved laughter in the crypt, the lighting of cigarettes which had been ignored until now. The air seemed easier to breathe.

"Here you are." Laura handed me my spectacles. "If you want them."

The glasses had survived the run, only to fall upon a worn seventeenth century gravestone beneath our feet. One lens was splintered.

"Thank you." I tucked them inside my suit jacket—double-breasted, brown, now stained with dust—and looked around for my hat. "I might need them later."

"For disguise? This close to Whitehall?" Those elegant lips curled into a smile. "Or have plain-glass lenses got some use I don't know about?"

"You're very observant."

"Not only that . . . I suspect we're headed for the same place, my love."

Then the all-clear sirens wailed, and it was time to go.

As we passed through the square, the skies were clear save for a distant observation-blimp, blue gills fluttering as it scoured enemy spyseeds and germspores from the air.

Hand in hand, Laura and I skirted still-moving sections of black rubbery Swastika Bomb carcasses, while bomb-disposal scarabs crawled around the debris, directed by their asbestos-suited masters. Clean-up dromedatanker crews were already spraying antiviral mist across the foul yellow fluids spattered everywhere.

We walked carefully, avoiding acid puddles and toxic pools, and turned into Whitehall. The long boulevard was remarkably untouched by the action. Tall white-gray buildings stood blocky and proud; their cross-taped Regency windows, with their heavy blackout curtains and sandbag reinforcements, concealed the smoke-filled rooms of the War Ministry, the Admiralty spill-over, and Military Intelligence.

They formed the intellectual center of the British war effort, in those darkest die-before-surrender days when it seemed certain the Blitzkrieg would destroy us all.

At a short flight of pale steps before tall iron-studded doors—we *were* headed for the same place—Laura kissed me lightly on the cheek. Then we passed inside, Laura returning the sentries' salutes, while I nodded politely, reinforcing my pseudo-civilian status.

In the foyer, as my heart shivered, we parted company for the first time.

Blue pipe-smoke wreathed the Old Man's office: a dark, mahogany-paneled chamber, heavy with stern predecessors' portraits. From the anteroom, I peered in, and waited while a group of women, half in uniform—WAFs and FANYs—exited in a clatter of high heels, a business-like bustle of long skirts, clutching their clipboards.

All intelligence personnel had antiallergen infusions and oncovaccination. Still, there were reddened eyes; everyone looked relieved to be out of the smoke.

"Come in, old chap." The admiral's voice boomed from behind his huge desk. "Take a pew."

"Sir."

I nodded automatically to his secretary, the formidable Miss Poundstone—chestnut brown eyes, so different from Laura—and passed inside, closing the heavy doors behind me. He indicated a chair with his pipe-stem.

Laura . . .

"Now then, Fleming—"

The Old Man's words snapped me back into the moment. "It sounded urgent, sir."

In the hard-backed chair, I waited for the fearful words.

"Time"—his big blunt fingers drummed on the leather-bound blotter—"that you went back into the field, don't you think?"

No. Too soon.

Part of me had had enough: of the twilight-sleep treatment in a Birmingham hospice on my return, drugged to the gills again, with morphine and God-knows-what; then of the endless retraining in the windy Rutland countryside, restringing my nerves in the echoing former public school where operatives underwent the harsh discipline designed to keep them alive. I had been teaching, too: as an old hand who had survived—flea-bitten and ragged-eared, but functioning—giving the cynical benefits of my hard experience to wide-eyed neophytes who revered me too much.

For their eyes were bright with youth's secret knowledge of their own immortality, secure in their iron-clad conviction that the torture victim's screams as Gestapo interrogators bent to work, the broken corpse splayed face-down in a dark puddle in some cobbled alleyway, were images from someone else's future, not from theirs.

"You're sending me into occupied territory?"

Part of me yearned to return: that desperate obsession with the brink. Yet all of me wanted Laura: my world was different now.

"Where else?" With a frown: "We can only mount this operation with a particular type of agent at the forefront. That means you, Fleming."

"Thank you, sir." I took it as a compliment.

"You know about nanoviral vectors. Well"—from under heavy white eyebrows, he glowered—"our cousins across the water are putting their best boffins—and I include the best who escaped Europe, not just Yanks—onto a single weapons program. The Brooklyn Project promises to end the war at a stroke."

I shifted. A feeling of dread slid across my skin.

"You don't want to hear this." For all his bluff manner, the Old Man could be sensitive to the point almost of telepathy. "Strategic context is hardly *de rigeur* in briefings."

Worrying about long-term implications could make your trigger-finger tremble at the wrong moment. Too much background was dangerous.

"The thing is"—with a granite smile—"you'll pick up the resonances soon enough, so I'm telling you right now."

His sympathy worried me.

And there's Laura to think of now.

But she was no more a civilian than I was. The war was bigger than me, or Laura, or any of us.

"What's wrong with this project?" I asked the Old Man then.

"Nothing, *per se*. But the Nazis have their own program running. If they beat us to it, the world will be under Adolf's jackboot before you know it. And we're not going to let that happen."

"No, sir."

Those two defiant words were my commitment: to the mission, to the future, to the decisions that changed our lives forever.

I had a pass which would let me through any Allied checkpoint, even if the name read H. Himmler and I was belting out the "Horst Wessel" song at full volume. That was the one I used now, accepting the sergeant-major's salute.

I waited while the megarhino-hide blast-doors slid open, then descended hard chitin steps into the Tac Bunker.

The observation balcony already held a visitor. I recognized

Admiral Quinn; it was not mutual. Instead, he nodded cautiously: a typical senior officer's greeting to a Whitehall man dressed in civvies.

He slid a cigarette half out of his packet of Senior Service, and proffered it.

"No thank you, sir."

"Fascinating." He closed the packet without taking one himself, slid it inside his dark braid-decorated jacket. "Don't you think?"

"Always."

Beneath us, the cavern stretched for two shadow-shrouded miles, upheld by massive columns, spanned everywhere by darkly glistening fibers which formed the Black Web. At the lowest levels, Strategic Command personnel were tiny uniformed figures scurrying amid overwhelming complexity, clutching their clipboards like talismans. Some walked with blue/scarlet messenger-transparrots perched upon their shoulders, ready to fly upon command.

But it was the Web itself that drew one's gaze.

Black hawsers as thick as Nelson's Column, a plethora of others merely as wide as my forearm, down to millions of near-invisible threads: all dark as night, catenary curves hanging in a three-dimensional maze, beyond any single person's comprehension.

And along those threads crawled, in every conceivable direction, the one army that might halt Hitler's destruction of Europe: dark microspiders, and their bigger, fist-sized counterparts whose swollen thoraxes would burst open to give birth to myriad offspring. Each tiny arachnid speck would already be imprinted with interaction-behavior; combined in their millions, the combination formed the Black Web's ghostly, disembodied *gestalt*: a para-mind that knew nothing of fatigue or fear or morality, but whose analytical powers might someday grant us victory.

"Excuse me, Admiral."

My footsteps sounded strangely hollow as I passed along the chitinous catwalk, descending to the North Atlantic display. A wide map-table tracked the vital Liberty Leviathan convoys, the U.S. lifeline that—bless their hearts!—was all that kept the British Isles from starvation.

But we had only patchy success in tracking the enemy's U-shark hunter-killer squadrons that preyed on merchant vessels from beneath the gray choppy waves, too often taking out the battleorca escorts that formed the backbone of His Majesty's Royal Navy.

And I thought of the Yanks' great behemoth-class carriers, burning and squealing in their death throes, trapped helplessly in the docks of Pearl Harbor beneath the Japanese hydra attack, the ravening dragonfire of Yamamoto's carrier-launched squadrons. We weren't the only ones to suffer in this war.

Military considerations fled my mind as I saw that elegant figure bending across the table, biting her lip as she used a long pointer to push a tiny model convoy onto revised coordinates.

Laura . . .

Her name was a prayer, a sigh.

When she looked up, a smile broke across her face, and she waved.

The tiny tea-room was spick and span—no ring-shaped stains, no chipped cups—with whitewashed bricks. Close heat emanated from large steam pipes running beneath the ceiling, occasionally knocking as if someone was trying to get out. The kettle's long flex ran across hooks above a poster reading: *The Enemy has Spiders everywhere.* Overstuffed armchairs and a tattered settee lent it the look of Senior Common Room, from the days of schoolboy innocence.

Before '38 . . .

Laura touched my arm. "Are you all right?"

"Just a touch of malaria." The usual excuse—but this was Laura. "Actually . . . A touch of memory. That's a whole lot worse."

November: a chill, fresh breeze blowing along Friedrichstrasse—

Even now, it haunted me.

—with morning sun glinting on the crystal shards.

"The Old Man's sending you back out."

I looked at her. "Just what did you say your assignment is, darling?"

"My current job involves technical background for someone who's on a trip to the American Southwest."

"Does it, indeed?"

I was destined to meet you, my love.

"Oh, yes." She handed me a cup, balanced on its ugly flower-decorated saucer. "Have you heard of Albert Einstein?"

"Well, yes. He's famous for—"

"The Project is his idea."

"I'm sorry?"

"He persuaded Roosevelt. Signed an open letter, with several of his colleagues from Princeton and elsewhere. The Brooklyn Project grew directly from that letter."

"I didn't know."

"Einstein's a true genius. Special multiplicity theory is what everyone knows him for—"

"DNA structure," I said. "Replicator-based evolution. Gene migration."

Laura, sitting with her knees primly together and her tea balanced atop, nodded as though everyone knew that. Above us, the steam pipes clanged.

"The point is—" she glanced up, waited for the noise to subside "—the special theory was inevitable. Yet *general* multiplicity theory is a stroke of genius, ahead of its time."

"If he hadn't been born . . . Or if he hadn't been Jewish, he might've been a Nazi."

"Don't say things like that." Laura shivered.

The tea in my mug had grown cold, and I set it down on the parquet floor. "Sorry."

She laid her hand on mine. "It was luck that you and I met now. We weren't supposed to . . ."

My world would have remained bleak and Laura-less, forever empty.

"Perhaps SOE didn't plan it, but Providence did."

Outside, footsteps sounded. We waited, but they walked on past the doorway.

Laura touched my cheek.

I leaned forward, and we kissed.

One week later, I was standing at the edge of a pink-orange desert, beneath a cloudless azure sky, a white-hot blazing sun.

The air's furnace-heat pressed upon me, squeezed me in its invisible fist.

A dark road arrowed across sands, disappeared over a low ridge. Behind me, straight railway lines—rail*road*: I should remember where I was—gleamed silver through the rippling air. The diminishing train slid through heat-haze, its chugging oddly flat in this dryness. I watched it disappear.

And then I was alone in a sere, endless landscape where human beings were never meant to live.

At my feet stood a battered suitcase that had been with me in the Far East and occupied Europe, though it bore no labels to mark its travels. My woolen suit, perfect for an English spring, was heavy upon me; folded atop my suitcase, the big overcoat looked ridiculous.

As was this rendezvous: away from the town, and the eyes of hypothetical fifth columnists. I could hardly be more conspicuous . . . should there be anyone here to observe me, before heat and dehydration took me.

I loosened my tie.

Off to one side, purple mountains shaded the horizon. Would there be snow upon their peaks? The thought of frozen water melting in cupped hands was almost overwhelming. Much closer, hundreds of saguaro cacti stood with upraised arms, as though caught in a hold-up: like green capital *psi*s.

Braithwaite's ruler snapped me across the knuckles as I stumbled conjugating my Greek verbs—

Those damned schooldays. They haunt you forever.

Stop whingeing.

In Africa, thousands of men were facing worse conditions than these. At least here, there was no threat of Rommel's rextanks suddenly appearing over the horizon, bringing their heavy armament to—

There.

A small dust cloud puffed upon the distant blacktop.

Deliberately unarmed, I waited in the heat. If this was an enemy of some kind, they would not know my face; at close quarters, the absence of a weapon might convince them I was harmless. And I always had my hands.

Half-fist to the gendarme's larynx. He falls, croaking, clutching his throat, eyes popping as he chokes . . .

A bad memory. But it had been a necessary killing, and I got away before the Waffen SS officers arrived: the ones I was sure—*almost* sure, that's what tortured me—the gendarme had notified. In the darkened alleyway, with the rain falling down in sheets—

Concentrate.

Here. Now.

Olive-colored, the jeepo was much closer now, revealing the driver: white shirt, broad scarlet tie blowing in the slipstream. I swallowed, wishing I could be that cool.

And then it was skidding to a halt, the jeepoceros bracing its squat, powerful legs, throwing up a cloud of dusty orange sand. Sunlight glinted—*watch out*—but it was not a weapon: the driver bore a polished steel hook in lieu of a left hand.

"Climb in, pal."

I controlled my breathing, ready for action. "It gets cold," I said casually, "in December."

"Yeah, right. Willya get in?"

I waited.

"Alright . . . Drops to seven below." Hawk-like features frowned. "Or is that nine? Like I should know Latin, too."

Parole-and-countersign were a random numerical reference, indirect if possible—I granted that *December* might be ambiguous—and a reply code that subtracted three. Where I came from, we took such things seriously.

Throwing my case and coat into the back, I slipped into the passenger seat (on the right) and held out my hand. "How do you do."

"Hi. The name's Felix. Felix Leichtner, though I'm thinking of changing the name. My old man will be pissed."

"I would think so. I'm—"

"I know who you are. Hang on."

He threw the switch, and the jeepo rumbled into life; then he swung it through an impossible turn—I glimpsed a small tan form watching us: ground-squirrel—and floored the accelerator.

Dashboard membranes flared red as we tore off along the lonely road, slipstream blowing, dust cloud billowing in our wake, while in every direction the orange sands stretched hot and majestic: a wilderness which could kill as surely as a hail of Wehrmacht bullets.

Vastness.

Overhead, a lone eagle wheeled in the deep azure sky. If the jeepo failed, would vultures make their own ghastly appearance? On every side, sandstone glowed; farther back, rocky outcrops bared strata: mint-green and sugary white, stippled with black.

Would Laura care to live here after the war, with me? Picture it: an adobe house near a small desert town, where I could paint New Mexico landscapes for a living, and share this beauty with a woman beyond compare.

In the midst of vastness, an outpost.

We shot under the candy-striped barrier before it fully lifted— Felix taking time to give a shoddy half-salute to the sentries, his hook-hand steering—and onto Main Street: the largest straight dusty track between wooden rows of whitewashed houses. Their plain exteriors held the charm of military barracks everywhere.

But soldiers in camp did not have individual homes, with slender wives in light cotton dresses—

"Eyes on the road, Limey."

"You're driving."

"But that's Mrs. Teller, and you don't want to start off on the wrong foot, my friend."

I shook my head. "I'm spoken for."

"Not what I heard." Felix glanced in my direction, then nodded as he span the jeepo to a screeching halt. "Good for you, though. And this"—with a blinding glint from his gesturing hook—"is home, sweet home."

Two badly upholstered armchairs sat in the too-hot lounge. We dragged them to face each other—I had unpacked bug-spray and used it: no eavesdrop-mites would survive the aerosol—so that Felix could brief me.

"First off, the Oppenheimers are throwing one of their parties tonight. You'll like Oppy. The Martians will be there—"

"I'm sorry?" This briefing had suddenly veered onto an unexpected track.

"Pet name. A bunch of Hungarian scientists: Wigner, Szilard, Teller, von Kármán. They're hoping to get Johnny von Neumann on board, from Princeton."

"I don't know him."

"Fun guy, sort of. Wife called Klara, a bit shrewish. He's something like your Turing, in his research interests. I think they met briefly."

I shrugged, but—inside—my nerves strung themselves tighter. *Plying me for info?*

"Come on, pal." Felix sighed. "Turing's geneticists at Bletchley Park are your major contribution to the war effort, and you've got the right level of clearance to know it. Without him, the Nazi commspiders' genomes and ganglionics would still be a mystery."

I relaxed, a little.

"It was *your* clearance I was worried about, old fruit."

Felix gave me a strange look.

"That's not an insult, is it?"

"God, no. Look, can we go somewhere to get a coffee?"

"Sure." And, as we stood: "I thought you Limeys only drank tea, old chap. Sorry . . . old *fruit.*"

I shook my head, but in fact I wished that Felix was not going to leave me here, among the boffins and their wives. I would rather spend my days swapping Yank-and-Limey humor than bashing my head against cutting-edge military research.

Laura . . . It's your company I need.

But if we survived this ongoing nightmare, formed the future we both wanted, it would be worth the wait.

Secrets within secrets.

Even in the long mess hall, we talked only of innocuous matters, not trusting the background chattering and clattering to hide our words. Felix noticed my interest when a platoon ran past outside, to cadence.

They were lean and fit to a man, and I needed to keep my own physical levels high. A tan would be suspect, once they dropped me into Europe; but melanin-reversers could wind back exposure-effects from the desert sun.

After we returned to my temporary home, Felix briefed me on base security.

"The core," he said, sitting down, "is a team of what are supposed to be Airborne Rangers."

"But . . . ?"

"They're some of Donovan's finest, and they keep closer track of both people and research than the intellectuals expect."

"I may not be intelligent"—I was quoting the Royal Navy gunners—"but I can lift heavy weights."

"Like that, yes. Easily underestimated."

So operatives from OSS were here. Very interesting.

"Can I train with them? I need to keep fit."

Dawn runs around Hyde Park, evening Indian club practice: they kept me going in London. But I needed more, and the Rutland training school was half a world away.

"If they can find you a uniform . . . They get up real early, you know?"

"Good. I'll be busy working my brain, the rest of the time."

"You don't know the half of it. Dick Feynman's a magician, literally and intellectually. He'll mentor you for an hour or two a day, but you'll be studying like crazy on your own."

"Good . . . What's he like?"

"Who, Dick? Quite the prankster. Cracked open the base commander's safe, left a birthday card, with a French letter tucked inside."

I rubbed my forehead with the heel of my palm. Travel-lag, after the long crossing in the deHavilland pteradrone, and the long train journey.

"This is supposed to be serious."

"Feynman's wife is in a sanatorium, near the town. Dying, apparently. The comedian act is partly a front."

I blinked and turned away. *Laura . . . I miss you.*

"Resistance-engineered bacterium. He hates the Nazis more than anyone I've met."

"All right." *But was he there for Kristallnacht?*

I said nothing, but my guard was down and Felix sensed the vibrations.

"Though you might give Dick"—his hawk-smile was humorless—"a run for his money."

"Chattanooga choo-choo" was blaring from the radiogram as we insinuated ourselves into the party. From their files—I'd been granted access; Felix stood over me in the base commander's office as I read—I recognized faces: Oppenheimer, Fuchs, Teller.

Off to one side, lean and quick-witted, Feynman was dazzling a group of his colleagues' wives with a conjuring trick. His sparkling eyes, more than sleight of hand, captivated them.

"Not a security risk, then?" I murmured.

"Probably not." Felix was looking at the buffet.

I knew what he meant. There was no reason for a fifth columnist to make himself conspicuous in quite that way: no reason to perpetrate double-bluff. But schizotypal behavior was common among academics . . .

Natural paranoia: discount.

A pretty woman offered us drinks. Her brilliant smile, directed at Felix's lean face, became fixed as he tapped the glass with his steel hook.

"Nice crystalware.".

"Um, thanks . . . " And then she was gone.

I looked at Felix. "That was a little coldhearted."

"Gets things out in the open." He gave the tiniest of shrugs. "It doesn't worry everyone."

"What do you tell them?"

"Just a wound I picked up in—Oh. Massive allergies, is all."

I nodded. OSS personnel were so thoroughly infused with antivirals that their bodies threw off clone-factor treatment.

"Why, *Fred*—"

There was another smiling woman in our path, looking impossible to faze. She used Felix's cover name with irony, as though aware it was not his real identity.

"How're you doing?" said Felix.

"Why don't you introduce me to your friend?"

Courtliness, not flirting.

"The name's Brand." I used my own cover ID. "James Br—"

"And he's a Limey," interjected Felix. "But he can't help it."

"Oh, that's wonderful."

"Jamie, this is Mrs. Oppenheimer."

She held out her hand to shake.

For a while we exchanged pleasantries, as she pointed out people of interest—"That's my husband, known as Oppy to these young people"—and made rueful observations about the poor facilities in their makeshift town.

"But we're coping," she said. "And it's important work, we know."

Then someone caught her attention, and she bade us a polite farewell and moved on. Felix and I remained standing, while a few of the more energetic men danced with their wives to Glen Miller. At home, they'd have been singing by now, about hanging out their washing on the Siegfried Line.

It was too hot to party. I was relieved when Felix took my elbow and steered me towards the screen door, passing close to Feynman and his admirers.

"—be kidding, Dick," one of the pretty women was saying. "That's disgusting."

"Nothing personal, ladies." Feynman grinned. "*Everybody's* body weight is ten percent bacteria. Not just yours. They're wriggling about, swapping genetic material like crazy—"

Shocked intakes of breath. Giggles.

"You look at the world, Dick"—the woman who spoke was pale-complexioned; she briefly touched Feynman's knee—"like nobody else."

(Was I the only one who saw the shadow pass behind his eyes, the thought of his dying wife?)

"But there's beauty in that dance of life, don't you see? You can understand the way things are built, and *still* enjoy the way they look esthetically."

"Uh, uh. You're just different from the rest of us."

"I'll say." One of the other women smiled.

Everybody laughed.

"Except that"—Feynman was excited now—"we can't be all that different from each other, or you couldn't build a human being by taking chemical fragments of two people—*unrelated* people, unless there's anyone here from Kentucky?—and fusing them together. That's exactly how babies are made."

"But Dick, I thought—"

And then we were past them, through the door, into the desert night.

Overhead, black velvet and a blazing multitude of silver stars such as one could never see in England. From behind us, a burst of laughter.

"Makes you realize," murmured Felix, "how insignificant we are. Maybe humanity deserves to go under."

I glanced back into the warm light, the partying scientists.

"And is our salvation really in there?"

"Getting drunk and flirting? Why not?"

We stepped into the middle of the pale moonlit dusty track which passed for a road.

"Y'know what?" Felix added. "A couple of them have calculated that, if the nucleic bomb goes off, the reaction could cascade through the biosphere. Wipe out all life in hours. And I mean *all* life."

I stopped. "You're jok—No. Is Feynman one of them? One of the doubters?"

"Oh, no. He thinks it's bound to work."

Looking up, I wondered how those distant, eternal suns burning in endless darkness might regard ephemeral mortals, who so easily contemplated their own destruction. And did they know how to laugh, those stars, or cry with pity?

Or would they even care?

Equations were scrawled across the dusty blackboard, alongside simplifying diagrams invented by Feynman purely to teach me things only the world's leading researchers comprehended. Einsteinian emergence-matrices measured base-base and gene-gene interdependence; Hamiltonians tracked evolutionary expansion through morphological phase-space . . .

And a pounding migraine, beginning over my right eye, spread inexorably inwards.

"—and then you depolarize the biflange confabulator, and the rekeezy blart destimblefies."

I wrote down half of that on my spiral-bound notebook, then stopped.

"Er, what—?"

"I had a feeling"—Feynman was grinning—"I might have lost you there."

I laid down my fountain-pen, rubbed my forehead. "There's a faint possibility," I told him, "that you might be correct."

"You're not alone. Einstein hates quantum evolution. With a vengeance."

"At least he understands it."

"I wouldn't go that far." Feynman perched himself on the nearest desk—the room was set up for twenty people, but he had requisitioned it for us two—then threw his chalk up in the air, caught it. "Nobody *understands* the theory. We just know how to use it."

I stared at him.

Feynman's intellect was magical. Whatever he explained became obvious, transformed me into a genius, torrents of energy coursing through my mind. Only later, alone in my room working through cell-function pathways, would I grind up against my own limitations.

"If you told me *why* you need to know this stuff"—gently—"we could focus on what's necessary."

And blow mission security?

But Feynman was correct. I could not manage this without rigorous and *specific* coaching.

I let out a slow breath.

"What I need"—I glanced out the window at sapphire sky—"is to recognize schematics for a nucleic bomb at a glance. Well enough to tell a fake from the real thing, or something that's *almost* a hundred percent correct."

The impish humor stopped dancing in his eyes. "You need to do this quickly?"

"Precisely."

"Under pressure, you mean."

"An awful lot, " I told him.

He mouthed the word *awful*.

"Well, then." Feynman jumped up from the desk, strode into a patch of sunlight, and began vigorously to wipe every equation from the board. "Let's get to work."

"You understand—"

"I've worked out *where* you'll be doing this, my friend." Feynman raised an eyebrow. "You're in the SOE, a real live spook, and you'll be examining enemy plans *in situ*. Is that how you say it in the King's English?"

"Close enough."

Feynman grinned, but I recognized the shadow which lurked behind his eyes.

"Well, then . . . " In an Eton-by-way-of-the-Bronx accent: "The best of British luck, old chap."

The Quonset hut's interior was dark and sweltering. Exertion threw off heat and humidity as we worked the drills. Palm-heels, elbow-strikes—blinking away salt-stinging sweat—side-kicks to knees.

"Harder!" barked Gunny Rogers.

Panting, my opponent tried for my wrist, but our bodies were slick with sweat—olive-green undershirts sopping wet, dark—and his hand slipped so I thrust up under his chin, swept his legs away.

"Come on, ladies. Let's *work*."

We pushed harder and harder, until we were barely standing, unable to see straight, and Gunny finally called a halt.

"Just take five," he said, as we breathed hard through open mouths.

In the corner, one of the Rangers was being discreetly sick.

Then I saw Gunny Rogers frown, looking over my shoulder. I turned around.

A big shaven-headed Ranger was throwing a punch—"Catch it!"—expecting his smaller partner to lock the wrist. Except that he came in too fast and hard, the short man failing to grab—

"*Damn it*," muttered Gunny.

—and the big man swung a long, deceptive uppercut, buried his fist. His victim dropped in a fetal position, gasping.

Gunny stepped forwards, but I was closer.

"Actually, old chap," I drawled, "I believe you're misinterpreting." I was still moving as I spoke.

"What do you—?"

Then I whipped both my hands against his big ham-fist and snapped him to the ground. His knees struck hard, pain brightening in his small eyes.

"Captain Fairbairn," I told him, "considers it an *attack*."

And I knew how devastating the wrist-throw could be.

I turned away, trying not to look at Gunny Rogers, who was struggling to hide his broad grin. The man who had been my partner raised his eyebrows, and whistled in appreciation.

"You've actually trained with—?"

He stopped, even as I felt the rush of air—*behind*—and I dropped, spinning—

But a big shadow moved past me, Gunny Rogers, and his huge arm shot out and the big man was down. Then Gunny was in the air, boots coming down together in a deadly bronco kick—

"No, Gunny!"

—but he separated his feet at the last moment, bootheels thudding into the mat either side of the downed man's head, raising puffs of dust instead of smashed bones, smeared blood.

"That"—Gunny grinned—"is what you might call the Applegate variation."

When the short, slim Captain Fairbairn demonstrated his combat skills before seated representatives of the U.S. Forces, he tossed a huge bear of a man called Rex Applegate straight into the laps of some very senior officers.

Applegate, at least, had been impressed. He now led the U.S. program teaching deadly combat skills—Japanese and Chinese warrior-techniques, by way of the Shanghai police—to elite forces and covert units.

And, so I had heard, to stay-at-home G-men. The FBI were worried about civilians—demobbed military men, once the war was over—possessing finely honed fighting techniques they did not know themselves; hence their own training. In Britain, we had too much on our rationed plates to worry about peacetime security.

"Not bad, Mr Brand." Gunny Rogers clapped me on the

shoulder afterwards, as we filed out of the Quonset glowing with exertion, strained and exhausted.

"Not bad yourself, Gunny."

Laughter and coarse jokes—some at the expense of the big man who now grinned ruefully: he had learned a lesson—rose up from the others as they headed to the showers. I slipped away, heading towards my small home.

Overhead, the empty early-morning sky gleamed, azure and serene.

Are we primitive animals, spilling each others' blood?

But I wondered, passing along the deserted dusty street, quiet before the working day, whether there were any rational conclusions to be drawn in a world where cosseted intellectuals, civilization's best, with their blackboards and chalk and scribble-filled notepads, could devise modes of devastation far deadlier than teeth ripping artery, blade slicing intestine in the thunder and stink and dirt of battle, and work their own cataclysm of torn DNA and ecodestruction, remotely tearing life asunder while holding themselves aloof from the stink and rawness and fear, at distant remove from the messy, bloody, excremental business of death.

Felix returned two days before my departure, purely to bid me farewell. We stood at the edge of the makeshift town which promised to change so much, and stared out at the dawn-smeared sky, the vast wide New Mexico desert, not needing to speak.

Finally, it was time for Felix to leave. A low-slung Ford, its black-green carapace filmed with desert dust, was waiting for him, a crop-haired driver at the wheel.

"Travelling in luxury," I said.

"Back to Washington, to fly a desk." Felix raised his left arm, watched liquid sunlight slide along the polished hook. "Just what I always wanted, I don't think."

"You'll do all right."

"Sure. I'll be training the neos." With a sudden grin: "They'll be impressed with this against their throats."

"They'll get the point."

"They surely will."

"Well—"

We shook hands.

"You watch your ass over there, Limey."

"Look after yourself, Yank."

He climbed into the back of his vehicle, and nodded as it slipped past me. I watched as it followed the arrow-straight road, black through Martian red, until the Ford grew tiny with distance, was lost from sight.

My final night. Restless, I walked the silvery, moonlit length of Main Street, wheeled left, passed the commander's cabin, Oppenheimer's—

Light.

Reflexively, I crouched. Torchlight flicked across the darkened window from inside, was gone.

A burglar? In Oppy's office?

Raising a hue and cry went against my nature and my training. An alert intruder might slip away. So I moved softly, heel-to-toe, creeping close to the wall until I reached the door.

The knob turned without a sound. Slowly, I passed inside, and closed the door against the night.

Farther inside, the hallway was dark. I crept forwards, reached a corner, peered around.

Not Oppy's room.

The burglar had passed on. Light flickered from a cross-corridor. Shadows and darkness were eerily confusing, but surely that was just an ordinary seminar room—

"Oh, very nice." The intruder's voice floated towards me: soft but unmistakable.

What the hell? Feynman?

I shrugged my shoulders once, flexed and released my hands, then crept forwards, ready to strike.

But when I stopped at the doorway and peered inside, Dick Feynman was cross-legged upon a desktop, diabolically impish as he played his torch's beam across a blackboard which held nothing that was secret from him.

In fact, I realized suddenly, he was due to attend the lecture which Teller was giving here tomorrow, and it was Teller's own equations that were scribbled across the board in preparation.

I cleared my throat.

"Doing some technical prep of your own, Mr. Feynman?"

He jumped, then slowly smiled, and pointed to an equation.

"I can solve this tonight," he said, "in about three hours. I know it took Ed and his pals the best part of a year. But if I do it in ten seconds, during the lecture tomorrow—"

I laughed silently, and shook my head.

"You don't need to impress anyone."

"I know. It's part of the fun."

After a moment, he slipped down from the desktop, tapped me on the upper arm. "Come on."

Then he led the way into the darkened corridor, as though there was nothing out of the ordinary in being caught sneaking around at night in a classified military installation. Perhaps, for Dick Feynman, it was the merest sidenote in an eventful life.

I had been right about an intruder in Oppenheimer's office. Feynman bent down at the lock, fiddled with it for a moment, then let the door swing open.

"That was locked, wasn't it, Dick?"

"Not well enough."

"Thank God you're on our side."

I had been in Oppy's office before, but not in the side-room which Feynman opened. Shelves bore glass display cases—strange shadows shifting in the light of Feynman's torch—and a small lab bench stood at the far end.

"Samples," Feynman pointed. "Don't open anything. We don't have isolation suits."

"Whatever you—"

I stopped, swallowing, and the darkness seemed to sway about me. My body shuddered, as though some outside agency controlled my nerves. I could do nothing but wait out the shaking-fit. Soon enough, it subsided.

Hand of glass.

That was what it looked like: glassine, perfectly sculpted, down to translucent bones and sinews and veins within. In other cases, different anatomical parts were likewise near-transparent, some shaded purple as though carved from quartz.

"Preservative stains," said Feynman. "I sometimes take a peek, just to remind myself how horrible our work is. And why we're doing it."

I shook my head, as though to deny the memories made tangible before me. Sweat coated my skin like a new, protective layer; I thought I might throw up. Neither the morphine treatment nor the long sessions with SOE padres had laid those ghosts to rest.

Nor could they ever.

"What's wrong, my friend? You know the kind of work we do."

I was an intelligence agent, trained to remain calm before interrogation, to pass unnoticed through foreign lands beneath the eyes of the enemy. But this . . .

Shards, glinting upon the cobblestones—

This, I would never forget.

"I was there," I whispered, ignoring the tears which tracked down my cheeks. "In Germany, on *Kristallnacht.*"

"Dear God."

I looked Feynman in the eyes.

"God," I told him, "was nowhere to be seen that night."

Memories, made indelible.

It was chilly, that ninth day of November in 1938. I was in Ravensbrück, but the exact location was irrelevant: for on that night, every city, town and village in Germany became aware of the diabolic movement which controlled the country; of the tiny, scarcely significant number of individuals who were clear-sighted and decent and courageous enough to speak out against it.

The squads wore heavy coats over their brown shirts, but only at first. As the night progressed, they grew warm with their work: dragging Jews from their homes, setting light to their businesses, bringing violence to the streets of Mozart's civilization, to Schopenhauer's culture, and whatever flared up in bedrooms would remain forever spoken only by women's remembered shrieks, by the sobbing of violated children.

Sturmabteilung thugs were everywhere, beating their victims in plain sight of any citizen who cared to draw back their heavy curtains or step outside, while the SA's infection squads screeched up in rented cars and trucks. Those who sprayed the victims were covered in protective gauntlets and hoods, as though unconvinced of their own purity, for the viral complexes were guaranteed harmless to the true Aryan genome.

Helpless, I watched.

Spray-victims scarcely screamed, for their vocal cords were one of the first parts to crystallize, as their panicked lungs sucked virus-laden mist inside, and doomed them. When the entertainment lessened, as struggling flesh became static glass and canisters ran out of fluid, the looting and burning started. Eventually, flushed with riotous violence and armed with pickaxe handles, with wood torn from destroyed store fittings, they returned to the corpses, now frozen like glass statues in the street, and put their backs into new work, swinging downwards, yelling curses, as they demonstrated their solution to the Jewish Question, the *Judenfrage*.

The next day, as the first groups of prisoners were forced aboard trucks to Dachau, I walked the streets, watching and listening, drinking in every detail of the fearful looks, the shared desperate supportive glee, even as my flesh crawled and every nerve screamed to get away, to forget that Crystal Night had ever happened.

While on the cobblestones, fragments glittered like diamonds in the watery winter sun.

The transatlantic flight, in the gray condragon's passenger womb, passed in fitful, sickening dreams—featuring Dick and Gunny, above all Laura, in strangely dark, surreal surroundings: good cheer turned to mockery amid chaotic dreamscape—as prep-infusions fought through my bloodstream, reset circadian rhythms, depleted skin melanin to a European pallor.

My escort, the young-looking SOE junior officer who had brought my infusions—were the Special Operations Executive recruiting from the schoolyards now?—said scarcely a word during my periods of lucidity.

It went against the paranoid grain to take debilitating treatment that left me barely conscious, unable to defend myself. But this was not a public flight; I had no right to refuse the treatment.

At one point I woke fully, stared through transparent membrane at the night sky, the silver-capped waves below, and laughed out loud. My junior officer looked worried, but I merely shook my head, unwilling to share the very real memory which had visited me.

Feynman—Dick—had led me into the comms room just before 11 A.M., when we would normally be finishing our intellectual sweat-session. I should have realized something was up from the grins the women gave him. As always, glistening black threads filled the room; on them crawled commspiders, pinhead-up to fingernail-sized, passing between nodelice whose thoraxes were swollen with the molecular-encoded fluids which technicians termed *infopus*.

And then, on the stroke of eleven, a sudden phase shift occurred. My neck prickled as half of the commspiders rose up on tiny rear legs, raised forelimbs in salute, and I realized the whole cross-and-diagonal formation was the Union Jack, instantiated in web arachnids.

Dick grinned as he, too, saluted.

Smiling, I slipped back into sleep, ignoring the nervous vibrations I was receiving from the youngster escorting me, aware they could mean only one thing: the mission pace was into overdrive; they were ready to send me in.

In London, I passed through Whitehall quicker than the proverbial dose of Andrew's Liver Salts. Final briefing, unusually, was to be in Baker Street; within twenty minutes I was there.

Even though they knew me, I went through full procedure at each of three checkpoints before I was in the heart of the great cubic warren. Formerly Marks & Spencer's corporate HQ, now more concerned with creating codes than selling winter woollies: either way, there was a grim, heartless, lightless efficiency to the place. A gray rectilinear warren, devoid of windows (save for the outer layer where no secret work was carried out), whose unending sameness made it easy to get lost.

"Fleming . . . How are you doing, old chap?"

"Not bad, Leo. Got a good one for me, have you?"

"Guaranteed unbreakable."

"Or my money back?"

We both laughed.

But that was only codes-and-ciphers; my briefing officer for the mission *per se* was a nervous-looking man with slicked-back hair and heavy glasses. His dark suit looked two sizes too big for his scrawny shoulders.

I did not know him well, but his name was Turner and his reputation among the field agents was of a ferocious intellect, second to none, whose planning paid as much heed to getting his people back as the initial access phase. They loved him for it.

But I knew that the powers-that-be used Turner sparingly, for the high-risk projects where potential gain outweighed perceived danger, in the opinion of Whitehall's desk-bound analysts.

He poked his head into the anteroom where I was waiting. "I'm ready for you now, old thing."

"Civil of you." I followed him into the windowless room and sat opposite his desk. "Lewis would've kept me kicking my heels for fifteen minutes, just to remind me who's boss."

"Ah." Turner removed the spectacles that I wasn't sure he needed, polished them on his wide silk tie, replaced them. "That's an Old Harrovian for you."

"You'd be an Eton man."

"Not quite." With a sly smile: "Barnsley Grammar School for Boys. On scholarship."

I wondered what Feynman would make of the social minefield which was our all-nurturing but ruthless class system.

"You could have fooled me," I told Turner, and hoped he would take it as a compliment.

"Language check." He steepled his fingers, getting to business. "You have fluent Polish?"

My personnel file lay on the desk, unopened.

"Rusty." This worried me.

"You don't have to pass for a native," Turner assured me. "You *will* have a German-national cover-ID, but I'm aware that's no problem. You can assume regional accents?"

I nodded, knowing that the real briefing was about to start.

"Very well. This"—Turner laid out a series of wide glossy black and white photographs: dark forest, slate-colored shore, choppy ocean waves—"is your target area. That's the Baltic Sea. And these men form your objective."

Two individuals, three photographs. Clear portraits of men in formal suits and bow ties; both of them scientists, I knew. Classic Aryan profiles.

"Codenames Wilhelm One," said Turner, "and Wilhelm Two. Their identities are hidden within the Reich, but they do in fact share first names. And the photographs, as you can see, post-date morphosurgery."

"Final cut?" I needed to know if their appearances might have changed since then, to move even closer to the Reich's cosmetic ideal.

"We think so. They're too busy for further surgery."

In the third photograph, taken upon an airfield with a drag-on squadron as backdrop, "Wilhelm One" was standing to the rear of a group dominated by Hermann Göring. Though the scientist was mostly obscured from view, his black SS uniform was unmistakable.

"Why two men?" I asked, knowing it doubled the risk.

Whistles. Men's shouts echoing in alleyways. Killer-dogs, barking.

I shook away the memory.

"This one"—Turner pointed at Wilhelm Two—"is designing what fly-boys call the payload. His institute in Berlin is carrying out the same work as our friends in New Mexico."

"You're sending me into *Berlin?*"

His gaze, dishwater gray, fastened on me for a long moment, and I wondered whether my show of nerves had blown the mission before the start.

"Access and egress," he said evenly, "would take too long. Not to mention the other difficulties. Wilhelm One, on the other hand, is developing long-range nymphcluster dragons on a genetically isolated development site in Usedom."

"All right. The Baltic, then."

Breathe. Stay calm.

"And this chap Wilhelm Two—Willi Zwei, we've begun calling him—is the one who appears to have made contact with us. I believe it's an insurance policy, in case his side loses the war. At the moment, it's a policy he probably thinks will never pay out."

Most Nazis would stake their life savings on all-out victory right now. These background ambiguities scared me.

"We're not sure"—I wanted to be clear on this—"who made the contact? They came to us first?"

"Not exactly. Polish Intelligence had already alerted us to the existence of this development base." Turner tapped the forest photograph. "The SS might have become aware of the partisans' surveillance, and set up a scam."

"Dear God."

"If I thought this was a likely scenario"—with frost in his tone—"I would not be sending you in. Is that clear?"

"Understood."

"Willi Zwei is due to visit the base from Berlin. I expect you and your team on the ground to make rendezvous with whichever Wilhelm is behind the message—"

"They made contact via a cut-out?"

"Of course. But the content indicates it must be either Wilhelm One or Two: they passed on info only one of them could have known."

No need to ask for details. If they were pertinent, he would tell me.

Turner talked me through the scenarios; none of them was pleasant. The worst possibility was that their project was stalled or fake, and I was falling into a trap specifically designed for someone with enough knowledge to verify nucleic bomb schematics at a glance.

"That's all," he said finally. "Thomas Cook's will see you through the rest."

Their official designation was Clothing, Travel and Firearms, but we called them Cook's Travel Agency because they sent us to such exotic places, where we could meet interesting people and with any luck not have to kill them.

Quite often, we came back.

"Thanks very much. I'll send you a postcard."

I tried the operator again.

"Whitehall one-four-nine-eight," I told her.

Once more, the empty ringing tone.

Before I left the Baker Street cube, Leo called out to me. He was waiting at the intersection of windowless corridors that I was most likely to take, grinning while a uniformed sergeant gave directions to a newly joined-up FANY who was obviously lost. She frowned prettily, unused to deciphering Geordie accents.

"Well, pet, first you go left—"

"Come on," said Leo. "There's someone you ought to meet."

I followed him back to his office, but it was empty. Leo surprised me by jamming a slightly disreputable trilby upon his head, then shrugging on his overcoat.

"We're going to Victoria."

"How's she doing, anyway?"

"Grow up, Fleming, why don't you?"

As we walked along Baker Street, it occurred to me that sandbag-manufacturers, to judge from the dirty piles around every doorway and window, were making a fortune. I looked up; the skies were clear of all but cream-and-gray cloud-masses. It would be nice to see some rain.

"How're your FANYs doing, Leo?"

"The resend rate is cut right down."

And agents blessed him for it. X-radiation checkpoints, sporemists, and natural hazards garbled many cryptocytes, whether avian-borne or carried by couriers beneath fingernails, or secreted in places it was best not to think about. If Leo's teams could decipher a part-randomized base sequence from the field— in effect, cracking a code that was not the one the agent had intended to use—it saved a second dangerous journey, with a vastly increased risk of capture.

"So who are we going to see?"

"Someone you'll like, I promise."

By this time the evening was growing cool, and we walked faster as we turned into Victoria High Street. Then we stopped opposite Westminster Cathedral, with its oddly pleasing mixture of brick-red and gray, and the bicolored tower rising upwards. Leo headed across the road, and I tagged along.

Inside, the cathedral looked soot-blackened but darkly impressive. I followed Leo through a discreet door at the side, nodded to a priest in vestments, and climbed a creaking wooden stairway. At the top, Leo rapped on a door.

"It's me."

"Come in, you."

Inside was a small, oak-paneled office whose shelves were crammed with books. A tall red-headed man rose from his bureau to greet us.

"This is Jack," Leo told me. "And I'll warn you now, he's a Jesuit. Don't expect to win any arguments."

I held out my hand, smiling.

"I won't. How do you, Father?"

"Jack. Please."

Leo peered at the shelves. "He's also the best geneticist we have."

"Second best." Jack waved me to a wooden chair. "You're too modest, Leo."

"I don't think so. There's something I could use your help with—"

As they launched into an arcane discussion of phage-borne randomizers, I walked over to the shelves that Leo had been examining. A small plain crucifix hung overhead, facing the picture of the Sacred Heart. Beneath lay a crammed mass of titles: Wallace's *Descent of Man*; Schrödinger's *Life Waves*; the complete Gibbon's *The History of the Decline and Fall of the Roman Empire*. Everything Immanuel Kant had written, in the original German. *Gray's Anatomy*. Hobbes' *Leviathan*. A slim volume of *Emergenic Transforms* by Riemann. Machiavelli's *The Prince*, in both English and Italian. *Tarzan of the Apes*, by Edgar Rice Burroughs.

Open on the desk, beside a cheap brown-robed statuette of some saint, was a copy of von Clausewitz's *On War*.

"Interesting," I murmured.

"St. Gregor Mendel?" asked Jack, mistaking my interest. "He's one of my heroes."

"Of course." I wondered in how high a regard he held von Clausewitz.

"Have you ever wondered how different the world might've been, if the Vatican legate hadn't plucked him from obscurity, and spread his work across the globe?"

"Um . . . "

"I'm afraid the Philistines have arrived," said Leo.

"Story of my life." Jack held out a small glob of blue gel towards me. "Here you are. It's a new antiviral. Best protection you can have."

So he knew I was going into occupied territory.

"Thanks, padre. I mean Jack."

At that point, Jack broke out a bottle of beaujolais which he assured us had not been consecrated, and we drank a small toast or two, and chatted about everything from girls—Jack laughed a lot—to Kant, to the war in Africa.

It was only later, at the end of our convivial evening when an SOE driver came to collect me and Leo, that I wondered what was really going on. Had Leo intended to cheer me up, the day before I went into danger? Or had he set up this distracting soirée purely to keep me busy?

Chatting beside me on the rear seat, Leo looked too fresh and innocent for the deceptive world in which we moved. But, even as I responded to his questions, all I could really think of was the one person who had come to matter, my small core of stability while everything around us slid into chaotic uncertainty.

Night flight.

Crouched in my transparent half-shell, ready to roll—

"Thirty seconds." The jumpmaster checked me, nodded.

A gunner peered back inside the long fuselage, grim-faced. Probably wondering whether I was worth it: there had been ack-ack on the way in, and Pterafighter or Falcon squadrons were probably already rising; the flight back was not going to be fun.

As for me . . .

"Ready—"

Slipstream, as the hatch furled back. The jumpmaster reached towards me.

"—Go!"

Then darkness and buffeting winds were all around, fear shrieking inside, as the half-shell completed itself, became a cocoon.

Darkest night above me, and below. Tumbling . . .

And drop.

Wet ripples on the silver moonlit grass: the drop-sphere and its chute-membrane were half-dissolved at the foot of a night-black hedge. I waited . . . then a soft whisper sounded and I dropped. Shadows against the night: four men, maybe six.

Wide-eyed, breathing fast and shallow, I crouched like a sprinter at the blocks, scared as hell and ready to explode into—

"Hello, darling."

Liquid words, sliding through the chill night air, struck straight through my trained defenses, and I nearly choked with shock.

Laura?

I should have realized. Even the initial infiltration, the set-up, would have needed specialized knowledge.

"*Dzien dobry* . . ." A male voice. I could just see the rifle-outline in his hands.

"*Milo mi pan poznać,*" I told him.

But it was the figure at the group's center I wanted to see.

Laura's here!

A week of dream and nightmare: of days holed up in safehouses—here an attic, while German voices rose up from the street below; there a deserted farm, the farmer's ruddy-faced wife giving cause for concern as she slipped away unannounced: we broke cover and made our way into the woods, just in case—and of the nights, traveling through heathland which became steep slopes blanketed with thick forest, filled with the rustle of tiny creatures, wind brushing branches, and the surprising hoot of a predatory owl.

And Laura, my Laura, was with me.

"You're good at keeping secrets, my darling," I told her. "I should've guessed why Leo kept me occupied in London."

"There's no secret how I feel about you, dear man."

Kindred spirits, and more.

When we traveled at night, we walked as one: each holding the other's hand, sometimes with our clasped hands in her coat pocket or mine, for warmth. Among the four Polish agents with us—who moved through darkness like pale, alert cats, their night vision enhanced even beyond mine—there was a calm acceptance of the relationship, with neither joking nor resentment.

They knew how easily lovers could be wrenched apart by the capricious, devastating daily tragedies of war.

Finally, after a cold few hours spent crouched beneath undergrowth while roving scanbats passed overhead—dark flutterings against a strangely golden moon—we trekked on through winding forest paths, finally descending to the town of Lubmin.

From the forest's edge, we watched. As false dawn smeared the eastern sky, stars glittering against a backdrop thickening into navy blue, our small group stood watchful, breathing pine-scented air, regarding the cobbled streets and peaked roofs. There were no patrols.

And then a window-shutter moved, just beneath a wooden eave, and someone laid a striped dishcloth across the granite sill. That was our signal.

One by one, we slipped across the open ground with nerves screaming against a hail of bullets that never came, boots in hand so that we walked on cold uneven cobblestones in silent socks, reached the back door leading to the safehouse's scullery, and slid inside.

The first morning was the worst.

In a threadbare coat and dirty shawl, head bent forward, Laura shuffled into a group of workers on the gray cobbles below, while I watched from the attic window. Then a dark green flatbed Volksnashorn transport pulled up, and one of the Wehrmacht soldiers jumped down, jackboots clattering on stone. He rapped the armored hide in a control sequence; the rear unfurled, formed a ramp up which the workers could drag themselves, ready for another long shift at The Keep.

I watched as they drove into a narrow street where houses leaned inwards, took a sharp turn at the far end, were lost from sight.

She's been doing this, I told myself, *for months.*

But even a long-established cover could be broken at any time.

For the rest of the day, nervous in my attic and unable to go out, I drove myself physically: stepping up and down from an old sturdy applecrate, performing sit-ups and press-ups, chin-ups from the rafters, striking empty air as I worked through the killing techniques of Fairbairn's system.

And then, when the nerves were finally quiescent, I lay prone on the floor with an imaginary long gun held in my hands, and mentally rehearsed the shot I was going to take. This visualization, entirely serious, was the only practice I would get.

When evening came and Laura climbed up to the attic, I took her in my arms, hugged her as though I could never let go, feeling the coldness of her skin, inhaling the faint laboratory scents clinging to her hair and clothes, too overwhelmed by her safe presence to speak.

She kissed me then, an explosion of warmth, and I abandoned thought to the immediacy of the moment, when communion needed no words.

It was on the fourth day, as I waited in the overfamiliar attic—dusty pale-amber collimated sunlight tracking the morning's progress across gray knotty floorboards—that a door banged below, and I jumped.

I waited for Elsa, the plump red-haired woman who owned this place, to call a greeting. Then softer footsteps rose upwards from the ladder-like stairs, and I crouched ready for combat—

"It's me."

—then relaxed, recognizing Piotr's voice. He was the team leader, whom Laura called Petya, but I used his proper name. The others—Zenon, Stanislaw and Karol—I had scarcely spoken to at all.

"Hello, Piotr. Everything okay?" My voice came out more stressed than I had intended.

"So far." His lean pale face betrayed little emotion: a face that had seen too much. "Everything is in place."

"Ready to go now?" My skin shrank.

"In a few hours. You're sure about the long shot?"

I understood: Piotr and the others were hunters; they did not trust me to make the kill.

"I placed second," I told him, "in Bisley, before the war."

"Bis—?"

"National rifle championships."

"Ah. Is good."

For Laura's sake, it had better be.

"You rest now," added Piotr, "and I call you when ready."

"I'll do my best."

Later, as the summer evening's sky finally darkened to gray, there was a knock from below, and Piotr's voice again:

"It's time."

People moved warily in the quaint streets, where inward-leaning houses with uneven leaded windows appeared to stare down at dark gray cobbles. Hunched shoulders betrayed the locals' awareness of constant observation: from spybats, from passing Waffen SS patrols, from each other. The landlady who wanted a new tenant; the disaffected pupil hating his teacher; the jealous neighbor bottling up resentment over the years: anyone might turn informer, spill out their suspicions to the *Sicherheitsdienst*, convince themselves of their countrymen's disloyalty.

And would they stand and watch afterwards, as their victims were taken away by stone-faced squads whose self-righteous force could not be denied? Or might they never stop to think of the suffering about to be inflicted on those who fell victim to the Reich's internal guardians of pure Aryan thought?

We're all products of the culture we—

I halted, just for a second, at the sight of gray uniforms ahead.

Don't stop.

Piotr, walking ahead of me, continued without reaction: showing more professionalism than I.

"*Papiere.*"

I ground to a halt, my guts tightening.

"*Ihre Papiere.*" Hand outstretched, impatience entering his tone. "*Schnell.*"

But it was his comrade's hand I noticed: flexing, itching to whip up the Mauser and squeeze the trigger for that momentary burst of flesh-destroying pleasure.

"*Bitte.*" I handed over my ID.

We used to say bad things, we agents, about Thomas Cook's, and the fussy matrons and old men who ran the section, but the documentation they produced was usually—

"*Also gut.*"

He handed them back, and *this* was the greatest danger: that I would reveal overwhelming relief, as my protective facade fell inwards, no longer shored up by fear-tension; relaxation would be my downfall.

For a moment I thought the other soldier was going to fire, and I prepared to claw at his eyes, to take some recompense with me to the grave—

But they were walking on now, not quite in step, and the sickening realization of my own mortality was washing through me in waves. For now, I was safe.

A scuffed footstep—Piotr, turning a corner up ahead— brought me back into reality. Here security was ephemeral, a guarantee of survival only until the next flashpoint, and I had better get a grip or we would be done for.

That included Laura.

Shards, on cobblestones—

For Laura's sake, I hunched my head forwards, tucked my false papers back in my too-thin jacket's pocket, walked on.

From a thicket beyond the town's edge, we stopped, stared back at armed curfew patrols heading into the alleyways, striding with a centered arrogance among ordinary people, knowing they could burst into homes upon a whim, always able to justify the violation of frail civilians in the name of the dark power which ruled their once-civilized selves.

A soft rain, like silent weeping, began to fall as we turned into the darkening forest, moving quickly now.

And then it was time for the long shot.

Damp grass lay beneath me, but the cold faded as I pulled

the hard butt into my shoulder, sighting the base of the tower that guarded the narrow defile, and began the breathing ritual. In the crosshairs, the sentinel was visible: a paler shadow inside his darkened booth.

"The other sentries," whispered Piotr, "are almost out of sight."
And breathe . . .
Behind me, though I could not turn around, I could sense the warmth of the other three Polish fighters, crouched in readiness.
"Three. Two. One. Gone."
I had twenty seconds exactly.
And hold.
Sweat on my finger, around my eye.
Ignore.
Centering the target's image—
Hold . . .
A wavering . . . Then steadiness.
Now.
Squeeze.
A shift in image, shadows in my sight, unable to tell if—
"He's down."
Success.

It was an airclaw, silent and accurate: a sniper's bullet. No ganglia to be disrupted by defensive sonic fields; no gunpowder whose crack would pull a thousand Wehrmacht troops and Waffen SS down upon our heads.

The rifle's weight lifted as strong hands tugged my shoulders.
"*Now go.*"
I was on my feet and moving.

The five of us ran like wraiths, up the slope with lungs and thighs burning in the cool night air, fast and silent. Beside me ran Stanislaw, the tallest of the Poles, carrying the heavy rifle one-handed, keeping pace despite the Browning's weight.

When we reached the tower, Stanislaw dropped back, and headed into the sentry's booth. He would strip the body and don the uniform.

"Two minutes," Piotr reminded him.

A change of guard had just occurred. From the info Laura had provided, the next perimeter patrol would not expect to recognize Stanislaw as the sentry on duty: from a different unit, newly posted to this place.

"No problem. Just go."

We moved on, into the narrow defile, cloaked by darkness at the rockface's base.

Rumble. Stink of sulfur.

Disgusting.

Hot breath played across my skin as the bulky hyperkomodo sniffed, licked my sweat with its reptilian tongue, then turned and lumbered away into shadows. Beside me, Piotr sagged: he had not been convinced the pherocipher would work; but we smelled like friend, not foe, to the ultrasensitive beast.

Then a wide flatosaur transport came into sight, moving along the defile with its scaly hide almost scraping the rock on either side. Counting carefully, I took a breath then rolled between two massive legs—it had twenty four in all—and whipped my hands up, hooking fingers desperately into ridged plates as it dragged me along the broken ground, and I swung up one foot—*missed*—then got the hold, pulled up the other, and then I was clinging on by all four limbs, like some desperate parasite hoping not to be shaken off.

When I could spare a glance, there were three other primate shadows—Piotr, Karol and Zenon—splayed against the underside with me, holding on while the lurching transport carried out us into the heart of the enemy's installation.

Through the internal checkpoint. Half-hearing the driver's chat with the guards.

"—*geht's mit dir?*"

"*Ausgezeichneit. Arnold hat ein neues Mädchen—*"

Then we were past, and I let go my hold.

Drop.

Stone thudded against my back. I timed the massive legs' movement, counting—

Now roll.

In the small courtyard, a wooden doorway swung open, and a blue firefly glimmered for an instant, before a small fist hid it once again.

Laura.

I was first into the narrow hallway, and I brushed Laura's cheek with my fingertips, but there was no time for any other greeting as we moved inside. The walls were lined with polished mahogany, from what I could glimpse in the firefly's blue-tinted illumination.

Then, at the hallway's end, we turned into a cross-corridor. This had been some landowner's grand house, but as the corridor's walls became bare stone and the air temperature dropped, it became obvious—even before the floor sloped downwards—that we were heading *into* the low craggy ground which splayed out, forming a headland, into the cold Baltic waves.

There was a weapons area filled with soldiers, swarming across the equipment, while officers barked out commands and a black-uniformed Gestapo colonel oversaw the activity. Ducking low, we used a wide pipeline for cover, passing into the barracks area—more soldiers, dining—then through an internal pherolocked door which responded to Laura's touch, into the cavernous pits.

A small catwalk, of wet-looking black chitin, extended bridge-wise across the pits, to an armored megarhino-hide door on the far wall. On either side of that door, in small recesses in the raw rockface, a big handle shone a dull, fluorescent red.

Laura leaned close to me.

"I'll go first, my love."

Her lips brushed my cheek, and then she was moving across the catwalk, in plain view of any sentries who might make an appearance below.

I held back, letting Karol and Zenon follow her—it would be their job to hold the deadman switches, keeping the armored door open—before making my own way onto the black chitinous catwalk, with Piotr close behind.

Small phosphorescent cocoons, adhered here and there to ceiling and walls, provided a hellish light. Far better, despite the moans which rose towards us, to keep the pits' poor dwellers hidden from human sight.

It was worse than *Kristallnacht.*

For the things that moved beneath me now, the once-human beings that fluttered and crawled and flowed in the cold pits, dragged slime-trails across broken rock or simply melded with it, were inflicted with something worse than agonizing death: a tortured ongoing pseudolife of glistening flesh and ever-raw wounds, of strange sprouting limbs—many-jointed protrusions, boneless ulcerated tentacles—and weeping, putrescent growths in an ongoing shamble of sickening flesh that could not die.

Behind me, a sharp inhalation, and a whispered name:

"*Brigitte . . .*"

Piotr, ashen-faced, was staring down at that jumble of animated meat, where a few strips of cloth—there, just visible, a dirty yellow star—remained, caught in folds as the hypertumorous growths had split clothing asunder. On a liquid protrusion which might once have been a head, a stretched mask, like a face impossibly distorted, pulled down and to one side, opened its pseudomouth in a silent plea, or recognition.

I caught Piotr's arm.

"The only thing we can do," I told him, "is avenge her."

A tense nod, sinews standing out like cables on his pale neck, and then he followed me.

But he looked back as he walked, keeping that tortured facsimile of life in view for as long as he could, until we reached the armored door.

Karol went to the right, Zenon to the left.

"*Jeden, dwa, trzy*—"

Simultaneously, each leaned down on a deadman handle. The door puckered, then slowly furled back, revealed the steel-lined passageway beyond.

Karol and Zenon would remain in place, for if either man released his hold the doorway would close. It could be opened normally only from the outside. Unauthorized egress was possible, in case of emergency; but using the interior handles would set off every alarm and klaxon in the installation, shutting down our mission in a matter of seconds.

"All right," said Laura. "We've made the rendezvous."
Let's hope Wilhelm manages the same.
We moved into the steel passageway.

Lab benches covered a factory-wide floor. Laura, Piotr and I walked the length of one aisle, to the flight of pinewood steps at the far end, where we stopped. The steps led up to a glass-walled cabin on a raised level, but the cabin—an isolation lab, perhaps—was unlit, as deserted as the ghostly expanse of benches, unoccupied stools and workplaces ranged across the wide, gloomy main chamber.

On one wall, high, hung a scarlet swastika-emblazoned banner. Below it, the only other door into this place slowly swung open.

"No . . . "

And *two* blond-haired figures, white lab coats over their impeccable suits, walked inside and stopped.

For a long moment, we stared at each other, locked in silence.

The contact, via a cut-out—a local schoolteacher with little knowledge of the Nazis who had contacted her, or of the resistance fighters with whom she engaged purely in writing, via a long-established letter-drop—had evinced knowledge of the long-range dragon program, and the nucleic bomb payload that their nymphclusters were designed to deliver. Whitehall's analysts had been certain that one or other Wilhelm was involved: no one had considered the possibility that *both* of them might be considering defection to the enemy. Especially now, as the Blitzkrieg was pulverizing England's cities, now that jackboots marched throughout Europe, once-free countries having fallen like dominoes before the encroaching Reich.

I don't like this.

It was too rich an offering to accept at face value.

"Let me show you something." The shorter of the two Wilhelms—Wilhelm One—gestured towards an opaque pearly panel upon the nearest wall. Speaking in English again: "Come here."

There was no point in shyness. I walked over to him, intending to offer my hand in greeting, but he turned away and dialed the panel into transparency.

Automatically, I moved to one side, but the lab surrounding me was shadow-shrouded, while the great hangar-chamber into which we looked was brightly lit with white incandescent arc-lamps. If the any of the groundcrew looked up, they were unlikely to spot us.

"Dear God," muttered Piotr.

For we were looking down upon the hugest dragons imaginable, their vast delta-wings filling the great shallow pits, stretching from wingtip to wingtip as wide as a row of houses. Nymphs, opalescent and spherical, their long tendrils neatly bundled up around great yolk-sacs, were being loaded into the dragon's cavities; once released over the target city, the ejected nymphs would blossom, shed their skins to become small adult dragons within seconds, swooping down in operant-conditioned precision to deliver their deadly payloads directly onto the soft civilian targets below.

"The first test-flights," said Wilhelm One in an even tone, "have proven satisfactory."

"What's their range?" I asked. And, when he did not answer: "*Was ist die Fliegweite?*"

"*Zwei tausand Kilometer.*" He shrugged. "*Vielleicht mehr.*"

With a two thousand kilometer range, they could launch from here—would not even have to relocate their facilities to occupied France, as I had expected.

Even without the nucleic bomb, if the Luftwaffe labs could spawn these hyperdragons fast enough, hatch them in sufficiently large batches to provide a dozen squadrons, maybe twenty, then the war against England would shortly be over, and Englishmen would be learning German in the same way our Saxon ancestors were once coerced into adopting Norman French. But the new regime would be something out of nightmare, such as the writers of medieval epics, for all their monsters and demons, could never have imagined.

"And you." I turned to face the other Wilhelm. "Just what are you hoping to get out of this?"

They wheeled blackboards on castors into place, near the pinewood steps that led to the isolation lab. Quickly, Wilhelm

Two scrawled equations in chalk while Wilhelm One, readying a glass dish upon an asbestos mat, gave a commentary.

"From what I understand"—he waited until I nodded: I knew he was not a specialist in quantum molecular evolution—"there are two problems. First is the bomb-core itself, with self-replicating attractor-strands designed to cascade through the atmosphere."

I felt myself grow cold.

"Second," Wilhelm One continued, "is the vector-trigger which energizes the process and carries the spawn outwards, enabling the cascade."

Even from party talk in Oppenheimer's house, I could have verified this much: that the Nazis were a long way down the line, to have gained insights into the trigger-mechanism, to have realized that it was as crucial to the weapon's operation as the nucleic core itself.

From the enzyme formulas currently growing upon the board—Wilhelm Two tossed one worn nub of white chalk aside, picked up a fresh stick—I could see, also, that they had at least the basics of core-construction techniques. Just as (contrary to Einstein's instincts) characteristics like intelligence had evolved in the natural world too fast for strict Wallacian macro-selection, so too could Wilhelm Two and his co-workers produce the necessary replicator-strands in far less time than the millennia which ordinary evolution would require.

As Schrödinger and Bohr had shown, enzymes act as chemical observers, forcing the collapse of molecular wave-functions—overlaid simultaneous possibilities—into one outcome. But an enzyme that repeatedly "observes" a molecule in the same position prevents it from once more entering a fuzzy, overlaid state, essentially freezing its configuration and energy forever.

But quantum biology had another, counterintuitive tenet: that the way in which a measurement is carried out partly determines the value that results.

And the New Mexico scientists made use of this. If the observing enzyme itself was slowly changing, then *it forced the observed molecule to evolve* in ways determined by the enzyme's own biochemical propensities.

"So what," asked Wilhelm Two, turning from the blackboard, "do you think, my friend?"

I tried to keep my face a frozen mask, but the Wilhelms exchanged a glance, and I knew that I had betrayed too much.

Whatever the results they had obtained so far, I knew now that the Nazi nucleic bomb project was a viable program, and that if they continued long enough they would succeed in destroying any ecosystem they targeted, including human life.

"*Also gut.*" Wilhelm Two nodded. "Good enough. Let me show you—"

A distant door clanged, and both Wilhelm's faces grew pale simultaneously.

They were not acting.

"Patrol," said Wilhelm One.

Obviously unscheduled.

"Quick." Wilhelm Two pointed up at the isolation lab. "Get inside."

Piotr reached inside his jacket.

No—

He must have hidden a revolver there, despite my orders. The idea was, no firearms to be brought inside the installation itself. If we had to shoot, we were dead, our mission a failure.

"Okay." Piotr looked at me, then took his hand out of his jacket, empty. "I agree."

Laura went first up the pinewood steps.

"*Hurry.*"

Inside the isolation lab, Wilhelm Two pointed at two booth-like reaction-cupboards built into the rear wall. He quickly pointed from Piotr to me.

"You two will, um, *Ihn verbergen . . .* "

"Hide," said Wilhelm One, staring through the window to the wider lab below.

Laura stared at me.

"No," I said.

But then, "You must." She reached up, brushed her fingertips across my lips. "There's room for you two, and I'm on the staff roster—"

"Quickly." Piotr grabbed my sleeve. "We must."

"All right."

Twisting a bakelite control-knob, Wilhelm nodded towards the transparent-fronted cupboards. The outer membrane slowly darkened to black opacity.

"Squid-ink derivative."

"I—"

But the doors outside were opening for the patrol, and there was no time to chat as I pushed myself inside, onto the waist-high surface, and pulled myself into a hunched position as the membrane hardened, trapping me inside the reaction-cupboard.

Laura—

But I could see out into the isolation lab, with Laura shivering as the patrol burst into the shadowed area outside, as the two Wilhelms briefly conferred. Sounds were muted, the words indecipherable, but the ink-soaked membrane was transparent from my side.

I let out a sound that was half a sob, then held myself still, breathing fast.

The isolation door opened, and an SS officer stepped inside, his black uniform magnificent with silver badges and decorations. His round face looked almost pleasant, save for the thin purple scar and the lifeless gaze that passed over the cupboard membrane—I shivered, unable to stifle the reaction—and continued on to Laura and the two Wilhelms.

"—*Sie hier?*" His voice raised high enough to penetrate my hiding-place.

Wilhelm Two muttered something, of which I could only decipher the word *arbeiten.* Claiming that they were working late on something important.

Did the SS distrust their own chief scientists this much?

Behind the officer, two gray-uniformed troopers took up position inside the doorway, hands upon their Mausers. But it was the SS man, with the fat white baton inserted in his shining belt, who scared me witless.

Laura, my love.

For a microsecond, her eyes flickered in my direction. Then she turned away, and looked down at the floor as she answered a direct question from the officer.

NO . . .

I saw then that she was holding the glass dish from the lab-bench where Wilhelm One had been standing; the scar bunched on his face as the SS man, too, noticed it. Off to one side, a small red light was blinking, and I wondered if Laura's taking the sample dish had triggered some kind of silent alarm.

The officer barked a question, but did not wait for Wilhelm One—already, to his credit, stepping forwards—to answer.

Instead, the baton slid from the black leather belt, its tapered nozzle just inches from Laura's fine face—

No! Laura!

And I clawed the membrane and might have yelled but it was already too late as the sporemist squirted and the woman I loved was a zombie before my fingers struck the membrane.

I stopped, frozen, unable to comprehend what I had just seen.

One of the troopers opened his mouth, about to speak—he might have heard me—but then he caught sight of the SS officer's creamy smile and subsided. He exchanged a glance with his comrade: I could see their unspoken decision to remain quietly inconspicuous.

Laura. Oh, my Laura.

Too late, now.

Expostulations, explanations. I could not care whether the Wilhelms cracked and gave me and Piotr away, or if they all walked away and left me here to suffocate and die. For Laura, the standing corpse of the woman I loved, was there before me: separated from my desperate grasp by a quarter-inch of impenetrable membrane and a lifetime of devastating regret.

When the membrane finally dissolved and hands helped me out, I could scarcely process the information that Wilhelms One and Two were here, that Piotr's hands were fastened on me like iron claws, and that the SS officer and his patrol were gone.

"Laura . . ." I said, to the one person who could not hear.

Who would never think a human thought again.

I reached out to touch her cheek, but held back from touching, in case of infection: a moment's cowardice that will never leave me. But there were tiny pustules already sprouting across that once-flawless ivory smoothness, precursors to the gross transformations which would soon render her fit company for the tormented monstrosities incarcerated in the pits outside.

And was that a glimmer of tortured awareness in those fine, dead eyes?

I hoped not. I prayed that she was truly gone.

Oh, my Laura.

Wilhelm One cleared his throat then, and said: "I am very sorry, sir."

Looking up, I saw him swallow, the same awareness registering in Wilhelm Two's face: the killing rage, the cacaphonic roar inside, inciting blood-vengeance in a wave of eye-gouges and throat-strikes. I could destroy them, tear them limb from—

"My friend." Piotr drew his revolver. "If you tell me, I will shoot them now."

The gunshot would be suicide, but I could not care. And the two Wilhelms, swallowing, dared not speak.

But finally I tore my gaze away from the one who mattered, and said: "What do you want? Really want?"

"You approve the bomb plans?" asked Wilhelm Two. "They are acceptable?"

"I—"

And *that* was the moment when the mission—and the world—could have come crashing down. Because there was another blackboard in here, another chalk diagram annotated with Wilhelm Two's scrawl, and its similarity to something Dick Feynman had shown me brought me to a halt.

"*I'm working on something,*" he had said, "*called Quantum Evolutionary Determinism. It's years from completion, but there's a technique you might use—*"

And so I used it now, in my head: Dick's integration-over-all-futures technique, as I stared at details of the enzyme whose job was to force-evolve the replicating core, and I knew now it would never work.

Before, I had given away my thoughts. But with emotions

burned away by Laura's zombie-death, I had no reactions to betray me. It saved me, now that life was no longer worth anything at all.

"—think they're fine. Whitehall would love to have you."

"But I would need to continue my work."

"You'll have a house in Oxford," I told him. "A big one. And you'll work with the finest minds we have."

A lie. Our scientists were not based in Oxford: too obvious a target.

"Very well, then," said Wilhelm Two.

A decision crystallized in Wilhelm One's eyes, and he nodded abruptly to his namesake.

"Good luck, my friend."

Then he wheeled on one heel, and walked quickly from the isolation lab. His footsteps clattered back from the pine steps, clacked across the polished parquet flooring, and then he was through the side-door beneath the scarlet banner, and lost from sight.

"I guess, my friend," I said to Wilhelm Two, "you'll be coming with us."

But there was one last development. Piotr, with a bottle of reagent in his hand which might have been hydrogen peroxide, pulled a lab-coat from its hook behind the door. He put down the stoppered bottle, and hauled on the white coat.

"You two get out of here."

"I—"

"The patrol might come back. If they don't look closely, they'll think"—with a gesture towards Wilhelm Two—"that I'm him."

I answered Piotr, though I could look only at Laura as I spoke.

"All right," I said. "We're going."

And, leaning closer: "*Goodbye, my sweet darling.*"

Then I walked away without looking back, leaving Wilhelm to follow me if he chose.

When we reached the far end of the steel passageway, Karol and Zenon were there, still leaning on the deadman-handle door-controls, looking at us curiously.

"Where—?"

Then a shot banged out, loud and flat, from the labs behind us.

Laura!

And I knew that Piotr had granted her rest in the only way possible.

"Come on." I took hold of Wilhelm's sleeve. "We're moving fast now."

For his own sake, he obeyed the implicit command, not knowing that I saw through the sham, would not reveal my knowledge of the program's uselessness.

Because if I did, I jeopardized everything: the fate of Britain, of the western world. Betrayed the cause that Laura had died for.

Oh, my love.

Saved the world for which I no longer gave a damn.

There were rushing patrols inside the grand house proper, heavy boots thudding on the carpeted hallways as they rushed to grab their weapons. But they allowed the senior scientist through, away from any danger that might have broken out inside the labs.

We were too far away to hear more gunfire, but I knew that Piotr would not sell his life cheaply.

Then out along the narrow defile, whose far end was marked by four bloody corpses—an entire patrol, dead—and our comrade Stanislaw, mortally wounded, white-faced and whimpering, inside his sentry-box.

Karol stepped inside with him, murmured comforting words, then used a Wehrmacht dagger to grant the only absolution possible.

I was too numb to feel anything as we trekked across open ground to the forest, to begin our long journey to the rendezvous point and freedom.

There must have been a flight, an RAF pick-up; but post-traumatic amnesia set in, they told me afterwards, for the reminder of the journey home remains forever lost in vacuum.

Little of the debriefing, in an isolated Wiltshire farmhouse, comes back to me, either. But I recall the conversation I finally had with the Old Man, when I returned to duty in Whitehall.

"Sit down." He pointed with his pipe-stem to the hard wooden chair before his desk. "And I'm sorry about Laura."

"Thank you, sir."

On the desk in front of him were typed papers, with diagrams annotated with ink in a tight, spiderly crawl I could not fail to recognize.

"Might as well burn them." I pointed at the schematics. "They're worthless."

His gray eyes appraised me. "Obviously, you did not reveal that at the time. Why did you bring him back?"

I closed my eyes.

Laura . . .

In my dreams, she always looked back at me.

"Perhaps it's too soon for you to—"

Opening my eyes: "I beg your pardon, sir." I needed to explain this. "It's my fault. *I knew too much.* I could have solved their problems, with what Feynman had shown me. I could have made the Nazi program work. Put it back on track. Wilhelm would have taken it from there."

"Surely you, of all people, would never—"

"I could, and I would have, sir."

The Old Man was shaking his head, showing too much faith in this poor operative.

I stood up, crossed to the window, and stared outside with hands clasped behind my back, staring at the black statue in the center of the road. Whitehall was a boulevard, I realized, which reminded me too much of Berlin before the war.

"The sporemist infection," I said softly, "is reversible, if caught in time. They would have offered me Laura, and I would have given them everything."

An avuncular hand descended on my shoulder: the first time the Old Man had touched me, since we had shaken hands on our first meeting three years and a lifetime before.

"It was why he wanted to come over. Wilhelm, I mean." I

sighed. "Too afraid of his masters to remain in place. He'd probably been exaggerating reports of his progress. But if he'd offered
them me—"

No need to point out the obvious.

"So our new Nazi friend is worthless," murmured the Old
Man.

The smell of wood-polish from the paneling; the redolence of
pipe-tobacco; the cry of a lone seagull gliding outside. None of it
made sense.

"You did the right thing," he said.

Wilhelm Two would never make it to the promised house in
Oxford. Instead, out walking on the Marlborough Downs,
accompanied by his SOE bodyguards, he would lose his footing
on a wet grassy slope, and tragically break his neck.

In Whitehall, nobody mourned.

Of course we won the war. The hyperdragons would have made
a difference, but for all Wilhelm One's successes, his masters
failed to mobilize the resources that would have swung the balance in their favor.

In the closing days, Stalin's forces suffered inordinately heavy
losses in their bid to be first into Berlin. To many tactically mind-
ed observers it seemed madness, since the Allied powers had
agreed to divide the conquered city between them. But to me, it
was obvious that the real target was the institute where Wilhelm
Two had worked. For Stalin wanted nucleic technology for himself: the weaponry that would later prove its power when the
Americans' bomb destroyed so much of the Japanese ecosystem.
I could have told Stalin that his men died in vain, but perhaps his
own project had been further behind, and whatever knowledge
his scientists gained might have been worth the price, in his eyes.

Afterwards, as the joy of V-E day swept through London's
thronged streets, it seemed almost impertinent to think of precious individuals lost during the years of darkness, when so many
millions, tens of millions, died.

But that was the point: of the Holocaust victims and the
Allied soldiers and the civilians caught in bombing raids, every

one had been a real life, defined a world of his or her own.

I tried to hand in my resignation, but where else would I go? To paint, in New Mexico? In that dream, there had been Laura to share my life. Alone, it was cold and pointless.

And so I stayed.

SOE slid into historical oblivion, reinventing itself in peacetime as DI6, then MI6. Even when the Old Man retired, I stayed on throughout the '50s, until I could stand the memories no more.

Every night, I dreamed of Laura.

One day, early in 1962, I resigned.

The next morning—in the intelligence community, no one works out their notice—I sat on a bench in St. James' Park, reading a *Daily Sketch* that someone had discarded, drinking in the scents of rhododendron I had been too busy to smell when I ran my five miles at dawn.

The newspaper headlines were large. After the western world's paranoia over orbiting Sputniks, this was the sentiment: *Time To Get Our Own Back.*

By "our" own, they meant the U.S.

Journalists focus on personalities, and the man in the spotlight was going to ride a fiery dragon up through the sky, and into the darkness beyond. But, behind the headlines . . . Well, since that notable absence from the Nuremberg trials, I had always known how things would play out.

It's been two decades.

I crumpled up the paper, and tossed it into a bin.

Trafalgar Square, when I walked through it, was scarcely changed from the day the Swastika Bomb dropped and Laura's life collided with mine, altering everything.

Whitehall, too, was the same. But, by the time I had passed through Parliament Square and was strolling down Victoria High Street, the buildings were transparent greens and blues and reds, slowly morphing as they cycled through their jelly-forms, while beneath them brightly dressed Londoners rode colorful trexes along boulevards that glistened like a dragonfly's wings.

I remembered Leo's friend Jack, the priest, talking about the importance of history's turning-points, and wondered if Mendel's legacy was only now coming into its own, truly defining the shape of modern times.

Westminster Cathedral, like Westminster Abbey at the road's far end, remained in its original form, surrounding by marvels of shifting bioarchitecture, while one- and two-man albatross-glides circled overhead, enjoying the view.

I went up the steps, moved quietly inside.

The high vaulted ceilings were as blackened as before the war, but candles shone brightly and the stained glass windows were magnificent in their rich-hued artistry. Incense was heavy upon the air, as the priest at the high altar celebrated the Mass. Not Jack: he was in South America, on missionary work.

"—art in Heaven, hallowed be thy—"

I turned away, retraced my steps to the entrance.

There was nothing for me here.

I used Thomas Cook's, the real travel agency, to make the booking. The SOE department was long defunct; few people in MI6 now would recognize the term.

Somehow, that made it seem even more appropriate.

Sweltering heat, though it was not yet spring. Blazing sun in a cloudless azure sky. Hotter than New Mexico, and humid.

I lay on straggly parched grass which struggled to grow through sandy ground. Using a soft cloth, I wiped the rifle's scope before putting my eye to the lens once more. A jumble of people: military uniforms, civilian suits. Women in candy-colored frocks, wide hats and short white gloves. No sign of the target.

Too soon.

I looked away, lay the rifle down, and lay back on the grass.

No blimps or scanbats overhead: they were steering clear of the area. The one security-hole I was able to exploit.

Florida, and hot: it was over three years since Felix and I had fished here last—he took a giant tuna despite his hook-hand—and I had avoided all contact with him since then. But through him I had made interesting contacts, which was how I was lying here now with an airclaw-loaded rifle, waiting for the moment.

Laura, my sweetest love . . .

Later. Concentrate now.

Huge and magnificent, the great silver hyperasaur stood waiting to lift: vastly bigger than any dragon-flyer built before, pregnant with massive energies, poised to burst upwards into sky, into space, to orbit our small planet with its brave lone pilot aboard.

His courage, I saluted.

Nearly time. Adjusting the scope . . .

There.

Among the dignitaries, on the official view-platform over-looking Cape Canaveral, was the one I was looking for. Dressed in a white linen suit, with the same white-blond hair—he had never bothered to have his appearance altered after the war—he took his place beside a five-star general.

The general clapped him on the back and handed over a cigar.

Riches, fame, and the chance to lead the free world into space. Ignoring his past: claiming that his wartime work was carried out in virtual captivity.

A blare of distant tannoys.

Countdown.

Distant roar, as the great hyperagon's engines burst into life, poured white flames downwards, blazing bright as the sun.

Crosshairs . . .

Ready to lift, mankind's future rising to the stars, but my focus now was on a single white-blond head.

Steady.

No Piotr to help me this time: the responsibility was mine alone.

Breathe in . . .

Lift off.

Even from here, the roar was deafening. Onlookers' cheers lost amid the hyperagon's thunderous rising.

And hold.

Centered.

It was, I admit it, a triumph for humankind. The first step in our species' fundamental destiny.

Hold . . .

Focus: face, hair, blond-white.

No mistaking the features.

And squeeze.

For Laura.

Turning away, as the speeding silver dragon arced higher, higher on its tail of fire, diminished in the azure sky, was gone.

Acid bubbling: self-destruct dissolved the rifle.

It's over now, my love.

I turned upon the sand-choked grass, and walked away.

JAILWISE

by Lucius Shepard

Lucius Shepard was easily the most prolific and consistently impressive short story writer of 2003. After returning from a self-described career "pause"—between 1992 and 1997 he published only a handful of stories—Shepard has delivered a series of major short stories, starting with "Crocodile Rock" in 1999, followed by the Hugo Award-winner "Radiant Green Star" in 2000, and culminating in the nearly 300,000 words of short fiction published this year. He had major stories in Asimov's, SciFiction, Polyphony, The Third Alternative, *and* The Dark, *a number of which were serious contenders for this volume, and his latest books are the novels* Colonel Rutherford's Colt *and* Floater, *an International Horror Guild Award nominee. Forthcoming are the novels* A Handbook of American Prayer *and* Viator, *a major new collection,* Trujillo, *and a shorter collection,* Two Trains Running.*

Shepard is an intensely romantic writer, and his work has always focused on how we see the world around us. The powerful look into the world of incarceration that follows says as much about freedom as it does about its lack.

DURING MY ADOLESCENCE, DESPITE being exposed to television documentaries depicting men wearing ponytails and wife-beater undershirts, their weightlifter chests and arms spangled with homemade tattoos, any mention of prison always brought to my mind a less vainglorious type of criminal, an image derived, I believe, from characters in the old black-and-white movies that prior to the advent of the infomercial tended to dominate television's early morning hours: smallish, gray-looking men in work shirts and loose-fitting trousers, miscreants who—although oppressed by screws and wardens, victimized by their fellows—

managed to express, however inarticulately, a noble endurance, a working-class vitality and poetry of soul. Without understanding anything else, I seemed to understand their crippled honor, their Boy Scout cunning, their Legionnaire's willingness to suffer. I felt in them the workings of a desolate beatitude, some secret virtue of insularity whose potentials they alone had mastered.

Nothing in my experience intimated that such men now or ever had existed as other than a fiction, yet they embodied a principle of anonymity that spoke to my sense of style, and so when I entered the carceral system at the age of fifteen, my parents having concluded that a night or two spent in the county lock-up might address my aggressive tendencies, I strived to present a sturdy, unglamorous presence among the mesomorphs, the skin artists, and the flamboyantly hirsute. During my first real stretch, a deuce in minimum security for Possession With Intent, I lifted no weights and adopted no yard name. Though I wore a serpent-shaped earring, a gift from a girlfriend, I indulged in no further self-decoration. I neither swaggered nor skulked, but went from cell to dining hall to my prison job with the unhurried deliberation of an ordinary man engaged upon his daily business, and I resisted, thanks to my hostility toward every sort of authority, therapy sessions designed to turn me inward, to coerce an analysis of the family difficulties and street pressures that had nourished my criminality, with the idea of liberating me from my past. At the time I might have told you that my resistance was instinctive. Psychiatrists and therapy: these things were articles of fashion, not implements of truth, and my spirit rejected them as impure. Today, however, years down the line from those immature judgments, I suspect my reaction was partially inspired by a sense that any revelation yielded by therapy would be irrelevant to the question, and that I already knew in my bones what I now know pit to pole: I was born to this order.

While I was down in Vacaville, two years into a nickel for armed robbery, I committed the offense that got me sent to Diamond Bar. What happened was this. They had me out spraying the bean fields, dressed in protective gear so full of holes that each day when I was done I would puke and sweat as if I had been granted a reprieve and yanked from the gas chamber with my lungs half full of death. One afternoon I was sitting by the access road, goggles around my neck, tank of poison strapped to my shoulders, waiting for the prison truck, when an old Volkswagen bus rattled up from the main gate and stopped. On the sliding panel was a detail from a still life by Caravaggio, a rotting pear lopsided on a silver tray; on the passenger door, a pair of cherubs by Titian. Other images, all elements of famous Italian paintings, adorned the roof, front, and rear. The driver peered down at me. A dried-up, sixtyish man in a work shirt, balding, with a mottled scalp, a hooked nose, and a gray beard bibbing his chest. A blue-collar Jehovah. "You sick?" he asked, and waggled a cell phone. "Should I call somebody?"

"Fuck are you?" I asked. "The Art Fairy?"

"Frank Ristelli," he said without resentment. "I teach a class in painting and sculpture every Wednesday."

"Those who can't, teach . . . huh?"

A patient look. "Why would you say that?"

"'Cause the perspective on your Titian's totally fucked."

"It's good enough for you to recognize. How do you know Titian?"

"I studied painting in college. Two years. People in the department thought I was going to be a hot-shit artist."

"Guess you fooled them, huh?"

He was mocking me, but I was too worn out to care. "All that college pussy," I said. "I couldn't stay focused."

"And you had places to rob, people to shoot. Right?"

That kindled my anger, but I said nothing. I wondered why he was hanging around, what he wanted of me.

"Have you kept it up? You been drawing?"

"I mess around some."

"If you'd like, I'd be glad to take a look. Why don't you bring me what you've been doing next Wednesday?"

I shrugged. "Sure, yeah. I can do that."

"I'll need your name if I'm going to hook you up with a pass."

"Tommy Penhaligon," I said.

Ristelli wrote it down on a note pad. "Okay . . . Tommy. Catch you Wednesday." With that, he put the van in gear and rattled off to the land of the free, his pluming exhaust obscuring my view of the detail from a Piero della Francesca painted on the rear.

Of course, I had done no drawing for years, but I sensed in Ristelli the potential for a sweet hustle. Nothing solid, but you develop a nose for these things. With this in mind, I spent the following week sketching a roach—likely it was several different roaches, but I preferred to think of it as a brother inmate with a felonious history similar to my own. I drew that roach to death, rendering him in a variety of styles ranging from realism to caricature. I ennobled him, imbued him with charisma, invoked his humble, self-abnegatory nature. I made him into an avatar among roaches, a roach with a mission. I crucified him and portrayed him distributing Oreo crumbs to the faithful. I gave him my face, the face of a guard to whom I had a particular aversion, the faces of several friends, including that of Carl Dimassio, who supplied the crank that kept me working straight through the nights. I taped the drawings on the wall and chuckled with delight, amazed by my cleverness. On the night before Ristelli's class, so wasted that I saw myself as a tragic figure, a savage with the soul of an artist, I set about creating a violent self-portrait, a hunched figure half buried in blackness, illuminated by a spill of lamplight, curled around my sketch pad like a slug about a leaf, with a harrowed face full of weakness and delirium, a construction of crude strokes and charred, glaring eyes, like the face of a murderer who has just understood the consequences of his act. It bore only a slight resemblance to me, but it impressed Ristelli.

"This is very strong," he said of the self-portrait. "The rest of them"—he gestured at the roach drawings—"they're good cartoons. But this is the truth."

Rather than affecting the heightened stoicism that convicts tend to assume when they wish to demonstrate that they have not been emotionally encouraged, I reacted as might a prisoner in one of the movies that had shaped my expectations of prison, and said with boyish wonderment, "Yeah . . . you think?," intending by this to ruffle the sensibilities of Ristelli's inmate assistant, a fat, ponytailed biker named Marion Truesdale, aka Pork, whose arms were inked with blue, circusy designs, the most prominent being a voluptuous naked woman with the head of a demon, and whose class work, albeit competent, tended to mirror the derivative fantasy world of his body art. In the look that passed between us then was all I needed to know about the situation: Pork was telling me that he had staked out Ristelli and I should back the fuck off. But rather than heeding the warning, I concentrated on becoming Ristelli's star pupil, the golden apple in a barrel of rotten ones. Over the next months, devoting myself to the refinement of my gift, I succeeded to such a degree that he started keeping me after class to talk, while Pork—his anger fermenting—cleaned palette knives and brushes.

Much of what I said to Ristelli during that time was designed to persuade him of the deprivation I faced, the lack of stimulation that was neutering my artistic spirit, all with an eye toward convincing him to do a little smuggling for me. Though he sympathized with my complaints, he gave no sign that he was ripe to be conned. He would often maneuver our conversation into theoretical or philosophical directions, and not merely as related to art. It seemed he considered himself my mentor and was attempting to prepare me for a vague future in which I would live, if not totally free, then at least unconstrained by spiritual fetters. One day when I described myself in passing as having lived outside the law, he said, "That's simply not so. The criminal stands at the absolute heart of the law."

He was perched on a corner of an old scarred desk jammed into the rear of the art room, nearly hidden by the folded easels leaning against it, and I was sitting with my legs stretched out in a folding chair against the opposite wall, smoking one of Ristelli's Camels. Pork stood at the sink, rinsing brushes in linseed oil, shoulders hunched, radiating enmity, like a sullen child forbidden the company of his elders.

"'Cause we're inside?" I asked. "That what you're saying?"

"I'm talking about criminals, not just prisoners," Ristelli said. "The criminal is the basis for the law. Its inspiration, its justification. And ultimately, of course, its victim. At least in the view of society."

"How the hell else can you view it?"

"Some might see incarceration as an opportunity to learn

criminal skills. To network. Perhaps they'd rather be elsewhere, but they're inside, so they take advantage. But they only take partial advantage. They don't understand the true nature of the opportunity."

I was about to ask for an explanation of this last statement, but Pork chose the moment to ask Ristelli if he needed any canvases stretched.

Ristelli said, "Why don't you call it a day. I'll see you next week."

Aiming a bleak look in my direction, Pork said, "Yeah . . . all right," and shambled out into the corridor.

"The criminal and what he emblematizes," Ristelli went on. "The beast. Madness. The unpredictable. He's the reason society exists. Thus the prison system is the central element of society. Its defining constituency. Its model." He tapped a cigarette out of his pack and made a twirling gesture with it. "Who runs this place?"

"Vacaville? Fucking warden."

"The warden!" Ristelli scoffed at the notion. "He and the guards are there to handle emergencies. To maintain order. They're like the government. Except they have much less control than the President and the Congress. No taxes, no regulations. None that matter, anyway. They don't care what you do, so long as you keep it quiet. Day to day it's cons who run the prisons. There are those who think a man's freer inside than out in the world."

"You sound like an old lifer."

Bemused, Ristelli hung the cigarette from his lower lip, lit up and let smoke flow out from his mouth and nostrils.

"Fuck you know about it, anyway?" I said. "You're a free man."

"You haven't been listening."

"I know I should be hanging on your every goddamn word. Just sometimes it gets a little deep, y'know." I pinched the coal off the tip of the Camel and pocketed the butt. "What about the death penalty, man? If we're running things, how come we let 'em do that shit?"

"Murderers and the innocent," Ristelli said. "The system tolerates neither."

It seemed I understood these words, but I could not abide the thought that Ristelli's bullshit was getting to me, and instead of pursuing the matter, I told him I had things to do and returned to my cell.

I had been working on a series of portraits in charcoal and pastel that depicted my fellow students in contemplative poses, their brutish faces transfigured by the consideration of some painterly problem, and the next week after class, when Ristelli reviewed my progress, he made mention of the fact that I had neglected to include their tattoos. Arms and necks inscribed with barbed-wire bracelets, lightning bolts, swastikas, dragons, madonnas, skulls; faces etched with Old English script and dripping with black tears—in my drawings they were unadorned, the muscles cleanly rendered so as not to detract from the fraudulent saintliness I was attempting to convey. Ristelli asked what I was trying for, and I said, "It's a joke, man. I'm turning these mutts into philosopher-kings."

"Royalty have been known to wear tattoos. The kings of Samoa, for instance."

"Whatever."

"You don't like tattoos?"

"I'd sooner put a bone through my nose."

Ristelli began unbuttoning his shirt. "See what you think of this one."

"That's okay," I said, suspecting now Ristelli's interest in my talent had been prelude to a homosexual seduction; but he was already laying bare his bony chest. Just above his right nipple, a bit off-center, was a glowing valentine heart, pale rose, with a gold banner entangling its pointy base, and on the banner were words etched in dark blue: The Heart Of The Law. The colors were so soft and pure, the design so simple, it seemed—despite its contrast to Ristelli's pallid skin—a natural thing, as if chance had arranged certain inborn discolorations into a comprehensible pattern; but at that moment I was less aware of its artistic virtues than of the message it bore, words that brought to mind what Ristelli had told me a few days before.

"The heart of the law," I said. "This mean you done crime? You're a criminal?"

"You might say I do nothing else."

"Oh, yeah! You're one of the Evil Masters. Where'd you get the tattoo?"

"A place called Diamond Bar."

The only Diamond Bar I'd heard of was a section of L.A. populated mainly by Asians, but Ristelli told me it was also the name of a prison in northern California where he had spent a number of years. He claimed to be among the few ever to leave the place.

"It's unlikely you've met anyone who's done time there," he said. "Until now, that is. Not many are aware of its existence."

"So it's a supermax? Like Pelican Bay? The hell you do to get put someplace like that?"

"I was a fool. Like you, stupidity was my crime. But I was no longer a fool when I left Diamond Bar."

There was in his voice an evangelical tremor, as if he were hearkening back to the memory of God and not a prison cell. I'd come to realize he was a strange sort, and I wondered if the reason he had been released might be due to some instability developed during his sentence. He started to button his shirt, and I studied the tattoo again.

"Doesn't look like a jailhouse tat . . . 'least none I ever saw," I said. "Doesn't even look like ink, the colors are so clean."

"The colors come from within," Ristelli said with the pious aplomb of a preacher quoting a soothing text. "There are no jails."

That conversation stayed with me. If Ristelli was not certifiably a wacko, I assumed he was well along the road; yet while he had given me no concrete information about Diamond Bar, the commingling of passion and firmness in his voice when he spoke of the place seemed evidence not of an unbalanced mind but of profound calm, as if it arose from a pivotal certainty bred in a quieter emotional climate than were most prison-bred fanaticisms. I believed everything he said was intended to produce an effect, but his motives did not concern me. The idea that he was trying to manipulate me for whatever purpose implied that he needed something from me, and this being the case, I thought it might be an opportune time to make my needs known to him.

I assumed that Pork understood how the relationship

between Ristelli and me was developing. To discourage him from lashing out at me, I hired a large and scarily violent felon by the name of Rudy Wismer to watch my back in the yard, at meals, and on the block, paying for his services with a supply of the X-rated Japanese comics that were his sexual candy. I felt confident that Wismer's reputation would give Pork pause—my bodyguard's most recent victim, a bouncer in a Sacramento nightclub, had testified at trial wearing a mask that disguised the ongoing reconstruction of his facial features; but on the Wednesday following our discussion of tattoos, Ristelli took sick midway through class and was forced to seek medical attention, leaving Pork and me alone in the art room, the one place where Wismer could not accompany me. We went about our cleaning chores in different quarters of the room; we did not speak, but I was aware of his growing anger, and when finally, without overt warning, he assaulted me, I eluded his initial rush and made for the door, only to find it locked and two guards grinning at me through the safety glass.

Pork caught hold of my collar, but I twisted away, and for a minute or so I darted and ducked and feinted as he lumbered after me, splintering easels, scattering palettes and brushes, tromping tubes of paint, overturning file cabinets. Before long, every obstacle in the room had been flattened and, winded, I allowed myself to be cornered against the sink. Pork advanced on me, his arms outspread, swollen cheeks reddened by exertion, huffing like a hog in heat. I prepared for a last and likely ineffective resistance, certain that I was about to take a significant beating. Then, as Pork lunged, his front foot skidded in the paint oozing from a crushed tube of cadmium orange, sending him pitching forward, coming in too low; at the same time, I brought my knee up, intending to strike his groin but landing squarely on his face. I felt his teeth go and heard the cartilage in his nose snap. Moaning, he rolled onto his back. Blood bubbled from his nostrils and mouth, matted his beard. I ignored the guards, who now were shouting and fumbling for their keys, and, acting out of a cold, pragmatic fury, I stood over Pork and smashed his kneecaps with my heel, ensuring that for the remainder of his prison life he would occupy a substantially diminished rank in the food chain. When the guards burst into the room, feeling charmed, blessed by chance, immune to fate, I said, "You assholes betting on this? Did I cost you money? I fucking hope so!" Then I dropped to the floor and curled into a ball and waited for their sticks to come singing through the air.

Six days later, against all regulation, Frank Ristelli visited me in the isolation block. I asked how he had managed this, and dropping into his yardbird Zen mode, he said, "I knew the way." He inquired after my health—the guards had rapped me around more than was usual—and after I assured him nothing was broken, he said, "I have good news. You're being transferred to Diamond Bar."

This hardly struck me as good news. I understood how to survive in Vacaville, and the prospect of having to learn the ropes of a new and probably harsher prison was not appealing. I said as much to Ristelli. He was standing beneath the ceiling fixture in my cell, isolated from the shadows—thanks to the metal cage in which the bulb was secured—in a cone of pale light, making it appear that he had just beamed in from a higher plane, a gray saint sent to illumine my solitary darkness.

"You've blown your chance at parole," he said. "You'll have to do the whole stretch. But this is not a setback; it's an opportunity. We need men like you at Diamond Bar. The day I met you, I knew you'd be a candidate. I recommended your transfer myself."

I could not have told you which of these statements most astonished me, which most aroused my anger. "'We?' 'A candidate?' What're you talking about?"

"Don't be upset. There's . . ."

"You recommended me? Fuck does that mean? Who gives a shit what you recommend?"

"It's true, my recommendation bears little weight. These judgments are made by the board. Nevertheless, I feel I'm due some credit for bringing you to their attention."

Baffled by this and by his air of zoned sanctimony, I sat down on my bunk. "You made a recommendation to the Board of Prisons?"

"No, no! A higher authority. The board of Diamond Bar. Men who have achieved an extraordinary liberty."

I leaned back against the wall, controlling my agitation. "That's all you wanted to tell me? You could have written a letter."

Ristelli sat on the opposite end of the bunk, becoming a shadow beside me. "When you reach Diamond Bar, you won't know what to do. There are no rules. No regulations of any sort. None but the rule of brotherhood, which is implicit to the place. At times the board is compelled to impose punishment, but their decisions are based not on written law, but upon a comprehension of specific acts and their effect upon the population. Your instincts have brought you this far along the path, so put your trust in them. They'll be your only guide."

"Know what my instincts are right now? To bust your goddamn head." Ristelli began to speak, but I cut him off. "No, man! You feed me this let-your-conscience-be-your-guide bullshit, and . . ."

"Not your conscience. Your instincts."

"You feed me this total fucking bullshit, and all I can think is, based on your recommendation, I'm being sent to walls where you say hardly anybody ever gets out of 'em." I prodded Ristelli's chest with a forefinger. "You tell me something'll do me some good up there!"

"I can't give you anything of the sort. Diamond Bar's not like Vacaville. There's no correlation between them."

"Are you psycho? That what this is? You're fucking nuts? Or you're blowing somebody lets your ass wander around in here and act like some kinda smacked-out Mother Teresa? Give me a name. Somebody can watch out for me when I get there."

"I wish I could help you more, but each man must find his own freedom." Ristelli came to his feet. "I envy you."

"Yeah? So why not come with me? Guy with your pull should be able to wangle himself a ride-along."

"That is not my fate, though I return there every day and every night in spirit." His eyes glistened. "Listen to me, Tommy. You're going to a place few will ever experience. A place removed from the world yet bound to it by a subtle connectivity. The decisions made by those in charge for the benefit of the population enter the consciousness of the general culture and come to govern the decisions made by kings and presidents and despots. By influencing the rule of law, they manipulate the shape of history and redefine cultural possibility."

"They're doing a hell of a job," I said. "World's in great god-damn shape these days."

"Diamond Bar has only recently come to primacy. The new millennium will prove the wisdom of the board. And you have an opportunity to become part of that wisdom, Tommy. You have an uncommon sensibility, one that can illustrate the process of the place, give it visual form, and this will permit those who fol-low in your path to have a clearer understanding of their purpose and their truth. Your work will save them from the missteps that you will surely make." Ristelli's voice trembled with emotion. "I realize you can't accept what I'm saying. Perhaps you never will. I see in you a deep skepticism that prevents you from finding peace. But accomplishment . . . that you can aspire to, and through accomplishment you may gain a coin of greater worth. Devote yourself to whatever you choose to do. Through devotion all avenues become open to the soul. Serve your ambition in the way a priest serves his divinity, and you will break the chains that weigh down your spirit."

On my first night in jail, at the age of fifteen, a Mexican kid came over to where I was standing by myself in the day room, trying to hide behind an arrogant pose, and asked if I was jailwise. Not wanting to appear inexperienced, I said that I was, but the Mexican, obviously convinced that I was not, proceeded to enlighten me. Among other things, he advised me to hang with my own kind (i.e., race) or else when trouble occurred no one would have my back, and he explained the diplomatic niceties of the racial divide, saying that whenever another white man offered to give me five, flesh-to-flesh contact was permitted, but should a Latino, an Asian, an Arab, an Afro-American, or any darkly hued member of the human troupe offer a similar encour-agement, I was to take out my prison ID card and with it tap the other man's fingertips. In every jail and prison where I did time, I received a similar indoctrination lecture from a stranger with whom I would never interact again. It was as if the system itself urged someone forward, stimulating them by means of some improbable circuitry to volunteer the fundamentals of survival specific to the place. Ristelli's version was by far the most unhelpful I had ever heard, yet I did not doubt that his addled sermonette was an incarnation of that very lecture. And because of this; because I had so little information about the prison apart from Ristelli's prattle; because I believed it must be a new style of supermax whose powers of spiritual deprivation were so ferocious, it ate everything it swallowed except for a handful of indigestible and irretrievably damaged fragments like Ristelli; for these reasons and more I greatly feared what might happen when I was brought to Diamond Bar.

The gray van that transported me from Vacaville seemed representative of the gray strangeness that I believed awaited me, and I constructed the mental image of a secret labyrinthine vastness, a Kafkaville of brick and steel, a partially subterranean complex like the supermax in Florence, Colorado, where Timothy McVeigh, Carlos Escobar, and John Gotti had been held; but as we crested a hill on a blue highway south of Mount Shasta, a road that wound through a forest of old-growth spruce and fir, I caught sight of a sprawling granite structure saddling the ridge ahead, looking ominously medieval with its guard turrets and age-blackened stone and high, rough-hewn walls, and my mental image of the prison morphed into more Gothic lines—I pictured dungeons, archaic torments, a massive warden with a bald head the size of a bucket, filed teeth, and a zero tattooed on his brow.

The road angled to the left, and I saw an annex jutting from one side of the prison, a windowless construction almost as high as the main walls, also of weathered granite, that followed the slope of the ridge downward, its nether reach hidden by the forest. We passed in among the ranked trees, over a rattling bridge and along the banks of a fast-flowing river whose waters ran a mineral green through the calm stretches, cold and clouded as poison in a trough, then foamed and seethed over thumblike boulders. Soon the entrance to the annex became visible on the opposite shore: iron doors enclosed by a granite arch and guarded by grandfather firs. The van pulled up, the rear door swung open. When it became apparent that the driver did not intend to stir himself, I climbed out and stood on the bank, gazing toward my future. The ancient stones of the annex were such a bleak corruption of the natural, they seemed to presage an imponderable darkness within, like a gate that when opened would prove the threshold of a gloomy Druid enchantment, and this, in conjunction with the solitude and the deafening rush of the river, made me feel daunted and small. The engine of the van kicked over, and the amplified voice of the driver, a mystery behind smoked windows, issued from a speaker atop the roof: "You have ten minutes to cross the river!" Then the van rolled away, gathering speed, and was gone.

At Vacaville I had been handcuffed but not shackled, not the normal procedure, and left alone now I had the urge to run; but I was certain that invisible weapons were trained on me and thought this must be a test or the initial stage in a psychological harrowing designed to reduce me to a Ristelli-like condition. Cautiously, I stepped onto a flat stone just out from the bank, the first of about forty such stones that together formed a perilous footbridge, and began the crossing. Several times, besieged by a surge of water, a damp gust of wind, I slipped and nearly fell—to this day I do not know if anyone would have come to my rescue. Teetering and wobbling, fighting for balance, to a casual observer I would have presented the image of a convict making a desperate break for freedom. Eventually, my legs trembling from the effort, I reached the shore and walked up the shingle toward the annex. The building terminated, as I've said, in an arch of pitted stone, its curve as simple as that of a sewer tunnel, and chiseled upon it was not, as might have been expected, Abandon Hope All Ye Who Enter Here or some equally dispiriting legend, but a single word that seemed in context even more threatening: WELCOME. The iron doors were dappled with orange patches of corrosion, the separate plates stitched by rows of large rivets whose heads had the shape of nine-pointed stars. There was no sign of a knocker, a bell, or any alarm I might engage in order to announce myself. Once again I gave thought to running, but before I could act on the impulse, the doors swung silently inward, and, moved less by will than by the gravity of the dimness beyond, I stepped inside.

My first impression of Diamond Bar was of a quiet so deep and impacted, I imagined that a shout, such as I was tempted to vent, would have the value of a whisper. The light had a dull golden cast and a grainy quality, as if mixed in with particles of gloom, and the smell, while it plainly was that of a cleaning agent, did not have the astringency of an industrial cleaner. The most curious thing, however, was that there were no administrative personnel, no guards, no term of processing and orientation. Rather than being kept in isolation until it was determined to which block or unit I would be assigned, on passing through the annex door I entered the population of the prison like a pilgrim into a temple hall. The corridor ran straight, broken every fifty yards or so by a short stairway, and was lined with tiers of cells, old-fashioned cribs with sliding gates and steel bars, most of them unoccupied, and in those that were occupied, men sat reading, wall-gazing, watching television. None of them displayed other than a casual interest in me, this a far cry from the gauntlet of stares and taunts I had run when I entered the population at Vacaville. Absent the customary rites of passage, undirected, I kept going forward, thinking that I would sooner or later encounter an official who would inscribe my name or open a computer file or in some other fashion notate my arrival. As I ascended the fourth stairway, I glimpsed a man wearing what looked to be a guard's cap and uniform standing at parade rest on the tier above. I stopped, expecting him to hail me, but his eyes passed over me, and without saying a word, he ambled away.

By the time I reached the sixth stairway, I estimated that I had walked approximately two-thirds the length of the annex, climbed two-thirds the height of the hill atop which the walls of the prison rested; and though I held out hope that there I might find some semblance of authority, I decided to ask for assistance and approached a lanky, pot-bellied man with a pinkish dome of a scalp that caused his head to resemble a lightly worn pencil eraser, an illusion assisted by his tiny eyes and otherwise negligible features. He was sitting in a cell to the right of the stairs, wearing—as was everyone within view—gray trousers and a shirt to match. He glanced up as I came near, scowled at me, and set down the notebook in which he had been writing. The gate to his cell was halfway open, and I took a stand well back from it, anticipating that his mood might escalate.

"Hey, brother," I said. "What's up with this place? Nobody signs you in and shit?"

The man studied me a moment, screwed the cap onto his pen. On the backs of his fingers were faint inky tracings, the ghosts of old tattoos. The precision of his movements conveyed a degree of snippishness, but when he spoke his voice was calm, free of attitude. "'Fraid I can't help you," he said.

I would have been on familiar ground if he had responded with a curse, a warning, or the fawning, fraudulent enthusiasm that would signal his perception of me as a mark, but this politely formal response met none of my expectations. "I'm not asking you to get involved, man. I just need to know where to go. I don't want to get my nuts busted for making a wrong turn."

The man's eyes fitted themselves to the wall of the cell; he seemed to be composing himself, as if I were an irritant whose presence he felt challenged to overcome. "Go wherever you want," he said. "Eventually you'll find something that suits you."

"Asshole!" I clanged my handcuffs against the bars. "Fuck you think you're talking to? I'm not some fucking fish!"

His face tightened, but he kept on staring at the wall. The interior of the cell had been painted a yellowish cream, and the wall was marred by discolorations and spots from which the paint had flaked away that altogether bore a slight resemblance to a line of trees rising from a pale ground. After a few seconds he appeared to become lost in contemplation of it. Some of the men in other cells on the ground tier had turned our way, yet none ventured to their doors, and I sensed no general animosity. I was accustomed to prisons filled with men on the lookout for breaks in the routine, any kind of action to color the monotony, and the abnormal silence and passivity of these men both intimidated and infuriated me. I took a circular stroll about the corridor, addressing the occupants of the cells with a sweeping stare, hating their mild, incurious faces, and said in a voice loud enough for all to hear, "What're you, a bunch of pussies? Where the hell I'm supposed to go?"

Some of the men resumed their quiet occupations, while others continued to watch, but no one answered, and the unanimity of their unresponsiveness, the peculiar density of the atmosphere their silence bred, played along my nerves. I thought I must have come to an asylum and not a prison, one abandoned by its keepers. I wanted to curse them further, but felt I would be slinging stones at a church steeple, so aloof and immune to judgment they seemed. Like old ladies lost in their knitting and their memory books, though not a man within sight looked any older than I. With a disrespectful, all-inclusive wave, I set out walking again, but someone behind me shouted "Bitch!" and I turned back. The baldheaded man had emerged from his cell and was glaring at me with his dime-sized eyes. He lifted his fist and struck down at the air, a spastic gesture of frustration. "Bitch!" he repeated. "Bitch . . . you bitch!" He took another babyish swipe at the air and hiccupped. He was, I saw, close to tears, his chin gone quivery. He stumbled forward a step, then performed a rigid half-turn and grasped the bars of his cell, pushing his face between—it appeared that he had forgotten that his gate was open. Many of the inmates had left their cells and were standing along the tiers, intent upon him—he covered his head with his hands, as if defending himself against the pressure of their gaze, and slumped to his knees. A broken keening escaped his lips. Trembling now, he sank onto his haunches. Shame and rage contended in his face, two tides rushing together, and the instant before he collapsed onto his side, he caught the race of one and said feebly and for a last time, "Bitch!"

Beyond the ninth stairway lay a deeply shadowed cellblock that had the musty, claustrophobic atmosphere of a catacomb. Walls of undressed stone set close together and mounted by iron stairs; the cells showing like cave mouths; dim white ceiling lights that had the radiant force of distant stars tucked into folds of black cloud. Fatigued and on edge, I was not up to exploring it. A cell stood open and untenanted just below the stairway, and deciding that my safest course would be to allow whoever was in charge to come to me, I entered it and sat down on the bunk. I was struck immediately by the quality of the mattress. Though it appeared to be the usual thin lumpy item, it was softer and more resilient than any prison mattress I had ever rested on. I stretched out on the bunk and found that the pillow was remarkably soft and firm. Closing my eyes, I let the quiet soothe me.

I must have been drowsing for several minutes when I heard a baritone voice say, "Penhaligon? That you, man?"

The voice had a familiar ring, and there was something familiar, too, about the lean, broad-shouldered man standing at the entrance to my cell. Framed by a heavy mass of greased-back hair, his face was narrow and long-jawed, with hollow cheeks, a bladed nose, and a full-lipped mouth. He might have been the love child of Elvis and the Wicked Witch of the West. I could not place him, but felt I should be wary.

He grunted out a laugh. "I can't look that different. Just shaved off the beard's all."

I recognized him then and sat up, alarmed.

"Don't get worked up. I'm not gonna fuck with you." He perched on the end of the bunk, angling his eyes about the cell. "You want to put up a picture or two 'fore your wall comes in; they got pretty much any kind you want in the commissary."

There were questions I might have asked concerning both the essence and the rather housewifely character of this last statement, but during my first month in minimum security, Richard Causey, then doing an eight-spot for manslaughter, had put me in the hospital for the better part of a month with injuries resulting from a beating and attempted rape; thus his comments on interior decoration sailed right past me.

"I 'spect it's been a while since anybody took the walk you did," Causey said with a trace of admiration. "Straight up from the door all the way to eight? I never saw anyone do it, that's for sure." He clasped his hands on his stomach and settled back against the wall. "Took me a year to move up here from six."

All my muscles were tensed, but he merely sat there, amiable and at ease.

"Most everybody stops somewhere along the first few

blocks," Causey went on. "They don't feel comfortable proceeding on 'til they nail down a crib."

"Is that right?"

"Yeah, they feel kinda how you felt when you got to nine. Like you best stop and give things a chance to sort themselves out. It's the same with everybody, 'cept you got a lot farther than most."

Though I may have made a neutral noise in response, I was intent upon Causey's hands, the muscles in his shoulders.

"Look here," he said. "I understand what you're feeling, but I'm not the man I used to be. You want me to leave, that's cool. I just figured you'd want to talk. I know when I came here, all I wanted was somebody to talk to."

"I'm not the man I was, either," I said, injecting menace into my voice.

"Well, that's good. Takes a different man than both of us were to do time in Diamond Bar."

I was beginning to think that, truly, Causey might have changed. No longer did he give off the hostile radiation that once he had, and his speech, formerly characterized by bursts of profanity commingled with butchered elisions, was now measured and considered by contrast. His manner was composed and the tattoo of a red spider that had centered his brow was missing. "Just wore away, I guess," he said when I asked about it. He told me what he could about Diamond Bar but cautioned that the prison was not easily explained.

"This'll piss you off . . . 'least it did me," he said. "But can't anybody tell you how to work this place. Things come to you as you need 'em. There's a dining hall and a commissary, like everywhere else. But the food's a helluva lot better and you don't need money at the commissary. The board handles everything. Supplies, discipline, recreation. We don't have any guards. I don't . . ."

"I saw a guard when I was walking up."

"Everybody sees that guy, but I never heard about him whupping his stick onto anybody. Could be he does his thing so's to give people something familiar to look at."

"You saying he's an inmate?"

"Maybe. I don't know. There's a lot I haven't figured out about, but it's coming." He tapped his temple and grinned. "Best thing about the place is the plumes. You gonna love them."

"What the hell's that?"

"The queens who get you off down in Vacaville? The plumes put them away. You can't hardly tell the difference between them and a real woman."

Anxious to steer the conversation away from the sexual, I asked who I needed to watch out for and he said, "Guys down on the first three or four blocks . . . some of them been known to go off. They're transferred out or given punishment duty. Mostly you need to watch out for yourself. Make sure you don't screw up."

"If there's no guards, people must just walk on out of here."

Causey gave me a penetrating look. "You crossed the river, didn't you? You entered of your own free will?"

"I thought the guards were watching."

"Might have been somebody watching. I couldn't tell you. All I know is, you and me and everyone else, we chose to be here, so we're not talking about a prison full of hard-core escape artists. And Diamond Bar's not so bad. Truth is, it's the best I've had it in a while. People say it's going to be even better once they finish the new wing. Escaping crossed my mind a time or two when I was first here. But I had the feeling it wasn't such a good idea."

What Causey said made me no more certain of my estate, and after he returned to his cell I remained awake, staring at the mysterious reach of the old prison that lay beyond the ninth stair, the dim white lights and anthracitic cell mouths. Everything I knew about Diamond Bar was cornerless and unwieldy, of a shape that refused to fit the logic of prisons, and this gave me cause to wonder how much more unwieldy and ill-fitting were the things I did not know. I was accustomed to prison nights thronged with hoots, cries, whispers, complaints, screams, an uneasy consensus song like the nocturnal music of a rain forest, and the compressed silence of the place, broken intermittently by coughs and snores, inhibited thought. At length I slept fretfully, waking now and again from dreams of being chased, hunted, and accused to find the silence grown deeper, alien and horrid in its thickness. But toward dawn—one I sensed, not witnessed—I woke to an outcry that seemed to issue from beneath the old prison, such a prolonged release of breath it could only have been the product of awful torment or extreme exaltation . . . or else it was the cry of something not quite human, expressing a primitive emotion whose cause and color is not ours to know, a response to some new shape of fear or a tidal influence or a memory from before birth, and following this I heard a whispering, chittering noise that seemed to arise from every quarter, like the agitated, subdued congress of a crowd gathered for an event of great and solemn gravity. While that chorus lasted I was full of dread, but once it subsided, almost stricken with relief, I fell into a black sleep and did not wake again until the shadows, too, had waked and the first full day of my true incarceration had begun.

During those early months at Diamond Bar I came to understand the gist of what Ristelli, Causey, and the baldheaded man had tried to tell me. Eventually one found what was suitable. Things came to you. Trust your instincts. These statements proved to be not the vague, useless pronouncements I had assumed, but cogent practicalities, the central verities of the prison. Initially I behaved as I had during my early days at Vacaville. In the dining hall, an appropriately cavernous room of cream-colored walls, with the image of a great flying bird upon the ceiling, dark and unfigured, yet cleanly rendered like an emblem on a flag . . .

In the dining room, then, I guarded my tray with my free arm and glanced fiercely about as I ate, warning off potential food thieves. When I discovered that the commissary was, indeed, a free store, I took to hoarding cigarettes, candy, and soap. It was several days before I recognized the pointlessness of these behavioral twitches, several weeks before I grew comfortable enough to forego them. Though I was not a heavy drug user, on those occasions that I grew bored, prior to beginning my work, I had no difficulty in obtaining drugs—you only had to mention your requirements to one of several men and later that day the pills or the powder would appear in your cell. I have no idea what might have occurred if I had developed a habit, but I doubt this was a problem at the prison. It was clear that the men on my block were all either above average in intelligence or skilled in some craft or both, and that most had found a means of employing their gifts and skills that left no time for recreational excess. As to the men housed in the cellblocks below the eighth stairway and how they managed things—of them I knew little. The men of different blocks rarely mingled. But I was told that they had a less innate grasp of Diamond Bar's nature than did we. Consequently their day-to-day existence was more of a struggle to adapt. In time, if they were not transferred, they—like us—would move into the old wings of the prison.

It did not seem likely that anyone could have less firm a grasp on the subject of Diamond Bar than I did, but I adapted quickly, learned my way around, and soon became conversant with a theory espoused by the majority of the men on my block, which held that the prison was the ultimate expression of the carceral system, a mutation, an evolutionary leap forward both in terms of the system and the culture that they believed was modeled upon it. They did not claim to understand the specifics of how this mutation had been produced, but generally believed that a mystical conjunction of event (likely a systemic glitch, an alchemy of botched paperwork and inept bureaucracy), natural law, and cosmic intent had permitted the establishment and maintenance of a prison independent of the carceral system or—so said the true believers—one that acted through subtle manipulation to control both the system and the greater society whose backbone the system formed. Though this smacked of Ristelli's cant, it was not so easy to dismiss now that I saw Diamond Bar for myself. The absence of guards, of any traditional authority; the peculiar demeanor of the inmates; the comfortable beds, decent food and free commissary; the crossing of the river in lieu of ordinary official process; the man dressed as a guard whom everyone had seen and no one knew; the rapid fading of all tattoos; the disturbing dawn cry and the subsequent mutterings, a phenomenon repeated each and every morning—what could be responsible for all this if not some mystical agency? For my part, I thought the theory a fantasy and preferred another, less popular theory—that we were being subjected to an experimental form of mind control and that our keepers were hidden among us. Whenever these theories were discussed, and they were often discussed, Richard

Causey, who had studied political science at Duke University prior to turning to a career of violent crime and was writing a history of the prison, would declare that though he had his own ideas, the answer to this apparently unresolvable opposition resided with the board, but that thus far their responses to his inquiries concerning the matter had been inadequate.

The board consisted of four inmates ranging in age from sixtyish to over seventy. Holmes, Ashford, Czerny, and LeGary. They met each day in the yard to, it was said, decide the important questions relating to our lives and—if you bought into the view that Diamond Bar was the purest expression of a carceral universe, the irreducible distillate of the essential human condition—the lives of everyone on the planet. To reach the yard it was necessary to pass through the old wing of the prison visible beyond the eighth stairway, and though in the beginning I did not enjoy the passage, made anxious by the gloomy nineteenth-century atmosphere of the wing's antiquated cells with their key locks and hand-forged bars, and the masses of rotting stone in which they were set, I grew accustomed to the sight and came to view the old sections of the prison as places of unguessable potential—it was there, after all, that I would someday live if I stayed at Diamond Bar. As I've noted, the prison straddled a ridge—the spine of the ridge ran straight down the middle of the yard. Most of the population would gather close to the walls or sit on the slopes, which had been worn barren by countless footsteps, but the members of the board met among the grass and shrubs that flourished atop the ridge, this narrow strip of vegetation giving the enclosed land the look of a giant's scalp pushing up from beneath the earth, one whose green hair had been trimmed into a ragged Mohawk. Rising beyond the west wall, several iron girders were visible, evidence of the new wing that was under construction. The new wing was frequently referenced in conversation as being the panacea for whatever problems existed in our relatively problem-free environment—it seemed an article of faith that prison life would therein be perfected. Again, this struck me as fiction disseminated by whoever was manipulating our fates.

Late one afternoon some four months after my arrival, myself and Causey—toward whom I had succeeded in developing a neutral attitude—and Terry Berbick, a short, thickset bank robber with a gnomish look, his curly black hair and beard shot through with gray, were sitting against the east wall in the yard, discussing the newcomer on our block, Harry Colangelo—this happened to be the baldheaded man whom I had confronted on the day I came to the prison. His furtive air and incoherent verbal outbursts had made a poor impression, and Berbick was of the opinion that Colangelo's move onto the block had been premature.

"Something confused the boy. Caught him at a crucial moment during his period of adjustment and he's never gotten squared away." Berbick glanced at me. "Might be that dust-up with you did the trick."

"It wasn't that big a deal."

"I don't know. Way he stares at you, seems like you got under his skin. It might be why he moved up to eight—so he can come back at you easier."

"I've seen it before," Causey said. "Something happens early on to fuck up a man's instincts, and next you know he goes to acting all haywire. Gets his ass transferred right out on outa here."

I was not certain that being transferred out of Diamond Bar was the bleak prospect that Causey and Berbick thought it, but saw no need to argue the point.

"There the fucker is." Causey pointed to the slope on our left, where Colangelo was moving crabwise down the ridge, his pink scalp agleam with the westering sun, eyes fixed upon us. "I think Terry nailed it. The man's all messed up behind you."

"Whatever." I turned my attention to the four old men who purportedly ruled the world. Doddering on their height, the wind flying their sparse hair up into wild frays. Behind them, the tops of the girders burned gold, like iron candles touched with holy fire. Several younger men stood near the four. When I asked who they were, Berbick said they spoke for the board.

"What?" I said. "The Masters of the Universe can't talk for themselves?"

Berbick rolled up to his feet, smartly dusted the seat of his trousers, acting pissed-off. "You want to find out about the board, let's go see them."

I looked at him with amusement.

"You act like you know something," he said. "But you don't know as much as we do. And we don't know dip."

"Ain't nothing," I said. "Forget it."

"Nothing bad'll happen. We'll go with you." He glanced at Causey. "Right?"

Causey shrugged. "Sure."

Berbick arched an eyebrow and said to me in a taunting voice, "It's just four old guys, Tommy. Come on!"

Colangelo, who had been sitting upslope and to the left of us, scrambled up and hurried out of our path as we climbed the ridge.

"Fucking freak!" said Berbick as we drew abreast of him.

The board members were standing in a semicircle just below the highest point of the ridge, which was tufted with two roughly globular, almost identically puny shrubs, so sparsely leaved that from a distance, seen against the backdrop of the stone wall, they looked like the models of two small planets with dark gray oceans and island continents of green. The steadfastness with which the board was contemplating them gave rise to the impression that they were considering emigration to one or the other. Drawing near, I saw that the oldest among them, Czerny, appeared to be speaking, and the others, their eyes wandering, did not appear to be listening. Holmes, a shrunken black man, bald except for puffs of cottony hair above his ears and behind his neck, was shifting his feet restlessly, and the other two, Ashford and LeGary, both grandfather-gray and gaunt, were posed in vacant attitudes. One of the younger men who shadowed them, a stocky Latino in his forties, blocked our path, politely asked what we wanted, and Berbick jerked his thumb toward me and said, "Penhaligon here wants to meet the board."

"I don't want to meet them," I said, annoyed. "I was just wondering about them."

"They're busy," the Latino said. "But I'll see."

"You trying to fuck me over?" I asked Berbick as the Latino man went to consult with the board.

He looked pleased with himself. "What could happen? It's only four old guys."

"Nothing to worry about," Causey said. "He's just giving you shit."

"I don't need you interpreting for me, okay?" I said. "You can quit acting like my fucking big sister."

"Damn!" said Berbick with surprise. "He's coming over."

With the Latino holding his elbow, Czerny was heading toward us, shuffling through the ankle-high grasses, wobbly and frail. His caved-in face was freckled with liver spots, and the tip of his tongue flicked out with lizardly insistence. He was small, no more than five feet five, but his hands were those of a much larger man, wide and thick-fingered, with prominent knuckles—they trembled now, but looked as if they had been used violently during his youth. His eyes were a watery grayish blue, the sclera laced with broken vessels, and the right one had a cloudy cast. When he reached us, he extended a hand and gave my forearm a tentative three-fingered pat, like the benediction of a senile pope who had forgotten the proper form. He mumbled something, barely a whisper. The Latino man gave ear, and when Czerny had finished, he said, "There's important work for you here, Penhaligon. You should set about it quickly."

It did not seem that Czerny had spoken long enough to convey this much information. I suspected that the Latino man and his associates were running a hustle, pretending to interpret the maunderings of four senile old men and in the process guaranteeing a soft life for themselves.

Czerny muttered something more, and the Latino said, "Come visit me in my house whenever you wish."

The old man assayed a faltering smile; the Latino steadied him as he turned and, with reverent tenderness, led him back to join the others. I framed a sarcastic comment but was stopped by Causey's astonished expression. "What's going on?" I asked.

"Man invited you to his house," Causey said with an air of disbelief.

"Yeah . . . so?"

"That doesn't happen too often."

"I been here almost five years, and I don't remember it ever happening," Berbick said.

I glanced back and forth between them. "Wasn't him invited me, it was his fucking handler."

Berbick made a disdainful noise, shook his head as if he

couldn't fathom my stupidity, and Causey said, "Maybe when you go see him, you'll . . ."

"Why the fuck would I go see him? So I can get groped by some old wheeze?"

"I guess you got better things to do," Berbick said. He was acting pissed-off again, and I said, "What crawled up your ass, man?"

He started to step to me, but Causey moved between us, poked me in the chest with two fingers and said, "You little hump! You walk straight up to eight from the door . . . You don't seem to appreciate what that means. Frank Czerny invites you to his house and you ridicule the man. I been trying to help you . . ."

"I don't want your help, faggot!"

I recognized Causey's humorless smile as the same expression he had worn many years ago prior to ramming my head into a shower wall. I moved back a pace, but the smile faded and he said calmly, "Powers that be got something in mind for you, Penhaligon. That's plain to everyone 'cept you. Seems like you forgot everything you learned about surviving in prison. You don't come to new walls with an attitude. You pay attention to how things are and behave accordingly. Doesn't matter you don't like it. You do what you hafta. I'm telling you, you don't get with the program, they gonna transfer your sorry ass."

I pretended to shudder.

"Man thinks he's a hardass," said Berbick, who was gazing up at one of the guard turrets, an untenanted cupola atop a stone tower. "He doesn't know what hard is."

"Thing you oughta ask yourself," Causey said to me, "is where you gonna get transferred to."

He and Berbick started downslope, angling toward an unpopulated section of the east wall. Alone on the height, I was possessed by the paranoid suspicion that the groups of men huddled along the wall were all talking about me, but the only evidence that supported this was Colangelo, who was standing halfway down the slope to my right, some forty feet away, almost directly beneath the spot where the board was assembled. He was watching me intently, expectantly, as if anticipating that I might come at him. With his glowing scalp, his eyes pointed with gold, he had the look of a strange pink demon dressed in prison gray, and my usual disdain for him was supplanted by nervousness. As I descended from the ridge top, he took a parallel path, maintaining the distance between us, and though under ordinary circumstances I would have been tempted to challenge him, having alienated Causey and Berbick, knowing myself isolated, I picked up my pace and did not feel secure until I was back in my cell.

Over the next several days, I came to recognize that, as Causey had asserted, I had indeed forgotten the basics of survival, and that no matter how I felt about the board, about the nature of Diamond Bar, I would be well served to pay Czerny a visit. I put off doing so, however, for several days more. Though I would not have admitted it, I found the prospect of mounting the iron stair to the tier where Czerny lived intimidating—it appeared that in acknowledging the semblance of the old man's authority, I had to a degree accepted its reality. Sitting in my cell, staring up at the dim white lights beyond the ninth stair, I began to order what I knew of the prison, to seek in that newly ordered knowledge a logical underpinning that would, if not explain everything I had seen, at least provide a middle ground between the poles of faith and sophism. I repaired my relationship with Causey, a matter of simple apology, and from him I learned that the prison had been constructed in the 1850s and originally used to house men whose crimes were related in one way or another to the boomtowns of the Gold Rush. The Board of Prisons had decided to phase out Diamond Bar in the 1900s, and at this time, Causey believed, something had happened to transform a horrific place that few survived into the more genial habitation it had since become. He had unearthed from the library copies of communications between the Board of Prisons and the warden, a man named McCandless Quires, that documented the rescinding of the phase-out order and conferred autonomy upon the prison, with the idea that it should become a penal colony devoted to reha-bilitation rather than punishment. During that period, every level of society had been rife with reformers, and prison reform was much discussed. In light of this, such a change as Diamond Bar had undergone did not seem extraordinary; but the fact that it had been given to Quires to oversee the change: that smacked of the bizarre, for he had been frequently reprimanded by the Board for his abuses of prisoners. Indeed, it was the atrocities perpetrated during his stewardship that had induced the Board to consider the question of reform. It was reported that men had been impaled, flayed, torn apart by the prison dogs. Quires' letters demonstrated that he had undergone a transformation. Prior to 1903, his tone in response to the Board's inquiries was defiant and blasphemous, but thereafter his letters displayed a rational, even a repentant character, and he continued to serve as warden until his retirement in 1917. There was no record of a replacement having been appointed, and Causey theorized that the board as we knew it had then come to power, though it was possible, given Quires' advanced age (88), that they had been running things for many years previously. From 1917 on, communications between Diamond Bar and the Board of Prisons steadily diminished, and in 1945, not long before VE Day, they apparently ceased altogether. It was as if the prison, for all intents and purposes, had become nonexistent in the eyes of the State.

Once Causey showed me a yellowed photograph he had unearthed from the prison archives. It had been shot in the yard on a sunny day in May of 1917—the date was inscribed on the back of the photo in a crabbed script—and it depicted a group of a woman and five men, four convicts, one of them black, and the last, an elderly man with white, windblown hair and a craggy, seamed face, clad in a dark suit and tie. Causey identified the elderly man as McCandless Quires, the warden. "And these here," he said, indicating the other four, "that's the board." He tapped each in turn. "Ashford, Czerny, LeGary, Holmes."

Judging by their faces, the men were all in their twenties. There was a rough similarity of feature between them and the old men who met each day in the yard, but the idea that they were one and the same seemed absurd.

"That's so, they'd all have to be more than a hundred," I said. "They're old, but not that old."

"Look at the shape of their heads," Causey said. "Their expressions. They all got that spacey smile. Look at Czerny's hands. See how big they are? It's them, all right."

"You need to take a breath, man. This isn't the fucking Magic Kingdom, this is prison we're talking about."

"This is Diamond Bar," he said sullenly. "And we don't know what the hell that is."

I studied the photograph more closely, concentrating on the woman. She was lovely, delicate of feature, with flowing blonde hair. Noticing my attentiveness, Causey said, "I believe that there's a plume. Quires didn't have no daughter, no wife, and she got the look of plume."

"What look is that?"

"Too perfect. Like she ain't a man or a woman, but something else entirely."

The photograph aside, what Causey told me lent a plausible historical context to the implausible reality of Diamond Bar, but the key ingredient of the spell that had worked an enchantment upon the prison was missing, and when at last I went to visit Czerny, I had retrenched somewhat and was content to lean upon my assumption that we knew nothing of our circumstance and that everything we thought we knew might well have been put forward to distract us from the truth. Climbing the stairs, passing meter after meter of stone, ash-black and broken like the walls of a mineshaft, I felt on edge. Up on the third tier, the ceiling lights shed a glow that had the quality of strong moonlight; the bars and railings were flaked with rust. Four prisoners were lounging against the railing outside Czerny's cell—the Latino who had spoken for him was not among them—and one, a long-limbed black man with processed hair, his sideburns and thin mustache giving his lean face a piratical look, separated from the rest and came toward me, frowning.

"You supposed to come a week ago and you just coming now?" he said. "That ain't how it goes, Penhaligon."

"He told me to come whenever I wanted."

"I don't care what he said. It's disrespectful."

"That kind of old school, isn't it?"

He looked perplexed.

"It's the kind of attitude you'd expect to find at Vacaville and San Q," I said. "Not at a forward-thinking joint like Diamond Bar."

The black man was about to speak, but turned back to the cell as Czerny shuffled onto the tier. I had no inclination to mock the old man. Surrounded by young men attentive as tigers, he seemed the source of their strength and not their ward. Though I did not truly credit this notion, when he beckoned, the slightest of gestures, I went to his side without hesitation. His eyes grazed mine, then wandered toward the dim vault beyond the railing. After a second, he shuffled back into the cell, indicating by another almost imperceptible gesture that I should follow.

A television set mounted on the wall was tuned to a dead channel, its speakers hissing, its screen filled with a patternless sleet of black, silver, and green. Czerny sat on his bunk, its sheets cream-colored and shiny like silk, and—since he did not invite me to sit—I took a position at the rear of the cell, resting a hand upon the wall. The surface of the wall was unusually smooth, and upon examining it I realized it was not granite but black marble worked with white veins that altogether formed a design of surpassing complexity.

During my first conversation with Causey, he had suggested I purchase some pictures from the commissary to decorate my cell "until your wall comes in." Though struck by this phrase, at the time my attention had been dominated by other concerns; but I had since discovered that once a cell was occupied, discolorations manifested on the wall facing the bunk, and these discolorations gradually produced intricate patterns reminiscent of the rock the Chinese call "picture stone," natural mineral abstractions in which an imaginative viewer could discern all manner of landscapes. The wall in my cell had begun to develop discolorations, their patterns as yet sparse and poorly defined; but Causey's wall, Berbick's, and others were fully realized. It was said these idiosyncratic designs were illustrative of the occupant's inner nature and, when reflected upon, acted to instruct the observer as to his flaws, his potentials, the character of his soul. None of them—at least none I had seen—compared to the elaborate grandeur of the one on Czerny's wall. Gazing at it, I traveled the labyrinthine streets of a fantastic city lined by buildings with spindly, spiny turrets and octagonal doorways; I explored the pathways of a white forest whose creatures were crowned with antlers that themselves formed other, even more intricate landscapes; I coursed along a black river whose banks were sublime constructions of crystal and ice, peopled by nymphs and angels with wings that dwarfed their snowy bodies like the wings of arctic butterflies. I cannot say how long I stared—quite a while, I believe, because my mouth was dry when I looked away—but from the experience I derived an impression of a convoluted, intensely spiritual intellect that warred with Czerny's drab, dysfunctional appearance. He was smiling daftly, eyes fixed on his hands, which were fidgeting in his lap, and I wondered if the audience was over, if I should leave. Then he spoke, muttering as he had out in the yard. This time I understood him perfectly, yet I am certain no intelligible word passed his lips.

"Do you see?" he asked. "Do you understand where you are now?"

I was so startled at having understood him, I could muster no reply.

He raised a hand, trailed his fingers across the bars of the gate, the sort of gesture a salesman might make to display the hang of a fabric. Assuming that he wanted me to inspect the bars, I stepped around him and bent to look at one. A bit less than halfway along its length the color and finish of the metal changed from rough and dark to a rich yellow. The join where the two colors met was seamless, and the yellow metal had an unmistakable soft luster and smoothness: gold. It was as if a luxuriant infection were spreading along the bar, along—I realized—all the bars of Czerny's cell.

I am not sure why this unsettled me more profoundly than the rest of the bizarre occurrences I'd met with at Diamond Bar. Perhaps it resonated with some gloomy fairy tale that had frightened me as a child or inflamed some even deeper wound to my imagination, for I had a sudden appreciation of Czerny as a wizardly figure, a shabby derelict who had revealed himself of an instant to be a creature of pure principle and power. I backed out of the cell, fetched up against the railing, only peripherally mindful of Czerny's attendants. The old man continued to smile, his gaze drifting here and there, centering briefly on my face, and in that broken muttering whose message I now comprehended as clearly as I might the orotund tones of a preacher ringing from a pulpit, he said, "You cannot retreat from the Heart of the Law, Penhaligon. You can let it illuminate you or you can fail it, but you cannot retreat. Bear this in mind."

That night as I lay in my cell, immersed in the quiet of the cell-block like a live coal at the heart of a diamond, growing ever more anxious at the thought of Czerny in his cell of gold and marble, an old mad king whose madness could kill, for I believed now he was the genius of the place . . . that night I determined I would escape. Despite the caution implicit in Czerny's final words, I knew I could never thrive there. I needed firm ground beneath my feet, not philosophy and magic or the illusion of magic. If I were to live bounded by walls and laws—as do we all—I wanted walls manned and topped with razor wire, written regulations, enemies I could see. Yet the apparent openness of the prison, its lack of visible security, did not fool me. Power did not exist without enforcement. I would have to ferret out the traps, learn their weaknesses, and in order to do that I needed to become part of the prison and pretend to embrace its ways.

My first step in this direction was to find an occupation, a meaningful activity that would convince whoever was watching that I had turned my mind onto acceptable avenues; since my only skill was at art, I began drawing once again. But making sketches, I realized, would not generate a *bona fide* of my submersion in the life of Diamond Bar; thus I undertook the creation of a mural, using for a canvas the walls and ceiling of an empty storeroom in one of the sub-basements. I chose as a theme the journey that had led me to the prison, incorporating images of the river crossing, of Frank Ristelli, the gray van, and so forth. The overall effect was more crazy quilt than a series of unified images, although I was pleased with certain elements of the design; but for all the attention it received, it might have rivaled Piero della Francesca. Men stopped by at every hour to watch me paint, and the members of the board, along with their entourages, were frequent visitors. Czerny took particular interest in my depiction of Ristelli; he would stand in front of the image for periods up to half an hour, addressing it with his customary vacant nods. When I asked one of his attendants the reason for his interest, I was told that Ristelli was revered for a great personal sacrifice made on behalf of us all and reflecting on the origins of our common home—he had been on the verge of being made a member of the board, but had forsworn the security and comfort of the prison and returned to the world in order to seek out men suitable for Diamond Bar.

Placing Ristelli's zoned piety in context with the psychological climate of the prison, it was not difficult to understand why they perceived him to be their John the Baptist; but in the greater context of the rational, the idea was ludicrous. More than ludicrous. Insane. Recalling how laughable Ristelli's preachments had seemed back in Vacaville reinforced my belief that the population of Diamond Bar was being transformed by person or persons unknown into a brain-dead congregation of delusionaries, and fearful of joining them, I intensified my focus on escape, exploring the sub-basements, the walls, the turrets, searching for potential threats. On one of these explorative journeys, as I passed through Czerny's block, I noticed that the massive oak door leading to the new wing, heretofore always locked, was standing partway open and, curious, I stepped inside. The space in which I found myself was apparently an anteroom, one more appropriate to a modern cathedral than a jail: domed and columned, with scaffolding erected that permitted access to every inch of the roof and walls. The door on the far side of the room was locked, and there was little else to see, the walls and ceiling being white and unadorned. I was on the verge of leaving when I saw a sheet of paper taped to one of the columns. Written in pencil upon it was the following:

This place is yours to paint, Penhaligon, if you wish.

A key lay on the scaffolding beside the note—it fitted the oak door. I locked the door, pocketed the key and went about my business, understanding this show of trust to signify the board's recognition that I had accepted my lot and that by taking up their charge I might earn a further degree of trust and so learn something to my benefit. To succeed in this I would have to do something that would enlist their delusion, and I immediately set about working on a design that would illustrate the essence of the delusion, The Heart of the Law. Though I began with cynical intent, as the weeks went by and my cell walls were covered with sketches, I grew obsessed with the project. I wanted the mural to be beautiful and strong to satisfy the artistic portion of my nature, my ego, and not simply to satisfy the board—in truth, I presumed they would approve of anything I did that hewed to their evangel. The dome and walls of the anteroom, the graceful volume of space they described, inspired me to think analytically about painting, something I had not done before, and I challenged myself to transcend the limits of my vision, to conceive a design that was somehow larger than my soul. I came to dwell more and more on the motive theory of Diamond Bar, that the criminal was the fundamental citizen, the archetype in whose service the whole of society had been created, and in the process I came obliquely to embrace the idea, proving, I suppose, the thesis that high art is the creation of truth from the raw materials of a lie, and the artist who wishes to be adjudged "great" must ultimately, through the use of passion and its obsessive tools, believe the lie he is intent upon illuminating. To augment my analytic capacities, I read books that might shed light on the subject—works of philosophy for the most part—and was astonished to discover in the writings of Michel Foucault a theory mirroring the less articulate theory espoused by the prison population. I wondered if it might be true, if delusion were being employed in the interests of truth, and, this being the case, whether the Secret Masters of Diamond Bar were contemplating a general good and the experiment of which we were a part was one that sought to evolve a generation in harmony with the grand design underlying all human culture. The books were difficult for me, but I schooled myself to understand them and became adept at knotting logic into shapes that revealed new facets of possibility—new to me, at any rate. This caused me to lose myself in abstraction and consequently diminished the urgency of my intention to escape. Like everyone who lived at Diamond Bar, I seemed to have a talent in that regard.

The design I settled upon owed more to Diego Rivera and Soviet poster art than to the muralists of the Renaissance. The walls would be thronged with figures, all reacting toward the center of the design, which was to occupy the dome and which I had not yet been able to conceptualize—I felt the image would naturally occur as a byproduct of my labors. It took three months of twelve-hour days to lay out the sketch on the walls, and I estimated that, if done properly, the painting would take a year to complete. Chances were I would be gone from Diamond Bar before then, and realizing this, when I began to paint, ensorcelled by my vision, driven by the idea of finishing in a shorter time, I worked fifteen and sixteen hours a day. Dangling in harness from the scaffolding, crouched over, forced into unnatural positions, I gained an appreciation for the physical afflictions that Michelangelo endured while painting the Sistine Chapel. Each night after work I tried to shake off the aches and pains by walking through the sub-basements of the prison, and it was during one of these walks that I encountered the plumes.

In prison, sex is an all-consuming preoccupation, a topic endlessly discussed, and from my earliest days at Diamond Bar the plumes had been recommended as a palatable alternative to self-gratification. The new wing, it was said, would house both women and men, thus ending the single unnatural constraint of prison life, and many held that the plumes would eventually become those women, evolving—as were we all—into their ideal form. Even now, Causey said, the plumes were superior to the sex available in other prisons. "It's not like fucking a guy," he said. "It feels, y'know, okay."

"Is it like fucking a woman?" I asked.

He hesitated and said, "Kinda."

"'Kinda' doesn't do it for me."

"Only reason it's different is because you're thinking about it not being a woman."

"Yeah, well. I'll pass. I don't want to think when I'm fucking."

Causey continued urging me to give the plumes a try, because—I believed—he felt that if I surrendered to temptation, I would become a complicitor in perversion, and this would somehow lessen the guilt attaching to his sexual assault on me.

That he felt guilty about what had transpired between us was not in question. As our relationship progressed, he came to speak openly about the event and sought to engage me in a dialogue concerning it. Therapy, I supposed. Part of his process of self-examination. At the time, I rejected his suggestions that I visit the plumes out of hand, but they may have had some effect on me, for in retrospect I see that my initial encounter with them, though it seemed accidental, was likely an accident I contrived. I was, you see, in a heightened state of sexuality. Immersed in my work, essentially in love with it, while painting I would often become aroused not by any particular stimulus—there were no visual or tactile cues—but by the concentrated effort, itself a form of desire maintained at peak intensity for hours on end. And so on the night I strayed into the section of the prison occupied by the plumes, I was, though tired, mentally and sexually alert. I was tempting myself, testing my limits, my standards, hoping they would fail me.

Three levels down from the main walls were dozens of rooms—bedchambers, a communal kitchen, common rooms, and so forth—an area accessed by a double door painted white and bearing a carved emblem that appeared to represent a sheaf of plumes, this the source of the name given to those who dwelled within. Much of the space had the sterile decor of a franchise hotel: carpeted corridors with benches set into walls whose patterned discolorations brought to mind *art nouveau* flourishes. The common rooms were furnished with sofas and easy chairs and filled with soft music whose melodies were as unmemorable as an absent caress. No barred gates, just wooden doors. The lighting was dim, every fixture limned by a faint halation, giving the impression that the air was permeated by a fine mist. I felt giddy on entering the place, as if I had stood up too quickly. Nerves, I assumed, because I felt giddier yet when I caught sight of my first plume, a slim blond attired in a short gray dress with spaghetti straps. She had none of the telltale signs of a transvestite or a transsexual. Her hands and feet were small, her nose and mouth delicately shaped, her figure not at all angular. After she vanished around a corner, I remembered she was a man, and that recognition bred abhorrence and self-loathing in me. I turned, intending to leave, and bumped into another plume who had been about to walk past me from behind. A willowy brunette with enormous dark eyes, dressed in the same fashion as the blond, her mouth thinned in exasperation. Her expression softened as she stared at me. I suppose I gaped at her. The memory of how I behaved is impaired by the ardor with which I was studying her, stunned by the air of sweet intelligence generated when she smiled. Her face was almost unmarked by time—I imagined her to be in her late twenties—and reminded me of the faces of madonnas in Russian ikons: long and pale and solemn, wide at the cheekbones, with an exaggerated arch to the eyebrows and heavy-lidded eyes. Her hair fell straight and shining onto her back. There was nothing sluttish or coarse about her; on the contrary, she might have been a graduate student out for an evening on the town, a young wife preparing to meet her husband's employer, an ordinary beauty in her prime. I tried to picture her as a man but did not succeed in this, claimed instead by the moment.

"Are you trying to find someone?" she asked. "You look lost."

"No," I said. "I'm just walking . . . looking around."

"Would you like me to give you the tour?" She put out her right hand to be shaken. "I'm Bianca."

The way she extended her arm straight out, assertive yet graceful, hand angled down and inward a bit: it was so inimitably a female gesture, devoid of the frilliness peculiar to the gestures of men who pretend to be women, it convinced me on some core level of her femininity, and my inhibitions fell away. As we strolled, she pointed out the features of the place. A bar where the ambience of a night club was created by red and purple spotlights that swept over couples dancing together; a grotto hollowed out from the rock with a pool in which several people were splashing one another; a room where groups of men and plumes were playing cards and shooting pool. During our walk, I told Bianca my life story in brief, but when I asked about hers, she said, "I didn't exist before I came to Diamond Bar." Then, perhaps because she noticed disaffection in my face, she added, "That sounds overly dramatic, I know. But it's more or less true. I'm very different from how I used to be."

"That's true of everyone here. The thinking you do about the past, it can't help but change you."

"That's not what I mean," she said.

At length she ushered me into a living room cozily furnished in the manner of a bachelorette apartment and insisted I take a seat on the sofa, then went through a door into the next room, reappearing seconds later carrying a tray on which were glasses and a bottle of red wine. She sat beside me, and as she poured the wine I watched her breasts straining against the gray bodice, the soft definition of her arms, the precise articulation of the muscles at the corners of her mouth. The wine, though a touch bitter, put me at ease, but my sense of a heated presence so near at hand sparked conflicting feelings, and I was unable to relax completely. I told myself that I did not want intimacy, yet that was patently untrue. I had been without a woman for three years, and even had I been surrounded by women during that time, Bianca would have made a powerful impression. The more we talked, the more she revealed of herself, not the details of her past, but the particularity of her present: her quiet laugh, a symptom—it seemed—of ladylike restraint; the grave consideration she gave to things I said; the serene grace of her movements. There was an aristocratic quality to her personal style, a practiced, almost ritual caution. Only after learning that I was the one painting a mural in the new wing did she betray the least excitement, and even her excitement was colored with restraint. She leaned toward me, hands clasped in her lap, and her smile broadened, as if my achievement, such as it was, made her proud.

"I wish I could do something creative," she said wistfully at one point. "I don't think I've got it in me."

"Creativity's like skin color. Everyone's got some."

She made a sad moue. "Not me."

"I'll teach you to draw if you want. Next time I'll bring a sketch pad, some pencils."

She traced the stem of her wine glass with a forefinger. "That would be nice . . . if you come back."

"I will," I told her.

"I don't know." She said this distantly, then straightened, sitting primly on the edge of the sofa. "I can tell you don't think it would be natural between us."

I offered a reassurance, but she cut me off, saying, "It's all right. I understand it's strange for you. You can't accept that I'm natural." She let her eyes hold on my face for a second, then lowered her gaze to the wine glass. "Sometimes it's hard for me to accept, but I am, you know."

I thought she was saying that she was post-operative, yet because she spoke with such offhanded conviction and not the hysteria-tinged defiance of a prison bitch, I also wondered, against logic, if she might be telling the truth and was a woman in every meaning of the word. She came to her feet and stepped around the coffee table and stood facing me. "I want to show you," she said. "Will you let me show you?"

The mixture of shyness and seductiveness she exhibited in slipping out of her dress was completely natural, redolent of a woman who knew she was beautiful yet was not certain she would be beautiful enough to please a new man, and when she stood naked before me, I could not call to mind a single doubt as to her femininity, all my questions answered by high, small breasts and long legs evolving from the milky curve of her belly. She seemed the white proof of a sensual absolute, and the one thought that separated itself out from the thoughtlessness of desire was that here might be the central figure in my mural.

During the night that followed, nothing Bianca did in any way engaged my critical faculties. I had no perch upon which a portion of my mind stood and observed. It was like all good nights passed with a new lover, replete with tenderness and awkwardness and intensity. I spent every night for the next five weeks with her, teaching her to draw, talking, making love, and when I was in her company, no skepticism concerning the rightness of the relationship entered in. The skepticism that afflicted me when we were apart was ameliorated by the changes that knowing her brought to my work. I came to understand that the mural should embody a dynamic vertical progression from darkness and solidity to brightness and evanescence. The lower figures would be, as I had envisioned, heavy and stylized, but those above demanded to be rendered impressionistically, gradually growing less and less defined, until at the dome, at the Heart of the Law, they became creatures of light. I reshaped the design accordingly and set to work with renewed vigor, though I did not put in so many hours as before, eager each night to return to Bianca. I cannot say I neglected the analytic side of my nature—I continued to speculate on how she had become a woman. In exploring her body I had found no surgical scars, nothing to suggest such an invasive procedure as would be necessary to effect the transformation, and in her personality I perceived no masculine defect. She was, for all intents and purposes, exactly what she appeared: a young woman who, albeit experienced with men, had retained a certain innocence that I believed she was yielding up to me.

When I mentioned Bianca to Causey, he said, "See, I told ya."

"Yeah, you told me. So what's up with them?"

"The plumes? There's references to them in the archives, but they're vague."

I asked him to elaborate, and he said all he knew was that the criteria by which the plumes were judged worthy of Diamond Bar was different from that applied to the rest of the population. The process by which they entered the prison, too, was different—they referred to it as the Mystery, and there were suggestions in the archival material that it involved a magical transformation. None of the plumes would discuss the matter other than obliquely. This seemed suggestive of the pathological myths developed by prison queens to justify their femininity, but I refused to let it taint my thoughts concerning Bianca. Our lives had intertwined so effortlessly, I began to look upon her as my companion. I recognized that if my plans for escape matured I would have to leave her, but rather than using this as an excuse to hold back, I sought to know her more deeply. Every day brought to light some new feature of her personality. She had a quiet wit that she employed with such subtlety, I sometimes did not realize until after the fact that she had been teasing me; and she possessed a stubborn streak that, in combination with her gift for logic, made her a formidable opponent in any argument. She was especially fervent in her defense of the proposition that Diamond Bar manifested the principle from which the form of the human world had been struck, emergent now, she liked to claim, for a mysterious yet ultimately beneficent reason.

In the midst of one such argument, she became frustrated and said, "It's not that you're a nonconformist, it's like you're practicing nonconformity to annoy everyone. You're being childish!"

"Am not!" I said.

"I'm serious! It's like with your attitude toward Ernst." A book of Max Ernst prints, one of many art books she had checked out of the library, was resting on the coffee table—she gave it an angry tap. "Of all the books I bring home, this is the one you like best. You leaf through it all the time. But when I tell you I think he's great, you—"

"He's a fucking poster artist."

"Then why look at his work every single night?"

"He's easy on the eyes. That doesn't mean he's worth a shit. It just means his stuff pacifies you."

She gave her head a rueful shake.

"We're not talking about Max Ernst, anyway," I said.

"It doesn't matter what we talk about. Any subject it's the same. I don't understand you. I don't understand why you're here. In prison. You say the reason you started doing crime was due to your problems with authority, but I don't see that in you. It's there, I guess, but it doesn't seem that significant. I can't imagine you did crime simply because you wanted to spit in the face of authority."

"It wasn't anything deep, okay? It's not like I had an abusive childhood or my father ran off with his secretary. None of that shit. I'm a fuck-up. Crime was my way of fucking up."

"There must be something else! What appealed to you about it?"

"The thing I liked best," I said after giving the question a spin, "was sitting around a house I broke into at three in the morning, thinking how stupid the owners were for letting a mutt like me mess with their lives."

"And here you are, in a truly strange house, thinking we're all stupid."

The topic was making me uncomfortable. "We're always analyzing my problems. Let's talk about you for a change. Why don't you confide your big secrets so we can run 'em around the track a few times?"

A wounded expression came to her face. "The reason I haven't told you about my life is because I don't think you're ready to handle it."

"Don't you trust me?"

She leaned back against the cushions and folded her arms, stared at the coffee table. "That's not it . . . altogether."

"So you don't trust me and there's more. Great." I made a show of petulance, only partly acting it.

"I can't tell you some things."

"What's that mean?"

"It means I can't!" Her anger didn't seem a show, but it faded quickly. "You crossed the river to come here. We have to cross our own river. It's different from yours."

"The Mystery."

She looked surprised, and I told her what I had learned from Causey.

"He's right," she said. "I won't talk about it. I can't."

"Why? It's like a vow or something?"

"Or something." She relaxed her stiff posture. "The rest of it . . . I'm ashamed. When I look back, I can't believe I was so disreputable. Be patient, all right? Please?"

"You, too," I said.

"I *am* patient. I just enjoy arguing too much."

I put my hand beneath her chin, trying to jolly her. "If you want, we can argue some more."

"I want to win," she said, smiling despite herself.

"Everything's like you say. Diamond Bar's heaven on fucking earth. The board's . . ."

"I don't want you to give in!" She pushed me onto my back and lay atop me. "I want to break you down and smash your flimsy defenses!"

Her face, poised above me, bright-eyed and soft, lips parted, seemed oddly predatory, like that of a hungry dove. "What were we arguing about?" I asked.

"Everything," she said, and kissed me. "You, me, life. Max Ernst."

One day while drinking a cup of coffee in the cafeteria, taking a break from work, I entered into a casual conversation with a dour red-headed twig of a man named Phillip Stringer, an ex-arsonist who had recently moved from the eighth tier into the old wing. He mentioned that he had seen me with Bianca a few nights previously. "She's a reg'lar wild woman!" he said. "You touch her titties, you better hold on, 'cause the next thing it's like you busting out of chute number three on Mustang Sally!"

Though giving and enthusiastic in sex, Bianca's disposition toward the act impressed me as being on the demure side of "reg'lar wild woman." Nevertheless, I withheld comment.

"She was too wild for me," Stringer went on. "It's not like I don't enjoy screwing chicks with dicks. Truth is, I got a thing for 'em. But when they got a bigger dick'n I got . . . guess I felt a tad intimidated."

"Hell are you talking about?" I asked.

He gazed at me in bewilderment. "The plume I saw you with. Bianca."

"You're fucked up, man! She doesn't have a dick."

"You think that, you never seen a dick. Thing's damn near wide around as a Coke can!"

"You got the wrong girl," I told him, growing irritated.

Stringer glowered at me. "I may not be the sharpest knife in the drawer, but I know who the hell I'm screwing."

"Then you're a goddamn liar," I said.

If it had been another time, another prison, we would been rolling around on the floor, thumbing eyes and throwing knees, but the placid offices of Diamond Bar prevailed, and Stringer dialed back his anger, got to his feet. "I been with that bitch must be fifty times, and I'm telling you she gets hard enough to bang nails with that son-of-a-bitch. She goes to bouncing up and down, moaning, 'Only for you . . .' All kindsa sweet shit. You close your eyes, you'd swear you's with a woman. But you grab a peek and see that horse cock waggling around, it's just more'n I can handle." He hitched up his trousers. "You better get yourself an adjustment, pal. You spending way too much time on that painting of yours."

If it were not for the phrase "only for you," I would have disregarded what Stringer said. Indeed, I did disregard most of it.

But that phrase, which Bianca habitually breathed into my ear whenever she drew near her moment, seeded me with paranoia, and that night as we sat on the sofa, going over the charcoal sketches she had done of her friends, I repeated the essence of Stringer's words, posing them as a joke. Bianca displayed no reaction, continuing to study one of the sketches.

"Hear what I said?" I asked.

"Uh-huh."

"Well?"

"What do you want me to say?'

"I guess I thought you'd say something, this guy going around telling everybody you got a dick."

She set down the sketchpad and looked at me glumly. "I haven't been with Phillip for nearly two years."

It took me a moment to interpret this. "I guess it's been such a long time he mixed you up with somebody."

The vitality drained from her face. "No."

"Then what the fuck are you saying?"

"When I was with Phillip, I was different from the way I am with you."

Irritated by the obliqueness with which she was framing her responses, I said, "You telling me you had a dick when you were seeing him?"

"Yes."

Hearing this did not thrill me, but I had long since dealt with it emotionally. "So after that you had the operation?"

"No."

"No? What? You magically lost your dick?"

"I don't want to talk about it."

"Well, I do! Hell are you trying to tell me?"

"I'm not sure how it happens . . . it just does! Whatever the man wants, that's how I am. It's like that with all the plumes . . . until you find the right person. The one you can be who you really are with."

I struggled to make sense of this. "So you're claiming a guy comes along wanting you to have a dick, you grow one?"

She gave a nod of such minimal proportions, it could have been a twitch. "I'm sorry."

"Gee," I said with thick sarcasm. "It's kinda like a fairy tale, isn't it?"

"It's true!" She put a hand to her forehead, collecting herself. "When I meet someone new, I change. It's confusing. I hardly know it's happening, but I'm different afterward."

I do not know what upset me more, the implication, however improbable, that she was a shapeshifter, capable of switching her sexual characteristics to please a partner, or the idea that she believed this. Either way, I found the situation intolerable. This is not to say I had lost my feelings for her, but I could no longer ignore the perverse constituency of her personality. I pushed up from the couch and started for the door.

Bianca cried out, "Don't go!"

I glanced back to find her gazing mournfully at me. She was beautiful, but I could not relate to her beauty, only to the neurotic falsity I believed had created it.

"Don't you understand?" she said. "For you, I'm who I want to be. I'm a woman. I can prove it!"

"That's okay," I said coldly, finally. "I've had more than enough proof."

Things did not go well for me after that evening. The mural went well. Though I no longer approached the work with the passion I had formerly brought to it, every brushstroke seemed a contrivance of passion, to be the product of an emotion that continued to act through me despite the fact that I had forgotten how to feel it. Otherwise, my life at Diamond Bar became fraught with unpleasantness. Harry Colangelo, who had more-or-less vanished during my relationship with Bianca, once again began to haunt me. He would appear in the doorway of the anteroom while I was painting and stare venomously until I shouted at him. Inarticulate shouts like those you might use to drive a dog away from a garbage can. I developed back problems for which I was forced to take pain medication, and this slowed the progress of my work. Yet the most painful of my problems was that I missed Bianca, and there was no medication for this ailment. I was tempted to seek her out, to apologize for my idiocy in rejecting her, but was persuaded not to do so by behavioral reflexes that, though I knew them to be outmoded, having no relation to my life at the moment, I could not help obeying. Whenever an image of our time together would flash through my mind, immediately thereafter would follow some grotesquely sexual mockery of the image that left me confused and mortified.

I retreated into my work. I slept on the scaffolding, roused by the mysterious cry that like the call of some grievous religion announced each dawn. I lived on candy bars, peanut butter, crackers, and soda that I obtained at the commissary, and I rarely left the anteroom, keeping the door locked most of the days, venturing out only for supplies. When I woke I would see the mural surrounding me on every side, men with thick arms and cold white eyes pupiled with black suns, masses of them, clad in prison gray, crowded together on iron stairs (the sole architectural component of the design), many-colored faces engraved with desperation, greed, lust, rage, longing, bitterness, fear, muscling each other out of the way so as to achieve a clearer view of the unpainted resolution that overarched their suffering and violence. At times I thought I glimpsed in the mural—or underlying it—a cohesive element I had not foreseen, something created *from* me and not by me, a truth the work was teaching me, and in my weaker moments I supposed it to be the true purpose of Diamond Bar, still fragmentary and thus inexpressible; but I did not seek to analyze or clarify—if it was there, then its completion was not dependent upon my understanding. Yet having apprehended this unknown value in my work forced me to confront the reality that I was of two minds concerning the prison. I no longer perceived our lives as necessarily being under sinister control, and I had come to accept the possibility that the board was gifted with inscrutable wisdom, the prison itself an evolutionary platform, a crucible devised in order to invest its human ore with a fresh and potent mastery, and I glided between these two poles of thought with the same rapid pendulum swing that governed my contrary attitudes toward Bianca.

From time to time the board would venture into the anteroom to inspect the mural and offer their mumbling approbation, but apart from them and occasional sightings of Causey and Colangelo, I received no other visitors. Then one afternoon about six weeks after ending the relationship, while painting high on the scaffolding, I sensed someone watching me—Bianca was standing in the doorway thirty feet below, wearing a loose gray prison uniform that hid her figure. Our stares locked for an instant, then she gestured at the walls and said, "This is beautiful." She moved deeper into the room, ducking to avoid a beam, and let her gaze drift across the closely packed images. "Your sketches weren't . . ." She looked up at me, brushed strands of hair from her eyes. "I didn't realize you were so accomplished."

"I'm sorry," I said, so overcome by emotion that I was unable to react to what she had said, only to what I was feeling.

She gave a brittle laugh. "Sorry that you're good? Don't be."

"You know what I mean."

"No . . . not really. I thought by coming here I would, but I don't." She struck a pose against the mural, standing with her back to it, her right knee drawn up, left arm extended above her head. "I suppose I'll be portrayed like this."

It was so quiet I could hear a faint humming, the engine of our tension.

"I shouldn't have come," she said.

"I'm glad you did."

"If you're so glad, why are you standing up there?"

"I'll come down."

"And yet," she said after a beat, "still you stand there."

"How've you been?"

"Do you want me to lie? The only reason I can think of for you to ask that is you want me to lie. You know how I've been. I've been heartbroken." She ran a hand along one of the beams and examined her palm as if mindful of dust or a splinter. "I won't ask the same question. I know how you've been. You've been conflicted. And now you look frightened."

I felt encased in some cold unyielding substance, like a souvenir of life preserved in lucite.

"Why don't you talk to me?" She let out a chillier laugh. "Explain yourself."

"Jesus, Bianca. I just didn't understand what was going on."

"So it was an intellectual decision you made? A reaction to existential confusion?"

"Not entirely."

"I was making a joke." She strolled along the wall and stopped to peer at one of the faces.

"I wasn't," I said. "What you told me . . . how can you believe it?"

"You think I'm lying?"

"I think there's drugs in the food . . . in the air. Or something. There has to be a mechanism involved. Some sort of reasonable explanation."

"For what? My insanity?" She backed against the wall in order to see me better. "This is so dishonest of you."

"How's it dishonest?"

"You were happier thinking I was a post-operative transsexual? It's my irrational beliefs that drove you away? Please!" She fiddled with the ends of her hair. "Suppose what I told you is true. Suppose who I am with you is who you want me to be. Who I want to be. Would that be more unpalatable than if my sex was the result of surgery?"

"But it's not true."

"Suppose it is." She folded her arms, waiting.

"I don't guess it would matter. But that's not . . ."

"Now suppose just when we're starting to establish something strong, you rip it apart?" A quaver crept into her voice. "What would that make you?"

"Bianca . . ."

"It'd make you a fool! But then of course I'm living in a drug-induced fantasy that causes you existential confusion."

"Whatever the case," I said, "I probably am a fool."

It was impossible to read her face at that distance, but I knew her expression was shifting between anger and despair.

"Are you okay?" I asked.

"God! What's wrong with you?" She stalked to the door, paused in the entrance; she stood without speaking for what seemed a very long time, looking down at the floor, then glanced sideways up at me. "I was going to prove something to you today, but I can see proving it would frighten you even more. You have to learn to accept things, Tommy, or else you won't be able to do your time. You're not deceiving anyone except yourself."

"*I'm* deceiving myself? Now that's a joke!"

She waved at the mural. "You think what you're painting is a lie. Don't deny it. You think it's a con you're running on us. But when I leave it'll be the only thing in the room that's still alive." She stepped halfway through the door, hesitated and, in a voice that was barely audible, said, "Goodbye, Tommy."

I experienced a certain relief after Bianca's visit, an emotion bred by my feeling that now the relationship was irretrievably broken, and I could refocus my attention on escape; but my relief was short-lived. It was not simply that I was unable to get Bianca out of my thoughts, or even that I continued to condemn myself both for abandoning her and for having involved myself with her in the first place—it was as if I were engaged in a deeper struggle, one whose nature was beyond my power to discern, though I assumed my attitudes toward Bianca contributed to its force. Because I was unable, or perhaps unwilling, to face it, this irresolvable conflict began to take a toll. I slept poorly and turned to drink as a remedy. Many days I painted drunk, but drunkenness had no deleterious effect on the mural—if anything, it sharpened my comprehension of what I was about. I redid the faces on the lower portions of the walls, accentuating their beastliness, contrasting them with more human faces above, and I had several small technical breakthroughs that helped me create the luminous intensity I wanted for the upper walls. The nights, however, were not so good. I went to wandering again, armed against self-recrimination and the intermittent appearances of Harry Colangelo with a bottle of something, usually home brew of recent vintage. Frequently I became lost in the sub-basements and wound up passed out on the floor. During one of these wanders, I noticed I was a single corridor removed from the habitat of the plumes, and this time, not deceiving myself as to motive, I headed for the white door. I had no wish to find Bianca. I was so debased in spirit, the idea of staining my flesh to match enticed me, and when I pushed into the entryway and heard loud rock and roll and saw that the halation surrounding the light fixtures had thickened into an actual mist that caused men and plumes to look like fantastical creatures, gray demons and their gaudy, grotesque mistresses, I plunged happily into the life of the place, searching for the most degrading encounter available.

Her name was Joy, a Los Angeleno by birth, and when I saw her dancing in the club with several men under a spotlight that shined alternately purple and rose, she seemed the parody of a woman. Not that she was unfeminine, not in the least. She was Raphaelesque, like an old-fashioned Hollywood blond teetering on the cusp between beauty and slovenly middle-age, glossy curls falling past her shoulders, the milky loaves of her breasts swaying ponderously in gray silk, her motherly buttocks dimpling beneath a tight skirt, her scarlet lips reminiscent of those gelatin lips full of cherry syrup you buy at Halloween, her eyes tunnels of mascara pricked by glitters. Drunk, I saw her change as the light changed. Under the purple she whitened, grew soft as ice cream, ultimately malleable; she would melt around you. Under the rose, a she-devilish shape emerged; her touch would make you feverish, infect you with a genital heat. I moved in on her, and because I had achieved an elevated status due to my connection with the board, the men dancing with her moved aside. Her fingers locked in my hair, her swollen belly rolled against me with the sodden insistence of a sea thing pushed by a tide. Her mouth tasted of liqueur and I gagged on her perfume, a scent of candied flowers. She was in every regard overpowering, like a blond rhinoceros. "What's the party for?" I shouted above the music. She laughed and cupped both hands beneath her breasts, offering them to me, and as I squeezed, manipulating their shapes, her eyelids drooped and her hips undulated. She pulled my head close and told me what she wanted me to do, what she would do.

Whereas sex with Bianca had been nuanced, passion cored with sensitivity, with Joy it was rutting, tumultuous, a jungle act, all sweat and insanity, pounding and meaty, and when I came I felt I was deflating, every pure thing spurting out of me, leaving a sack of bones and organic stink lying between her Amazon thighs. We fucked a second time with her on top. I twisted her nipples hard, like someone spinning radio dials, and throwing back her head she spat up great yells, then braced both hands on the pillow beside my head and hammered down onto me, her mouth slack, lips glistening with saliva poised an inch above mine, grunting and gasping. Then she straightened, arched her back, her entire body quaking, and let out a hideous groan followed by a string of profane syllables. Afterward she sat in a chair at her dressing table wearing a black bra and panties, legs crossed, attaching a stocking to her garter belt, posing an image that was to my eyes grossly sexual, repellently voluptuous, obscenely desirable. As she stretched out her leg, smoothing ripples in the silk, she said, "You used to be Bianca's friend."

I did not deny it.

"She's crazy about you, y'know."

"Is she here? At the party?"

"You don't need her tonight," Joy said. "You already got everything you needed."

"Is she here?"

She shook her head. "You won't be seeing her around for a while."

I mulled over this inadequate answer and decided not to pursue it.

Joy put on her other stocking. "You're still crazy about her. I'm a magnet for guys in love with other women." She admired the look of her newly stockinged leg. "It's not so bad. Sad guys fuck like they have something to prove."

"Is that right?"

"You were trying to prove something, weren't you?"

"Probably not what you think."

She adjusted her breasts, settling them more cozily in the brassiere. "Oh, I know exactly what you were trying to prove." She turned to the mirror, went to touching up her lipstick, her speech becoming halting as she wielded the applicator. "I am . . . expert in these matters . . . like all . . . ladies of the evening."

"Is that how you see yourself?"

She made a kissy mouth at her reflection. "There's something else in me, I think, but I haven't found the man who can bring it out." She adopted a thoughtful expression. "I could be very domestic with the right person. Very nurturing. Once the new wing's finished . . . I'm sure I'll find him then."

"There'll be real women living in the new wing. Lots of competition."

"We're the real women," she said with more than a hint of irritation. "We're not there yet, but we're getting there. Some of us are there already. You should know. Bianca's living proof."

Unwilling to explore this or any facet of this consensus fantasy, I changed the subject. "So, what's your story?" I asked.

"You mean my life story? Do you care?"

"I'm just making conversation."

"We had our conversation, sweetie. We just didn't talk all that much."

"I wasn't finished."

She looked at me over her shoulder, arching an eyebrow. "My, my. You must really have something to prove." She rested an elbow on the back of the chair. "Maybe you should go hunt up Bianca."

It was a thought, but one I had grown accustomed to rejecting. I reached down beside the bed, groping for my bottle. The liquor seemed to have an immediate effect, increasing my level of drunkenness, and with it my capacity for rejection. The colors of the room were smeary, as if made from different shades of lipstick. Joy looked slug-white and bloated, a sickly exuberance of flesh strangled by black lace, the monstrous ikon of a German Expressionist wet dream.

She gave what I took for a deprecating laugh. "Sure, we can converse some more if you want." She started to unhook her brassiere.

"Leave that shit on," I said. "I'll work around it."

Not long after my night with Joy, a rumor began to circulate that one of the plumes had become pregnant, and when I discovered that the plume in question was Bianca, I tried to find her. I gave the rumor little credit. Yet she had claimed she could prove something to me, and thus I could not completely discredit it. I was unsure how I would react if the rumor reflected the truth, but what chance was there of that? My intention was to debunk the rumor. I would be doing her a favor by forcing her to face reality. That, at any rate, is what I told myself. When I was unable to track her down, informed that she was sequestered, I decided the rumor must be a ploy designed to win me back, abandoned my search, and once again focused my energy upon the mural. Though a third of the walls remained unfinished, I now had a more coherent idea of the figures that would occupy the dome, and I was eager to finalize the conception. Despite this vitality of purpose, I felt bereft, dismally alone, and when Richard Causey came to visit, I greeted him effusively, offering him refreshment from my store of junk food. Unlike my other visitors, he had almost nothing to say about the mural, and as we ate on the lowest platform of the scaffolding, it became obvious that he was preoccupied. His eyes darted about; he cracked his knuckles and gave indifferent responses to everything I said. I asked what was on his mind and he told me he had stumbled upon an old tunnel beneath the lowest of the sub-basements. The door leading to it was wedged shut and would take two people to pry open. He believed there might be something significant at the end of the tunnel.

"Like what?" I asked.

"I ran across some papers in the archives. Letters, documents. They suggested the tunnel led to the Heart of the Law." He appeared to expect me to speak, but I was chewing. "I figured you might want to have a look," he went on. "Seeing that's what you're painting about."

I worried that Causey might want to get me alone and finish what he had started years before; but my interest was piqued, and after listening for several minutes more, I grew convinced that his interest in the tunnel was purely academic. To be on the safe side, I brought along a couple of the chisels I used to scrape the walls— they would prove useful in unwedging the door as well. Though it was nearly three in the morning, we headed down into the sub-basements, joined briefly by Colangelo, who had been sleeping in the corridor outside the anteroom. I brandished a chisel and he retreated out of sight.

The door was ancient, its darkened boards strapped with iron bands, a barred grille set at eye level. It was not merely stuck, but sealed with concrete. I shined Causey's flashlight through the grille and was able to make out moisture gleaming on brick walls. With both of us wielding chisels, it required the better part of an hour to chip away the concrete and another fifteen minutes to force the door open wide enough to allow us to pass. The tunnel angled sharply downward in a series of switchbacks, and by the time we reached the fifth switchback, with no end in view, I realized that the walk back up was going to be no fun whatsoever. The bricks were slimy to the touch, rats skittered and squeaked, and the air . . . dank, foul, noisome. None of these words or any combination thereof serve to convey the vileness of the stench it carried. Molecules of corruption seemed to cling to my tongue, to the insides of my nostrils, coating my skin, and I thought that if the tunnel did, indeed, lead to the Heart of the Law, then that heart must be rotten to the core. I tied my shirt across the lower half of my face and succeeded in filtering the reek, yet was not able to block it completely.

I lost track of the passage of time and lost track, too, of how many switchbacks we encountered, but we traveled far beneath the hill, of that much I am certain, descending to a level lower than that of the river flowing past the gate of the prison annex before we spotted a glimmer of light. Seeing it, we slowed our pace, wary of attracting the notice of whatever might occupy the depths of Diamond Bar, but the space into which we at length emerged contained nothing that would harm us—a vast egglike chamber that gave out into diffuse golden light a hundred feet above and opened below into a black pit whose bottom was not visible. Though the ovoid shape of the chamber implied artificiality, the walls were of natural greenish-white limestone, configured by rippled convexities and volutes, and filigreed with fungal growths, these arranged in roughly horizontal rows that resembled lines of text in an unknown script; the hundreds of small holes perforating the walls looked to have been placed there to simulate punctuation. A considerable ledge rimmed the pit, populated by colonies of rats, all gone still and silent at the sight of us, and as we moved out onto it, we discovered that the acoustics of the place rivaled that of a concert hall. Our footsteps resounded like the scraping of an enormous rasp, and our breath was amplified into the sighing of beasts. The terror I felt did not derive from anything I have described so much as from the figure at the center of the chamber. Dwarfed by its dimensions, suspended from hooks that pierced his flesh at nine separate points and were themselves affixed to chains that stretched to the walls, was the relic of a man. His begrimed skin had the dark granite color of the prison's outer walls, and his long white hair was matted down along his back like a moldering cape; his limbs and torso were emaciated, his ribs and hipbones protruding and his ligature ridged like cables. Dead, I presumed. Mummified by some peculiar process.

"Quires!" Causey's whisper reverberated through the chamber. "Jesus Christ! It's Quires."

The man's head drooped, his features further hidden by clots of hair. I had no evidence with which to argue Causey's claim and, indeed, not much inclination to do so. Who else, according to the history of the prison, merited the torment the man must have experienced? It did not seem possible. Quires had been in his eighties when he stepped down as warden more than eighty years before. But the existence of the chamber undermined my conception of the possible. Its silence was so liquid thick and chilling, it might have been the reservoir from which the quiet of the prison flowed. A brighter fear flickered up in me.

"Let's go back," I said. "We shouldn't be here."

At the sound of my voice, the rats offered up an uneasy chittering chorus that swirled around us like the rushing of water in a toilet. Causey was about to respond to my urging when Quires—if it was he—lifted his head and gave forth with a cry, feeble at first, but swelling in volume, a release of breath that went on and on as if issuing not from his lungs but from an opening inside him that admitted to another chamber, another voice more capable of such a prolonged expression, or perhaps to a succession of openings and voices and chambers, the infinitely modulated utterance of a scream proceeding from an unguessable source. The chittering of the rats, too, swelled in volume. Half-deafened, hands pressed to my ears, I sank to my knees, recognizing that the cry and its accompanying chorus was pouring up through the holes that perforated the walls and into every corner of the prison, a shout torn from the Heart of the Law to announce the advent of a bloody dawn. Quires' body spasmed in his chains, acquiring the shape of a dark thorn against the pale limestone, and his face— Even at a distance I could see how years of torment had compressed his features into a knot of gristle picked out by two staring white eyes. I felt those eyes on me, felt the majestic insistence of his pain and his blissful acknowledgment that this state was his by right. He was the criminal at the Heart of the Law, the one in whom the arcs of evil and the redemptive met, the lightning rod through which coursed the twin electricities of punishment and sacrifice, the synchronicity of choice and fate, and I understood that as such he was the embodiment of the purpose of Diamond Bar, that only from evil can true redemption spring, only from true redemption can hope be made flesh. Joyful and reluctant, willing servant and fearful slave, he was thaumaturge and penitent, the violent psychotic saint who had been condemned to this harsh durance and simultaneously sought by that service to transfigure us. Thus illuminated, in that instant I could have translated and read to you the fungal inscriptions on the walls. I knew the meaning of every projection and declivity of stone, and knew as well that the Heart of the Law was empty except for the exaltation of the damned and the luminous peace of the corrupted. Then Quires' cry guttered, his head drooped. The rats fell silent again, returned to their petty scuttling, and all but a residue of my understanding fled.

I staggered up, but Causey, who had also been borne to his knees by the ferocity of the cry, remained in that posture, his lips moving as though in prayer, and it occurred to me that his experience of what had happened must have been far different from mine to produce such a reverent reaction. I turned again to Quires, realizing I could not help him, that he did not want my help, yet moved to give it nonetheless, and thus I did not see Colangelo break from the tunnel behind us . . . nor did I see him push Causey into the pit. It was Causey's outcry, shrill and feeble in contrast to Quires', but unalloyed in its terror, that alerted me to danger. When I glanced back I saw that he had vanished into the depths, his scream trailing after him like a snapped rope, and on the spot where he had knelt, Colangelo stood glaring at me, Causey's chisel in his right hand. Had he forced a confrontation in the anteroom, anywhere in the upper levels of the prison, I would not have been so afraid, for though he was taller and heavier, I was accustomed to fighting men bigger than myself; but that dread place eroded my confidence, and I stumbled away from him, groping for my own chisel. He said nothing, made no sound apart from the stentorian gush of his breath, pinning me with his little eyes. The wan light diminished the pinkness of his skin. His lips glistened.

"The hell is your problem?" I said; then, alarmed by the reverberations of my voice, I added in a hushed tone, "I didn't do shit to you."

Colangelo let out an enervated sigh, perhaps signaling an unraveling of restraint, and rushed at me, slashing with the chisel. I caught his wrist and he caught mine. We swayed together on the edge of the pit, neither of us able to gain an advantage, equal in strength despite the difference in our sizes. The excited squeaking of the rats created a wall around us, a multiplicity of tiny cheers hardened into a shrill mosaic. At such close quarters, his anger and my fear seemed to mix and ferment a madness fueled by our breath, our spittle. I wanted to kill him. That was all I wanted. Everything else—Quires, Causey, the panic I had previously felt—dwindled to nothing.

Colangelo tried to butt me. I avoided the blow and, putting my head beneath his chin, pushed him back from the pit. He went off-balance, slipped to one knee. I wrenched my left arm free and brought my elbow hard into his temple. He slumped, still clutching my wrist, preventing me from using my chisel. I threw another elbow that landed on the hinge of his jaw, an uppercut that smacked into the side of his neck and elicited a grunt. He sagged onto his side as I continued to hit him, and when he lost consciousness I straddled his chest and lifted the chisel high, intending to drive it into his throat; but in straightening, I caught sight of Quires hanging at the center of his chains. He did not look at me, but I was certain that in some way he was watching, aware of the moment. How could he not be? He was the substance of the prison, its spirit and its fleshly essence, the male host in whom the spider of female principle had laid its eggs, and as such was witness to our every thought and action. I sensed from him a caution. Not reproval, nothing so pious. In the thin tide of thought that washed between us there was no hint of moral preachment, merely a reminder of the limit I was on the verge of transgressing. What was it Ristelli had said? "Innocents and murderers. The system tolerates neither." Madness receded, and I came to my feet. Prison logic ordained that I should push Colangelo into the pit and spare myself the inevitability of a second attack; but the logic of Diamond Bar, not Vacaville, commanded me. Numbed by the aftershocks of adrenaline and rage, I left him for the rats or whatever else fate might have in store, and with a last glance at Quires, suspended between the light of heaven and the pit, like the filament in a immense bulb, I began my ascent.

I had in mind to seek out Berbick or someone else whom Causey had befriended, to tell them what had become of him and to determine from their advice whether or not to make the events of the night and morning known to the board. Perhaps, I thought, by opening the sealed door I had violated an inviolate taboo and would suffer as a result. I might be blamed for Causey's death. But as I trudged wearily up along the switchbacks, the emotion generated by my fight with Colangelo ebbed away, and the awful chamber in which we had struggled began to dominate my thoughts. Its stench, its solitary revenant, its nightmarish centrality to the life of the prison. With each step, I grew increasingly horrified by my acceptance of the place and the changes it had worked in me. It had neutered my will, obscured my instincts, blinded me to perversity. The things I had done . . . Bianca, Joy, my devotion to that ridiculous mural. What had I been thinking? Where the fuck had Tommy Penhaligon gone? I wanted to be who I was at that precise moment: someone alert to every shadow and suspicious presence; open to the influence of emotion and not governed by a pathological serenity that transformed violent men into studious, self-examining drones and, were you to believe the plumes, less violent men into women. If I returned to my cell and confided in Berbick, thereby obeying the rule of the prison, sooner or later I would be sucked back in and lose this hard-won vantage from which I could perceive its depravity and pathetic self-involvements. I had no good prospects in the world, but all I could aspire to in Diamond Bar was that one day I would go shuffling through the yard, an old man dimly persuaded that he had been gifted with the grasp of a holy principle too great for the brains of common men to hold, a principle that was no more than a distorted reflection of the instrumentality responsible for his dementia. Instead of heading to my cell, when I reached the eighth stair I kept walking down through the hill toward the annex gate, past the cells of sedate men who had grown habituated to the prison, past those of agitated new arrivals; and when I reached the gate—it was, of course, unlocked—I threw it open and stood on the threshold, gazing out upon a beautiful spring morning. Cool and bright and fresh. A lacework of sun and shadow under the dark firs. The river running green with snowmelt. I had no fear of the quick-flowing current; I had crossed it once in handcuffs, and unfettered I would cross it all the more easily. Yet I hesitated. I could not, despite my revulsion for what lay behind me, put a foot forward on the path of freedom. I felt something gathering in the woods, a presence defined by the sound of rushing water, the shifting boughs and pouring wind. A wicked immanence, not quite material, needing me to come out from the gate a step or two in order to be real. I berated myself for a coward, tried to inject my spine with iron, but second by second my apprehension grew more detailed. I had a presentiment of jaws, teeth, a ravenous will, and I backed away from the gate, not far, but far enough to slow my pulse, to think. No one walked out of prison. There must be watchers . . . a single watcher, perhaps. A mindless four-footed punishment for the crime of flight. I told myself this was the same illusion of threat that had driven me inside the walls many months before, but I could not disregard it. The beckoning green and gold of the day, the light rippling everywhere—these had the insubstantiality of a banner fluttered across a window, hiding a dreadful country from my sight.

Once kindled, fear caught in me and burned. The flickering of sun on water, the stirring of fallen needles, mica glinting on the face of a boulder: these were unmistakable signs of an invisible beast who slumbered by the steps of the prison. I heard a noise. It may have been someone starting a chainsaw downriver, a car engine being revved, but to my ears it was a growl sounded high in a huge throat, a warning and a bloody promise. I sprang to the gate and slammed it shut, then rested against the cold metal, weak with relief. My eyes went to the second level of the tier.

Gazing down at me was a man in a guard's uniform, absently tapping the palm of his hand with a nightstick. I could hear the slap of wood on flesh, counting out the time with the regularity of a metronome, each stroke ticking off the ominous fractions of his displeasure. Finally, as if he had become sure of me, he sheathed the nightstick and walked away, the sharp report of his boot heels precisely echoing the now-steady rhythm of my heart.

I spent the remainder of the day and half the night staring at the discolorations on the wall opposite my bunk—they had never come in fully, never developed into a complicated abstraction as had the walls of my fellow prisoners, possibly because the walls upon which I expended most of my energy were the ones in the anteroom of the new wing. Yet during those hours I saw in their sparse scatter intimations of the scriptlike fungus inscribed upon the walls of the chamber at the Heart of the Law, indecipherable to me now as Arabic or Mandarin, tantalizingly inscrutable—I suspected they were the regulations by which we lived, and contemplating them soothed me. I could not avoid recalling the chamber and the man suspended therein, but my thoughts concerning these things were speculative, funded by neither fear nor regret. If it had been Quires, one hundred-and-sixty years old and more, tortured for half that span, this lent credence to Causey's assertion that Czerny, LeGary, Ashford, and Holmes were the original board of Diamond Bar who had been photographed with the warden in 1917 . . . and what did that say about the potentials of the prison? Time and again I returned to the truths I had sensed as Quires cried out from his chains, the dualities of punishment and sacrifice he seemed to incorporate. It was as if he were a battery through which the animating principle of the place was channeled. This was a simplistic analogy, yet when coupled with the image of a Christlike figure in torment, simplicity took on mythic potency and was difficult to deny. Now that I had proved myself unequal to traditional freedom, I was tempted to believe in the promised freedom of the new wing, in all the tenuous promise of Diamond Bar. The illusion of freedom, I realized, was the harshest of prisons, the most difficult to escape. Ristelli, Causey, Czerny, and Bianca had each in their way attempted to lead me to this knowledge, to demonstrate that only in a place like Diamond Bar, where walls kept that illusion at bay, was the road to freedom discernable. I had been a fool to disregard them.

Near midnight, a skinny, towheaded man stopped in front of my cell door and blew cigarette smoke through the bars from his shadowed mouth. I did not know him, but his arrogance and deferential attitude made me suspect he was a familiar of the board. "You're wanted at the annex gate, Penhaligon," he said, and blew another stream of smoke toward me. He looked off along the corridor, and in the half-light I saw the slant of a cheekbone, skin pitted with old acne scars.

In no mood to be disturbed, I asked, "What for?"

"Man's being transferred. Guess they need a witness."

I could not imagine why a transfer would require witnesses, and I felt the creep of paranoia; but I did not think the board would resort to trickery in the exercise of their power, and, reluctantly, I let the man escort me down through the annex.

The gate was open, and gathered by the entranceway, in partial silhouette against the moonstruck river, was a group of men, ten or twelve in all, consisting of the board and their spokesmen. Their silence unsettled me, and once again I grew paranoid, thinking that I was to be transferred; but then I spotted Colangelo off to one side, hemmed in against the wall by several men. His head twitched anxiously this way and that. The air was cool, but he was perspiring. He glanced at me, betraying no reaction—either he did not register me or else he had concluded that I was only a minor functionary of his troubles.

Czerny, along with LeGary, Ashford, and Holmes, was positioned to the left of the entrance. As I waited for whatever ritual was to occur, still uncertain why I had been invited, he came a tottering step toward me, eyes down, hands fingering his belt, and addressed me in his usual muttering cadence. I did not understand a single word, but the towheaded man, who was sticking to my elbow, said in a snide tone, "You been a bad boy, Penhaligon. That's what the man's telling you. You seen things few men have seen. Maybe you needed to see them, but you weren't prepared."

The towheaded man paused and Czerny spoke again. I could find nothing in his face to support the sternness of his previous words—he seemed to be babbling brokenly, as if speaking to a memory, giving voice to an imaginary dialogue, and thinking this, I wondered if that was what we were to him, memories and creatures of the imagination: if he had gone so far along the path to freedom that even those who lived in Diamond Bar had come to be no more than shadows in his mind.

"This is the edge of the pit," the towheaded man said when Czerny had finished. "The one you saw below is only its metaphor. Here you were closest to peril. That's why we have summoned you, so you can watch and understand."

Another spate of muttering and then the towheaded man said, "This is your final instruction, Penhaligon. There are no further lessons to be learned. From now on we will not protect you."

Czerny turned away, the audience ended, but angered by his claim that the board had protected me—I had no memory of being protected when I fought with Colangelo—and emboldened by the certainty that I was not to be transferred, I said to him, "If the pit I saw below was a metaphor, tell me where Causey is."

The old man did not turn back, but muttered something the towheaded man did not have to translate, for I heard the words clearly.

"If you are fortunate," Czerny said, "you will meet him again in the new wing."

The towheaded man nudged me forward to stand by Czerny and the rest of the board, inches away from the line demarcating the limits of the prison and the beginning of the world, a dirt path leading downward among boulders to the river flashing along its course. I have said the river was moonstruck, yet that scarcely describes the brightness of the landscape. The light was so strong even the smallest objects cast a shadow, and though the shadows beneath the boughs quivered in a fitful wind, they looked solid and deep. The dense firs and the overhang of the entrance prevented me from seeing the moon, but it must have been enormous—I pictured a blazing silvery face peering down from directly above the river, pocked by craters that sketched the liver spots and crumpled features of a demented old man. Sprays of water flying from the rocks in midstream glittered like icy sparks; the shingle on the far shore glittered as though salted with silver. Beyond it, the terrain of the opposite bank lay hidden beneath a dark green canopy, but patches of needles carpeting the margins of the forest glowed a reddish-bronze.

Who it was that shoved Colangelo out onto the path, I cannot say—I was not watching. It must have been a hard shove, for he went staggering down the slope and fell to all fours. He collected himself and glanced back toward us, not singling anyone out, it seemed, but taking us all in, as if claiming the sight for memory. He wiped dirt from his hands, and judging by his defiant posture I expected him to shout, to curse, but he turned and made for the river, going carefully over the uneven ground. When he reached the river's edge, he stopped and glanced back a second time. I could not make out his face, though he stood in the light, but judging by the sudden furtiveness of his body language, I doubted he had believed that he would get this far, and now that he had, the idea that he actually might be able to escape sprang up hot inside him, and he was prey to the anxieties of a man afflicted by hope.

Oddly enough, I hoped for him. I felt a sympathetic response to his desire for freedom. My heart raced and my brow broke a sweat, as if it were I and not that ungainly pinkish figure who was stepping from rock to rock, arms outspread for balance, groping for purchase on the slick surfaces, wobbling a bit, straining against gravity and fear. I had no apprehension of an inimical presence such as I had detected that morning, and this made me think that it had been nerves alone that had stopped me from escaping, and increased my enthusiasm for Colangelo's escape. I wanted to cheer, to urge him on, and might have done so if I had not been surrounded by the silent members of the board and their faithful intimates. That Colangelo was doing what I had not dared caused me envy and bitterness but also infected me with hope for myself. The next time I was alone at the gate, perhaps I would be equal to the moment.

The wind kicked up, outvoicing the chuckling rush of the river, sending sprays higher over the rocks, and along with the wind, the brightness of the river intensified. Every eddy, every momentary splotch of foam, every sinewy swell of water glinted and dazzled, as if it were coming to a boil beneath Colangelo. He kept going past the midpoint, steadier, more confident with each step, unhampered by the buffets of the wind. Close by the gate the boughs bent and swayed, stirring the shadows, sending them sliding forward and back over the dirt like a black film. The whole world seemed in motion, the atoms of the earth and air in a state of perturbation, and as Colangelo skipped over the last few rocks, I realized there was something unnatural about all this brilliant movement. The shapes of things were breaking down . . . briefly, for the merest fractions of seconds, their edges splintering, decaying into jittering bits of bright and dark, a pointillist dispersion of the real. I assumed I was imagining this, that I was emotionally overwrought, but the effect grew more pronounced. I looked to Czerny and the board. They were as always—distracted, apparently unalarmed—but what their lack of reaction meant, whether they saw what I did and were unsurprised, whether they saw something entirely different, I could not determine.

Colangelo let out a shout—of triumph, I believed. He had reached the shore and was standing with a fist upraised. The sand beneath his feet was a shoal of agitated glitter, and at his back the bank was a dark particulate dance, the forms of the trees disintegrating into a rhythm of green and black dots, the river into a stream of fiery unreality. How could he not notice? He shouted again and flipped us off. I realized that his outlines were shimmering, his prison garb blurring. Everything around him was yielding up its individuality, blending with the surround, flattening into an undifferentiated backdrop. It was nearly impossible to tell the sprays of water from sparkling currents in the air. The wind came harder, less like a wind in its roaring passage than the flux of some fundamental cosmic force, the sound of time itself withdrawing from the frame of human event, of entropy and electron death, and as Colangelo sprinted up the bank into cover of the forest, he literally merged with the setting, dissipated, the stuff of his body flowing out to be absorbed into a vibratory field in which not one distinguishable form still flourished. I thought I heard him scream. In all that roaring confusion I could not be certain, but he was gone. That much I knew. The world beyond the annex gate was gone as well, its separate forms dissolved into an electric absence of tremulous black, green, and silver motes, depthless and afire with white noise, like a television set tuned to a channel whose signal had been lost.

The board and their retainers moved away, talking softly among themselves, leaving me on the edge of the prison, of the pit, watching as—piece by piece—the forest and river and rocks reassembled, their inconstant shapes melting up from chaos, stabilizing, generating the imitation of a perfect moonlit night, the air cool and bracing, the freshness of the river sweetly palpable, all things alive with vital movement—boughs shifting, fallen needles drifting, light jumping along the surface of the water with the celerity of a charge along a translucent nerve. Even after what I had seen, I stood there a long while, tempted to run into the night, disbelieving the evidence of my senses, mistrusting the alternatives to belief, and so oppressed in spirit that I might have welcomed dissolution. A step forward, and I would be free one way or another. I stretched out a hand, testing its resistance to the dissolute power of the world beyond, and saw no hint of blurring or distortion. Yet still I stood there.

The anteroom is empty of scaffolding, swept clean of plaster dust, and I am sitting in a folding chair beneath the domed ceiling, like—I imagine—a gray-clad figure escaped from the lower portions of my mural. Years down the road I may look back and judge my work harshly, but I know at this moment I have achieved my goal and created something greater than myself. The mural rises up from solidity into the diffuse, from dark specificity into layered washes of light from which less definite figures emerge . . . less definite, at least, from this vantage. At close quarters they are easily identifiable. Bianca is there, a golden swimmer in the air, and at her side our son, her proof made flesh, born five months after our conversation in this very room. When told of his birth I went to visit her in the newly designated maternity ward of the prison hospital. Sleeping, she looked exhausted, her color weak and cheeks sunken, yet she was beautiful nonetheless. The child slept beneath a blanket in a crib beside her bed, only the back of his head visible. My emotions seemed to be circling one another like opponents in a ring. It was so strange to think of her with a child. Now that she had established the ultimate female credential, the freak detector in my brain emitted a steady beep. It was as if I were determined to paint her with a perverse brush, to view her condition and her Mystery in terms of an aberration. At the same time, I was drawn to her as never before. All my old feelings were reinvigorated. I decided to seek a reconciliation, but when I informed her of this she told me it was not what she wanted.

"You can't hide what you feel," she said. "You're still conflicted." She gave "conflicted" a distasteful reading and closed her eyes. "I'm too tired to argue. Please go."

I sat with her a bit longer, thinking she might relent, but when she fell asleep again I left the room. We see each other on occasion. Each time we meet she searches my face but thus far has found no apparent cause for confidence there. I have little hope she will ever find me other than wanting, and the prospect of life without her grows more difficult to bear. It seems I cannot shake the skepticism that Frank Ristelli correctly attributed to me, for despite everything I have experienced at Diamond Bar, I continue to speculate that our lives are under the influence of a powerful coercive force that causes us to believe in unrealities. My chest, for instance. Some weeks ago I noticed a scatter of pale discolorations surfaced from the skin thereon, their hues and partly rendered shapes reminiscent of the tattoo on Ristelli's chest, and yet when that tattoo achieves final form, as I assume it must, I will with part of my mind seek an explanation that satisfies my cynic's soul. If the birth of a child from a woman once a man fails to persuade me of the miraculous, is there anything that will overwhelm my capacity for doubt? Only when I paint does the current of belief flow through me, and then I am uncertain whether the thing believed is intrinsic to the subject of the work or a constant of my ego, a self-aggrandizing principle I deify with my obsessive zeal.

Ristelli, too, occupies a place in the dome of the anteroom, a mangy gray ghost slipping back into the world, and Causey is there as well, tumbling toward its center where, almost buried in light, Quires hangs in his eternal torment, a promethean Christ yielding to a barbaric sacrifice. I have pored over Causey's notes and rummaged the archives in an attempt to learn more about Quires, to understand what brought him to this pass. A transcendent moment like the one that left Saul stricken on the road to Damascus, an illumination of blinding sight? Or did Quires gradually win his way to a faith strong enough to compel his redemptive act? I have discovered no clue to explain his transformation, only a record of atrocities, but I think now both answers are correct, that all our labors are directed toward the achievement of such a moment, and perhaps therein lies the root cause of my skepticism, for though an illumination of this sort would remove the barriers that keep me from my family, I fear that moment. I fear I will dissolve in light, grow addled and vague, like Czerny, or foolishly evangelical like Ristelli. The abhorrence of authority that pushed me into a criminal life resists even an authority that promises ultimate blessing. I am afflicted with a contrarian's logic and formulate unanswerable questions to validate my stance. I poison my feeble attempts at faith with the irrationalities and improbabilities of Diamond Bar.

Pleased by my celebration of their myth, the board has offered me another room to paint, and there I intend to celebrate Bianca. I have already sketched out the design. She will be the sole figure, but one repeated in miniature over and over again, emerging from flowers, aloft on floating islands, draped in shadow, dressed in dozens of guises and proximate past forms, a history of color and line flowing toward her twice lifesized image hovering like a Hindu goddess in an exotic heaven populated by her many incarnations. That I have relegated her to the subject of a painting, however contemplative of her nature, suggests that I have given up on the relationship, turned my obsession from the person to the memory of the person. This distresses me, but I cannot change the way things are. My chains still bind me, limiting my choices and contravening the will to change. In recent months, I have come to envision a future in which I am an ancient gray spider creaking across a web of scaffolding that spans a hundred rooms, leaking paintlike blood in his painful, solitary progress, creating of his life an illuminated tomb commemorating folly, mortal confusion, and lost love. Not so terrible a fate, perhaps. To die and love and dream of perfect colors, perfect forms. But like all those who strive and doubt and seek belief, I am moving rapidly in the direction of something that I fear, something whose consolations I mistrust, and am inclined to look past that inevitability, to locate a point toward which to steer. My son, whom Bianca has named Max, after—she says—her favorite painter, Max Ernst, an implied insult, a further dismissal from her life . . . I sometimes think my son might serve as such a point. My imagination is captivated by the potentials of a man so strangely born, and often I let myself believe he will be the wings of our liberty, the one in whom the genius of our home will fully manifest. Since he is kept apart from me, however, these thoughts have the weight of fantasy, and I am cast back onto the insubstantial ground of my own life, a gray silence in which I have rarely found a glint of promise. Tears come easily. Regrets like hawks swoop down to pluck my hopeful thoughts from midair. And yet, though I am afraid that, as with most promises of fulfillment, it will always hang beyond our grasp, an eidolon, the illusion of perfection, lately I have begun to anticipate the completion of the new wing.

JUST LIKE THE ONES
WE USED TO KNOW

by Connie Willis

Connie Willis was born in 1945 and lives in Greeley, Colorado. Her first story, "The Secret of Santa Titicaca," appeared in 1971, but she only began publishing regularly in the early '80s. She is best known for her short fiction, which has been gathered in three volumes, Fire Watch, Impossible Things, *and* Miracle and Other Christmas Stories. *Her early stories include the time-travel story "Fire Watch," "All My Darling Daughters," "A Letter from the Clearys," "The Sidon in the Mirror," "Blued Moon," and "The Last of the Winnebagos."*

Willis's first book was the science fiction novel Water Witch *(with Cynthia Felice), which was followed by her solo debut,* Lincoln's Dreams, *which won the John W. Campbell Memorial Award. Her second novel,* Doomsday Book, *sharing the same mid-21st-century time-travel framing device as "Fire Watch," is more typical of Willis's fiction, and won both the Hugo and Nebula Awards. It was followed by the short novels* Uncharted Territory, Remake, *and* Bellwether, *and a major novel,* Passage. *Willis has become one of the most celebrated writers in modern science fiction, and to date her fiction has won the Hugo Award eight times, the Nebula Award six times, the Locus Award nine times, the John W. Campbell Memorial Award, and many other honors.*

Willis has spoken in interviews of her love of Christmas and she has regularly written holiday stories for Asimov's Science Fiction Magazine. *The story which follows, the latest in this vein, takes a look at what happens when we all dream of a white Christmas.*

THE SNOW STARTED AT 12:01 A.M. Eastern Standard Time just outside of Branford, Connecticut. Noah and Terry Blake, on their way home from a party at the Whittiers' at which Miranda Whittier had said, "I guess you could call this our Christmas Eve *Eve* party!" at least fifty times, noticed a few stray flakes as they turned onto Canoe Brook Road, and by the time they reached home, the snow was coming down hard.

"Oh, good," Tess said, leaning forward to peer through the windshield. "I've been hoping we'd have a white Christmas this year."

At 1:37 A.M. Central Standard Time, Billy Grogan, filling in for KYZT's late-night radio request show out of Duluth, said, "This just in from the National Weather Service. Snow advisory for the Great Lakes region tonight and tomorrow morning. Two to four inches expected," and then went back to discussing the callers' least favorite Christmas songs.

"I'll tell you the one I hate," a caller from Wauwatosa said. "'White Christmas.' I musta heard that thing five hundred times this month."

"Actually," Billy said, "according to the St. Cloud *Evening News,* Bing Crosby's version of 'White Christmas' will be played 2150 times during the month of December, and other artists' renditions of it will be played an additional 1890 times."

The caller snorted. "One time's too many for me. Who the heck wants a white Christmas anyway? I sure don't."

"Well, unfortunately, it looks like you're going to get one," Billy said. "And, in that spirit, here's Destiny's Child, singing 'White Christmas.'"

At 1:45 A.M., a number of geese in the city park in Bowling Green, Kentucky, woke up to a low, overcast sky and flew, flapping and honking loudly, over the city center, as if they had suddenly decided to fly farther south for the winter. The noise woke Maureen Reynolds, who couldn't get back to sleep. She turned on KYOU, which was playing "Holly Jolly Oldies," including "Rockin' Around the Christmas Tree" and Brenda Lee's rendition of "White Christmas."

At 2:15 A.M. Mountain Standard Time, Paula Devereaux arrived at DIA for the red-eye flight to Springfield, Illinois. It was beginning to snow, and as she waited in line at the express check-in (she was carrying on her maid-of-honor dress and the bag with her shoes and slip and makeup—the last time she'd been in a wedding, her luggage had gotten lost and caused a major crisis) and in line at security and in line at the gate and in line to be de-iced, she began to hope they might not be able to take off, but no such luck.

Of course not, Paula thought, looking out the window at the snow swirling around the wing, because Stacey wants me at her wedding.

"I want a Christmas Eve wedding," Stacey'd told Paula after she'd informed her she was going to be her maid of honor, "all candlelight and evergreens. And I want snow falling outside the windows."

"What if the weather doesn't cooperate?" Paula'd asked.

"It will," Stacey'd said. And here it was, snowing. She wondered if it was snowing in Springfield, too. Of course it is, she thought. Whatever Stacey wants, Stacey gets, Paula thought. Even Jim.

Don't think about that, she told herself. Don't think about anything. Just concentrate on getting through the wedding. With luck, Jim won't even be there except for the ceremony, and you won't have to spend any time with him at all.

She picked up the in-flight magazine and tried to read and then plugged in her headphones and listened to Channel 4, "Seasonal Favorites." The first song was "White Christmas" by the Statler Brothers.

At 3:38 A.M., it began to snow in Bowling Green, Kentucky. The geese circling the city flew back to the park, landed, and hunkered down to sit it out on their island in the lake. Snow began to collect on their backs, but they didn't care, protected as they were by down and a thick layer of subcutaneous fat designed to keep them warm even in sub-zero temperatures.

At 3:39 A.M., Luke Lafferty woke up, convinced he'd forgotten to set the goose his mother had talked him into having for

Christmas Eve dinner out to thaw. He went and checked. He *had* set it out. On his way back to bed, he looked out the window and saw it was snowing, which didn't worry him. The news had said isolated snow showers for Wichita, ending by mid-morning and none of his relatives lived more than an hour and a half away, except Aunt Lulla, and if she couldn't make it, it wouldn't exactly put a crimp in the conversation. His mom and Aunt Madge talked so much it was hard for anybody else to get a word in edgewise, especially Aunt Lulla. "She was always the shy one," Luke's mother said, and it was true, Luke couldn't remember her saying anything other than "Please pass the potatoes," at their family get-togethers.

What did worry him was the goose. He should never have let his mother talk him into having one. It was bad enough her having talked him into having the family dinner at his place. He had no idea how to cook a goose.

"What if something goes wrong?" he'd protested. "Butterball doesn't have a goose hotline."

"You won't need a hotline," his mother had said. "It's just like cooking a turkey, and it's not as if you had to cook it. I'll be there in time to put it in the oven and everything. All you have to do is set it out to thaw. Do you have a roasting pan?"

"Yes," Luke had said, but lying there, he couldn't remember if he did. When he got up at 4:14 A.M. to check—he did—it was still snowing.

At 4:16 Mountain Standard Time, Slade Henry, filling in on WRYT's late-night talk show out of Boise, said, "For all you folks who wanted a white Christmas, it looks like you're going to get your wish. Three to six inches forecast for western Idaho." He played several bars of Johnny Cash's "White Christmas," and then went back to discussing JFK's assassination with a caller who was convinced Clinton was somehow involved.

"Little Rock isn't all that far from Dallas, you know," the caller said. "You could drive it in four and a half hours."

Actually, you couldn't, because I-30 was icing up badly, due to freezing rain that had started just after midnight and then turned to snow. The treacherous driving conditions did not slow

Monty Luffer down as he had a Ford Explorer. Shortly after five, he reached to change stations on the radio so he didn't have to listen to "those damn Backstreet Boys" singing "White Christmas," and slid out of control just west of Texarkana. He crossed the median, causing the semi in the left-hand eastbound lane to jam on his brakes and jackknife, and resulting in a thirty-seven-car pileup that closed the road for the rest of the night and all the next day.

At 5:21 A.M. Pacific Standard Time, four-year-old Miguel Gutierrez jumped on his mother, shouting, "Is it Christmas yet?"

"Not on Mommy's stomach, honey," Pilar murmured and rolled over.

Miguel crawled over her and repeated his question directly into her ear. *"Is it Christmas yet?"*

"No," she said groggily. "Tomorrow's Christmas. Go watch cartoons for a few minutes, okay, and then Mommy'll get up," and pulled the pillow over her head.

Miguel was back again immediately. He can't find the remote, she thought wearily, but that couldn't be it, because he jabbed her in the ribs with it. "What's the matter, honey?" she said.

"Santa isn't gonna come," he said tearfully, which brought her fully awake.

He thinks Santa won't be able to find him, she thought. This is all Joe's fault. According to the original custody agreement, she had Miguel for Christmas and Joe had him for New Year's, but he'd gotten the judge to change it so they split Christmas Eve and Christmas Day, and then, after she'd told Miguel, Joe had announced he needed to switch.

When Pilar had said no, he'd threatened to take her back to court, so she'd agreed, after which he'd informed her that "Christmas Day" meant her delivering Miguel on Christmas Eve so he could wake up and open his presents at Joe's.

"He can open your presents to him before you come," he'd said, knowing full well Miguel still believed in Santa Claus. So after supper she was delivering both Miguel *and* his presents to Joe's in Escondido, where she would not get to see Miguel open them.

"I can't go to Daddy's," Miguel had said when she'd explained the arrangements, "Santa's gonna bring my presents *here*."

"No, he won't," she'd said. "I sent Santa a letter and told him you'd be at your daddy's on Christmas Eve, and he's going to take your presents there."

"You sent it to the North Pole?" he'd demanded.

"To the North Pole. I took it to the post office this morning," and he'd seemed contented with that answer. Till now.

"Santa's going to come," she said, cuddling him to her. "He's coming to Daddy's, remember?"

"No, he's not," Miguel sniffled.

Damn Joe. I shouldn't have given in, she thought, but every time they went back to court, Joe and his snake of a lawyer managed to wangle new concessions out of the judge, even though until the divorce was final, Joe had never paid any attention to Miguel at all. And she just couldn't afford any more court costs right now.

"Are you worried about Daddy living in Escondido?" she asked Miguel. "Because Santa's magic. He can travel all over California in one night. He can travel all over the *world* in one night."

Miguel, snuggled against her, shook his head violently. "No, he can't!"

"Why not?"

"Because it isn't *snowing!* I want it to snow. Santa can't come in his sleigh if it doesn't."

Paula's flight landed in Springfield at 7:48 A.M. Central Standard Time, twenty minutes late. Jim met her at the airport. "Stacey's having her hair done," he said. "I was afraid I wouldn't get here in time. It was a good thing your flight was a few minutes late."

"There was snow in Denver," Paula said, trying not to look at him. He was as cute as ever, with the same knee-weakening smile.

"It just started to snow here," he said.

How does she do it? Paula thought. You had to admire Stacey. Whatever she wanted, she got. I wouldn't have had to mess with carrying this stuff on, Paula thought, handing Jim the hanging bag with her dress in it. There's no way my luggage would have gotten lost. Stacey wanted it here.

"The roads are already starting to get slick," Jim was saying. "I hope my parents get here okay. They're driving down from Chicago."

They will, Paula thought. Stacey wants them to.

Jim got Paula's bags off the carousel and then said, "Hang on, I promised Stacey I'd tell her as soon as you got here." He flipped open his cell phone and put it to his ear. "Stacey? She's here. Yeah, I will. Okay, I'll pick them up on our way. Yeah. Okay."

He flipped the phone shut. "She wants us to pick up the ever-green garlands on our way," he said, "and then I have to come back and get Kindra and David. We need to check on their flights before we leave."

He led the way upstairs to ticketing so they could look at the arrival board. Outside the terminal windows snow was falling, large, perfect, lacy flakes.

"Kindra's on the two-nineteen from Houston," Jim said, scanning the board, "and David's on the eleven-forty from Newark. Oh, good, they're both on time."

Of course they are, Paula thought, looking at the board. The snow in Denver must be getting worse. All the Denver flights had "delayed" next to them, and so did a bunch of others: Cheyenne and Portland and Richmond. As she watched, Boston and then Chicago changed from "on time" to "delayed" and Rapid City went from "delayed" to "cancelled." She looked at Kindra's and David's flights again. They were still on time.

Ski areas in Aspen, Lake Placid, Squaw Valley, Stowe, Lake Tahoe, and Jackson Hole woke to several inches of fresh powder. The snow was greeted with relief by the people who had paid ninety dollars for their lift tickets, with irritation by the ski resort owners, who didn't see why it couldn't have come two weeks ear-lier when people were making their Christmas reservations, and with whoops of delight by snowboarders Kent Slakken and Bodine Cromps. They promptly set out from Breckenridge with-out maps, matches, helmets, avalanche beacons, avalanche probes, or telling anyone where they were going, for an off-limits backcountry area with "totally extreme slopes."

At 7:05, Miguel came in and jumped on Pilar again, this time on her bladder, shouting, "It's snowing! Now Santa can come! Now Santa can come!"

"Snowing?" she said blearily. In L.A.? "Snowing? Where?"

"On TV. Can I make myself some cereal?"

"No," she said, remembering the last time. She reached for her robe. "You go watch TV some more and Mommy'll make pancakes."

When she brought the pancakes and syrup in, Miguel was sitting, absorbed, in front of the TV, watching a man in a green parka standing in the snow in front of an ambulance with flashing lights, saying, "—third weather-related fatality in Dodge City so far this morning—"

"Let's find some cartoons to watch," Pilar said, clicking the remote.

"—outside Knoxville, Tennessee, where snow and icy conditions have caused a multi-car accident—"

She clicked the remote again.

"—to Columbia, South Carolina, where a surprise snowstorm has shut off power to—"

Click.

"—problem seems to be a low-pressure area covering Canada and the northern two-thirds of the United States, bringing snow to the entire Midwest and Mid-Atlantic States and—"

Click.

"—snowing here in Bozeman—"

"I told you it was snowing," Miguel said happily, eating his pancakes, "just like I wanted it to. After breakfast can we make a snowman?"

"Honey, it isn't snowing here in California," Pilar said. "That's the national weather, it's not here. That reporter's in Montana, not California."

Miguel grabbed the remote and clicked to a reporter standing in the snow in front of a giant redwood tree. "The snow started about four this morning here in Monterey, California. As you can see," she said, indicating her raincoat and umbrella, "it caught everybody by surprise."

"*She's* in California," Miguel said.

"She's in northern California," Pilar said, "which gets a lot colder than it does here in L.A. L.A.'s too warm for it to snow."

"No, it's not," Miguel said and pointed out the window, where big white flakes were drifting down onto the palm trees across the street.

At 9:40 Central Standard Time the cell phone Nathan Andrews thought he'd turned off rang in the middle of a grant money meeting that was already going badly. Scheduling the meeting in Omaha on the day before Christmas had seemed like a good idea at the time—businessmen had hardly any appointments that day and the spirit of the season was supposed to make them more willing to open their pocketbooks—but instead they were merely distracted, anxious to do their last-minute Mercedes-Benz shopping or get the Christmas office party started or whatever it was businessmen did, and worried about the snow that had started during rush hour this morning.

Plus, they were morons. "So you're saying you want a grant to study global warming, but then you talk about wanting to measure snow levels," one of them had said. "What does snow have to do with global warming?"

Nathan had tried to explain *again* how warming could lead to increased amounts of moisture in the atmosphere and thus increased precipitation in the form of rain and snow, and how that increased snowfall could lead to increased albedo and surface cooling.

"If it's getting cooler, it's not getting warmer," another one of the businessmen had said. "It can't be both."

"As a matter of fact, it can," he'd said and launched into his explanation of how polar melting could lead to an increase in freshwater in the North Atlantic, which would float on top of the Gulf Stream, preventing its warm water from sinking and cooling, and effectively shutting the current down. "Europe would freeze," he'd said.

"Well, then, global warming would be a good thing, wouldn't it?" yet another one had said. "Heat the place up."

He had patiently tried to explain how the world would grow both hotter and colder, with widespread droughts, flooding, and a sharp increase in severe weather. "And these changes may happen extremely quickly," he'd said. "Rather than temperatures gradually increasing and sea levels rising, there may be a sudden, unexpected event—a discontinuity. It may take the form of an abrupt, catastrophic temperature increase or a superhurricane or other form of megastorm, occurring without any warning. That's why this project is so critical. By setting up a comprehensive climate data base, we'll be able to create more accurate computer models, from which we'll be able to—"

"Computer models!" one of them had snorted. "They're wrong more often than they're right!"

"Because they don't include enough factors," Nathan said. "Climate is an incredibly complicated system, with literally thousands of factors interacting in intricate ways—weather patterns, clouds, precipitation, ocean currents, manmade activities, crops. Thus far computer models have only been able to chart a handful of factors. This project will chart over two hundred of them and will enable the models to be exponentially more accurate. We'll be able to predict a discontinuity before it happens—"

It was at that point that his cell phone rang. It was his graduate assistant Chin Sung, from the lab. "Where *are* you?" Chin demanded.

"In a grant meeting," Nathan whispered. "Can I call you back in a few minutes?"

"Not if you still want the Nobel Prize," Chin said. "You know that hare-brained theory of yours about global warming producing a sudden discontinuity? Well, I think you'd better get over here. Today may be the day you turn out to be right."

"Why?" Nathan asked, gripping the phone excitedly. "What's happened? Have the Gulf Stream temp readings dropped?"

"No, it's not the currents. It's what's happening here."

"Which is what?"

Instead of answering, Chin asked, "Is it snowing where you are?"

Nathan looked out the conference room window. "Yes."

"I thought so. It's snowing here, too."

"And that's what you called me about?" Nathan whispered. "Because it's snowing in Nebraska in December? In case you haven't looked at a calendar lately, winter started three days ago. It's *supposed* to be snowing."

"You don't understand," Chin said. "It isn't just snowing in Nebraska. It's snowing everywhere."

"What do you mean, everywhere?"

"I mean everywhere. Seattle, Salt Lake City, Minneapolis, Providence, Chattanooga. All over Canada and the U.S. as far south as—" there was a pause and the sound of computer keys clicking "—Abilene and Shreveport and Savannah. No, wait, Tallahassee's reporting light snow. As far south as Tallahassee."

The jet stream must have dipped radically south. "Where's the center of the low pressure system?"

"That's just it," Chin said. "There doesn't seem to be one."

"I'll be right there," Nathan said.

A mile from the highway snowboarders Kent Slakken and Bodine Cromps, unable to see the road in heavily falling snow, drove their car into a ditch. "Shit," Bodine said, and attempted to get out of it by revving the engine and then flooring it, a technique that only succeeded in digging them in to the point where they couldn't open either car door.

It took Jim and Paula nearly two hours to pick up the evergreen garlands and get out to the church. The lacy flakes fell steadily faster and thicker, and it was so slick Jim had to crawl the last few miles. "I hope this doesn't get any worse," he said worriedly, "or people are going to have a hard time getting out here."

But Stacey wasn't worried at all. "Isn't it beautiful? I wanted it to snow for my wedding more than anything," she said, meeting them at the door of the church. "Come here, Paula, you've got to see how the snow looks through the sanctuary windows. It's going to be perfect."

Jim left immediately to go pick up Kindra and David, which Paula was grateful for. Being that close to him in the car had made her start entertaining the ridiculous hopes about him she'd had when they first met. And they were ridiculous. One look at Stacey had shown her that.

The bride-to-be looked beautiful even in a sweater and jeans, her makeup exquisite, her blonde hair upswept into glittery snowflake-sprinkled curls. Every time Paula had had her hair done to be in a wedding, she had come out looking like someone in a bad 1950s movie. *How does she do it?* Paula wondered. *You watch, the snow will stop and start up again just in time for the ceremony.*

But it didn't. It continued to come down steadily, and when the minister arrived for the rehearsal, she said, "I don't know. It took me half an hour to get out of my driveway. You may want to think about canceling."

"Don't be silly. We can't cancel. It's a Christmas Eve wedding," Stacey said, and made Paula start tying the evergreen garlands to the pews with white satin ribbon.

It was sprinkling in Santa Fe when Bev Carey arrived at her hotel, and by the time she'd checked in and ventured out into the plaza, it had turned into an icy, driving rain that went right through the light coat and thin gloves she'd brought with her. She had planned to spend the morning shopping, but the shops had signs on them saying "Closed Christmas Eve and Christmas Day," and the sidewalk in front of the Governor's Palace, where, according to her guidebook, Zunis and Navajos sat to sell authentic silver-and-turquoise jewelry, was deserted.

But at least it's not snowing, she told herself, trudging, shivering, back to the hotel. And the shop windows were decorated with *ristras* and lights in the shape of chili peppers, and the Christmas tree in the hotel lobby was decorated with kachina dolls.

Her friend Janice had already called and left a message with the hotel clerk. *And if I don't call her back, she'll be convinced I've taken a bottle of sleeping pills,* Bev thought, going up to her room. On the way to the airport, Janice had asked anxiously, "You haven't been having suicidal thoughts, have you?" and when her friend Louise had found out what Bev was planning, she'd said, "I saw this piece on *Dateline* the other night about suicides at Christmas, and how people who've lost a spouse are especially vulnerable. You wouldn't do anything like that, would you?"

They none of them understood that she was doing this to save her life, not end it, that it was Christmas at home, with its lighted trees and evergreen wreaths and candles, that would kill her. And its snow.

"I know you miss Howard," Janice had said, "and that with Christmas coming, you're feeling sad."

Sad? She felt flayed, battered, beaten. Every memory, every thought of her husband, every use of the past tense even— "Howard liked . . . ," "Howard knew . . . ," "Howard was . . . ,"— was like a deadly blow. The grief-counseling books all talked about "the pain of losing a loved one," but she had had no idea the pain could be this bad. It was like being stabbed over and over, and her only hope had been to get away. She hadn't "decided to go to Santa Fe for Christmas." She had run there like a victim fleeing a murderer.

She took off her drenched coat and gloves and called Janice. "You promised you'd call as soon as you got there," Janice said reproachfully. "Are you all right?"

"I'm fine," Bev said. "I was out walking around the Plaza." She didn't say anything about its raining. She didn't want Janice saying, I told you so. "It's beautiful here."

"I should have come with you," Janice said. "It's snowing like crazy here. Ten inches so far. I suppose you're sitting on a patio drinking a margarita right now."

"Sangria," Bev lied. "I'm going sightseeing this afternoon. The houses here are all pink and tan adobe with bright blue and red and yellow doors. And right now the whole town's decorated with *luminarias*. You should see them."

"I wish I could," Janice sighed. "All I can see is snow. I have no idea how I'm going to get to the store. Oh, well, at least we'll have a white Christmas. It's so sad Howard can't be here to see this. He always loved white Christmases, didn't he?"

Howard, consulting the *Farmer's Almanac*, reading the weather forecast out loud to her, calling her over to the picture window to watch the snow beginning to fall, saying, "Looks like we're going to get a white Christmas this year," as if it were a present under the tree, putting his arm around her—

"Yes," Bev managed to say through the sudden, searing stab of pain. "He did."

It was spitting snow when Warren Nesvick checked into the Marriott in Baltimore. As soon as he got Shara up to the suite, he told her he had to make a business call, "and then I'll be all yours, honey." He went down to the lobby. The TV in the corner was showing a weather map. He looked at it for a minute and then got out his cell phone.

"Where *are* you?" his wife Marjean said when she answered.

"In St. Louis," he said. "Our flight got rerouted here because of snow at O'Hare. What's the weather like there?"

"It's snowing," she said. "When do you think you'll be able to get a flight out?"

"I don't know. Everything's booked because of it being Christmas Eve. I'm waiting to see if I can get on standby. I'll call you as soon as I know something," and hung up before she could ask him which flight.

It took Nathan an hour and a half to drive the fifteen miles to the lab. During the ride he considered the likelihood that this was really a discontinuity and not just a major snowstorm. Global warming proponents (and opponents) confused the two all the time. Every hurricane, tornado, heat wave, or dry spell was attributed to global warming, even though nearly all of them fell well within the range of normal weather patterns.

And there had been big December snowstorms before. The blizzard of 1888, for instance, and the Christmas Eve storm of 2002. And Chin was probably wrong about there being no center to the low pressure system. The likely explanation was that there was more than one system involved—one centered in the Great Lakes and another just east of the Rockies, colliding with warm, moist air from the Gulf Coast to create unusually widespread snow.

And it *was* widespread. The car radio was reporting snow all across the Midwest and the entire East Coast—Topeka, Tulsa, Peoria, northern Virginia, Hartford, Montpelier, Reno, Spokane. No, Reno and Spokane were west of the Rockies. There must be a third system, coming down from the Northwest. But it was still hardly a discontinuity.

The lab parking lot hadn't been plowed. He left the car on the street and struggled through the already knee-deep snow to the door, remembering when he was halfway across the expanse that Nebraska was famous for pioneers who got lost going out to the barn in a blizzard and whose frozen bodies weren't found till the following spring.

He reached the door, opened it, and stood there a moment blowing on his frozen hands and looking at the TV Chin had stuck on a cart in the corner of the lab. On it, a pretty reporter in a parka and a Mickey Mouse hat was standing in heavy snow in front of what seemed to be a giant snowman. "The snow has really caused problems here at Disney World," she said over the sound of a marching band playing "White Christmas." "Their annual Christmas Eve Parade has—"

"Well, it's about time," Chin said, coming in from the fax room with a handful of printouts. "What took you so long?" Nathan ignored that. "Have you got the IPOC data?" he asked.

Chin nodded. He sat down at his terminal and started typing. The upper left-hand screen lit up with columns of numbers.

"Let me see the National Weather Service map," Nathan said, unzipping his coat and sitting down at the main console.

Chin called up a U.S. map nearly half-covered with blue, from western Oregon and Nevada east all the way to the Atlantic and up through New England and south to the Oklahoma panhandle, northern Mississippi, Alabama, and most of Georgia.

"Good Lord, that's even bigger than Marina in '92," Nathan said. "Have you got a satellite photo?"

Chin nodded and called it up. "And this is a real-time composite of all the data coming in, including weather stations, towns, and spotters reporting in. The white's snow," he added unnecessarily.

The white covered even more territory than the blue on the NWS map, with jagged fingers stretching down into Arizona and

Louisiana and west into Oregon and California. Surrounding them were wide uneven pink bands. "Is the pink rain?" Nathan asked.

"Sleet," Chin said. "So what do you think? It's a discontinuity, isn't it?"

"I don't know," Nathan said, calling up the barometric readings and starting through them.

"What else could it be? It's snowing in Orlando. And San Diego."

"It's snowed both of those places before," Nathan said. "It's even snowed in Death Valley. The only place in the U.S. where it's never snowed is the Florida Keys. And Hawaii, of course. Everything on this map right now is within the range of normal weather events. You don't have to start worrying till it starts snowing in the Florida Keys."

"What about other places?" Chin asked, looking at the center right-hand screen.

"What do you mean, other places?"

"I mean, it isn't just snowing in the U.S. I'm getting reports from Cancun. And Jerusalem."

At eleven-thirty Pilar gave up trying to explain that there wasn't enough snow to make a snowman and took Miguel outside, bundled up in a sweatshirt, a sweater, and his warm jacket, with a pair of Pilar's tube socks for mittens. He lasted about five minutes.

When they came back in, Pilar settled him at the kitchen table with crayons and paper so he could draw a picture of a snowman and went into the living room to check the weather forecast. It was really snowing hard out there, and she was getting a little worried about taking Miguel down to Escondido. Los Angelenos didn't know how to drive in snow, and Pilar's tires weren't that good.

"—snowing here in Hollywood," said a reporter standing in front of the nearly invisible Hollywood sign, "and this isn't soapflakes, folks, it's the real thing."

She switched channels. "—snowing in Santa Monica," a reporter standing on the beach was saying, "but that isn't stopping the surfers. . . ."

Click. "—*para la primera vez en ciencuenta anos en* Marina del Rey—"

Click. "—snowing here in L.A. for the first time in nearly fifty years. We're here on the set of *XXX II* with Vin Diesel. What do you think of the snow, Vin?"

She gave up and went back in the kitchen where Miguel announced he was ready to go outside again. She talked him into listening to Alvin and the Chipmunks instead. "Okay," he said, and she left him warbling "White Christmas" along with Alvin and went in to check the weather again. The Santa Monica reporter briefly mentioned the roads were wet before moving on to interview a psychic who claimed to have predicted the snowstorm, and on a Spanish-language channel she caught a glimpse of the 405 moving along at its usual congested pace.

The roads must not be too bad, she thought, or they'd all be talking about it, but she still wondered if she hadn't better take Miguel down to Escondido early. She hated to give up her day with him, but his safety was the important thing, and the snow wasn't letting up at all.

When Miguel came into the living room and asked when they could go outside, she said, "After we pack your suitcase, okay? Do you want to take your Pokémon jammies or your Spider-Mans?" and began gathering up his things.

By noon Eastern Standard Time, it was snowing in every state in the lower forty-eight. Elko, Nevada, had over two feet of snow, Cincinnati was reporting thirty-eight inches at the airport, and it was spitting snow in Miami.

On talk radio, JFK's assassination had given way to the topic of the snow. "You mark my words, the terrorists are behind this," a caller from Terre Haute said. "They want to destroy our economy, and what better way to do it than by keeping us from doing our last-minute Christmas shopping? To say nothing of what this snow's going to do to my relationship with my wife. How am I supposed to go buy her something in this weather? I tell you, this has got Al Qaeda's name written all over it."

During lunch, Warren Nesvick told Shara he needed to go try his business call again. "The guy I was trying to get in touch with wasn't in the office before. Because of the snow," he said and went out to the lobby to call Marjean again. On the TV in the corner, there were shots of snow-covered runways and jammed ticket counters. A blonde reporter in a tight red sweater was saying, "Here in Cincinnati, the snow just keeps on falling. The airport's still open, but officials indicate it may have to close. Snow is building up on the runways—"

He called Marjean. "I'm in Cincinnati," he told her. "I managed to get a flight at the last minute. There's a three-hour layover till my connecting flight, but at least I've got a seat."

"But isn't it snowing in Cincinnati?" she asked. "I was just watching the TV and . . ."

"It's supposed to let up here in an hour or so. I'm really sorry about this, honey. You know I'd be there for Christmas Eve if I could."

"I know," she said, sounding disappointed. "It's okay, Warren. You can't control the weather."

The television was on in the hotel lobby when Bev came down to lunch. "—snowing in Albuquerque," she heard the announcer say, "Raton, Santa Rosa, and Wagon Mound."

But not in Santa Fe, she told herself firmly, going into the dining room. "It hardly ever snows there," the travel agent had said, "New Mexico's a desert. And when it does snow, it never sticks."

"There's already four inches in Espanola," a plump waitress in a ruffled blouse and full red skirt was saying to the busboy. "I'm worried about getting home."

"I'd rather it didn't snow for Christmas," Bev had teased Howard last year, "all those people trying to get home."

"Heresy, woman, heresy! What would Currier and Ives think to hear you talk that way?" he'd said, clutching his chest.

Like she was clutching hers now. The plump waitress was looking at her worriedly. "Are you all right, *señora?*"

"Yes," Bev said. "One for lunch, please."

The waitress led her to a table, still looking concerned, and handed her a menu, and she clung to it like a life raft, concentrating fiercely on the unfamiliar terms, the exotic ingredients:

blue corn tortillas, quesadillas, chipotle—

"Can I get you something to drink?" the waitress asked.

"Yes," Bev said brightly, looking at the waitress's name tag. "I'd like some sangria, Carmelita."

Carmelita nodded and left, and Bev looked around the room, thinking, I'll drink my sangria and watch the other diners, eavesdrop on their conversations, but she was the only person in the broad tiled room. It faced the patio, and through the glass doors the rain, sleet now, drove sharply against the terracotta pots of cactus outside, the stacked tables and chairs, the collapsed umbrellas.

She had envisioned herself having lunch out on the patio, sitting in the sun under one of those umbrellas, looking out at the desert and listening to a mariachi band. The music coming over the loudspeakers was Christmas carols. As she listened, "Let It Snow" came to an end and the Supremes began to sing "White Christmas."

"What would cloud-seeding be listed under?" Howard had asked her one year when there was still no snow by the twenty-second, coming into the dining room, where she was wrapping presents, with the phone book.

"You are *not* hiring a cloud seeder," she had laughed.

"Would it be under 'clouds' or 'rainmaker'?" he'd asked mockseriously. "Or 'seeds'?" And when it had finally snowed on the twenty-fourth, he had acted like he was personally responsible.

"You did *not* cause this Howard," she had told him.

"How do you know?" He'd laughed, catching her into his arms.

I can't stand this, Bev thought, looking frantically around the dining room for Carmelita and her sangria. How do other people do it? She knew lots of widows, and they all seemed fine. When people mentioned their husbands, when they talked about them in the past tense, they were able to stand there, to smile back, to talk about them. Doreen Matthews had even said, "Now that Bill's gone, I can finally have all pink ornaments on the Christmas tree. I've always wanted to have a pink tree, but he wouldn't hear of it."

"Here's your sangria," Carmelita said, still looking concerned. "Would you like some tortilla chips and salsa?"

"Yes, thank you," Bev said brightly. "And I think I'll have the chicken enchiladas."

Carmelita nodded and disappeared again. Bev took a gulp of her sangria and got her guidebook out of her bag. She would have a nice lunch and then go sightseeing. She opened the book to Area Attractions. "Pueblo de San Ildefonso." No, that would involve a lot of walking around outdoors, and it was still sleeting outside the window.

"Petroglyphs National Monument." No, that was down near Albuquerque, where it was snowing. "El Santuario de Chimayo. 28 mi. north of Santa Fe on Hwy. 76. Historic weaving center, shops, chapel dubbed 'American Lourdes.' The dirt in the ante-room beside the altar is reputed to have healing powers when rubbed on the afflicted part of the body."

But I hurt all over, she thought.

"Other attractions include five nineteenth-century reredos, a carving of Santo Nino de Atocha, carved wooden altarpiece. (See also Lagrima, p. 98.)"

She turned the page to ninety-eight. "Chapel of Our Lady of Perpetual Sorrow, Lagrima, 28 mi. SE of Santa Fe on Hwy 41. Sixteenth-century adobe mission church. In 1968 the statue of the Virgin Mary in the transept was reported to shed healing tears."

Healing tears, holy dirt, and wasn't there supposed to be a miraculous staircase right here in town? Yes, there it was. The Loretto Chapel. "Open 10-5 Apr-Oct, closed Nov-Mar."

It would have to be Chimayo. She got out the road map the car rental place had given her, and when Carmelita came with the chips and salsa, she said, "I'm thinking of driving up to Chimayo. What's the best route?"

"Today?" Carmelita said, dismayed. "That's not a good idea. The road's pretty curvy, and we just got a call from Taos that it's really snowing hard up there."

"How about one of the pueblos then?"

She shook her head. "You have to take dirt roads to get there, and it's getting very icy. You're better off doing something here in town. There's a Christmas Eve mass at the cathedral at midnight," she added helpfully.

But I need something to do this afternoon, Bev thought, bending over the guidebook again. Indian Research Center— open weekends only. El Rancho de las Golondrinas—closed Nov-Mar. Santa Fe Historical Museum—closed Dec 24-Jan 1.

The Georgia O'Keeffe Museum—open daily.

Perfect, Bev thought, reading the entry: "Houses world's largest permanent collection of O'Keeffe's work. A major American artist, O'Keeffe lived in the Santa Fe area for many years. When she first arrived in 1929, she was physically and psychologically ill, but the dry, hot New Mexico climate healed and inspired her, and she painted much of her finest work here."

Perfect. Sun-baked paintings of cow skulls and giant tropical flowers and desert buttes. "Open daily. 10 A.M.–6 P.M. 217 Johnson St."

She looked up the address on her map. Only three blocks off the Plaza, within easy walking distance even in this weather. Perfect. When Carmelita brought her enchiladas, she attacked them eagerly.

"Did you find somewhere to go in town?" Carmelita asked curiously.

"Yes, the Georgia O'Keeffe Museum."

"Oh," Carmelita said and vanished again. She was back almost immediately. "I'm sorry, *señora,* but they're closed."

"Closed? It said in the guidebook the museum's open daily."

"It's because of the snow."

"Snow?" Bev said and looked past her to the patio where the sleet had turned to a heavy, slashing snow.

At 1:20, Jim called from the airport to tell them Kindra's and David's planes had both been delayed, and a few minutes later the bakery delivered the wedding cake. "No, no," Stacey said, "that's supposed to go to the country club. That's where the reception is."

"We tried," the driver said. "We couldn't get through. We can either leave it here or take it back to the bakery, take your pick. If we can *get* back to the bakery. Which I doubt."

"Leave it here," Stacey said. "Jim can take it over when he gets here."

"But you just heard him," Paula said. "If the truck can't get through, Jim won't be able to—" The phone rang.

It was the florist, calling to say they weren't going to be able to deliver the flowers. "But you have to," Stacey said. "The wedding's at five. Tell them they have to, Paula," and handed the phone to her.

"Isn't there any way you can get here?" Paula asked.

"Not unless there's a miracle," the florist said. "Our truck's in a ditch out at Pawnee, and there's no telling how long it'll take a tow truck to get to it. It's a skating rink out there."

"Jim will have to go pick up the flowers when he gets back with Kindra and David," Stacey said blithely when Paula told her the bad news. "He can do it on his way to the country club. Is the string quartet here yet?"

"No, and I'm not sure they'll be able to get here. The florist said the roads are really icy," Paula said, and the viola player walked in.

"I told you," Stacey said happily, "it'll all work out. Did I tell you, they're going to play Boccherini's 'Minuet No. 8' for the wedding march?" and went to get the candles for the altar stands.

Paula went over to the viola player, a lanky young guy. He was brushing snow off his viola case. "Where's the rest of the quartet?"

"They're not here yet?" he said, surprised. "I had a lesson to give in town and told 'em I'd catch up with them." He sat down to take off his snow-crusted boots. "And then my car ended up in a snowbank, and I had to walk the last mile and a half." He grinned up at her, panting. "It's times like these I wish I played the piccolo. Although," he said, looking her up and down, "there are compensations. Please tell me you're not the bride."

"I'm not the bride," she said. Even though I wish I was.

"Great!" he said and grinned at her again. "What are you doing after the wedding?"

"I'm not sure there's going to be one. Do you think the other musicians got stuck on the way here, too?"

He shook his head. "I would have seen them." He pulled out a cell phone and punched buttons. "Shep? Yeah, where are you?" There was a pause. "That's what I was afraid of. What about

Leif?" Another pause. "Well, if you find him, call me back." He flipped the phone shut. "Bad news. The violins were in a fender bender and are waiting for the cops. They don't know where the cello is. How do you feel about a viola solo of 'Minuet No. 8'?"

Paula went to inform Stacey. "The police can bring them out," Stacey said blithely and handed Paula the white candles for the altar stands. "The candlelight on the snow's going to be just beautiful."

At 1:48 P.M. Eastern Standard Time, snow flurries were reported at Sunset Point in the Florida Keys.

"I get to officially freak out now, right?" Chin asked Nathan. "Jeez, it really *is* the discontinuity you said would happen!"

"We don't know that yet," Nathan said, looking at the National Weather Service map, which was now entirely blue, except for a small spot near Fargo and another one in north-central Texas that Nathan thought was Waco and Chin was convinced was the president's ranch in Crawford.

"What do you mean, we don't know that yet? It's snowing in Barcelona. It's snowing in Moscow."

"It's supposed to be snowing in Moscow. Remember Napoleon? It's not unusual for it to be snowing in over two-thirds of these places reporting in: Oslo, Kathmandu, Buffalo—"

"Well, it's sure as hell unusual for it to be snowing in Beirut," Chin said, pointing to the snow reports coming in, "and Honolulu. I don't care what you say, I'm freaking out."

"You can't," Nathan said, superimposing an isobaric grid over the map. "I need you to feed me the temp readings."

Chin started over to his terminal and then came back. "What do *you* think?" he asked seriously. "Do you think it's a discontinuity?"

There was nothing else it could be. Winter storms were frequently very large, the February 1994 European storm had been huge, and the one in December 2002 had covered over a third of the U.S., but there'd never been one that covered the entire continental United States. And Mexico and Manitoba and Belize, he thought, watching the snowfall reports coming in.

In addition, snow was falling in six locations where it had

never fallen before, and in twenty-eight like Yuma, Arizona, where it had snowed only once or twice in the last hundred years. New Orleans had a foot of snow, for God's sake. And it was snowing in Guatemala.

And it wasn't behaving like any storm he'd ever seen. According to the charts, snow had started simultaneously in Springfield, Illinois; Hoodoo, Tennessee; Park City, Utah; and Branford, Connecticut; and spread in a completely random pattern. There was no center to the storm, no leading edge, no front.

And no let-up. No station had reported the snow stopping, or even diminishing, and new stations were reporting in all the time. At this rate, it would be snowing everywhere by—he made a rapid calculation—five o'clock.

"Well?" Chin said. "Is it?" He looked really frightened.

And him freaking out is the last thing I need with all this data to feed in, Nathan thought. "We don't have enough data to make a determination yet," he said.

"But you think it might be," Chin persisted. "Don't you? You think all the signs are there?"

Yes, Nathan thought. "Definitely not," he said. "Look at the TV."

"What about it?"

"There's one sign that's not present." He gestured at the screen. "No logo."

"No what?"

"No logo. Nothing qualifies as a full-fledged crisis until the cable newschannels give it a logo of its own, preferably with a colon. You know, *O.J.: Trial of the Century* or *Sniper at Large* or *Attack: Iraq*. He pointed at Dan Rather standing in thickly falling snow in front of the White House. "Look, it says *Breaking News,* but there's no logo. So it can't be a discontinuity. So feed me those temps. And then go see if you can scare up a couple more TVs. I want to get a look at exactly what's going on out there. Maybe that'll give us some kind of clue."

Chin nodded, looking reassured, and went to get the temp readings. They were all over the place, too, from eighteen below in Saskatoon to thirty-one above in Ft. Lauderdale. Nathan ran them against average temps for mid-December and then highs and lows for the twenty-fourth, looking for patterns, anomalies.

Chin wheeled in a big-screen TV on an AV cart, along with Professor Adler's portable, and plugged them in. "What do you want these on?" he asked.

"CNN, the Weather Channel, Fox—" Nathan began.

"Oh, no," Chin said.

"What? What is it?"

"Look," Chin said and pointed to Professor Adler's portable. Wolf Blitzer was standing in the snow in front of the Empire State Building. At the lower right-hand corner was the CNN symbol. And in the upper left-hand corner: *Storm of the Century.*

As soon as Pilar had Miguel's things packed, she checked on the TV again.

"—resulting in terrible road conditions," the reporter was saying. "Police are reporting accidents at the intersection of Sepulveda and Figueroa, the intersection of San Pedro and Whittier, the intersection of Hollywood and Vine," while accident alerts crawled across the bottom of the screen. "We're getting reports of a problem on the Santa Monica Freeway just past the Culver City exit and . . . this just in, the northbound lanes of the 110 are closed due to a five-car accident. Travelers are advised to take alternate routes."

The phone rang. Miguel ran into the kitchen to answer it. "Hi, Daddy, it's snowing," he shouted into the receiver. "We're going outside and make a snowman," and then said, "Okay," and handed it to Pilar.

"Go watch cartoons and let Mommy talk to Daddy," she said and handed him the remote. "Hello, Joe."

"I want you to bring Miguel down now," her ex-husband said without preamble, "before the snow gets bad."

"It's already bad," Pilar said, standing in the door of the kitchen watching Miguel flip through the channels:

"—really slick out here—"

"—advised to stay home. If you don't have to go someplace, folks, don't."

"—treacherous conditions—"

"I'm not sure taking him out in this is a good idea," Pilar said. "The TV's saying the roads are really slick, and—"

"And I'm saying bring him down here now," Joe said nastily. "I know what you're doing. You think you can use a little snow as an excuse to keep my son away from me on Christmas."

"I am not," she protested. "I'm just thinking about Miguel's safety. I don't have snow tires—"

"Like hell you're thinking about the kid! You're thinking this is a way to do me out of my rights. Well, we'll see what my lawyer has to say about that. I'm calling him *and* the judge and telling them what you're up to, and that I'm sick of this crap, I want full custody. And then I'm coming up there myself to get him. Have him ready when I get there!" he shouted and hung up the phone.

At 2:22 P.M., Luke's mother called on her cell phone to say she was going to be late and to go ahead and start the goose. "The roads are terrible, and people do *not* know how to drive. This red Subaru ahead of me just *swerved* into my lane and—"

"Mom, Mom," Luke cut in. "The goose. What do you mean, start the goose? What do I have to do?"

"Just put it in the oven. Shorty and Madge should be there soon, and she can take over. All you have to do is get it started. Take the bag of giblets out first. Put an aluminum foil tent over it."

"An aluminum-foil what?"

"Tent. Fold a piece of foil in half and lay it over the goose. It keeps it from browning too fast."

"How big a piece?"

"Big enough to cover the goose. And don't tuck in the edges."

"Of the oven?"

"Of the tent. You're making this much harder than it is. You wouldn't *believe* how many cars there are off the road, and every one of them's an SUV. It serves them right. They think just because they've got four-wheel drive, they can go ninety miles an hour in a *blizzard*—"

"Mom, Mom, what about stuffing? Don't I have to stuff the goose?"

"No. Nobody does stuffing inside the bird anymore. Salmonella. Just put the goose in the roasting pan and stick it in the oven. At 350 degrees."

I can do that, Luke thought, and did. Ten minutes later he

realized he'd forgotten to put the aluminum foil tent on. It took him three tries to get a piece the right size, and his mother hadn't said whether the shiny or the dull side should be facing out, but when he checked the goose twenty minutes later, it seemed to be doing okay. It smelled good, and there were already juices forming in the pan.

After Pilar hung up with Joe, she sat at the kitchen table a long time, trying to think which was worse, letting Joe take Miguel out into this snowstorm or having Miguel witness the fight that would ensue if she tried to stop him. "Please, please . . ." she murmured, without even knowing what she was praying for.

Miguel came into the kitchen and climbed into her lap. She wiped hastily at her eyes. "Guess what, honey?" she said brightly. "Daddy's going to come get you in a little bit. You need to go pick out which toys you want to take."

"Hunh-unh," Miguel said, shaking his head.

"I know you wanted to make a snowman," she said, "but guess what? It's snowing in Escondido, too. You can make a snowman with Daddy."

"Hunh-*unh*," he said, climbing down off her lap and tugging on her hand. He led her into the living room.

"What, honey?" she said, and he pointed at the TV. On it, the Santa Monica reporter was saying, "—the following road closures: I-5 from Chula Vista to Santa Ana, I-15 from San Diego to Barstow, Highway 78 from Oceanside to Escondido—"

Thank you, she murmured silently, thank you. Miguel ran out to the kitchen and came back with a piece of construction paper and a red crayon. "Here," he said, thrusting them at Pilar. "You have to write Santa. So he'll know to bring my presents here and not Daddy's."

By ordering sopapillas and then Mexican coffee, Bev managed to make lunch last till nearly two o'clock. When Carmelita brought the coffee, she looked anxiously out at the snow piling up on the patio and then back at Bev, so Bev asked for her check and signed it so Carmelita could leave, and then went back up to her room for her coat and gloves.

Even if the shops were closed, she could window-shop, she told herself, she could look at the Navajo rugs and Santa Clara pots and Indian jewelry displayed in the shops, but the snowstorm was getting worse. The luminarias that lined the walls were heaped with snow, the paper bags which held the candles sagging under the soggy weight.

They'll never get them lit, Bev thought, turning into the Plaza.

By the time she had walked down one side of it, the snow had become a blizzard, it was coming down so hard you couldn't see across the Plaza, and there was a cutting wind. She gave up and went back to the hotel.

In the lobby, the staff, including the front desk clerk and Carmelita in her coat and boots, was gathered in front of the TV looking at a weather map of New Mexico. ". . . currently snowing in most of New Mexico," the announcer was saying, "including Gallup, Carlsbad, Ruidoso, and Roswell. Travel advisories out for central, western, and southern New Mexico, including Lordsburg, Las Cruces, and Truth or Consequences. It looks like a white Christmas for most of New Mexico, folks."

"You have two messages," the front desk clerk said when he saw her. They were both from Janice, and she phoned again while Bev was taking her coat off.

"I just saw on TV that it's snowing in Santa Fe, and you said you were going sightseeing," Janice said. "I just wondered if you were okay."

"I'm here at the hotel," Bev said. "I'm not going anywhere."

"*Good,*" Janice said, relieved. "Are you watching TV? The weathermen are saying this isn't an ordinary storm. It's some kind of extreme mega-storm. We've got three feet here. The power's out all over town, and the airport just closed. I hope you're able to get home. Oops, the lights just flickered. I'd better go hunt up some candles before the lights go off," she said, and hung up.

Bev turned on the TV. The local channel was listing closings: "The First United Methodist Church Christmas pageant has been cancelled and there will be no *Posadas* tonight at Our Lady of Guadalupe. Canyon Day Care Center will close at 3:00 P.M. . . ."

She clicked the remote. CNBC was discussing earlier Christmas Eve snowstorms, and on CNN, Daryn Kagan was standing in the middle of Fifth Avenue in a snowdrift. "This is usually the busiest shopping day of the year," she said, "but as you can see—"

She clicked the remote, looking for a movie to watch. Howard would have loved this, she thought involuntarily. He would have been in his element.

She clicked quickly through the other channels, trying to find a film, but they were all discussing the weather. "It looks like the whole country's going to get a white Christmas this year," Peter Jennings was saying, "whether they want it or not."

You'd think there'd be a Christmas movie on, Bev thought grimly, flipping through the channels again. It's Christmas Eve. *Christmas in Connecticut* or *Holiday Inn*. Or *White Christmas*.

Howard had insisted on watching it every time he came across it with the remote, even if it was nearly over. "Why are you watching that?" she'd ask, coming in to find him glued to the next-to-the-last scene. "We own the video."

"Shh," he'd say. "It's just getting to the good part," and he'd lean forward to watch Bing Crosby push open the barn doors to reveal fake-looking snow falling on the equally fake-looking set.

When he came into the kitchen afterward, she'd say sarcastically, "How'd it end this time? Did Bing and Rosemary Clooney get back together? Did they save the General's inn and all live happily ever after?"

But Howard would refuse to be baited. "They got a white Christmas," he'd say happily and go off to look out the windows at the clouds.

Except for news about the storm, there was nothing at all on except an infomercial selling a set of Ginsu knives. How appropriate, she thought, and sat back on the bed to watch it.

At 2:08, the weight of the new loose snow triggered a huge avalanche in the "awesome slopes" area near Breckenridge, knocking down huge numbers of Ponderosa pines and burying everything in its path, but not Kent and Bodine, who were still in their Honda, trying to keep warm and survive on a box of Tic-Tacs and an old donut found in the glove compartment.

By two-thirty, Madge and Shorty still weren't there, so Luke checked the goose. It seemed to be cooking okay, but there was an awful lot of juice in the pan. When he checked it again half an hour later, there was over an inch of the stuff.

That couldn't be right. The last time he'd gotten stuck with having the Christmas Eve dinner, the turkey had only produced a few tablespoons of juice. He remembered his mom pouring them off to make the gravy.

He tried his mom. Her cell phone said, "Caller unavailable," which meant her batteries had run down, or she'd turned it off. He tried Aunt Madge's. No answer.

He dug the plastic and net wrapping the goose had come in out of the trash, flattened it out, and read the instructions: "Roast uncovered at 350 degrees for twenty-five minutes per pound."

Uncovered. That must be the problem, the aluminum foil tent. It wasn't allowing the extra juice to evaporate. He opened the oven and removed it. When he checked the goose again fifteen minutes later, it was sitting in two inches of grease, and even though, according to the wrapping, it still had three hours to go, the goose was getting brown and crispy on top.

At 2:51 P.M., Joe Gutierrez slammed out of his house and started up to get Miguel. He'd been trying to get his goddamned lawyer on the phone ever since he'd hung up on Pilar, but the lawyer wasn't answering.

The streets were a real mess, and when Joe got to the I-15 entrance ramp, there was a barricade across it. He roared back down the street to take Highway 78, but it was blocked, too. He stormed back home and called Pilar's lawyer, but he didn't answer either. He then called the judge, using the unlisted cell phone number he'd seen on his lawyer's palm pilot.

The judge, who had been stuck waiting for AAA in a Starbuck's at the Bakersfield exit, listening to Harry Connick, Jr., destroy "White Christmas" for the last three hours, was not particularly sympathetic, especially when Joe started swearing at him.

Words were exchanged, and the judge made a note to himself to have Joe declared in contempt of court. Then he called AAA to see what was taking so long, and when the operator told him he was nineteenth in line, and it would be at least another four hours, he decided to revisit the entire custody agreement.

By three o'clock, all the networks and cable newschannels had logos. ABC had *Winter Wonderland,* NBC had *Super Storm,* and Fox News had *Winter Wallop.* CBS and MSNBC had both gone with *White Christmas,* flanked by a photo of Bing Crosby (MSNBC's wearing the Santa Claus hat from the movie.)

The Weather Channel's logo was a changing world map that was now two-thirds white, and snow was being reported in Karachi, Seoul, the Solomon Islands, and Bethlehem, where Christmas Eve services (usually cancelled due to Israeli-Palestinian violence) had been cancelled due to the weather.

At 3:15 P.M., Jim called Paula from the airport to report that Kindra and David's flights had both been delayed indefinitely. "And the US Air guy says they're shutting the airport in Houston down. Dallas International's already closed, and so are JFK and O'Hare. How's Stacey?"

Incorrigible, Paula thought. "Fine," she said. "Do you want to talk to her?"

"No. Listen, tell her I'm still hoping, but it doesn't look good."

Paula told her, but it didn't have any effect. "Go get your dress on," Stacey ordered her, "so the minister can run through the service with you, and then you can show Kindra and David where to stand when they get here."

Paula went and put on her bridesmaid dress, wishing it wasn't sleeveless, and they went through the rehearsal with the viola player, who had changed into his tux to get out of his snow-damp clothes, acting as best man. As soon as they were done, Paula went into the vestry to get a sweater out of her suitcase. The minister came in and shut the door. "I've been trying to talk to Stacey," she said. "You're going to *have* to cancel the wedding. The roads are getting really dangerous, and I just heard on the radio they've closed the interstate."

"I know," Paula said.

"Well, she doesn't. She's convinced everything's going to work out."

And it might, Paula thought. After all, this is Stacey.

The viola player poked his head in the door. "Good news," he said.

"The string quartet's here?" the minister said.

"Jim's here?" Paula said.

"No, but Shep and Leif found the cello player. he's got frost-bite, but otherwise he's okay. They're taking him to the hospital." He gestured toward the sanctuary. "Do you want to tell the Queen of Denial, or shall I?"

"I will," Paula said and went back into the sanctuary. "Stacey—"

"Your dress looks beautiful!" Stacey cried and dragged her over to the windows. "Look how it goes with the snow!"

When the bell rang at a quarter to four, Luke thought, Finally! Mom! and literally ran to answer the door. It was Aunt Lulla. He looked hopefully past her, but there was no one else pulling into the driveway or coming up the street. "You don't know anything about cooking a goose, do you?" he asked.

She looked at him a long, silent moment and then handed him the plate of olives she'd brought and took off her hat, scarf, gloves, plastic boots, and old-lady coat. "Your mother and Madge were always the domestic ones," she said, "I was the theatrical one," and while he was digesting that odd piece of information, "Why did you ask? Is your goose cooked?"

'Yes," he said and led her into the kitchen and showed her the goose, which was now swimming in a sea of fat.

"Good God!" Aunt Lulla said, "where did all that grease come from?"

"I don't know," he said.

"Well, the first thing to do is pour some of it off before the poor thing drowns."

"I already did," Luke said. He took the lid off the saucepan he'd poured the drippings into earlier.

"Well you need to pour off some more," she said practically, "and you'll need a larger pan. Or maybe we should just pour it down the sink and get rid of the evidence."

"It's for the gravy," he said, rummaging in the cupboard

under the sink for the big pot his mother had given him to cook spaghetti in.

"Oh, of course," she said, and then thoughtfully, "I *do* know how to make gravy. Alec Guinness taught me."

Luke stuck his head out of the cupboard. "Alec Guinness taught you to make *gravy?*"

"It's not really all that difficult," she said, opening the oven door and looking speculatively at the goose. "You wouldn't happen to have any wine on hand, would you?"

"Yes." He emerged with the pot. "Why? Will wine counteract the grease?"

"I have no idea," she said. "But one of the things I learned when I was playing off-Broadway was that when you're facing a flop or an opening night curtain, it helps to be a little sloshed."

"You played off-Broadway?" Luke said. "Mom never told me you were an actress."

"I wasn't," she said, opening cupboard doors. She pulled out two wine glasses. "You should have seen my reviews."

By 4:00 P.M., all the networks and cable newschannels had changed their logos to reflect the worsening situation. ABC had *MegaBlizzard,* NBC had *MacroBlizzard,* and CNN had *Perfect Storm,* with a graphic of a boat being swamped by a gigantic wave. CBS and MSNBC had both gone with *Ice Age,* CBS's with a question mark, MSNBC's with an exclamation point and a drawing of the Abominable Snowman. And Fox, ever the responsible news network, was proclaiming, *End of the World!*

"*Now* can I freak out?" Chin asked.

"No," Nathan said, feeding in snowfall rates. "In the first place, it's Fox. In the second place, a discontinuity does not necessarily mean the end of the wo—"

The lights flickered. They both stopped and stared at the overhead fluorescents. They flickered again.

"Backup!" Nathan shouted, and they both dived for their terminals, shoved in zip drives, and began frantically typing, looking anxiously up at the lights now and then.

Chin popped the zip disk out of the drive. "You were saying that a discontinuity isn't necessarily the end of the world?"

"Yes, but losing this data would be. From now on we back up every fifteen minutes."

The lights flickered again, went out for an endless ten seconds, and came back on again to Peter Jennings saying, "—Huntsville, Alabama, where thousands are without power. I'm here at Byrd Middle School, which is serving as a temporary shelter." He stuck the microphone under the nose of a woman holding a candle. "When did the power go off?" he asked.

"About noon," she said. "The lights flickered a couple of times before that, but both times the lights came back on, and I thought we were okay, and then I went to fix lunch, and they went off, like that—" she snapped her fingers. "Without any warning."

"We back up every five minutes," Nathan said, and to Chin, who was pulling on his parka, "Where are you going?"

"Out to my car to get a flashlight."

He came back in ten minutes later, caked in snow, his ears and cheeks bright red. "It's four feet deep out there. Tell me again why I shouldn't freak out," he said, handing the flashlight to Nathan.

"Because I don't think this is a discontinuity," Nathan said. "I think it's just a snowstorm."

"Just a snowstorm?" Chin said, pointing at the TVs, where red-eared, red-cheeked reporters were standing in front of, respectively, a phalanx of snowplows on the Boardwalk in Atlantic City, a derailed train in Casper, and a collapsed Wal-Mart in Biloxi, "—from the weight of a record fifty-eight inches of snow," Brit Hume was saying. "Luckily, there were no injuries here. In Cincinnati, however—"

"*Fifty-eight* inches," Chin said. "In *Mississippi*. What if it keeps on snowing and snowing forever till the whole world . . . ?"

"It can't," Nathan said. "There isn't enough moisture in the atmosphere, and no low pressure system over the Gulf to keep pumping moisture up across the lower United States. There's no low pressure system at all, and no ridge of high pressure to push against it, no colliding air masses, nothing. Look at this. It started in four different places hundreds of miles from each other, in different latitudes, different altitudes, none of them along a ridge of high pressure. This storm isn't following any of the rules."

"But doesn't that prove it's a discontinuity?" Chin asked

nervously. "Isn't that one of the signs, that it's completely different from what came before?"

"The *climate* would be completely different, the *weather* would be completely different, not the laws of physics." He pointed to the world map on the mid-right-hand screen. "If this were a discontinuity, you'd see a change in ocean current temps, a shift in the jet stream, changes in wind patterns. There's none of that. The jet stream hasn't moved, the rate of melting in the Antarctic is unchanged, the Gulf Stream's still there. El Niño's still there. *Venice* is still there."

"Yeah, but it's snowing on the Grand Canal," Chin said. "So what's causing the mega-storm?"

"That's just it. It's not a mega-storm. If it were, there'd be accompanying ice-storms, hurricane-force winds, microbursts, tornadoes, none of which has shown up on the data. As near as I can tell, all it's doing is snowing." He shook his head. "No, something else is going on."

"What?"

"I have no idea." He stared glumly at the screens. "Weather's a remarkably complex system. Hundreds, thousands of factors we haven't figured in could be having an effect: cloud dynamics, localized temperature variations, pollution, solar activity. Or it could be something we haven't even considered: the effects of de-icers on highway albedo, beach erosion, the migratory patterns of geese. Or the effect on electromagnetic fields of playing 'White Christmas' hundreds of times on the radio this week."

"Four thousand nine hundred and thirty-three," Chin said.

"What?"

"That's how many times Bing Crosby's 'White Christmas' is played the two weeks before Christmas, with an additional nine thousand and sixty-two times by other artists. Including Otis Redding, U2, Peggy Lee, the Three Tenors, and the Flaming Lips. I read it on the internet."

"Nine thousand and sixty-two," Nathan said. "That's certainly enough to affect something, all right."

"I know what you mean," Chin said. "Have you heard Eminem's new rap version?"

By 4:15 P.M., the spaghetti pot was two-thirds full of goose grease, Luke's mother and Madge and Shorty still weren't there, and the goose was nearly done. Luke and Lulla had decided after their third glass of wine apiece to make the gravy.

"And put the tent back on," Lulla said, sifting flour into a bowl. "One of the things I learned when I was playing the West End is that uncovered is not necessarily better." She added a cup of water. "Particularly when you're doing Shakespeare."

She shook in some salt and pepper. "I remember a particularly ill-conceived nude *Macbeth* I did with Larry Olivier." She thrust her hand out dramatically. "'Is that a dagger that I see before me?' should *not* be a laugh line. Richard taught me how to do this," she said, stirring the mixture briskly with a fork, "It gets the lumps out."

"Richard? Richard *Burton?*"

"Yes. Adorable man. Of course he drank like a fish when he was depressed—this was after Liz left him for the second time—but it never seemed to affect his performance in bed *or* in the kitchen. Not like Peter."

"Peter? Peter Ustinov?"

"O'Toole. Here we go." Lulla poured the flour mixture into the hot drippings. It disappeared. "It takes a moment to thicken up," she said hopefully, but after several minutes of combined staring into the pot, it was no thicker.

"I think we need more flour," she said, "and a larger bowl. A much larger bowl. And another glass of wine."

Luke fetched them, and after a good deal of stirring, she added the mixture to the drippings, which immediately began to thicken up. "Oh, good," she said, stirring. "As John Gielgud used to say, 'If at first you don't succeed . . .' Oh, dear."

"What did he say that for—oh, dear," Luke said, peering into the pot where the drippings had abruptly thickened into a solid, globular mass.

"That's not what gravy's supposed to look like," Aunt Lulla said.

"No," Luke said. "We seem to have made a lard ball."

They both looked at it awhile.

"I don't suppose we could pass it off as a very large dumpling," Aunt Lulla suggested.

"No," Luke said, trying to chop at it with the fork.

"And I don't suppose it'll go down the garbage disposal. Could we stick sesame seeds on it and hang it on a tree and pretend it was a suet ball for the birds?"

"Not unless we want PETA and the Humane Society after us. Besides, wouldn't that be cannibalism?"

"You're right," Aunt Lulla said. "But we've got to do something with it before your mother gets here. I suppose Yucca Mountain's too far away," she said thoughtfully. "You wouldn't have any acid on hand, would you?"

At 4:23 P.M., Slim Rushmore, on KFLG out of Flagstaff, Arizona, made a valiant effort to change the subject on his talk radio show to school vouchers, usually a sure-fire issue, but his callers weren't having any of it. "This snow is a clear sign the Apocalypse is near," a woman from Colorado Springs informed him. "In the Book of Daniel, it says that God will send snow 'to purge and to make them white, even to the time of the end,' and the Book of Psalms promises us 'snow and vapours, stormy wind fulfilling his word,' and in the Book of Isaiah . . ."

After the fourth Scripture (from Job: "For God saith to the snow, Be thou on the earth") Slim cut her off and took a call from Dwayne in Poplar Bluffs.

"You know what started all this, don't you?" Dwayne said belligerently. "When the commies put fluoride in the water back in the fifties."

At 4:25 P.M., the country club called the church to say they were closing, none of the food and only two of the staff could get there, and anybody who was still trying to have a wedding in this weather was crazy. "I'll tell her," Paula said and went to find Stacey.

"She's in putting on her wedding dress," the viola player said.

Paula moaned.

"Yeah, I know," he said. "I tried to explain to her that the rest of the quartet was *not* coming, but I didn't get anywhere." He looked at her quizzically. "I'm not getting anywhere with you either, am I?" he asked, and Jim walked in.

He was covered in snow. "The car got stuck," he said.

"Where are Kindra and David?"

"They closed Houston," he said, pulling Paula aside, "and Newark. And I just talked to Stacey's mom. She's stuck in Lavoy. They just closed the highway. There's no way she can get here. What are we going to do?"

"You have to tell her the wedding has to be called off," Paula said. "You don't have any other option. And you have to do it now, before the guests try to come to the church."

"You obviously haven't been out there lately," he said. "Trust me, nobody's going to come out in that."

"Then you obviously have to cancel."

"I know," he said worriedly. "It's just . . . she'll be so disappointed."

Disappointed is not the word that springs to mind, Paula thought, and realized she had no idea how Stacey would react. She'd never seen her not get her way. I wonder what she'll do, she thought curiously, and started back into the vestry to change out of her bridesmaid dress.

"Wait," Jim said, grabbing her hand. "You have to help me tell her."

This is asking way too much, Paula thought. I want you to marry me, not her. "I—" she said.

"I can't do this without you," he said. "Please?"

She extricated her hand. "Okay," she said, and they went into the changing room, where Stacey was in her wedding dress, looking at herself in the mirror.

"Stacey, we have to talk," Jim said, after a glance at Paula. "I just heard from your mother. She's not going to be able to get here. She's stuck at a truck stop outside Lavoy."

"She can't be," Stacey said to her reflection. "She's bringing my veil." She turned to smile at Paula. "It was my great-grandmother's. It's lace, with this snowflake pattern."

"Kindra and David can't get here either," Jim said. He glanced at Paula and then plunged ahead. "We're going to have to reschedule the wedding."

"Reschedule?" Stacey said as if she'd never heard the word before. Which she probably hasn't, Paula thought. "We can't reschedule. A Christmas Eve wedding has to be on Christmas Eve."

"I know, honey, but—"

"Nobody's going to be able to get here," Paula said. "They've closed the roads."

The minister came in. "The governor's declared a snow emergency and a ban on unnecessary travel. You've decided to cancel?" she said hopefully.

"*Cancel*?" Stacey said, adjusting her train. "What are you talking about? Everything will be fine."

And for one mad moment, Paula could almost see Stacey pulling it off, the weather magically clearing, the rest of the string quartet showing up, the flowers and Kindra and David and the veil all arriving in the next thirty-five minutes. She looked over at the windows. The snow, reflected softly in the candlelight, was coming down harder than ever.

"We don't have any other choice than to reschedule," Jim said. "Your mother can't get here, your maid of honor and my best man can't get here—"

"Tell them to take a different flight," Stacey said.

Paula tried. "Stacey, I don't think you realize, this is a major snowstorm. Airports all over the country are closed—"

"Including here," the viola player said, poking his head in. "It was just on the news."

"Well, then, go get them," Stacey said, adjusting the drape of her skirt.

Paula'd lost the thread of this conversation. "Who?"

"Kindra and David." She adjusted the neckline of her gown.

"To *Houston*?" Jim said, looking helplessly at Paula.

"Listen, Stacey," Paula said, taking her firmly by the shoulders. "I know how much you wanted a Christmas Eve wedding, but it's just not going to work. The roads are impassable. Your flowers are in a ditch, your mother's trapped at a truck stop—"

"The cello player's in the hospital with frostbite," the viola player put in.

Paula nodded. "And you don't want anyone else to end up there. You have to face facts. You can't have a Christmas Eve wedding."

"You could reschedule for Valentine's Day," the minister said brightly. "Valentine weddings are very nice. I've got two weddings that day, but I could move one up. It could still be in the evening," but Paula could tell Stacey had stopped listening at "you can't have—"

"*You* did this," Stacey snapped at Paula. "You've always been jealous of me, and now you're taking it out on me by ruining my wedding."

"Nobody's ruining anything, Stacey," Jim said, stepping between them. "It's a snowstorm."

"Oh, so I suppose it's *my* fault!" Stacey said. "Just because I wanted a winter wedding with snow—"

"It's nobody's fault," Jim said sternly. "Listen, I don't want to wait either, and we don't have to. We can get married right here, right now."

"Yeah," the viola player said. "You've got a minister." He grinned at Paula. "You've got two witnesses."

"He's right," Jim said. "We've got everything we need right here. You're here, *I'm* here, and that's all that really matters, isn't it, not some fancy wedding?" He took her hands in his. "Will you marry me?"

And what woman could resist an offer like that? Paula thought. Oh, well, you knew when you got on the plane that he was going to marry her.

"Marry you," Stacey repeated blankly, and the minister hurried out, saying, "I'll get my book. And my robe."

"Marry you?" Stacey said. "*Marry you*?" She wrenched free of his grasp. "Why on earth would I marry a *loser* who won't even do one simple thing for me? I *want* Kindra and David here. I *want* my flowers. I *want* my veil. What is the *point* of *marrying* you if I can't have what I want?"

"I thought you wanted me," Jim said dangerously.

"*You*?" Stacey said in a tone that made both Paula and the viola player wince. "I *wanted* to walk down the aisle at twilight on Christmas Eve," she waved her arm in the direction of the windows, "with candlelight reflecting off the windowpanes and snow falling outside." She turned, snatching up her train, and looked at him. "Will I *marry* you? Are you *kidding*?"

There was a short silence. Jim turned and looked seriously at Paula. "How about you?" he said.

At six o'clock on the dot, Madge and Shorty, Uncle Don, Cousin Denny, and Luke's mom all arrived. "You poor darling," she whispered to Luke, handing him the green bean casserole and the sweet potatoes, "stuck all afternoon with Aunt Lulla. Did she talk your ear off?"

"No," he said. "We made a snowman. Why didn't you tell me Aunt Lulla had been an actress?"

"An *actress*?" she said, handing him the cranberry sauce. "Is that what she told you? Don't tip it, it'll spill. Did you have any trouble with the goose?" She opened the oven and looked at it, sitting in its pan, brown and crispy and done to a turn. "They tend to be a little juicy."

"Not a bit," he said, looking past her out the window at the snowman in the backyard. The snow he and Aunt Lulla had packed around it and on top of it was melting. He'd have to sneak out during dinner and pile more snow on.

"Here," his mom said, handing him the mashed potatoes. "Heat these up in the microwave while I make the gravy."

"It's made," he said, lifting the lid off the saucepan to show her the gently bubbling gravy. It had taken them four tries, but as Aunt Lulla had pointed out, they had more than enough drippings to experiment with, and, as she had also pointed out, three lardballs made a more realistic snowman.

"The top one's too big," Luke had said, scooping up snow to cover it with.

"I may have gotten a little carried away with the flour," Aunt Lulla had admitted. "On the other hand, it looks exactly like Orson." She stuck two olives in for eyes. "And so appropriate. He always was a fathead."

"The gravy smells delicious," Luke's mother said, looking surprised. "*You* didn't make it, did you?"

"No. Aunt Lulla."

"Well, I think you're a saint for putting up with her and her wild tales all afternoon," she said, ladling the gravy into a bowl and handing it to Luke.

"You mean she made all that stuff up?" Luke said.

"Do you have a gravy boat?" his mother asked, opening cupboards.

"No," he said. "Aunt Lulla wasn't really an actress?"

"*No.*" She took a bowl out of the cupboard. "Do you have a ladle?"

"No."

She got a dipper out of the silverware drawer. "Lulla was never in a single play," she said, ladling the gravy into a bowl and handing it to Luke, "where she hadn't gotten the part by sleeping with somebody. Lionel Barrymore, Ralph Richardson, Kenneth Branagh . . ." She opened the oven to look at the goose. "And that's not even counting Alfred."

"Alfred *Lunt*?" Luke asked.

"Hitchcock. I think this is just about done."

"But I thought you said she was the shy one."

"She was. That's why she went out for drama in high school, to overcome her shyness. Do you have a platter?"

At 6:35 P.M., a member of the Breckenridge ski patrol, out looking for four missing cross-country skiers, spotted a taillight (the only part of Kent and Bodine's Honda not covered by snow). He had a collapsible shovel with him, and a GPS, a satellite phone, a walkie-talkie, Mylar blankets, insta-heat packs, energy bars, a thermos of hot cocoa, and a stern lecture on winter safety, which he delivered after he had dug Kent and Bodine out and which they really resented. "Who did that fascist geek think he was, shaking his finger at us like that?" Bodine asked Kent after several tequila slammers at the Laughing Moose.

"Yeah," Kent said eloquently, and they settled down to the serious business of how to take advantage of the fresh powder that had fallen while they were in their car.

"You know what'd be totally extreme?" Bodine said. "Snowboarding at night!"

Shara was quite a girl. Warren didn't have a chance to call Marjean again until after seven. When Shara went in the bathroom, he took the opportunity to dial home. "Where *are* you?"

Marjean said, practically crying. "I've been worried sick! Are you all right?"

"I'm still in Cincinnati at the airport," he said, "and it looks like I'll be here all night. They just closed the airport."

"Closed the airport . . ." she echoed.

"I *know*," he said, his voice full of regret. "I'd really counted on being home with you for Christmas Eve, but what can you do? It's snowing like crazy here. No flights out till tomorrow afternoon at the earliest. I'm in line at the airline counter right now, rebooking, and then I'm going to try to find a place to stay, but I don't know if I'll have much luck." He paused to give her a chance to commiserate. "They're supposed to put us up for the night, but I wouldn't be surprised if I end up sleeping on the floor."

"At the airport," she said, "in Cincinnati."

"Yeah." He laughed. "Great place to spend Christmas Eve, huh?" He paused to give her a chance to commiserate, but all she said was, "You didn't make it home last year either."

"Honey, you know I'd get there if I could," he said. "I tried to rent a car and drive home, but the snow's so bad they're not even sure they can get a shuttle out here to take us to a hotel. I don't know how much snow they've had here—"

"Forty-six inches," she said.

Good, he thought. From her voice he'd been worried it might not be snowing in Cincinnati after all. "And it's still coming down hard. Oh, they just called my name. I'd better go."

"You do that," she said.

"All right. I love you, honey," he said, "I'll be home as soon as I can," and hung up the phone.

"You're married," Shara said, standing in the door of the bathroom. "You sonofabitch."

Paula didn't say yes to Jim's proposal after all. She'd intended to, but before she could, the viola player had cut in. "Hey, wait a minute!" he'd said. "I saw her first!"

"You did not," Jim said.

"Well, no, not technically," he admitted, "but when I did see her, I had the good sense to flirt with her, not get engaged to Vampira like you did."

"It wasn't Jim's fault," Paula said. "Stacey always gets what she wants."

"Not this time," he said. "And not me."

"Only because she doesn't want you," Paula said. "If she did—"

"Wanna bet? You underestimate us musicians. And yourself. At least give me a chance to make my pitch before you commit to this guy. You can't get married tonight anyway."

"Why not?" Jim asked.

"Because you need two witnesses, and I have no intention of helping *you*," he pointed at Jim, "get the woman *I* want. I doubt if Stacey's in the mood to be a witness either," he said as Stacey stormed back in the sanctuary, with the minister in pursuit. Stacey had on her wedding dress, a parka, and boots.

"You can't go out in this," the minister was saying. "It's too dangerous!"

"I have no intention of staying here with him," Stacey said, shooting Jim a venomous glance. "I want to go home *now*." She flung the door open on the thickly falling snow. "And I want it to stop *snowing!*"

At that exact moment, a snowplow's flashing yellow lights had appeared through the snow, and Stacey had run out. Paula and Jim went over to the door and watched Stacey wave it down and get in. The plow continued on its way.

"Oh, good, now we'll be able to get out," the minister said, and went to get her car keys.

"You didn't answer my question, Paula," Jim said, standing very close.

The plow turned and came back. As it passed, it plowed a huge mass of snow across the end of the driveway.

"I mean it," Jim murmured. "How about it?"

"Look what I found," the viola player said, appearing at Paula's elbow. He handed her a piece of wedding cake.

"You can't eat that. It's—" Jim said.

"—not bad," the viola player said. "I prefer chocolate, though. What kind of cake shall we have at our wedding, Paula?"

"Oh, look," the minister said, coming back in with her car keys and looking out the window. "It's stopped snowing."

"It's stopped snowing," Chin said.

"It has?" Nathan looked up from his keyboard. "Here?"

"No. In Oceanside, Oregon. And in Springfield, Illinois."

Nathan found them on the map. Two thousand miles apart. He checked their barometer readings, temperatures, snowfall amounts. No similarity. Springfield had thirty-two inches, Oceanside an inch and a half. And in every single town around them, it was still snowing hard. In Tillamook, six miles away, it was coming down at the rate of five inches an hour.

But ten minutes later, Chin reported the snow stopping in Gilette, Wyoming; Roulette, Massachusetts; and Saginaw, Michigan; and within half an hour the number of stations reporting in was over thirty, though they seemed just as randomly scattered all over the map as the storm's beginning had been.

"Maybe it has to do with their names," Chin said.

"Their names?" Nathan said.

"Yeah. Look at this. It's stopped in Joker, West Virginia; Bluff, Utah; and Blackjack, Georgia."

At 7:22 P.M., the snow began to taper off in Wendover, Utah. Neither the Lucky Lady Casino nor the Big Nugget had any windows, so the event went unnoticed until Barbara Gomez, playing the quarter slots, ran out of money at 9:05 P.M. and had to go out to her car to get the emergency twenty she kept taped under the dashboard. By this time, the snow had nearly stopped. Barbara told the change girl, who said, "Oh, good. I was worried about driving to Battle Mountain tomorrow. Were the plows out?"

Barbara said she didn't know and asked for four rolls of nickels, which she promptly lost playing video poker.

By 7:30 P.M. CNBC had replaced its logo with *Digging Out,* and ABC had retreated to Bing and *White Christmas,* though CNN still had side-by-side experts discussing the possibility of a new ice age, and on Fox News, Geraldo Rivera was intoning, "In his classic poem, 'Fire and Ice,' Robert Frost speculated that the world might end in ice. Today we are seeing the coming true of that dire prediction—"

The rest had obviously gotten the word, though, and CBS

and the WB had both gone back to their regular programming. The movie *White Christmas* was on AMC.

"Whatever this was, it's stopping," Nathan said, watching "I-80 now open from Lincoln to Ogalallah," scroll across the bottom of NBC's screen.

"Well, whatever you do, don't tell those corporate guys," Chin said, and, as if on cue, one of the businessmen Nathan had met with that morning called.

"I just wanted you to know we've voted to approve your grant," he said.

"Really? Thank you," Nathan said, trying to ignore Chin, who was mouthing, "Are they giving us the money?"

"Yes," he mouthed back.

Chin scribbled down something and shoved it in front of Nathan. "Get it in writing," it said.

"We all agreed this discontinuity thing is worth studying," the businessman said, then, shakily, "They've been talking on TV about the end of the world. You don't think this discontinuity thing is that bad, do you?"

"No," Nathan said, "in fact—"

"Ix-nay, ix-nay," Chin mouthed, wildly crossing his arms.

Nathan glared at him. "—we're not even sure yet if it is a discontinuity. It doesn't—"

"Well, we're not taking any chances," the businessman said. "What's your fax number? I want to send you that confirmation before the power goes out over here. We want you to get started working on this thing as soon as you can."

Nathan gave him the number. "There's really no need—" he said.

Chin jabbed his finger violently at the logo *False Alarm* on the screen of Adler's TV.

"Consider it a Christmas present," the businessman said, and the fax machine began to whir. "There *is* going to be a Christmas, isn't there?"

Chin yanked the fax out of the machine with a whoop.

"Definitely," Nathan said. "Merry Christmas," but the businessman had already hung up.

Chin was still looking at the fax. "How much did you ask them for?"

"Fifty thousand," Nathan said.

Chin slapped the grant approval down in front of him. "And a merry Christmas to you, too," he said.

At seven-thirty, after watching informercials for NordicTrack, a combination egg poacher and waffle iron, and the revolutionary new DuckBed, Bev put on her thin coat and her still-damp gloves and went downstairs. There had to be a restaurant open somewhere in Santa Fe. She would find one and have a margarita and a beef chimichanga, sitting in a room decorated with sombreros or piñatas with striped curtains pulled across the windows to shut the snow out.

And if they were all closed, she would come back and order from room service. Or starve. But she was *not* going to ask at the desk and have them phone ahead and tell her the El Charito had closed early because of the weather, she was not going to let them cut off all avenues of escape, like Carmelita. She walked determinedly past the registration desk toward the double doors.

"Mrs. Carey!" the clerk called to her, and when she kept walking, he hurried around the desk and across the lobby to her. "I have a message for you from Carmelita. She wanted me to tell you midnight mass at the cathedral has been cancelled," he said. "The bishop was worried about people driving home on the icy roads. But Carmelita said to tell you they're having mass at eight o'clock, if you'd like to come to that. The cathedral's right up the street at the end of the plaza. If you go out the north door," he pointed, "it's only two blocks. It's a very pretty service, with the luminarias and all."

And it's somewhere to go, Bev thought, letting him lead her to the north door. It's something to do. "Tell Carmelita thank you for me," she said at the door. "And *Feliz Navidad.*"

"Merry Christmas." He opened the door. "You go down this street, turn left, and it's right there," he said and ducked back inside, out of the snow.

It was inches deep on the sidewalk as she hurried along the narrow street, head down, and snowing hard. By morning it would look just like back home. It's not fair, she thought. She turned the corner and looked up at the sound of an organ.

The cathedral stood at the head of the Plaza, its windows glowing like flames, and she had been wrong about the luminarias being ruined—they stood in rows leading up the walk, up the steps to the wide doors, lining the adobe walls and the roofs and the towers, burning steadily in the descending snow.

It fell silently, in great, spangled flakes, glittering in the light of the street lamps, covering the wooden-posted porches, the pots of cactus, the pink adobe buildings. The sky above the cathedral was pink, too, and the whole scene had an unreal quality, like a movie set.

"Oh, Howard," Bev said, as if she had just opened a present, and then flinched away from the thought of him, waiting for the thrust of the knife; but it didn't come. She felt only regret that he couldn't be here to see this and amusement that the sequined snowflakes sifting down on her hair, on her coat sleeve, looked just like the fake snow at the end of *White Christmas*. And, arching over it all, like the pink sky, she felt affection—for the snow, for the moment, for Howard.

"You did this," she said, and started to cry.

The tears didn't trickle down her cheeks, they poured out, drenching her face, her coat, melting the snowflakes instantly where they fell. Healing tears, she thought, and realized suddenly that when she had asked Howard how the movie ended, he hadn't said, "They lived happily ever after." He had said, "They got a white Christmas."

"Oh, Howard."

The bells for the service began to ring. I need to stop crying and go in, she thought, fumbling for a tissue, but she couldn't. The tears kept coming, as if someone had opened a spigot.

A black-shawled woman carrying a prayer book put her hand on Bev's shoulder and said, "Are you all right, *señora?*"

"Yes," Bev said, "I'll be fine," and something in her voice must have reassured the woman because she patted Bev's arm and went on into the cathedral.

The bells stopped ringing and the organ began again, but Bev continued to stand there until long after the mass had started, looking up at the falling snow.

"I don't know how you did this, Howard," she said, "but I know you're responsible."

At eight P.M., after anxiously checking the news to make sure the roads were still closed, Pilar put Miguel to bed. "Now go to sleep," she said, kissing him good-night. "Santa's coming soon." "Hunh-unh," he said, looking like he was going to cry. "It's snowing too hard."

He's worried about the roads being closed, she thought. "Santa doesn't need roads," she said. "Remember, he has a magic sleigh that flies through the air even if it's snowing."

"Hunh-*unh*," he said, getting out of bed to get his Rudolph book. He showed her the illustration of the whirling blizzard and Santa shaking his head, and then stood up on his bed, pulled back the curtain, and pointed through the window. She had to admit it did look just like the picture.

"But he had Rudolph to show the way," she said. "See?" and turned the page, but Miguel continued to look skeptical until she had read the book all the way through twice.

At 10:15 P.M. Warren Nesvick went down to the hotel's bar. He had tried to explain to Shara that Marjean was his five-year-old niece, but she had gotten completely unreasonable. "So I'm a cancelled flight out of Cincinnati, am I?" she'd shouted. "Well, I'm canceling you, you bastard!" and slammed out, leaving him high and dry. On Christmas Eve, for Christ's sake.

He'd spent the next hour and a half on the phone. He'd called some women he knew from previous trips but none of them had answered. He'd then tried to call Marjean to tell her the snow was letting up and United thought they could get him on standby early tomorrow morning and to try to patch things up— she'd seemed kind of upset—but she hadn't answered either. She'd probably gone to bed.

He'd hung up and gone down to the bar. There wasn't a soul in the place except the bartender. "How come the place is so dead?" Warren asked him.

"Where the hell have you been?" the bartender said and turned on the TV above the bar.

"Most widespread snowstorm in recorded history," Dan Abrams was saying. "Although there are signs of the snow beginning to let up here in Baltimore, in other parts of the country they weren't so lucky. We take you now to Cincinnati, where emergency crews are still digging victims out of the rubble." It cut to a reporter standing in front of a sign that read *Cincinnati International Airport.* "A record forty-six inches of snow caused the roof of the main terminal to collapse this afternoon. Over two hundred passengers were injured, and forty are still missing."

The goose was a huge hit, crispy and tender and done to a turn, and everyone raved about the gravy. "Luke made it," Aunt Lulla said, but Madge and his mom were talking about people not knowing how to drive in snow and didn't hear her.

It stopped snowing midway through dessert, and Luke began to worry about the snowman but didn't have a chance to duck out and check on it till nearly eleven, when everyone was putting on their coats.

It had melted (sort of), leaving a round greasy smear in the snow. "Getting rid of the evidence?" Aunt Lulla asked, coming up behind him in her old-lady coat, scarf, gloves, and plastic boots. She poked at the smear with the toe of her boot. "I hope it doesn't kill the grass."

"I hope it doesn't affect the environment," Luke said.

Luke's mother appeared in the back door. "What are you two doing out there in the dark?" she called to them. "Come in. We're trying to decide who's going to have the dinner next Christmas. Madge and Shorty think it's Uncle Don's turn, but—"

"I'll have it," Luke said and winked at Lulla.

"Oh," his mother said, surprised, and went back inside to tell Madge and Shorty and the others.

"But not goose," Luke said to Lulla. "Something easy. And nonfat."

"Ian had a wonderful recipe for duck a l'orange Alsacienne, as I remember," Lulla mused.

"Ian McKellen?"

"No, of course not, Ian Holm. Ian McKellen's a terrible cook," she said. "Or—I've got an idea. How about Japanese blowfish?"

By 11:15 P.M. Eastern Standard Time, the snow had stopped in New England, the Middle East, the Texas panhandle, most of Canada, and Nooseneck, Rhode Island.

"The storm of the century definitely seems to be winding down," Wolf Blitzer was saying in front of CNN's new logo: *The Sun'll Come Out Tomorrow,* "leaving in its wake a white Christmas for nearly everyone—"

"Hey," Chin said, handing Nathan the latest batch of temp readings. "I just thought of what it was."

"What what was?"

"The factor. You said there were thousands of factors contributing to global warming, and that any one of them, even something really small, could have been what caused this."

He hadn't really said that, but never mind. "And you've figured out what this critical factor is?"

"Yeah," Chin said. "A white Christmas."

"A white Christmas," Nathan repeated.

"Yeah! You know how everybody wants it to snow for Christmas, little kids especially, but lots of adults, too. They have this Currier-and-Ives thing of what Christmas should look like, and the songs reinforce it: 'White Christmas' and 'Winter Wonderland' and that one that goes, 'The weather outside is frightful,' I never can remember the name—"

"'Let It Snow,'" Nathan said.

"Exactly," Chin said. "Well, suppose all those people and all those little kids wished for a merry Christmas at the same time—"

"They *wished* this snowstorm into being?" Nathan said.

"*No.* They *thought* about it, and their—I don't know, their brain chemicals or synapses or something—created some kind of electrochemical field or something, and that's the factor."

"That everybody was dreaming of a white Christmas."

"Yeah. It's a possibility, right?"

"Maybe," Nathan said. Maybe there was some critical factor that had caused this. Not wishing for a white Christmas, of course, but something seemingly unconnected to weather patterns, like tiny variations in the earth's orbit. Or the migratory patterns of geese.

Or an assortment of factors working in combination. And

maybe the storm was an isolated incident, an aberration caused by a confluence of these unidentified factors, and would never happen again.

Or maybe his discontinuity theory was wrong. A discontinuity was by definition an abrupt, unexpected event. But that didn't mean there might not be advance indicators, like the warning flickers of electric lights before the power goes off for good. In which case—

"What are you doing?" Chin said, coming in from scraping his windshield. "Aren't you going home?"

"Not yet. I want to run a couple more extrapolation sets. It's still snowing in L.A."

Chin looked immediately alarmed. "You don't think it's going to start snowing everywhere again, do you?"

"No," Nathan said. Not yet.

At 11:43 P.M., after singing several karaoke numbers at the Laughing Moose, including "White Christmas," and telling the bartender they were going on "a moonlight ride down this totally killer chute," Kent Slakken and Bodine Cromps set out with their snowboards for an off-limits, high-avalanche-danger area near Vail and were never heard from again.

At 11:52 P.M., Miguel jumped on his sound-asleep mother, shouting, "It's Christmas! It's Christmas!"

It can't be morning yet, Pilar thought groggily, fumbling to look at the clock. "Miguel, honey, it's still nighttime. If you're not in bed when Santa comes, he won't leave you any presents," she said, hustling him back to bed. She tucked him in. "Now go to sleep. Santa and Rudolph will be here soon."

"Hunh-unh," he said and stood up on his bed. He pulled the curtain back. "He doesn't need Rudolph. The snow stopped, just like I wanted, and now Santa can come all by himself." He pointed out the window. Only a few isolated flakes were still sifting down.

Oh, no, Pilar thought. After she was sure he was asleep, she crept out to the living room and turned on the TV very low, hoping against hope.

"—roads will remain closed until noon tomorrow," an exhausted-looking reporter said, "to allow time for the snow plows to clear them: I-15, State Highway 56, I-15 from Chula Vista to Murrietta Hot Springs, Highway 78 from Vista to Escondido—"

Thank you, she murmured silently. Thank you.

At 11:59 P.M. Pacific Standard Time, Sam "Hoot'n'Holler" Farley's voice gave out completely. The only person who'd been able to make it to the station, he'd been broadcasting continuously on KTTS, "Seattle's talk 24/7" since 5:36 A.M. when he'd come in to do the morning show, even though he had a bad cold. He'd gotten steadily hoarser all day, and during the 9:00 P.M. newsbreak, he'd had a bad coughing fit.

"The National Weather Service reports that that big snowstorm's finally letting up," he croaked, "and we'll have nice weather tomorrow. Oh, this just in from NORAD, for all you kids who're up way too late. Santa's sleigh's just been sighted on radar over Vancouver and is headed this way."

He then attempted to say, "In local news, the snow—" but nothing came out.

He tried again. Nothing.

After the third try, he gave up, whispered, "That's all, folks," into the mike, and put on a tape of Louis Armstrong singing "White Christmas."

GREETINGS

by Terry Bisson

Terry Bisson was born in February 1942, in Owensboro, Kentucky. After receiving a B.A. from the University of Louisville in 1964, he lived in New York, scripting comics, editing, and writing for tabloids. He lived four years in the Red Rockers hippie commune in the Colorado mountains, working as an auto mechanic, then returned to New York in 1976, serving as an editor and copywriter at Berkley and Avon until 1985. For the next five years he ran "revolutionary mail-order book service" Jacobin Books, and in the mid-'90s he was a consultant with a major publisher.

His first novel was fantasy Wyrldmaker, *followed by novels where Americana blends with magical/SFnal themes,* Talking Man *and* Fire on the Mountain. *His short story "Bears Discover Fire" won the 1991 Hugo, Nebula, Locus, and Sturgeon Awards, and is collected in* Bears Discover Fire and Other Stories. *Later novels—*Voyage to the Red Planet, Pirates of the Universe, *and* The Pickup Artist—*combined serious SF with satire. Bisson was also chosen to complete Walter M. Miller Jr.'s sequel to* A Canticle for Leibowitz, Saint Leibowitz and the Wild Horse Woman. *His short story "macs," which won the Hugo, Nebula, and Locus Awards, appears in the collection* In the Upper Room and Other Likely Stories (2000). *His most recent book is the short novel* Dear Abbey.

Bisson published several impressive works this year, most notably Dear Abbey *and this story, a powerful and disturbing look at just how the Western world may deal with an increasingly aged population.*

Most things may never happen: this one will
            —Philip Larkin, "Aubade"

1

It started out with a tangle, which should have been a sign. Tom's first concern, after his initial raw animal terror, was how to break the news to Ara; so he called Cliff and asked for help, telling him not to tell anyone, at least until he got there. But Cliff was already on the phone with Pam, who was meeting Arabella at the farmers market, and so by the time Tom got to Cliff's (walking across the golf course, even though it was prohibited) "the girls" had already dropped their bikes in the yard and were waiting in the kitchen.

They were all best friends, old friends ("At our age," Tom liked to joke, "all your friends are old"), and so Tom wasn't surprised or, after he thought about it, even annoyed to see them. It made it like an event, a ceremony of sorts, which seemed proper. And the terror had receded to a dull dread: a fear no less animal, but more domesticated, which he was to learn to live with over the next ten days, like a big, ugly, dun-colored dog.

"What's this, Cliff, an intervention?" he asked.

"Don't make this into a joke," Arabella warned. She was known for bursting into tears but only for the little things: a fender bender, a dropped dish, a goldfish floating on the top of the water. Her hand was damp as it found Tom's under Cliff and Pam's old-wood kitchen table.

"Start at the beginning," said Cliff, who was a lawyer, though he didn't practice anymore. "Guess he finally got it down," Tom liked to joke; though he didn't feel like joking this morning. It was 11:25, almost lunchtime. It was mid-October, and most of the leaves that were due to go that year were gone.

"It's pretty simple," Tom said, though pretty wasn't exactly the word. "I got it an hour ago, when I checked my mail. Certified. Here, I printed it out."

He laid it on the table, flattening it with the heel of his hand. Under the official U.S. logo, it read:

GREETINGS Thomas Aaron Clurman (401-25-5423)
YOU HAVE BEEN CHOSEN BY LOTTERY FOR
INDUCTION INTO THE OREGON SUNSET BRIGADE.
CONGRATULATIONS ON YOUR SACRIFICE. YOU ARE
TO REPORT TO CASCADE CENTER 1656, 18767 WEST
HELLEN ST, AT 10 AM, OCTOBER 22, 20—. IF YOU WISH
TO DISCUSS OTHER ARRANGEMENTS, AS PROVIDED
BY LAW, PLEASE CALL 154 176 098 8245.

"That's only ten days from now," Pam said. "The bastards."

"They don't want to give you time to think about it," said
Cliff, who was serving coffee to everyone.

Arabella burst into tears.

"Come on, honey. What am I, a goldfish?"

"I don't get it," said Cliff, sitting down. The coffee was
imported directly from the growers in Costa Rica. "I thought they
weren't drafting anyone under seventy-five."

"Guess now they are." Tom folded the notice and put it into
the pocket of his L.L. Bean chamois shirt. "The law says three
score and ten, doesn't it?"

"The bastards," said Pam.

"That's the Bible, not the law," said Cliff. "Maybe it's the
death rate in Africa. I read where some new vaccine has lowered
the infant mortality rate by thirty-four percent."

"Whatever," said Tom, suddenly irritated by Cliff's interest in
world events. "At any rate, last summer we talked about what we
would do, remember? No way I'm marching off with the Sunset
Brigade, so I'll need your help; Ara and I will need your help."
He squeezed Arabella's hand.

Arabella was slow in squeezing back.

"Well, of course," said Pam. "But isn't there something we
need to do first, some . . . ?"

"There's no appeal process," Cliff said. "There are options, of
course. And we're with you a hundred percent, Tom. We all feel
the same way you do."

Do you really? thought Tom. "Right. Anyway, maybe
Arabella and I should talk first, and see you guys later."

"Yes, later," said Pam. "Tonight's card night anyway. Come early for dinner."

"Should we bring anything?" asked Arabella.

"Just yourselves," said Pam. "The bastards."

Walking home, around the golf course, Tom and Arabella were silent. He walked her bike, which was, he thought, sort of like holding hands. Now, when there was everything to talk about, there was nothing to say. How come the world looks so bright? Tom wondered. So various, so beautiful, so new . . .

"You and Cliff were stoned that night at Holystone Bay," said Arabella. "It isn't all that easy to, you know, do it yourself."

"Stoned but sincere," said Tom. "What do you want me to do, join the Brigade?"

"I don't want any of it. There must be something we can do. We should call the kids."

"Not yet," said Tom. "It's not their problem. Besides, Gwyneth was just here last week. Thomas is another matter altogether."

"Thomas always was."

That night Pam cooked pasta. Cliff brought out a bottle of wine from his own vineyard.

"It must have been Africa," he said. He showed them the article in *The Economist.* A new vaccine had reduced the infant mortality rate and therefore, it was speculated, adjustments would have to be made in the death rates in the "developed" countries.

Tom had never had a problem with this before. Neither had Cliff. America had reaped the benefits of selective underdevelopment for hundreds of years. Now they were making up for it.

But tonight, drinking Cliff's Willamette Valley pinot noir and looking out over the golf course, Tom found it alarming that someone else's good fortune was his bad luck. Did this mean that life was a zero-sum game after all, and that the humanistic, liberal philosophy that had guided him and Cliff for most of their fifty-odd years as friends, was false, based on a false premise—that the greatest good for all and the greatest good for one were in some sort of deep, unwritten, unspoken but unbreakable harmony?

Now the world, lopsided or not, was about to spin on without him.

It was, quite literally, unimaginable.

"I think they're after the opposition," Pam was saying. "The bastards."

"We're hardly the opposition," Cliff pointed out. "In fact, you might recall we're among those who supported the hemlock laws as a progressive move; a willingness to think and act in global terms."

"But not the Brigades," said Tom. "Not those smiling, marching fuckers with their little flags."

"What about the Resistance?" Pam asked.

"That's an urban legend," said Cliff.

"Wishful thinking," said Tom. "A token opposition at best. Look, there's no point in talking about how to beat this. We're not kids. I'll be seventy-one in August. I've had my three score and ten."

"So has Cliff," said Pam, who was sixty-six herself. "I still say there's something fishy about it. How many friends do we have who've gotten Greetings?"

"Guy Frakes, from the firm," said Cliff.

"Not exactly a friend. And he was almost eighty," said Pam.

"Seventy-seven," said Cliff.

"That's what he told you."

"You're not going to get that many anyway," said Cliff. "The Brigades are just a symbol, showing our willingness to adjust the death rate rationally. Most of the quota is made up by DNRs and end-term care reductions."

"And it's all guys," said Tom. "That was a great victory of the women's movement."

"Huh?" said Pam, showing her teeth.

"Look, it's a law of nature. All this does is put us into some sort of compliance," Tom said. He was amazed, listening to himself, at how self-assured he sounded. "Besides, we already decided what to do about this. Remember? We talked about it."

"You mean last summer, at the beach house," said Pam. "You guys were stoned."

"What does being stoned have to do with it?" Cliff protested. "It was after we watched that PBS special on the Brigades, before they had their weekly show."

"It was disgusting," said Tom. "Enlightening, really. All those geezers in their orange uniforms marching off into the sunset."

"Some were even volunteers," said Cliff.

"Cancer patients," said Tom. "They joined for the last cigarette."

"I don't see why you have to make a joke of it," said Arabella.

"It's no joke," said Tom. "It's my life, and I want to go out like I lived, with my friends, with dignity. With some dignity, anyway. At home. Listening to Coltrane, or Bob Dylan."

"And stoned," said Cliff. "Why not. I'll take care of that part."

"We'll all do our part," said Pam. She reached out for Arabella's hand. "You can count on us."

"Me, too," said Tom. "I'll check out. End of story. That'll be it."

It. They were all silent. Tom reached for the wine bottle, and saw that it was empty.

"It's just that we never really thought it would happen," said Arabella.

"No, but how many people live to be this old anyway? Better than dying of cancer." Although Tom wasn't as sure as he sounded. At least cancer didn't give you a date.

"It's even legal," said Cliff, "not that that matters. Oregon has a law making it legal to do it at home. Every state except Kentucky and Arkansas has them—it was a rider that defused some of the opposition to the Brigades."

"So what do we—do?" Arabella asked, pouring herself the last few drops of wine.

"We open another bottle," suggested Tom.

"I checked out the law at lunch," said Cliff. "All you have to do is show the Greetings, and you get the hemlock kit. It can all be done at the drugstore."

"How convenient," said Pam. "The bastards."

2

The next morning, Tom, Pam and Arabella went to Walgreens for the kit. They were sent to the pharmacy counter at the back of the store.

The pharmacist was a young man of about forty-five. He had a Sunset Brigade Certificate on the wall: a picture of his father, the former owner of the store, saluting a sunset. Living Forever In Our Hearts, it said.

"Can I help you?" he asked.

Tom seemed to have lost his voice.

"We need one of those kits," Pam said, because Arabella wasn't speaking up either. It seemed that she had lost her voice, too.

"One of those what?"

Pam took the induction notice from Tom's hand; she unfolded it and spread it out on the counter. "They sent us back here to get it."

"Oh, the home kit." The pharmacist looked at Tom. "It's $79.95."

"Jesus," said Pam. "Eighty bucks? What do you get?"

"You get an IV rack," the pharmacist said. "You get the three chems, the sharps, and the sterile solution; cotton swabs; death certificate, plastic bags . . ."

Arabella looked sick. "I'm going to wait in the car," she said.

Tom started to follow her, but something held him back. This is my show. The pharmacist reached under the counter and set a beige box on the counter. "There's a DVD, too," he said. "Do you have a DVD player?"

"Everybody has a DVD player." Tom's voice was back.

"Well, there's a DVD that comes in the kit. And this 800 number here on the side is for the monitor. But you don't have to worry about that; he'll be calling you. As soon as I make this sale, your number goes into the database."

"Monitor?" Pam sounded suspicious.

"There has to be someone there from the government," the pharmacist said. "You're using lethal drugs."

"But they're supposed to be lethal," said Tom.

"Doesn't matter," the pharmacist said. "It's the law. It's not an extra cost. Although I hear some people tip him."

"Ring it up," said Tom.

Arabella was waiting by the car, in the parking lot. "Cliff just called," she said.

"And?"

"Better let him tell you." And she burst into tears, for the second time.

Cliff had gotten his notice at the office. He went in two days a week. He wasn't practicing, but mentoring a younger attorney.

"This makes things simpler," he said, spreading it out on his kitchen table. It looked exactly like Tom's, except that the date was three days later.

GREETINGS William Clifford Brixton III (401-25-5423)
YOU HAVE BEEN CHOSEN BY LOTTERY FOR INDUCTION INTO THE OREGON SUNSET BRIGADE. CONGRATULATIONS ON YOUR SACRIFICE. YOU ARE TO REPORT TO CASCADE CENTER 1656, 18767 WEST HELLEN ST, AT 10 AM OCTOBER 25, 20—. IF YOU WISH TO DISCUSS OTHER ARRANGEMENTS, AS PROVIDED BY LAW, PLEASE CALL 154 176 098 8245

"Simpler!?" said Pam.

"I mean, now it's unanimous, or something."

"Like, we don't count?" said Arabella.

"That's not what I said," said Cliff. "Not what I meant."

"Do you really want to count?" Tom asked. "I mean, this is one battle the women's liberation movement didn't want to win."

"Leave the women's liberation movement out of this," said Pam. "So what do we do now?"

"The same thing we were already doing," said Cliff. "Same time, same station. Another kit."

"Jesus! Isn't one enough?" Tom asked. "We've always shared everything before."

"And we're sharing this," said Cliff. "But it's the law. You have to have one for each—inductee."

3

The next day, a Wednesday, Tom went with Cliff and Pam to pick up the second kit at the drugstore. This time they got another pharmacist; a more sympathetic, older man—African-American.

Was it just a convention of the movies, or were African-Americans always more sympathetic? Tom wondered. It was always either that or angrier, never both at once, as in real life.

Real life. It has a beginning. It has an end. It's almost over.

"There are several alternate exit program DVDs," the pharmacist was saying. "Made to coordinate with the official kit. You can get them at Tower Records or order them from Amazon. Or your church may provide one. It's more personal."

"Two by two," said Cliff, laying the two kits side by side on the kitchen table. "Like Noah's ark."

"Not exactly," said Tom.

The woman were away, at the Aerobics for Seniors class that they shared. Life had to go on, after all.

It will go on, Tom thought. Without me. It was, quite literally, inconceivable.

"Let's smoke a joint," said Cliff. He pulled out the silver cigarette case he had received after twenty years at his law firm. In it were six neatly rolled joints, the finest sinsemilla, a week's supply.

That afternoon, as luck would have it, the Brigades had their weekly show. It was afternoon TV; not quite ready for prime time. The celebrity guest was introduced to do the invocation. It was almost always a woman.

This week it was Hillary Clinton.

The Sunset Brigade, in rose-colored coveralls, were lined up on a hill overlooking the sea. Their eyes were shining; their jaws were firm. The veterans got to wear their military braid. The theme was a frenchhorn/piano concerto especially written for the Brigades by Randy Newman.

Tom turned off the sound.

"You get an extra four days," he said, looking at Cliff's induction notice.

"Three," said Cliff. "I'm not going to take them, though. We'll go together. It'll be easier on the girls that way."

"You think so?"

"I know so." Cliff passed Tom the joint. Hillary got thin, scattered applause. The Brigade saluted the flag and started up the hill. Judging from the vegetation, this induction was taking place somewhere in the East. Massachusetts? New Jersey? The East, like the West, looked all alike.

There was nothing to distinguish the draftees from the volunteers, except for the few who were in wheelchairs with IVs on little masts. They marched (or rolled) off shoulder to shoulder in their rose uniforms and easy-off slippers, following the color guard off to the departure site, which was always over a hill and never seen. They carried little individualized flags their wives and grandchildren had made. The flags would be returned to the loved ones.

When the last of the men disappeared over the hill, Cliff turned the sound back on. The closing theme was by Elton John: another version of "Candle in the Wind."

Tom turned it off.

"Better to do it our own way," said Cliff.

"Anything is better than that clown show," said Tom.

"What are you guys watching?" Pam asked, bursting through the door like Kramer, as she always did.

Always, thought Tom. Always was almost over. For him, anyway. And for Cliff, too.

"Nothing," said Cliff, turning off the TV. "Some dumb reality show."

Tom and Arabella had never had trouble making love, even though the frequency had dropped. Once they had gone for a whole year. But when he turned sixty-five, Tom had decided that they were going to set aside a day every two weeks for sex play, like it or not. It turned out that they liked it; liked being freed of the need to think about it and initiate it. At least he did.

But today something was wrong.

"Not a problem," said Arabella.

"Easy for you to say," said Tom.

Ara saw no point in arguing. She got out of bed and undressed, pulling on her regular panties, the ones he hated, that made her look like an old lady. "How about I make us some coffee?"

"Later," said Tom. "First I got to go see Ray."

Ray was Tom's lawyer. His office was in a trendy new shopping center overlooking the Rose Garden. His desktop was of recycled barn wood. Odd, thought Tom, how many things in the new world get more valuable as they get older.

Everything but us.

"What can I do you for?" asked Ray.

They were old movement comrades, if not exactly friends. They had once been adversaries, since Ray was of the electoral persuasion, and Tom and Cliff were Direct Action.

But that was long ago.

Tom unfolded his induction notice and flattened it along Ray's desk, looking out for splinters.

"Jesus fucking Christ," said Ray. "Are you sure this isn't a mistake. I thought they weren't calling anyone under seventy."

"I'm seventy," said Tom, refolding the paper. For the first time he noticed its color and shape, like a tiny tombstone. "So are you."

"Well, you get certain advantages," said Ray. "There's the bonus. And there is no probate, which means you won't have to worry about Arabella. I mean, in terms of the house and stuff."

"We don't get the bonus," said Tom. "We're not doing it."

"Not doing it?" Ray looked uncomfortable.

"Not doing the Brigade thing. There's a provision in the law that allows you to do it yourself, at home. We're going to do it at our summer place, down at Holystone Bay."

Ray nodded. He had done the paperwork on the partnership twelve years before, when Tom and Ara had bought the house with Cliff and Pam. Ray had provided for every possible disagreement. There had been none. If anything, the two families were closer now than they had been then, when they had been cautiously, consciously, determinedly recovering from Cliff and Arabella's foolish, brief, unhappy affair.

"I want you to make sure Arabella is covered. And one other thing: I want you to have my Steve Earle records."

"Jesus, man. That's huge. But what about Cliff?"

"Cliff, too. Cliff's going with me."

"Jesus fucking Christ. Cliff, too! I've always hated these

Brigades, even though I agree with the idea, I guess. But this stinks."

"I don't know why you say that," said Tom. "We've always felt that it wasn't right for the developed countries to use all the resources. Well, here it is: population control. It's not abortion or infanticide. It's voluntary. Or sort of, anyway."

"Nobody fucking volunteers," said Ray. "Not for—this."

"Well. Let's not abandon all our principles just because our number came up."

Ray was silent. Tom realized he had been lecturing him. It was an old habit he had never managed to lose. "Sorry," he said. "I was on a high horse."

"It's okay," Ray said. "I've always rather liked your high horse. And now—"

He blushed and shuffled through a stack of papers.

"You need to sign a power of attorney for Arabella," he said. "I have one on boilerplate. It will avoid probate. Especially since you and Arabella aren't actually married."

"What about the domestic partners' law?"

"They still contest that occasionally," said Ray. "What if they wanted to get even?"

"For what?"

"For doing things your own way. Here. You sign it, and I'll get Arabella's signature after. I mean, later."

Tom signed the papers and got up to leave. Ray came around his desk and stopped him at the door.

"I don't know what to say, man."

"I'm sorry I lectured you. It's just, a shock, you know."

"It is to me, too. I don't know what to say, man."

"That's okay. Just so long, I guess."

"It's been great knowing you."

"Likewise," Tom said. And he meant it. It was his first good-bye. "So long."

When Tom got home, Cliff and Pam were at the house. Cliff laid a ticket on the glass-topped table. It had a red-white-and-blue border.

"What's that?" asked Tom.

"Your airline pass," said Cliff. "I figured you might want to see your kids."

"What about your kids?"

"We just saw them last month," Pam said.

The pass was good for one round trip in the continental U.S.A.

"I thought we didn't get them if we did it ourselves."

"I fooled them," said Cliff. "I turned my kit back in, told them I'd changed my mind."

"You didn't—"

"No, no. I'll go back and get it again. Change my mind again. I have ten days to decide, remember?"

"I could have done that," said Tom.

Cliff shook his head. "You're not a good liar," he said. "I'm a lawyer, remember? Or didn't you notice that big car parked outside?"

After Cliff left, Arabella asked: "Who are you going to see?"

"Thomas," he said.

"I thought so," she said.

4

Tom and Arabella had two kids. Thomas, from Tom's first marriage, was a loan officer in Las Vegas. Thomas and his wife, Elaine, had two kids. If it had been possible, they would have had 1.646, thought Tom—the national average. The only child actually born of Tom and Arabella was Gwyneth, thirty, a kindergarten teacher in San Francisco.

She was Tom's favorite, but he had seen her just the week before. She knew he loved her.

Thomas was more of a problem.

On Monday, with four days left to go, Tom caught a flight for Las Vegas. It felt strange to be leaving Arabella, this close to the end of everything. Tom, who used to be terrified of landings, noticed as the plane descended that he wasn't nervous anymore. Everything in the world looked so temporary—what was a plane filled with people, more or less?

He was a little disappointed when the landing, like the twenty-three that had preceded it that day, or the two hundred twenty-three that had preceded it that week, went off without a hitch.

Thomas met him at the gate, looking worried. "Something wrong?" he asked.

"Why should something be wrong?"

"You don't usually come and visit us here except on holidays," said Thomas. "In case you didn't notice. And Arabella usually comes with you."

"I just felt like seeing the grandchildren," said Tom. "And you and Elaine, of course."

Traffic in Las Vegas was even slower than Tom had remembered. The leather seats and quiet ride of the big Mercedes made it worse, not better.

Thomas and Elaine put him in the guest room, which had its own bath.

"Makes it feel like a motel," he said to Arabella, on his cell phone.

"It's their world," said Arabella. "People want to have their own bathroom. Sharing a bathroom seems old fashioned, and probably a little unsanitary, I guess."

"Makes it feel like a motel," Tom said again.

"Just be nice," she said, "and hurry home."

The next afternoon, Tom took his grandchildren to the zoo.

Tara wanted to see the gorilla that had died the month before. She naively thought its body would still be on display. Eric wanted to talk about his day at school. Tom was impressed—how many kids want to talk about school? Until he heard what it was.

"We got a visit from the Sunset Brigade," Eric said. "Two men came by the school in their uniforms and told us to take good care of the planet because they were leaving it to us, to take good care of it. We got a signed certificate. It was cool."

"I'll bet," said Tom.

"Will you join the Brigade when you get old, Grandpa?"

"I'm already old," said Tom. "And I think the Brigades are horseshit."

"Grandpa said the S-word today," said Tara at the dinner table, right after Thomas had said grace. "Pass the mashed potatoes."

"Say please," said her mother, Elaine.

"I was overexcited," said Tom. "It must have been the gorilla."

"There wasn't any gorilla," said Eric.

That evening Tom gave the grandchildren a good-night kiss, and Thomas took him to the airport to catch the red-eye back to Portland. There is always a red-eye to everywhere from Vegas.

"Dad," said Thomas. "The kids aren't old enough to share your values. I mean about the Brigades and the government."

"They may never get that old," Tom said. "You didn't."

"You may recall, I was never given the chance," said Thomas.

Tom had abandoned his first family when he had gone underground with the Red Storm.

"That was my mistake," said Tom. "It doesn't mean I don't love you today."

"I know, Dad. And I know how you feel about the Brigades."

"You do?"

"Sure. It's how you feel about everything. Resistance. Rejection. Rebellion. Is there something you wanted to tell me?"

"Just that—I am proud of you, you know. You're a much better father than I ever was."

"Not such a stretch," said Thomas; then he laughed and clapped his father on the shoulder, a glancing blow. "I noticed you didn't say, 'better man'."

"I meant that, too."

"I know, I know. Well, Dad, this is as far as I can go without a ticket."

They hugged and parted. Tom had taken great pains not to show his son his red-white-and-blue ticket. He waved good-bye and disappeared down the tunnel, through the gauntlet of bored security guards.

5

"Wainwright is opening the house," said Pam, when she met Tom at Portland International. "We're all set up to head down tomorrow."

"Tomorrow?"

"Well, we all thought we could go down early and get a day at the beach before, you know . . ."

"Before we do it," said Tom. He was finding a perverse pleasure in reminding others what this was all about. Even Arabella. Even though he didn't want to say what "it" was any more than the others did.

He slept late. When he got up, Ara was packing groceries, tears running down her face.

"We knew this had to happen," he said, putting his arms around her from behind.

"That doesn't make it any easier," she said.

While she finished packing, he found himself walking through the rooms, saying good-bye to the Salter Street house. It wasn't as hard as he would have thought. He had said good-bye to lots of houses in his day. And this house was more Arabella's than his anyway, even though they had bought it together, almost twenty years before.

It was Ara's garden he found hardest. She made sure it was all watered before she left. These plants will continue to grow, he thought. They will still be growing in their mindless, stupid way, while I will be no more.

No more.

"Heere's Johnny!" said Cliff, pulling up in his yellow Cadillac.

The drive from Portland to Holystone Bay was three hours, over the dark, tangled ridges of the Coast Range. It was a quiet drive. The four of them, who had talked nonstop about everything for twenty years, couldn't think of anything to say.

It was raining when they crossed the last ridge and saw the ocean with the great holed rock that gave the bay, and its smattering of a town, its name. The house was cold. The wind rattled through the boards. Tom fired up the wood stove while Cliff hauled in the groceries and Arabella and Pam put them away.

"Brrrr," said Cliff. "This house was never designed for winter."

"It's fall," said Pam.

"It was never designed for any of this," Tom said grimly.

"Well, it'll have to do," said Cliff. He set the beige box on the table, which was made of driftwood planks, salt-whitened—like bone, Tom thought.

"Stop it," he said, to himself.

"Huh?" asked Pam from the kitchen door. "What?"

"Nothing."

There was knock at the front door. Tom opened it, and stepped back—shocked at the figure on the stoop.

Death, in a yellow hood. No—

Not yet.

A young woman was on the stoop, dressed in a yellow raincoat, hood up, dripping wet.

"Can I help you?"

"I'm Karin," the young woman said. "With an I. Your midwife."

"Midwife?"

"I mean M-monitor," she said, standing first on one foot and then the other. "Monitor. For the induction."

"That's not until tomorrow," said Cliff.

"I know, but I thought I . . ."

"Come in out of the rain," said Arabella from the kitchen door.

Tom closed the door behind her, and she stood, dripping all over the rag rug. Arabella took her raincoat and gave her a towel. Instead of drying her hair with it, she put it around her shoulders like a shawl. She was very tall and thin.

"You must be Arabella," she said, using two fingers to squeeze the rain out of her stringy blond hair; it fell, hissing, onto the wood stove. "I know all your names from the social security database. My name is Karin, with an I. I know it's not until tomorrow—"

Even they call it "it," thought Tom, with a certain grim satisfaction.

"—but I came early, because I've never seen the Oregon coast," she said, "and I thought I would make it sort of a little vacation. The state pays for three days for out-of-the-way places. I'm staying up the road at the Spyglass Lodge."

"The only place around," said Cliff. "Wainwrong's place."

"How did you get here?" asked Pam, looking outside for a car.

"I walked. They don't give us a car. They give us cab fare, but there are no cabs. There's no anything here."

"You got that right," said Tom.

"I didn't mean to intrude," Karin said. "I just came by to say hello and introduce myself. I don't usually do . . . this sort of thing."

"We don't either," said Tom.

"Sit down," said Pam. She set an extra place for dinner. Ara cooked frozen shrimp imported from South Carolina, and Cliff opened a bottle of Willamette Valley pinot noir.

"This is my government service," Karin said, after she had stopped shivering. "I still have eight months to go. I haven't done too many of these."

"Then we're even," said Tom.

"What's this about being a midwife?" Arabella asked. "Is that what they call it?"

"Oh, no, no!" said Karin with a laugh, which she quickly stifled, turning it into a polite cough. "I was training to be a midwife when they called me up. That's what I still hope to do full time. This is very good wine for Oregon."

"Pinot noir," said Cliff. "I own an interest in the vineyard."

"An interest!" Pam said, with a bitter laugh. Cliff had invested a hundred thousand in the vineyard; he often joked that the wine was twelve hundred dollars a bottle. It was Pam's least-favorite joke.

"Let me guess," said Tom. "You're from California."

"Los Angeles. But my boyfriend is from Oregon. He told me it was beautiful here."

"It's a lot nicer here in the summer," said Arabella. "But we like it all the time."

"Does it always rain like this?"

"No, no. Sometimes it rains sideways," said Tom.

They finished the bottle, and Cliff opened another. The presence of the girl at the table made it somehow easier to talk. She was a dishwater blonde with sallow skin but perfect, if slightly small, teeth. Her eyes were a washed-out blue.

"We bought this place for twenty grand twenty years ago," said Cliff.

"Twenty-one five," said Pam.

"We were in the army together," said Cliff. Tom, Arabella,

and Pam all looked at him, puzzled. "The anti-war army," he said. "Back in the day."

"He told me all about you, the man at the motel," Karin said.

"Wainwrong," said Cliff.

"Wainwright," said Karin, looking confused.

"Cliff's little joke," said Pam. "He has several of them. Anybody want to play cards?"

"We're not allowed to play cards," said Karin. "And I guess I should be heading back."

It had almost stopped raining, so they let her walk. Her raincoat was still wet, but her hair was almost dry. It was only a quarter mile up the steep, slick, empty street, to Wainwright's Spyglass Lodge.

6

Sunrises are sneaky in Holystone Bay. The sun lingers behind the fog-topped ridges to the west until the world is lit by a gradual pearly glow, and then it appears unannounced and unheralded, except by shadows, and somehow less than surprising. Two long shadows on the sand announced the arrival of the sun over the ragged line of Georgia-Pacific Ridge, named after the company that owned it.

My last sunrise, thought Tom, and I missed it. He and Ara were walking on the beach. It was too cold and windy to talk. They stopped and stood, holding hands, watching the sea patiently enlarging its hole in the great stone offshore. One, two, three: it was like watching a clock.

"Do you think we should call Gwyneth?" asked Arabella.

"Let's leave her in peace," said Tom, "till after. I know her; she'll feel something is required of her, and it isn't."

"Maybe it's something required of us," said Arabella.

"Let's think about it for another day or so," said Tom. "Look, isn't that the girl?"

It was indeed the girl, stringy blond hair and all.

"What are you doing here?"

"Just taking a walk," Karin said. "I didn't mean to intrude on anyone."

"You're not intruding," said Arabella. "This is a public beach."

"Does this job always make you cry?" asked Tom.

"I'm sorry; it's not you," Karin said. "It's me. A personal loss. My boyfriend. We just broke up."

She lit a cigarette—an American Spirit. She offered Tom one, but Arabella turned it down for him.

"He doesn't smoke."

"I'm thinking of starting again," said Tom.

"Can I use your phone?" asked Karin. Tom's was in a mesh pocket on his windbreaker. "I can't use mine, because I don't want him to know where I am. I promised myself I wouldn't call him. But he broke every promise to me. I can break one."

"Then make the call, dear," said Arabella, handing her Tom's phone.

"Feel free," Tom said. "I have some extra minutes I'm never going to use."

"You shouldn't be so hard on her," said Arabella, as they watched her walk away, dialing. "She's exactly Gwyneth's age."

"How can you tell?"

"A mother can tell."

When Tom and Ara got back to the house, there was a car pulled up in front. A Ford Expedition, the ice-blue Shackleton model, with a blue light on top.

"Oh no," said Tom. "Wainwrong."

"Do you want me to tell him to go away?" asked Arabella, taking Tom's hand again; she had dropped it back on the little wooden stair that led up the last dune.

"No, of course not."

Wainwright was in the kitchen, having a cup of coffee with Cliff. Pam was scowling at them both.

"Wainwright wants to handle the arrangements," she said.

"The what?"

"The arrangements," said Wainwright, standing up and extending his giant paw. "In addition to being the mayor and the head Homey, and of course the handyman and hotelier, I operate the only licensed funeral home on this section of the coast. But aren't we getting ahead of ourselves? I came by to extend my sympathies to you all. And to offer my services, of course."

"Of course," said Tom. "How did you find about about this, anyway?"

"The girl," said Wainwright. "It's a terrible thing. It's on the Homeland Security database, too. All this stuff is tracked."

"We don't need any services," said Tom. "We're handling this on our own."

"Of course you are," said Wainwright, pulling at his beard. "But you can't do everything by yourselves. If you don't go through the Brigade, the government doesn't cover the funeral costs."

"No funeral," said Tom. "We're saying our good-byes as we go."

"No funeral, then. But what about cremation? You can't do that yourself."

"He's right, Tom," said Cliff. "He already gave us a price. It makes it easier on the girls."

"There are no girls here," said Pam.

"I want to be as helpful as I can," said Wainwright. "This is a courageous thing you're doing."

"What's courageous about it?" said Tom. "We have no choice."

"But to do it alone, like this."

"I'm not doing it alone," said Tom. "I'm with my family and friends. And Cliff is doing it, too."

"Cliff!" Wainwright looked at Cliff, shocked. "I had no idea. She didn't tell me that. You're both sidetracking the Brigade, giving up the bonus?"

"Sidestepping," said Tom. It sounded like a dance.

"I don't need no stinkin' bonus," said Cliff. "I'm a wealthy lawyer. Perhaps you haven't noticed my car, parked just outside."

"You already gave us a price," said Pam.

"That was for one," Wainwright said. "The problem is, there are regulations. Even if I could technically stuff two . . ."

"Can we talk about this later?" said Arabella.

"Of course," said Wainwright, brightening. "I'll see what I can do. Meanwhile . . ."

"Meanwhile, we who are about to die salute you," said Tom, lifting Cliff's coffee cup.

Wainwright shuffled toward the door. "Meanwhile, there's a

big storm coming on. There's a pressure dome moving in. I have to get back up to the lodge and look after the shutters. You should close yours."

"One of them is broken," said Cliff. "On the ocean side. Remember, you were going to fix it?"

After Wainwright had driven away in his Ford Expedition, Tom turned to Cliff. "You never got the hemlock kit?"

"One is enough," said Cliff. "They still think I'm showing up at the Brigade. I want to surprise them."

"For real? For sure? You still want to go early with me?"

"Come on, of course for real. Isn't that what we decided? Case closed. Where are you going?"

"Give me the card to your Caddy. I'm going for a drive."

Arabella stayed to help Pam with lunch while Cliff closed the shutters, all but the one that was broken. Tom drove out to the headland and parked, and watched the sea through the windshield, like a drive-in movie.

Tomorrow that stone will still be here, and so will the sea. So will the seagull, floating on the wind, looking for something to eat. While I will be—

Something to eat.

No more Tom. No more nothing.

All hole and no stone. Over. Fini.

He started the car. If there was a storm coming, it wasn't showing yet. The waves were smaller than usual, moving the tangles of seaweed in and out, like a big mop. A big fucking mop. Tom decided to skip lunch. He drove up the coast six miles toward Seal Cove, the first real town.

There was hardly any traffic. Tom passed a state trooper. As always, he felt illegal, today more so than ever. Do they know I'm going to die tonight? he thought. It gave him a great freedom: It's like, I can do anything. The ultimate outlaw, beyond the reach of the law.

He resisted the impulse to wave.

He was thinking of calling Gwyneth, dreading it. Had he left his phone with the girl on purpose? He even stopped and swiped his card at the phone on the edge of the parking lot of Seal Cove

Liquors. She knows we love her, he said to himself. Then he hesitated. Why add this to her troubles?

Then he dialed anyway. He was relieved when he got
Gwyneth's machine. "If you don't know what to do now, you
have no business using a phone."

"Gwyn, honey," he said. "It's your dear old dad. I'm calling
from Holystone Bay. Your mother and I are here at the house
with Pam and Cliff. It's beautiful."

It wasn't particularly beautiful, especially not in the parking
lot of Seal Bay Liquors, but honesty was not among Tom's purposes.

"I just called to say that I'm thinking of you, and I love you.
Your mother, too. Bye!"

There. That done, he went inside and rewarded himself with
a pack of American Spirits, the brand the girl had smoked. And
on second thought, a bottle of whiskey.

When he got back to the house, the afternoon was almost
gone. Cliff and Pam were playing a version of two-handed soli-
taire Pam had invented.

"Old Grand-Dad," said Cliff admiringly. "What's the occasion?"

"Very funny. Where's Ara?"

"She went for a walk," said Pam.

The wide beach was empty, and the sea was strangely still. There
was no surf at all, just a smooth glassy plate rising and falling, in
and out. A windsurfer heading toward the stone was the only solid
thing—his sail was transparent, so that he looked like a walker on
the water, striding the waves like the gulls strode the wind.

The sea is calm tonight. The tide is full, the moon lies fair
upon the straits. The Sea of Faith was once—

He couldn't remember the rest of the words. It didn't seem to
matter. There was no moon anyway. It was the ending he remembered: Ah, love, let us be true to one another!

"There you are. I found you."

It was Arabella. He had gone looking for her, and she had
found him. As usual; as always. Looking at her slight form in her
sweatshirt and jeans, heavy breasted, narrow in the hips, her

short hair faded gray but still full, he felt a tremendous rush of love, even more powerful than the sexual desire that had drawn him to her thirty years before when he had first seen her across the room at a World Bank protest.

Thirty-two.

Is this what's love is? he wondered. Not what's left after sex, and sex's promises, and sex's betrayals, but what grows from them all, like a bright plant from dark soil.

"I called Gwyneth," he said. "And left a message. Okay?"

"Does that mean I have to call her tomorrow?"

"I guess."

"She'll be angry."

"Maybe that's the best way," said Tom. "Anger." He skipped a stone across the glassy sea. "Funny. There are no waves today."

"It's the pressure dome," said Arabella. "Wainwright says it means a storm is coming."

"Wainwright's a weatherman, too?" The waves that usually boomed through the rock, cutting the hole bigger every day, every year, every century, were lapping gently. The rock was getting the evening off. The windsurfer cut through the hole, an unheard-of maneuver. "He looks like a jesus bug," said Tom. "Walking on the water."

"A what?" Ara took his hand.

"A jesus bug. When I was a kid there were lots of jesus bugs on the pond behind my grandparents' barn. I used to shoot at them with my BB gun. I didn't think anything about it."

"He made it through," said Arabella. The windsurfer caught the wind again, and headed out to sea.

"Good for him." Tom had forgotten the American Spirits. He opened the pack and lit one, while Arabella looked on disapprovingly.

He waited for her to say something.

"It's all organic," he said finally. "Indian approved."

"Are you okay?" Ara asked.

He looked at her sharply and exhaled, then said, "No."

"Me, neither."

"I love you," he said finally. "I really do."

"I know."

"You and me, Ara, we've had a great run. I don't regret a bit of it. I mean that. Not even the hard parts. I mean that."

"I know," she said. "There've been some hard parts."

"That's okay."

"This is one of them."

"Oh, honey." She was crying. "Maybe we should go back to the house."

"This one is different," she said. "This one we can't make better."

He sat with her on a rock while she cried softly. He held her hand, but after a while he felt nothing. He was like the stone on which they sat. When you throw a stone into the water, it disappears without a trace, as if it had never been.

"It's getting dark," he said finally. "Let's go in."

7

Theirs was the only house in the row of beach houses that was lighted. The lighted window drew Tom and Arabella like a beacon—a little spot of life on a dark, silent coast. And as they approached, the light went out.

It was Cliff, nailing a plywood sheet over the window.

"Wainwrong's back," he said. "Bearing plywood, and other gifts."

Wainwright was in the kitchen with Pam.

"I brought some lasagna," he said. "From the restaurant. Mirta made it special. And the plywood, to replace the broken shutter. By the way, have you seen the girl?"

"Karin?" asked Pam. "No. Not since this morning."

"I was supposed to give her a ride down here, but I couldn't find her."

"She likes to walk on the beach," said Arabella.

"She's got my cell phone," said Tom.

"Well, I hope she's got her raincoat, too," said Wainwright. "There's a massive pressure dome off the coast. That's why there are no waves. It'll bring a big storm later tonight."

"You mentioned that already," said Tom.

"Well, I just felt the need to remind you. And I brought you this." He held up a DVD.

"A going away present?" Tom asked.

"It's called EZ-Exit," Wainwright said. "It replaces the DVD in the kit, which is sort of religious. With this one, you can make it the way you want it to be. There are eight programs on the disk. Different kinds of music, visuals . . ."

"You've tried them?" asked Tom, taking the plastic case and setting it on the coffee table next to the plain beige box. The DVD's cover showed an angel in a tie-dyed smock, playing a guitar. He looked a lot like Jerry Garcia.

"I was curious," said Wainwright. "I inherited it from York."

"Yorick?"

"The uncle who left me the funeral home. He had cancer, so he did himself in. Some of them are pretty cool. My favorite is number four, which is all Jerry Garcia."

"The Dead."

"It's a solo thing. But you get the idea. They are designed to be combined with acid or dope, or maybe even heroin; the Garcia one, who knows? I'm not saying this officially, of course."

"Of course not," said Cliff. Wainwright was the local Homeland Security Chief.

"We need to be getting ourselves ready," said Pam.

"Ever hear of the Last Supper?" asked Tom.

"I understand," said Wainwright, standing. His gray ponytail almost brushed the little house's low ceiling. He held out his big hand, first for Cliff, then for Tom. "If anybody could turn water into wine, it's you guys. I mean that."

"Thanks," said Tom.

"Thanks," said Cliff.

"It takes real courage to laugh in the face of death."

Death. There was a long silence. It was the first time anyone in the house had said the word.

"Well," said Wainwright. "Don't let the lasagna get cold. I had Mirta make it special. And Cliff, I hope you nailed that plywood down good. This is what they call the calm before the storm. You probably thought that was just a saying."

"Like death and taxes," said Tom.

"I'll never forget the last time we had a pressure dome off shore like this. It was back when Doc Azarov's boat was in my marina. Remember that Boston Whaler? That old son of a bitch had it insured for twice as much as . . ."

"Good night, Wainwright," said Pam, opening the door. Outside, the night was strangely still. "Thanks for the lasagna."

"And the plywood," said Cliff.

"And the Grateful Dead," said Tom.

"It's solo Garcia," Wainwright corrected. "But great stuff. There's also some jazz, if that's your thing. And Yanni. Yuck. Meanwhile, before I go, can I ask one question?"

"Shoot," said Cliff.

"You guys have never been really sick or anything, have you? Like a heart attack or cancer or something?"

Tom and Cliff both shook their heads.

"I didn't think so. You're lucky you can laugh."

"What do you mean?" Arabella asked.

"Because death is not just some abstract nothing," Wainwright said, stopping in the doorway. "It's not like a hole you fall into. It's a thing. I learned that from York. It comes after you. It's like a mad dog. It's irresistible."

"Thanks and good night," said Pam, shutting the door in his face.

"Wow," said Tom.

"What was that?" said Arabella, pouring herself another Old Grand-Dad.

"An asshole," said Pam.

"*Quod erat demonstrandum,*" said Cliff. "What say we retire to the deck and watch the sunset?"

"Wow," said Tom, again.

The wind had come up, and the sea was getting choppy. Big slow rollers boomed. The windsurfer was long gone; even the birds were gone. Cliff poured everyone a double shot of Old Grand-Dad, and they arranged themselves facing west. Tom and Arabella shared one chair.

The sunset wasn't a disappointment like the sunrise had been. It was in fact a winner. A huge, and hugely distant, ball of fire sank slowly into a black band of cloud, turning it rose, then bright red, like a bloodstain. They watched silently until the wind came up. The waves were back. The hole in the rock looked like a wound, red against the black of the stone.

Cliff poured another round. "Quite a show," he said. "Don't guess we get to ask for an encore."

Nobody felt like talking. They just sipped their drinks and stared at the red streak where the sun had been, growing darker and darker. The wind came up, cold and smelling of rain.

Tom lit an American Spirit. It took three matches.

"I wish you wouldn't do that," said Ara. Tom threw the cigarette away and wrapped his arms around her. The first raindrops arrived, one by one, sounding like stones hitting the plywood.

Pam stood up. "It's about that time," she said.

Both Tom and Cliff looked up, suddenly, like two deer caught in headlights.

"For supper, I mean, before the lasagna gets any colder."

Supper was surprisingly easy, almost normal. Cliff opened a twelve hundred dollar bottle of pinot noir and they ate with a candle on the table. It was almost like the old, good times. Yesterday.

The lasagna wasn't bad, either.

"Here's to good friends," said Cliff. He twirled his glass and watched the wine slip down from the sides. "Can I get serious?"

"Beats me. Have you ever tried?" Tom immediately wished he hadn't said it when Cliff took his hand. They had been friends for twenty, no, thirty years, but they had never held hands.

"There's something I want to say," said Cliff. "Which is, thank you. It has really been a privilege to be part of this foursome. I truly love you guys. My family. All of you."

"And we love you," said Arabella.

"And we love you," said Tom. He took Pam's hand; she was crying. "It's hard to leave this sweet old world. But the hardest thing is leaving friends."

"I still don't think it's fair," said Pam, breaking the circle and standing up. "I'm not going to pretend it's all right."

"No, it's not all right," said Arabella, pouring herself another drink.

"The undiscovered country," said Tom, lighting a cigarette. "Funny how we think of it that way. And yet it's the most famil- iar thing of all. We spend a third of our lives unconscious, in that little death called sleep."

There. He had said the word.

"We have been dead since Time began, for half of eternity, and alive for a only a few brief moments, and yet we fear what we know better than life itself. A kind of going home, back, to what we always were."

Ashes.

"That's a pretty speech," said Pam. "But you still can't smoke in the house."

"Pam!" said Cliff.

"It's okay," said Tom. "I want to step outside anyway, and watch the storm come in."

Cliff joined him. They stood in the lee of the house, out of the rain, almost.

"Are you scared, Tom?"

"I wasn't. I really wasn't. Until now. Now I'm scared shitless."

"Me, too. But we can't let the girls know. We can't lay that on them, too."

"No, no. Cliff, are you sure you want to do this?"

"I got the greetings, too, remember, buddy?"

"I mean now, tonight, with me."

"Sure. What's three days?"

"It seems like a lifetime from here."

"Damn, it does, doesn't it? But no, I'm too scared to do it alone. And can you imagine the girls having to do it twice?"

"They probably make it easy in the Brigade. I mean, with the group dynamics and all."

"Fuck that. Don't we have group dynamics here? What, are you saying you want to go join the geezers? Or that I should?"

"Neither."

"So shut the fuck up, please. What are you, chain smoking?"

"Why not? Want a drag?"

"Why not. Jesus, what is this shit! No wonder the Indians died out."

"Better not let Pam hear you say that."

"I may be old, but I'm not stupid. They'll be all right, won't they, Tom? The girls?"

"They'll be fine," said Tom. "That's the one thing I'm sure of. If it was them leaving us, we would stick together and survive, wouldn't we?"

"I just worry about Pam. Arabella is so level-headed. Pam is always lashing out at one thing or another."

"Ara will keep her on track. They're good together. They were always the real couple, you know. You and me were just the support system."

Cliff looked hurt. "That's sort of true, isn't it?"

Tom put his arm around Cliff's waist. "No. But we have to do our best and trust them to do the same. Right?"

"Right," said Cliff. "Stiff upper lip."

"Absolutely colonial," said Tom. "And now I'm getting wet. Let's go inside, buddy."

Pam and Arabella were doing the dishes. "You guys get the night off," said Pam. It was her first attempt at a joke, and they all honored it with a laugh.

Arabella dried her hands and poured another Old Grand-Dad. The bottle was half gone. Tom lifted it, worried. "I thought you were leaving the bourbon alone," he said.

"I thought you didn't smoke," Arabella said. She gave him a peck on the cheek; it was almost girlish. "Don't look so worried; it's just for tonight. I am not about to become an old drunk."

"I have something better anyway," said Cliff, sitting back down at the table and opening his silver case. "Enough talk about death—"

There, thought Tom. We have both said it. Suddenly it seemed easy.

"—let's talk about life!" Cliff lit a joint and passed it to Tom. "All our favorite things. Ice cream, whiskey, good friends, good dope."

"This is certainly good dope," said Tom.

"Lawyer dope," said Cliff.

Tom passed the joint to Pam while Cliff put a CD in the player. Coltrane: *My Favorite Things.*

Pam passed the joint to Arabella, but she waved it away.

Tom was relieved, until he saw her fill her glass again.

"What were your favorite things?" Cliff asked.

Past tense already?

"My favorite thing was sunrise from the top of Mt. Hood," Cliff said, exhaling a huge Jamaican-style cloud toward the ceiling.

"You never went there," said Pam. "You only talked about it."

"Just knowing it was there was enough. What a run. What a stage on which to strut."

Cliff got up from the table and went into the living room. Remembering the beige box on the coffee table, Tom got a chill. "Where are you going?"

"I'm looking for my Shakespeare. There's an index."

"He's going to look up Death," said Pam, groaning.

Now they had all said it; all except Arabella.

"I don't need no stinkin' index," said Cliff, coming back into the room empty-handed. "Out, out damned spot!"

"That's not about death," Tom said. "That's about murder."

"So?" said Pam, suddenly serious.

"So? Everything in *Hamlet* is about death," said Cliff. "Good night, sweet prince."

"That's from *Macbeth*," said Arabella.

"I beg your pardon!" said Cliff.

"I mean the spot," said Arabella, giggling. "I know because my grandmother used to say it when she was washing the dishes. She was an actress until she met my grandfather. They were married for fifty years. Can you imagine?"

"Almost," said Tom. He pulled her down beside him on the couch.

"Well, it's a *Macbeth* sort of night," said Cliff. "To be or not to be. The undiscovered country."

"That's from *Star Trek*," said Tom, to lighten the mood.

"*Quod erat demonstrandum*," said Cliff. "Habeus corpus and all that. Listen to that wind howl."

They fell silent and listened to the wind howl. It was not a pretty sound.

"We have time for one more game of cards," said Pam. She knocked the cards on the table three times, preparing to shuffle.

As if in answer, there were three raps on the door.

Pam froze; they all froze.

Had it been imagined? There was no sound but the shrieking of the wind and the rattling of the rain on the plywood.

Then there it was again: RAP RAP RAP . . .

"Fucking Wainwrong's back," said Cliff.

You wish, thought Tom. He got up and opened the door. Who would have thought Death would appear as a tall, skinny girl in a yellow hood, carrying an attaché case instead of a scythe, and asking:

"Can I come in? Are you ready?"

8

Karin took off the slicker, which made her look a little less like Death, and dried her stringy blond hair with the towel Arabella provided. She was wearing a forest-green uniform: Youth Service Corps. It didn't do much for her figure. While Pam made sassafras tea for everyone, Karin set her attaché case down on the coffee table, between the beige kit and the EZ-Exit DVD.

"What's this?" she asked.

"Your hotelier gave it to us," said Cliff. "It replaces the DVD in the kit."

"This is all new to me," said Karin. "You'll have to forgive me; all I know is the medical procedure."

"We'll forgive you," said Tom. Forgive them, Lord, they know not what they do. "Want a cigarette? I have your brand."

"I can't smoke in uniform," said Karin.

"You can't smoke in the house anyway," said Pam. "Do you want some sassafras tea?"

Tom opened the beige kit. It contained a bottle of pills, a DVD in a plastic slipcase with an angel (not Jerry Garcia) waving an American flag, and a red-white-and-blue death certificate.

"This is all you get for $79.95?" he said. "They could at least give you a little gun."

"No guns in the house," Pam reminded him.

"The kit is really just for the death certificate," said Karin. She didn't seem to mind saying the word anymore; in uniform, she was all business. "Where's the other one?"

"It's in the mail," Cliff lied smoothly. "They said you could write in both names on that one."

"I didn't know you could get them by mail," said Karin, unlocking her attaché. "Anyway, I have everything I need here." She took out a little plastic device that looked like a toy pipe organ. It was three upright plastic tubes in ascending sizes, each one filled with a fluid: one pink, one amber, and one yellow. "The amber one is a tranquilizer. The yellow is a muscle relaxant, very powerful and smooth acting. The pink contains the actual . . ."

"We don't need to know the details," said Pam.

"That's true," said Karin. "Sorry." Each tube was connected to a clear plastic IV line; the lines were tangled. Karin set the little device on the piano, which had come from Arabella's grandmother's house in Corvallis, and began the process of untangling the lines.

Meanwhile, Cliff put the EZ-Exit DVD into the player and started navigating through the menu. The first image that came up was clouds, and the Yanni soundtrack.

He skipped to Track Two: Jerry Garcia facing a huge crowd in a sunny meadow. "Was Jerry Garcia at Woodstock?"

"It was raining at Woodstock. See what the next one is," said Tom.

Arabella poured herself another bourbon. Pam was sipping sassafras tea.

Track Three was Coltrane: "My Favorite Things" over a picture of dunes and the sea.

"Let's do the dunes," said Tom.

"Done," said Cliff, hitting pause. "Now what?"

Karin arranged them on the couch, girl-boy-boy-girl. Tom and Cliff were sitting side by side, between their two wives. Cliff held the remote and laid it on his lap while he pulled a fat joint out of his silver case.

"I don't think that's allowed," said Karin.

"I think it is," said Cliff. "I'm a lawyer, or haven't you seen my car outside?" He lit the joint and passed it to Tom. "It comes under medicinal, and we're all terminal here, right?"

"Well, I don't know," said Karin, who was still trying to untangle the IV lines. She looked, to Tom, like Penelope undoing her weaving. Is that what death is like? he wondered. Instead of your life flashing before your eyes, a string of classical references.

"Don't we get a few minutes to say our good-byes?" Pam asked.

Karin shook her head. "We're already in overtime," she said. "This was supposed to happen at sunset."

She pulled two syringes from her attaché case. She swabbed each man's arm with alcohol.

"Wouldn't want to get an infection," said Tom. He closed his eyes as Karin put the needle in his arm. Cliff left his open.

When both needles were inserted, she hooked the IV lines up to a coupler, which connected both men to all three lines. The lines were still tangled, but the loose ends were free, and each one found a connection.

Karin seemed satisfied. "Now, before I release the fluids, I have to note the exact time. Does anybody have a watch?"

"Aren't you supposed to have that?" asked Cliff. "Here, take my Rolex. But you can't keep it. Pam gets it in my estate."

"Rolex!" said Pam. "Don't let him make you nervous. He bought it on Canal Street in New York last year."

They were all nervous. Karin's hands shook as she slipped the watch onto her skinny wrist. Tom felt suddenly sorry for her. Arabella was leaning back on the couch with her eyes half closed. I'm glad we've said our good-byes, Tom thought. The whole point of all this is to make you eager to get it over with. "Let's get it over with," he said.

As soon as Karin had turned her back to write down the time, Tom felt Cliff tapping his hand.

He looked down and saw an orange tab of LSD in his palm. "Wainwright?" he whispered.

"No way, man. Clifford select. I've been saving this for a special occasion. I think this qualifies."

Cliff swallowed his.

Tom squeezed Cliff's hand but didn't take the acid. He pretended, and dropped it into his pocket. "I'm with you, man," he said.

"All I have to do is push this plunger down," Karin said. "It's better if I'm behind you and you aren't watching. The idea is . . ."

RIING

Karin jumped and pulled a cell phone from her pocket.

"That's my phone!" said Tom. He had forgotten it. He reached for the phone, but Karin pulled it back.

"I don't think . . ."

"Better answer it," said Cliff, grinning. "It might be the governor."

Karin reluctantly handed Tom his phone.

"Daddy?"

"Gwyn?"

"Daddy! What are you doing!"

"Gwyn, honey . . ."

"I can't believe this. This is crazy. You can't do this!"

Tom got up from the couch. He looked at Arabella. "It's Gwyneth. I want to take this outside."

Even more reluctantly, Karin unhooked Tom's IV from the coupler, and he stepped outside the door. The wind had dropped. He lit a cigarette.

"Daddy!" Gwyneth's voice sounded far away. "This is crazy. You can't do this."

"How did you find out what I was doing?"

"Thomas called me after your visit. He thought you were acting strange. Daddy, you can't do this. There are other ways."

"You mean the Brigade?"

"No! There's an underground. A Resistance! I thought you of all people would know enough to know about that. I called them. They are on their way. They can help."

"Help with what? Honey, this is already happening." Tom looked down at the needle dangling from his arm. "We're already into the procedure."

"Fuck the procedure," Gwyneth said. "You can't just abandon us this way. We have a right to be there."

"Gwyn, honey, believe me, you don't want to be here. This isn't *Little House on the Prairie*."

"This is too cruel. Let me talk to mother."

"Your mother is okay. She's—busy," said Tom.

"She's drunk, right? I can't believe you let her start drinking again! I can't believe you two!"

Tom looked up. They were in the eye of the storm. A few stars showed overhead, and among them, a single blinking light—a plane far overhead, coming from Japan, bypassing Oregon, heading for Chicago or Toronto or New York or . . .

"Put her on, maybe I can talk some sense to her," said Gwyneth. "This is just too ZZXXXZZZ—"

"You're breaking up," said Tom. The stars overhead seemed cold and far away. They were lost in a sea of blackness. Floating in a sea of death.

It's all death out here. Come and join us.

He felt it pulling at him. But the tiny spark of life was still pulling harder. Wainwright was wrong. Death wasn't a mad dog; it was more like gravity: everywhere, but weak. Nothing escaped it in the long run, but everything, even a few cells, could resist it for a while.

For a while, but time is up. "I have to go back in," he said.

"You can't do this to me," Gwyneth said. "Are you saying I'll never talk to you again? You're my father! You can XXZZXXZZX—"

"You're breaking up," Tom said again. "I love you, honey. I'll always love you." A lie. Always was all but over. He clicked his phone shut and walked back into the house.

"Gwyneth," he said, putting the phone on the table.

"Let me talk to her," Arabella said woozily.

"She says she'll call you tomorrow," said Tom, sitting back down on the couch and holding up his arm for the connection. "Let's get on with this."

"Let's get it on . . ." Cliff sang; he was smiling. The acid, Tom thought. Maybe I should have taken it, too. While Karin reconnected the lines to his IV, he leaned over and gave Arabella a kiss. Her lips were cold. Her eyes were closed. She seemed as far away now as she would ever be.

"It's been a pleasure working with you all," said Karin. "Thanks for all your help."

"Think nothing of it," said Tom. "Should we start the DVD?"

"Go," said Karin.

Cliff was holding the remote. Tom leaned over and pressed

PLAY. The TV showed a picture of the dunes, wavering, like from a rocking boat. The tall grass was dancing to the familiar sounds of "My Favorite Things."

The camera was a handheld, lurching through the dunes toward the bright blue sea. Maybe I'm getting a rush, Tom thought. It was almost as if he had taken the acid. There was Coltrane, then Bill Evans. No, it was the triads of McCoy Tyner.

These are a few of my favorite things . . .

"You will feel sleepy," said Karin, from far away. "Whatever you do is okay now. Just relax, go to sleep if you want to."

Sleep? Is that what they call it?

The camera was a handheld, bobbing up and down through the low, no, high dunes. Ocean and sky met in a faraway blue/blue line. Ahead, there was something sticking up. It was bright orange. The trick, Tom thought, is to pretend to walk, to pretend to be there. He pretended to run toward the top of the dune, but the sand was soft and his feet were numb with cold, and clumsy. He slowed to a walk, and there it was, a small hang-glider with a seat hanging under it. It was already in the air, hovering. He sat down on the seat and scooted over to make room for Ara, and someone was beside him. Too heavy, though; it was Cliff. Tom pushed off with one foot and the glider soared upward, over the dunes. The clumsiness was gone, though his feet were still cold.

My favorite things.

"Hey, this is great," he said to Cliff, but it was Pam who answered. "Cliff is gone."

Where was Ara?

The little glider was sailing higher and higher and higher, caught in an updraft. "I can't turn this thing," said Tom. Leaning from side to side did nothing; it was as if he had no weight at all.

Higher and higher.

The dunes were gone, and it was all sea and sky.

Coltrane, soprano, blue blues blue. My favorite things.

Tom squeezed Arabella's hand, and she squeezed back. She had never understood his thing about music, about Coltrane, but she was getting it now, at last.

"Oh, honey," Tom said, but she was gone again, and he was alone on the wide under-glider seat, descending.

It was going down.

The water looked solid, like a sheet of blue light.

There was an island ahead, tiny but getting bigger. He tried to turn, but the glider was heading straight for it. They know what they are doing, Tom thought.

The island had a hole in it, like a little pond. Someone was standing beside it, waving him in.

Ara?

The glider tipped, and he hit the water, and the water was hard. Tom closed his eyes, and they opened instead. He was on the floor, looking up at the low, patched ceiling of the summer house he had bought twenty years ago with Arabella and Cliff and Pam. The IV stung in his arm, and his arm was bleeding. Karin was on the couch, kneeling between Pam and Cliff. She was pulling a plastic bag over Cliff's head. Arabella was slumped over sideways.

Tom gulped for air but nothing came. He clutched his face, and it was covered with clear plastic. He ripped off the plastic bag. The rush of air felt like water, waking him.

"Hey!" Karin was taping the plastic bag around Cliff's neck. Cliff's hand was raised, bobbing up and down, as if he were hoping to be called on.

Objection, Your Honor.

"Hey!" Pam sat up and started beating on Karin's back. "What the hell are you doing?"

"It's not working right," Karin cried. "I must have crossed the lines."

Tom stood up and pushed them both aside and ripped the bag off Cliff's head. "He can't breathe! You're trying to kill him!"

Cliff's mouth was lopsided, and he was drooling. His right hand was still bobbing up and down.

"Do something!" Pam was hitting Tom in the back now. "He's had a stroke. Do something!"

"I'm trying," said Tom. He pushed on Cliff's chest, but Cliff just sank deeper into the couch.

"We have to continue the procedure," said Karin. "We can't stop now."

"Somebody do something!" said Pam.

Tom stood back, confused. Where had the island gone? Ara was sleeping peacefully on the couch, her head to one side. She was the only one in the room who looked dead.

Karin traced the tubes into Cliff's arm. "Oh no!"

"What?" asked Tom and Pam together.

"I misrouted the tubes," said Karin, pulling two more plastic bags out of her case. "We have to use the bags. They're the backup."

"What do you mean, 'misrouted'?" Pam stopped her with a strong hand on her skinny little arm.

"He got two of the relaxants," Karin said, pointing at Cliff. "Double yellow. The whole thing has to start over."

"What?" Tom looked around the room. It was like waking up. He was in the beach house he had bought twenty years ago with Arabella and Cliff and Pam. He had survived Death. He wasn't dead at all.

He stood up, reaching down to the coffee table to steady himself. "Everybody slow down," he said calmly. "Let's all have a drink of sassafras tea—or whiskey."

"She can't drink on the fucking job!" said Pam. "All she can do legally is kill you."

"We've run out of time" said Karin, looking at Cliff's watch. "The deadline was nine o'clock!"

Deadline.

"Give me that," said Pam, grabbing at the watch. It slipped off Karin's wrist and hit the floor with a loud crack.

"The whole thing was supposed to be over twenty minutes ago," Karin said, starting to cry. "I messed it up entirely. Now I'll lose my certification for sure."

"Tough shit," said Pam. "I'm calling 911. We need an ambulance. Tom, where's your phone?"

"On the table," said Tom. He pulled the IV from Cliff's arm, then pulled Cliff down from the couch, onto the floor. He knelt over him and pushed down on his chest.

"Your IV is bleeding," said Karin. "There's not supposed to be any blood. That means it's out of the vein."

"It's out for sure now," said Tom, pulling his needle free.

"You can't do that!" said Karin. "You're not medical personnel."

"Personnel?" Tom had always hated the word. "Nobody's personnel here," he said, tossing the IV to the floor. "But Pam's right about one thing: this whole business is over. Now we have to get Cliff to a doctor."

"Nobody's going to any doctor," Karin said grimly. She was rummaging around in her attaché case. For what? Tom wondered: Instructions? A noose? A gun?

He grabbed her arm. "Sit down!"

"You can't order me around!"

"I can't?" He pushed her down on the couch beside Arabella. "Because I'm dead? Well, I'm not dead anymore. In fact, I've lost all interest in being dead. Arabella!"

He slapped her face, gently at first, then harder. "Wake up, it's over."

"It's not over!" said Karin. It was in fact a gun. She pulled it out of the attaché case: a tiny 9 mm automatic, matte-black, as black as a little hole in the Universe.

"He's choking!" said Pam. She was kneeling over Cliff, banging on his chest with her fists.

"It's the muscle relaxant," said Karin. "Let it do its work. It relaxes the diaphragm." She pointed the gun at Pam, then at Tom. "I'm sorry, but I can't allow you to interfere."

"Give me that," said Tom. He reached for the gun, and she handed it to him, surprising them both. It fit into his hand just right. He pointed it at her. "Now do something for Cliff."

He clicked the safety off, then on again. Karin hadn't known that it was on.

"This is all wrong," said Karin, kneeling down over Cliff and pushing Pam aside. "It's his diaphragm, it's not his lungs. You have to press down, here, hard."

Cliff gasped, then took a single loud breath.

"It was supposed to be yellow to yellow," said Karin. "But the pink looked yellow in the tubes. The light was bad!"

She pressed down on Cliff again, and he took another breath. "Now we have to start over."

"No way," said Tom. "This show is over."

"What do you mean?"

"What I said. Over. We have to get Cliff to the doctor in

Tillamook. No point calling an ambulance. That will take forever."

"I can't allow this," said Karin, standing up. "I have already signed the papers."

"Shut up," said Pam, pushing down on Cliff's diaphragm. "It's not working. He's not breathing again."

"You do it," said Tom.

"I can't," said Karin. "If we just let the muscle relaxant work, it will . . ."

"It will kill him, I know," said Tom. "But we don't want to kill him anymore, do we? What you have to do is help him breathe."

"No."

Tom clicked the safety off, then on again. It made a wicked little noise, like a gun on TV. "Yes."

Karin knelt back down on the floor. She pressed down on Cliff's diaphragm, and he took another breath. "You're making a big mistake," she said. "I'm a federal employee on duty. This is terrorism."

"Terrorism is about innocent people. I don't see any of them here. Pam, see if you can wake Arabella up. She's passed out from the fucking whiskey. Then we have to get Cliff into the car. Do you have the card?"

"You do," said Pam, dragging Cliff by his armpits toward the door.

The storm was back. When Pam opened the door, a flood of rain and wind filled the room. Tom felt a moment's nostalgia for the peaceful sea he had been flying over. It had been replaced by a raging storm.

Arabella got to her feet on her own. "What's going on?" she asked. "Tom?"

"It's over," said Tom. "Get in the car. We have to get Cliff to the doctor."

"I can't allow this," said Karin. "It's terrorism."

"Get in the car!" said Tom. He pointed the gun toward the open door.

"No."

"Stay here, then." Each taking an arm, Pam and Tom dragged Cliff out the door, into the rain, across the gravel drive, to the yellow Cadillac.

"The card, the card," said Tom.

"You have it," said Pam.

They dragged Cliff into the back seat while Ara wobbled woozily around the car and into the right front seat. "Going for a ride in the car car . . ." she sang.

Jesus! thought Tom. The rain was pounding down, and he was soaked. Karin was standing on the doorstep in her yellow raincoat, hurriedly punching numbers into Tom's cell phone.

"She's calling the police," said Pam.

"You were about to call them a minute ago," Tom reminded her. "Get in the back with Cliff."

Tom got into the driver's seat and slipped the card through the slot on the dash. The Cadillac started with a smooth whine.

"Let's go, let's go! He's not breathing again!"

Dead again.

"I'm going," said Tom. "But first—"

He got out of the car and grabbed Karin by the arm. "You're going with us," he said, dragging her toward the car.

"No!" She pulled away, holding onto the doorknob of the little house they had bought twenty-five years ago. It was raining then, too . . .

"Let her go!" said Pam. "Get back in the car. Cliff is barely breathing. Are you sure you can drive? Your arm is still bleeding."

"Only a little," said Tom. "But I'm woozy." When he closed his eyes he could still see the island perched on the edge of earth and sea, and the glider descending. "Hell, I was dead a little while ago."

"Let me drive," said Pam. She got out of the car and put Tom into the back with Cliff. Then she got into the driver's seat.

Tom leaned forward over the seat back. Rain was streaming down the windshield, out-running the wipers. "It's raining," Arabella said, opening her eyes.

"No shit," said Pam, slipping the Cadillac into gear. She started out the drive, then slammed on the brakes. Karin was standing in front of them, carrying her raincoat wadded up, like a yellow ball. "What's that crazy little bitch up to now?"

"Crazy little bitch," said Arabella, giggling.

"I'm going, too," said Karin, pulling the back door open.

"No way!" Tom pushed her away.

Karin threw her wadded-up slicker into his lap as she fell backward and sat down heavily in a puddle on the drive.

"Go!" Tom said.

"I'm going, I'm going." Pam floored the gas, and the Cadillac spun out onto the highway, spraying gravel and mud behind it, and roared up the hill toward the meager lights of the town.

9

Pam raced through the town's single street. "Where are we going?" she cried.

"Tillamook, Tillamook," Tom said. The word was like a mantra. It was the biggest town around; it would have a hospital with an emergency room.

"Uh oh!" A Ford Expedition sped past them with a blue light flashing. "Wainwright," said Pam.

"Where's he going?"

"After us," said Pam. "That little bitch called the cops, remember? Well, that includes him. He's got his Homeland Security light on."

Tom looked back. The Ford's taillights were bright. "He's stopping; he saw us."

"Of course he saw us!" said Pam. "How many yellow Caddies are there around here this time of year? Now what?"

"He thinks we're going to Tillamook. Step on it till we're out of sight, then turn right."

Pam understood perfectly. She topped the hill, then slowed, skidding on the wet asphalt, and turned into a narrow street leading up into the pines.

"Now stop and turn off the lights. Put her in PARK and take your foot off the brake."

"Why are cars always 'her'?"

"You should be flattered."

They watched out the rear window, through the streaming rain, holding their breaths as the Ford Expedition raced past on the highway, heading for Tillamook.

"Dumb shit," said Pam. "How's Cliff?"

Cliff was slumped against the door. "He's breathing. How's Ara? I've seen her drunk, but I've never seen her drunk like this."

"I gave her a tranq," said Pam. "She must have taken two. They interact with the whiskey, making me the designated driver. Now what?"

"I'm thinking." Tom shook an American Spirit out of the pack and fished through his pockets for a match.

"Wainwright will figure out we're not ahead of him," Pam said. "He'll turn around and come back. They've probably got the state troopers out, too, by now."

"I know, I know." Tom found matches in Karin's slicker, next to a lump that might have been a phone—or another gun.

"You can't smoke in the car," said Pam.

"Oh, for Christ's sake!" Tom shoved the slicker onto the floor. He rolled down his window and lit the cigarette, taking two drags before tossing it out into the rain.

Another car sped by on the highway. A state trooper, blue light flashing, heading down the hill toward the beach and the house.

"Damn that little bitch," said Pam. "She must have called every cop in the country. What do we do now?"

"We can't go to Tillamook. We have to stay off the highway. Go to the end of this street and turn left. We'll go to Azarov's."

"That quack?"

"He'll have to do. Cliff's breathing, but only about once or twice a minute."

"Damn that little bitch." Pam put the car into gear and roared off, spraying gravel—no lights. "This is Bonnie and Clyde time."

"Clyde?" asked Arabella, sitting up. "Who's Clyde?"

"Nobody, honey," said Tom. "Fasten your seat belt."

Pam drove without headlights, from streetlight to streetlight through the dark town. She saw Azarov's driveway almost too late; she barely made the turn, and skidded to a stop in a circular gravel driveway behind a Boston Whaler on a trailer, white as a ghost in the steel gray rain.

A light came on, revealing a stubby unpainted porch.

The door opened, and a man stepped out, holding an umbrella.

"Doc, it's Cliff, he's . . ."

"I know, I know," said Azarov, a middle-aged Iranian with a pepper and salt beard. A blond woman was standing in the doorway behind him, talking on a cell phone.

"I cannot treat him," said Azarov.

"He's having trouble breathing!"

"You do not understand," said Azarov. He walked out to the car, under his umbrella, and bent down to the open window. "I cannot treat him. There is an all-points DNR out on him, and on you too, Tom."

"Nice to see your ass, too," Tom muttered.

"You must go now, before the authorities get here!"

"They don't know where we are."

"They will puzzle it out. I am the only doctor for miles."

"Chiropractor," said Pam.

Azarov ignored her. "It is on the TI-hotline, Tom. Assault, terrorism, kidnapping."

"Kidnapping?"

"But the main thing is the termination. Interfering with a termination is a federal offense."

"We didn't interfere; she fucked it up."

"Emily is on the phone with Homeland Security right now," Azarov said, pointing back over his shoulder. "They will be all over you like fleas in shit."

"It's flies on shit," said Tom. "At least take a look at Cliff."

The doctor shook his head. "If I even look at him, I will have to put a bag over his head. Yours too, Tom. Try Portland. Take the old highway. They may not be watching that."

"Damn!" said Pam.

"Just go!" Azarov pleaded.

"Let go of the car, then," said Pam.

"It must look like I am trying to stop you. Go!"

Pam hit the gas and turned sharply around the Boston Whaler. Azarov went flying, into the shrubbery by his porch.

Was that for real? Tom wondered. Or for show?

The old highway was a concrete slab, cracked and repaired in so many places that it looked like an asphalt highway patched with concrete.

It was dark in the pines. Pam turned on the headlights. The rain slacked up, but there were wisps of fog tangled in the trees like ghostly Spanish moss. The road was slick with leaves and an occasional tiny, battered corpse.

Roadkill. We are the Universe's roadkill.

In the car, there was silence. Pam drove; Arabella slept; Tom watched the road grimly, with his gun in his hand; and Cliff breathed, once every mile or so.

They were almost at the top of the pass when they saw the roadblock. The road was filled with lighted flares and plastic cones.

"Shit."

Two figures stood beside a blue Ford Expedition, waving lights in the air. One of them wore a trooper hat over a ponytail.

"Wainwright!" said Pam, slowing. "And his Homies. How did they find us here?"

"Slow down," said Tom. "Stop. I'll talk to him."

"Are you kidding? They'll shoot."

"Not if we stop. Just do it." Tom pulled Karin's little gun out of his pocket as Pam rolled to a stop. He rolled down the window. The flares hissed. "Wainwright, is that you?"

"Tom, Cliff? Step out of the car, please." Wainwright started toward them, a stungun held across his chest. He looked stern.

Tom stuck the pistol out of the window and fired twice into the air.

BAM BAM

Wainwright hit the ground rolling, just as he'd been trained to do. Pam stepped on the gas without being told, scattering flares and cones.

"He'll be right behind us," she said, as she rounded the first curve, into the trees.

"Not him. He'll leave it to the state troopers now," said Tom. "Let's just try and get to the interstate before they block it."

"How's Cliff?"

"Still breathing."

The road corkscrewed down the mountain and followed a rocky little creek. Pam drove expertly; Tom could feel the rear end of the Cadillac sliding on the turns but always returning to true.

Cliff was slumped against the door. His eyes were open. He looked terrified.

"We're taking you to a doctor," Tom said.

"What?" asked Pam from the front.

"It's Cliff. His eyes are open."

"Habeus corpus," said Cliff.

"What?" demanded Pam.

"He's talking in his sleep," Tom said. "Just drive!"

Pam drove. The road left the creek bed and switchbacked up another long hill. They were almost at the top when they saw the SUV parked across the road—another Ford Expedition.

Pam slowed. A man got out of the SUV and stood on the highway in the rain, waving his arms. He wore a ponytail under a wide-brimmed hat.

"Wainwright," said Pam. "How the hell did he get ahead of us?"

"That's not Wainwright," said Tom. "That's a Tilly hat. And that's not the Shackleton model."

"Must be one of his Homies," said Pam.

"Just go around him."

"I hear you. Hang on! The shoulder looks soft."

It was indeed soft. As soon as the Caddy hit it, it crumbled.

"Uh oh." In the back seat, Tom could feel the rear of the car sliding sideways, off the edge. Pam overcorrected with the wheel, and the car nosed down, into a grove of trees so black they looked like they had erased the world. Tom closed his eyes and heard wood snapping, first small branches, then bigger and bigger; then nothing at all.

Tom was surprised to find eyes behind his eyes. He opened them both. He was looking up out of a car window. It was like when he was a kid and lying in the back of his father's Oldsmobile watching the long riverbottoms pass under the wide Indiana sky. Except he wasn't a kid anymore.

He was seventy-one.

He sat up.

There was darkness and leather all around. He was between the seats; they were jammed together.

Cliff's door was open. He was out of the car; only his feet were up on the seat. One shoe was missing. Then both feet were gone, and Cliff had slipped away.

Passed away.

Arabella!

"Ara!" Tom tried to get up, but he was wedged tightly. He wriggled free, out Cliff's door, and tried to open Arabella's door.

It was jammed. He climbed back into the car and leaned over the back of the front seat.

Pam was slumped against the window, which was smeared with blood. Arabella was leaning forward with her head in her hands, as if in thought. Tom put his hand on the back of her head. Her hair was wet and cold. His hand was sticky. "Ara!"

"Tom," said a voice. Someone was pulling at his arm. "There's no time. Come on."

"No!" said Tom. No time? Someone had him by the arm, pulling him out of the car. He jerked his arm free and tried to stand and fell to his knees on cold, wet stones. "Who are you? What are you doing here?"

"A friend."

"Arabella," Tom said. There was blood on his hand; he wiped it on his shirt. So much blood!

He tried to get to his feet and fell again; then he felt something cold—a cold, soft, wet rag, like a dirty diaper—pulled across his mouth and nose.

"Ara," he said out loud, and the night went gray, then white: a brilliant cold bone white.

10

The island was a hole of sand in a wall of water. Tom was circling down toward it, down, down, down. The island was bright, too bright; sunny, too sunny.

The lawn chair swung under the glider's wing, but the wing was too square, like a door or a window.

Tom opened his eyes. He was in a lawn chair, but inside, by a window. The window was bright, too bright.

"Arabella?"

She was gone. The car was gone, the night was gone, the rain was gone.

He looked at his hand. The blood was gone.

"Habeus corpus," said a familiar voice.

It was Cliff. He was sitting in a wheelchair, between two single beds. They were in a motel room. The wallpaper was a black-and-white pattern of interlocked birds flying in two directions at once; an Escher, wall to wall.

Cliff's right arm was lifting and dropping, lifting and dropping. His face looked weird; his mouth was slack. Tom panicked for a moment; then he looked into Cliff's eyes and saw that he was still there.

"Cliff, you're alive," he said, amazed. "We're both alive."

Shit, he thought meanwhile. He's had a stroke or something. And where are the girls?

Then he remembered.

He remembered it all, from the scene in the beach house, to the chase, to the crash.

"Where are the girls?" He got up, unsteadily. He was wearing pajamas. "Where are we?"

"Habeus corpus," said Cliff.

"You're awake," said a woman's voice.

Tom stood and turned and saw her standing in the doorway, all in white, like an angel. It was not Arabella, though.

"Who are you?"

"You can call me Tanya," she said. She was young and skinny, with limp blond hair, like Karin, the Angel of Death. "Don't worry, you're safe here. But I think you're not ready to be walking around yet."

She was right. Tom felt dizzy. "Where's my wife? Is she here?" He sat back down. The lawn chair creaked.

"The Super will explain it all," Tanya said. "In the meantime, you get some rest. You're not ready to be walking around yet."

"What day is it?"

But she was gone. Tom turned back to Cliff. "What happened? Where are the girls?"

"Habeus corpus," said Cliff. He lifted his arm and dropped it, twice.

"How long have we been here?"

"Habeus corpus," said Cliff.

Shit, man. Is that all you can say? Cliff looked bad, but that was to be expected. What about Pam? What about Arabella?

Tom got up, still dizzy, and opened the door. Looking out, he saw a long hallway past other doors, most of them closed. He could hear shouting at the far end of the hall. Steadying himself against the wall, he walked toward the sound.

A TV was blaring in a room filled with old people; it was a small room, and it only took six to fill it, four of them in wheelchairs, like Cliff.

The shouting was a talk show. A fat white girl in a halter top was shouting at a skinny black man with three gold teeth. He made the ancient, universal, hands-up gesture of helplessness, but it only made her shout louder.

Maybe we're dead after all. And here we are in Hell.

"Tom!" It was the woman in white, Tanya; she was feeding an old man with a long spoon. "You should wait in your room. I'll bring your lunch there."

Tom didn't have to be told twice. In Hell you do what they tell you.

He shuffled back to his room and sat down and closed his eyes. He didn't want to look at Cliff. His mouth was too slack and his eyes, though bright, were too wide. He looked like an old baby.

"You can call me Tanya."

Huh? Tom opened his eyes. The woman in white was feeding Cliff with a long spoon; the same long spoon. It was a terrible spoon. "Are you hungry?"

Tom shook his head, too hard: it hurt.

"You probably still have the chemicals in your bloodstream. We thought there for a while last night we were going to lose you."

"Please," said Tom. "Start at the beginning. What happened? Where am I? Where's my wife, Arabella?"

"There was an auto accident," said Tanya. "The Super is checking our sources, trying to find out about your wife. I told her of your concern. In the meantime, just relax and let your body heal itself."

"What about Cliff? Is his body healing its fucking self?"

"He has apparently had some kind of stroke. The doctor will be here tomorrow to look at him. I can understand why you would be upset. Meanwhile, you are safe here with us."

"Who is us?"

"I'm not allowed to talk about that. But you know who we are. You know you do."

The Resistance? "This is all a mistake," said Tom.

"There." Tanya wiped Cliff's chin and stood up, smiling. "Meanwhile, don't worry about a thing. The Super will let you know as soon as she finds out something."

"The Super?"

"You can call her Dawn." Tanya left, closing the door behind her.

Dawn. Tom felt strangely relieved. Maybe it was all a mistake, my mistake, he thought. Maybe his memory of Arabella and her head all sticky with cold blood was a dream. He checked his hands again. They were clean.

Maybe I just dreamed I saw Arabella dead.

"Cliff, do you remember anything about the wreck?"

"Habeus corpus."

Shit. Poor fucking Cliff. Tom lay down on the bed closest to the door and closed his eyes, determined to search his memory ruthlessly and confront whatever he found. Instead, he went to sleep.

When Tom woke up, it was dark. He turned on the light beside his bed and studied the wallpaper birds. Were they landing or taking off? He was still trying to decide when there was a knock at the door.

"Tom? Do you mind if I call you Tom? We like to call everyone by their first names. You can call me Tanya, remember?"

She was at the door, all in white, like an angel.

"I remember." Tom closed his eyes. The last thing he wanted to see was an angel.

"I'm afraid I have bad news. Your wife and her friend have passed away."

"Passed away? What?"

"There were fatalities in the accident. The Super asked me to tell you, since I'm a more familiar face. She will be here in the morning to speak with you directly, if you want to know the details."

"Arabella? Passed away." Tom couldn't bring himself to say the word. The word would make it real.

"I'm so sorry," Tanya said and closed the door again.

Tom swung his feet off the bed. He tried to stand up, but he was dizzy; he sat back down.

He could reach the door from the bed; the room was that small. He put his hand on the knob, but he didn't want to open it. Not now, not yet. Through that door, Arabella was dead.

Maybe this is the dream. He lay back down and closed his eyes and willed the world to go away, and before very much hateful time had passed, it did.

11

When Tom woke up, light was streaming in the window. It was morning. He was alive.

Arabella was dead.

He stood up. Cliff was asleep on the other bed. Just as well. Tom wasn't dizzy any more. He looked for his clothes and found them in a paper bag at the foot of the bed. They smelled of smoke and rain. His hands were shaking, but he managed to put on his shirt and button it. One sleeve was stiff with dried blood.

Arabella's? Better not to think. He had to sit down to pull on his pants, first one leg and then the other. Arabella had always hated these pants. Arabella—

"Habeus corpus," said a calm, untroubled voice.

Cliff wasn't asleep after all; his eyes were wide open and his hand was plucking at the covers. In the morning light, he didn't look like an old baby anymore. He looked like an old man.

"Back in a minute," Tom said. "I'm going down the hall to figure out what's happening."

"Habeus corpus," said Cliff in the same calm voice as before, but his big eyes were brimming with tears.

He knows.

"It'll be all right" Tom said. What a stupid fucking remark! "Be right back." He squeezed Cliff's hand and slipped out the door, into the dark hallway.

Tanya was in the dayroom, feeding one of the old folks through a tube. It was thicker than the IV tubes Karin had tangled. "Tom, good morning," she said. "Where are you going in those clothes?"

"The Super. Her office?"

"You really shouldn't wear those clothes around here, they're covered with blood and dirt."

Tom nodded. "Sure thing. Where's her office?"

The Super's office was another motel room off another hallway on the other side of the TV room. Instead of beds, it had two desks and two swivel chairs. A woman sat in one, at a computer screen. She looked up when she saw Tom in the doorway.

"You must be Tom." She also wore white.

Tom nodded.

"I'm sorry to say your wife has been in an accident."

"I know. I was in the same god-damned accident. And who the hell are you, anyway?"

"You can call me Dawn. I'm the Super of this site. Look, I'm on your side, okay? Why don't you sit down so we can talk."

Tom sat down in the other swivel chair. The wallpaper was the same Escher birds, either landing or taking off.

"I know this is all a shock. This whole operation has been difficult."

"You can say that again. Who are you people, anyway? Where am I?"

"You know who we are, Tom. We feel the same way you do about the Brigades, the kevorkians, the involuntary suicides. We have devoted our energies to doing something about it."

"This is all a mistake," Tom said. "None of this was supposed to happen."

"Of course not," Dawn said, shaking her head sympathetically. She had long hair tied back in a ponytail, like Wainwright's. She looked to be in her mid-forties. "We know that you didn't volunteer for the Brigade; that's why we intervened. We don't intervene when there is a terminal illness or a voluntary cessation."

"Nobody intervened in anything. You must have picked me up on the highway, after the accident. My wife—"

"I'm afraid your wife didn't survive the accident," said Dawn. "Nor did her friend, Cliff's wife."

"Pam," said Tom. "Pam and Arabella." Saying the names somehow made them more alive. Less—dead.

"I'm sorry for your loss," said Dawn.

"I need to call my daughter," Tom said. "This is a family emergency."

"I understand, certainly, but that's not possible right now," said Dawn. "You are still under the influence of the drugs, and we are in a crisis situation here. There's an all-points out on you and your friend."

"And he needs to see a doctor."

"That's going to happen. We're doing the best we can in the face of a Homeland Security Blue Alert. Usually they ignore us; this is a new development. But with any luck, the doctor will be here tonight. He's the one who rescued you, in fact. But delete that; I'm not sure you're supposed to know that."

"He's the doctor who treated Arabella? My wife?"

"I really can't say," said Dawn. "I'm sure we'll know more by tonight. Can you wait until then?"

Tom suddenly felt very tired. He was relieved to be relieved of the necessity of doing anything. "Sure," he said, getting up. "But Arabella—"

"There's nothing any of us can do for her now. And one other thing. Please don't wear those clothes here. They will freak out the others."

On his way down the hallway toward his room, Tom passed a door that opened to the outside. He opened it and saw a yard of yellow clay with patches of grassy sod, like hairplugs. Beyond the yard was a dark forest of shaggy pine trees. They were moaning, as if in a wind, though their limbs were still. The sky overhead was filled with thin, high clouds. At the coast the clouds were low and thick; here they were wraiths, like ghosts.

He found the American Spirits in his shirt pocket. Matches, too, all crumpled and black with blood. He lit one; there was no one to tell him no.

Arabella is gone.

The taste was sweet. Almost like a friend. Or a betrayal.

He looked down at his hand. It was wrinkled and old. He could almost see right through it, to the ground. He was seventy-one. He was old.

"Tom? That door's alarmed." It was Tanya, all in white.

"Alarmed?"

"You can look out, but don't go through. It's not to keep people in; it's to keep intruders out."

"Okay."

"Plus, you can't smoke here, you know. The others."

"I understand," he said, taking a long drag. He flipped the cigarette out and hit a bare spot. An easy shot, since most of the lawn was bare.

Cliff was lying on his back, looking up at the ceiling and the birds.

Tom sat on the bed beside him and took his hand so that it stopped fluttering.

"It's bad, Cliff," he said. "We didn't think it could get any worse, but it did. Ara and Pam were killed. There was a wreck. Both killed. But you already knew, didn't you?"

"Habeus corpus."

"You remember everything that happened, don't you?" Tom was surprised at the anger in his voice. Was he mad at Cliff for understanding or for not understanding?

"Habeus corpus."

Tom had never felt so alone. He lay down on the other bed and closed his eyes.

It was afternoon when he awakened. He could tell by the shadows, even though he didn't know which way was east and which was west. There was something about the shadows, about the slow dropping of the birds . . .

"That's it," he thought. I can tell time by them. In the morning they are taking off and in the afternoon they are dropping back down. It was easy. Everything was easy; too easy.

He fell back asleep. He dreamed of Arabella. He was walking in big circles on the sand, looking for her.

He awoke in a panic. Arabella was gone.

Cliff was gone.

He found Cliff down the hall in the TV room, lifting and dropping his arm. How did he get back and forth? Did someone push him?

"That's better," said Tanya.

Huh? Then Tom realized she was referring to his outfit. He was wearing pajamas. Someone had changed his clothes while he slept.

"Would you like to join us?"

No, he wouldn't. But he did. She brought him some tuna salad on a tray. He hadn't realized he was hungry before. It tasted good.

On the TV a judge was berating an overweight man for allowing his dog to ruin his girl friend's carpet. The judge and the defendant were black; the girl friend, also overweight, was white. The dog was white. Tom watched for a while, then went down the hall to the motel room/office where Dawn was pecking at a keyboard.

"The doctor?" he asked hopefully.

"He's on his way," she said. "I can't give you an arrival time because we're not in contact. Too dangerous. The phones are all monitored, and a call would lead them here. But don't worry; he will be here, and he will have news."

News? Tom went back to the TV room hoping to watch the news. But there was nothing on except judges and game shows.

"Is there anything to read?" he asked.

"Of course," said Tanya. Her smile and her tone made it clear that she approved of reading. She gave him a stack of magazines. One was about golf; another was about yachts for sale. He never got to the others. He must have fallen asleep, for when he opened his eyes he saw the lights of a car on the window; that's how he knew it was dark outside.

He heard a car door slam. That's how he knew the doctor had arrived.

"Where are you going?" Tanya asked. She was playing checkers with an old woman, moving for both of them.

"The office."

"It's right down the hall."

"I know where it is."

There was a man in the office in Dawn's chair. He had a ponytail like Wainwright's, and he wore a Tilly hat. Tom recognized it from *The New Yorker* ads.

"You must be Tom," the man said. "Come in and sit down."

"That was you," Tom said, as he sat down in Dawn's empty chair. "Flagging us down."

"Sorry I'm late," the man said. "I had to take a circuitous route to get here. They're on us like ticks on a hound. I'm afraid I don't have much to tell you yet. I'm trying to get through to certain people. Everybody's gone to ground. The Homies are swarming like bees."

"Are you the doctor?"

"One of them. You can call me Lucius. We don't use our real names here. And of course I can't tell you where you are. I'm not even supposed to know myself. As you have probably determined, you are safe here with the Resistance. I'm sorry about your wife."

"Where is she?"

"She didn't make it out of the wreck. There was nothing we could do for her, and we barely had time to pull you and Cliff free before the Homies got there."

"No, I mean where is she now?"

"That's what we're trying to find out."

"We thought you were the Homies. We tried to get around."

"The shoulder was soft, from the rain. The embankment gave way. You went all the way down into the ravine."

"You caused the wreck," Tom said, standing. "We were getting away."

"The rain caused the wreck," Dawn broke in. She was standing in the doorway. "The government and its inhuman policies caused the wreck."

"You only thought you were getting away," said Lucius. "They had roadblocks up all over the place. Still do. DNR and APB and whatever else they can think of. And you still had Karin's GPS sender in the car." He saw Tom's confusion. "Oh, yeah. It was in her raincoat; that's how I was tracking you, too."

"Karin? The monitor? She was in on this?"

"Not that she knew of."

Tom sat back down. "You are the boyfriend. She told Arabella you had broken up with her."

"It was she who broke up with me. She learned that I was using her to track the involuntary kevorks. I think she was pretty ambivalent about the whole business anyway."

"She was just doing her job. Not too fucking ambivalent, either. She tied a plastic bag over Cliff's head, which is why he's the way he is now. Are you going to do something for him?"

"I'm going to look at him while I'm here. But don't expect too much, Tom. The muscle relaxant knocks out the blood supply to the brain; stroke symptoms are fairly common among survivors."

"I have to find my wife. Is there a phone? I have to speak with my daughter."

"That can happen," said Lucius. "Your daughter knows about all this; she's the one who called and put us on the trail. Gwyneth? But it can't happen yet. You have to give it a few days."

"Days?"

"Come, I have something I have to show you, so you know the situation, the real deal."

The real deal. Tom followed Lucius and Dawn into the TV room. Lucius took a remote from a drawer under the TV (so that's where it was hidden!) and switched to CNN. If the old folks staring at the screen noticed the change, none of them showed any sign of it. Only Cliff seemed interested, with his bright eyes and his right hand fluttering up and down.

"It's been on all the networks," Lucius said. He sampled through memory, backing up through the evening news, until a familiar face filled the screen.

Tom's own. His mouth was open, as if he were about to speak. It was a picture Gwyneth had taken last summer on the deck. Wainwright must have picked up the picture in the house. Had they left it open? But of course, Wainwright had a key. The Homies had a key.

"Sought on terrorism charges, plus attempted murder and flight to evade prosecution," said the broadcaster. "Shoot-out in a sleepy seaside resort town of—" The words were unconnected but powerful.

There were pictures of rotating lights and a wrecked car being winched up a steep embankment, onto a rain-dark highway.

Then a Brigade, marching under an American flag. A sturdy, weathered face, looking resolutely into the sunset.

Then Tom's face again. He was surprised by how decrepit, how depraved, how old and wicked he looked. Could they have tampered with the photo? Did they need to?

"Aggravated terrorism and kidnapping—"

"Terrorism? Kidnapping?" Tom said. "All I did was pull an IV out of my arm!"

"And take a shot at a federal employee on duty, according to them. Which makes it a Homeland Blue Alert."

"Wainwright? I shot in the air, and the idiot hit the dirt. He's just a fucking handyman anyway."

"He's a Homey on alert," said Lucius. "Or maybe they meant Karin; who knows?"

"I never shot at her. She pulled a gun on me!"

Lucius shrugged. "Whatever. The kidnapping charge may refer to Cliff here. Apparently he's still under Brigade induction. You guys didn't even get your paperwork right."

"I've seen enough," said Tom. "I need to call my daughter and tell her where I am."

"We're taking care of that," said Dawn. "We're trying to get through to her. It has to be done in a secure way that doesn't endanger the others."

The others again.

"You have to understand," said Lucius. "It's not really you they are after. It's us." He tapped himself on the chest. "By putting out an APB-DNR on you, they are admitting that we exist."

"That there is alternative to involuntary suicide," said Dawn. "That there is an active, effective Resistance."

"I still need to contact my daughter. Are the cops looking for her, too?"

"I'm sure she's being watched," said Lucius, "in the hope that she will lead them to you—and to us. That's why the important thing now is to lay low and remain cool. Surely you of all people can understand that."

"What do you mean?"

"I mean, we know about you and Cliff and your history in the movement. We know we can trust you to maintain security until this cools down."

"If it ever does," said Dawn. She raised her chin slightly, as if prepared to take a blow.

Lucius shot her a look. "Meanwhile, I need to take a look at Cliff, and you need to go back to your room and relax until morning. I promise to let you know as soon as we find out anything. Okay?"

"Okay," said Tom.

12

Tom's clothes were still in his room, in the paper bag. He knew better than to put them on. He fished out the American Spirits. There were only four left in the pack; they were all bent. And there was something else in the bottom of the bag, something heavy.

It was Karin's little matte-black 9 mm automatic. He wrapped the shirt around it and put it back.

He straightened out one of the last American Spirits and took it down the hall to the outside door before lighting it.

The stars looked very cold and very small and very far away.

Tom wondered how he would ever get to sleep with Arabella gone, lost, closed up in a morgue drawer somewhere.

"Tom? Do you mind if I call you Tom?"

It was a girl in white, a black girl, not Tanya. She was pushing Cliff through the hall in his wheelchair. "You can call me Butterfly. You know, you can't smoke here."

"Sorry," said Tom. He threw away the cigarette and followed them to his room.

The next morning, Dawn's office was closed. Breakfast was pancakes, with sausage. Some of the old folks in the TV room even smiled when they smelled the sausage.

Tanya's replacement had a sweet, wide smile and fluttering hands that almost matched Cliff's. "You can call me Butterfly," she said.

"I know," said Tom.

She was combing Cliff's hair over his bald spot, tenderly. Tom helped put the breakfast dishes away and checked the office again. Still closed.

He was watching a morning talk show when Lucius came in and pulled the remote from the drawer. "The Resistance is no longer a myth," he said, switching to CNN.

The TV showed two young people in chains, a man and a woman. They were both smiling and holding up their fists as they were led to a waiting Homeland Security van.

"This story has broken the silence," said Lucius. "Now the whole country knows there is a Resistance and it is active. The government has stopped trying to hide it. They are of course trying to paint us as murderers and criminals, but the people will know the difference. Most of them, anyway."

"How about Cliff?" Tom asked.

Lucius shook his head. "Not so good. I examined him last night. There's no change, and there's not likely to be change. We can take care of him, of course. That's why this place is here."

"He doesn't want to be here," Tom said. "Neither do I. We need to be with our families."

"I understand how you feel," said Lucius. "But you can't really speak for Cliff, can you? It would be suicide for you or him to leave here, and we can't allow that. Plus, it would endanger the others. Wait until you have thought it over and things have cooled down a little."

"What would your wife think?" It was Dawn, in the doorway.

"I'm sure she wouldn't want you to throw away your life after all the efforts that have been taken to save it. Think of the thousands who are risking their own careers to put up a resistance to the involuntary suicide and judicial murder that is the Brigades and the kevorkian laws."

"This has all been a mistake," Tom said again. "We appreciate what you are doing, but . . ."

"Not a mistake," said Lucius. "An inevitability. Sooner or later they would have to realize we existed. Now the fight has been joined. It's more important than ever that we keep you hidden and help you survive this assault."

"Let me call my daughter, at least."

Lucius put a hand on Tom's shoulder. "I understand, and we're on it. We have to patch in the call from the Netherlands, so they can't trace it. We've gone from symbolic resistance to real Resistance. We need your total cooperation."

"Doing what?"

"Laying low. Being cool. Chilling, I believe was once the word."

Tom spent the morning "chilling" in the TV room with Cliff. The morning was filled with talk, then with games where people won money and then leaped about.

After a particularly big win, with much leaping about, Tom went back to his room to get an American Spirit out of the paper bag. There were three left, all crooked. The black gun was still safe, wrapped in the shirt in the bottom of the bag.

He unwrapped it and put on the shirt. The blood on the sleeve cracked off and fell to floor as dark powder.

He went back down the hall to the open door and lit the cigarette. The forbidden taste, the betrayal, was sweet—but where was the betrayed? Arabella, I didn't mean to leave you there alone. I didn't mean for any of this to happen.

The long bare lawn, with a few patches of grass, ended abruptly at a row of shaggy pines; dark, thoughtless, still-living trees.

Tom tried to remember Arabella's face, her voice, but they both were dim. Like seeing through fog.

"Remember, Tom, you can't smoke here."

It was Butterfly, Tanya's replacement. Darker skin, brighter eyes, all in white like—

"Oh, yeah, I forgot," said Tom, flipping the cigarette out onto the lawn, hitting a bare spot. "What's that noise out there?"

"What noise? Out where?"

"Beyond the trees. I thought it was the wind, but there's no wind."

"A highway, I think," Butterfly said. "I don't know which one, of course. We come here blindfolded, for security. That way if we're arrested, like the ones this morning, we can't betray anything because we don't know anything."

"I thought it was the wind," Tom said. A highway was better.

When Tom got back to the room, Cliff was there, sitting in his wheelchair by the window. Tanya was feeding him lunch with a long spoon. "There's a sandwich for you on the bed," she said. "I'm sorry we're out of juice."

"I thought you had gone," Tom said.

"We're all stuck here until the alert is lifted," she said. "We can't all get arrested, can we?"

She made it sound like a privilege. As soon as she had wiped her spoon and left, Tom unwrapped his sandwich and ate it. Tuna fish.

"This is fucked," he said. "It's an old folks home. Assisted living. We go from assisted dying to assisted living. Fuck!"

"Habeus corpus," said Cliff.

"It's a bunch of kids taking care of old people. But I'm talking to Gwyneth this afternoon. I'm going to figure out a way to get us out of here."

"Habeus corpus," said Cliff.

"I don't know where. Just somewhere. Anywhere."

Tom lay down on his bed and closed his eyes. He wanted to see the island again, but he couldn't find it, even in his imagination. Sleep wouldn't come; it was neither morning nor afternoon. He opened his eyes and watched the birds, caught in the wallpaper's beige universe, neither landing nor taking off.

Finally he got up and went down the hall to the TV room. The old folks were dozing, tomato soup dribbling down their chins. On the TV a judge was listening to the excuses of a black man whose dog had ripped down the wash from a neighbor's yard. "He didn't know it was wash, Your Honor. Who hangs out wash anymore?"

The judge seemed unsympathetic. Just as she was about to announce her verdict, Tom felt a hand on his shoulder. He jumped, startled; he had been imagining he was the defendant.

It was Lucius, looking pleased. "Tom, your call. As promised."

Tom followed him to the office down the hall. "Make the best of it," Lucius said. "It took a lot of doing. We have people in Europe, too. We learned a lot from you and Cliff."

"From me and Cliff?"

"From your generation. From people with a personal history of resistance. From all those who would not go gently into that good night. There's the phone. Remember, it's international." He turned and left the room.

Tom was both eager and reluctant to pick up the phone. "Gwyn?"

"Dad!"

"It's me. Are you all right, honey?"

"Yes, they can't prove anything. Oh, it's so good to hear your voice."

"What do you mean, they can't prove anything? Have you been arrested?"

"Only detained for an hour or so yesterday. They're so stupid."

"What about your mother?"

"She's at Wainwright's."

Tom felt a moment's surge of hope. Then he realized what she meant. "Funeral home?"

"He won't release her body. They say it's evidence."

Her body. It used to mean something else.

"I'll take care of it, Dad. I promise. It's what mother would have wanted."

"What? That?"

"For you to be okay. Don't do something foolish like I know you're thinking about."

"Like what?"

"Everyone is looking for you. You and Cliff are heroes. You have to lay low."

"Heroes, hell. Gwyneth, this is no good. This is an old folks home."

"What's wrong with that?"

"Nothing, but I'd rather have joined the fucking Brigade. Cliff is here, too. He's had some kind of stroke."

"Daddy, talk sense. It's not fair to Mom. It's not fair to me!"

"You're breaking up," Tom said. "I love you."

"I don't want to be an orphan!"

"I love you," said Tom, hanging up.

"She's right, you know," said Lucius. He was standing in the doorway.

"What the hell do you know! You were listening to my phone call?"

"Of course not." Lucius sat in the chair across from Tom and placed his two thick hands between his knees. "But I know what she was saying. I know this place looks bad. We have people here who were injured by the kevorkian chemicals. But you don't belong here. At the other centers, in California and back East, you will find people you will want to be with. Maybe even work with. You may even want to work with us. Now you have a choice. That's the whole point."

"What about Cliff?"

"He belongs here. He'll have to make his own choices. You can't make his choices for him."

And you can? "What about my wife? They won't release her to my daughter."

"And they sure as hell won't release her to you. Tom, you're a wanted man. You're part of the Resistance, whether you like it or not."

"Ara wasn't supposed to die."

"Tom, you have to give her up. She was ready to give you up. Can't you do the same for her?"

"I don't want to talk about it," said Tom, getting up.

"I understand," said Lucius. "You've been through a lot. Get some rest and think about it and we'll talk tomorrow."

13

Outside, the sun was going down. Tom found Cliff in the TV room. He pulled the remote out of the drawer and found CNN. The rest of the old folks either didn't notice or didn't mind; most of them were dozing.

"Arrested in Eugene and Northern Washington," said the announcer. The TV showed four young people in chains, being loaded into a red-white-and-blue ashcroft van. They were smiling and holding up their fists.

"More arrests," said Dawn. She was standing in the doorway again; she seemed to like doorways.

"How many of you are there?" Tom asked.

"I don't actually know," Dawn said. "And of course, I wouldn't say if I did. The Resistance is nationwide. Some are medical students, some are religious activists, some are volunteers like Tanya and Butterfly. We come from every sector of society, just like the opposition to the death penalty, or the right-to-life movement in your day."

"But those were two entirely different sets of people and politics," Tom said.

"Things change. The enemy of my enemy is my friend. We unite all those who are dedicated to fighting a society that discards old people when their usefulness is done. We fight for the dignity of old age and the rejection of suicide as a social policy. Surely you, with your history of political activism, can understand that."

"Not exactly. I supported the idea of voluntary termination at first," said Tom. "It seemed like a socially desirable thing, especially since the life span is so long in the developed world."

"Isn't that a little racist," said Dawn, with a tight smile. "Isn't suicide itself a little arrogant, with a hint of noblesse oblige? It's not just about you anyway. The Resistance is more than just a haven for those who are escaping the kevorkian laws. It's a mechanism for those who want to put their principles into action, like the Underground Railroad."

"But the Underground Railroad wasn't set up for the benefit of those who ran it," Tom protested.

Or was it? He looked up, and she was gone.

Cliff was getting stronger. His arm was rising farther and falling more slowly. His eyes seemed brighter, more . . . understanding.

"Where are you taking him?" asked Butterfly.

"For a walk," said Tom. "Is that allowed?"

"Of course, but don't go outside. We don't know who might be watching through the fence."

"There's a fence?"

"It's not to keep people in," said Tanya, who was helping with the evening feeding. "It's to keep people out. Security."

Tom rolled Cliff down the empty hall. He stopped by their room and got the next-to-last American Spirit out of the bag. Then he smoked it, half in and half out of the open back door, while Cliff looked on in his now customary silence.

"It's all backward," said Tom. "More than backward. Twisted almost totally around."

"Habeus corpus," said Cliff.

"Young people dedicating their lives to keeping old people alive. Risking their lives, or at least their freedom, so . . . what? So we can watch talk shows and eat tuna? Most of us don't even know what we are watching on TV. Or maybe we do. That's worse."

"Habeus corpus," said Cliff.

"They see this as their big shot. By repressing them, the government is finally taking them seriously. And in a weird way, they dig it! I can see it in their eyes, hear it in their voices. Remember all the people in the movement who didn't care about winning, who just wanted to fight the good fight?"

"Habeus corpus."

"You can't win, and therefore you never have to take responsibility for actually changing anything. You just get to feel good about making the fucking effort. Moralism in arms. They're not fighting the Brigades; they're fighting Death itself. Moralism's ideal strategy: pick a fight you know beforehand you can't possibly win. But what am I saying—it's not just them. All our lives, we are fighting Death. That's what life is, I guess: a slow holding action against entropy."

"Habeus corpus," said Cliff.

"Tom, you know you can't smoke here." It was Butterfly. "Think of the others."

"They can't smell it," Tom said. "They don't know what the hell's going on anyway. Tell me, Butterfly, why do you do this?"

"This?"

"All this. Taking care of all these old people. Of us."

"Old age deserves dignity," Butterfly said.

"No, it doesn't," Tom said, throwing out his cigarette and closing the door. "Take it from one who knows."

Tom was alive, in a motel room. Arabella was dead, in a drawer.

It was backward. Worse than backward. But what could he do? He was a prisoner here, and Dawn was right: it was the fault of the government. The whole business was fucked.

He lay down on the bed and closed his eyes. He had a gun, in the bag. He could end it for himself and Cliff. But what would that do to the kids here, who had saved them; or who thought they had saved them? It would be worse than betrayal.

He was trapped. He was in a drawer like Arabella.

Only worse: alive. With no one to talk to, except Cliff, who had forgotten how to talk back.

It was over, but it still went on. It was just as his grandfather had said, back in Indiana: "The problem is, life goes on after it's over."

He closed his eyes, hoping the world would go away again, like before. But it didn't. Tom was no longer tired, no longer dizzy. He tried counting sheep, and it was going okay, until suddenly someone pulled at his sleeve.

"There you are. I found you."

He opened his eyes. He was in the bed alone. But it was Arabella's voice. He started to cry, for the first time in years, and closed his eyes.

"I found you," she said again.

14

There was a quarter moon. The clouds continued their march eastward, into nothingness. They dissipated over the unseen desert, leaving not a trace: no rain, no shadow, and finally, no cloud.

Tom stood in the doorway smoking the last American Spirit,

all the way down, until it would have burned his fingers if it were not for the filter. He tossed it away and went back inside and put on his clothes, stiff shirt and all. There was the gun, in the bottom of the bag. The safety was off. Had it been off all along?

He switched it on and stuck the gun into his belt.

He felt like an outlaw. An American Spirit Outlaw. An old fucking outlaw.

"Habeus corpus," said Cliff.

"You awake? We need to talk," said Tom. He sat down on the bed and took Cliff's hand. "I have to get out of here," he said. "I have to deal with Gwyneth and with Arabella, and Pam, too. Everything is fucked. They don't need me here. You don't need me here."

"Habeus corpus," said Cliff.

"Gwyneth will help me. I will come for you when all this is over. I'll try. I'll do what I can. But first I need to get far enough away so if I get caught they can't trace me back to these kids."

"Habeus corpus," said Cliff.

He knows I'm lying, Tom thought. Then he saw that Cliff was looking at the gun in his belt.

"It's the one I took from Karin," he said. "With an I. Don't worry, I'm not going to use it. If I can get to the highway, I can trade it for a ride to Portland."

"Habeus corpus."

"Seattle, then. Hell, Eugene. I know we're in Oregon, somewhere on the western side of the Cascades; I can tell by the clouds." He put his hand on the doorknob. "So long, buddy. So long again."

Cliff raised his arm and held it, almost steady. A salute? A plea? "Habeus corpus," he said.

Tom took his hand off the door. He couldn't go through. Not alone, anyway. "Okay, okay," he said.

If the alarm went off, Tom didn't hear it. Perhaps the alarm had been a bluff, he thought, as he pushed the wheelchair through the door and onto the long, patched lawn. Then he turned it around: it was easier to pull than to push. Cliff was facing backward, saluting or waving steadily, as Tom pulled him into the woods.

Just inside the trees, there was a steep bank. At the bottom was a chainlink fence, taller than a man, with three strands of barbed wire at the top. Beyond the fence there was a dirt road. Tom could barely make it all out in the moonlight.

He heard a bell ringing behind him.

"Habeus corpus," said Cliff.

"The alarm," said Tom. "I thought they were bluffing."

"Tom? I know you're there!" Lucius was speaking through a bullhorn. "I'm on your side. I want to bring you back safely, in a way that doesn't endanger you or us. Is Cliff with you?"

Tom didn't answer. That meant they couldn't see him, even in the moonlight. He heard a door open and shut; he heard muffled voices.

"We know he's with you. That's okay. Just don't go any farther. There's a fence. It's electric."

You're bluffing, Tom thought.

"It's not to keep you in. It's to keep them out. Come back before you bring the Homies down on us all."

Tom studied the fence. There was no way he was going to get through it with a wheelchair, even if it wasn't electric, which it probably wasn't. Plus, the bank was too steep here; there was no way down.

"Tom, it's me, Lucius. I'm coming to bring you back."

Tom pointed the gun straight up, toward the sky, and pulled the trigger. He had forgotten the safety was on. He clicked it off and pulled the trigger again.

BLAM!

"Whoa! What was that?"

He fired again: BLAM!

"Damn, Tom, I hope you're not shooting at me," Lucius shouted through the bullhorn. "Because I'm not going to shoot back, if that's what you want."

Tom decided it was best not to answer.

"Habeus corpus," Cliff whispered. Tom was surprised. Had he been able to whisper before, or was this a new power? Cliff was leaning forward in his wheel chair, his right hand plucking at the rim of the right wheel. Suddenly Tom realized what was happening.

Too late.

Before he could grab the chair, Cliff had rolled it over the edge of the bank. It pitched forward, spilling him out and rolling down on top of him. Cliff and the chair hit the fence at the same time.

There was a crackling sound, and a wad of dry grass burst into flame.

"Shit! It is electric!" Tom slid down the bank, holding the gun in one hand and slowing himself with the other.

The grass was still burning, but the fence was no longer crackling.

Cliff was half in and half out of the chair, wedged between the bottom of the bank and the fence. The wire was sparking where it crossed the spokes of the wheel. Cliff's arm was rising and falling rapidly.

Tom grabbed Cliff's hand, and it shocked him.

"Damn!" He tried it again; this time it was barely a tingle. He grabbed Cliff's wrist and pulled him out of the chair. But there was nowhere to go. They were both wedged in the tiny space between the steep bottom of the bank and the fence.

"Habeus corpus," said Cliff.

"I know," said Tom. "It wasn't supposed to be like this, old buddy. We did our best, didn't we?

"Habeus corpus."

Tom could hear doors slamming in the distance. Floodlights came on, lighting the tops of the trees, high above.

"Tom, don't do this! You're giving us no choice."

No choice? Tell me about it.

He could see silhouettes at the top of the bank. They were looking down. A light shone in his face.

He raised the gun and fired again.

BLAM!

The light went out.

"Go ahead, you old fool," said Lucius. "I can wait till morning. You're trapped there. We tried to work with you, but you're determined to put us all in danger. Well, we can wait you out."

Tom thought it best not to answer. At least the light was out. He tried to move the chair, but it was wedged against the fence. His hands tingled again when he touched it. It wasn't a shock, really; more of a warning.

Cliff was folded up in a fetal position on the ground. His left leg was moving in unison with his arm, back and forth.

Shit. Tom turned over and lay on his back and looked up.

The clouds swept across the moon like cotton swabs, big and incredibly beautiful, faster and faster—eastward, toward the still faraway dawn. They disappeared behind the trees.

"Habeus corpus," said Cliff.

"I know."

Tom put the gun against the side of Cliff's head. It wasn't supposed to be like this, but no one had to look. He could keep his eyes closed.

"So long again, old buddy."

BLAM!

"Tom! If you're firing at me, you're wasting your shots. I won't fire back."

Tom put the gun against his own temple. As he searched for the familiar little indentation, he saw the island again, finally. There was one tree on the center, just like in the cartoons. The hang glider was descending, too fast. There was Arabella, all in silhouette, all in black, but sweetly familiar.

"I found you."

Then there was nothing at all.

> *This grave partakes the fleshly birth,*
> *which cover lightly, gentle earth.*
> —Ben Jonson

AWAKE IN THE NIGHT

by John C. Wright

*John C. Wright was born in 1961 and graduated from the William
& Mary School of Law in 1987. He was admitted to practice law in
New York in 1989, but became a journalist for* St. Mary's Today
*in Virginia before becoming a full-time writer. He lives in
Centreville, Virginia, with his wife and their two children.*

*Wright's first published fiction was "Farthest Man from Earth"
in* Asimov's Science Fiction, *which was followed by a handful of
stories, most notably "Guest Law." His most significant work to date
is the far future romance* The Golden Age, *published in three volumes as* The Golden Age, The Phoenix Exultant, *and* The
Golden Transcendence. *Upcoming is a major new fantasy novel,*
The Last Guardian of Everness.

In 1912 William Hope Hodgson published The Night Land, *a
dark, strange tale of a far future dying earth where vast malign forces
stared inimically down on the Last Redoubt of Man. In 2003
Wright published two long stories set in the Night Land for Andy
Robertson's* The Night Land *website: "The Last of All Suns" and
the moving romance that follows. We hope for more.*

YEARS AGO, MY FRIEND PERITHOÖS went into the Night Lands. His
whole company had perished in their flesh, or had been Destroyed
in their souls. I am awake in the night, and I hear his voice.

Our law is that no man can go into the Night Lands without the
Preparation, and the capsule of release; nor can any man with
bride or child to support, nor any man who is a debtor, or who
knows the secrets of the Monstruwacans; nor a man of unsound
mind or unfit character; nor any man younger than twenty-two
years; and no woman, ever.

The last remnant of mankind endures, besieged, in our invulnerable redoubt, a pyramid of gray metal rising seven miles high above the volcano-lit gloom, venom-dripping ice-flows, and the cold mud-deserts of the Night Lands. Our buried grain fields and gardenlands delve another one hundred miles into the bedrock.

Night-Hounds, Dire Worms, and Lumbering Behemoths are but the visible part of the hosts that afflict us; monsters more cunning than these, such as the Things Which Peer, and Toiling Giants, and Those Who Mock, walk abroad, and build their strange contrivances, and burrow their tunnels. Part of the host besieging us is invisible; part is immaterial; part is we know not what.

There are ulterior beings, forces of unknown and perhaps unimaginable power, which our telescopes can see crouching motionless on cold hillsides to every side of us, moving so slowly that their positions change, if at all, only across the centuries. Silent and terrible they wait and watch, and their eyes are ever upon us.

Through my open window I can hear the roar and murmur of the Night Lands, or the eerie stillness that comes when one of the Silent Ones walk abroad, gliding in silence, shrouded in gray, down ancient highways no longer trod by any man, and the yammering monsters cower and hush.

Before me is a brazen book of antique lore, which speaks of nigh-forgotten times, now myth, when the pyramid was bright and strong, and the Earth-Current flowed without interruption.

Men were braver in those days, and an expedition went north and west, beyond the land of the abhumans, seeking another source of the Earth-Current, fearing the time when the chasm above which our pyramid rests might grow dark. And the book said Usire (for that was the name of the Captain), had his men build a stronghold walled of living metal, atop the fountain-head of this new source of current; and they reared a lofty dome, around which was set a great circle charged with spiritual fire; and they drove a shaft into the rock.

One volume lies open before me now, the whispering

thought-patterns impregnated into its glistening pages murmuring softly when I touch the letters. In youth, I found this book written in a language dead to everyone but me. It was this book that persuaded the lovely Hellenore (in violation of all law and wisdom) to sneak from the safety of the pyramid into the horror-haunted outer lands.

Perithoös had no choice but to follow. This very book I read slew my boyhood friend—if indeed he is dead.

Through the casement above me, the cold air blows. Some fume not entirely blocked by the Air-Clog that surrounds our pyramid stings my nose. Softly, I can hear murmurs and screams as a rout of monsters passes along a line of dark hills and crumbling ruins in the West, following the paths of lava-flows that issue from a dimly-shining tumble of burning mountains.

More softly, I can hear a voice that seems human, begging to be let in. It is not the kind of voice that one hears with the ear. I am not the only thing awake in the night.

Scholars who read of the most ancient records say the world was not always as it is now. They say it was not always night, then; but what it may have been if it were not unending night, the records do not make clear.

Certain dreamers—once or twice a generation we are born, the great dreamers whose dreams reach beyond the walls of time—tell of aeons older than the scholars tell. The dreamers say there was once a vapor overhead, from which pure water fell, and there was no master of the pump-house to ration it; they say the air was not an inky darkness whence fell voices cry.

In those days, there was in heaven, a brightness like unto a greater and a lesser lamp, and when the greater lamp was hooded, then the upper air was filled with diamonds that twinkled.

Other sources say that the inhabitants of heaven were not diamonds at all, but balls of gas, immeasurably distant, but visible through the transparent air. Still others say they were not gas, but fire. Somehow, despite all these contradictory reports, I have always believed in the days of light.

No proofs can be shown for these strange glimpses of times agone, but, when great dreamers sleep, the instruments of the

Monstruwacans do not register the energies that are believed to accompany malign influence from beyond our walls. If it is madness to have faith in what the ancients knew, it is a madness natural to human kind, not a Sending meant to deceive us.

As I nodded, half-awake, softly there came what seemed to be the voice of Perithoös into my sad and idle thoughts. I was called by my name.

"Telemachos, Telemachos! Undo for me the door as once I did for you; return the good deed you said you would. If vows are nothing, what is anything?"

I did not move or raise my head, but my brain–elements sent this message softly out into the night, even though my lips did not move: "Perithoös, closer than a brother, I wept when I heard your company was overwhelmed by the monsters. What became of the maiden you set out to rescue?"

"Maiden no more I found her. Dead, dead, horribly dead, and by my hand. Herself and her child; and I had not the courage to join them."

"How are you alive after all these years?"

"I cannot make the door to open."

"Call to the gate-warden, Perithoös, and he will lower a speaking tube from a Meurtriere and you may whisper the Master-Word into it, and so prove your human soul has not been destroyed, and I will be the first to welcome you."

The Master-Word did not come. Instead, mere words, such as any fell creature of the night could impersonate, now whispered in my brain: *"Telemachos, son of Amphion! I am still human, I still remember life, but I cannot say the Master-Word."*

"You lie. That cannot be."

And yet a felt a tear stinging in my eye, and I knew, somehow, that this voice did not lie: he was still human. But how could he forget the Word?

"Though it has never been before, in the name of the blood we shed together as boys, the gruel in which we bound our silly oath, I call on you to believe and know that a new sorrow has appeared in this old, sad world, like fresh blood from an old scar; it is possible to forget what it means to be a man, and yet remain one. I have lost the Master-Word; I have lost my very self. Let me through the door. I am so cold."

I did no longer answer him, but stirred my heavy limbs.

Though my hands and feet felt like lead, I moved and trembled and slid from my desk where I slumbered, and fell to the floor heavily enough to jar myself awake.

How long I lay I do not know. My memory is dark, and perhaps time was not for me then flowing as it should have been. I remember being cold, but not having the strength to rise and shut the window; and this was an old part of the library, so there were no thought-switches I could close just by wishing them closed.

My thoughts drifted with the cold wind from the window.

This wing of the library had been deserted for half a million of years. No one came into this wing, since no one could read the language, or understand the thoughts, of the long-forgotten peoples who had sent Usire out to found a new stronghold. Only I knew the real name of those ancient folk; modern antiquarians called them the Orichalcum people, because they were the only ones who knew the secret of that metal, and no other trace of them survived.

And so the Air Masters, during the last two hundred years of power-outages, had lowered the ventilation budget in this wing to a minimum. I had needed a vasculum of breathing-leaf just to get in here, and would have fainted with the window shut.

Nor were failures of the ventilations rare. Most windows of most of the middle-level cities stood open, these days, no matter what the wise traditions of elder times required.

It was two miles above the Night Land. No monster could cross the White Circle, and nothing has climbed so high since the Incursions of four hundred thousand years ago; and even if they did, this window was too small to admit them.

I remembered wings. In my dreams I see doves, or the machines used by ancient men to impersonate them. But the air is thin, and even the dark and famished things have no wings to mount so high.

I thought there was no danger to have the window open. Stinging insects, vapors or particles would be surely stopped by the Air-Clog. But what if the power losses over the last few centuries were greater than is publicly admitted by the Aediles or the

Castellan? It had not stopped the Mind-Call, as it should have done.

Many Foretellers have dreamt that it is five million years before the final extinction of mankind. Most of the visions agree on certain basic elements, though much is in dispute. Five million years. We are supposed to have that long. I wondered, not for the first time, if those who say that they can see the shape of fate are wrong.

I came awake when there was a movement, a clang, behind me as the hatch swung open. Here was a Master of the Watch, clad from head to toe in full armor, and carrying in hand that terrible weapon called the Diskos.

I knew better than to wonder why a Watchman was here. He came into the chamber, his blade extending before him as he stepped, and his eyes never left me. The shaft was extended. The blade was lit and spinning. The furious noise of the weapon filled the room. Flickering shadows fled up and down the walls and bookshelves as eerie sparks snapped, and I felt the hair on my head, the little hairs on my naked arms, stir and stand up. I smelled ozone.

Without rising, I raised my hands. "I am a man! I am human!"

His voice was very deep, a rumble of gravel. "They all say that, those that talk."

Slowly, loudly, clearly, I said the Master-Word, both aloud with reverent lips, and by sending it with my brain-elements.

It seemed so dark in the chamber when he doused his blade, but his smile of relief was bright.

My youth had been a solitary one. To hold one's ancestors in honor, and to love the lore of half-forgotten things, has never been in fashion among schoolboys. The pride of young men requires that they seem wise, despite their inexperience, and the only way to appear all-knowing without going to the tedium of acquiring knowledge is to hold all knowledge in weary-seeming contempt. Students and apprentices (and, yes, teachers also) bestowed on me their well-practiced sneers; but when my dreams began, and ghosts of other lives came softly into my brain as I slept, then I was marked as a pariah, and was made the butt of every prank and cruelty boyish imagination could invent.

Perithoös was as popular as I was unpopular. He was an alarming boy to have as a schoolmate, for he had the gift of the Night-Hearing, and could hear unspoken thoughts. All secrets were open to him; he knew passwords to open locked doors and cabinets, and could avoid orderlies after lights-out. He knew the answers to tests before the schoolmasters gave them, and the plays of the opposing team on the tourney field. He was good at everything, feared nothing, and anarchy and confusion spread from his wake. What was there for a schoolboy not to love?

Once, when the Head Boy and his gang had me locked in the cable-wheel closet, so that I would be absent from the feast-day assembly and gift-giving, Perithoös left the assembly (a thing forbidden by the headmaster's rules), took a practice blade from the arms-locker and spun the charged blade against the closet door hinges, shattering the panel with a blast of noise.

Not just school proctors, but civic rectors and men of the Corridor Guard arrived. To use one of the Great Weapons while inside the pyramid was a grave offense; and neither one of us would admit who did it, even though they surely knew.

We both were scourged by the headmaster and given triple-duty, and had porridge for our holiday feast, while the other boys dined on viands and candied peaches.

Perithoös and I ate alone in the staff commissary, our shirts off (so that our backs would heal) and shivering in the cold of the unheated room. We were not allowed to speak, but I tipped my bowl onto the board and wrote in the porridge letters from the set-speech: *shed blood makes us brothers—I shall return this deed.*

Even at that age, he was taller than the other lads, broad of shoulder and quick of eye and hand, the victor of every sport and contest, the darling of those who wagered on gymnastics games. He was as well-liked as I was ill-liked. So I expected to see doubt, or, worse, a look of patronizing kindness in his eye.

But he merely nodded, wiped away the porridge-stain with his hand quickly, so that the proctor would not see the message. Under the table, with perfect seriousness, he clasped my hand with his, and we shook on it. Porridge dripped through our fingers, but, nonetheless, that handclasp was sacred, and he and I were friends.

At that time, neither one of us knew Hellenore of High Aerie.

I had been found in the library by proctors of the Watch, whose instruments had detected the aetheric disturbance sent by the voice in the Night.

The Monstruwacans kept me for a time as a guest in their tower, and I drank their potions, and held the sensitive grips of their machines, while they muttered in their white beards and looked doubtful. More than once I slept beneath their oneirometers, or was examined inch by inch by a physician's glass.

I told them many times of my mind-speech with Perithoös, and they did not look pleased; but the physician's glass said my soul was without taint, and my nervous system seemed sound, and besides, both the Archivist (the head of my guild) and the Master of Architects (the head of my father's) sent letters urging my release, or else demanding that an inquest be convened at once.

I spent the remainder of my convalescence in Darklairstead, my father's mansions on level Fourscore-and-Five. Ever since, a generation ago, the power failed along this stretch of corridor (half the country receiving from the sub-station at Bountigrace is dark) it has been a quiet and restful place.

Among my very earliest memories was one dream, repeated so many times in my childhood that I filled a whole diary with scrawled words and clumsy sketches trying to capture what I saw.

When I was seven years, my mother died, and her shining coffin was lowered into the silvery rays of the Great Chasm. My father became strange and cold. He sent my brother Arion to prentice with the Structural Stress Masters. Tmelos (who is younger than I) was sent to the quarters of my Aunt Elegia, in Forecourtshire, for her to raise. Patricia took holy orders, and Phthia stayed with Father to run the house and rule the servants. Me, I was sent to board at a school in Longnorthhall of Floor 601, where the landing of the Boreal Stair reaches for many shining marble acres under lamps of the elder days, and potted Redwoods grow. When I left home for school, the dream left me.

As I recovered at my father's manse, the dream came once again, and it no longer frightened me, for nothing that reminds one of childhood, even ill things, can be utterly without a certain charm.

It was a dream of doors.

I saw tall doors made of a substance that gleamed like bronze and red gold (which I later found to be the metal called *Orichalcum*, an alloy made by a secret only the ancients knew). The doors were carven with many strange scenes of things that had been and things that would be.

In the dream I would be terrified that they would open.

Father and I would dine alone, without servants. The dining chamber is a pillared hall, wide and gloomy. Out of the hatch window, I would often see, across the air shaft from me, little candles dancing in the hatches of some of my neighbors. Once, candles had been used only for the most solemn ceremonies, back when the ancient rules against open flames in the pyramid had been enforced: the sight of candles used as candles always saddened me.

Some nights there was a hint of music from some city far overhead echoing down the shaft, and, once, the hiss of a bat-winged machine carrying a Currier-boy (only boys are small enough) down the airshaft on some business of the Life Support House, or perhaps the Castellan, too urgent to wait for the lifts.

Our table was made from a tree felled down in the under-ground country, by a craftsman whose art is the cutting and jointing of living material, an art called Carpentry. Such is Father's prestige he can have such things brought up the lifts for him, but he has never moved the family to better quarters.

My father is a big, tall man, with fierce, penetrating eyes in an otherwise very mild face. He shaves his chin, but has a moustache that bristles, and this gives his penetrating eyes a strange and savage look.

I have dreamed of other lives, and once, in a prehistoric world, a dusky savage who was me, strong and lean of limb, and braver than I ever hoped to be, died beneath the claws of a tiger. The great cat was more bright of hue than anything in our world is, shining orange and black as it slunk through dripping jungles beneath a sun as hot as the muzzle of a culverin. I wonder what became of that species, that lived on some continent long since swallowed by the seas, before the seas dried up, before the sun died. I have always though that extinct beast looked something like my father.

His bald head was growing back in new hair, as sometimes happens to men of his order, for men who work near the Earth-Current, their vitality was greater than normal.

After dinner, we brought out carafes of water and wine, which glistened in the candle-light, and mixed them in our bowls. I am sparing with the wine and he is sparing of the water; but he is sober even when he drinks deep, and shows no levity nor thick-wittedness. Perhaps exposure to the Earth-Current helps here too.

He sat with his bowl in his hand, staring out the air-shaft. He spoke without turning his head. "You know the tale of Andros and Naäni. You were raised on it. I am sure I hate it as much as you adore it."

I said, "Andrew Eddins of Kent, and Christina Lynn Mirdath the Beautiful. The tale shows that, even in a world as dark as ours, there is light."

Father shook his head. "False light. Will-o'-Wisp light! I do not blame the hero for his deeds. They were great, and he was a mighty man, high-hearted and without vice. But the hope he brought served us ill. Perithoös was no Andros, gone into the Night. And that high-born girl who toyed with your affections; Hellenore. She was no Mirdath the Beautiful. Hellenore the Vain, I should call her."

"Please speak no ill of the dead, father. They cannot answer you."

He raised his bowl with a graceful gesture and took a silent sip, and paused to admire the taste. "Hm. Neither can they hear me, and so they will not flinch. She is not the first of the dead who have served the living poorly. He did us ill, whichever forefather first thought it would be wise to leave us tales and songs that tell young boys to go be brave and die, or to perish for a gesture."

I said, "Keeping a promise counts for more than mere gesture, Father."

"Does keeping a promise count more than preserving flesh or soul?"

I said, "Those who study such matters say that souls are born again in later ages, even if the conscious memories are lost; poets claim that oath-breakers are reborn into lives accursed with turmoil and bitter anguish. If so, then each man in his present life must take care to die spotlessly, his soul still pure."

Father smiled bitterly. He did not read poets. "What point is the punishment, if, in his next life, each criminal has forgotten what crime he did?"

I said, "So that even men who are stoical and hard in this life will fear to break their word; for, in their next, they will be young and green again; and suffering that comes unannounced, for reasons that seem reasonless, is surely the hardest pain of all to bear."

"A pretty tale. Must you die for an idle fiction?"

"Sir, it is not a fiction."

He said: "Must you die, fiction or not?"

"I had no other friend in my school days."

"Perithoös was no true friend!"

"And yet I gave my word to him, friend or not. Now I am called to fulfill it."

"Who calls? There are Powers in the dark who can mock our voices and our thoughts, and deceive even the wisest of us. Only the Master-Word is one the Horrors cannot utter, for it represents a concept that they cannot understand, an essence that does not dwell in them. If what called to you did not call out the Master-Word, you know our law commands you not to heed it."

I answered: "Despite the law, despite all wisdom, still, a hope possesses me that he is alive, and undestroyed, somehow."

He said grimly: "A true man would not call out to you."

I did not know if he meant that a man of honor would die before he let himself be used to lure a friend out into the darkness; or if he meant that what called out to me had not been human at all. Perhaps both.

I said: "What sort of man would I be, if it truly were Perithoös calling, and I did not answer?"

He said: "It is your death calling."

And I had no answer back for that. I knew it was so.

After a space of silence, eventually he spoke again: "Do you see any cause for the hope you say has taken possession of you?"

"I see no cause."

"But—?"

"But hope fills me up, father, nonetheless, and it burns in my heart like a lamp, and makes my limbs light. There are many ugly things we do not see in this dark land that surrounds us, father, horrors unseen. And there are said to be good powers as well, whose strange benevolence works wonders, though never in a way humans can know. And they also are not seen, or only rarely. There are many things, which, although unseen, are real. More real than the imperishable metal of our pyramid, more potent that the living power of the Earth-Current. More real than fire. So, I admit, I see no cause for hope. And yet it fills me."

He was silent for a while, and sipped his wine. He is a rational man, who solved problems by means of square and chisel, stone and steel, measured currents of energy, knowing the strengths of structures and what load each support can bear. I knew my words meant little to him.

He reached out his hand and doused the lantern, so that I could not see the pain in his face. His voice hovered in the dark, and he tried to make his words cold: "I will not forbid you to venture into the Night Lands—"

"Thank you, Father."

"—Since I have other sons to carry on my name."

Visions, pulmenoscopy, and extra-temporal manifestations were not unknown to the people of the Last Redoubt. The greatest among us are known to have the Gift; and at least one of the Lesser Redoubt also was endowed with the Night-Hearing, and memory-dreams. Mirdath the Beautiful is the only woman known to have crossed the Night Lands, and her nine scrolls of the histories and customs of the Lesser Redoubt are the only record of any kind we have for the history, literature, folkways and sciences of that long-lost race of mankind. All the mathematical theories of Galois we know only from her memory; the plays of Euryphaean, and the music of an instrument called a pianoforte; the infinite resistance coil and the sanity glass, and all the inventions that sprang from them, are due to her recollection. Her people were a frugal folk, and the energy-saving circuits they used, the methods of storing battery power, were known to them a million years ago, and greatly conserved our wealth. Much of what she knew of farming and crops we could not use, for the livestock and seed of our buried fields were strange to her. She knew more of the lost aeons than even Andros, and was able to tell tales from the time of the Cities Ever Moving West, of the Painted Bird, and of the Gardens of the Moon; she knew something of the Failures of the Star-Farers, and of the Sundering of the Earth. More, she also had the gift of the Foretelling, for some of the dreams she had were not of the past, but of the future, and she wrote of the things to come, the Darkening, the False Reprieve, the disaster of the Diaspora into the Land of Water and Fire, the collapse of the Gate beneath the paw of the South Watching Thing, the years of misery and the death of man, beyond which is a time from which no dreams return, although there is said to be a screaming in the aether, dimly heard through the doors of time, the time-echo of some event after the destruction of all human life. All these things are set out in the Great Book, and for this reason Mirdath is also called The Predictress. Mirdath and Andros had fifty sons and daughters, and all the folk of High Aerie claim descent from them, some truly, and some not. Hellenore of High Aerie was one of those who made that claim truly.

When I was a young man, a time came when my future had disturbed those whose business it is to seek foreknowledge from dreams, and I was summoned to an audience.

For many generations the Foretelling art had fallen into disrepute, and charlatans rose to deceive the common people; but then a girl of the blood of Mirdath was born whose gift was proven by many sad events, and the Library of Ages-Yet-To-Be was reopened. The Sibylline Book had more treatises of prophecy added to it, and eschatologists compared dream-journals and revised their estimates. Even I had heard of her: the hour-slips said she was sure to be the next Sibyl.

I don't recall the date. It must have been soon after my Initiation, for I wore my virile robe, and my hair was cropped short as befits a man. The blade that was ever after to be partnered with my life, I had hung over the narrow door to my cell in the journeymans' room of the Librarians' Guild-house, as only those beyond their fourteenth year are permitted. I remember that the squire sent to come fetch me called me "Sir" instead of "Lad," even though he (to my young eyes) seemed incredibly old.

I remember the Earth-Current was running strong that year. It was my first time at the Great Lift Station for my floor. Invisible forces lifted the platform in a great surge of wind off the deck. Maidens clutched their bonnets and squealed, and many a young gallant (for a strong flow of the Earth-Current makes lads more bold and amorous) took the opportunity to put an arm around fair shoulders to steady a maiden making her first voyage away from her level. Some of the more daring boys learned over the rail, and waved their caps at the rapidly dwindling squares and rooftops of the city, before, like an iron sky, the underside of the next deck upwards swallowed the lift platform. I rode the axial express all the way to the utmost level. I remember I had to drink a potion made by the apothecary, because of the thinness of the air.

Fate House sits atop the highest stories of the highest city; the hanging gardens of High Aerie sit between the shining skylights of West Cupola and the pleasances and airy walks of Minor Penthouse. There are floral gardens here, under glass, as well as pools and lakes amid the rooftop-fields of the long-empty aerodromes built by ancient peoples.

The domes of Fate House were dusky blue, inscribed with gold, and, above the roof-tiles, many a monument of ancient hero or winged genius of the household stood on slender pillars among the minarets. All within was as somber and august as a fane.

Here was Hellenore daughter of Eris. I see again the sheen of her satiny dress, as she sat beneath the rose lamp on a Lector's chair too large for her delicate frame. How like a swan's, her neck; all her mass of ink-black hair was gathered up and held in place with amethyst pins, jewel-drops like the stars the ancients knew, within the clear darkness of their temporary nights. I recall the delicate small hairs, wanton and wild, that had strayed from the strictness of her coiffure and kissed the nape of her neck.

None of our pyramid has eyes like that, hair like that, save those descended from the strange blood of Mirdath the Beautiful. And none but me remembered the grace of the swan, and so none but me could see it in her.

Her voice was soft music, each word careful and light, like a brushstroke of calligraphy laid in the air. With what delicate tones she spoke of the grim horrors in the night, the grim future she foresaw nightly in her dreams!

We spoke for a time, of the horrors of the Deception two million years hence (slightly less than halfway between now and the Extinction), when colonies of man leaving the Great Pyramid would go to dwell in what seemed a fair country to the West, even as certain legends said, not knowing that the House of Silence had already cursed and undermined the whole of that land, and merely held their influence at bay for millennia, waiting for the memory of these prophecies of Hellenore to be forgotten. Whole cities, pyramids and domes as great as ours, would be swallowed and cracked open, and multitudes would die, one entire branch of the human family wiped out; the survivors to be changed into something not human.

Then we spoke of my fate.

"My visions revealed hundreds shall die because of some ill-considered act you set in motion; first one, then many more, will go pelting out into the darkened world to perish amid the ice, or be ripped to bloody rags by Night Hounds, to be sucked clean of their souls and left as husks, grinning mouths and eyes as dry as stones. Heed me! I see many prints of boots across the icy dust of the Night Land, leading outward from our gates; I see but one set coming in."

I asked: "Must these things come to pass?"

"No human power can alter what must be."

"And powers more than human?"

She said softly: "We foreseers behold the structure of time; there are creatures not quite wholly inside of time, powers of the Night Land, whose malice we cannot foretell, since they are above and alien to the rules of time and space that bind all mortal life; there are said to be good powers, too."

"A riddle! Man's fate can be changed, but men cannot change fate," I said.

Her full lips toyed with a smile, but she did not allow the smile to appear. "We are but drops in a river, young man," she said. "No matter what one drop might wish or do, the river course is set, and all waters glide to the ocean."

These words electrified me. "Ah!" I said, forgetting my manners, jumping up and taking her hand. "Then you have seen them too! Rivers and oceans! In visions, I have seen and heard the waters flowing, ebbing, pulled by tides, crashing by the shore. There is no sound alike it in the world, now."

She was startled and displeased, and favored me with a look of ice as she drew her fair and slender hand from mine. "Strange boy—what is your name again?—I spoke a line from old poetry. My people in the high-most towers are learned in such lore, and know old words like *river* and *sea*; but no one has seen them, except in the decorations of volumes none can read."

I did not say that there was one who could read what others had forgotten. I spoke stiffly, "My apologies, high born one. Your comment thrilled my heart, for I had thought you meant to say that we would do great deeds in times to come, to defy that ocean that must swallow of human lore and history, so that the water-course down which the current takes us might be ripped free of its bed, and set to a new path."

"Strange boy! What strange things you say!" She recoiled, one slim hand on her soft bosom, her lovely long-lashed eyes looking at me askance. Even in surprise, even when showing disdain, how elegant her every gesture!

"There was a time when all men spoke thus, and did deeds to match."

"Only men?" But she was not looking at me. Her eyes were turned sideways, and she stared at some spot on the walls of her family's presence chamber. There were many busts, portraits and engraved tablets along the walls—I don't know which ancestor her gaze was resting on. In hindsight, it surely was Mirdath.

I said, "Can you tell me what this ill-considered act might be?"

Her eyes were elsewhere; she spoke airily, unheeding: "Oh, some chance remark spoken to some girl you fall in love with."

My voice was hollow, and my stomach was empty. What? Must I vow to be silent, to speak never more to any woman? It took me a moment to rally my courage. I drew a breath, and spoke. "If that is my doom, I will learn to welcome it. If I must, I will take the vow, and go to some monastery in the buried basements, forbidden to woman, that I might never meet my love."

Her glittering eyes returned to me, and now a girlish mischief was in them. She said archly: "You will defy the structures of time and destiny, and rip up the pillars of the laws of nature, but you will meekly foreswear love and speech, merely because you are ordered to it? Backward boy! You would challenge what we cannot change, but would submit to what we can!"

That made me smile. "Perithoös says the same thing of me. Always looking backwards! We were walking at the Embrasures, and he joked once that—"

Hellenore sat upright, eyes shining. She said, "You know Perithoös, the athlete? What hour does he stroll upon the balcony, what level, where?"

A glow of joy lived in her face; and then she blushed and my heart ached with pleasure to see her cheek glow; but the thought of meeting Perithoös was such that she could not put away her smile, so she lifted her slender hand to hide it. If you have seen young maidens in the grip of first love, you know the sight; if not, my poor pen cannot mark it.

I told her I would arrange a meeting, and the smile came out again.

Beautiful, was that smile; though not for me.

And yet so lovely!

They met, at first, with chaperones.

At first. One of them could see the future and the other could see thoughts; both were bold, nobly born, and love-drunk. How was a duenna to keep them under watch?

They died swiftly, those who died, when the three hundred suitors set out to rescue Hellenore.

The company had been divided into three columns of one

hundred men each. Before five-and-twenty hours of march, the rearguard column had driven off a host of troll-things from the ice hills, and stopped to rest and tend their wounds. From the balconies, and from the viewing tables, we watched them make a camp. It was hard to see, for it was well camouflaged; the tents and palisade were mere shadows among shadows, even under the most powerful magnification; and the sentries at the picket moved without making noise, warily.

But then they did not stir again. Either a sending from the House of Silence, or an invisible fume leaking from the ground, made the sleepers not to wake. Long-range telescopes glimpsed the survivors, perhaps the sentries who did not lay down, trying to carry one or two men to higher ground. The rest were left behind. A pallid slug a thousand feet long oozed into view near the last known position of those men; the Monstruwacan instruments recorded tiny Earth-Current discharges at about that same time, so it was thought that the survivors swung their weapons once or twice before they died.

At about seventy hours, the main column was beset by the Great Gray Hag, mate of the monster slain by Andros, and her fleshy fingers pushed men into the sagging hole that formed her maw, armor and all. The column was routed, and fled into the Deathly Shining Lands to escape her. They did not emerge. The Shine is opaque, and nothing has been seen again of those men. The scouts accompanying the main column were eaten by Night Hounds, one by one.

The vanguard column lasted until the end of the second week, when the Bell of Darkness descended from the cloud, and tolled its dire toll. Only seven out of those hundred had the presence of mind, or strength of will, to bare their forearms and bite down on the Capsule of Release. Those whose nerve failed them, and who did not slay themselves in time, were drawn silently up into the air, their eyes all empty, and strange little vulgar grins upon their lips, and their bodies floated upward into the mouth of the Bell.

We all watched from the balconies. I heard from underfoot, like an ocean, the sound of mothers and wives weeping, men shouting, children crying, and the noise was like the oceans of the ancient world, but all of grief.

The shattering noise of the Home-call echoing from the upper cities interrupted, ordering all the millions to shut their windows; and lesser horns were sounded on the balconies to pass the warning to the lower cities. The watchmen ordered the Blinds raised up on their great pistons to block the windows and embrasures of every city and hamlet dug into the northeastern side of the pyramid; and the towers and dormer windows lowered their armor.

I remember hearing, before the Blinds closed over us, the whispering murmur of the Air-Clog, straining under double power, raising an unseen curtain to deflect the malice of the tolling bell, lest the sound of it drive mad the multitudes.

Perithoös had been in the vanguard. The Monstruwacans studied blurry prints made from long-range telescopes, and tried to confirm each death, what little comfort that might have been to the grieving families. Not every corpse was accounted for.

My cousin Thaïs came to see me while I was undergoing Preparation. She is pretty and curt, with a sly sense of humor and a good head for chess and math. Thaïs did not, aloud, try to argue me out of my venture, but she showed me her calculation: the expected average lifespan of men who went forth to save Hellenore worked out to an hour, twelve minutes.

By traditions so ancient that no record now recalls a time when they were not, those who venture into the Night Land do not carry lamps. It is too well known, too long confirmed by experience, that a traveler cannot resist the temptation to light such lamps, when the darkness has starved his eyes for too many fortnights.

And so it is thought that since the weapons we carry give off light when they are spun, those who walk in the Night will have light when and only when it is needful: that is, namely, when one of the monstrosities is no further off from us than a yard or two; for then we must strike, we must see to make the stroke.

Our craftsman could make lamps to burn a million years or more. We will not carry them into the Dark. A man who will not trust his soul to warn him of unseen dangers coming silently upon him is the only kind who needs a lantern in the Night. But would such a man, too unsure to trust his soul, be man enough to beat back all the horrors his lantern would attract?

We carry also a dial of the type that can be read by touch, for to lose track of hours, and proper times for rest and sup, is to court madness.

There is a scrip for toting the tablets, made of solidified vital nutrients, which is the traveler's sole food—for there is nothing wholesome in the Night Lands to eat, and more solid food, even a bite from an apple, might bring too much belly-cheer, and relax the discipline of the Preparation.

Likewise, water is condensed out of the atmosphere in a special cup by a powder made by the Chemists' Guild. The new-water is pure and clear, but bitterly cold, and the cup has that virtue that anything placed in it is cleansed of venom or morbific animacules. Some travelers hold the cup over mouth and nose when treading lands were the air is bad.

The mantle is woven of a fiber that, though it is not alive, is wise enough to shed heat more or less as the deadliness of the chill grows more or less, depending on the amount heat escaping from the ground.

The armor is so stern, and made so cunningly, that even monsters many times the strength of a man cannot dint it, and the joints are fitted at a level too fine for the eye to see. A blessing in the metal, an energy not unlike what throbs so purely in the fires of the White Circle, is impregnated into the helm and breastplate, to help slow those particular influences that attack the brain and freeze the heart.

Arms, armor, mantle, are made by craft a million years has perfected; and they are fair to the eye, but grim and without ornament, as befits the sobriety of the undertaking.

At last the torment of the Preparation Chambers ended. I was oddly clear-headed after the fasting and the injections, and I had endured the test of being forced to view that which still lives, pinned to a slab and sobbing, within the refrigerated cell at the center of the secret museum of the Monstruwacans. I had read the bestiaries of former travelers returned sane from outer voyaging, and learnt what they said of the ways and habits of the night-beasts; and I understood why such journals are not shown to any save those whose quest carries them outside our walls.

The Capsule of Release still ached within the tender flesh of my forearm; and the hour of parting was come.

The lamps of the Final Stair were darkened. The watchmen, armed with living blades and armored in imperishable gray metal, stood for a time in silence, composing their thoughts, so that no disturbance in the aether, no stray gleam of thought or metal or sudden noise, would tell the waiting horrors of the Night Lands that a child of man had strayed among their cold hills.

I stood with my face pressed to the periscope for many minutes, and the escort with me showed no impatience, for they knew it was my life I staked at hazard on my judgment of the ground.

At last I raised my hand.

The Master of the Gatehouse saluted me with his dark Diskos, and the door-tender closed the switch that sent power to the valves. The metals leaves of the inner gate swung shut behind me, and then the outer leaves swung open, very swiftly and silently.

Out I stepped. The ashy soil crunched beneath my boot. The air was as chill as death. The outer valve was already shut behind me, and two layers of armor heavily closed back over it, locking pistons clicking shut almost without noise. If a monster were to lunge across the Circle from the all-surrounding darkness now, or a Presence to manifest itself, the door wardens were obliged to do nothing but guard the door. I was already beyond rescue.

None within would come out for me, as I was now going out for Perithoös, and he had gone out for his fair Hellenore. Prudent men, they all.

A few minutes into the walk—no more than half a mile—I crossed the place where a hollow tube of transparent metal, charged with holy white energies, makes a circle around the vast base of the pyramid. It is held to be one of the greatest artifacts of ancient times, the one thing that keeps all the malefic pressures, the eerie calls and poisonous clouds and groping fingers of subtle forces at bay. The hollow tube is two inches in diameter, hardly higher than my boot-top. It only took a single step to cross it, but I must clear my mind of all distempered thought before the unseen curtain would part for me. My ears popped with the change in pressure.

It is customary not to look back when one steps across the line of light. I was inclined to follow the custom.

My father had not been present to see me off.

We who live within this mountain-sized fortress of a million windows of shining light, we cannot see, where flat high rocky plains lift their faces into our light, the long dark shadows cast by the rocks and hillocks and moss-bushes radiating away from the pyramid; darkness that never moves, straight and level as if drawn by a ruler. Even the smallest rock has a train of shadow trailing away from it, reaching out into the general night, so that, looking left and right, the traveler sees what seem to be a hundred hundred long fingers of gloom, all pointing straight toward the Last Redoubt of Man.

But no traveler is unwise enough to step into such a high plain lit so well. The bottom mile of the pyramid is darkened, her base-level cities long abandoned, and the lower windows covered over with armor plate. A skirt, as it were, of shadow surrounded the base of the pyramid, and one must travel away from the pyramid to expose oneself to the shining of the many windows of the Last Redoubt; even before leaving the protection of the skirt of shadow, there are many places where the ground has been tormented into crooked dells and ragged shapes, dry canyons, or deep scars from the ancient glaciers or the far more ancient weapons of prehistory. Such broken ground I sought.

I entered the canyons to the west within the first two hours of traveling, and encountered no beasts, no forces of horror.

My way was blocked by a river of boiling mud shown on none of our maps. The telescopes and viewing tables of our pyramid had never noted it, despite that it was so close to us, for ash floated in a layer atop the mud-flow, and was the same hue as the ground itself. It was not visible to me until my foot broke the sticky surface and I was scalded. Perhaps it was newly erupted from some fire-hole; or perhaps it had been here for centuries. We know so little.

This mud river drove me south and curving around the side of the pyramid, and I marched thirty hours and three. I ate twice of the tablets, and slept once, finding a warm space behind a tall rock where heat and some uncouth vapor escaped from a rent in the ground.

Before I slept, I probed the sand near the rent with the hilt of my Diskos, and a little serpent, no more than an ell in length, reared up. It was a blind albino worm, of the kind called the amphisbaena, for its tail had a scorpion's stinger. I slew it with a fire-glittering stroke from my roaring weapon; the heavy blade passed through the worm as if it were made of air, and the halves were flung smoking to either side. It was with great contentment I slept, deeming myself to be a mighty hero and a slayer of monsters.

The encampment and stronghold of Usire, I knew from my books, and from my memory-dreams, lay to the North by Northwest beyond the shoulders and back of the Northwest Watching Thing. There are other watchers more dreadful, but none is more alert, for the ground to the Northwest is wide and flat in prospect, and it is lit by the Vale of Red Fire; and there is neither a crown nor eye-beam nor wide dome of light to interfere with the view the monster commands.

To go to the country beyond the creature, my way must go far around, for the North way was too well watched. To my West was the Pit of Red Smoke itself, a land of boiling chasms and lakes of fire, impassible. To the East of me, I could see the silhouette of the Gray Dunes: and here was a sunken country populated by thin and stilt-legged creatures, much in shape like featherless birds, and they carried iron hooks, and they were very careful never to expose themselves to the windows of the pyramid as they stirred and crawled from pit to pit. The canyon-walls were riddled with black doorways, from whence, now and again, the Wailing which gives the Place of Wailing its name would rise from these doorways, and the bird-things would caper silently and flourish their hooks. To the East I would not go.

I went South.

Each time I rose after snatched sleep, the shapes of two of the

Great Watching Things, malign and silent, were closer and clearer to my gaze.

First, to my right, rising, vast and motionless, the Thing of the Southwest was but a dim silhouette, larger than a hill. It was alive, but not as we know life. There was a crack in the ground at its feet, from which a beam of light rose, to illume part of that monster-cheek, and cast shadows across its lowering brow. Its bright left eye hung in the blackness, slit-pupilled and covered with red veins, seemingly as big as the Full Moon that once hung above a world whose nights came and went.

Some say this eye is blinded by the beam, and that the beam was sent by Good Forces to preserve us. Others say the beam assists the eye to cast its baleful influence upon us, for it is noted by those whose business it is to study nightmares, that this great catlike eye appears more often in our dreams than any other image of the Night Lands.

I remember my mother telling me once, how a time came when that great eye, over a period of weeks, was seen to close; and a great celebration was held in the many cities of the pyramid, and they celebrated for a reason they knew not why. They knew only that the eye had never before been known to close. But the lid was not to stay closed forever and aye, in eleven years' time a crack had appeared between the upper and nether lid, for the monster was only blinking a blink. Each year the crack widened. By the time I was born, the eye was fully opened, and so it had been all of my life.

Second, to my left was the great Watching Thing of the South, which is larger and younger than the other Watching Things, being only some three million years ago that it emerged from the darkness of the unexplored southern lands, advancing several inches a decade, and it passed over the Road Where the Silent Ones Walk between twenty-five and twenty-four hundred thousand years ago.

Then, suddenly, some twenty-two hundred thousand years ago, before its mighty paws, there opened a rent in the ground, from which a pearl or bubble of pure white light rose into view. Over many centuries the pearl grew to form a great smooth dome some half a mile broad. The Watching Thing of the South placed its paw on the dome, and it rises no further, but neither has the Watching Thing advanced across that mighty dome of light in all these years.

It is known from prophecy that this is the Watcher who will break open the doors of the Pyramid with one stroke of its paw, some four and a half million years from now, but that the death of all mankind will be prevented for another half million years by a pale and slender strand of white light that will emerge from the ground at the very threshold of the great gates. More than this, the dreams of the future do not tell.

Between the Watching Thing of the South and of the Southwest, the Road Where the Silent Ones Walk runs across a dark land. The Road was broad, and could not be crossed except in the full view of the Watching Things to the South and the Southwest. But the ground on the far side of the Road is dim, lit by few fire-pits, and coated with rubble and drifts of black snow, where a man could hide.

In this direction was my only hope. Suppose that the eye-beam does indeed blind the right eye of the Watching Thing of the Southwest, and suppose again that the dome of light troubles the vision of the Great Watcher of the South more than the Monstruwacans have guessed; I could cross the Great Road on the blind-side of the Southwest monster, and sneak between him and his brother, perhaps to hide among the black snow-drifts beyond. I would then follow the road as it wound past the place of the Abhumans, and then leave the road and venture North, into the unknown country called the Place Where the Silent Ones Kill.

Many weeks of terror and hardship passed, and my supplies grew sparse.

Once a party of abhumans came upon me by surprise; I slew two of them with my Diskos, though it was a near thing, and I fled when the others stopped to chew their comrade.

Once a luminous manifestation meant to wrap me in her misty arms; but the fire which spun from my weapon could do hurt to subtle substances even when there was no material substance for the blade to bite; swirled lightning dispelled part of the tension that held her cloudy fingers together, and she flew off, maimed and sobbing.

Once a Night-Hound ran at me suddenly from the darkness, and I chopped him in the neck before he could rend me; the blade of the Diskos shot sparks into the smoldering wound, and the monster's huge limbs jerked and danced as it fell, and it could not control its jaws enough to bite me. A soft voice from the corpse called me by name and spoke words of ill to me, but I fled. I will not write down the words in this place: it is not good to heed things heard in the Night Land.

As I passed through the abhuman lands, they grew aware of me, and hunted me.

I was driven far away from the Road into lands that grew ever colder. Each time I lay down to sleep, the hills between me and the Pyramid were higher. A time came when I passed beyond the sight of the Last Redoubt; even the tallest tower of the Monstruwacans was not tall enough to see into this land where I now found myself. I was beyond all maps, all reckoning.

At first, I walked. Each score of hours my dial counted, I slept four. Because there were crevasses, I struck the ice before me with the haft of my weapon as I walked. Then I grew aware of how loudly the echo of my metallic taps floated away across the utter darkness of the icy world, and I grew very afraid.

After this, I crawled across the ice in utter blackness. I surely crawled in circles.

After four score more hours, about half a week of crawling, I felt a pressure in the air. It was so malign that I was certain one of the Outer Presences must be standing near. All was utter black, and I saw nothing but the ghosts of light starved eyes create.

For about an hour I crouched with my forearm bare, my hand numb without my gauntlet, and the capsule touching my lips; but the pressure against my spirit grew no greater. I heard no sound.

So I crawled away. Over many hours I crawled and slept and crawled again, but whatever stood on the ice behind me, I could sense its power even as a blind man can feel when the door of an oven is opened across the room. I took my bearings from this, and kept the power forever behind me.

A time came when I saw light in the distance. I went toward it, and, over very many hours, I began to sense the downward slope of the ice. The path soon became broken, and I crawled from crag to crag, from high hill to low hill of ice.

The light grew clearer as I trudged down the mighty slope of ice, and I could see the footing well enough to walk. I put my spyglass to my eye, and scanned the horizon.

Here I saw, looming huge and strange, the head and shoulders of the Northwest Watching Thing. The crown of its head was mingled with the clouds and smokes of the Night Land; and to the left and right of his shoulders, like wings, I saw long, streaming shafts of pure and radiant light. This was the reflected glow of the Last Redoubt, bright in the dark air of the night world.

I was behind the Watcher; seeing it from an angle no human person had ever seen it. The Last Redoubt was blocked from view; I was in the shadow of the monster.

A cold awe ran through me then, as if a man from the ancient times were to wake to find himself on the side of the moon (back when there was a moon) that forever turned its face away from Earth.

I had come into the Place Where the Silent Ones Kill.

When Hellenore's father forbad the courting of Perithoös to go forward, they began to meet by secret, and my father's mansions, the darkened passages of Darklairstead, were used for the rendezvous. I helped Perithoös because he asked it of me, and I felt obligated to do him a good turn, even though it troubled me. As for Hellenore, she was beautiful and I was young. She barely knew I existed, but I could deny her nothing. She had many suitors; how I envied them!

Once, not entirely by accident, I came across where Perithoös and Hellenore sat alone in a bower before a fountain in the greenhouse down the corridor not far from the doors of my father's officer's country house. The greenhouse was built along the stairs of Waterfall Park, downstream from where a main broke a thousand years ago. Near the top, it is a sloping land of green ferns under bright lamps, and the water bubbles white as it tumbles from stair to stair, with small ponds shining at the landings. Near the bottom, the ceiling is far away, and the lamps were dim. At the bottom landing is a statue of the Founder's Lady, surrounded by naiads, and water poured from their ewers into a pond bright with dappled fish whose fins were fine as moth-wings.

Through the obscuring leaves that half-hid them, I saw Perithoös sitting on the grass, his back resting on the fountain's raised lip, and one arm around Hellenore's bare shoulders. In his other hand, he held a little book of metal, of the kind whose pages turn themselves, and the letters shined like gems; ferns and flowering iris grew to their left and right, half-surrounding the pair in flowery walls. Her head was on his shoulder, and her dark hair was like a waterfall of darkness, clouding his neck and chest.

In this wing of the greenhouse, many of the lamps had died a century ago, and so the air was half as bright here as elsewhere. To me, the view seemed like a cloudy day, or a sunset; but I was the only one in all mankind who knew what twilight was. How strange that, so many millions of years after it could not ever be found again, lovers still sought twilight.

As I approached, I heard Hellenore's soft laugh—but when she spoke, her whisper was cross. "Here he comes, just as I foresaw."

Perithoös whispered back, "The boy is sick for love of you, but too polite to say aloud what is in his mind."

"But not polite enough to stay where he is welcome!" she scolded.

"Hush! He hears us now."

I pushed aside the leafy mass of fern. Crystal drops, as small as tears, clung to the little leaves, and wetted me when I stepped forward.

Now she was primly kneeling half a yard from him, and her elbows were in the air, for she had pulled her hair up, and, in some fashion I could not fathom, fixed it in place with a swift and single twist of her hands. The same gesture had drawn her silken sleeves (that had been falling halfway to her elbow) back up to cover her shoulders.

Perithoös, one elbow languidly on the fountain lip, waved his book airily at me, the most casual of salutes. "Telemachos! The lad who lived a million lives before! What a surprise this would have been, eh?" And he smiled at Hellenore.

I bowed toward her and nodded toward him. "Milady. Perithoös. Excuse me. I was just . . ."

Hellenore favored me with one cool glance from her exotic, tip-tilted eyes, and turned her head, her slender hands still busy pinning her hair in place. If anything, her profile was more fair than her straight glance, for now she was looking down (I saw that there were amethyst-tipped hair-pins driven point-first in the soil at her knees), and the drop of her lashes gave her an aspect both pensive and demur, achingly lovely.

Seeing himself ignored, Perithoös plucked up a fern-leaf, and reached over to tickle Hellenore's ear. She frowned (though, clearly, she was not displeased) and made as if to stab his hand with one of her jeweled pins.

Perithoös playfully (but swifter than the eye could see) grabbed her slender wrist with his free hand before she could stab him, and perhaps would have done more, but he saw my eyes on him, and casually released her. I wondered how he dared be so rough with a woman so refined and reserved; but she was smothering a smile, and her dark eyes danced when she looked on him.

I said awkwardly in the silence, "I had not expected to find you here."

Perithoös said, "By which you mean, you expected us to flee before we let ourselves be found. Come now! There is no need to be polite with me—I see all your dark thoughts. You came to gaze on Hellenore. Well, who would not? She knows it as well. How many suitors have you now, golden girl? Three hundred?"

My heartbeat was in my face, for I was blushing. But I said merely, "I hope you see my brighter thoughts as well. Of the three of us, surely one should be polite."

Perithoös laughed loudly, and was about (I could see from his gesture) to tell me to go away; but Hellenore, her calm unruffled, spoke in her voice that I and I alone knew had the cooing of doves in it: "Please sit. We were reading from a new book. There are scholars in South Bay Window, on level 475, who have challenged all the schoolmen, and wish to reform the ways the young are taught."

I did sit, and I thought that Hellenore must have been well-bred indeed to invite so unwelcome an intruder as I was to consume the brief time she had to share with her young wooer.

She passed the book to me, but I read nothing. Instead, I was staring at sketches that had been penned into the flyleaves. "Whose hand is this?" I said, my voice hoarse.

Hellenore tilted her head, puzzled, but answered that the drawings were her own, taken from her dreams.

"I know," I said, my head bowed. And by the time I raised my eyes, I had remembered many strange things, things that had happened to me, but not in this life.

They both looked so young, so achingly young, so full of the pompous folly and charming energy of youth. So inexperienced.

Perithoös was looking at me oddly. Though I do not have his gift, I would venture that I knew his thought, then: he saw what I was thinking, but did not know how someone my age could be thinking it.

Perithoös said, "Telemachos will be against it, no matter what the South Bay Window scholars suggest. All new things pucker up his mouth, for they are sour to his taste."

"Only when they are worse than the old things." I said.

Perithoös tossed a leaf at me. "For you, that is each time."

"Almost each time. Mostly, what is called 'new' is nothing more than old mistakes decked out in new garb."

"The New Learning is revolutionary and hopeful. Come! Shake off the old horrors of old dreams! The world is less hideous than we thought. These studies prove that the outside was never meant for man; do you see the implication?"

I shook my head.

He said happily, "It implies that our ancestors did not come from the Night Lands. We are not the last of a defeated people, no, but the first of a race destined to conquer! The Bay scholars claim that we have always dwelt in this pyramid, and deny what the old myths say. Look at the size and shape of the doors and door-handles. It was clear that men first evolved from marmosets and other creatures in the zoological gardens. Our ancestors kept other creatures who bore live young, cats and dogs and homunculi, you see, in special houses; this was back before the Second

Age of Starvation. I assume our ancestors ate them to extinction."

I blinked at him, wondering if he had lost his mind, or if I had lost my ability to tell when he was joking. "'Evolved'?"

"By natural selection. Blind chance. We were the first animals who were of a size and stature to pass easily down these corridors and enter and exit the places here. Other creatures were too large or too small, and these were cast out in the Night Land after many unrecorded wars of prehistory. The New Learning allows us hope to escape from the promise of universal death for our race: we need merely wait for the time when we will evolve to be suited to fit the environment outside, and we will be changed; and those horrors will no longer seem hideous to the changed brains of the creatures we shall become."

I said sternly, "The Old Learning speaks of such a possibility as well. It is hinted that the abhumans were once True Men, before the House of Silence altered them. The tradition of the Capsule of Release is not without roots."

"Prejudice! Antique parochialism! The only reason why what we think of as True Men prevailed, is because our hands were best fitted to work the controls of the lifts and valves, our eyes best adapted to the lighting conditions, and we were small enough to enter the crawlspaces if giants chased us. Those giants outside are outside because they were too big for these chambers."

"And if we never dwelt in any place except this pyramid, whence came the ancestress of Hellenore? Whence came Mirdath? Or does your book prove she does not exist as well?"

He opened his mouth, glanced at Hellenore (who gave him an arch look), and closed it again. He dismissed the question with an airy wave of his hand. "Whatever might be the case here, skepticism will break down all the old rules and old ways, and leave us free. To live as we wish and love as we wish! Who could not long for such a thing?"

"Those who know the barren places where such wishful thinking leads," I said heavily, climbing to my feet.

Unexpectedly, Perithoös seemed angry. He shook his finger at me. "And where does thinking like yours lead, Telemachos? Are we always to be frozen in place, living the lives our ancestors lived?"

I did not then guess (though I should have) what provoked him. The traditional way of arranging a marriage, and so, by extension, the traditional way of doing anything, could not have had much appeal for him, not just then.

I spoke more sternly than I should have: "We are men born in a land of eternal darkness. We grope where we cannot see clearly. Why mistrust what ancient books say? Why mistrust what our souls say? Our forefathers gave us this lamp, and the flame was lit in brighter days, when men saw further. I agree the lamp-light of such far-off lore is dim for us; but surely that proves it to be folly, not wisdom, to cast the lamp aside, for then we are blind."

He said, "What use is light to us, if all it shows us are images of horror?"

I said, "There are still great deeds to be done; there will be heroes in times to come." And I did not say aloud, but surely Perithoös saw my thought: *unless this generation makes all its children to forget what heroism is.*

"Bah!" said Perithoös. His anger was hidden now, smothered somewhat beneath a show of light-heartedness. He smiled. "Will our writings be published in any other place than within these walls? Why will we do praiseworthy acts, when we know there will be nothing and no one left to sing our praises? Even you, who claims you will be born once more, will have no place left to be born into, when this redoubt falls."

I said, "Do not be jealous. I am not unlike you. This life could be my final one. You both have had others you forget; but this could be the first you will remember next time."

Perithoös looked troubled when I said this; I saw on his face how eerie my words (which seemed so normal to me) must have sounded to him.

Hellenore said eagerly, "What do you remember of us? Were Perithoös and I—" But then she broke off and finished haltingly, "How did the three of us know each other before?"

I said, "You were one of Usire's company, and lived in a strong place, a place of encampment, in a valley our telescopes no longer see, for the Watching Thing of the Northwest moved to block the view, once the House of Silence smothered the area with its influence. You, milady, were an architect, for women studied the liberal arts in those strange times; and you were possessed of the same gift you have now. In those times, you saw these ages now, and you sculpted one of the orichalcum doors before the main museum of Usire's stronghold, and wrought the door-panels with images of things to come."

Perithoös smiled sourly. "What Telemachos is not willing to say is—"

I interrupted him. "Madame, I was favored by you then, though I was of high rank and you were not. I helped sculpt the other door with images of things that had been."

Hellenore looked embarrassed. I hope my face did not show the shame I felt.

I turned to Perithoös, but I continued speaking to Hellenore, though I did not look at her. "What Perithoös is not willing to say is—since we are being honest and free with each other's secrets—he cannot fathom why I am not jealous of your love for him, even though he can see in my mind that I am not. He sees it, but he does not believe it. But that is the answer. Last time, he lost. This time, me. It does not mean we are not friends and always will be."

Hellenore was disquieted: I could see the look in her eye. "So I have not loved the same man in all ages, in every life . . ."

She was no doubt thinking of Mirdath the Beautiful, whose own true love was constant through all time.

I said awkwardly, "You have always loved noble men."

But she was looking doubtfully at Perithoös, and he was looking angrily at me. Odd that he was now angry. Surely I had said no more than what he had been about to say was in my mind. But perhaps he did not expect Hellenore to take seriously the thought that they were not eternal lovers.

Perithoös said, "No doubt if we three are born in some remote age in the future, and find ourselves the very last left living of mankind, you will seek to do the noble deed of poisoning minds against me, and worming your way into intimacies where you are not wanted! Is this the kind of praiseworthy and noble things you practice, Telemachos?"

Angry answers rose to my lips, but I knew that, even if I did not say them aloud, Perithöos would see them burning in my heart. With no more than a nod, and a muttered apology (how glad I was later to have uttered it, even if they did not hear!) I spun on my heel and marched from the grove, dashing the wet ferns away from my face with awkward gestures. The scattered drops dripped down my cheeks.

Behind me, I heard Hellenore saying, "Don't speak ill of Telemachos!"

Perithoös spoke in a voice of surprise. "What is this?"—which I took to be a sign that she had not had in her mind what to say before she spoke.

She said, "I foresee that my family will bring more pressure to bear against Telemachos, for my father suspects he knows the secret places where we meet. He will bear it manfully, and not betray us, though his family will suffer for it—you have chosen your friend well, Perithoös."

Perithoös said, "Ah. Well, he actually chose me."

She murmured something softly back. By then I was out of earshot.

My dial marked sixty hours passing while I descended the icy slope into this land, the Place Where the Silent Ones Kill, and I slept twice and ate of the tablets three times. The altimeter built into the dial measured the descent to be twenty-two thousand feet. During the middle part of that time, I passed through an area of cold mists where the air was unhealthy, and left me dazed and sick.

This area of bad mist was a low-hanging layer of cloud. The cloud formed an unseen ceiling over a dark land of ash cones, craters, and dry riverbeds, lit now and again by strange, slow flares of gray light from overhead. The ash cones in this area were tall enough to be decapitated by the low-hanging clouds. I spent another thirty hours wandering at random in this land, hoping to stumble across some feature or landmark I would know from my memory-dreams.

Once, a flickering gray light of particular intensity trembled through the clouds above. I saw the silhouette of what I thought (at first) was yet one more ash cone; but it had a profile: I saw heavy brows, slanting cheeks, the muzzle and mouth-parts of a

Behemoth, but huge, far more huge than any of his cousins ever seen near the Last Redoubt. A new breed of them, perhaps? It was as still as a Watching Thing, and a terrible awareness, a sense of sleepless vigilance came from it. It was taller than a Fixed Giant, for the dread face was wrapped partly in the low-hanging clouds, and wisps blew across its burning, horrible eyes. How one of that kind had come to be here, or why, was a mystery before which I am mute.

I looked left and right. In the dim and seething half-light of the cloud overhead, it seemed to me that there were other Behemoths here; two more I saw staring North, their eyes unwinking. I traveled along the bottoms of the dead river-beds after that, hoping to avoid the gaze of the Behemoths; but now I knew the place I sought lay in the direction the giant creatures faced.

The gray light faded, and I walked in darkness for thirty-five hours. A briefer flare of gray light came again and I saw, in the distance, a great inhuman face gazing toward me; and yet I saw, nearer at hand, another Behemoth to my left facing toward him. By these signs, I knew the massive shadow rising between me and that far Behemoth was what I sought.

The colorless light-flare ended, and all was dark as a tomb. But I felt a faint pressure, as of extraterrestrial thought reaching out, and I feared the Behemoth facing me, over all those miles, had seen me.

I crept forward more warily. The ground here was becoming irregular underfoot, sloping downward. I walked and crawled across the jagged slabs of broken rock I found beneath my feet and fingers, ever downward. I could not see enough to confirm whether this was a crater-lip.

After another mile, the ground changed under my hands. Here there was ash and sand underfoot, for soft debris, over the aeons, had filled this crater-bottom. I was able to stand and move without much noise, and I waved the haft of my weapon before me in the dark as I walked, the blade unlit, like a blind-man's cane, hoping it would warn me of rocks or sudden pits or the legs of motionless giants.

After an hour's walk or two, under my boot I felt smooth and hard stones. Stooping, I traced their shape in the dark. They were square, fitted together. Manmade. A road. A few more steps along I felt something looming from the utter dark near me; by touch, I found it was a stele, a mile-stone cut with letters of an ancient language.

I knew the glyphs from former lives: the name spelled USIRE.

One hundred, two hundred paces further on, and my fingers touched the pillars and post of a great gate. I touched a bent shape that had once been a hinge; I touched the broken gate-bars, the shattered cylinders that had once been pistons holding these doors shut against the night.

Beyond the doors, I felt nothing but more sand, and here and there a slab of stone or a huge column of bent and rusted metal. I sensed nothing alive here, no Earth-Current pulsing through power-lines, no throb of living metal. The place where whole-some men dwell often will carry a sense in the aether, like the perfume of a beautiful woman who has just left the chamber, a hint that something wholesome and fair had once been here—there was nothing like that here.

Instead, I felt a coldness. I felt no horror or fear in my heart, and I realized how strange that must be.

I was surely near the center of where a ring of the Behemoths bent their gazes; even in the dark, I should have felt it as a weight on my heart, a sense of suffocation in my soul. Instead I was at ease.

Or else benumbed.

How very silent it was here!

Slowly at first, and then with greater speed, I backed away from the broken gates that once had housed the stronghold of Usire. Blind in the utter dark, I ran.

I was still in the open when the gray light came again, and slowly trembled from cloud to cloud overhead, lighting the ground below with fits and starts, a dull beam touching here, a momentary curtain of light falling there, allowing colorless images to appear and disappear.

I beheld a mighty ruin where once had been a metropolis; its dome was shattered and rent, and its towers were utterly dark.

Here and there among the towers were shapes that were not towers, and their expressionless eyes were turned down; watching the ruins at their feet, waiting with eternal, immortal patience, for some further sign of the life that had been quenched here, countless ages ago.

More than merely giants stood waiting here. The gray light shifted through the clouds, and beams fell near me.

A great company of hooded figures, shrouded in long gray veils, stood without noise or motion facing the broken walls. They were tall as tall men, but more slender. The nearest was not more than twelve feet from me, but its hood was facing away.

There next two of the coven stood perhaps twenty feet from me, near the broken gate; it was a miracle I had not brushed against them in the dark as I crept between them, unknowing of my danger. Even as quiet as I was, how had they not heard the tiny noises I had made, creeping in their very midst?

Then I knew. It was not the noise carried by the air they heeded. It was not with ears they heard. They were spirits mighty, fell, and terrible, and they did never sleep nor pause in their watch. A hundred years, a thousand, a million, meant nothing to them. They had been waiting for some unwise child of man to sneak forth from the Last Redoubt to find the empty house of Usire, dead these many years. They had been waiting for a thought of fear to touch among them—fear like mine.

With one accord, making no sound at all, the dozens of hooded figures turned, and the hoods now faced me.

I felt a coldness enter into my heart, and I knew that I was about to die, for I felt the coldness somehow (and I know not how this could be, and I know not how I knew it) was swallowing the very matter and substance of my heart into an awful silence. My cells, my blood, my nerves, were being robbed of life, or of the properties of matter that allow physical creatures such as man to be alive.

I turned to flee, but I fell, for my legs had turned cold. I made to raise my forearm to my lips and bite down on the capsule, but my arm would not obey. My other arm was numb also, and the great weapon fell from my fingers. Nor could my spirit sense the power in the metal any longer, despite that the shaft and blade were still whole. The Diskos was still alive, but I wondered if its soul had been Destroyed, and feared I was to follow.

Then I could neither move my eyes nor close them. Above me there was only black cloud, lit here and there with a creeping gray half-light. A sharp rock was pushed into the joint between my gorget and the neck-piece of my helm, so that my head was craned back at a painful angle; and yet I could not lift my head.

The Silent Ones made no noise, and I could not see if they approached, but in my soul I felt them drifting near, their empty hoods bent toward me, solemn and quiet.

Then the clouds above me parted.

I saw a star.

Whether all the stars had been extinguished; or whether the zone of radiation that surrounds our world, transparent in former ages, had grown opaque; or whether there was merely a permanent layer of cloud and ash suffocating our world, helping to slow the escape of heat, had been debated for many an age among savants and knowledgeable people. Of these three, I had always inclined to the last opinion, thinking the stars too high and fine to have been reached by the corrupt powers of the Night Land.

That the Night had power to quench the stars was too dread to believe; but that the stars should have the grace to push aside the smog and filth of the Earth, and allow one small man one last glimpse of something high and beautiful, was too wondrous to hope.

I cannot tell you how I knew it was a star, and not the eye of some beast leaning down from a cliff impossibly high above, or some enigmatic torch of the Night World suspended and weightless in the upper air, bent on strange and dreadful business.

And yet more than my eye was touched by the silvery ray that descended from that elfin light; I saw it was a diamond in heaven, indeed, but somehow also a flame and a burning ball of gas, immensely far away; and how such a thing could have a mind, and be aware of me, and turn and look at me, and come to my aid in my hour of need, I cannot tell you, for diamonds and flames and balls of gas do not have souls; but neither can I tell you how a hill, shaped like unto a grisly inhuman thing, could sit and watch the Last Redoubt of Man without stirring and flinching for a million years. Is the one more unlikely than the other?

I felt strength burning in me, human strength, and I raised my head.

The coven of Silent Ones was here, but the blank hoods were lifted and turned toward the one star. The thoughts, the cold thoughts of the Silent Ones were no longer in me.

A fog was rising. As mild and as little as the light from the star might have been, it somehow made little fingers of white mist seep up from the sand.

There may have been a natural, rather than a supernatural explanation for this; but I doubt it. Like a veil, the pure cloud rose to hide me from the enemy; the delicate rays of this one star still shined through these pearly curtains, and illuminated them, and made every bead and hanging breath of the mist all silvery and fair to see.

If this were not supernatural, then the supernatural world should be ashamed that such wonders can be wrought by merely natural means, by star-light, and little water-drops.

While the Silent Ones were closed off behind a wall of fog, I picked up my weapon and crept away. I was blinded, so I followed the star. Here and there about me in the silvery mists, I could see looming shadows of the Silent Ones, terrible and motionless. And yet they did not sense me, or do me hurt, which I attest is starkly impossible, unless but that one of the Good Powers that old tales said sometimes save men from the horrors of the Night had indeed suspended the normal course of time, or relaxed the iron laws of nature out of mercy. No one knows these things.

The star led me to where a little stand of moss-bush spread. Beneath the bush was hid a door, set flat into the rock underfoot; and one of the leaves of the door had been forced inward a little way against its hinges. The crooked opening was large enough perhaps to admit a man—or the small nasty crawling things and vermin of the Night Lands, stinging snakes and centipedes—but too narrow to let any of the larger brutes or monsters pass in.

The star went out, and the mists that hid me began to part. I saw tall shadows slanting through the mists, and feared the Silent Ones were drifting near.

I doffed my helm and breastplate and undid my vambraces, that I might be lithe and small enough to squeeze in through this crack. It might have been wise to drop my armor into the crack before I went in; but wisdom also warned me not to make a clatter, so I pushed the armor plates beneath a moss-bush, where (I hoped) they would not be seen.

The edges of the door scraped and cut me; I was blood-streaked when I fell into the dark place beneath.

Of the wonders of the city of Usire, I have not space to say. Let it suffice that there were many miles of rock that had been mined out to form the fields and farms beneath the dome, and that the dome itself, even broken, was a mighty structure, many miles across, and half a mile high. There were places where the feet and legs of the Behemoths had broken through the roof, and I would peer out across a shattered balcony to see the knees and thighs of rough and leprous hide, knowing that somewhere, far below, were feet; and the palaces and museums, fanes and libraries of Usire, a great civilization of which the folk of the Last Redoubt know nothing, lay trampled underfoot. Many layers of roof and hull had been shattered in the footfalls of the giants, back, ages ago, when the giants walked; darkness and cold had entered in.

I found the doors of orichalcum I had seen so often in my dreams.

The images carved into the right-hand leaf of the door were as I had seen them, exactly (now that the memory came back to me) as I had carved them in a former life.

The right-hand door was of the past: here were sculpted images of star-farers landing their winged ships on worlds of bone and skull, horror on their faces as they came to know our Earth was the only world remaining in all the universe not yet murdered. The fall of the Moon was pictured, and the sundering of the earth-crust. Here were the Road-Makers, greatest of all the ancient peoples; and there were the Cliff-Dwellers, whose mighty cities and empires clung to endless miles of chasm walls, during the age when the upper surface of Earth was ice, but the floor of the great rift was not yet cooled enough for men to walk upon it. Here was an image of the Founder, tracing the boundaries where the Last Redoubt would rise with a plow pulled by a type of beast now long extinct; this was a legend from the first aeon of the Last Redoubt and twenty aeons and one have passed since that time.

The left-hand door held images from the end of time: the Breaking of the Gate was pictured here, and the severing of man into two races, those trapped far below ground, and those trapped in the highest towers, when all the middle miles of the Last Redoubt were made the inhabitation of unclean things that wallowed in the darkness. The tragedy of the Last Flight was pictured, millions women and children of the Upper Folk attempting escape by air, in a winged vehicle like those used by our earliest ancestors; the image showed the winged ship, buoyancy lost, falling among the waiting tribes of sardonic abhumans, the loathly gargoyles, and furious Night Hounds.

The time of the Final Thousand was shown, when all living humans would know not just their own lives, but the lives of all who came before, so that each man was a multitude; each woman, all her mothers.

Here was a picture of the Last Child, born by candle-light in her mother's ice-rimmed coffin; there was an icon of the Triage. Three shades, representing all the dead fated to fade from the world's dying aura, were bowing toward the wise-eyed child, proffering their ghostly dirks hilt-first. Any shade the Last Child shunned had no hope of further human vessels for its memories.

The final panel of the furthest future, which formed the highest part of the left-hand door, showed the Archons of High Darkness, Antiseraphim and other almighty powers of the universal night, seated on thrones among the ruins of the Last Redoubt; and while Silent Ones bowed to them, and the Southern Watching Thing fawned and licked their dripping hands, all the books and tools and works of man were pictured heaped upon a bonfire around which abhumans cavorted, and the greater servants were shown eating the lesser servants at feast.

These images were fanciful, mere iconography. The Ulterior Beings have no form or substance, no shape that can be drawn with pencil or carved in stone. Nonetheless, the door-maker carved well the nightmare scene, and I knew what she meant to portray.

There was on the right, in the past, at the highest part of the door, an image directly opposite the image of the triumphant powers of darkness at feast. Here, golden, was the many-rayed orb which was meant to represent the Last Sunset, which was the earliest legend of the earliest time, and, in the foreground, here was the mother and father of mankind, holding hands sadly and watching the dusk; the man was pictured with one hand raised, as if to salute, or bid farewell, whatever unimaginable age of gladness had ruled the upper air before that time.

I was cheered to think that, even then, my ancient self who made these doors had not considered the days of light to be a myth to be ashamed of.

I put my shoulder to the cunningly carven panels and pushed.

They were the doors to a museum, of course.

Here I found the dusty and rusted wreckage of broken stalls and looted displays: tarnished machines, broken weapons, dead glasses, and empty bookshelves. But in the ruin was one machine, shaped like a coffin, still bright. Light came from its porthole.

This casket was a type long forgotten in the Last Redoubt, able to suspend the tiny biotic motions we call life, each cell frozen, and carefully thawed again by an alchemy that revives each cell separately. These once had been used in aeons when men ventured into the Void, but those who slept too long in them came out changed, troubled by strange dreams sent to them from minds that roamed the deepest void between the stars, and loyal to things not of Earth.

Inside the casket was Perithoös.

I wiped the frost from the porthole to peer inside. He was horribly maimed; scar tissue clotted his empty eyesockets; his left arm was off at the elbow, a mere stump. No wonder he had never attempted to find the Last Redoubt again: blind, maimed, and without the Capsule.

A few minutes search allowed me to find a spirit glass in an alcove; I brought it back and connected it to the physician's socket by means of a thinking-wire cannibalized from an inscription machine. I tilted the glass until I caught an image of Perithoös in it. And there, shining at the bottom of his soul, tangled in a network of associations, dreams, fears, and other dark things, like a last redoubt, besieged by fear yet unafraid, was the thing in us that knows and recognizes the Master-Word.

I whispered the Master-Word. The shining, timeless fragment in his soul pulsed in glad recognition.

Human. Perithoös was human.

The Master-Word stirred something in him. Even though he was frozen, his blood and nerves all solid, there was sufficient action in his brain to allow his thought to reach through the armor of the coffin and touch my brain:

You came!

"I came."

It was not unexpected that even a frozen man could still send and hear thoughts. If this method of suspending life could have also suspended the spiritual essences of life, and kept them safe, the star-voyages of early man would not have ended in such nightmarish horror, for the space-men would have been deaf to the things that whisper in the dark of the aetheric spaces, and would have returned from the void whole and sane.

Slay me and then slay yourself. We are surrounded by the powers from the House of Silence.

"I came to save you, not to kill you."

I merit death. I slew Mirdath.

"Mirdath? She lived and died many generations ago."

Hellenore. I mean Hellenore. My only love; the fairest maid our pyramid ever knew. She was to be my bride. And I also slew her child. The child in the womb reached out and touched my mind, and told me things I should not have heard.

"Your child?"

No. A creature carried her off to the Tower-Without-Doors and violated her; things were done to her womb to permit her to conceive a nonhuman.

I winced at the thought. "What creature? An abhuman?"

No, though it answered to them. The bridegroom was a thing bred or made by the arts of the House of Silence, in the centuries since the fall of the Lesser Redoubt.

I knew that when that Redoubt fell, out of all those millions, only Mirdath had been saved. Of the rest, not all of them had been allowed to die without suffering, especially not the women, and most were put to pain of the type death does not ease.

"You call it a bridegroom? She married it?"

The abhumans mock our sacraments. You know why.

I nodded. It is not enough that we die; that will not satisfy them. They must make the things we deem precious seem grotesque and ugly, even to us, so that there is nothing fair left in the world. (I speak of the lesser servants, the ones once human—we are not in the thoughts of the greater ones.)

The bridegroom bit my weapon out of my hand, and tore off my arm, but the capsule buried in my forearm broke beneath its iron teeth, and venom filled its mouth.

"It died instantly?"

No. Its unnatural life stayed in its frame long enough to slay the rest of my men.

I killed the child with my thoughts, for its life was weak; but Hellenore, by then, had no soul to slay, and I strangled her one-handed while she clawed out my eyes. Such was my last sight.

Slay me, that I may cease from seeing it ever and again forever.

"Many a weary mile I have walked to save you, Perithoös, for I will not fail of the promise we made as children. Why did you call out to me, across all the miles of the Night-Lands, if you did not wish me to bring you back into the warmth and human comfort of our mighty home?"

I cannot open the door.

"Do you mean the casket lid?"

The door that opens to escape from a life that grows intolerable. The door that honor commands men to use when all other doors are shut. You must open the door for me. You of all men know that there is something beyond that door, and that it opens back into this life again, but with forgetfulness, blessed forgetfulness, to quench the pain of memory. There is much I must forget.

A picture came from his brain-elements into the visual centers of my brain. It was an image of Hellenore, her eyes filled with childish faith in the man she loved. She raised a gauntlet too large for the slender hand that bore it, and tilted back a helmet too large for her, and raised her mouth for one last kiss, before she slid down a rope from a small window in the postern gate.

Away across the black and grainy soil of the Night Land she walked; and there she was, outlined for a moment against the glow of the Electric Circle; then she was gone.

She had not been moving as those who are Prepared are trained to move, skulking from rock to rock, or standing motionless to let one's gray cloak blend with the gray background, avoiding discolored patches of ground. She did not know how to walk.

And she dragged the great weapon behind her, for the weight was more than she could bear, and she wheeled it like a wheelbarrow on its blade; an image that would be comical, were it not so horrifying.

His thoughts were clear as crystal, sharp as knives:

She will not be born anew. The darkness consumed her. I have destroyed her forever. I sent her into the Night without a capsule, without the words and rites, without the exercises of the soul and mind, carrying a weapon she had never swung before, in armor too big for her.

More images. Perithoös had sent her out. He lowered her on a rope from a window in the postern gate and watched her walk away. His gift allowed him to chose a time when the portreve was one who admired his fame too much to turn him in, and the gatewarden he could blackmail with knowledge taken from the man's own guilty mind.

The enormity of the crime was too great for me to take in. I was overcome with emotion at that moment. The strength left my legs, and I sat. My weapon I put down, the first time it had left my grip in weeks. I put my head in my hands.

"Madness!" I said. "Madness. There were simpler ways to die, and ways that do not carry hundreds of dead down with you! Was she so jealous of Mirdath, did the law that forbids women to walk the Night Land offend her so much? Did she so much want to be thought more manly than a man? It was not enough for her that she was more fair than women?"

That was not the reason.

Eventually, I said softly, "Why?"

For love.

"What?"

Love. Surely that emotion excuses us from all limits, all law. We thought we could be together, here. We thought the stronghold of Usire would provide us some sanctuary against the Night, but that we would be far from the Pyramid, free to live as we wished . . .

"Madness! Would she step to the bottom of the sea without a suit, or play with lepers without an immunity? Ah, but you don't know about oceans or lepers, do you? All old things are dead to you, including the wisdom of our laws!"

Some old things I know. I gave her a harquebus from a museum, and brought it to life with the Earth-Current. I rendered it obedient to her with my thought. The piece was able to discharge a streamer over 900 yards, carrying a charge enough to kill a Dun Giant.

"You know why the ancients forbade us to use such weapons. The energy can be sensed from miles away, even of a single shot. Or do you? How little do you know of the world you live in, of what has come before? Why trick her into killing herself in such a foolish fashion? Surely it would have been simpler to throw her from an embrasure, or dash out her brains against a post, or bury her alive. Did you want to feed them? Feed the horrors?"

I was imagining her, surprised by a petty-worm or scorpion, touching off the voltage, and sending a lightning-bolt echoing across the darkened land. I imagined the thing we see shadowed in one of the windows of the House of Silence tilting its dark head toward the source of the energy-noise. I imagined Night Hounds, pack upon pack, swarming down from the Lesser Dome of Far Too Many Doors, baying as they came.

I spoke in a voice made hollow and weak from despair and disgust. How could he overlook what was so plain to see?

"No woman, ever, must travel in the Night Lands. Here are monsters to slay us."

She thought she would foresee them, or that my spirit would warn me ere they came near. And . . . And . . .

"And what?"

I had prepared everything for us, a capsule she could carry in her poke, an instrument that would lead us to where the Stronghold of Usire was, by the traces of Earth-Current it still gave off. If the instrument sensed nothing, we would turn and come back home; and so there was no risk—we thought that the monsters would stay clear of any land were the Earth-Current was running. And if we found this place, we could reconnect the White Circle to the Current, sanctify the ground, and erect an Air-Clog of our own, stronger than that we had left. It would have been, not as safe as Home, but safer!

"You sent her off by herself? By herself?!"

I meant to meet her before the hour was gone! Less! Forty minutes, no more! Time enough for me to descend and escape out of a wicket, carrying the other gear. I had to stay behind to joggle the power, or else the Air-Clog would not have parted for us.

From a low window, we had together picked the rock where she was to hide and wait for me; it was less than eighty yards from the gate! Eighty yards! She could not have mistaken the rock; we had studied every feature lovingly. She could not have mistaken the rock! It was cleft like a miter, and one part jutted like my sister Phaegia's nose.

He said more, much more, then; many excuses, much sophistry. I could not make myself heed his thoughts. My own thoughts were too loud: I kept picturing what it must have been like for her.

To be trapped in the darkness of the outer lands, being hunted by Night-Hounds, to have the eyes of inhuman beings searching the unending night—and then—after hunger and weariness and nightmares and false hopes—to be found by the Cold Ones, and taken to their secret places, and to have one's nervous system laid open, and all one's intimate thoughts laid bare. And then to be raped by unclean creatures, and then to marry one's rapist. And all this time to wonder why one's own beloved, one's true love, the beloved trusted and cherished above all others, to have him merely abandon you to this fate . . .

I was walking up and down the aisles of the ruined museum, looking for an axe or heavy bar. It was not something I meant to think, but I was looking for something to smash in the casket lid, and expose the freezing innards to the air. (Even in my anger and turmoil, I note that it never occurred to me to use the Diskos on him: it is something we only ever swing against monsters. I do not know if any human person has ever been struck with one.)

Perithoös broke into my endless circle of thought: *I tried! I was prevented! I wanted to come after her immediately. That was our plan, but—*

I pounded my fist against the portal where his frozen, maimed face was held in ice. The noise was loud, but the glass held, despite the hardness of my gauntlets.

Like water bubbling from a holed jug, my anger left me. Men who have eaten nothing but the tablets for weeks do not have stomach enough to stay angry.

I sat down again.

"But you were arrested by the magistrates, weren't you?"

Yes.

I said, "They granted clemency on your promise that you would venture out after her. Has the world gone mad? You mocked the law that says no woman ever may venture into the Land; they mocked that law that forbids a man of unsound mind or unfit character to go. You were but a callow youth, perhaps that can excuse; but they were judges. Men of the law!"

The judges thought that no punishment the hand of man could mete out would match this.

"And no one else could trace the screaming, her voice you could hear in your head, back to the source: they needed you to find her."

The Silent Ones let her scream so that others would come forth from the Pyramid and be destroyed. They opened their barrier to let my call reach you for the same reason.

I nodded sadly. And the Silent Ones would have had me, had not one of those Powers that no one can explain intervened.

You know I betrayed you.

"You were afraid the Silent Ones would destroy you unless you called other children of men out from the Last Redoubt. It is an old, old trick. An old fear."

A fear you do not share. What is wrong with your thoughts? Why are you not afraid?

"I was spared."

≫ 504 ≪

The Silent Ones will not permit us to leave this place! I am wounded and blind—how can you hope we can cross the Night Land together? Hellenore said she saw many pairs of boot-prints leading out, but only one coming back in. You will live; not me. It is fated.

I said "Fated. I don't understand why Hellenore went forth. Were her visions of the future unclear? Did she have some vision that told her she was to be a wife and mother, but it cruelly deceived her?"

I deceived her. She saw what was to come. I told her not to believe her visions.

"Why did she listen to such a stupid idea?"

Because you deceived her. You convinced her that fate could be changed.

"I said the opposite; that we must endure what could not be changed."

She was convinced of that, too. Even when I talked her into venturing forth, in her mind there was nothing but grim resolve. Women sacrifice much and suffer much to become our wives, to bear our children; nature inclines them to endure great sacrifice.

"A sacrifice for what? For what gain? She knew that bloodshed and destruction would spring from her going-forth. What—"

Something like laughter came from his frozen brain. *She saw far, far into the future. Isn't it obvious? I found the shaft. I reconnected the main leads. I restored the power. As I had planned from the start. But it took me months.*

"What do you mean? What . . . ?"

Are you an idiot? The casket is powered. The Earth-Current is alive here, still strong, but deep, deep beneath the rock. And so the victory of the dark powers here is not complete.

You must return to the Last Redoubt with this news: if they drive a shaft deep enough, and at an angle to find the sources directly beneath this spot, the Last Redoubt will live out its promised span of life five million years hence; otherwise we fail within a few hundred years.

The engineering needed to drive a shaft so many miles to find so small a place might be beyond the powers of the present generation of men; but there would be generations to come. The gardens, and fields, and mines beneath the Great Redoubt were so extensive that, compared to that work, what Perithoös proposed was not an insurmountable matter.

I cannot explain why I laughed. The laughter was bitter on my tongue. I said, "So all our proud and vain dreams of returning as heroes will come true, won't they? We will be lauded. I can think of no more just punishment for folly, than to have a foolish wish come true."

We?

(I admit the word surprised me as well. It just slipped out; but, once I had said it . . .)

"We."

I am blind and crippled, and wicked besides.

"You are coming with me."

If I return to the pyramid, the magistrates will condemn me to death.

"And so your wish shall be granted! Or perhaps the law that you may not stand twice for the same offense will forbid a new hearing. If judges still uphold our laws, which seems not the fashion among these modern folk. In any case, it is their affair, not mine."

Why do you not bestow the death my acts have merited? Have you no sense of justice?

"Well, obviously, not so much as I should have. A just man would have not answered your plea."

I felt a stirring in the aether, as if he were gathering his brain-elements to send a thought, but the thought was too confused, too full of shame, to send. Had his face not been frozen, I wonder what his expression might have given away.

"You put me on trial, didn't you? You pretended to misplace the Master-Word. If I had been a man of justice, obedient to our laws, I would have been safe, and never answered you. I failed your trial and you condemned me to death and annihilation at the hands of the Silent Ones. Your justice condemned me; but something spared me. I wonder why. Why was I spared?"

You knew you should not come. Why did you come?

I came because I am a romantic fool, the kind of fool it is easy to fool. But he had asked the wrong question.

"Don't ask why I came. Ask why I had been permitted to come. Ask why the cunning of the House of Silence did not prevail. A miracle was wrought to permit me to be here. My certain destruction and doom was set aside. Why?"

I saw now why the star had parted the clouds to touch me, and to restore my life to me.

It was, at once, a reprieve and a punishment heavier than I could imagine; for my punishment was to stand, in relation to Perithoös, as that star had stood to me, and save him. To be his friend, despite all his crimes, all his foolish pride and boastful madness, to be his friend nonetheless, and save him.

Perhaps the Good Power that had saved me meant to save the Last Redoubt as well, to let the message go though telling where another vein of the Earth-Current could be found in the shrinking core of the planet. But, somehow, I doubted it. The things that seem great and momentous to men, I am sure are of little matter to the Ulterior Powers who sometimes protect Life.

I knew the words to start the rebirth-cycle for the coffin, and how to adjust the feeds to bring the Earth-Current back into his body, so that uneven thawing would not mar him.

I picked up my weapon again, and leaned on it. The Earth-Current within the haft was aware of the current flowing in the casket—a phenomenon spiritualists call affected resonance. It felt good to have the warlike spirit of my Diskos propping me up at that moment; in a former life I owned a boarhound, and his loyalty had been not unlike this.

Perithoös touched his mind to mine again, but weakly. His spirit was faint, for his aura was being drawn back close to his flesh in preparation for the decanting; he would sleep many hours before the lid would open and he would wake. But I heard him.

I don't understand.

"How can you not understand me? You see my thoughts."

I see your thoughts, but they are senseless.

Strange. My thoughts seemed perfectly clear to me.

The same madness that droves Perithoös into the night was the only thing that might save him from it. The love that binds friends or brothers is no less real than that which binds wooer and beloved. The power that saved me surely knew what a boastful and foolish man I was, but mothers do not strangle their babies if they are born lame; the stars do not cease to shine on us if we men cripple ourselves.

And I should not abandon my friend, whether he was a true friend to me, or not.

Men's souls are crooked and unsound things, not good materials out of which to build friendships, families, households, cities, civilizations. But good or no, these things must be built, and we must craft them with the materials at hand, and make as strong and stubborn redoubt as we can make, lest the horrors of the Night should triumph over us, not in some distant age to come, but now.

We are surrounded by the Silent Ones. We are fated to die. One of us will perish before we regain the pyramid; Hellenore saw only one pair of footprints leading back. How is it possible that we both shall live?

But by then the cycling process was too advanced, and his thoughts lost focus. Many hours must pass before I would open the lid, and answer his question.

As I carried him on my back, out past the golden doors, I led his blind hand to touch the bas-relief on the left panel of the golden doors.

Here was the panel carven long ago by Hellenore in a former time, a small depiction of one small event in what, to her, had been the future—now our present. Here was a man without a breastplate or helm, wearing only gauntlets and greaves, carrying a one-armed man on his back; a blindfold (but I knew now it was a bandage) covered his eyes.

The image showed a star shining down on them, and the gates of the Last Redoubt opening to receive them. Only one pair of footprints led in.

⋮⋮⋮⋮⋮
●●●●●●●●

OFF ON A STARSHIP

by William Barton

William Barton was born in Boston in 1950 and worked as an engineering technician before switching to information technology. He has been employed by the Department of Defense and worked on the U.S. nuclear submarine fleet, and is currently a freelance writer and software architect.

Barton started his career in the early '70s with two novels, Hunting on Kunderer *and* A Plague of All Cowards, *before a long hiatus from publishing that ended with two novels written with Michael Capobianco,* Iris *and* Fellow Traveler, *in the early '90s. They were followed by the novels* Dark Sky Legion, When Heaven Fell, The Transmigration of Souls, Acts of Conscience, *and two further novels with Capobianco,* Alpha Centauri *and* White Light. *His most recent novel is* When We Were Real.

Barton has published a series of increasingly impressive short stories, starting with 1993's "Almost Forever," and culminating in the recent stories "Heart of Glass" and "The Engine of Desire." In 2003 he published two strong novellas, "The Man Who Counts" and the story that follows. It is the kind of story that will always resonate with science fiction readers, touching on why we read it and why we love it. It is, in a sense, a loving salute to the dreams we had of the way the future was.

I<small>T WAS THE BEST OF TIMES.</small> I<small>T WAS</small> the worst of times. Isn't that how it's supposed to go?

It was, oh, I guess the middle of November 1966, that night, maybe seven P.M., dark out, of course, cold and quiet. The sky over Woodbridge, Virginia, was flooded with stars, so many stars the black night, clear and crisp, had a vaguely lit-up quality to it, as if ever so slightly green. Maybe just the lights from the gas stations and little shopping centers lining Route 1, not far away.

I was walking home alone from the Drug Fair in Fisher Shopping Center, up by the highway, where I'd read comic books and eaten two servings of ketchupy French fries, moping by myself. I'd stayed too long, reading all the way through the current *Fantastic Four* so I could put it back and not pay. I was supposed to have been home by six-thirty, so my mom could head out on her date.

Out with some fat construction worker or another, some guy with beery breath and dirty hair, the sort of guy she'd been "seeing" (and I knew what was meant by that), one after another, in the two years since she'd run off my dad, leaving me home alone to look after my two little sisters, ages three and seven.

I remember thinking how pissed off she was going to be.

I was standing on the east rim of Dorvo Valley, looking down into the shadows, thinking about how really dark it was down there, an empty bowl of land, looking mysterious as ever. Murray and I named it that when we'd discovered it three years ago, maybe a half-mile of empty land, cleared of underbrush, surrounded by trees, called it after a place in the book we'd been trying to write back then, *The Venusians,* our answer to Barsoom, though we'd kind of given it up after *Pirates of Venus* came out.

Murray. Prick. That was why I was at Drug Fair alone. There'd been a silence after I called his house, then his mother had said, "I'm sorry, Wally. Murray's gone off with Larry again tonight. I don't know when he'll be home. I'll tell him you called."

I felt hollow, remembering all the times we'd sat together at Drug Fair, reading comics for free, drinking cherry cokes and eating those ketchupy French fries. Remembered last summer, being here in Dorvo, the very last time we'd "played Venus" together, wielding our river-reed swords, lopping the sentient berry clusters from the Contac bushes we called Red Devils, laughing and pretending we'd fallen into a book. Our book.

Murray's dad was the one named them Contac bushes, telling us they were really ephedra, and that's where the stuff in allergy medicines came from.

But then school started, eleventh grade, and we'd met Larry. Larry, who was going steady with Susie. Pretty blonde Susie, who had a chunky girlfriend named Emily, who wore glasses.

Something like this had happened before, when we were maybe ten or eleven, and Murray had joined Little League, telling me it would help him find his way as an "all-around boy." This time, I think, the key word would be pussy, instead of baseball.

I stood silent, looking out across the dark valley; the black silhouette of the woods beyond; above them, the fat golden spire of Our Lady of Angels Catholic Church, floodlit from below, where I'd been forced to go before my parents split up. In the Dorvo Valley mythos, on our wonderfully complete Venus, lost Venus, we'd called it the Temple of Venusia, and the city at its feet, no mere shopping center, but the Dorvo capitol, Angor: portmanteau'd kiddy-French Angel of Gold.

I realized I'd better get going. Through the black woods, down the full length of Greenacre Drive, past Murray's house, where his parents would be sitting, silent before the TV, drinking Pabst Blue Ribbon beer, across the creek, up Staggs Court to my furious, desperately horny Mom.

If I was lucky, she'd spend the night with whoever it was, and I wouldn't have to lie in bed in the dark by myself, listening to their goings-on.

I blew out a long breath, a long wisp of warm condensation flickering like a ghost in the bit of light from the sky full of stars, and stopped, eyes caught by some faint gleam from deep in the valley of the shadow. I felt my heart quicken, caught in a mythopoeic moment. Look, Murray. A cloud skimmer . . . !

Yeah. Right. Where's Murray now? In a dark movie theater somewhere, with his hand groping up a girl's dress, like a real grown-up boy.

But the gleam was there, really there, and, after another moment, I started walking down through the long grass, stumbling over Red Devils and weeds, skirting around holes I could barely see but remembered from long familiarity with the place, night vision growing keener as I went down in the dark.

Looking toward the phantom gleam, I thought to shade my

eyes with one hand, occluding the Golden Angel, cutting off more light from the stars.

Stopped walking.

Thought, um, *no.*

I looked away, blinking like a moron. Looked back.

The flying saucer was a featureless disk, not quite sitting on the ground, maybe sixty feet across. The size of a house, anyway. Not shiny or it would've reflected more starlight. There were things in the deeper shadows underneath it, landing legs maybe, and other shadows, moving shadows, rustling in the brush nearby.

Near me. Something started to squeeze in my chest.

Something else started to tickle between my legs: a need to pee.

I slowly walked the rest of the way down the hill, until I was standing under its rim. The moving shadows in the underbrush were things roughly the size and shape of land crabs, a little bigger maybe, with no claws, though I couldn't make out what was there in their place.

They seemed to be taking hold of the Red Devils, bending them down, pulling off the little berry clusters. What the hell would clawless land crabs want with Contac berries?

Robots. In a comic book, these would be robots.

Anyway, they seemed to be ignoring me.

I felt unreal, the way you feel when you've taken two or three Contac capsules, or maybe drunk an entire bottle of Vicks Formula 44 cough syrup.

There was a long, narrow ramp projecting from the underside of the saucer, leading up to an opening in the hull, not dark inside but lit up very dim indigo, perhaps the gleam I'd seen from the valley's rim. I walked up to it, heart stuttering weirdly, walked up it and went inside.

In movies, flying saucers have ray cannons, and they burn down your city. And in my head I could hear Murray, jealous Murray, girl on his fingers forgotten, wondering where I'd gotten the fucking nerve.

But I went inside anyway.

It turned out the thing was like the saucer-starship from *The Day the Earth Stood Still.* There was a curved corridor, one wall solid, the other lattice, wall sloping slightly inward. A little vertical row of lights here, beside something that looked like a door. Around the curve . . .

I caught my breath, holding stock-still, heart racing up my throat.

Held still and wondered again at finding myself here.

The thing didn't look much like Gort from the movie. Not so featureless. Real joints at elbows, wrists, knees, hips, but there was nothing where its face should be either, just a silvery shield, a curved pentagonoid roughly the shape of an urban policeman's badge, like the Boston metro badge my Uncle Al wore.

I stood in front of it, looking up. No taller than my dad, so only an inch or two taller than me—looking had to be an illusion. It looked a little bit like the robots I used to draw as part of the Starover stories I once tried to write, the ones that filled the background of all those drawings I did, of hero Zoltan Tharkie, policeman Dexteran Kaelenn, and all the odds-and-sods villains they faced together.

I remember Murray and I used to sit together at Drug Fair, tracing pictures from comic books and coloring books, filling in our own details, Tharkie and Kaelenn and the robots, Älendar and Raitearyón from Venus. I remember those two had had girlfriends, and . . .

Stopped myself, shivering.

I reached out and touched the thing.

Cold. Motionless.

My voice sounded rusty as I whispered, "Klaatu, barada . . ." Strangled off a fit of giggles with something like a sneeze. Patricia Neal, I remembered, couldn't pronounce the words the same way as Michael Rennie, substituting *Klattu, buŕodda* in her quaint American drawl. Quit it! *Jesus!*

Nothing.

I turned away from the silvery phantasm—maybe nothing more than an empty suit of armor?—slid my fingers along the light panel. Just as in the movie, the door slipped open, and I went on through.

"Ohhhhh . . . !"

I could hardly recognize my own voice, shocky and faint.

There was another corridor beyond the door, and its far wall was transparent, like heavy glass, or maybe Lucite. There was smoky yellow light in the room beyond, lots of water, things like ferns. *Something* in the steamy mist . . .

I put my nose to the warm glass, bug-eyed, remembering the scene from near the end of *Tom Swift in the Race to Moon*, maybe my favorite book from the series, where they finally get aboard the robot saucer sent by the Space Friends.

Little dinosaurs. Little tyrannosaurs. Little brontosaurs. Little pteranodons winging through the mist.

"Not quite a brontosaurus," I told myself, voice quiet, but louder than a whisper. "Head's too long and skinny. Not a diplodocus either. Nostrils in the wrong place." There were other things moving back in the mist. Babies, maybe? Hatchlings? Would that be the right word?

I walked on, slowly, going through another door, walking along another hallway. After a while, I began to wonder how they got all this space folded up into a flying saucer little enough to fit in Dorvo Valley.

Another robot, yet another door, and I found myself in a curved room with big windows on the outside. Ob Deck, the voice in my head called it, pulling another word from another book, as I pressed to the glass, cold glass this time, looking out on greenish night.

Dorvo Valley. Little landcrab robots. Brilliant green light flooding up from the ground beyond the forest. Something odd. It isn't that bright outside. Can't be much more than eight P.M.

Little frozen image of my mother.

How long before she calls the police?

Thought dismissed.

What should I do?

Get out of here! Run home. Call the cops yourself.

I pictured that. Pictured them laughing at me as they hung up, as I turned to face my raging mother. "You little bastard!" she would say. "Bob didn't even *wait* for me."

Pictured that other scenario: the cops come, we go to Dorvo

Valley. Nothing, not even a circle of crushed vegetation. And, either way, I go to school in the morning. Word would get out, one way or another.

The lights flickered suddenly, and a soft female voice said, "Rathan adun dahad, shai unkahan amaranalei." More flickers. Outside, I could see the little land crabs were making their way downhill, dragging their loads of harvested Red Devils.

Cold clamp in my bowels.

I turned and ran, through the door, down one corridor, through the next door, up another, around a curve, back through . . . Ob Deck! Turned back, found myself facing a faceless robot, still motionless. Started to whimper, "Please . . ." There was a rumbling whine from somewhere down below, spaceship's structure shivering. The lights flickered again, the lady's voice murmuring, "Ameoglath orris temthuil ag lat eotaeo." More flicker. Something started to whine, far, far away, like the singsong moan of a Mannschenn drive.

I felt my rectum turn watery on me, clenched hard to stop from shitting myself, and snarled, "That's just a fucking story! Think! *Do* something, you friggin' idiot!" As if my father's words could help me now.

I turned and looked out the window, just in time to see the ground under the saucer drop away. Suddenly, surrounding the dark woods, the map of Marumsco Village was picked out in streetlights. There was Greenacre Drive, where Murray's parents would be finishing up their beer. Beyond the dark strip of the creek, halfway up Staggs Court, had to be the porch light of my house, where, by now, my mom would be about ready to kill me.

It shrank to a splatter of light, surrounded by the rest of Woodbridge, little Occoquan off that way. I squashed my face to the glass, looking north, and was elated to see, from twenty-two miles away, you could still make out the lights of the Pentagon, could see the floodlit shape of the Capitol Dome, the yellowish spike of the Washington Monument.

City lights everywhere I looked. Speckles and sparks and rivers of light, brighter and more numerous than the stars in the sky. I'd never flown on a plane at night before. I'd never . . .

I felt my face grow cool.

Watched the landscape shrink.

Suddenly, light appeared in the west, like sunrise.

No! I'm high enough up the sun is shining from where it's still daytime!

Turned toward the blue. On the horizon, the curved horizon, there was a band of blue, above it only black, sunlight washing away the stars.

Curved?

Bolt of realization.

I can see the curvature of the Earth. That means . . . I shivered again. And then I wondered, briefly, if Buzz Aldrin and Jim Lovell were somewhere nearby, peering out through the tiny rendezvous windows of Gemini XII, watching my flying saucer rise.

Whole Earth bulging up below now, looking for a moment like the pictures sent down from Gemini XI, which had gone all the way up to an 850-mile apogee. It turned to a gibbous blue world, getting smaller, then smaller still.

Something flashed by, huge and yellow-gray.

Moon! It's the *Moon!*

How fast?

That was no more than a five-minute trip.

I tried to do the calculation in my head; couldn't quite manage. I'd never been any good at math. A lot slower than the speed of light, anyway.

I remembered the final scene from *Invaders from Mars*, where the little boy wakes up from his dream, and felt a cold hand on my heart. If I wake up now and it's time for school, why don't I just kill myself and get it over with?

But the ship flew on into the black and starry sky, and I realized, after my moment of inattention, I could no longer find the Earth *or* Moon. Where am I going?

And why?

I awoke from a dreamless sleep, and opened my eyes slowly, lying on my side, cramped and cold, against the curved Ob Deck bulkhead, staring at the motionless gort by the door. Whispered, "Gort. Merenga." Nothing.

I always wake up like that, always knowing where I am,

never confused. Maybe because there's that little re-entry period, those few seconds between waking up and opening my eyes, when I remember where I was when I went to sleep, so I know where I'll be when I awaken.

I pushed myself to a sitting position, back to the wall, something in the back of my neck making a little gurgle as I stretched, like my spine was knuckles wanting to crack.

Seemed more real, now that I'd been asleep, putting a bracket around the night before. I was here. Period. Unlike the hazy wonder of the dream where we flew past Jupiter, some time around midnight. It'd been a fat, slightly flattened orange ball, not at all the way I would've expected.

Three hours, I remember thinking. That's fast. What, fifty thousand miles a second? More? We went by something that looked like a ball of pink twine, and that's when I discovered if I put my finger against the window glass and circled something, it'd get bigger, that another tap would make it small.

I'd picked out five little crescents. Circled and tapped. Figured out the red potato must be Amalthea, the pink ball Europa. Maybe the scabby yellow one was Io? Those other two, two similar-looking gray cratered bodies, looking pretty much like the Moon, those would be Ganymede and Callisto, but I couldn't figure out which was which.

Murray would know. Murray out at night in the summertime, pointing at this star and that one, naming names, mythological and scientific, every kid in the neighborhood but me impressed as all hell. Once, I'd caught him in a mistake.

And he'd said, "I don't know if I want you for a friend anymore."

After that, I kept my mouth shut.

The lights flickered and the woman's soft voice said, "La grineao druai lek aporra . . ." Trailing off, like she had something else to say, but couldn't quite get it out.

I stood, turned and looked out the window.

It was like a featureless yellow ball, hazy maybe, circled by a striated yellow-white ring, grooved like a 45 rpm record. Colored like those records I'd had as a child, like the one with "Willie the Whistling Giraffe." I'd loved that song, and listened to it so much

I could still sing all the words. I was startled to find out, years later, it was written by Rube Goldberg.

Saturn was growing in the window, growing slowly and . . . I realized it should already be going past, shrinking away. "We're slowing down." I glanced at the robot, as if looking for confirmation.

Nothing.

When I looked back, a smoky red ball was in the window, starting to slide past. It stopped and stabilized when I circled it with a quick fingertip, movement transferring to the sky beyond, Saturn starting a slow slide across the fixed stars.

"Titan."

Nothing.

"Goddamn it, *Titan!*"

Like I wanted something from myself then. But all I could do was remember, remember Captain Norden from *The Sands of Mars* reminiscing about the cold, howling winds of Titan, remember Tuck and Davey from *Trouble on Titan* and their homebuilt oxygen-jet, flying the methane skies.

What would I remember about all this, years from now?

I had a glimpse of the man I might have become, some fat guy in a crumpled suit, selling who-knows-what. All the men on Staggs Court. All the men in America in 1966.

The woman's voice said, ". . . kag at vrekanai seo ke egga." The lights flickered again, like punctuation. I tapped Titan to release the image and pressed my nose to the glass.

Ought to feel colder than this. Saturn's pretty far from the sun.

There. A spark of pale yellow light.

It grew swiftly, filling the window without interference from me, gliding to a stop just outside. It was a cylinder of gray rock, things visible on its surface, structures, and I could see it was revolving slowly around its long axis.

Revolving so there'd be artificial gravity inside, centrifugal force. It'll be hollow, I thought. Maybe this was what Isaac Asimov had termed a "spome," short for "space home," in some *F&SF* column or another? No, that's not right. Where the hell . . . Asimov's article was in that book my dad brought home, Kammermeyer something . . . "There's No Place Like Spome"? Dad had gone to a meeting of the American Chemical Society a year or two earlier, had come home snickering about the little fat man with what he'd term "a thick New York Yid accent."

I remembered him saying, "*Asimov?* Now I see him in a *different* light!" When I was little, we'd lived in a neighborhood full of Russian Jews, somewhere in Boston, Brookline maybe, and he'd done a good job of picking up the accents, and those special cadences. It'd become the basis for some family in-jokes.

The thing rotated toward us, though it had to be my flying saucer flying around I guess, then a four-mandibled parrot's beak opened, spilling bright yellow light, and we flew right in.

Flew right in, swooped over green landscape, found a flat white field, concrete I figured, and slotted in to a landing, one of the few vacant spaces in a parking lot full of flying saucers just like mine.

A flicker of lights.

A womanly voice, full of warmth and welcome, "Todos passageiros said . . ." Then the saucer groaned and shivered as the boarding ramp slid down. It only took me a minute to realize that if I could find a land crab, I could follow it down to the hatch; maybe fifteen minutes after that, I was standing outside.

There was a cool breeze blowing across the concrete apron, and it smelled sweet here, making my nose itch. Alien pollen? I'm allergic to a lot of stuff. I whispered, "What if I get sick?" My voice sounded funny, here in the silence. I shouted, "*Hello-oh?*"

Not even an echo, my voice carried away to nowhere by the breeze. "Anybody . . ." Of course not. I started forward, walking between two other saucers, stopped suddenly, feeling a cold knot in my guts, looking back toward my saucer, realizing how easy it would be to get lost here.

Does it matter?

How would I know if *my* saucer is ever going back to Earth?

From where I stood, I could see beyond the last row of saucers. There was a tall chain link fence, topped by razor wire; beyond it, a dark green forest.

Nothing moving.

No dinosaurs, big or little in the woods, no pteranodons in the sky.

Sky? Well, not exactly.

Overhead, the main thing was a long yellow stick of bright light. In a story, that'd be a fusion tube or something, an "inner sun" for this long, skinny ersatz Pellucidar. Beyond, to the left and right, were two green bands, the same color as the forest. Between them were three more bands of black.

In one of them, you could see Saturn, its brightly backlit rings looking like ears, or maybe jug handles. And that bright star? That'd be the sun I guess. Glass? So how come I didn't notice any windows from the outside? How come it just looked like rock?

My memory started picking through stories, right then and there.

Something moved in the distance. I looked, and felt cold when I saw what it was. One of those brontosaurus-things, full size I think, but with a too-skinny head, snaky neck dipping so it could browse among the treetops. Glad for the razor wire. Cold but elated. As if . . . As if!

There was a deep bass thrumming noise, almost like a long, low burp. The bronto looked up. The inner sun suddenly brightened, filling the landscape with a violet dazzle.

I blinked hard, eyes watering, looked up again and realized that Saturn was gone, that I felt something else in my guts, a pulling and twisting. Dizzy. I'm dizzy. Like the ship is maneuvering violently, and I just can't see it because there's nothing to see.

Then there was a great big ripping sound.

A white zigzag crack appeared in the windows, going from one to the other, as if it were a rip in the sky itself, though my mind served up an image of what it would be like as the glass blew out and the air roared away to space, carrying off forest and trees, brontos, flying saucers, Wally and all.

The crack opened like white lips, revealing a blue velvet throat beyond, into which, somehow, the ship seemed to plunge; then the fusion tube dimmed, back to yellow again, back to being a soft inner sun, all the odd twisting and pulling stopped, and there was only the soft breeze.

In a story, I thought, we'd be going faster than light now.

And then I said, "Damn! This is the coolest thing that ever happened to *any*one! Murray would be *so* fucking jealous!"

Yeah, right. I could almost see his bemused, angry smirk, fading into the blue velvet hypersky as he turned away, forgetting about me, about Venus, about all the things we'd done together, all the dreams we'd had.

On Earth, in only a little while, people would stop wondering what'd become of me, and go on with their lives.

Some days later, I couldn't tell you how many days, already a good bit skinnier than I was the night I'd decided to cut through Dorvo Valley on my way home from Drug Fair, I sat beside a little deadwood campfire on the concrete apron beside my trusty flying saucer, roasting up a few fresh breadfruit for supper.

Mangosteen! That, I'd remembered, was from a kiddie book I'd found in my grandfather's attic, when we went up for the funeral, four, five years before: *The Hurricane Kids in the Lost Islands.* I'd been looking for the sequel ever since, where Lebeck and DuBois send their boys off to the Land of the Cave Dwellers.

Breadfruit? Probably not. Probably no breadfruit back in the Jurassic.

Sudden image of myself finding the little gate, sneaking out into the edge of the Big Woods, finding all sorts of stuff. Nuts mainly, and these things. Ferns. A tree I recognized had to be a gingko. Little lizards, maybe skinks, anoles, some kind of snake.

I fished one of the breadfruits out of the fire with a stick, held it down and cut it open with another stick I'd managed to break off at an angle and sharpen by rubbing on the pavement. It had mealy yellow-white flesh inside, like badly overcooked baked potato, steamy now, odorless, smelling just the way it would taste when it cooled enough to eat.

This was the last of them. Tomorrow I'd have to go out again and . . . I felt a little sick. Last time, blundering around in the woods, picking nuts and berries and whatnot, there'd been that soft rumble, I'd looked up, and suddenly wet my pants.

The allosaurus didn't even notice, didn't look up as I'd crept away, back through the gate, closing it carefully behind me. I'd cooked and eaten, silent with myself, sitting bareass while my underpants and jeans dried by the fire, draped over my constant companion.

I looked at it now, little humanoid robot, two feet tall, looking just like a toy from Sears I'd had when I was eight or nine, electric igniter in one hand, fire extinguisher in the other. It'd come toddling up just as I'd burst into tears beside my pitiful pile of dry sticks, just as I'd screamed, "Fuck it!" and thrown my pathetic attempt at a fire drill as hard as I could at the nearest flying saucer hull.

I said, "What d'you think, Bud? Why's this starship got a Jurassic biome inside?"

Silence.

"Yeah. Me too."

I picked up the now merely hot breadfruit and scooped out some tasteless muck with my upper front teeth. "Mmmmm . . ." blech. Even butter, pepper, and sour cream wouldn't've helped. Not much, anyway.

"What d'you think, Buddy? Thanksgiving yet?" Probably not. It hasn't even been a week. But I pictured my little sisters, Millie and Bonnie, sitting down to turkey dinner with Mom. Bonnie probably misses me. Millie was probably glad just to get my share.

Christmas. I wondered what Dad would get me? I'd asked for a copy of *Russian in a Nutshell*. Two years. Then what? No college for me. Bad grades and no money.

Vietnam?

Maybe. Some of my friends' older brothers had gone. At least one boy who'd picked on me when I was little was dead now. I remembered reading an article in the *Post* a while back, about how so many good American boys were being corrupted by little brown Asian prostitutes, which made me think about *Glory Road*.

Murray and I had talked about that the next day, and he'd given me a funny look, kind of a sneer, before changing the subject. Remember when we debated Vietnam in eighth-grade Social Studies class? I'd said I wasn't worried. It'll be all over, long before I turn draft age, toward the end of 1969. Yep. All over.

And, just like that, there was a deep bass thrum, like a gong gone wrong. When I looked up, the blue velvet sky was broken by a long white crack, white lips opening, spitting us out into a sky full of stars.

I got up, throwing the half-eaten breadfruit aside, running for the flying saucer's ramp. Behind me, I could hear the sharp, fizzy hiss of my little buddy's fire extinguisher, as it sprayed away the flames.

Down on the yellow-gray world, I crouched in the shade of the flying saucer's hull, looking out toward the horizon, across a flattish landscape under a pale, blue-white sky. I'd run off the bottom of the ramp when we landed, had run right out there, bounding high, realizing the surface gravity of this place was maybe no more than half that of Earth.

But then the light from the vivid spark of a tiny blue sun had turned to pins and needles in my November-white skin, forcing me back into the shade. My face, when I touched it, was already starting to peel.

Jesus. Stupid.

And what if? What if a lot of things. What if the air here had been deadly poison? What if there's some disease here a human being could catch? What if I'm already dead and merely waiting to fall down?

Yeah, yeah, I know. The guy in the story never dies. Except the one in that Faulkner story the teacher made fun of, when we studied it in tenth grade English Lit class. "What're we supposed to imagine?" she'd said. "He's carrying paper and pen, taking notes as he jumps in the river and drowns?"

From space, the planet had looked like a yellow-gray ball, almost featureless. Oh, there was a tiny white ice cap at the visible pole. A few pale clouds near what looked like some isolated mountain peaks. A canyon here, a dune-field there. Mars without the rust?

Arrakis, I thought. I'd enjoyed the five-part serial in *Analog,* though I was mighty pissed off about the stupid format changes Campbell was playing with, going from digest to some standard magazine size, then back again, fucking up my collection. I remember I wondered if the Dune world had started out as Mars, if maybe Herbert realized at some point that the solar system was too small for the story.

I thought about my bedroom. My bed. The little desk. Bookcases full of children's hardcovers, the stuff from Grandpa's attic, the paperbacks and magazines I was buying down at Drug Fair, *Amazing* and *Fantastic, Worlds of If* . . .

Out in the sun, the land crabs had buckets and little self-propelled wheel barrow things, were shoveling up patches of mauve sand. Melange? What ever it was, it went no more than a few centimeters deep. I sniffed, but couldn't smell anything like cinnamon. Whatever this place was, it mainly smelled like fireworks. Gunpowder. It smells like gunpowder.

From the Ob Deck, I'd been able to see something that looked like a city, way off on the horizon, low white buildings, dazzling in the sun. A circle of my fingertip had brought them close. Adobe? No sign of movement, some of the buildings looking weathered and worn, the ruins of Koraad perhaps.

Miles off, anyway. I could wait 'til nightfall, and it'd take maybe three or four hours to get there, tops. Yeah? And what if the starship leaves without you? What then? I thought about *Galactic Derelict* suddenly. No. I never wanted to be one of Andre Norton's dickless boys. Let's have a Heinlein adventure, at least.

Or maybe I can grow up to be John Grimes after all? Is there a beautiful spy somewhere waiting for me? Jesus. Grow up. At this rate, I'll be lucky to last another week!

What if this was a Larry Niven story? What if we land on a planet that has a habitable *point?* I pictured myself running down the ramp, out onto the sand. Then the deadly winds of We Made It would come up and there I'd be, on my way to fucking Oz.

After a bit, I turned and went on up the ramp. Look out the window. Watch the baby dinosaurs or something. One thing you know: the saucer will leave, the starship will fly, and, sooner or later, we'll be somewhere else. And another thing: who owns all this shit? The robots? Not bloody likely, cobber. Maybe this thing is like some super-sophisticated Mariner probe. And, sooner or later, it'll take its samples on home.

What happens when they find *me* in the collection bag?

Watching the land crabs gather up Spice, I suddenly wished for . . . something. Anything. Wished I'd see a sandworm in the distance. Wished for Paul Atreides to come riding up? No. Chani, maybe?

I'm guessing it was maybe three weeks before we made the next landfall—no, planetfall's the right word—three weeks in which I got *really* sick of plain breadfruit. Somewhere along the way, I got up the nerve to cook and eat a few little lizards, which turned out to be mainly bones, and salty as kippered herring snacks, finally moving on to a two-foot brown snake I'd caught.

Didn't taste like chicken, more like fish I guess, but the oily juice that cooked out of it made the breadfruit taste okay.

The next planet was . . . what'd we used to say in Junior High? Cool as a moose. I crept down the ramp, uselessly cautious, and stood there with my mouth hanging open. What can I say? Earthlike but alien?

The spaceport, if that's what it was, was just a plain concrete apron, not much bigger than the helicopter pad next to the Pentagon, sitting next to what looked like a walled city. Not a Medieval city, not an ancient Roman city. The walls were plain and unadorned, no crenellations, no battlements, no towers. White concrete walls, pierced by a few open gates on the side I could see. Egyptian Memphis, I remembered, had been called something like *Ineb-Hed* by the natives. White Walls.

The buildings I could see over the wall were low and white and square.

Overhead, the sky was dark green, green as paint, with little brown clouds floating here and there. The sun, if sun it was, was a dim red ball, halfway up the sky, banded like Jupiter, with mottled splotches here and there. Sunspots? Starspots? Maybe it's a planet, and that's reflected light.

Away from the city, the land was all low forest, things not much like trees, grayish, bluish, a reddish-purple that I realized with a flush of pleasure might be the heliotrope of Amtor. Things moving in the shadows, inside the forest. Pod-shaped things. Plants with lips.

The land crab robots were coming out of the saucer now, forming up by rank and file, so when they set off, heading for the nearest city gate, I walked along beside. What the hell? If they start to leave, I'll follow them back. Safe enough.

It was gloomy in the city, a city full of gray-green shadows. Gloomy and motionless, reminding me of the scene where

Gahan of Gathol walks into a seemingly deserted Manator. Sure. And the landcrabbots'd make pretty good Kaldanes?

That filled up my head with long-running images of Ghek, crawling through the Ulsio warrens of Manator.

I looked in an open doorway, yelped, tripped over my own feet, and wound up on my knees, staring, heart pounding. Jesus Christ! Well, at least it wasn't moving.

The thing, when I got close to it, was about three feet tall, looking like it was made of black leather. There were staring black leather eyes. Black leather fangs. Black leather hands shaped like a three-fingered mechanical grab.

I touched it, wondering what the hell I'd do if it woke up and turned out to really *be* a thrint. Fuck. I'd do whatever it wanted, I guess, and that would be that. It didn't budge, no matter how hard I pushed, nor did it have a bit of give to it. Cold black metal, glued to the ground.

Statue, maybe? Or just another switched-off robot?

What the hell is going on here?

Where is everyone?

Back out on the street, the land crabs were gone. Okay. Look around a bit more, then get the hell on back to the saucer. I went on up the street to the end, where it came to some kind of octagonal plaza. There was something that looked like an empty fountain in the middle, beyond it a domed building made mostly of glass, lots of tempting shadows inside.

The glass doors, when I tried them, swung right open, so I went on in.

Inside it was all broad aisles, floor carpeted in a patterned nappy monochrome the same color as the sky, and lining the aisles were . . . I don't know. Exhibits? Things like pictures anyway. Dioramas. Blocks of stuff like glass or Lucite, with motionless objects inside. Animals, I think. Some things that could only have been machines. Things that were clearly paintings of the "thrintun," looking like they were walking around the city, doing whatever.

So are those the aliens? Are they all in some kind of stasis? Suspended animation?

I suddenly found myself wishing there'd been more variability in the stories I'd been reading since I learned how to read. But the stories had been pretty much self-similar, as though the writers, without any source of new ideas, could only copy each other, over and over again.

In the middle of the building, taking up a big space under the dome, was a flat, tilted spiral shape, made of what looked like metallic dust, hanging motionless in the air. Like the Andromeda galaxy, blue and red and white and . . . my mouth went dry. Star map!

I walked round and round the thing, peering inside, trying to recognize something, anything, but it looked like every spiral galaxy illustration I'd ever seen. All of them. Or none. For all I knew, it could be NGC 7006 and here I was, beyond the farthest star.

On the other side of the spiral was an aisle lined with things that looked like model spaceships. Some of them looked pretty much like what humans were building, back on Earth. Look here. It's a couple of thrintun sitting in a sort of Gemini capsule. Not quite, but close. And this? A thrint climbing down on the dusty surface of some moon or another?

The ships got more and more advanced, until I suddenly wondered where the flying saucers were. Ah. Right here. Right at the end. Here's a flying saucer, surrounded by thrintun with things like guns, surrounded by thrintish tanks and cannons . . . surely, standing on the rim of the saucer, I'd see one of my familiar gorts?

On the ground under the rim of the saucer were models of about two dozen creatures, every one of them different.

Yep. That'd be the thrintun being welcomed to the Galactic Federation, right? Pleased at how clever I was, I started walking back toward the useless star map. Hey, if I'm lucky, it's *my* galaxy, and I'm not so far from home after all. Right. What the fuck am I going to do, *walk* back to Earth?

I stopped by the model of the moon lander. Maybe that was their moon? It was a pretty primitive spaceship, looking a lot like the earliest designs of the Apollo lunar excursion module. Moon. I tipped my head back, trying to look out through the dome, wondering if I'd spot a crescent somewhere in the dark green sky.

Very dark green sky.

Felt my mouth go drier than I would've thought possible. No sun, though I could see a flush of red in the sky, off to one side. So how the fuck long have I been in here, anyway?

I walked back up the aisle, around the spiral galaxy, back down the other aisle and out the door. Despite the fact that it was starting to get a little cool out, I felt myself start to sweat, armpits suddenly growing spongy and damp. Well. Started to walk back the way I thought would lead to the spaceport. Just get outside the walls. You'll find it.

I started to run, making little gagging sounds, throat suddenly sore, feeling like I was going to start crying, like a little kid lost in a supermarket.

And my little flying saucer popped up above the walls right in front of me, hung there for just a second, then dwindled away into the dark green sky and was gone.

I stood there, looking up, feeling the hot tears start down my cheeks, vision blurring, and whispered, "I always do something stupid, don't I? Just like Daddy says." I rubbed the tears from my eyes, suddenly angry, and thought, There you go, champ. Murray'll be *so* fucking jealous now, won't he?

I awoke, opening my eyes on a flood of vermilion sunshine coming in through the window, falling on me like a spotlight, and wished, just this once, I could be one of those people who wake up confused, not knowing where they are. I couldn't really remember the dream—something about school, I think—and had a nice hard-on, probably nothing to do with any images I'd seen in my sleep.

Christ. Mouth *so* fucking dry.

I rolled over on my side, feeling dizzy, headachy, hungry, looking around the room. The wall-to-wall carpet I'd slept on was pale gray, softer and fuzzier than the stuff in my parents' house. Mom's house, nowadays. Dark green walls, with brown trim. Stuff like furniture, odd-shaped couches and chairs and little tables I was kind of afraid to touch, for no reason I could put my finger on.

Stories. Too many stories. What if.

I'd wandered around for a while as it'd gotten darker, wondering what the fuck I was going to do, watching the sky fill up with unfamiliar stars. Finally knelt and drank some water from the gutter. Bitter metallic stuff, tasting way worse than the water in Marumsco Creek. And I'd gotten sick as a dog the last time I'd drunk from the creek, coming down with a high fever that resolved into tonsillitis, resulting in a shot and some pills and five days of missed school.

I remembered Murray looking at me with bemused contempt. Home come you're sick all the time, Wally?

I don't know.

After a while, in the dark, it started to rain, hot stuff that scalded in my eyes, burned on my scalp, making me run for the nearest shelter, which happened to be something like a porch, on something like a house, in something like a suburban neighborhood. No, not suburban. Small town. Like the neighborhoods in 1930s movies. Judy Garland and Mickey Rooney. When I'd tried the door, it'd opened, and I'd gone in, sat down in the middle of the floor, just sat there in the dark, listening to the rain, wondering if they had thunder and lightning here.

I got up, feeling stiff and tired, rubbing my empty stomach. Almost flat now. At this rate, I'd soon be as skinny as when I was a little kid. I'd always wanted that. What had made me get fat anyway? Starting to hang around with Murray and eat whatever and whenever he ate? I remember Mom was glad when I stopped being so thin.

There was a little room off what I thought of as the parlor, small, windowless, airless, and in the light of day I could see there was something like a stone sink, beside a little hole in the floor. Maybe the thrintun couldn't sit down and just squatted over the hole? No, wait. Thrintun regurgitate their waste, so they'd lean over the hole and . . .

I felt my intestines cramp. So now I've got to shit. Great.

One step forward and I stopped, sweat beading on my brow, asshole clenching. I was *afraid* to squat over the hole. What if I slipped and fell in and couldn't get out? What if it flushed with a death ray? No, wait. Shit's not alive enough to merit a death ray. Disintegrator? "Man, how did I get so goofy? No wonder nobody at school likes me."

I'll go outside and do it on the sidewalk, I guessed.

Next to the toilet hole, there was an obvious bathtub, made of the same gray stone as the sink, with a little row of glassy "buttons" above one end. Light panel controls? I touched one. There was a hiss, and the tub started to fill up—though I couldn't see anything like a faucet—smoky fluid welling up from nowhere, filling the room with a familiar sharp, ugly smell.

Sulfuric acid? I certainly recognized the smell from first-period Chemistry class. Wonder how that's going? My lab partner had been a big beefy guy named Al, full of dumb jokes, who was a shot-putter and discus-thrower on the track-and-field team.

There was another room that looked like a kitchen, by what had to be the back door, though it was on the side of the building, just like the back door to my parents' house. Something like a little oven sitting on the counter, an oven with a door. When I opened it, no gas jets or electric resistance heating elements, only a skinny light bulb thingy.

Right. I remembered my sister Millie's Easy-Bake Oven cooked perfectly well with a hundred-watt light bulb. Scrambled eggs. Teeny-tiny biscuits. A birthday cake the size of a deck of cards. If I knew you were comin' I'd've . . .

Nothing like a refrigerator? There was a long, narrow trough under the one window, the kitchen sink maybe? A roll of plain white paper towels hanging from the wall next to it. Great. Murray's mom had started using them, though at my house we still used cloth dish towels that would start to stink long before they went in the hamper. Dishrags, my mom said.

When I touched one of the glass buttons over the trough, it quickly filled up with a bubbly gray, acid-smelling sludge. I stood there, paralyzed, knowing not to touch it, and thought, Right. *Destination: Universe!* "The Enchanted Village."

Is that where I am now, in an A. E. Van Vogt story?

Angry at myself, I tore the paper towels from their holder and went back through the house to the living room, intending to go out the front door. Hell, at least I've got toilet paper now and . . .

"*Yow!*" I hit my head on the wall as I stepped back, turning, trying to run. Stopped, willing my heart to quiet down, making myself turn back and look.

It was a bipedal man-shape, not quite a gort but similar, no more than four feet tall, standing beside the open front door, staring at me with two glowing red glass eyes. No, not really like a gort. Feet like a bird. Three-fingered hands. No, two fingers and a thumb, just like a thrint, but far, far more gracile.

Is the damned thing humming? No. Silent.

I stammered, swallowed, then said, "Henry Stanley, I presume?"

Nothing.

"Hey, buddy. Sorry to have to tell you I'm not David Livingstone. Just a lost little dipshit has got himself in a *pile* of trouble."

The head turned just a bit, red lenses focusing on my face, seeming to look right into my eyes. Then it said, "Beeoop-click, zing?"

Really. I said, "Pleased to meetcha."

Oh, hell. My guts cramped hard, released from terror, and I quickly walked to the door, the robot turning to face me as I edged around it. I walked out onto the sidewalk, avoiding the stringy blue and yellow grass of the lawn, which had wriggled and tried to grab my shoes as I'd walked across it last night, got out into the street and started to pull down my pants. Thought better of it, kicked off my shoes and pulled my pants off entirely.

I squatted on the pavement, suddenly really glad I had the paper towels. The mossy stuff from the woods I'd used on the starship had been really scratchy. Jesus, I wish I could have a fucking bath!

When I looked up, the robot was standing on the porch, watching me.

By the time dusk came round again, dark green sky flushed red in what I thought of as the west as the fat red planet-star sank through the horizon, I was exhausted, dragging my ass out one of the deserted city's radial roads, away from downtown, back out into the burbs. We'd been out to the spaceport with its little patch of empty, unmarked concrete, then back to the museum, where we'd looked at every fucking exhibit, looking for a clue. Any clue.

We. Me and my little robot pal, which followed me all around, like a quiet puppy, plodding along in my wake, little metal bird feet clicking discretely on pavement and bare floor, soundless on the carpet that pretty much lined every building we'd visited so far.

"Pipe dream," I whispered, voice rasping like a cartoon character, mouth dry as dust.

The robot made some little *oot-boop* sound or another, as if a sympathetic noise. There were always plenty of puddles around in the morning, but by noon they'd mostly dried up. I found one now, kind of oily and sludgy looking, knelt beside it, and leaned down.

"Foooo?" Slim metal fingers on my shoulder.

I looked up. "Man, if you know where there's any real water, this is the time."

Its head cocked to one side, not so much like it understood, as the way a dog looks at you when you talk to it. They want to understand, but they don't. I turned away, leaned down again and took a sip. Gagged. Spat. "Jesus."

Rubbing my hand back and forth across tingling lips, I picked a house, went up on the porch, robot clicking along behind me, opened the door and went inside, where it was already gloomy, only light coming from the windows. Finally, I sat down on the carpet, wondering what next.

"What did I think I was going to find in the fucking museum?"

The robot was standing there, looking down at me, red eyes bright, as if concentrating. Does it *really* want to understand? How the hell would I know? Just a robot. A robot made by aliens, rather than some little guy from the Bronx.

I had a vision of me and the robot, finding some way to mark down Earth in the big star map, then mark it out again on the dome of night. Of the robot leading me to some ancient apparatus in some old thrintun exhibit.

"Wally to Earth! Wally to Earth! Hey, can you hear me guys?"

The robot just stood there, continuing to stare. "Right. Only in stories . . ."

But this . . . but *this* . . . !

I whispered, "So what the hell should I call you? Friday? Nah, too obvious."

It made some random fluty sounds, like the ones Millie made on the recorder she'd gotten last Christmas.

"Tootle?" Like the train in the story. "I think I can, I . . ."

It suddenly reached out and tried to stick a metal finger in my mouth.

"Hey!"

It froze in position, then said, "Whee-oo. Dot-dot."

Mournful and sad. I lay back on the rug, curled up in a little ball, put my hands over my face and made some stupid little sobbing sounds. No tears though. Probably too dried out to cry. Rolled onto my back, stretching out, looking up at meaningless black shadows, my throat making a little clucking noise as I tried to swallow.

Well. There would be water in the morning. Hot, bitter water, but it hadn't killed me so far. I looked up at the robot. "You know how to turn on the lights, buddy? Is there a fucking TV here anywhere?"

Shit. I missed TV. When was I going to see *Gilligan's Island* again? What the hell would the Professor do in my shoes? Or Mr. Wizard? No, not that one. The owl one. Drizzle, drazzle, druzzle, drome, time for zis vun to come home . . . ?

Jesus, I miss a lot of things. Things I thought I hated. Mom and Dad. My sisters. My so-called friends. Murray. Even school. Maybe. Some time or another, still bullshitting myself as the room grew darker and darker, 'til all I could see were the robot's staring red eyes, I must have fallen asleep.

Woke up suddenly, opening my eyes on grainy darkness, pain roaring in my arm, sitting up, struggling to figure out . . . to find . . . my voice, yelling, echoing, something like a scream that'd started in my sleep.

The robot's bright red eyes were near me, making enough light so that I could see the gleam of its body, arms and legs and featureless face, could see the reddish-black outlines of things in the room, thrintun furniture.

I tried to stand, stumbling, twisting to look at my upper arm, pain radiating away from a black smear. Black and wet. Blood! I'm bleeding! I made some weird gargling sound, looking back at the robot, which seemed to be holding something in one hand, pinched daintily by its few fingers.

The clenched hand went to its featureless face, briefly, as if eating the whatever-it-was, though it had no mouth, then reached out and grabbed me by the arm, just below the bloody spot.

"No! No! Lemme go!" Shrieking, voice breaking.

Its other hand reached out and touched the wound.

Flare of white light.

Sear of pain.

Just like that, I blacked out.

And awoke again, clear-headed, salmon-pink sunshine flooding the room. The robot was standing over me, motionless, red eyes staring. No eyelids. Right. I sat up, no stiffer than usual, mouth still dry, dull ache like a bruise in my left upper arm.

Memory.

"Kee-rist . . ." still whispered.

Dream?

No. The sore spot on my arm was marked by a skinny white scar, like a really bad cut from a long time ago. Right. Fresh scars are red, then pink for a while. One that big would take months to fade. I touched it. Tender, but not too bad.

"What the hell . . ."

When I stood up, licking my lips, the robot backed off a few paces, staring right into my eyes. Then it lifted a hand and seemed to beckon. This way. This way. Come on. Turned and walked slowly to the bathroom door. Turned to face me. That hand motion again. Come on. What the fuck are you waiting for?

I followed it into the bathroom. "Well?"

When it reached out and tapped a glass button, the little room filled with pale pastel pink light, making my skin seem to flush with health and well being. I thought, If there's light at night, I'm going to wish for a book. It tapped a button on the wall over the hole in the floor. There was a flicker of dim blue light somewhere down the hole, a faint sizzle, a faint electric smell.

Yah. Disintegrator.

Why the hell didn't I just tap all the buttons in the house myself? Was I afraid? Jeez, I'd filled the tub, and the kitchen sink thingy . . .

It tapped the button over the tub, the same one I'd tried, the one that'd gotten me a tub full of battery acid. This time, some clear, smokeless stuff began welling up. All I could do was stare, watching it fill up, rubbing the scar on my arm, feeling my heart pound.

"All right," I said. I glanced at the robot, no expression possible, red eyes on me. "Something's going on. What? Ah, fuck." I reached out and stuck my finger in the stuff. No sizzle. No burn. Warm, though. Cupped a handful, brought it dripping to my face. Sniffed. Odorless. Put it in my mouth. Tasteless. Swallowed.

"Water."

Some little parrot-voice repeated, "Waw. Tur."

There was a prickling in the back of my neck, as if something were crawling in my dirty hair. I turned and looked at the robot. "You say something, buddy?"

"Beeee-oooo."

"Oh." Turned back to the tub, swallowing hard. Then I pulled off my filthy clothes, stepped over the rim and sat down. Sat down in warm water, leaned forward and plunged my face, rubbing my cheeks, where a scruffy, patchy, half-silky, half-rough beard had grown out maybe a quarter-inch or so, opened my mouth and tried to swallow, came up gasping, choking, laughing.

I looked up at the robot, and shouted, "Jesus! This is wonderful!"

It said, "Waw. Tur. Wun. Dur. Full." Turned suddenly and walked away, leaving me alone in the tub.

I leaned back against the rim and sank down, feeling the water prickle all over, lifting scales of dead skin, old sweat, grime and dirt and who-knows-what, suddenly wishing for shampoo, for soap, toothpaste and toothbrush.

How the hell did it know I needed water? Sudden memory, me, screaming, trying to get away, blood on my arm, robot touching whatever to its face, the sizzle of the fleshwelder that made this scar on my arm.

I touched the scar, and thought, *Sample.* It took a sample for analysis. What was it they said in science class? We're seventy percent water? Something like that.

I wished for the bottle of nasty blue Micrin mouthwash sitting by the bathroom sink at home. I'd asked Mom to buy Scope, like Murray's parents, but it was green, you see, and Mom always liked blue stuff best.

I guessed if I washed my clothes in plain water, it'll help a little bit. Wouldn't it?

Better than nothing, anyway.

The robot came back, carrying a stone plate heaped with some smoky, steamy brown stuff, filling the bathroom with a smell like pork chops. Plain pork chops, no Shake 'n Bake or anything . . . my mouth suddenly watered so hard I started to drool.

The plate, when I balanced it on the rim of the tub, was full of something that looked like very coarsely ground hamburger, closer to shredded than anything else, a lighter shade of brown than you see in cooked ground beef. I touched it with my finger tip, getting a little juice on my skin. Sniffed. Licked.

Yah. Pretty much like pork chop grease and . . . jerked. Looked up at my staring robot. "Synthesized from . . . ?" Nothing.

Smart. Smart as hell. Smarter than me. What else should I have expected from a star-faring civilization? A little thrill from somewhere inside. Better than *Arsenal of Miracles.* 'Cept, of course, for the parts about Peganna of the Silver Hair.

I picked up a chunk of crumbly meat and popped it in my mouth. Chewed. Swallowed. Took another. Not really much like pork. Kind of gamey, but not venison either. Suddenly, the plate was half empty, and my stomach wasn't growling anymore.

I said, "So. Ground Wally tastes pretty good. You got any Worcestershire sauce? I like Lea & Perrins best."

It said, "Ground. Wally. Good. No. Sauce."

"Oh, that's okay, I . . ." Stopped. Stared at those red eyes, realizing my nameless little robot pal had just said an original sentence.

Some time in the night I awoke, swimming up from a dream, knowing it was a dream, hating it, but knowing. Face wet, cooling, fingers gentle in my hair. I jerked the rest of the way awake, eyes opening on dim pink light, light coming from nowhere, everywhere, certainly not the square black windows.

There was a soft sizzling outside as the hot acid rain came down, tonight as every night.

The robot stroked its two skinny fingers and long thin thumb through my hair, animate, but hardly alive. "Wally. Wake. Up. Now."

I whispered, "Yeah." Started shivering, wishing for . . . something. Anything.

"Wally. Crying. In. Sleep." Still that jerky delivery, though it'd improved sharply as the day wore on. Saying words as words now, rather than crude, isolated syllables.

What the hell had I been dreaming about? It was already getting away, the way dreams so often do. Something about my parents, some fight they'd had only a few weeks before Dad had moved out. I remember Mom said "scumbag" and Dad countered with "whore." I remember their arguments were always like that, like they were playing some stupid game of one-upmanship.

I said, "Can you make me something to eat?"

"What. To. Eat." No intonation, but it'd picked up on infinitives now.

What, then? So far, it'd been able to make ground meat and cups of some sweet, fatty yellow milk. Wally milk? This count as cannibalism? I had a sudden pang of longing, realizing I missed Brussels sprouts, of all things. "Ice cream?"

"What. Ice. Cream."

What indeed. "Uhhhh . . . Milk. Sugar. Ummm . . ." Why the fuck don't I *know* this stuff? I could picture it in my head. Taste it. Desperately taste it. Vanilla. I love vanilla ice cream. I could even call up an image of a vanilla bean. But I don't think you could manufacture a vanilla bean out of the contents of Wally Munsen's carcass.

The robot reached out and slowly stroked my hair one more time.

I said, "It's cold. Frozen. Not hard like ice . . ." realizing it wasn't cold here, that the robot might not know what ice was.

"Soft. Mushy." I shrugged helplessly. "Maybe it's the fat that gives it that texture?"

I followed the robot out to the kitchen, curious about what it planned to do. Hell, maybe I could learn to run the synthesizer myself? All it did was put its fingers over four nodes, two on one side of the panel, two on the other. They lit up blue, and it stood there, motionless, for maybe a minute.

There was a soft gurgle, and a blob of white ice cream suddenly extruded from the bottom of the trough. Maybe a quart. The robot got a plate from the cupboard, reached in, scooped the ice cream onto it, and handed it to me.

"Ice. Cream."

I took the plate, sniffing at the blob. "Maybe." But it didn't smell like ice cream. Not quite. "You got a spoon?"

"No. Spoon."

I sighed. Might as well ask it to get me a McDonald's. I stuck out my tongue and licked the surface of the stuff. No. Not ice cream. More like heavy cream. Maybe the way ice cream would taste if you left out all the flavoring. "Good enough. Thanks." I took a bite, getting it all over my face, and thought, "Anyway, the texture's perfect."

Afterward, I washed my face in the bathroom sink, went back to the living room and curled up again, wanting to sleep. Some time before I drifted off, the robot came back and squatted by my side, reaching out and slowly stroking my hair. Cold metal fingers, but nice enough for all that.

There were days now when I awoke with a sensation of intense well-being. Fed. Rested. Someone to talk to. Sort of. The light flooding in the window slanted sharply downward, as if I'd overslept, looking almost orange on the gray carpet.

I got up, stretching, listening to the gristle in my back make its little sounds, realizing I felt better sleeping on the floor than I ever had on any of the too soft mattresses my parents had bought me over the years. Mom likes soft mattresses, so that's what everyone must like, hmm?

I remembered my dad stretching in the morning, frowning as he arched his back. Not a clue.

I went to the door and out onto the porch. It was warm, soft breeze gentle on my bare skin. I walked over to where my clothes were draped over the railing and felt them. Dry, but stiff. I'd tried washing them in plain water, which turned out to be useless. Tried to get the robot to make soap, but it could only come up with something like Crisco, something that smelled and tasted good enough that I finally just ate it.

I'd put them outside to dry and forgotten them, acid rain leaching some of the color out of my pants, leaving little white streaks here and there.

Jesus. Mom will kill me.

I'd kept my shoes inside, and it was warm enough to go naked here. For now, anyway. I stretched again, peed over the railing into the grass, which wriggled and squirmed like it was trying to get away, then went back in the house.

"Robot?"

Nothing.

Awful damn quiet in here.

Went into the kitchen.

There was a plate of cold, pale brown meatloaf and a stone mug of yellowish wallymilk beside the trough.

"Robot?"

Felt my heart maybe pounding a little bit. No robot in the backyard. No robot in the bathroom. No robot in any of the other rooms, mysterious rooms, of the house I was making my home base. No robot in the street outside, or much of anything else moving. Grassy stuff stirring. Clouds in the sky drifting slowly, that was it.

No birds here.

No rats. No bugs.

I went back to the kitchen and slowly ate my cold breakfast. Thoughtful of robot to leave something. Thoughtful of it to let me sleep.

Goddamn it.

After breakfast I went to the bathroom and filled up the tub, trying not to feel scared.

Noontime. No lunch. No robot.

Finally, I put on my shoes and socks, went naked on out to

the street and began to make my usual rounds, keeping my mouth shut, unwilling to make speech sounds that would go unanswered. Went out through the nearest city gate and walked to the empty spaceport, stood looking up at the grass-green sky, shading my eyes from the reddish-orange light of the brilliant noonday sun. No saucers. And no robot. Went back to the house and checked in.

No robot.

Very slowly walked downtown, walked to the museum, wondering what the fuck I was going to do if it was gone for good. Sure, I had a sink, a toilet, and a bathtub. I'd got water to drink, I could stay clean, I could take a crap indoors.

On the other hand, I never had figured out how to run the synthesizer. I'd stood there with my fingers on the right nodes, stood there feeling silly, wishing it to work, muttering "Abracadabra, open sesame, you fucking piece of shit . . ."

The robot had stood watching, red eyes on me, and finally said, "Wally no can do." Getting good now, it was, though still with nothing like inflection.

"Go ahead you little bastard. Laugh!"

It said, "No can do, Wally."

No can laugh. What means word laugh, Wally?

And every night, it would sit beside me and stroke my hair while I fell asleep. I was going to miss that, even if I didn't starve to death. I went into the museum, willing myself not to cry. Anyway, what if it *does* come back? What if the ships never come again? What if I have to stay here forever? All by myself? Me and, maybe, if I'm lucky, the damn robot?

No, not forever.

I was barely sixteen years old, though.

What if I had to stay here for fifty years?

Fifty years eating my own synthetic flesh.

I got goose bumps, standing under the museum dome, standing in front of the useless goddamned star map. "Where the fuck *am* I?" My voice echoed under the dome, silencing me.

I walked over to the history section, to where I'd left off on the first day, to the aisles that dealt with what'd happened after the thrintun had made first contact, had been welcomed into the

Galactic Federation, if that's what it was. There was a whole section of cool little dioramas there, each one showing a single thrint surrounded by another sort of being, behind them all, a deep image of another world, pink suns and green, yellow skies, blue, purple, gold, you name it. Usually, there was stuff like vegetation in a color complementing the sky, as with Earth, with its blue sky and green trees.

Like God had a plan of some kind.

My favorite diorama was a world with a pale, pale yellow sky, just a hint of yellow, a world that seemed to be all tall buildings and not much else, the aliens' version of Trantor, maybe? There were lots of different beings here, scattered among them a lot of land crab robots, which helped to give it scale. In the sky over the buildings was a flying saucer, and when you looked closely, very deep in the sky, shadowed by its color, there was a spome, obviously hanging in space, so big you could see it in orbit from the ground.

Are they all still out there? I wondered.

Or are they all gone?

What if all these worlds are as empty as this one, as the others I'd seen so far? I'd started thinking of it as the Lost Empire sometimes, wondering what could possibly have happened. Did the robot know? I'd asked, more than once, but had so far gotten no answer.

Either it didn't know, or didn't know how to tell.

Then a piping voice said, "Wally?"

My heart seized in my chest, then I spun around, "You're . . . *uh.*"

I'd been going to say, *You're back!*, but the thing before me . . . was not a robot at all. Certainly not *my* robot. About the same size, but . . . pale gray skin. Big black eyes, slightly slanted. Noseless face. Lipless mouth. Two fingers and a thumb on each hand. Fleshy bird-feet.

More or less, I thought, like the beings they put on those Saucer books, paperbacks at Drug Fair competing for rack space with the science fiction I read. Who was it read that stuff? Kenny. Kenny, who would get something by Charles Fort when Murray and I would be buying *Prince of Peril* or whatever Andre Norton title was out. What'd that book been called? *Lo!?* Something like that.

The being stepped toward me, lifting one of those peculiarly familiar hands. "I'm sorry I startled you."

"Who . . ." What?

It said, "It's me, Wally."

Uhhh . . . "Robot?"

The gash of a mouth seemed to smile. "Well, you can still call me that if you want, but I went for an upgrade. I'm really more of an artificial man now."

Artificial . . . an inane voice yammered in my head: What, then? Tor-Dur-Bar? Pinocchio? I remembered the joke about "my only begotten son" and sort of snickered.

The robot said, "Come on, Wally. Let's go home. You must be starving." Its intonation, I noticed, had suddenly gotten much better.

So. Nighttime. I lay on the floor, wrapped up in a blanket Robot'd produced from who knows where or God knows what, listening to the hiss of the evening rain, alien room suffused with a soft orange light. Even if I had a book, I wouldn't have been able to read it in this.

But I wanted a book anyway.

I kept my head down, chin tucked in, trying to lose myself somehow. Think about all the books you've read. Jesus. I'd read *thousands* of books, it was practically all I did! Why couldn't I remember them better?

I started again, imagining myself to be Ghek, slinking alone through the darkness below the pits of Manator, drinking the Ulsios' blood, finding myself on the cliff over the subterranean river, the one he assumed might wind up flowing toward . . . Omean? The Lost Sea of Korus? Hell. Started to drift back . . .

But I was Tars Tarkas, struggling to get my fat ass through the hole in the base of the tree, while John Carter defended me from the Plant Men, no wait, Carthoris . . . the pimalia blossoms, the garden in Ptarth, Thuvia . . .

No use, me again, though now wondering about the reproductive systems of the Red Martians. Monotremes, obviously. I remembered we'd seen this film in science class one time, the biologist in the film flipping over a platypus, everyone in the class giggling nervously at the hairy slit on its belly. He'd pried open the slit, to more giggles, then . . . *damn!* There's an *egg* in there! So, what then? When John Carter fucks Dejah Thoris, does he find himself bumping into an egg? What'll we call it, my incomparable princess of Helium? In my imagination, while they talked, old Johnny kept on humping her and . . .

Oh, great. Now I had a hard-on. One of those real tingly ones meaning I'd probably come even if I kept my hands off it. On the other hand . . . right.

I flipped back the blanket, rolling onto my back, wrapping my fingers around the damned thing and . . . stopped, stock still. Robot was standing impassively over by the bathroom door, arms folded across its pale gray chest, featureless black eyes glinting in the orange light.

After a minute, it said, "Is something wrong, Wally?"

I could feel the nice hard-on start to go spongy on me.

Then it said, "Would you like me to help?"

To my horror, my dick hardened right back up, Dejah Thoris's weird monotreme crotch displaced by an image of two-fingers-and-thumb reaching for me, as I remembered doing myself in the tub only a few days before, bright steel robot watching impassively from the door, red eyes motionless, expressionless, merely light bulbs stolen from a Christmas tree.

It said, "Your facial skin is changing color, Wally. Turning pink. That never happened before."

My dick shrank out of my hand, suddenly soft and little again. Littler than usual. Kind of puckered. I said, "Uh. Sorry. It's . . . kind of different now. I . . ."

What *did* I want? Did I *want* it to help? A sudden vision of a difficult reality. The one where I live here, along with this thing, until I was old and dead. No pussy for you, dude.

Robot seemed to smile, making me think of all those jokes I'd been hearing at school for years. It. *It.* Not *he* for gosh sakes. It'd be like jerking off in a sock. A very friendly and helpful sock. It said, "I'll be in the kitchen if you need me. Call out when you're done. I'll bring some warm milk to help you sleep."

Then it was gone.

I wrapped the blanket around myself, suddenly feeling very cold indeed.

Did you ever wake up directly from a dream? No, that's not right. Did you ever wake up *in* a dream? The dream is running along, telling its tale, real as life, and suddenly you're there as *you*, knowing it's a dream, thinking about it *as* a dream, while the story continues to run.

In my dream, it was summer, June I think, and I was maybe ten or eleven years old. Fifth or sixth grade, so maybe it was 1961 or 1962? Maybe school was just about to end, or just over, which'd put it no later than maybe June 8 or thereabouts.

We were down by the big clearing, big patch of bare dirt down by the end of Carter Lane, across from Kenny's house, where, sometimes, we could get together enough boys to play a real sandlot baseball game, back where the creek came in sight of the road, where they'd build that big private pool, the one where my parents refused to buy a family membership in time for the summer of 1963. Right now, it was just scraggly woods and swampy ground, bare dirt ending suddenly where the ground sloped off down to the creek.

The little blonde girl and I were sitting on the horizontal trunk of a not-quite-fallen tree, looking at each other. What was her name? Of course I remember. It was Tracy, my age, in my grade and school, though not in my class. I only saw her out on the playground, at recess, and here on weekends.

Blonde, blue eyes, pale face, searching look. Thin, no sign of the adult she might one day become. Not yet. Her hair was done up in long braids that were wrapped round and round and pinned at the crown. Once, I'd asked her how come she always wore it that way.

"You'd be so pretty with your hair worn long and brushed out."

That searching look, blue eyes reaching for my childish soul. "My mom thinks it makes me look too grown up."

"Would you take it down for me now?"

I don't remember that I ever saw her smile. Not a sad little girl, just so serious. More like me than anyone else I'd ever met.

She said, "I can't get it back like this by myself. Mom would kill me." For once, the frown faded away. "I wish I could though. I'd do it for you, Wally."

I could smile, and I did.

In dreams, you can see a future that didn't happen.

A couple of eleven year olds fall in love, despite the fact that her mom didn't want her "too grown up," despite the fact she never said a word about her dad, or just why she was so . . . not sad. Just so serious. Whatever it was, it made her see right into me. Maybe those two eleven year olds could've waited out the decade it would take, and, free at last, live happily ever after?

In real life, that was the day she told me her dad had been transferred, that she'd be moving away to Texas. When? Tomorrow. In the morning.

Then she'd looked up at the sun, shading her eyes, and said, "I better get on home. Mom doesn't know I'm out here." To my astonishment, when we stood up, she gave me a hug, fierce and strong, then turned and ran.

I'd walked home in the noonday sun, feeling that burn in my throat that means you want to cry, but can't. Mom was making lunch when I got there, tuna salad sandwiches with too much chopped celery. She'd looked at me, and said, "What's wrong?" Felt my head, looking for a fever.

I opened my eyes on the pink light of a Lost Empire morning, and Robot was sitting cross-legged by my side, slowly stroking my hair, which was getting pretty long, and rather greasy from the lack of shampoo. How do primitives clean their hair? I . . .

Rolled away hard, heart pounding.

It said, "I'm sorry, Wally. I won't do that anymore, if it bothers you."

I swallowed, wishing I'd stop waking up with an erection. Futile hope. "No. No. You just startled me. I can't get used to you like that."

"I'm sorry. It's not reversible."

I felt my face flush. "Never mind. It's okay."

"You want breakfast now?"

"Sure." Tuna fish sandwiches? Surely we can figure this out? As it stood up, I found myself looking at its featureless crotch.

Not quite featureless. Kind of a faint divided bump, like you see on some of the neighborhood moms in their tight, white summer shorts.

Unbidden, as Robot turned away, heading for the kitchen, I wondered about "upgrades." Even from the back, you could see the shape was there, if not the details. Like a girl in gray coveralls.

The image of Tracy came up, briefly, from the dream. Not the shape of her, which, at that age, hadn't been much different from mine. Just the face, the eyes, the hair.

So. Robot can give me a hand job. It's already volunteered. And you've already managed to think of a blow job on your own, you sick bastard. What kind of upgrades are available? Just stuff thrintun would know about? What good is that? Other races of the Lost Empire?

Maybe the Saucer People from those paperbacks were real, and this was the closest thing to a human Robot could get for itself, from its stash of upgrades? So it tried hard for me when I describe food and stuff I'd like it to make. Remember the ice cream? Not to mention the "soap."

Heh.

That tasty soap. I'd had it again already, for dessert.

So what if I asked it to grow a pussy for me, as an upgrade?

What would I ask for?

I'd seen my sisters in the bathtub from time to time. Not much to work with there. An accidental glimpse of my mom one summer, changing her clothes in a room with the door open, her not knowing she was reflected in a mirror. Hell, I was maybe five years old back then. She probably didn't care if I saw her. Not yet.

I remembered I'd been startled by the black hair.

What else?

Well, there was a diagram in one of our encyclopedias. A line drawing labeled "vulva" that didn't make much sense.

Those magazines, the ones Murray's dad kept down in the basement? Nothing. I knew enough about human anatomy and the mechanics of commercial art to know those women's pussies had been swept away by something called an airbrush.

I snickered, and thought, Jesus. Maybe I'd better just stick with soap? Maybe when I can get it to make me a cake of

Lifebuoy, we'll try something more complicated?

Out in the kitchen, it was just finishing up making me some sliced meat, solid this time, rare and juicy, to go with my mug of milk. We'd tried for bread a few times, and wound up with something like grayish Play-Doh that tasted more like soap than the soap had.

I put my hand gingerly on its shoulder, realizing that I was really tired of this bland diet of sweet milk and venison-pork. "Robot?"

"Yes, Wally."

"Can you help me get back home?"

It turned toward me, giving me a long, long look out of those empty black eyes. "Are you so lonely, Wally?"

I swallowed past a tight spot in my throat and nodded, unable to speak. Yes, damn you. I miss everything about my nasty little life. Even the bad stuff. That hurt too. I wouldn't have imagined I would, just like I didn't imagine I'd miss my dad 'til he was gone.

It said, "How much do you know about accelerated frames of reference, and probabilistic space-time attractors?"

"Well . . ."

That same long look continued. "Eat your breakfast, Wally. Take your bath, then we'll see what we can do."

By midmorning, it'd led me back through the town and out to the so-called spaceport once more. Led me out onto the empty concrete apron, off to one side, reddish-yellow sunshine warm and smarmy on my bare skin. I almost skipped my shoes this time, but Robot told me not to.

"No sense getting a stubbed toe, is there?"

Which made me remember when I was a little kid, pre-school, going to the beach with my mother's family. We'd lived in Massachusetts then, some little town outside Boston, and the beaches of New England are rocky indeed. Where did we used to go? Not Nantucket. That's an island where rich bastards live. Nantasket? That's it. I remember Grandpa took me to see a beached freighter one time.

Anyway, stubbed toes. Lots of them.

Robot said, "Stand over here, Wally. Right by me."

Then it raised its hands, making a slow sort of Gandalfish gesture.

My stomach lurched as we suddenly rose in the air, taking a patch of concrete with us. "*Hey!*"

"Stand still, Wally."

As the thing on which we stood went up and up, things like antennae, like giant radiotelescopes, like Jodrell Bank, like stuff on TV, began unfolding down below, swinging up into sight.

I whispered, "'Open, sez me.'" What's that from? A Popeye cartoon?

The upward movement stopped, and suddenly a hatchway opened in the concrete between us. Robot gestured toward it, "Shall we, Wally?"

"What is this?"

"The spaceport information nexus and interstellar communications center."

"Oh." Muted.

Down inside was a room just like the main room of an airport control tower, complete with outward leaning windows and things like radar screens. Lots and lots of twinkly little lights, too. Red, green, blue, yellow, you name it.

It started waving its fingers at the lights and, outside, various antennae started groaning around, aiming this way and that, nodding upward to the great green sky.

"What're you going to do? Are you calling Earth?"

The empty black eyes fixed on me again. "No, Wally. I can only call installations with the same sort of subspace communication systems as these."

"Oh. Then . . ."

It said, "I need to find out what's happened, Wally, before I can know what's to be done, if anything." *If anything?* I felt sick. Then it said, "This will take a while. I assume you can find your way to the museum from here?"

"Well, of course." Robot thought I was stupid, did it? Maybe so. How many people accidentally stow away on an automated space probe and wound up stranded on a deserted planet?

"I'll meet you there in time for supper. That elevator cage

over there will take you down to ground level." Then it turned away and resumed playing with all the little lights, while the big antennae creaked and moaned.

I stood and watched for a while, at a loss. What do I want? Do I really want to go home again, back to a pathetic little life that showed no promise of ever getting better? What if the Empire's *not* Lost? What if the saucers come again, this time full of light and life, full of things ever so much better than people?

What if there's *real* adventure to be had?

Eventually, I got in the elevator cage and went on my way, wondering if I could find something to do.

Take a while turned out to be an understatement. Two, three, four days and I gave up going out to the spaceport, gave up watching the antennae wig-wag around, gave up watching the little lights twinkle, reflected in Robot's slanty goggle eyes.

Eyes like fucking sunglasses.

What's under them, ole buddy, ole pal?

It'd make me breakfast, make me something I could save for lunch, and would head on out, leaving me alone for the day, like a man going off to work, leaving his wife alone to fend for herself.

I remember my mom used to scream about that, back before the breakup. Dad'd come home from work, wanting nothing more than his supper and a quiet evening in front of the TV, and Mom would snipe and snipe, "I sit here all day long, looking at these same four goddamned walls. I want to get *out* once in a while!"

He'd look at her, lying on the couch in his boxer shorts, bleary eyed. "I'm tired."

You could see a kind of red light behind her eyes then. "Tired? Well, you won't be quite so tired later on tonight, I know that."

"Bitch."

Now he was gone, and Mom had a job of her own from which to come home tired. We were eating a lot of macaroni and cheese then. Macaroni and cheese, and meatloaf. I wondered if she thought about him sometimes, about how tired he'd been, and how she felt now?

On day five, it got dark before Robot came home. I was getting hungry, starting to worry, just the way Mom seemed to worry when Dad would be late getting home from work on nights when the traffic on U.S. 1 clogged to a standstill. Should I go on out to the spaceport and see what was up? What if it wasn't there? What if it started to rain while I was out?

Then the door opened and Robot came in, moving rather slowly, it seemed. "Sorry I'm late. I'll get your supper now."

I followed it out to the kitchen, and, as it touched the blue lights over the trough, beginning the process that would extrude my meat, would fill my mug with milk, it seemed to move as though exhausted.

"Are you all right?"

Scooping hot meatloaf onto a plate, it said, "This organic form is difficult to master. It seems I required another minor physiological upgrade." Then it pulled a second steaming plate from the trough, more meatloaf just like the first, and two cups of cool yellow milk. "Come on, we'll eat together."

We settled on the living room floor and I started in. Robot picked up a chunk of meat in its hand, turning it over and over, as if nonplused.

That's me, I thought. "What's wrong?"

It looked at me. "I have some inhibitions about eating what seems like it must come from a living being."

"Synthetic."

"When I was really a robot, I knew that. The organic processor seems to have a little difficulty with the concept."

"Hey, if I don't mind eating myself, why should you?"

"True." It popped the glob of ground wally in its mouth and started to chew. And I felt myself grow goose bumps.

Afterward, we had ice cream, sweeter now than before, with something very much like the vanilla flavor I'd been wanting. Robot took a taste, and said, "This is good. Maybe next time I can make it better, now that I'm getting some idea of what it's supposed to be like."

But it put the plate down, hardly touched.

I put out my hand, not quite touching its arm. "Tell me what's really wrong."

Something very like a sigh. "Oh, many things, Wally."

I felt chillier inside than the ice cream would account for. "Such as?"

"I can't figure out how to get you home."

"Oh."

"And I can't figure out what's happened to my civilization, either. I don't know where they've gone. Or why they're gone." It pushed the other plate of ice cream toward me. "You have this please."

"Sure."

After a while, I said, "Do you even know where we are?"

"Yes. My galaxy. My world."

"In the same galaxy as Earth?"

"I don't think so, Wally."

"Oh."

I finished the ice cream and Robot took the dishes away, walking slowly. By the time it got back, I was shaking out my blanket, starting to settle down to sleep, wishing again I had a book, any book. Christ, I'd settle for *Green Mansions* or *Lord Jim* now. Even *The Red Badge of Courage*.

Robot stood there, looking down on me, arms hanging loosely by its sides, looser than I'd ever seen, more than just exhausted. I threw back the blanket and patted a spot on the floor by my side. "Come on. If you need to eat now, maybe you need to sleep too."

It curled up with me under the blanket. After a minute, it grew warm, than another minute and I guess I went to sleep.

I awoke, eyes shut, not quite knowing what I'd been dreaming. Some real-life thing, I suppose, nothing bad, or the dream would still be a vivid shape in my heart. Something warm on my chest, not quite like hugging my extra pillow. And, of course, the usual hard on, but somehow compressed and tight, pushed against the base of my belly.

Oh, God. I'm hugging Robot!

I started to let go, trying not to panic, wondering what the hell was tickling the end of my nose.

Forced my eyes open. There was a neck right in front of my face. A skinny neck with Caucasian-white skin, rising into wisps of pale blonde hair. Long blonde hair drawn up into tight braids, braids wrapped round and round . . .

I think every muscle in my body went into some tetanus-like spasm. I took a deep breath, so fast and tight my voice made this weird, high-pitched whoop, recoiled, rolling away, up onto my hands and knees, taking the blanket with me, crouching there, bug-eyed again, heart pounding like mad.

Pulling the blanket away like that spilled the naked girl over onto her face. She lifted her head and looked at me, out of bleary blue eyes, and whispered, "Wally . . . ?" her voice sounding tired and confused.

And I made that exact same sound Jackie Gleason used to make, dumbfounded in almost every *Honeymooners* episode, *humminahummina* . . .

She sat up slowly, turning to face me, sitting cross-legged, eyes brightening as she woke up, just the way a human wakes up. Pale skin, smooth all over, little pink nipples on a smooth, flat chest, snub nose with a little pale spray of freckles, big, *big* blue eyes, naked as a jaybird, but for the brass-colored bobby pins holding up her braids.

"Good morning, Wally!"

I sat down hard. Swallowed. Or tried to, anyway. "*Tracy?*"

She cocked her head to one side and smiled, filling the room with sunshine. "I think so, Wally. Anyway, this is the girl you've been dreaming about."

"My . . . *dreams.*"

Funny thing. Usually when your mouth goes dry, it just *is* dry, all at once, or maybe before you notice it. This time, I felt my spit absorbed by my tongue, like water sucked into a dry sponge.

She said, "Yes, Wally."

What was the name of that story? Silverberg, was it? In the *Seventh Galaxy Reader* or maybe *Best from F&SF,* Seventh Series. The one where the telepath sees peoples' thoughts as run-on sentences connected by ampersand characters.

"You can . . . read my mind." Flat. Nervous. Sick.

She stood slowly, stretching like a real human, as though stiff from sleep, hips slim, just the littlest bit of fine blonde pubic hair in a patch above that little pink slit.

Eleven years old, I thought. I remembered most of the girls in junior high started to grow tits when they were in seventh grade.

She saw where I was looking and smiled, then said, "Sort of. Not as well as I'd like to." Then gave me a funny look. "How do you think I learned to speak English? From listening to you chatter?"

I snatched my eyes away, feeling my face heat up. Yes. That's *exactly* what I'd thought. "Uh. Does that bother you? My talking all the time?" It bothered a lot of people, including my parents. I think it even bothered Murray, though most of the time he was willing to listen.

She said, "Oh, no, Wally! I love talking to you!" Eyes brightening. I suddenly remembered Tracy'd said that to my eleven-year-old self, once upon a time. Then this Tracy—*Robot* a hard voice in my head snarled—said, "This is the coolest thing that's ever happened to me!"

Ever happened to Tracy? Or to Robot? I said, "Yeah, me too." I curled myself into a seated ball, knees against my chest, heels pressed together, wishing the goddamned hard-on would go away. Bathroom. You just need to take a piss, that's all.

Tracy . . . No! For Christ's sake. *Robot!* Robot's bright blue eyes were on my face, filled with something that could pass for empathy. The empathy in a story, anyway. She came over to where I sat, kneeling down, put a warm gentle hand on one of my knees, leaning so she could look right into my eyes.

It. It, not *her*.

I don't think there's a word for how scared I was, right then.

She said, "Would you like to try the thing you've been dreaming about, Wally? There's not enough detail in your dreams for me to work with, but your genetic matrix may have contributed enough X-chromosome-based hardware and instinctual behaviors to get us started."

I flinched, aghast, at Robot, at myself. Stuttered hard, finally got out, "But . . . you're still a *child!*" The real Tracy, my Tracy, would be sixteen right now, more or less grown. This . . . *thing* . . .

She sank back on her heels, looking sad, just the way the real Tracy had looked sad, sad and serious. "I'm sorry, Wally. I didn't know that would matter."

For breakfast, Robot managed something a lot like bland French toast, with a lemon-yellow glob of something I suppose you could call wallybutter, though nothing like maple syrup, not even the imitation nasty Mrs. Butterworth's crap my sisters demanded, just so they could see the bottle and repeat the "when you bow down this way!" line from the commercial.

Every time they did that, I'd remember my own infatuation with the Log Cabin tin less than a decade earlier. It seemed different, somehow.

Robot brought the plate to me as I soaked in the tub, chirping, "See, Wally? I'll figure out a way to make you real bread yet!" Then she stepped over the rim of the tub and sank down at the opposite end with a cozy little grin, chin barely clearing the surface of the water.

"Uh." I looked at the pile of sticky squares, steam rising, yellow butter-stuff slumping as it melted. "Is some of this yours?"

She took a square, dipped one corner in the butter, and took a bite. "Mmmmm . . ."

Afterward, clean and dry after a fashion, Robot's hair clean anyway, since it was brand new, we set out, I in my grubby shoes and socks because Robot insisted, though she herself was barefoot, feet slapping quickly on the pavement to match my pace. I'd thought about putting on my clothes, but they were still draped over the railing, so weathered and stiff now I suppose they would've felt like crumpled newspaper on my skin.

I settled for keeping my eyes to myself as I followed her down the road. "Where're we going, Robot?" She turned suddenly, stopping before me in the street, looking up at my face, eyes bigger still, going back to looking . . . not sad. Wistful? Maybe that was the way Tracy had looked, not sad, not serious, and the eleven-year-old me just hadn't known any better?

Softly, she said, "I'd like it if you call me Tracy."

Thunderstruck, I thought, This is a *robot*. Not a little girl. Not Tracy. Tracy, *my* Tracy, is sixteen years old, somewhere on Earth, probably still in Texas, and I . . . that other voice, dark voice that sounded to me like my dad's voice, whispered, It's just a robot. And *if* it's just a robot, what difference does it make if . . . ? I slammed the door on that one.

Then I said, "I'm sorry. Tracy."

She smiled. Brightening the day.

"So. Where're we going?"

She pointed to the dome of the museum, not far away in the middle of the town, where all the radial streets came together.

Inside, she led me right to the big blue-white-red spiral galaxy hanging under the dome, standing beside it with hands on hips, head tipped back, looking up. I wondered briefly where the bobby pins had come from, other than my memory, my dreams. From the hemoglobin in my blood? And what about the brassy color? Shouldn't they be steely-looking? Tracy's bobby pins had been brassy, though. Maybe there were copper molecules in the tissue sample.

Tracy started manipulating a panel of sequins down by the pedestal, and the galaxy vanished, replaced by a shapeless, irregular splash of light and dark that looked almost like an explosion.

She looked up at me. "This is what your culture has just begun to conceptualize as a Supercluster, Wally. It's a map of the entity you've been referring to as the Lost Empire."

My scalp prickled briefly at that reminder, but . . . hell. I was *used* to the idea of telepaths. Maybe that's what made it more all right for me than it would have been for somebody else. I imagined my mom thinking someone could look into her head.

It didn't look like anything I remembered hearing about. Still, if she knew the term, it had to be in my head, somewhere. Some article in *Scientific American,* maybe? I'd always been glad the Prince William County Public Library took it. "How big?"

She said, "Oh, it's about three hundred million light years across, maybe." Off to one side, a pinpoint sparkled, catching my eye. "That's where we are right now."

"And . . . Earth?"

She said, "You don't know enough about the structure of the universe for me to tell."

"Uh. Sorry."

She grinned, then made another pinpoint twinkle, way off to the other side, pretty much outside the edge of the great splash of light. "Your Local Group might be right there. There are five galaxies matching what you know as the Milky Way, Andromeda, Triangulum, and the Magellanic Clouds, in roughly the right positions, though you're awfully hazy about where they really are, and exactly how big."

"Sorry."

"And there are at least twenty other galaxies mixed in with them that your astronomers must have noticed."

"But not me."

"No, Wally."

"Well, even if that *was* Earth, there's no way . . ."

She made a third spot sparkle, this time deep ruby-red, deep in the heart of the Lost Empire Supercluster. "There's a research facility here, at one of the Empire's main educational institutions, where we can . . . figure it out, one way or another."

"But . . ."

She said, "If we could get a starship, we could get there in just a few weeks, Wally."

I suddenly felt odd. "And . . . Earth?"

That wistful look. "If that's really your Local Group, not much longer."

"Where else would Earth be?"

She said, "Wally, the thing you were on was an automated space probe, just like you thought. We'd been exploring the other superclusters for a long time."

"So Earth could be anywhere?" For some reason, that made me feel . . . I don't know. Lighter. More carefree?

She said, "Yes."

"What if it's somewhere on the other side of the universe?"

She laughed. "There's no 'other side,' Wally."

"Very far away, anyhow. Your ships seem so fast."

She said, "If Earth's not somewhere nearby, we may never find it. You seem to have no idea how big the universe really is."

"One of your probes found it."

"Yes. And that may be our only hope. The probes didn't have infinite range."

"Anyway, we don't have a starship."

She turned away from me then, looking out through the dome of the museum, up at the deep green sky. "I don't know where everyone's gone, or why, but the communication network is running just fine. I've been able to wake up some sleeping nodes here and there, send out program code, get a few things moving. Our ride will be here soon."

Then she looked at me and laughed again, I suppose, at the expression on my face.

And so the empty world of the dark green skies was gone, never to be seen again, Tracy and I now camped out by a bubbling stream in the soft garden wilderness of a pale orange spome, pale orange landscape separated by broad stripes of blue velvet hyperspace sky. There were no dinosaurs here, and I was, in a way, sorry for that, because I'd liked them, liked the idea of them; but red-silver butterfly-bats floated through the air over-head, perched in the pale orange trees, while spidermice crept through the pale orange grass, speaking to us in gentle whispers.

Only little things, gentle things, safe things.

Arriving here, we'd walked away from the field of saucers, this one without fence or razor wire, while the Green Planet shrank away to nothing in the starry sky, and Tracy said to me, "No, look, you got it all wrong, Wally. *Thrintun* was the name of their planet. The Slavers just called themselves Thrint."

"Are you sure?"

She smiled. "That's what's in your long-term memory. Your short-term memory just reloaded it wrong. Of course, I can't guarantee it's what was really in the story."

"Um."

She'd led me to a long, low, warehouse-like building, where we picked up magic toys, then walked away into the woodland while the starship groaned off into hyperspace and the windows above us turned soft blue, in perfect contrast to the landscape, both around us and overhead. Eventually, we came to a meadow: orange grass, widely separated orange trees, kind of like gnarly little crabapple trees, complete with little orange fruit, a scatter-ing of ruddy yellowish flowers, tiny creek chuckling over bits of round brown stone.

We set up the tent, spread our picnic blanket, and one of the magic toys Tracy had taken turned out to be something like a hibachi, complete with built-in burgers, already smoky hot, smell making my mouth water.

I touched one, and found it cool enough to pick up, the perfect temperature for eating. "What are these things?"

She said, "I don't know. But they're chemically compatible with our bodies."

When you looked close, they weren't really hamburgers. Bready disks of some kind, nicely toasted. I took a little bite. "Ukh . . ."

A fleck of concern lit in her eyes. "Not good?"

I took another, bigger bite, chewed and swallowed. "Weird. Mustard and cinnamon don't really go together."

She smiled. "I notice it's not stopping you, though."

"No." I finished it, and took another. "Can this thing make hot dogs?"

"Probably."

Hot dogs with integrated buns. Great. In what book did I read the phrase, *societé anonyme d'hippophage?* I gave my head a shake, trying to banish nonsense. If possible. Christ. Me. Anyway, I'm not eating wally anymore. Good enough.

I said, "Who used to live in this place, Tracy? I mean, orange grass and all . . . ?"

She said, "Nobody ever lived in these things, Wally. They were part of an automated transport system, and I think what happened is, the sample ecologies spread out in here. The spomes have been wandering around on their own for a very long time."

"How long?"

A thoughtful look. "Well, from the time the first star-faring civilization got started to my manufacture date, something like a billion of your years."

My mouth got that familiar dry feeling. "That's not what I meant."

She said, "Based on astronomical evidence, I think I was asleep in storage for a significant fraction of that. Perhaps a hundred million years?"

"From before the end of the Cretaceous, and whatever killed off the dinosaurs?" And clearly why the robot spomes could have them in their possession. I remember some scientists theorized about a supernova.

She said, "I don't think there was any relationship. Wherever Earth is, it must be outside the range of the event that . . . got rid of everyone." A momentary look of intense brooding in the eyes of a china doll, quickly banished.

"And you have no idea how the Lost Empire got lost."

"Not yet. It's illuminating that only the organic intelligences were lost."

"It's hard for me to believe this," I waved my hand around the spomey landscape, "all this, all the stuff on all the planets, has survived, intact, for a hundred million years or more."

Another smile. "Not unattended, Wally. Just unpeopled."

"Oh. Right."

I lay back and looked at the sky again, staring at blue hyperspace, wondering what would become of me. What if we find Earth? What then? Just go home? I tried picturing that, imagined myself appearing, bareass, back in Dorvo Valley, with a naked little blonde girl holding my hand: "Hi, Mom! Sorry I'm late! Hey, look what I found!"

Tracy said, "You have an erection again, Wally."

I rolled away from her, curling up around myself, facing down slope, toward the trees and little creek. "Sorry."

She said, "Look, I know we can't do the thing you've been dreaming about, not without risking damage to some components of this immature body, but I can still help with those other things."

I thought, "What about damage to me?"

After a long moment, she reached out and touched my back softly, making me flinch. Then she said, "I *will* grow up, you know. This body is as real as your genome could make it."

I said, "You're eleven, Tracy. It'll be a while before you're all grown up."

She said, "I'll be physically mature enough for successful intercourse in no more than twelve to eighteen months, if you really want to wait."

I looked over my shoulder at her, baffled. "I can't believe I'm talking about this stuff with a little girl."

Softly, she said, "I'm not a little girl, Wally. I'm a robot, remember?"

I looked away again, remembering she'd wanted to be called Tracy, rather than Robot.

Another girlish sigh. "It's so hard for me to know what's right, Wally. Your memories of your real cultural surround are all mixed up with what was in those stories you loved. As if your culture itself were somehow confused. As if it couldn't distinguish between dream and reality."

That made me laugh. Really laugh.

To Tracy's disappointment, what she called the Master Planet seemed to lie in ruins. And *what* ruins!

Ruins, real ruins, were thin on the ground for an American boy in the 1960s. I remember Murray and I used to argue about that, as we tried to write stories about our imaginary Venus, Murray wanting ruins to be like Pompeii, like the Coliseum, seen in books, in movies, on TV. Like one of Burroughs's African lost cities, or like Koraad on Barsoom. Murray'd never seen a real ruin, having traveled so little, having lived only in New York City and the suburbs of Washington, D.C. I'd lived in the Southwest, and my parents had taken me to see Mesa Verde, to visit Chaco Canyon.

Real ruins, of real abandoned cities, sitting out in the weather for hundreds of years, are different from maintained ruins, like the Coliseum, or cities preserved under volcanic ash for thousands of years. Burroughs was in the Army in the 1890s and served in the Southwest. Why didn't he know that?

The cityscapes of the Master Planet were like that: stumps of buildings with their foundations exposed; crumbled, fallen walls; a sense of haze and dust everywhere.

We stood by our flying saucer, and Tracy said, "Whatever happened, happened here. And there was nothing left behind to keep things up."

Keep things up, I thought, awaiting the owners' return.

In the end, a few days later, we wound up on something Tracy referred to as a "substation," some adjunct of the Master Planet, one of many apparently scattered round the Lost Empire. From space, seen out the saucer window, it looked like a little blue moon, hardly a planet at all, a little blue moon surrounded by ghostly white radiance, and, though I looked and looked, nothing else nearby. No sun. Not even an especially bright star. No gas giant for it to orbit. No nothing.

On the ground—well, no; not ground—the place was like a cityscape, but the buildings were made of something like sheet metal, tin, copper, zinc, varicolored anodized aluminum, streets paved with sheets of rolled gold, nothing but metal everywhere but the sky.

From under the saucer's rim, I just stood there, looking up, at a pitch-black sky flooded with so many stars it lit up the landscape, making a million little shadows in every dark corner.

"*Man . . .*"

Every now and again, there'd be the quick yellow streak of a meteor.

"Where the hell are we?" Up in the sky, it was as if there were some shapes hiding behind the stars, faint washes of light that disappeared when I looked at them.

Tracy put one cool hand on the small of my back, making my neck hair tingle. "We're in an irregular galaxy. There's a lot of dust. Nebulae. Lots of really young stars."

Like a Magellanic Cloud. I, uh . . . "Was this galaxy even here a hundred million years ago?"

"Yes. These galaxies evolve fast and don't last as long as the spirals, but they're not ephemeral. They also don't have much in the way of naturally habitable planets. We used them as resource centers. Industrial complexes."

We. My little Tracy, the Space Alien.

She said, "I've got a lot of work to do, Wally. Why don't you go sight-seeing? I'll find you later."

"Uh . . ." I felt a sudden chill, turning to look up at our saucer.

She smiled. "I won't let it go anywhere, Wally." She patted me on the arm, then turned and quickly walked away into the shadows.

Sight-seeing. Was there anything here to see? I started walking, but there wasn't much. Metal buildings. No, not even that. This kind of looked like the stuff inside a machine of some kind. Maybe an old TV. Except no vacuum tubes or anything. Like lifting the hood of a car and not knowing what you're looking at.

I remembered I always resented those boys who knew what cars were about. Resented that I couldn't learn, that Dad wouldn't let me help with our car. Goof, he'd say. You'll either break something or hurt yourself. When I was missing Dad, I wouldn't remember stuff like that.

Everybody was always mad at me about something.

There was something kind of like a lake. No, more like a pool. Round, but full of cool, fresh water, surrounded by a soft area. I wished for grass, but this stuff was more like a satin comforter stapled to a slanting floor. Nice to sit on naked, though.

A little too cool to sit here naked.

I went back to the saucer and got one of the picnic blankets we'd taken from the spome, came back to the little pool and sat again, all wrapped up, looking out over the ersatz cityscape, remembering that where my dad had taken German in college, Murray's dad had taken French, so Murray would say *faux*, where I said *ersatz*.

What if I could pick and choose my companions? Who would I bring here now?

Murray? Would I want Murray here with me now? My best friend since second grade, my best friend ever, maybe my only friend? I remember the day before I left, running into Murray in the high school corridor. Larry was standing with him, the two of them talking about something. They shut up when they saw me, Larry smiling, Murray's eyes full of that now-familiar contempt.

What the hell did I do to make this happen, Murray?

The longer I stared at the sky, the easier it was to see those shapes embedded in the deeper dark. All I had to do was not quite look at them, pretend to be looking at something else, but pay attention to the corners of my eyes, and shapes of wan light would pop out of nowhere.

If Murray was here, I guess I'd get some lecture about "averted vision," his eyes full of amusement as he showed me, once again, how really cool he was, how smart, how much better than me at everything and anything.

I felt my eyes start to burn, and had to put away all those

questions. Except: there's no one I want with me. No one at all to go back to. Why is that?

Three meteor trails burned overhead, dazzling yellow, side by side in the sky, like a long, hot cat-scratch. Maybe I dozed after that.

—Came back from wherever, not knowing if I'd slept or not, for the sky was unchanged. Darkness, stars, and the faint shapes beyond. Jumped slightly at the shadow standing by the rim of the pool's little arena, girl-shape looking down at me.

"Tracy?"

She walked down across the satin groundcover, until she was close enough to see by starlight, eyes vast, face so soft and lovely. What would've happened if you hadn't moved away, five years ago? Nothing. Your mom would've found out about us, would've talked to my mom, and we'd've been ordered apart, "just to be safe." Boys and girls that age aren't allowed to like each other.

Something wrong though, here and now.

I said, "Are you all right? You look sick."

She kneeled down beside me, and I could see there was a shine of sweat on her.

"What's wrong?"

She said, "I'll be all right. I had to have a little more work done on myself, while I was at it. They have much better equipment here than back on the Green Planet." She seemed to shiver.

"Oh, Tracy . . ." I gathered her in and wrapped the blanket about us both. She was hot and clammy, not that dry heat like when you have a fever; more like something inside was heating her up, making her sweat, making the night feel cold.

When I was about five, my grandpa, who died drunk, got me to drink a glass of whiskey, laughing when he saw I could get it down without gagging. It made me sweat like that, once it was inside. I remember my mom went apeshit over it, cussing Grandpa like I'd never heard before, but there was nothing to be done. All I did was go to sleep, and wake up the next day feeling like I was full of helium and ready to float away.

She snuggled in close, arms around the barrel of my chest, her sweat getting on me, starting to run down in my lap, making me shiver too. "I'll be all right. Really." Hardly more than a whisper.

Well, then.

She said, "I found the Earth."

Smarmy pang of fear. "Um . . ."

She said, "Really not that far. No more than two hundred million parsecs. On the far side of the next supercluster from here."

"How long?"

I could feel her face change shape against my chest. A smile? She said, "Well that depends."

"On?"

She squeezed me a little bit, shivering a little harder. "Well, it only took you a few weeks to reach the Green Planet, so that's all it'll take to get back . . ."

Damn. Mom. School. Murray.

And no way I can explain where I've been, much less who this little girl might be. Sudden cold horror. When I get off the saucer in Dorvo Valley, Tracy, *my* Tracy now for sure, will get back aboard and go away?

There was a brief clicking sound, then she said, "But the hyperdrives are not immune to Relativity, Wally."

I thought about my homecoming, in those stiff old clothes waiting for me in the saucer, turning up at Mom's house on Staggs court, in, what? Maybe March 1967? By now, Apollo 1 will have flown. And I'll have to repeat the eleventh grade.

Yep, *that*'ll make Murray jealous, all right.

Then I said, "Huh?"

More clicking. "You left Earth twenty-three years ago, Wally." More clicking. "Some of that was lost in local travel." Clicking. "If I take you straight home from here, it's only another twenty." Clicking. "But only three weeks, starship time." She started to shudder really hard against me, and I realized the clicking sound was the chatter of her teeth. "God, you are really sick!"

Sweat was pouring off her now, running down between my legs and pooling on the satin. She said, "Just hold me, Wally. I'll be all right in the morning. I promise."

I wrapped the blanket tight around us both, feeling the heat increase, and just sat there, staring at the sky, while Tracy shivered and chattered, murmuring to herself, sometimes real words, sometimes things that sounded like foreign languages, nothing that made any sense.

Twenty-three years, I thought. 1989? And then another twenty?

Up in the sky, the stars marched slowly overhead, old ones setting, new ones rising, showing me the orientation of the blue moon's axis. Meteors would burn by ones and twos and threes, until I paid attention and found the swarm's radiant. That, I thought, must be the direction of our travel through interstellar space.

Once, something like a pink Bonestell moon appeared out of nowhere, just a dot in the sky at first, then swelling to a huge, pockmarked balloon, before shrinking away to nothing again.

After a long, long while, Tracy's shivering started to die down, her skin to cool. Maybe, I thought, the worst is over? After another long while, despite my determination to stay awake, to hold her, guard her, protect her, I fell asleep.

It was, of course, still dark when I awoke.

I was lying on my side under a sky full of stars, arms wrapped around Tracy, her back pressed to my chest, my face buried in the tickle of her hair, which had come loose from her braids. It wasn't wet with sweat any more, but seemed greasy, with a funny smell to it, not much like the dry wispy hair she'd had since she so magically appeared.

I had my usual erection, pressed up against her, painfully hard, harder than usual, in fact.

No more fever.

Her skin, rather cool, was no longer drenched with sweat either, and not dry. Kind of oily. Or greasy, like her hair.

Very cool. So very cool that . . .

I felt my heart start to thud in my chest.

Oh, Christ.

Something wrong with the way she feels, too, as if she's suddenly gotten fat. Or, loose. No more muscle tone, I . . .

I started to reach for her heart, holding my breath, terrorized, suppressing my thoughts, not wanting to know until I *knew*. What the hell will I *do*?

She stirred in my arms, taking a deep breath, making me

freeze. Took a deep breath, stiffened, seemed to stretch, then curled up a little tighter, flabby chest skin settling across one of my arms, the one that'd been reaching to feel for her heartbeat.

I whispered, "Tracy . . ."

Her voice was hoarse, and foggy, as if she were very, very tired. "Here, Wally."

I cupped part of her chest in my hand, and thought, "Wait just a second here . . ."

She twisted then, twisted over onto her back so she could turn toward me, eyes shining in starlight, teeth a flash of white in the shadows of her face. And then she said, "Accelerated maturation. Oh, I know I'm still a little small. I can't add mass overnight, but the machinery did figure out how to get me to end-stage pretty quickly."

She took me by the wrist, pulled my hand off her breast and dragged it down between her legs, down into the hot and wet of her, and said, "No more excuses, Wally."

To my amazement, I knew exactly what to do.

We stayed down by the lake, tangled together under the stars, until I got so hungry I started to get dizzy, even lying down. It was hard walking back to the saucer, not just leaving the magic shore, but because Tracy tried walking so close to me I kept tripping over her.

Finally, we settled for holding hands as we walked, and I couldn't stop smiling, feeling like I was flying through the air. Different. Different. This was . . .

I said, "I feel like a grown-up now! How can just one fuck make me feel so different?"

Tracy laughed, stopping and turning to face me, looking up, holding both of my hands in hers. "Well, more than one . . ."

Technically speaking, I guessed that was right.

"Do you want to go home now?"

My smile must have gone out like a light.

"Wally?"

I said, "Unless you've got time travel, my home's gone. I can't *imagine* what Earth must be like in 2009. Maybe there's been an atomic war by now."

I remember I'd tried to write a story when I was in the eighth grade, a story I called "Bomblast," set in the far future year of 1981. I'd known roughly how many nuclear weapons America had in 1963, then tried to extrapolate forward a couple of decades, and come up with something like thirty thousand warheads. Okay. So give the same to the Russians. Then I'd tried to imagine a war in which sixty thousand hydrogen bombs went off all on the same day.

I couldn't write the story, but I could imagine it.

Tracy said, "All those stories, and you still can't imagine 2009? What good were they?"

"I don't know."

She said, "If we don't take you home, then what do you want to do?"

I ran my hand down her bare back, and discovered she wasn't tall enough, or my arms long enough, to grab her by the ass.

She giggled. "If you don't think of anything else, that's all there *is* for us to do."

"Suits me."

She gave me a squeeze. "You'll get sick of it, sooner or later, Wally."

"Impossible."

"Well, let's go. We'll think of something, some day."

As we walked the rest of the way back to the saucer, I thought of something else. "Tracy?" She looked up. "Did you ever find out what happened to your people?"

She looked away for a second, putting her face in shadow. "I wasn't really *people*, Wally."

I felt bad for making her think like that. "You are now."

She smiled then, just the way I'd always wanted the original Tracy to smile. "Yes. Thanks to you."

Me?

She said, "But I found something, Wally. You know how I told you the hyperdrives experience time dilation?"

I nodded.

"Well, the citizens of the Empire lived a long time, compared to humans, largely from perfected medical treatment, but they were hardly immortal. The universe was, in a sense, closed to them, just the same way the stars are closed to Earth."

Right. Apollo/Saturn would get us to the Moon by the end of the decade, to Mars by 1984 or thereabouts, maybe even to the moons of Jupiter by the end of the century. But the stars? Never.

There was that alternative vision of 2009. The good one. Rather than an Earth blasted away to slag by tens of thousands of nuclear explosions, maybe Murray did get to be the first man on Mars, the way he said he would be: Murray on Mars in his mid-thirties. Maybe I'd go home and there he'd be, commanding the first expedition to Saturn.

Jealous?

No. *I* was holding hands with Tracy.

She said, "I think they were working on a new type of space drive, one that would have been virtually instantaneous, given them access to all places and all times, all at once."

What the hell book had I read where they had some kind of instantaneous radio? One of those Ace Doubles? *Rocannon's World*, maybe.

"The evidence is spotty, but it looks like the event sequences all stop when they switched on the test unit."

"So . . . ? Where'd they all go?"

More shadow, this time deep in her eyes. "I don't know, Wally. I think maybe they went to the Omega Point."

I waited for a minute, but she didn't offer any more, and I decided not to ask. After a bit, we went up the ramp and into the saucer, lifting off for our spome.

Sightseeing.

Sightseeing and fucking.

So much fucking, I probably would've lost another twenty pounds and gotten as skinny as a rock star, except that Tracy insisted she had to eat if she was ever going to grow. I didn't mind her only being four-foot-nine, but it didn't seem fair to make her stay little, and since I had to hang around while she was eating, I guessed I might as well eat too.

Eventually, we wound up going to a world Tracy found in one of those magical electronic information nodes she could access, something she said would interest us both, and it did: a planet-sized museum that'd been the Lost Empire's biggest tourist attraction. Like the Smithsonian and the Guggenheim and the Louvre and everything else you could possibly think of, all rolled into one and then enlarged a million, billion times.

What can I tell you about the history of a billion years? A billion years, a hundred billion galaxies, all of it stuffed into a tiny corner of an incomprehensibly larger universe?

I remember standing in a hall with more square footage then the Pentagon, detailing the history of a nontechnological race, a people who looked a little like vast shell-less oysters, slimy and featureless gray, who'd devoted a hundred thousand years to perfecting an art form that looked like nothing so much as boiling bacon grease.

The stories got it wrong, I remember thinking. All those story aliens were nothing more than Chinamen and Hindoos in goofy rubber suits pretending to be wonderful and strange. Even the best of them . . . Dilbians? Talking bears from a fairy tale. Puppeteers? Kzinti? I remember I'd liked all that stuff, but what's a few more intelligent cows and giant bipedal housecats among friends?

Tracy and I walked the halls, and fucked and ate and sight-saw, and one day wound up in a great dark cavern of the winds, in which were suspended ten thousand interstellar warships, bristling with missile launchers and turrets and ray projectors.

The Chukhamagh Fleet, the narrative node named them, most likely inventing a word I could pronounce, at Tracy's behest. They'd been hit by the expanding wave-front of the Lost Empire, and, being a martial people, had decided to make a fight of it. The local police force, if you can call them that, dragged the fleet straight here to the museum, where they made the crews get out and take public transportation home.

So there we were, sprawled on the floor on a picnic blanket, dizzy from exertion, sweat still evaporating, in front of a kilometer-long star-battleship that looked better than anything I'd ever seen in a movie.

Look at the goddamned thing! What a story *that* would've made!

Hell, maybe somebody did think of it.

Maybe it was written and published, and I just missed it. Maybe . . .

I rolled on my side then, looked at Tracy and smiled.

You could see she was expecting me to crawl right back on top of her, but what I said was, "Hey, I've got an idea! Tell me what you think of *this* . . ."

The automatic pilot dropped us out of hyperspace just outside Jupiter's orbit, just as planned, and gave a delicate little chime to get our attention. I guess we were about done anyway, getting up off the command deck floor, using the blanket to dry off a bit, plopping down bareass in those nice leather chairs the Chukhamagh had been so proud of.

Not really comfortable, especially the way my nuts kept winding up in the crevice the Chukhamagh made for their beavertails, but good enough.

"Let's see what we got here."

I let the autopilot find Earth with the telescope optics, frosted blue-white marble swelling to fill the vidwall. Hmh. Not exactly the way I expected. I guess I didn't really pay attention on the way out, so I'd keep expecting to see the continents on a globe instead of blue with white stripes and a hint of tan here and there. What's that white glare? Antarctica?

I said, "No atomic war, I guess."

Tracy said, "It's not that common, anyway. Judging from the early history of the Lost Empire, not one culture in a million blows itself to bits on the way to star travel. Ecological misadventure is much more common."

Like wiping out an entire intergalactic civilization while you're looking for a quicker way to get around? She still wasn't talking about that. Not telling me what an Omega Point might be, or why it'd taken the organic sentiences but left the robots behind. Maybe someday. Maybe not.

I polled the electromagnetic spectrum. Lots of noise from Earth, just like you'd expect. Try a sample. "Jesus."

Tracy cocked her head at the two sailors on the screen. "Something you recognize."

"Yah. I guess I didn't expect *Gilligan's Island* would still be in reruns after half a century."

"Not your language, though."

"Maybe it's dubbed in Arabic or Japanese or something."

I sampled around the solar system, trying to figure out . . . "Almost nothing. A couple of satellites around Jupiter and Saturn. Hell, I figured on a Mars base by now, at least."

Not a peep from the Moon. No Moonbase? What the fuck . . .

There was a tinkertoy space station in very low Earth orbit, not even half way to Von Braun's celebrated two-hour orbit. No space-wheel. No spin. No artificial gravity. On the other hand, I was impressed by the big delta-winged shape docked to one end. "At least they've got real space ships now!"

Tracy said, "The remotes show eleven humans aboard."

Eleven. Better than Von Braun's projected seven-man crew for those 1950s ships. "How many aboard the station?"

"Eleven total, between the station and ship." She went deeper into the scan data, and then said, "I think the station is set up to house a three-man crew. That little thing with the solar panels down there is the escape capsule, I guess."

I looked, but didn't recognize it. Smaller than an Apollo, bigger than a Gemini. Kind of, I thought, like a Voskhod with two reentry modules, all wrapped up in some green crap.

I flopped back in the command pilot's chair, and said, "Man, what a bunch of fuckin' duds! They might just as well have had the goddamn atomic war and got it over with!"

Tracy smiled, and said, "Maybe you're being a little hard on them."

Getting a little bossy, now that she's full size. Although having her five-feet-eight to my six-foot-nothing made for a *much* more comfortable fuck.

She said, "Are we ready, then?"

I gave the pathetic old Earth a long, long look, thought about Murray, down there somewhere, pushing sixty, and said, "Sure. Let's do it." Get it over with, and get back to something worthwhile.

I sent the signal, dropping the main fleet out of hyperspace, bringing it swinging on in, wave on wave of robot-crewed battleships, wondering what they'd make of it down there, when, in just a minute, the radar screens began to go wild.

And then, not just on every TV, not just on every movie screen, not just on every audio tape, but in the printed words of every book, magazine, and newspaper, on every billboard, on the signs by the side of every road that should've given speed limits and directions, the labels on bottles, the images and text on the boxes of all the breakfast cereals, on magical things Tracy explained to me, the little display windows on electronic calculators(!), on these shiny little thingies called CDs that'd displaced our old LPs, on every page in every browser (not a clue! something to do with "peecees" and what she termed "the Internet"?), all over the world, there was nothing but the face of a fiery God, and the words of his message:

"Behold," he said. "I am coming to punish everyone for what he has done, and for what he has failed to do."

I took a moment to imagine the look on Murray's face right now, another moment to wonder if he even remembered me. When the moment was over, we got down to work.

And so the seed of mankind was parceled out to the trillion worlds of the Lost Empire, a family here, a neighborhood there, this one with a whole nation, that one with no more than a township, a few with no more than a single man or woman, left to wonder just what they'd done to merit such a nightmare punishment, or such a grand reward.

It was a long while before they understood what'd been done to them, longer still before they began to look for one another.

"But that, Little Adam, is another story."